PENNY
SAVANNAH

PENNY SAVANNAH

A Tale of Civil War Georgia

To Sam

Happy Birthday
Jan. 5, 2017

Jim Jordan

JIM JORDAN

Penny Savannah: *A Tale of Civil War Georgia*

Published by:
Pulaski Square Press
78 Winding Oak Drive
Okatie, SC 29909
843-987-0408

Edited by Stephen G. Hoffius

Cover illustration, book design, and Georgia map by Paul F. Rossmann

ISBN: 978-0-9983426-0-3

In memory of
Henry Jordan, Sidney Friend,
and Michael Thomas Donofrio

TABLE OF CONTENTS

INTRODUCTION

Penny Savannah is a work of historical fiction about the War Between the States in Georgia, and particularly Savannah. It is told from the perspectives of southern characters, black and white. The narrative tries to convey the style and norms of that time. For example, the word "negro" is used rather than "African American," and it is not capitalized, as it wasn't at the time.

Many of the characters are enslaved, and I have tried to recreate their dialect in the narrative. I relied mostly on the phonetic wording as related in newspaper accounts of the day mimicking the patois (for one example, see the *Crisis* (Columbus, Ohio), November 25, 1862); personal reminiscences of white people; and the *Slave Narratives*, a collection of interviews with former slaves conducted from 1936 to 1938 by the Federal Writers' Project. These narratives are available online at: https://memory.loc.gov/ammem/snhtml/snhome.html. The words are easily understood if read aloud.

Almost all persons of color, enslaved or free, were uneducated; they spoke with a rich language, but it wasn't proper English. However, a few blacks received some form of schooling. Examples include ministers who were trained in and could read the Bible, and black children, such as Susie King Taylor, who grew up in the company of white children, borrowed their books, and attended illegal schools for blacks. See Patricia W. Romero, ed., *A Black Woman's Civil War Memoirs* (Princeton, N. J.: Marcus Wiener Publishing, Inc., 1988), 29-30. In *Penny Savannah*, slaves who have close associations with whites speak proper, or close to proper English.

The "n" word was rarely used by upper-class southern whites in the antebellum and Civil War eras. After reading hundreds of letters written by members of the southern aristocratic class, I have never seen it invoked. As one Georgia woman wrote in her reminiscences, "The word 'nigger' was not acceptable in polite speech, tho it was a term much in use among the negroes themselves." See Julia E. Harn, "Old Canoochee—Ogeechee Chronicles," *Georgia Historical Quarterly* 16 (June 1932): 150. However, the word was used by most other whites and I have employed it as it would have been spoken at the time. Generally, the use of the word was not frowned upon, and newspapers, both South and North, printed it freely. For example, a Savannah paper in 1857 ran an advertisement for a play called "The Niggers in the Wilderness." See the *Daily Morning News*, December 23, 1857. For examples of use of the word in northern newspapers, see the *New York Herald*, December 1, 1858 and the *Weekly Wisconsin Patriot*, April 26, 1862. The terms "Sambo," as it was a common name for slaves, and "darkey," were often used, as were "colored person" and "person of color."

Masters would not normally refer to their bondsmen as slaves (except in political discussions or referring to the law), but rather as negroes or servants. See Harn, "Old Canoochee—Ogeechee Chronicles": 150.

Appendix A provides the author's comments, notes, and research references. Appendix B lists the characters' names with a brief discription of each. ◈

ACKNOWLEDGEMENTS

I would like to thank the following individuals and institutions for their assistance in researching and writing this book.

I am especially grateful to those folks who read the manuscript and provided so many valuable insights: Steve Hoffius of Charleston, my indispensable editor; Hugh Harrington, Gainesville, Georgia author and historian; Mary Sykes of Okatie, South Carolina; Jewell Anderson of Savannah; Kris Lehman of Callawassie Island, South Carolina, and Kathleen Jordan, my understanding wife.

Several individuals provided valuable expertise and information: Hugh Harrington for firearms and other weaponry; author and Victorian era reenactress Kim Poovey of Beaufort, South Carolina for women's fashions and social customs; Saul Jacob Rubin, former rabbi of Congregation Mickve Israel of Savannah for insights into the Jewish experience in Savannah during the Civil War; Jay Jones of Custom Wagons in Nicholasville, Kentucky for vehicles of the era; Bob Goss and Carolyn Patterson of Charlottesville, Virginia, proprietors of The Inn at Monticello, for sharing the diary of Private William H. Smith, Bob's great-great-grandfather, a prisoner at Andersonville in 1864; and Anne Buckner Burgamy of Milledgeville, Georgia for details about military camp life.

Employees and volunteers at historical sites and historical societies were especially helpful: Gloria Swift of the Fort Pulaski National Monument; Trevor Johnston of Fort McAllister State Park; Abbie Parks of the Cobb Landmarks and Historical Society in Marietta, Georgia; Elaine DeNiro of the Roswell Historical Society; Alan Marsh, chief of resource management at the Andersonville National Historic Site; Muriel Jackson of the Genealogy and Historical Room at the Washington Memorial Library in Macon, Georgia; Lynette Stoudt, Katharine Rapkin, and Lindsay Sheldon of the Georgia Historical Society in Savannah; Luciana Spracher of the City of Savannah Library and Archives; Susan Hoffius of the Waring Historical Library, Medical University of South Carolina; Lou Benfante and staff of the Heritage Library of Hilton Head Island; Ephraim J. Rotter of the Thomas County Historical Society in Thomasville, Georgia; and the staffs at the Lane Library at Armstrong State University, the Zach S. Henderson at Georgia Southern University, the Reese Library at Georgia Regents University in Augusta, the University of South Carolina, Beaufort and Bluffton campuses, and the Thomas, Georgia County Public Library, Thomasville branch.

Dr. John Duncan, professor emeritus at Armstrong State University and proprietor of V & J Antique Maps, Prints & Books in Savannah, provided excellent maps and other reference materials.

Special thanks are due to Paul Rossmann of Charleston, who did the cover illustration, and friend and neighbor Melinda Welker for my photo.

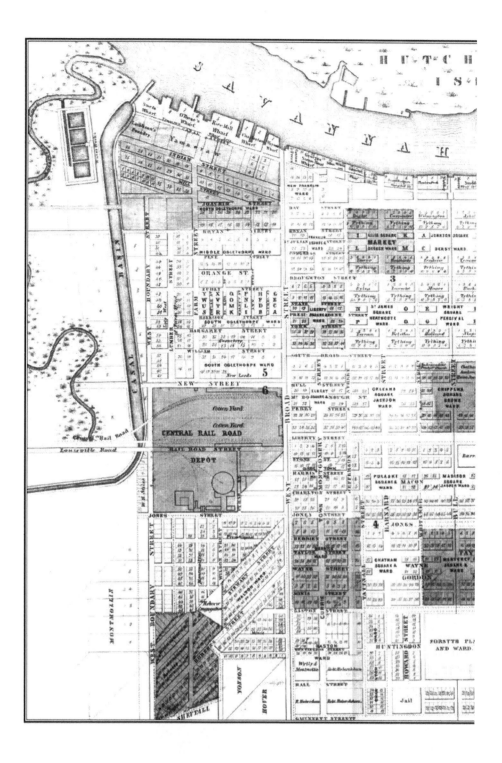

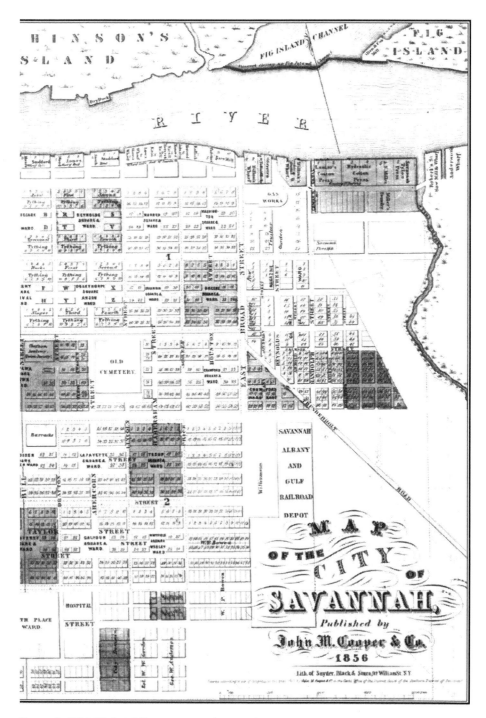

Savannah, 1856, Waring Collection 1018, volume 2, plate no. 26,
courtesy of the Georgia Historical Society

MAP OF GEORGIA

◦◦

CHAPTER ONE

Penny Savannah

July 1862

Willie Sloan nursed a whiskey in the Marshall House Hotel bar and bemoaned his streak of bad luck, which he traced back to the night fourteen months earlier when he shot a damned darkey on a Savannah pier. Willie rarely patronized fancy saloons, but he needed money fast, and this was one place where he might find it. Robbing inebriated businessmen was not his preferred line of work—he was a thief. But he had few other options that promised a quick payoff. Not that it was an easy job. With the war reducing commerce to a trickle, there were far fewer guests at the hotels, and finding a suitable mark—a well-dressed, free-spending drunk—was a challenge in itself.

However, this night's prospects were looking up. A bald, pot-bellied man a little over five feet tall in a business suit stood at the far end of the bar and bragged to anyone within earshot about all the goods he was importing on blockade runners and selling as fast as he could. He even bought drinks for Willie and the three other patrons. Willie prayed that the blowhard wasn't staying at the Marshall House, as he preferred molesting someone on a dark, deserted street rather than in a hotel hallway or room, near so many other people.

Finally, at 10:30 the man slid off his stool, staggered through the lobby, and, as Willie's ill fortune would have it, up the stairs. Willie followed. He kept one floor behind his prey to avoid suspicion and planned to wait in the stairwell until he heard the sound of a key in a door lock. Then he would charge, push his victim into the room, beat him senseless, and take his valuables.

The man exited on the third floor and turned left. Willie waited a few steps from the landing. He heard a male voice slur "Good evening." Willie peeked around the corner and saw a cleaning woman in the hall watching the patron dig through his pockets. Willie cursed under his breath. He couldn't attack the man with someone present. When the guest pulled the key from his jacket, several things fell to the floor, but he was too intoxicated to notice. After four unsuccessful jabs, he finally inserted the key into the lock and stumbled into his room.

The cleaning woman stepped to the door, picked up the dropped items, and slipped them into her apron pocket. She hesitated, as if she were about to knock, then turned around and walked up the hall. Willie pulled back, tiptoed down one flight, and waited by the entrance to the stairwell. When he heard her footsteps reach the second floor, he moved into the landing and said, "Hello."

She yelped, dropped the broom and dust pan, and held her hand over her chest. "Goodness, sir. You startled me." The girl picked up the cleaning implements and tried to walk around Willie. He blocked her path.

She was young, no more than eighteen years old, and attractive, with strawberry blond hair under her work bonnet. He said in a hoarse whisper, "I sat in the bar downstairs for two hours, waiting for that drunk to leave. I followed him, but you ruined my plans. Now hand over what you picked up."

The girl's face flushed red. "I . . . I don't know what you're talking about."

Willie dropped his fake smile and growled, "Don't play games with me, girl, or I'll pull you by your hair to the manager, have him search you, and get that man to identify his possessions. You'll be in jail before you can wink those pretty green eyes."

The young lady's jaw muscles tightened. "Sir, you lay a hand on me and I'll scream for help and tell the manager that I was turning in some valuables I found on the floor when you appeared and tried to take them from me. Who will he or the police believe? I belong here. My guess is you don't."

Willie wondered if she was bluffing, but he didn't want a confrontation in the hotel and a possible chat with the police, not with his background. "All right," he grumbled, "we'll be partners. What did we get?"

The girl looked down the stairs for other people. She met his gaze and whispered, "Twenty dollars and a watch. You can have the watch."

"Let me see it." She removed the item from her apron and Willie snatched it. He narrowed one eye to inspect the German-made timepiece, grinned, and put it in his jacket pocket. He tipped his hat, revealing grey, callous eyes and straight black hair parted in the middle and plastered to his head. "It was a pleasure." He hopped down the stairs, knowing he would soon be about fifty dollars richer. His luck had finally changed.

As soon as he reached the street, Willie got an idea. The girl would make an ideal partner, finding easy marks for him. He would break into their rooms when they weren't there and give her a small cut. Willie waited a half block away from the hotel. Twenty minutes later, at eleven o'clock, the girl walked through the door and in his direction. He stepped from the shadows and said, "Good evening. We meet again." She glanced at him, flinched, and continued on, her eyes fixed straight ahead. Willie kept up. "My name's Willie. What's yours?" She didn't reply.

He said, "My guess is that you're in the same boat as me—down on your luck and trying to survive. We could do real good working together."

She quickened her pace and spoke without looking at him. "Sir, I've never stolen anything in my life. I fully intend to find out the man's name and repay him when I'm in better circumstances."

Willie laughed. "Sure you will. Look, you shouldn't feel bad. Men who get that careless deserve to lose their money. If you didn't take it, I would have. And if I hadn't, someone else on some other night would." The girl didn't respond. "Slow down. I don't bite. If you don't mind me asking, how old are you? You don't look more than eighteen. And why is a beautiful young girl working as a maid in a hotel at night?"

She wrapped her arms around herself as she maintained her stride. Willie tried again. "I'm just trying to help. You need friends in this business. What's your name?" The girl ignored the request. "I can always go to the hotel and get it."

The girl froze at the threat. She realized that he could make life difficult for her at her job, and she couldn't afford to lose it. Though it didn't pay enough to cover her bills, it was the best she could find considering her age of seventeen and lack of experience. She decided to try to placate the man. "Penny," she said, without looking at him.

"Penny what? Like a penny for your thoughts?"

The girl gazed silently at the ground. She wasn't going to give him a last name, even a phony one. He said, "All right. I'll call you Penny Savannah."

She finally looked at him. "Willie, this is as far as you go. Goodbye."

Willie tipped his hat. "Have it your way, Penny Savannah. If you change your mind, you can find me at Fowler's Saloon. I like you—you're tough and smart. We could make a lot of money together. Think about it." He walked away.

The girl watched him fade into the darkness until she was certain he wasn't going to turn around and follow her. She regretted giving him a name, even though it was fake. But he knew where she worked, and that was worse.

Penny proceeded to her boarding house by Washington Square. She stopped at the door to her room to count her haul—forty Confederate dollars and forty greenbacks. Dumb Willie hadn't even asked to see the cash. Although she was certain that he still got the better of the deal, Penny now had enough to pay her past-due balance and have a roof over her head for a few more weeks. Despite feeling guilty for her actions, she breathed a sigh of relief and entered the room. ◈

PART 1

∿

General Lee's Mistake
May 1861 – April 1862

CHAPTER TWO

❧

Blind Tom

May - July 1861

James McBain jerked up from a daydream and knocked the top hat off his lap. His wife Sarah stroked his arm, knowing that his thoughts on that warm July evening were on a battlefield in Virginia and not in the Masonic Hall. He tried to blink his way back into the moment as he scanned the packed auditorium, which buzzed in anticipation. The fluttering of hundreds of hand fans looked like a swarm of large white butterflies descending on the chests of the patrons.

The crowd hushed. McBain squinted at a lanky man with snow-white hair and goatee holding the arm of a black boy, escorting him to the center of the stage. The twelve-year-old, with close-cropped black hair atop a low forehead, in a buttoned-up, black cloth jacket with a white shirt collar skirting over, appeared to be sleepwalking. His chin almost touched the top of his chest. The pair stopped by the shiny mahogany Steinway & Sons piano. The man released his grip, slid back the bench, guided the boy to a seated position, and patted his shoulder.

The man ran his palms over the front of his grey suit jacket to smooth out any wrinkles, faced the sea of faces, spread his arms, and announced, "Ladies and gentlemen of Savannah, patriots of the glorious South. My name is General James Bethune. I need not remind you of our great struggle for freedom now taking place. Just yesterday our boys met and defeated the Lincolnites on the battlefield at Manassas." A cheer rose from the audience. "Early reports suggest that the fighting was fierce and the casualties great. Many of them hail from this beautiful city. Some paid with their lives, others suffered serious wounds." McBain closed his eyes and massaged his temples, thinking of his son, wherever he might be. Bethune continued, "We showed the abolitionists that we can never be defeated, that we will never submit. In honor of that great victory, and in tribute to our valiant husbands, sons, and brothers, I am proud to say that all proceeds from these three concerts are being donated to the Soldiers' Relief Fund of Savannah."

The general bowed to the applause. When he resumed, he gradually elevated his voice until he shouted. "And now, fellow Southrons, it is my great honor to present to you tonight THE MARVEL OF THE MUSIC WORLD—THE ONE

AND ONLY—BLIND TOM BETHUNE!" The crowd responded with polite hand clapping. The boy sat still, his shoulders slumped. The man stepped behind him, said, "Show 'em, Tom," and walked to the side of the stage.

James and Sarah stretched in their seats to get a better look. They had trouble believing the newspaper reports of a negro boy blind from birth and with the mentality of a five-year-old who was a musical genius. The youngster sat straight, raised his chin, and began to play "Oliver Galop," reputed to be one of his earliest compositions. The moment he hit the first note, his lips widened, revealing a smile as white as the keys. His fingers flowed like small waves on a beach. The tinkling sound and triple-meter beat had James and Sarah tapping their armrests. The man in front of them bobbed his head from side to side in time with the music. Sarah thought that it would be nice to dance to the tune. Tom finished and the crowd greeted him with louder and longer applause than at his introduction. After one piece he had transformed himself from a novelty to an authentic musician. McBain leaned towards his wife and said, "The rumors are true." Sarah nodded her agreement.

Tom bowed while sitting, then started his second song, another dance tune. James saw all the legs in his row pumping up and down to the music. He and everyone in the hall knew that the talents of a blind black boy could only have been encouraged to develop in the benevolent South, and not in the hypocritical North. The performance magnified the patrons' euphoria from the recent victory over the Yankees, and renewed their hope that the North, having tasted the South's steely resolve, would soon fold up its tents, put away its guns, and leave the slave states alone to live in peace. Still, families agonized over the fate of their loved ones who had fought at Manassas.

Tom swept into the military marching piece, "La Marseillaise," and finished with an exclamation point, the fingers of both hands extended, stabbing into the keys. He then turned towards the crowd, beaming widely, and joined in their applause. General Bethune walked behind him and squeezed his shoulders, a gesture that bespoke the master's affection.

James McBain recalled all he had read about Tom's amazing journey to fame. When General James N. Bethune of Columbus, Georgia, a lawyer and newspaper editor, purchased Tom's parents Domingo and Charity Wiggins in 1850, he acquired their blind, feeble baby as well. As a toddler Tom was allowed to stumble and bump his way about the big house where his mother worked. He spent many afternoons sitting on the floor in the parlor while Bethune's two daughters practiced their piano lessons. Tom amused the girls with his ability to repeat words they had just spoken, though he had no idea what they meant. He could even mimic noises, like chirping birds.

One evening as the Bethunes sat for supper they heard someone plunking a tune on the piano. The daughters looked at each other. They had been practicing the same melody that very afternoon. The general's eyes darted from child to child, trying to determine if they were playing a practical joke on him. He walked from the room with his wife and the girls close behind. The general peeked into the parlor and murmured, "Well, I'll be." The family stepped in and gawked at the sightless four-year-old standing on the piano bench, banging away.

Tom turned his head towards the voice and grinned. "Tom play piano."

The general acknowledged, "Yes, Tom, and quite well." It didn't take long for Bethune to realize that he could capitalize on the boy's talent. He hired instructors, who played compositions that Tom instantly repeated. In time, Tom started composing his own melodies, inspired by the sounds he heard about him, like the wind and rain.

In 1857, at age eight, Tom gave his first public performance in Columbus and became an overnight sensation in the city. Two years later a celebrated Portuguese pianist gave a concert there and performed "Fantasy of the Bohemian Girl." To the astonishment of the crowd and, even more, the pianist, Tom took the stage and repeated the entire piece. Bethune then took him on tour through the South, and the shows earned thousands of dollars. Master and slave were in Kentucky when Georgia seceded, and Bethune hustled the boy back home. Tom had remained in Dixie ever since, dazzling audiences wherever he went.

⚜

Bethune waited for the applause to recede and called out, "Thank you, thank you, loyal Savannah. Now, even though you just saw and heard a young blind boy play a piano as well as anyone, I know there are a few folks here who probably think there's some trickery going on. I can't have that. Tom can't have that. So I'm asking for a volunteer, one adept at the piano, to come up and play a piece, and Tom will prove conclusively that he is genuine. Can I have a volunteer please?"

Ten rows back an arm shot up. Bethune waved the man to the stage. Many knew the thin, partially bald, bespectacled gent and watched him glide up the stairs. Bethune asked him, "My good sir, please tell us your name."

The man replied, "I am Mr. Louis, a music and dance teacher here in Savannah."

The colonel raised his eyebrows. "Then you must be familiar with many compositions. Can you think of a piece which is little known?"

Mr. Louis nodded so quickly that his eye glasses slid down his nose. "Yes, sir. My associate, Mr. James Lord Pierpont, completed 'We Conquer or Die' a day ago. Only I have heard it."

Bethune pointed to the bench. "Please sit next to Tom and play it, sir." Tom swiveled over and patted the bench for Mr. Louis, drawing laughter from the folks.

The music teacher bowed to the audience and sat. He rubbed his hands together, placed them on the keys, cleared his throat, threw back his shoulders, and began to play the patriotic ode. Tom tilted his head upwards with his mouth opened slightly, as if he were catching raindrops. Then he tapped the top of the piano with his finger tips as if they were marching to the music. The gentleman played for about two minutes before Bethune said, "Thank you, Mr. Louis."

The teacher played a few last notes and finished by singing:

And this is our watchword,
We conquer or die.

The audience applauded as Mr. Louis stood and Tom slid to the center of the bench. Bethune asked, "Tom, have you ever heard that composition?" The negro shook his head. "Tom, do you think you can play it?" The boy grinned, gave a short laugh, and hit the keys, repeating the composition note for note, rocking his shoulders in time, and ended by dragging the knuckles of his right hand along the entire keyboard. Mr. Louis stared at the top of the piano, and then underneath, as if looking for an elf who might be playing from within. Shocked at Tom's performance, the teacher clapped slowly, as if he were underwater. Tom pushed away the bench, stood, and turned around with his back toward the piano. He bent his knees slightly, placed his hands on the keys, and plunked the tune again.

Bethune grabbed the stunned music teacher's hand and pumped it. "Thank you, again, Mr. Louis. I think everyone is a believer now."

The audience burst into cheers. The general said, "Tom, please resume the performance."

The boy grinned and said, "Tom like that. Yes, indeed." He proceeded to play "Yankee Doodle" for a minute with his left hand and looked towards the crowd, which clapped along. Then Tom placed his right hand on the keys and played "Fisher's Hornpipe" at the same time. The audience was too awed to cheer.

James McBain turned to his wife and said, "Two songs at once! I've never seen anything like it. Danny would love to see him. Joseph, too." McBain quieted at the mention of his son. His mind wandered back two months—to the last time he had seen Joseph. It was a day that no one in Savannah would ever forget.

For pomp, the procession that sent Second Lieutenant Joseph McBain and one hundred other men of Company A of the Oglethorpe Light Infantry to Virginia equaled any ever held in Savannah. After mustering into Confederate service on the morning of May 21, 1861, the soldiers, with luggage, knapsacks, haversacks, bedrolls, rifles, and other belongings, convened at their parade ground at the corner of Whitaker and South Broad streets. At noon, nine other Savannah militia companies in full dress formed a column along South Broad. The Oglethorpes, with their four commissioned officers on horseback followed by the non-commissioned officers and privates on foot, marched through, receiving crisp, coordinated salutes from the other unit, all to the tune of "Bold Soldier Boy" being oompahed by a brass band.

One by one the companies fell in behind the Oglethorpes and trudged in step through the town's sandy thoroughfares. As they turned onto Bull Street and passed by the Independent Presbyterian Church, where most of the Oglethorpes worshipped, Joseph looked to the sidewalk and saw his six-year-old son Danny, with dark brown eyes and blond-brown hair covering his ears, perched upon his grandfather's shoulders. The smiling boy waved a small Georgia flag as if he were trying to swat a fly. Earlier that day, tears ran down Danny's face as he sat on Joseph's bed in his grandparent's house on Pulaski Square, watching his father pack. "When will you be back, Pa?" he sniffled.

Joseph zipped up his carpetbag. "As soon as I can, Danny. Maybe in a few months." He stepped over and kissed the top of the boy's head. "I want you to be brave and listen to Grandpa and Grandma while I'm gone. And don't cry. Southern boys don't do that." Danny nodded, wiped the tears on his shirtsleeves, and forced a big grin, exposing crooked white teeth. Joseph laughed. "That's better."

Now, seeing his father on horseback near the head of the parade, in a dark blue shirt with a buff-colored bib design bordered by shiny brass buttons, dark blue trousers, and a shako hat with a silver shield and plume of white feathers in front, Danny couldn't seal his smiling lips on a bet.

Sixty-nine-year-old, six-foot-tall James McBain stood as straight as a statue, even with Danny sitting on his shoulders, holding his grandfather's shoulder-length silver hair with one hand as if he were riding a horse. James's Heritage plantation produced Savannah Grey bricks, and also had a lumber mill and an iron foundry. Few structures in Savannah could be built without using at least one of his products. But despite his financial success, turmoil saturated McBain's life. He had suffered a stroke two years earlier, from which he had mostly recovered, though he had not regained all his energy. His forty-two-year-old daughter Amy had married a northern newspaper reporter and, fearing for his life in Savannah, they had moved to New York City. When Joseph's Yankee wife Emily and their baby daughter Charlotte traveled to New York City to visit her family in December 1860, her parents had convinced her, with a war looming, not to return to the evil, slave-holding South. And now forty-one-year-old Joseph, who should be running the plantation, was going to war, leaving James to carry that burden. Danny remained the one shining light in James and Sarah's lives.

Sarah, standing to the left of her husband, looked resplendent in her dark blue skirt over hoops and beige bodice, colors that matched her son's uniform. Her white sun bonnet covered her grey-streaked hair. She pressed her hands together, as if in prayer. Sarah Potter of the Coleraine plantation—just a few miles west of the Heritage on the Savannah River—had met James McBain in 1817, at the age of twenty, and they married one year later. She had Amy in 1819 and Joseph a year later, but despaired at her inability to have more children. She raised her daughter and son and ran the Heritage household with the help of a dozen servants. Now, after forty-three years of marriage, she spent most of her time at their Savannah house, helping to raise Danny and volunteering at several organizations to support the war effort. She did not want her husband worrying over the plantation. They had enough wealth. He could hire someone to run it, or he could sell it. God would provide guidance. At that moment, her one concern, as for all mothers of soldiers, was her son's safe return.

Thirty-year-old Patience McBain, recently widowed, and wearing a black dress and turban slightly darker than her skin, stood on the other side of James McBain. Her six-year-old son, James Vitruvius, known to all as Truvy, perched on her shoulders so he could sit beside his friend, Danny. Fourteen-month-old Gully Palladio sat at her feet, trying to pound a palmetto bug into the brick sidewalk with the heel of his hand. Patience's parents were slaves of a local cotton merchant. Patience had been working in the kitchen when, at sixteen years of age, she fell in love with Andrew, Joseph McBain's closest friend and a slave of James McBain. On James McBain's petition, the state legislature manumitted Andrew at age thirty, and he and Patience married in March 1851. Patience's owner then sold her to Andrew for the bargain price of five hundred dollars so she could be owned by her husband. When Andrew died, he left all of his possessions to Joseph McBain, including his house, since his wife, as a piece of property, could not legally own property. Joseph also inherited Patience, but he allowed her to continue to live in the house that Andrew had built, let her have access to all of Andrew's assets, and hired her out as a cook and gave her all the wages.

With his grandson on his shoulders and the vibrations of brass instruments in his ears, James McBain followed the soldiers, many of whom he knew. They marched along Bull Street, around Chippewa, Madison, and Monterey squares— three of the twenty-four fenced-in, grassy, symmetrically placed parks that made the town so unique—to Gaston Street, and then back to Whitaker. There, from the front steps of his house, the mayor presented the Oglethorpes with a silk Confederate flag made by the ladies of Savannah. After local dignitaries gave several speeches calling for all Savannahians to unite behind their sons, the parade snaked back through town to the railroad terminus.

The officers dismounted and gave their horses to the company quartermaster to board in the stock car. Joseph hugged and kissed his mother and son, shook hands with his father, wished the servants well, and walked down the boarding path to a large group of soldiers waiting to enter a car. He turned and waved to his family just as James set Danny on the ground. The boy sprinted the thirty yards to his father and jumped into his unsuspecting arms, causing Joseph's shako hat to slide over his forehead. The men who witnessed the incident got a good laugh, with one shouting, "Good catch, sir!" Second Lieutenant Hamilton Couper reached over and adjusted Joseph's hat. Joseph gave Danny a final hug and put him on the ground. The boy wrapped his arms around his father's thigh and yelled, "Please come home soon, Pa. Promise me!"

Joseph squatted and placed his hands on his son's shoulders. "I promise. Now, remember what I said about being brave." Danny bowed his head, trying to remember. Then he ran back to his grandparents, turned around, and saluted his father, his flattened right hand resting horizontally on the crook at the top of his nose. Joseph and the other Oglethorpes returned proper salutes. Joseph gave a final wave and climbed the three steps into the car.

The band did not stop playing nor did the crowd disperse until the train—its engine belching black smoke and its whistle screeching like a hungry hawk—disappeared from sight. Then the praying began.

James looked up and saw everyone around him, including Sarah, rising to their feet, applauding Blind Tom. He stood and joined in. The general walked to the middle of the stage and shouted above the cheering crowd, "Blind Tom Bethune, fellow Georgians! Thank you! Long live Jefferson Davis and our glorious Confederacy!" The negro stood, faced the audience, and bowed three times. Bethune walked to the boy's side, laid his arm around his shoulders, and they bowed together. The clapping and whistling continued, and the man and boy remained in place, soaking in the adulation. The general finally raised his arms and the crowd hushed. "Ladies and gentlemen, Tom has asked me to allow him to play one more song." A patron yelled, "Bravo!" and the crowd sat.

Tom returned to the piano, removed a white kerchief from his jacket, and wiped his brow. The hall hushed in anticipation. Tom reared back and poked a finger at the G key, repeating it for fifteen seconds, raising and lowering the volume with the force of his touch. The people began to squirm in their seats, wondering if the simple boy had forgotten the song. Then Tom changed to the E key and repeated it for fifteen seconds. The folks looked to the side of the stage for General Bethune to break Tom out of his rut. But Bethune stood motionless. Tom switched to the C key, and just when the collective murmur of concern was loud enough for him to hear, he started to play ever so slowly, G, E, C, C, C, D, E, F, G.

I...wish...I...was...in...the...land...of...cotton

Tom picked up the pace.

old...times...there...are...not...forgotten

A man leapt to his feet and started to sing. Like mushrooms, others popped up and joined in until the entire audience, including James and Sarah McBain, sang as one.

look away…look away…look away…Dixieland.
I wish I was in Dixie, away, away,
In Dixieland, I'll take my stand,
To live and die in Dixie

Men whistled, tossed their hats in the air, and raised their arms in triumph. Tom played the refrain again and again, looking towards the people with a smile as wide as Dixie itself.

The boy finished the tune, stood, and waved. The crowd remained on its feet, cheering him and the South and its institutions. Bethune took Tom's arm and the pair walked off the stage. The McBains left the hall exhilarated, but as soon as they reached the street, James's thoughts returned to where they were when he entered—to a battlefield in distant Virginia. ❧

CHAPTER THREE

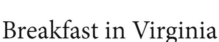

Breakfast in Virginia

May – July 1861

As the train pulled from the station on the long journey to Virginia, the soldiers leaned out the windows and waved to their families. Hamilton Couper, the former United States district attorney for Georgia, sat with Joseph. The two men, whose fathers had been friends for decades, discussed the latest rumor—that the Yankees planned to attack Richmond, the new capital of the Confederacy, and put a quick end to the rebellion. The first great battle of the war would probably take place along one of the routes from Washington to Richmond. Joseph tried to involve First Lieutenant Joseph J. West in the conversation, but the medical doctor, sitting across the aisle, kept to himself and studied Hardee's Tactics, a primer on military organization and operation.

Soon Couper closed his eyes and nodded off, and Joseph gazed out the window at the green marsh land and checkerboard rice fields of the South Carolina lowcountry. He thought of Andrew and felt a dull throb in his head at his friend's murder on a Savannah pier two weeks earlier. He vowed to track down the killers the moment he returned home.

Loud voices pulled Joseph from his thoughts. Company Captain Francis S. Bartow, Savannah lawyer and representative to the Confederate Congress, entered the car. Bartow was a hero to Georgians for defying Governor Joseph Brown's order to keep the Oglethorpes in Savannah to protect the city in case of a Yankee attack. Bartow wanted his men to fight on the front lines in Virginia, and offered the company's services directly to the Confederate States military. They were accepted by the secretary of war.

Bartow patted the backs of the young privates, who averaged nineteen years of age, saying that they had carried themselves like true warriors and made all Savannah proud. Joseph heard Private Hamilton Branch, the youngest of three Branch brothers in the company, reply, "I'll follow you to the gates of hell, Captain."

Joseph admired Bartow for the stand he took against Brown and the respect he received from the young Oglethorpes. The two men, however, had differed on the issue of secession. Bartow, like most Savannahians, believed that Georgia had to leave the Union after Lincoln's election. Joseph thought that Georgia first should have tried to negotiate its differences with the North or wait until Lincoln deprived the South of some rights. War was too high a price to pay and the republic was too sacred to break up. But now that the conflict had begun, Joseph's loyalty to his state overrode all other considerations.

Hundreds of people greeted the Oglethorpes at each city along the route, cheering their defiance of Governor Brown. The company finally reached Richmond on the night of May 25 and marched to a field three miles outside of town. In darkness illuminated by a full moon, they received equipment from the quartermaster and made camp.

There had been a shortage of tents in Savannah and the sleeping arrangements were tight. The first morning, during reveille, as Joseph walked by the tents of the enlisted men, he heard someone call, "Help! We can't get out." Joseph squatted, pulled back the front flap, and saw seven soldiers packed so tightly that they were unable to move without pushing a hand into someone else's face or body. Hamilton Branch stuck out his head like a turtle from its shell and called, "Lieutenant McBain, we're trapped in here!" Joseph poked his head inside the tent, winced at the odor, grabbed Branch by the feet, and pulled him out on his stomach. The others began to squirm like fishing worms in a can. Joseph grabbed another pair of ankles when one of the boys released a deafening blast of wind that would have sent a valley full of grazing cows on a stampede across Virginia. Five soldiers knocked Joseph to the ground in their frantic escape from the tent.

As Joseph struggled to his feet, he heard a voice from inside say, "Thanks, Lieutenant. I have some room now." Joseph didn't attempt to identify the culprit. He slapped the dirt from his hands and pants, picked up his mess kit, and went to the quartermaster's wagon to collect his rations. He received three days worth of bacon, salt pork, corn meal, fat, beans, coffee, sugar, and molasses. The men in each company formed messes, usually with their tent mates, and cooked their meals in a group. Officers messed together and, fortunately, First Lieutenant West brought a servant, who cooked for them, as well as washed his master's clothes, cleaned his tent, and tended to his horse.

Over the ensuing days Joseph witnessed companies of between sixty-five to one hundred men pour into camp in uniforms that represented almost all the colors of the rainbow. A carnival-like atmosphere prevailed, with soldiers marching from the railroad depot in formation, led by a standard bearer, and welcomed along the route by the local residents and a band. Ladies attended daily inspections and afterwards thanked the men for their courage. Joseph felt like a hero without having fired a shot.

Daily life, however, quickly became routine. Soldiers rose at sunrise, attended roll call, drilled, performed fatigue duty, sharpened knives and bayonets, checked cartridge boxes, cleaned firearms, occasionally bathed in a nearby creek, and endured inspection. Joseph passed his free time by writing to his parents and Danny. He would have written to his wife and fourteen-month-old daughter, Charlotte, but postal services to New York from the South no longer existed. Still, he thought of them, especially Charlotte, daily.

After supper the men discussed the latest rumors that deluged the camp. One disturbed them more than any other—that a peaceful settlement with the North would soon be reached and war avoided.

Within a week several thousand soldiers had crammed into the grounds and the commanding general organized regiments of ten companies from each state. One evening Captain Bartow called the Oglethorpes together to tell them that they were now Company B of the Eighth Georgia Regiment and that he was its colonel. He added, "We've been ordered to join the eleven-thousand-man Army of the Shenandoah, commanded by General Joseph E. Johnston, stationed to the north near Harpers Ferry." The men cheered the news. One private stood and danced a jig. "An eighteen-thousand-man Union army is hunting General Johnston. We will see to it that those Yankees never hunt again." The men shouted huzzahs.

Company B then elected its officers: Dr. Joseph West as captain, Hamilton Couper as first lieutenant, and Joseph McBain and John Branch as second lieutenants. The Eighth Georgia left Richmond on June 5 and arrived at Johnson's camp after four days of sweaty, dirt-choking train rides and marches. Their excitement quickly evaporated as they settled into camp routine.

Ten days later General Johnston raised the hopes of the men by moving the camp to Winchester, about thirty miles to the west. He organized his army into four brigades, each one consisting of three-to-five regiments and an artillery unit. He assigned the Eighth Georgia to the Second Brigade and named Francis Bartow as its commanding officer and William Montgomery Gardner of Augusta, a veteran of the Mexican-American War, as the lieutenant colonel of the Eighth Georgia. West, Couper, Branch, and Joseph kept their commissions in Company B. Within weeks Bartow had risen from a company captain to a brigade commander, generating great pride in the Oglethorpes, who were not reluctant to tell anyone that they had served under him since Savannah.

Again they waited, and the men came to believe that they would never fight. One night Bartow and Gardner sat with the officers of the Eighth Georgia and unrolled a map of Virginia, Maryland, and Washington City. Bartow tapped the location of General Pierre G. T. Beauregard's twenty-two-thousand-man Confederate Army of the Potomac on the south side of Bull Run, a creek that snaked from east to northwest across northeastern Virginia. He also pointed out the location of Union General Irvin McDowell's thirty-five-thousand-man army at Fairfax Court House, a town between Bull Run and Washington that the federals had recently captured. "McDowell has to cross Bull Run if he wants to march to Richmond," explained Bartow. "The question is, where will he do it?"

The men stared at the map. One captain said, "They could come over any-where. Doesn't much matter, we'll send them back howling." Another captain tapped his pipe on the map and said, "My guess is that they'll try at Blackburn's Ford on the east, the shortest route to Richmond."

Joseph suggested, "McDowell might navigate Bull Run on the western side, move west, and try to take control of our railroads at Manassas Junction. If he does that, he'll cut the supply lines to our forces in the area. Then he'll proceed to Richmond."

Colonel Gardner nodded. "That looks like a possibility. I'm sure General Beauregard is considering it."

In fact, Beauregard, who had commanded the Confederate forces at Charleston during the attack on Fort Sumter, did not want to give the federals the opportunity to get near Bull Run. He asked President Jefferson Davis for permission to consolidate with Johnston's army, ford Bull Run, and attack McDowell at Fairfax Court House. Davis rejected the plan, leaving Beauregard no choice but to dig in and await a Yankee attack. The fate of the fledgling Confederacy lay in the balance.

On July 17, almost two months after the Oglethorpes left Georgia, Beauregard received reports that McDowell had started marching towards Bull Run and sent word to Johnston at Winchester to reinforce him immediately. That night Captain West told the Oglethorpes, "We're marching tomorrow to Manassas Junction where we'll take the cars to General Beauregard at Bull Run. Cook three days' rations and be prepared to depart first thing. I don't want any other company beating us to the front of the line!"

The next morning the Eighth Georgia Regiment organized first and Company B led the procession with a coordinated bounce in its step. An Oglethorpe private started to sing and soon the entire regiment joined in:

> *You are going to the wars, Willie boy, Willie boy,*
> *You are going to the wars far away,*
> *To protect our rights and laws, Willie boy, Willie boy,*
> *And the banner in the sun's golden ray.*

They sang for hours until they came upon a negro man in a white apron standing in the middle of the road, by a large Georgian brick house with a two-story central unit and matching one-story flanking wings, set back about fifty yards. The servant held up his hand and called to Colonel Gardner. "Missus say come up tuh breakfus', all ub you. Come on up." The black man turned and walked up the circular driveway. After twenty steps he twisted his head and saw the startled troops frozen in place. He put his hands on his hips and said, "Massa, come on up. Ain' you mens hungry?"

Colonel Gardner swiveled in his saddle and stretched to view the long line of his regiment. He told the negro, "I have seven hundred men with me."

The negro nodded. "Dat all right. Missus know it. Now don' go makin' she sad." He waved his arm and continued towards the house.

Gardner called out, "Men, stack your arms. We've been invited to breakfast. Follow your officers in single file and be on your best behavior."

Gardner and the officers dismounted, gave their horses to a guard, and followed the negro to a stone pathway that led to the back of the house and a lawn as big as Johnson Square, bordered on three sides by leafy, bulging boxwoods. The servant climbed a flight of three steps and held open a door to the house. The officers stepped up the stairs as if they were traversing a field of torpedoes, careful not to scuff a board. They removed their hats and entered at one end of a room that seemed as large as a barracks. Tables were lined up end-to-end on either side of the room, set with white linen, and covered with wagon-wheel-sized platters piled high with steaming biscuits, bread, sliced ham, bacon, chicken, pies, and cakes. Ten smiling white women stood at the far side of each set of tables, ready to serve the food with foot-long silver forks and spoons. The officers stared in disbelief. Joseph knew that most of them came from wealthy families, but he'd bet that none had ever seen a spread equal to this. He certainly hadn't.

A woman about twenty-five years of age with brunette hair parted in the middle, pulled back, and set in buns on either side of her head, stepped over to Gardner and said, "Good morning, Colonel. I'm Miss Blakely. You have many brave, hungry boys outside and I bet they'd enjoy some home cooking. Please have them come in."

Gardner answered as a private would a general: "Yes, ma'am. Right away, ma'am. And thank you so much, ma'am." The officers stood aside while the privates and non-commissioned officers entered the house, their eyes bugging out of their heads at the elegantly dressed women, the rich, gold-embroidered draperies, the immense chandeliers that looked like giant jellyfish with tentacles of sparkling glass, the smoky smell of the ham and bacon and the sweet, buttery odor of the biscuits and cakes. They walked along the tables, accepting the delicacies, which the women wrapped in newspaper and placed in their haversacks, with "Thank you, ma'am." A constant stream of servants entered a side door with replacement platters. As the soldiers left the dining room, they were handed cans of hot, sweet coffee.

One private told a server not to bother wrapping his food as he was going to sit and eat it as soon as he went outside. She replied, "You haven't time, young man. You're going to Manassas to help General Beauregard. The Yankees attacked him yesterday. You must get there as soon as possible." The soldiers froze at hearing the news. They told the men next to them and word spread as fast as a spring flood. Soon they would be fighting.

After two hours Miss Blakely rejoined the thirty officers of the Eighth Georgia. She laid a bound book on a nearby table, and asked them to sign it with their name, rank, and regiment, "for the historic occasion." When Joseph's turn came, she caught his eye and smiled. Joseph, with dark blond hair parted in the middle and half way down his neck, hazel eyes, and a smile that revealed white teeth and dimples, often drew coy, inviting looks from women. He tried to think of something to say, but the lady's beauty had him tongue-tied. He heard Captain West from behind. "Lieutenant, if you've forgotten your name, I will fill in the information for you." Joseph heard the other officers trying to stifle their laughter.

Red-faced, Joseph said, "That's thoughtful of you, Captain, but I believe I can handle the challenge." Joseph wrote, handed back the pen, and said, "Miss Blakely, I'll never forget this generosity. I would be honored to thank you and the other women more formally after we've taken care of the Yankees."

The lady never took her eyes off of Joseph. "It would be so nice to hear from you again, Lieutenant, to see how you are getting on. Please write to me at Cornwall plantation. Do you need to write it down?"

"Certainly not. I shall never forget it." Joseph heard an officer clear his throat. He said, "So nice to meet you," and moved to the serving tables.

After the officers received their food, thanked the women, and walked back to their horses, First Lieutenant Couper called to Gardner, "Colonel, Lieutenant McBain has requested permission to remain here and personally guard this house. He fears the Yankees will attack it first." Joseph exhaled in disgust as the men bellowed.

By afternoon the Eighth Georgia and a few of the regiments of Bartow's Second Brigade and General Barnard Bee's Third Brigade reached the desolate Piedmont Junction. The tracks were barren and the men rested in an adjoining field. At seven o'clock in the evening a train finally arrived and took the soldiers to Manassas, an agonizingly slow twenty-five-mile ride. Due to a shortage of cars the lagging regiments, with thousands of men, had to wait for the snail-paced train to return.

During the ride Bartow informed his officers that the Union army had progressed from Fairfax Court House to Centreville, just a few miles northeast of Bull Run Creek. The federals then tested the rebel defenses by sending a skirmishing unit of three thousand men to Blackburn's Ford at the eastern end of the creek, on the Confederate right, near a route to Richmond. The rebels repulsed the attack, but everyone expected a full-scale onslaught to follow.

The Eighth Georgia finally arrived at Manassas Junction at seven o'clock in the morning of July 20 and, with the officers leading the way on horseback, General Bee's and Bartow's troops marched three miles and camped near the top of a hill, close to the anticipated battlefield. The officers then rode to the crest and observed the Bull Run Creek basin. Joseph studied the eight-mile expanse that looked like a watercolor, with huge, open green fields divided in half by a silver, sparkling, fresh-water creek, winding like a snake. He felt as if he had a seat in an amphitheatre, waiting for a performance to begin. He saw Beauregard's Army of the Potomac, dug in behind the natural mounds and breastworks by the five fords, or crossings, in the creek.

The twenty-seven-hundred men of Bee's and Bartow's regiments were placed behind and between two of Bull Run Creek's fords, in reserve to support forces at either position. To the left, on an adjoining hill, the First Brigade, commanded by Colonel Thomas J. Jackson, an instructor from the Virginia Military Institute, sat in reserve at two other fords. Joseph used his field glass to observe the Warrenton Turnpike further left of Colonel Jackson. This was the road that Joseph had thought the Union troops would take to attack Manassas Junction. It crossed a stone bridge over Bull Run Creek, and Joseph could see some of the twelve-hundred Confederates, commanded by Colonel Nathan "Shanks" Evans, waiting on a hill overlooking the bridge.

After reviewing their position, the officers returned to camp. That evening Colonel Bartow addressed the Oglethorpes. Joseph watched the boys in the firelight—the shadows dancing across their faces made them seem so much older. "Men, the time has come. All the drills are about to be put to the test. I know you're anxious, but remember, war means death and by sunset tomorrow some of you will not be with us. Soldiering is the ultimate responsibility, and our freedoms and rights, everything we, our families, and fellow Southerners hold dear, depends on us. I know you're up to the challenge and I consider it the highest honor to lead you into battle. I will see you tomorrow." The men applauded Bartow and then lay awake to boast of how they were going to punish the enemy.

Eventually, the young warriors drifted off to sleep. Joseph listened to their snoring as he stared at the pin holes of light in the black Virginia sky and wondered where he would be at sunset the next day. He opened his eyes when he heard the officer of the guard. It was five o'clock. Thirty minutes later, as they were finishing breakfast, the men heard the pop, pop, pop of distant rifle fire and the boom, boom, boom of small cannons.

The battle had begun.

They checked and rechecked their weapons and aimed their rifles at imaginary Yankees in the trees. They moved to their positions on the other side of the hill. Joseph observed the battlefield in the early light of day and, through his field glass, saw Union troops advancing on his left on the Warrenton Turnpike.

At eight o'clock a soldier on horseback charged up to General Bee and Colonel Bartow, panting as if he had run on foot. He delivered a message and galloped back down the hill. Bee and Bartow rode to their officers. Bartow pointed north. "Men, earlier this morning the enemy, about fifteen hundred in number, marched on our extreme left from Centreville along the Warrenton Turnpike towards the stone bridge, which Colonel Evans is defending. That's the gunfire we've been hearing. He sent his infantry to the bridge to halt their advance. Evans just reported to General Beauregard that this attack is a diversion and that the enemy is sending the main part of its army through the woods further left in a flanking

movement. Evans and nine hundred of his men went to greet them. We're following General Bee to reinforce the three hundred men still guarding the stone
bridge. We can't allow the enemy to cross it. This is it. We're going to war!"

The officers ordered the soldiers in formation and then led them, their firearms held diagonally across their chests and running on the double-quick, towards hell. ☙

CHAPTER FOUR

"Never Give Up the Field, Boys"
July 21, 1861

An hour after General Barnard Bee's and Colonel Frances Bartow's men left to support Colonel Shanks Evans and defend the stone bridge, the flanking Union soldiers—fifteen thousand of them—started to emerge from the woods at an area known as Sudley Springs, about two miles north of the stone bridge on the Confederate side of Bull Run Creek, and marched towards the Warrenton Turnpike. Evans had anticipated this and placed his nine hundred men and a two-piece artillery battery on the heavily treed Matthews Hill overlooking the road.

When the federals came into range, the rebels opened fire and the stunned Yankees fell back, hiding in the pine thickets on either side of the road. They quickly regrouped and returned fire. Men on both sides started falling.

The Second and Third brigades heard the battle raging as they arrived at the bridge. Bee told Bartow to have the Eighth Georgia follow his men to reinforce Evans. They raced one-half mile and ascended the hundred-foot-high Henry House Hill—so named because the Henry family lived there—to a large plateau partially covered by dense pine thickets for a view of the battle. Through field glasses, Joseph and the other officers watched Evans retreat from Matthews Hill to Buck Hill, next to Henry House Hill. Bee led his fighters towards Buck Hill to slow the Union advance while Bartow kept his troops in reserve. But the federals continued to flow from the woods at Sudley Springs and, with their superior numbers, they punished the rebels. Bee called for the Eighth Georgia.

Joseph checked his rifle and revolver one last time and felt electricity—generated by extreme excitement and anxiety—course through his fingers.

The troops charged to the base of Buck Hill, through woods, and into an open field. Colonel Gardner stopped his men while he determined the position of the enemy. They heard a high-pitched buzz from above and looked skyward. An object streaked about twenty feet over their heads. Gardner screamed, "Everyone, down! They've spotted us." Joseph jumped from his horse and fell flat on his stomach as a shell exploded in the field about thirty yards away, pelting the soldiers with huge clumps of turf and scattering the officers' horses. Joseph's heart pounded so hard that he thought he was bouncing. The men lay flat for fifteen minutes as cannon shells blasted around them, sending vibrations through their bodies, splitting their ear drums, and testing their courage.

When the bombardment slowed, Bartow rode onto the field and called, "Colonel, a battery on this hill has your range. Take them out!" Gardner gave the order to advance to a pine thicket about two hundred yards closer to the battery. The men charged as a blizzard of bullets pierced the air about them. Joseph thought he was trapped in a giant beehive. He reached the rear of the thicket and darted from tree to tree to the front, behind a wide pine. He set the rifle hammer at half-cock and held the five-foot-long weapon close to his body. As he peeked around the tree to find a target, the bark above him shattered, and a piece sliced across his face. He touched his cheek. It stung as if he had cut himself while shaving. His fingers were covered in blood. He wiped them on his trouser legs, dropped to his knees, and tried again to locate the enemy.

Non-stop gunfire cracked and boomed all around Joseph. He saw two large pine thickets further up the hill, on the left and on the right, both about one hundred yards away, and spotted Yankee heads sticking out from behind the trees on the left. He pulled the hammer to full-cock, aimed, and fired. He rolled on his back, rested the butt of the rifle on the ground between his feet, and held the barrel above his head with one arm. With the other hand he grabbed a paper cartridge from his box, bit off the end with his teeth, dumped the powder into the barrel, lodged the paper and ball into its mouth with his thumb, rammed them down, pulled the hammer to half-cock, and placed a percussion cap on the nipple. Then he rolled over to a kneeling position, pulled the hammer to full-cock, aimed, and fired. The maneuver, used by all the soldiers, took less than a minute. The floor of the woods around Joseph looked like a pulsating carpet of humanity.

The enemy returned fire from further up the hill. A shell exploded near Joseph and shook the ground so hard that he almost dropped his rifle. As he reloaded and aimed, sweat and blood dripped off his nose and chin and onto the stock. The Yankee fire became so intense that it tore off a branch hanging a few feet over Joseph and dropped it on his head. He saw stars and had to sit for a minute to regain his senses. He felt a lump the size of a small egg and then continued shooting.

The onslaught momentarily slowed and Gardner, seeing that the federals had retreated from the thicket on the left, ordered his men to advance to the trees on the right. The soldiers charged in a crouch, running like geese. At that moment, one thousand more Union soldiers found an unguarded crossing over Bull Run and entered the Buck Hill battlefield. They started firing on the Georgians, forcing them back to the pines that they had just departed.

Joseph hid behind a tree and tried to aim, but his view was blocked by hundreds of retreating Confederates and he held his fire. He hollered, "Run, men, run!" One rebel fell, then another, and then another. Joseph saw Lieutenant John

Branch, the oldest of the three brothers, running towards him. With just yards to the thicket, Branch doubled over like a triggered raccoon trap, and dropped to the ground, clutching his gut. Corporal Sanford Branch, the middle brother, Captain West, and three soldiers crawled from the thicket to John's side. West spoke to the stricken man, touched his forehead, and returned to the trees. As he passed Joseph he said, "Lieutenant Branch will be dead in minutes."

Colonel Gardner jumped off his horse and urged his men on, whistling and waving his right arm in a circular motion, when he screamed in pain, flipped in the air, and landed on his back. He grabbed his ankle with one hand and crawled on his side like a snake to the shelter of a tree.

The survivors of the Eighth Georgia finally made it back to the thicket and started returning fire at the advancing Yankees. The enemy began falling like corn stalks at harvest. Gunpowder smoke hovered over the battlefield like a dense grey cloud and smelled like dozens of fireworks shows. Every time Joseph aimed, he saw that the federals had inched closer and realized his regiment could not stop them. The notion that the slick Union city boys would turn and run once they faced the leather-tough rebel country boys turned out to be a fantasy. They were fierce as tigers.

Bartow charged onto the battlefield and ordered the Eighth Georgia back to Henry House Hill. Joseph zigzagged to the back of the thicket while looking over his shoulder at the placement of the enemy, and SLAM—he tripped face-first into the dirt, his rifle flying from his grasp. He rose onto his elbows and saw that he had stumbled over the body of an Oglethorpe private, spread-eagled on the ground, his eyes and mouth open, and a crimson blot on the buff bib of his uniform slowly spreading.

Joseph heard a non-human squeal above the din of blasting rifles. A horse was lying on the ground, kicking its legs, but unable to rise. Colonel Bartow writhed underneath the dying animal, trying to claw his way out. Joseph crawled on his chest to his commander, grabbed him under his arms and pulled him free. The horse let out a loud snort and its body went limp. Bartow jumped to his feet and thrust his sword towards the hill. Joseph retrieved his Enfield and wondered if any living thing would survive this day.

A new storm of artillery and musket fire thundered. Joseph dropped on his belly. He rolled over, loaded, and aimed his rifle, but saw the Union troops pulling back. He looked in the opposite direction to the crest of Henry House Hill and spotted thousands of rebel soldiers firing over the Eighth Georgia at the federals, giving him and his comrades cover to retreat. They ran to the plateau of the hill and collapsed on the ground, gasping, their legs having given out and their lungs on fire. A boy next to Joseph gulped too quickly from his canteen and began coughing uncontrollably, puking water all over himself.

General Beauregard arrived from Bull Run Creek and took charge. He placed the remnants of Bartow's brigade on the left of the plateau in a pine thicket, General Jackson's brigade of five Virginia regiments and eleven artillery pieces in the center, and General Bee's and a South Carolina brigade's forces on the right to protect against assault from the stone bridge. He kept two companies of cavalry in reserve and sent General Johnston to get the reinforcements still arriving at the train depot.

Joseph realized that the Yankees had inflicted huge losses on the rebels and Union General McDowell would undoubtedly launch another attack. A victory would give them clear access to Manassas Junction, control of the railroads, and a direct route to Richmond. The rebellion might be over in weeks.

As Joseph inspected his cartridge box, the Yankees began an artillery barrage that shattered trees and blew holes in the earth all around the Henry House Hill defenders. One shell hit near Joseph and an arm in a grey sleeve landed in front of him. White stringy tissue and a bone stuck out one end. A piece of human matter the size of a fist that looked like a damp pink sponge stuck to the front of his shirt. He swiped at it three times until it flew off. Joseph crawled to a tree, sat against it and bowed his head, fighting the urge to vomit. He took a deep breath and looked at the Henry house just as the roof blew apart, with wood and debris shooting skyward and thudding to the ground in clouds of dirt. He knew that anyone inside it was dead.

Blasts of gunfire again filled the air. The Union charge had begun. Joseph heard screams every time a Minie ball ripped into a man's flesh and shattered his bones. Despite a furious, ear-ringing return volley, the Yankees inched closer. Joseph slithered on his belly towards the front of the thicket, fired his rifle from one knee, and began the maneuver of rolling, reloading, and firing. After an hour of mutual slaughter, the federals retreated.

Joseph drank from his canteen and poured water over his steaming head. The hot July air was thick enough to chew. He heard gun reports about a quarter of a mile away and pulled out his field glass. A Union advance on the Confederate center had gained the plateau, and about one thousand of the enemy in red uniforms, bayonets fixed, charged into hundreds of crouched rebel defenders, who fired their rounds at men no more than twenty feet away. The shrieks of the maimed, Union or Confederate, sounded the same. Joseph and the other Oglethorpes stood, ready to rush to the aid of Jackson's men, but Bartow came by and shouted from a new horse, "Hold your places, men. We can't leave here. The Yankees will be back."

As Bartow predicted, a new round of artillery shells and rifle fire ripped into them. Someone shouted, "They're over here!" and the men rushed through the pine thicket to see the hillside swarming with soldiers. The rebels fired volley after volley, and men on both sides kept dropping.

The Yankees' numerical advantage proved too great and each charge took more casualties and penetrated deeper into rebel lines. Bartow witnessed the enemy's progress and rode near the thicket with the flag of the Eighth Georgia Regiment in his hand. He pleaded to his troops, "Hold your position, men! I appeal to you to hold it!" He barely finished his sentence when he dropped the banner, grabbed his chest, tumbled off his horse, and thudded onto his side. He struggled to his knees. Joseph and several others ran to Bartow, who gasped with blood flowing over his fingers, "Never give up the field, boys, never," and then pitched forward. Their commanding officer was dead.

The men scrambled back to the thicket and continued battling, but the federals gained the edge of the plateau and charged towards them. Bartow's warriors let off a huge volley, clouds of smoke everywhere, and the enemy fell en masse, but still more kept coming until it became obvious that surrender or death were the rebels' only options. Joseph looked for a higher-ranking officer to wave the white flag when he heard a new burst of gunfire and shouts to his right. General Jackson charged his regiment into the center of the Union line. Explosions boomed, bayonets plunged, and soldiers screamed.

Thousands of Confederate reinforcements, just arrived by train, sprinted towards the center and right, diving into the fray. The Yankees, now outmanned and exhausted, couldn't hold off the onslaught. They broke and ran for their lives down the hill and towards the stone bridge.

The survivors of Bartow's Brigade, just minutes from defeat, emerged out of the thicket and chased after the enemy. They had done it—they defeated the Lincolnites. Joseph pumped his rifle high over his head in victory and ran towards Captain West to congratulate him when an artillery shell exploded nearby, propelling him into the air, and slamming him headfirst into the turf. A white-hot pain seared into the back of his left leg. He grabbed at the wound and cried out. Through watery eyes he got a worm's view of the open plateau littered with bodies. He reached out and clutched grass, grimacing with each effort, pulling himself forward—to where, he had no idea. He called for help but couldn't hear his own words.

Unconsciousness offered no relief. Joseph dreamed that railroad workers were driving spikes into the back of his thigh. He couldn't breathe and screamed to open his lungs. He reared up on his stomach, gulping air. Sweat soaked his shirt. He raised himself on his elbows, looked around, and saw stained-glass windows ringing the upper wall of a long room. There were about one hundred men on cots. They all wore soldiers' uniforms, with bandages and rags covering their heads and parts of their bodies. A surgeon and two nurses stood by the cot next to his. He closed his eyes and tried to roll onto his back but the pressure on the wound caused him to clench his teeth and gasp.

Moments later, someone asked him for his name, rank, regiment, and place of residence. He opened his eyes and saw the surgeon and nurses hovering over

`26                                            CHAPTER FOUR`

him. He forced a hoarse reply. One nurse said, "Good Lord, another from the Eighth Georgia."

The other nurse, holding a pair of scissors, told Joseph, "Hold still, Lieutenant." He cut off the leg of the uniform from the crotch, and although the scissor never touched him, Joseph moaned. The aide threw the bloody material aside.

The surgeon said, "Lieutenant, the nurses are going to hold you down. Don't resist." He held a blood-soaked towel and patted around the wound. He dipped the towel in a basin, squeezed it until Joseph's blood clouded the water, and continued to clean around the gaping wound. Joseph rolled his head from side to side and breathed through his teeth. The doctor said to an aide, "This cut is very deep. I believe it has done damage to the tissue and muscle." The surgeon kept cleaning the wound, little by little. He then announced, "This leg must come off."

Joseph shouted, "No!"

The nurse scribbled in his book. The surgeon understood that any man hearing this prognosis would be filled with fear and dread, but he had other soldiers to see and didn't have time to try to save the limb. The amputation would only take fifteen minutes. He said to the nurses, "Take him to the operating table."

CHAPTER FIVE

The Wagon

July - November 1861

The nurses hoisted Joseph onto his good leg, and with his arms draped around their shoulders, dragged him out the back door to a tent with the side flaps rolled up. As they helped him onto a long table, Joseph saw a pile of arms and legs in a wheelbarrow a few yards away and his head started to spin. A man wiping down a blood-smeared handsaw stepped to his side. In a raspy voice, Joseph pleaded, "Please, doctor, save my leg."

Exhausted by ten straight hours of amputations caused by the destructive power of the Minie ball, the surgeon placed the handsaw on a smaller table with other medical instruments. They reminded Joseph of the blacksmith's stall at the Heritage. The doctor replied, "If amputation will save your life, I have no choice, Lieutenant. Let me have a look." In the late afternoon sunlight that flooded into the tent, the doctor lifted a towel from a basin of water, wrung it out, and dabbed at the eight-inch-long slice, moving his head to inspect it from every angle. He gently touched the skin bordering the wound to open it, trying not to tear it further. Joseph buried his face in his arms, the veins in his temples and neck bulging just short of the bursting point. The doctor pressed down firmly on the sides of the thigh, searching for broken bones. He mumbled, "Nasty gash, probably caused by a piece of shrapnel. The wound is long and deep, there might be tissue damage, and you've lost a lot of blood, but I don't feel any broken bones, or see any debris. I can sew it up, but if gangrene sets in, we'll have to amputate if it doesn't kill you first. Do you want to take the risk?"

"Yes!"

"All right. Let's get you sewn up."

Joseph gasped, "Thank you, doctor." The nurses held his lower body down and the doctor stitched the wound using silk thread and a sewing needle.

For five days Joseph lay in his cot, listening to the sounds of a war-time hospital—the cries, moans, and prayers of seriously injured soldiers—while waiting for his leg to heal. Then, needing to free the bed, the surgeon-in-charge transferred him by wagon to a hospital in Richmond. By early August Joseph could take a few one-legged steps with crutches, but he couldn't put any weight on his left leg, and the area around the wound remained sore. At the end of the month the stitches were removed and Joseph was able to hobble on crutches around nearby streets. By mid-September the doctors believed that he had healed without infection and could go home, though he would no longer be able to march, drill, or run. He would always walk with a severe limp and require a crutch. They issued him medical furlough papers for the remainder of the war. Although devastated by the end of his active service, his spirits were lifted when he learned that Colonel Gardner had recommended him for a promotion to brevet first lieutenant—an increase in rank without pay—for his conduct during the battle at Manassas.

A few days later Joseph exited the cars in Savannah and saw Danny running down the boarding path to greet him. He dropped the right crutch and leaned forward to receive his son, but when Danny jumped into his arm, Joseph lost his balance and fell backwards, with the boy sprawled on top of him. Other passengers ran over and helped the pair to their feet. One handed Joseph his crutches and said, "God bless you, sir."

Danny hugged his father's right leg and cried, "I'm sorry, Pa!"

Sarah came up, said, "Oh, my dear son," and embraced him, trapping Danny in between. James waited for his wife and grandson to release their grips before shaking Joseph's hand. The McBains had been informed of Joseph's injury but didn't know what to expect. They were just happy that he had returned alive. James dusted off Joseph's jacket as Hercules, the family coachman, greeted him and took his luggage to the coach.

During the ride home Danny hugged his father around the waist. Joseph said, "It's good to see you, son."

When they arrived at Pulaski Square, Joseph, who had lived with his parents and not in his own house on Monterey Square since his wife had left him, led the family up the front stairs. William the butler, dressed in a black suit, opened the door, bowed, revealing a bald, glistening head, and said, "Welcome home, Master Joseph." Joseph limped into the foyer and froze. The house servants were lined up in the hall. The kitchen help, Jinny, Patty, and Lilly, donning black dresses with white lace collars and white work caps, were on the left. The house maids and seamstresses, Nannie, Dolly, and Chloe, similarly dressed in grey, were on the right. Jefferson, who worked under Hercules in the stables and coach house in Savannah, and his helper Barney stood at attention at the end of the hall. They all shouted in unison, "Welcome home, Master Joseph!" Joseph laughed and greeted each one. He couldn't have been happier.

Joseph spent the next week doing what he had dreamed of when in the hospitals in Virginia—being with Danny. Although he tired easily and his leg constantly ached, Joseph couldn't let the boy think that he had slowed down. The family, with Hercules close by, went fishing, boating, and picnicking—activities that did not tax Joseph. Whenever they were in town, acquaintances and strangers alike, having heard of Joseph's heroism, stopped and thanked him. Danny repeated every such incident to his classmates at the Chatham Academy. Life seemed to be getting back to normal.

⁂

"Ah belieb de Lawd jes' send down one ub he angels, mussy boo coo," the grinning man quipped as he stopped in front of Masonic Hall on Broughton Street, using one of several French phrases he had learned from a Haitian chef years earlier. He was hoping to charm a pretty lady with a sweetgrass basket filled with yarn at her feet. She stood five feet tall, wore a brown work dress with a white apron, and, at twenty-five, looked many years younger than the male stranger. She had a large chest with matching hips and her round face framed a flat nose. A thick braid of hair stuck through the back of her orange head scarf, as if trying to escape from the others.

"Ah belieb de Lawd jes' slam you in de head wid uh hammuh!" the young woman shot back.

The man giggled and held his arms at his sides as if he were being tickled. He was thirty-eight years old, five feet seven inches tall, thin except for an emerging belly, had long black hair crowning a narrow head whose eyes were not quite level, nor fully open, presenting a sleepy demeanor. He replied, "Ah know uh angel when ah see she. An' ah see she right now, see boo play. I sho' hope she don' fly way intuh de sky."

The woman rolled her eyes and shook her head. "I ain' flyin' no place, mistuh crazy man." She folded her arms and appraised the stranger. "You got uh name?"

The man bowed. "Ub cause. Pahdin muh rudity. Dey call me Dante, bes' chep in all Sabannah."

James McBain owned Dante, who had entered this world two years after Joseph McBain. Dante's mother Handy was the meanest person at the Heritage, perhaps in all Georgia. When her anger bubbled to the surface, a common occurrence, she beat up on Dante or her husband, whoever happened to be nearest. When Dante was twelve his father ran away, whether from slavery or Handy, no one knew. Two days later he lay dead in a field outside of Beaufort, South Carolina, shot by a planter who caught him stealing from his vegetable garden. Handy blamed Dante and slapped him silly at every opportunity. One night, while sitting around a communal fire in the slave quarter, Handy accused another woman of casting a spell on her husband, which made him flee. A fight ensued, a knife appeared, and Dante became an orphan. The killing caused him little grief.

Unbeknownst to the folks at the Heritage, Handy had taught Dante, who had a reputation for being lazy, a petty thief, and untrainable, how to cook. When

Jinny, the head cook, discovered this, she took him under her wing. Several years later he was preparing meals for the McBains at their new Savannah house on Pulaski Square. When Amy, James McBain's daughter and Joseph's older sister, opened a restaurant in town, she hired Dante.

Within the context of the peculiar institution, Dante lived as well as a bonds-man could. He worked at his trade, for which he received pay—less a twenty percent commission taken by James McBain—and shared a room with Hercules next to the stables at the McBain house in Savannah. Starting in 1861, however, things started to crumble. When Amy married a New Yorker, she sold the restau-rant and moved north; some fool white Southerners attacked a fort in Charleston harbor and started a war; and three white men shot and killed his friend Andrew.

"Who you cook fuh, mistuh massa chep?" the black girl challenged, her chin slightly upraised.

"Fuh Massa Boo No. He own de City Hotel."

The black girl raised her eyebrows, impressed by Dante's employment. She didn't know the owner, but she had seen white men in suits and top hats walk in and out of the hotel. She adjusted her head scarf and felt the renegade braid. Her fingers moved quickly, as if shuffling a deck of cards, and tucked it back in.

Dante asked, "Do angels hab names?"

The girl cocked her head as if she didn't hear him properly. "Ub cause dey do. You ebuh read de Bible, go tuh chu'ch? Ebuh hey'uh ub Gabriel an' he hawn?" The girl didn't wait for Dante to reply. "Ah ain' no angel, but momma call me Isetta."

Dante repeated the name by syllable. "AH-SET-TUH." He was making prog-ress. He eyed the yarn in the basket and asked, "You uh seamstress?"

"Ah knittin' fuh de soljuhs." Everyone in town contributed to the war effort. White women had their female servants make clothes for the boys and bandages to patch them up.

Dante started to ask Isetta if he could call on her next Sunday when he looked toward the street and saw a wagon roll by with what appeared to be an image of a horse on the right side. He froze, then turned to her and stammered, "Ah, ah, ah gotta go, gotta run. Ah see you agin, ah prumise." Dante spun around and took off after the wagon.

Isetta put her hands on her hips and watched Dante dash away. A brown-haired, middle-aged white woman the same height as Isetta, and wearing a red hoop skirt, matching long-sleeve bodice, and white-lace bonnet walked up to her. "Who was that?"

Isetta faced the woman. "Some man who say he de bes' chep in all Sabannah, Missus. Call hese'p Dante."

Caro Lamar watched the negro trot eastward on Broughton Street, carefully side-stepping white people. "Come, Isetta. Mr. Lamar will be joining the girls and me for supper tonight. I want everything to be perfect."

Few things could have pulled Dante away from Isetta, but a wagon just like that one almost ran over him last May as he walked home from work at night. A few minutes before the near-collision, Dante heard a gunshot from the direction of the river, but thought little of it. Then, as he crossed State Street, the wagon charged towards him. Dante jumped back and, in the dim glow of the gas-fueled lamplight, he spotted three men in the wagon with a marking on its side that resembled a horse rearing up on its hind legs. One-half hour later, Dante dropped to his knees in tears as he learned that Andrew had been shot and killed at the river. He knew that that wagon carried the murderers and vowed revenge, even if it meant his own demise.

In the six months since Andrew's death, Dante followed the same daily routine. When he walked to work, he stared at the right side of every open wagon, looking for that image. When he returned to his room after work, he slid a wooden case from under the bed, opened it, and admired the Colt revolver with the dark-brown oak grip that he had bought to use on Andrew's killers. He purchased it for fifty dollars, his life savings, from another slave, who had stolen it. Of course, negroes were strictly prohibited from possessing guns, and if it were ever found in his room or on him, Dante would go to jail for a long time, after a serious whipping. But he had to keep his promise. Andrew's murder would not go unanswered.

Dante crossed Habersham and walked about fifteen paces behind the wagon, trying to avoid notice. The driver sat hunched over on the bench, wearing a floppy-brimmed leather hat, and holding the reins loosely in his hands. Dante couldn't see his face, but he hadn't seen the faces of the men that night. He needed to get a better look at that image and find out where the man lived.

As the wagon traveled through the east side of town, Dante's hands turned as clammy as a dish rag. He had never before been in this area, which was inhabited by poor whites, and the strangeness frightened him even more. There were no people about, just a few chickens pecking at the road. He dropped further back.

A barking dog ran up to Dante, who froze, as he was deathly afraid of canines. The black, brown, and white mongrel sniffed his leg and crotch, growled, and ran off. Dante resumed his pace and watched the vehicle turn right onto Anderson Street. When he reached the corner, he saw the back of the wagon disappear behind a wooden fence half-way down the block on the right. He shivered in fear, but also felt a jolt of excitement as he realized that he might have discovered the house of Andrew's killers. He walked on eggshells past the sagging, unpainted, wooden cottages, to the edge of the fence. His teeth began chattering like castanets when someone behind him shouted, "POW, POW," lifting him inches off the ground. Two white boys, about ten years old, with small sticks in their hands, pointed like pistols, ran past him. "Pow, pow, you're dead." Dante leaned against the fence and waited for his innards to settle into place. He inched his head around the fence and saw the back end of the wagon jutting out behind the house on the left side of the driveway. On the right side was an open yard with a wooden stable, a watering trough, and scattered piles of yellow hay.

Dante had often dreamed of catching Andrew's killers, cornering them, laughing as they pleaded for their lives, and blasting lead balls into their heads. But now that he may have found them, he was so scared he needed to visit a privy. He hadn't been in a fight since his boyhood and carefully avoided confrontation. Besides, he didn't have his gun. Still, he needed to make sure that this was the correct wagon so he could return later. A voice in his head said, "Go on—for Andrew!"

Dante slunk along the sandy driveway and stopped at the edge of the house. He closed his eyes, took a deep breath, and poked his head around the corner. Pain shot through his scalp as he flew through the air, hit the side of the wagon, and landed belly first in the yard. He raised himself on his elbows and shook the sand from his face. A tug on his shirt flipped him onto his back. He stared up at the wagon driver, who held a whip in his hand. Dante rolled over onto his hands and knees and started to crawl towards the horse pasture. A boot on his back pressed him flat into the earth, and a kick into his side turned him on his back.

"Well, boy, you followed me here, what do you want?" The man, whose leather hat and brown-and-grey whiskers could not conceal a three-inch scar on his left cheek, raised the whip over his head and cracked it in the air.

Dante held up his hands for protection. "No, massa. Ah ain' lookin' fuh nuttin! Ah jes' loss, see boo play."

The whip cracked and tore Dante's shirt without hitting his skin, exhibiting the man's skill. "You'll feel the next one, boy. That's a promise, so fess up!"

Dante rolled his head to the side, searching for an excuse. "Ah jes' lookin fuh wu'k. Kin you he'p dis po' nigguh?"

The man turned his ear towards Dante. "Looking for work? You followed me here for a job? What kind of . . . . Why, you lying son of a. . . ." The man raised the whip and Dante's body tensed like a cornered cat.

"What's going on, Harold?" a voice called from the back door of the house.

The man suspended his assault and pointed at the prone trespasser. "Sam, this darkey followed me here all the way from town. Says he's lost or looking for work. He's confused. I'm unconfusing him."

Sam, shorter and stockier than Harold, with red pimples on his pale white face, a bald pate, and hair on the sides of his head that stuck out like the wings of a bird, walked down the back stairs and rested his foot on Dante's stomach. "This sure is a sorry looking specimen. If he don't tell you the truth, no one will miss him." Sam pushed his foot down and air whooshed from Dante's mouth.

The slave tried to rise up on his elbows, but the man's foot kept him down. All he noticed was the sun glaring off the man's belt buckle with an insignia of an eagle landing on a branch. Sam said, "He's all yours, Harold. Just make it quick. We have work to do." Sam returned to the house.

Dante's mind raced. He turned over, got to his hands and knees and crawled to the other side of the wagon. The whip cracked and cut into his backside, causing him to scream and drop on his stomach. He smelled something awful, looked up, and came eye-to-eye with a pile of fresh horse dung.

Harold walked behind him. "Get up, boy, or the next one will be a lot harder."

Dante pushed up and rested on one knee with his back to Harold. "Yassuh, massa, yassuh." Dante turned his head and his jaw dropped when he saw a faded painting of a horse rising up on its hind legs on the side of the wagon. He continued, "Massa, ah tell you ebryting. No need tuh whup me agin, no suh, mussy boo coo."

Harold eased the whip to his side. "Just get up and start talking. NOW!"

Dante leaned forward, readying himself to stand, scooped up the pile of horse poop, leaped in the air, whirled like a dervish, and smashed it in Harold's face just as he was saying, "What the . . . !" Dante fled for the street as Harold, retching and spitting out horse droppings, ran after him, but stopped at the gate. He couldn't give chase in this condition. He shook his fist and yelled, "I'll kill you when I get my hands on you, you damned nigger! And I will find you!"

Dante ran to East Broad and then slowed to a brisk walk. A black man running through town would arouse suspicion in any white person. He headed for the McBain house on Pulaski Square, zigzagging through the lanes of the city, unable to wipe the smell of horse waste from his hands. He charged up the driveway and crashed through the carriage-house doors so loudly that Hercules turned around with clenched fists, ready to defend himself. He saw Dante wiping at his pants. "What in damnation? You smell like horse shit and you look worse!"

Dante panted like a hunting dog at the end of a chase. "Huhclees, ah see 'em, ah see de mens dat kill Andrew. Ahm gwine tuh kill 'em! You comin'?"

The coachman leaned against the gig. "Slow down, nigger, and make sense!"

Dante repeated the day's events. "Dat's de wagon, an' dey de killuhs. Ahm gittin' muh gun!"

Hercules grabbed Dante's arm. "Don't be an idiot. You git caught with that gun, you'll rot in jail the rest of your life. You never even fired it. You'll blow off your own balls before you hit one of them men. You want 'em dead, let Master Joseph do it. He wants 'em as bad as we do. Tell him what you saw, but you better catch him quick. He's at his army headquarters today and word is he's leavin' for Fort Pulaski in a few days."

Dante stared at the ground. Hercules had a point—Master Joseph loved Andrew like a brother, and he had searched for the killers for weeks before leaving for Virginia. Joseph would surely hunt them down, though Dante wanted to pull the trigger himself and watch them squirm in death. Heartened by Hercules's solution to his dilemma, Dante headed for the door. "Ah got tuh git tuh wu'k. Ah see Massa Joesup in de mawnin'."

Hercules wrinkled his nose. "You better clean up good and git some other clothes. A snake wouldn't bite you if you stepped on him, the way you smell."

After washing from a wooden tub in back of the coach house, and wincing at the touch of his cut backside, Dante donned clean clothes and left for the City Hotel. He wore a cap and avoided the main streets, but still looked for the wagon with a horse on its side. When he returned from work that night, he went to his room, careful not to wake Hercules, and inspected his gun. He then lay in bed and thought of Harold and Sam, cornered and pleading for their lives as he emptied his repeater into them. He couldn't wait to see Master Joseph the next morning.

⚬❦⚬

That same early November day, three weeks after his return, Joseph sat with his father after supper on the back piazza. James asked, "When do you think you'll be able to return to work?"

Joseph lit a Montecristo and puffed slowly, knowing that his answer would not be well received. "Father, we're at war. Every man who can carry a gun is fighting. I can't sit idly by."

James's voice rose an octave. "Sit idly by? You fought and almost had your leg blown off. The doctors furloughed you for the rest of the war. That's not sitting idly by."

Joseph brushed a few ashes from his sleeve. "I'm a Georgian, Father, and I'll fight for her, no matter what price. I learned that from you, and I'm glad I did. Right now, others are risking their lives for me and my family. It's my battle as much as anyone else's." Joseph grimaced and rubbed the back of his leg. "Bartow and Bee are dead. So are John Branch and five Oglethorpe privates. Thirty-eight others are in Richmond hospitals. Santy Branch is in a Yankee prison. Over two hundred of the five hundred men in the Eighth Georgia were killed or wounded. I must continue in some role, for my family, and for theirs."

A green gecko ran along the piazza railing, catching the eye of both men. James stared at the reptile as he spoke, "I admire your patriotism, Joseph, but you're not fit to serve. The Oglethorpes won't take you back, even if they wanted."

The gecko looked at the men with round, protruding, black eyes, expanded its neck into a red ball larger than its head, and scampered off. "You're partly right, Father. Company A can't. They're still in Virginia preparing for the next battle. But I've spoken to Frederick Sims, the captain of Company B. They've been mustered into Confederate service for twelve months and are stationed at Fort Pulaski. I told Sims that I still want to serve in some capacity and he said that there are things I can do to help, even in my condition. He's cleared it with Charles Olmstead." Joseph gave a short laugh. "Can you believe it, Charlie Olmstead, just twenty-five-years-old, a major and commander of the regiment at the fort? He's written to Joseph West of Company A to inform him of the transfer. I'll be stationed here at Pulaski, close to home and perfectly safe."

James looked towards Madison Square and the goatees of Spanish moss hanging from the branches of the live oak trees, set aglow by the dull light from the street lamps. The beauty, however, could not temper his disappointment. He knew his son's mind was made up. He asked, "When do you report?"

"Any day now, as soon as Sims finishes the paperwork." Joseph saw his father staring at the square. "I can't think of any other event that could separate us, except for this war. I'm fighting for our future."

James sighed. He had other plans for his elder years. He wanted to spend time with his grandchildren; travel to Scotland to see the homeland of his grandfather, who came to Georgia in 1736 looking for a better life; and tour America, the country he loved. The elder McBain placed his segar on the ashtray, stood, and said, "I'm very tired, Joseph. I'm glad you're home, even for such a short period of time. So are your mother and Danny."

Joseph grabbed onto the arms of the chair, pushed himself up, and balanced himself on his good leg and the toes of the injured one. "I love you, Father." The men embraced. James then started for the door.

Joseph said, "Father, one last thing." James stopped. "Hercules said Dante wants to see me in the morning. It's an emergency. Do you know anything about that?" James shook his head, bid goodnight, and left Joseph alone with his thoughts. ◈

CHAPTER SIX

Port Royal

November 7-8, 1861

At eight o'clock the next morning Dante appeared in the doorway of the family parlor, which Joseph was using as his office. Joseph looked up from the writing desk and leaned back in his chair. "Come in, Dante. Hercules said you wanted to see me?"

Dante jumped into the room like he was crossing a three-foot-wide creek. "Massa, ah see dem mens dat kill Andrew. Ah see dey house."

Joseph pushed himself up and leaned on the desk. "Are you sure?" Dante repeated the events of the prior day. Joseph asked, "You're absolutely certain that's the wagon?"

"Ah suhtin, Massa. An' dems de mens. Dey call deyselbes Harole an' Sam."

Joseph ran his fingers through his hair. Harold, Sam, and Willie were the names of the three men on the wharf that night. He whispered, "Holy Mother of God." He thought that he and Charlie Lamar had driven down that street and past that house when they were searching for the murderers in the days following the act, but couldn't be sure. In any case, it didn't matter. He told Dante, "Tell Hercules to get the wagon. We're going to pay those men a visit. The third one, Willie, who fired the shot, can't be far away."

Exalted at the prospect of revenge, Dante shouted, "Yassuh, Massa!" and dashed from the room. He returned five minutes later to tell Joseph that Hercules was ready but stopped outside the door when he saw Joseph loading a revolver at his desk. Dante stood still and watched him perform the task that he hoped to do himself one day soon.

After Joseph finished, he looked up and saw the negro staring at him. "Yes, Dante?"

"De wagon ready, Massa."

Joseph shoved the gun in his holster, grabbed a crutch, and headed out the front door. He tossed the crutch into the bed and hopped up, squeezing Dante between him and Hercules. They moved ten yards when distant, unmistakable explosions engulfed the air. Joseph held up his hand and said, "Do you hear that?"

Hercules said, "Yes, sir. Someone is shootin' mighty big guns."

Every white person and many of the blacks in Savannah knew that a federal fleet of about seventy ships had gathered along the coast between South Carolina and Georgia in recent days. Military authorities had heard that the Yankees planned to strike the rebel fortifications on Hilton Head and take control of the island and Port Royal Sound. Those explosions could only mean that the attack had begun and Joseph would soon be ordered to Fort Pulaski. He had no time to lose. "Let's get going."

Hercules snapped the reins. They went only a few more streets when a soldier on horseback galloped up to them. "Lieutenant McBain! Union ships are bombing our forts on Hilton Head. Commodore Tattnall thinks they'll come up the Savannah River next. Captain Sims wants you at the wharf in an hour to take the *Ida* to Fort Pulaski."

Joseph cursed, "Damnation!" He took a deep breath and said, "Thank you, Corporal. I'll be there in an hour." The soldier charged off. As they rode back to the house, Joseph told Hercules and Dante, "We'll have to wait until I return."

Hercules replied, "Yes, Master Joseph," as Dante groaned.

The sound of "THUD, THUD, THUD," vibrated through the men's bodies. Joseph said, "Dante, thank you for finding those men. I promise you both, they'll pay for Andrew. But while I'm gone, Dante, don't do anything stupid. Do you understand me?" Dante nodded slowly, without conviction. Joseph said to Hercules. "I'll be back in a few minutes." He climbed down from the wagon, took his crutch, and hobbled to the house.

❧

Those explosions on the morning of November 7 could also be heard at the Heritage. James McBain had been talking to his black overseer, Isaac, near the kiln when Jehova, an eighteen-year-old, ran up to them. McBain liked the boy and thought he could be a driver of a gang once he gained some maturity. "I don't like the look on your face, Jehova. What's wrong?"

The young negro glanced over his shoulder towards the avenue of oaks, the tree-lined road that connected the plantation to the Augusta Road. Then he asked, "Massa, kin ah speaks wid you?"

McBain looked at Isaac before responding. "You're speaking with me now."

"Yassuh, Massa. 'Member dat pass you gib me two day ago?"

James folded his arms across his chest, preparing himself for some unwelcome news. "Of course. Why?" Masters often allowed their slaves to visit relatives and friends on nearby plantations during their free time, usually on Saturday evenings and Sundays, by signing passes that allowed blacks to travel on the roads after dark. The "patrol," a group of local white men, policed the area at night, looking for runaways and troublemakers. Any negro caught without a pass received a sound whipping followed by an escort home.

"Ah go tuh visit a gu'l at Brampton plantation yestiddy ebnin, an' Massa Wul-lieson come up behind me an' grab me an' say he gwine tuh whup me fuh bein' dere. Ah tell he dat ah ain' doin' nuttin', and he say dat's why he gwine tuh whup me, cause ah should be back here, doin' sumptin'. He pull he whip, an' ah runs fuh home, tru de woods. He come aftuh me, screamin' dat he gwine tuh whup muh black arse, but he trip in a gully an fall on he face an' cry out, 'Good Lawdy!'" Al-though any potential conflict with a neighbor had to be taken seriously, McBain had to run his hand over his face to stop from laughing. "Den he yell, 'Ah git you tuhmorruh, you damned nigguh!' Dat's wut ah got tuh say, Massa."

The three men turned toward the sound of a gig bumping down the feeder road from the avenue of oaks. The vehicle skidded to a stop, shooting up dirt, and causing the horse to neigh. Patrick Williamson grabbed a whip, jumped off, and stomped over to McBain. He saw Jehova and shouted, "You!"

James said, "Good morning, Mr. Williamson. You look upset."

"You're darned right, Mr. McBain, pardon my language. I'm upset because of this darkey of yours!" Williamson then recounted his version of the story, which essentially matched Jehova's. "I aimed to whip him last night, and failing because of his rascality, I'm going to do it right now." Williamson uncoiled the whip with the shake of his hand.

McBain stepped in front of Jehova. "I'm sorry, Mr. Williamson, but you're not going to do anything of the kind. You had an opportunity last night on your land. Had you whipped him then, I would have judged your actions and, if I had objected, spoken to you. But you didn't, and now that he's on my land, you have no right to touch him. You know that. To put your mind at ease, I will make sure that he doesn't visit your plantation again." McBain turned to Jehova and noticed that every slave working at the kiln was looking at them. McBain refocused on Williamson. "Will that be all, sir?"

Williamson trembled with anger. "Mr. McBain, I'll . . . ."

"BOOM … BOOM … BOOM" shook the air. All heads turned east. Both men knew the source of the noise. They had been expecting it for days.

Williamson said. "I believe the attack has started, Mr. McBain."

"Yes, I guess it has. The war is on our doorstep, not just in far-away Virginia."

Williamson glared one last time at Jehova and said, "I'd best be going. If you hear any news, please let me know. I'll do the same."

The two men, at odds a moment ago, but now drawn together by a larger, shared problem, shook hands. Williamson boarded his gig and left as quickly as he had arrived.

James McBain closed his eyes and prayed for the rebel forces to repel the in-vaders. He knew that Joseph would be called to Fort Pulaski and wanted to return to Savannah before his son left. He then scolded Jehova. "Get back to work. And don't ever visit Brampton again."

The boy muttered, "Yassuh, Massa," and ran to the kiln.

With the sound of artillery fire blanketing the river basin, McBain asked Isaac, "When will the brick burn be finished?"

"She peaks tomorrow night. Then we'll start bringing her down. Two or three days after that."

McBain stood closer to Isaac. "Good. I have to go into town for a day or two. Keep a close eye on things. Tell everyone that there's nothing to worry about. They'll be safe here. Make sure that they understand I'll protect them from the Yankees."

Isaac glanced at the slaves working at the kiln and assured McBain, "No need to worry, Massa. You can depend on me."

McBain patted Isaac on the shoulder. He knew that he took a gamble years before when he selected a black man to be his overseer. Only a few planters did— mainly to save the salary of a white overseer. But Isaac knew more about brick production than any white man and, as McBain had no white candidates to replace the previous overseer, he took a chance, hoping that Isaac's religious bent would ensure his loyalty. In fact, as the plantation minister, Isaac had always been accepted by the other slaves as their leader and followed his orders. On Sundays his deep baritone voice hammered the word of God into their souls. Isaac's physical presence added to his stature. He stood five-feet, six-inches tall with a body shaped like a tree trunk and just as solid. He had a full, snow-white head of hair in the shape of an inverted bowl, and a neatly trimmed, white beard and moustache. McBain once overheard Jehova say about Isaac, "De Lawd hese'p don' look no bettuh." Now McBain wondered if Isaac would be able to calm the slaves and squelch any notions of freedom they might have if the Union attack proved successful.

⸙

When James returned to Savannah that afternoon, he learned from a neighbor that the Yankees had chased away the rebel defenders and controlled Hilton Head Island and Port Royal Sound. He also found out from a frowning Danny that Joseph had already departed for Fort Pulaski. To lift the boy's spirits, Chloe, one of the house servants, came by, put him on her shoulders, and paraded up and down the hall while Danny shot an imaginary gun. James retired to the library and poured himself a small shot of whiskey.

That evening he explained the situation to Sarah as she walked in the door from volunteering at the Savannah Poor House and Hospital. "This certainly is distressing news," he said. "Now we have to wait to see how our military and fellow citizens react to our new vulnerability."

The next day James watched in shock as many neighbors packed their belongings and headed with their slaves to towns in the interior. It wasn't a full-scale panic, but the fleeing wagons clogged enough streets to qualify as a small stampede. That evening, as James told Sarah about his day, they heard a knock at the front door. Seconds later their butler William stuck his head in James's study. "Master Lamar here to see you, sir."

James said, "Show him in."

James and Sarah greeted Gazaway Lamar, and then Sarah excused herself to get ready for supper. Lamar was one of the most successful businessmen in Georgia, making his mark in shipping, banking, insurance, and trading cotton. He had lived in New York from 1846 to 1861 while he served as president of a bank and traded cotton. After the war broke out he moved back to Savannah, became the president of a local bank, and did all in his power to help the new Confederacy.

James poured a snifter of brandy for his guest and they sat. Lamar said, "Terrible situation, this. We had no defense against the Yankee ships. And now they're lodged on our coast, but that's as far as they'll get. We may not be able to match the firepower of their navy, but at some point they'll have to venture onto our soil, and when they do, they'll re-learn the lessons of Manassas."

McBain shook his head. "Gazaway, I'm afraid most people here don't share your view. I already know men who are sending their families inland, afraid that Savannah will be attacked next. I'm thinking of sending Mrs. McBain and my grandson to stay with her sister in Roswell, outside of Atlanta, until things are safe again. This town has changed in the past two days. The excitement of those rallies after Lincoln's election and secession, the cheering as our boys marched off to war, the celebrating after Manassas, they're all gone. I feel it walking in the streets, talking to merchants and bankers. Few of us thought that the Yankees could get this close to here. Now, three months after Manassas, they're in a position to blockade and attack us."

Lamar sipped his drink. McBain's concerns didn't dampen his optimism. "England and France won't tolerate the shortage of cotton and will join us. The Yankees will run like dogs back to their borders."

James refilled Lamar's glass. "Until that happens, if it ever does, we have to be able to circumvent the blockade. Edward Anderson's mission will be a good test."

Lamar nodded. "Yes, and it had better be successful. We need those guns."

Just weeks after the attack on Fort Sumter, the Confederate government sent Major Edward C. Anderson, a forty-six-year-old army officer and Savannah native on a secret mission to England. While there, he received instructions to purchase much-needed arms for the Confederacy. Using funds sent to him by the secretary of war and Georgia Governor Joseph Brown, Anderson bought eleven thousand Enfield rifles, other armaments and munitions, and a ship, the *Fingal*, to transport them back home. Union agents, aware of the mission, tried unsuccessfully to bribe British officials to deny the *Fingal* customs clearance. The vessel, masquerading as a merchant ship, departed in mid-October for Georgia and stopped at Bermuda to take on coal and water. On November 7 the vessel secretly sailed out of Bermuda harbor, unaware that Union warships were bombarding Confederate positions in Port Royal Sound and would soon have complete control of the coastline to which they were steaming.

Lamar said, "James, let me tell you why I stopped by. I just left Mayor Holcombe's office. He informed me that the new commander for the Department of the South, General Robert E. Lee, has arrived. He set up his headquarters at Coosawhatchie, on the rail road line, to have access to both Savannah and Charleston. He's in town tonight and is going to Fort Pulaski tomorrow to make an inspection. The mayor is certain that Lee will want to know about the availability of bricks and lumber to strengthen the fort and would like you to accompany the party. Are you free?"

"Yes, Gazaway, I'll be honored to meet the new general," James said, knowing that it would be an excellent opportunity to see Joseph. "Have you met him yet?"

Lamar shook his head. "I'm not excited about West Pointers. Give me a hardened soldier who learned to be a leader by fighting Indians and Mexicans. Besides, Lee was recently defeated by the Yankees at Cheat Mountain in western Virginia. I think Richmond could have served us better with another man."

James replied, "I must disagree, Gaz. He performed valiantly in Mexico and he captured John Brown at Harpers Ferry. I don't need to remind you that Lincoln wanted him to take command of the federal army. He's an excellent engineer—just what we need to strengthen our forts and batteries. He served here thirty years ago on the construction of Fort Pulaski. He knows the area."

Lamar shrugged, unconvinced. "Perhaps, but he's still a West Pointer. Too much time in the classroom. I'll see you tomorrow at seven-thirty at the *Ida*." The two men shook hands and Gazaway left. James drained his brandy and realized that he'd better start planning his course of action in case the Yankees attacked Savannah. ✑

CHAPTER SEVEN

❧

"They Cannot Breach Your Walls"

November 9, 1861

The early November morning sunlight barely began to illuminate the study when Danny charged in wearing a dark blue jacket, white shirt, and light brown breeches, and carrying a black and yellow wooden rifle in his hands. "What are you doing, Grandpa?"

McBain looked up from his desk and laughed at the little soldier. "Work, so I can go to Fort Pulaski today with the new general."

The rifle hit the floor. "You're gonna see Pa? Can I come, please, please?"

"I'm sorry, Danny. This is official business." Danny stomped the floor and scrunched up his lips. James hated to disappoint his grandson. "Would you like to come with me to the boat before you go to school? Maybe you can see the general."

The boy jumped in the air. "Yes, sir!" He picked up his rifle, laid it across his shoulder, stood ramrod straight, and marched in place—stopping only to scratch an itch on his bottom.

McBain pulled a watch out of his vest pocket. "All right, soldier. I'll get my jacket and we'll be on our way in five minutes."

Danny almost fell over performing an about-face, and marched from the room, his right arm swinging to and fro.

❧

Dante held the heavy pistol in both hands as he closed his left eye and aimed at the wall in his room. He pulled back the hammer with his thumb to half-cock, held his breath, set the hammer to full-cock, and slowly tugged the trigger with his index finger. "Click!" He exhaled and smiled at the sound. Dante had evaluated the situation as he lay in bed the previous night and made up his mind to take care of Andrew's killers before they disappeared again. First he had to load the weapon as he saw Joseph do it a few days earlier and as had been explained to him by the seller. It seemed complicated but he had no choice if he were to fulfill his mission.

Dante sat on the bed, put the case between his legs, and removed the contents. He pulled the gun's hammer to half-cock, held the weapon by the barrel, and rested the grip on the case. After taking a deep breath, the slave inserted the thin nozzle of the brass powder flask into one of the six chambers and depressed the lever on the neck until the chamber was three-quarters full. A loud noise from the driveway caused him to jerk up and almost drop the flask. Dante waited a minute, wiped his brow with the back of his hand, turned the cylinder with his thumb, and repeated the process for each chamber. He took a metal ball from a pouch, placed it on the mouth of an open chamber, and turned the cylinder with his thumb until the ball lined up with the loading rammer underneath the barrel. A strong pull on the rammer squeezed the ball into the chamber. Dante returned the loading lever to its original position, turned the cylinder with his thumb, and repeated the process until the revolver was fully loaded.

The negro gently released the hammer and brought the weapon a few inches from his face to examine the shiny, nine-inch-long barrel. Dante felt like his muscles had doubled in size. He closed his eyes and imagined the look on the faces of Harold and Sam when they saw him and his gun. He then counted out six percussion caps and put them in his pocket.

Dante donned a two-sizes-too-big frock coat that Master Joseph had handed down to him ten years before and stuck the gun in the inside pocket. If he were caught with it, he would say that he had just found it in an alley and was returning it to Massa. He pulled his cap low to hide his face and walked from his room, down the driveway, and onto Macon Street. He planned to go to the killers' backyard, announce to Harold that he was sorry he threw horse dung in his face, and, when they came after him, he would complete the deed. Then he wondered—what if he fired and missed and they pulled guns? His head began to spin.

"Dante!" The negro nearly jumped out of his shoes. Massa McBain and Danny were sitting in the family gig on the street. He thought about the weapon he was carrying and tried to swallow, but couldn't.

Massa said, "Didn't mean to scare you. Hop on. I need you for an hour or two. Hercules went to the Heritage and Jefferson and Barney are in town."

Danny clapped his hands at seeing the servant. The two had a mutual affection for each other and often played quoits and town ball with Truvy in Pulaski Square. Dante hoisted himself onto the gig. McBain said, "You look like a buck coming face-to-face with a shotgun."

Danny swiveled closer to his grandfather and sang, "Hi, Dante!"

"Hey, Massa Danny."

McBain told Dante, "I'm going to Fort Pulaski for the day. I'm bringing Danny to the wharf to meet the new general. After I leave I want you to drive him to school and then bring the gig back to the house. Hercules will pick me up later."

"Yassuh, Massa." Dante turned away and watched the sandy street roll by with a ringing in his head. If he were caught with a gun near a general, he would be hanged on the spot.

Danny said, "Dante, what's that in your pocket sticking into my side?"

Dante jerked up, raised his backside off the seat, wrapped the frock tighter about him, and inched away from Danny, not daring to catch Massa's eye. "T'ain' nuttin'. Jes' uh hammuh. Bin wukin' in de coach house."

Fortunately, Massa drove on, unaware of the beads of sweat running down Dante's cheeks. Fifteen minutes later he pulled up to the foot of the wharf where the steam tug *Ida* was docked. McBain told Dante to wait for Danny and walked with the boy towards a group of twenty city officials, businessmen, and military officers. Dante breathed a sigh of relief as the two left the gig.

Mayor Thomas Holcombe stepped forward to welcome McBain and introduce him to General Lee, six feet tall, with thinning grey hair, and a grey beard in a grey military uniform. James had never seen a man stand so straight yet appear so relaxed. Lee's smile seemed to welcome an old friend, though they had never met. Lee had arrived at his headquarters at Coosawatchie on November 7, just as the Union guns were blasting the rebel positions in Port Royal harbor—too late to be of any help. The next day the general informed the secretary of war that the Union had complete possession of the coastal waters, inland waterways, and all the coastal islands, and threatened Charleston and Savannah. McBain felt that if anyone could save Savannah, it was General Lee.

McBain placed his hand on Danny's back and presented him to the general, who bent from the waist and offered his hand. Instead of taking it, Danny stood at attention and saluted, resting his flat, right hand on the bridge of his nose. He said, "General Lee, I want to join the army now, but my pa says I have to finish school first. That won't be until June." Danny released his salute.

The onlookers laughed as Lee straightened and returned the salute. "That's very wise of your father, Danny, but I think he meant until you finish all your school, including college."

Danny said, "General Lee, my pa is at Fort Pulaski. Please say hello to him for me. I miss him a lot."

The general stooped again and asked, "What's your father's name, Danny?"

"First Lieutenant McBain, sir."

Lee patted the boy's shoulder. "I promise, Danny. I know he misses you."

"Thank you, sir. He fought at Manassas. He's real brave. He was injured and walks with a crutch, but he can do anything he did before, just with a limp. The day before he left for Fort Pulaski, we were throwing the ball in the square when. . . ."

The *Ida*'s high-pitched whistle stopped the little chatterbox. McBain hugged the boy and pointed towards Dante. Danny ran to River Street, jumped onto the gig, and saluted the boat. When he thought his grandfather and General Lee couldn't see him, he grabbed Dante's hat from his head and waved it back and forth like a shipwrecked man who has spotted a boat on the horizon.

Dante tapped his foot at a woodpecker's pace, wanting to get away and drop off Danny so he could find Harold and Sam. "Dey gone, Massa Danny. Time fuh school." The boy sat with Dante's hat on his lap. Dante whistled as he drove up the Whitaker Street ramp and over to Bull Street. He didn't see the man in a floppy leather hat ride past him from the other direction, nor did he see the horse turn around and follow him to the Chatham Academy and then to the McBain house. Only the appearance of Jefferson and Barney in the driveway prevented Harold from exacting his revenge right then and there.

As Dante unharnessed the horse from the gig, he saw that Danny had left his hat on the seat. He put it on and left the carriage house, but could tell by the sun that he didn't have enough time to walk to the east side of town, deal with Harold and Sam, and get to work by three o'clock. He'd try again the next day. He also realized that he now had a loaded gun which he could not unload other than by firing it. He went to his room, placed the gun and caps in the case, and slid it under the bed. He felt more confident than ever that he would find and kill those men.

◦✦◦

The structure that General Lee had helped plan after he had graduated from West Point had become an impregnable, five-faced, brick bastion. A drawbridge over an encompassing moat provided entry. The rooms or casemates within the longest fort wall—known as the gorge—contained the officers' and enlisted men's quarters, kitchen, storerooms, and ammunition magazines. The casemates in the four shorter walls, two each facing the north and south channels of the Savannah River, housed the heavy guns. Perched atop the casemates on the ramparts, another tier of guns on platforms, partly shielded by the parapet, threatened to rain destruction on enemy ships entering the river.

McBain, Gazaway Lamar, the fort officers, and other invited guests followed Lee and Major Charles W. Olmstead during the inspection, which lasted five hours. The general seemed to examine every gun, brick, and blade of grass. When he looked up, everyone looked up. When he stepped forward, the entourage followed. When he stopped, they all stopped. Lee pointed and explained to Olmstead how to strengthen the fort by building traverses on the ramparts between the guns; digging long, parallel ditches on the parade ground to trap incoming, rolling cannon balls; and erecting shields of heavy timber in front of the casement entryways. After each dictate, McBain and Lamar nodded at each other, impressed by the general's engineering knowledge and thoroughness. James was able to fall back from the pack and walk with Joseph, but they had little time to chat as no one spoke when General Lee did.

At the end of the tour, Lee declared that no guns in the enemy's arsenal could breach Fort Pulaski's seven-foot-thick walls, and that the defenders were perfectly safe within them. Everyone breathed more easily. General Lee then asked to be introduced to Lieutenant McBain. Surprised at being called out, Joseph limped forward on his crutch and saluted. Lee studied Joseph's gait and inquired of the injury. Joseph explained the Eighth Georgia's role in the battle of Manassas, his wound and medical furlough, and volunteering to serve as an officer of the guard. Lee thanked Joseph for his service, and, when he spotted James standing at the back, thanked him for the sacrifice of his family. The seventy-year-old Scotsman's chest puffed up in pride, though he knew every man present who had a son of military age was making the same sacrifice. Lee told Joseph of his earlier meeting with Danny and predicted that one day the boy would be a general. Joseph told Lee that Danny believed he already was, which drew laughter from the crowd. Lee smiled and replied, "I look forward to serving under him."

During the ride back to Savannah, James McBain's spirits picked up. Fort Pulaski was declared impregnable by the best engineer in the South, perhaps in all America. The Yankees couldn't overrun it, nor could they get their ships past it to attack Savannah. He felt sure that his family and property were safe for the foreseeable future. ❧

CHAPTER EIGHT

"If Only for One Day"
November 10-14, 1861

"You awake?" Isaac called across the bedroom to Delpha, his wife of forty-six years, mother of their three grown boys, and grandmother to seven. Delpha, who as a seamstress had worked all day sewing uniforms for soldiers, yawned from her bed, "Yes."

"Hercules told me he spoke to one of the riverboat pilots in town. The Yankees captured Hilton Head a few days ago. They control the coast and already have ships at the mouth of the river."

Delpha could hardly open her eyes. "So?"

"The ocean is only eighteen miles from here by boat. We kin reach it in one night with a strong tide."

Delpha sat up. "What you sayin', Isaac?"

The overseer remained on his back, his hands folded on his chest. "I'm saying that we're only one night away from freedom."

In the darkness Delpha stepped over the cold wood floor and sat on the edge of Isaac's bed. "You mean run away? Leabe Massa?"

Most of the Heritage slaves thought Master McBain was a fair man. Although he demanded hard work, he fed, housed, and clothed them well, and, when warranted, he stood up for them against the likes of Mr. Williamson, the neighbor who wanted to punish Jehova. McBain usually took Isaac's advice regarding Heritage operations, and Isaac appreciated the trust placed in him. But Isaac was still enslaved, and no amount of good treatment could make up for the loss of freedom. He didn't think Massa or any other white man could understand that. Isaac sat against the wall. "Delpha, we're somewhere in our sixties. We been slaves all our lives. I want to be a free man, if only for one day. I want to walk roads and streets at night without a pass, to own a house, a wagon, a mule, and tools. I don't want to worry about being sold or auctioned."

"Massa don' nebuh sell us. You know dat."

"Yes, but he's gettin' old and Master Joseph don't have the same love for the plantation. He might go to New York to live with his wife and baby. If Joseph sells the place, we get a new massa who don't know or care about us."

The moonlight beamed through the window and illuminated Isaac's hair. Delpha believed that over their years together she had watched each strand turn white. She thought that people ran away because they could no longer tolerate cruel treatment, not because they yearned to be free. She also knew that they were usually caught and punished with a severe whipping. Now her husband, who had been treated kindly by McBain smelled the freedom so close to them. She had her reservations. "Us don' know what dem Yankees do wid us. Dey might make us dey own slabes. Massa say dey sells black folk tuh Cooba tuh pick suguh cane."

Isaac reached out his hand and touched his wife's arm. "If I was younger I'd wait for the Yankees to take Savannah. But if they get run off, we lose this chance."

Words escaped her. She lay back next to her husband and closed her eyes. The room started to spin. "What 'bout us boys an' dey famblies?"

"It's too dangerous to take them. Once we're free I'll come back for them." Isaac knew that over the many years of slavery in the South, most runaways were males because they were physically able to make the long, arduous, and dangerous journey to free territory. With freedom just eighteen miles away, Isaac felt confident bringing his wife in one boat, but he couldn't transport his entire family with grandchildren. That was too risky.

Delpha held her husband's hand. "When, Isaac?"

"We tell the boys tomorrow night and leave the night after. The tide starts at the right time, one o'clock. It'll carry us down the river in darkness. We're in the middle of a brick burn and there'll be activity at the kiln. We kin walk to the wharf and no one will pay us no mind. Solomon is workin' that night. We need his help."

In the distance, one of the hunting dogs started to bark, and then all the others joined in. Delpha sat up and stared at the floor. She thought of reminding her husband that she couldn't swim, but he knew that. "Ahm 'fraid, Isaac."

Isaac leaned over and hugged his wife. "The Lord will protect us. In His hands we have nothing to fear."

Delpha nodded, but she wasn't entirely convinced.

Confederate Major Edward Anderson snorted like an angry bull as he stood with his hands on his hips on the deck of the *Fingal*. He had been in England since May and had faced seemingly insurmountable obstacles raising money; procuring a ship; purchasing rifles, heavy guns, and other supplies; avoiding the surveillance of Union spies; and sailing back to Georgia. Now, shortly before midnight on November 12, not far from the Georgia coast, when he needed the pilot he had hired in Bermuda to take the ship to the Savannah River, Anderson was fit to be tied. The navigator was spread out on a chair, his head rolling over the backrest, with a bottle of liquor dangling from his hand. Anderson stomped over and, with an upward swipe of his foot, flipped the chair, and sent the man sprawling. The pilot struggled to his feet just as a wave rocked the boat, flopping him on his back. Anderson dumped a bucket of water on the drunkard, who coughed, spit, stood, and weaved to his quarters to change his clothes.

Major Anderson and Lieutenant James Bulloch had to pilot the ship themselves for the time being. Upon approaching the coast, they spotted a warship in their way, silhouetted against a full moon. Certain that it was a Union frigate acting as a blockader, Anderson gave the order to blow by it. The *Fingal* steamed up to twelve knots, and the major heard the confused yells of the Union lookouts as the rebels sped past. In a minute they had lost sight of the enemy.

At about 2 a.m. on November 13, the *Fingal* came to seven fathoms. An exhausted Anderson turned the ship over to the hung-over pilot, who promptly grounded her on the Wassaw shoals. Amid curses and threats barked by Anderson and Bulloch, the pilot backed her off and dropped anchor at seven fathoms. The men waited for daybreak and prayed that the blockader would not come searching for them.

⚬⚭⚬

The night after Isaac revealed to Delpha his plan to escape, he called his sons to the overseer's house to inform them. At first they stared blankly at their father. Kitt, at twenty-four the youngest and unmarried, said he would go with them. Isaac put his hand on the boy's shoulder, peered into his eyes, and said, "No, son. You stay put and listen to what I say." Kitt looked to his brothers for support. Getting none, he hung his head.

Noah, the middle son, knew that his father's word was final. He hugged his mother. She stepped away, wiped a tear from her cheek, and tried to light a candle. He saw her hand shake and helped her. Noah's wife, who insisted on accompanying him to this meeting, said she heard a screech owl that very evening, which meant that somebody would soon die. Noah told her to hush her mouth. Isaac laughed and said that he would shoot the bird before he left, ensuring that only it would die.

Solomon, at thirty, had inherited his father's devoutness, and, as words escaped him, clutched the Bible that he always carried. He knew that he might never see his parents again, but such was the reality of slavery. He was confident that Isaac could make the escape successfully, having met every challenge in running the Heritage for so long. He held his mother and gave her his Bible, explaining that it was her chariot to freedom.

Isaac told Solomon that he would need his help camouflaging Massa's boat with branches prior to their departure. As Solomon was the driver of the brick operation, he could easily walk to the wharf, which could not be seen from the kiln. The family knelt and held hands in prayer. Then the sons returned to their cabins.

Just before midnight on November 13, Isaac and Delpha left the overseer's house with a fishing pole and their personal belongings tied up in a blanket. They walked to the wharf and, as they passed the road to the kiln, Solomon joined them.

Delpha's stomach began to churn as she climbed down the ladder to one of McBain's smaller rowboats, ten feet long, and grabbed the side to steady herself. Solomon handed her the bundled blanket, fishing pole, and Bible, which she laid on the deck under the front bench seat. Isaac retrieved the leafy magnolia tree branches he had left near the wharf that day and handed them down to Solomon, who laid them cross-wise, leaving enough space over the two benches for humans to sit. In the moonlight, the rowboat looked like a fallen tree. Solomon hugged his mother and told her in a cracking voice that he loved her. He climbed the ladder, embraced his father, handed him a palm-sized wooden cross that he had carved that evening, and returned to the kiln. Isaac dropped the cross into his shirt pocket and patted it.

At 12:30 a.m., at the end of the incoming tide, Isaac got in the boat and rowed west. After a few minutes he spoke softly to Delpha, who was sitting on the front bench, facing him. "Noise carries over water, so always whisper. I'm rowing to the creek that cuts between Argyle and Hutchinson islands to get to the back river. Few folks live on that side and we can't be seen from Savannah or Fort Jackson. We should get to the ocean no later than daybreak. Union ships there will pick us up."

Despite the moderate temperature, Delpha shivered. She picked up Solomon's Bible and held it to her chest. She looked up at the full, silver moon, with wisps of clouds floating by, and thought she had never seen a night so beautiful. She began to relax, closed her eyes, and breathed in the pungent odor of the loamy marsh. Isaac continued, "If I see a boat, I'll pull in the oars and we'll lie under the branches. The tide will pull us."

Delpha hummed, "Yes, Jesus Loves Me."

They reached the north channel at the start of the outgoing tide which ran at three knots. They passed Hutchinson Island and the harbor by 2:30 a.m., and Smith's Island and Fort Jackson by three. Isaac pulled in the oars and rested for a few minutes, having negotiated the most dangerous part of the journey. He closed his eyes and started to thank God when Delpha hissed, "Isaac! In back of you!" He turned and saw a ship just yards away. He grabbed the oars and pulled furiously with the right to steer towards the south channel. Their boat swung within feet of the ship before skidding away. Isaac prayed that sentries hadn't seen or heard him. When they reached the south channel Delpha crawled under the branches and lay on the deck, breathing its fishy smell and praying for the journey's end.

Isaac had heard of the Mosquito Fleet, the small navy of four converted river steamers and steam tugs, each with one or two mounted field artillery pieces, charged with defending the coast and Savannah River against the mighty Union navy. He never considered that it would be patrolling the river that night. After a short rest he retook the oars and passed Elba Island by four o'clock. He steered back towards the north channel but spotted a ship bobbing in the water between Elba and Bird islands and returned to the south channel. He maintained his course past Long and Cockspur islands.

He took out an old pocket watch that Massa had given him. It was 6:30 a.m. The first glimmer of dawn allowed Isaac to see the outline of Fort Pulaski. He pulled in the oars and spread some branches over him. The tide still ran strong enough to sweep the boat past the fort. He whispered under the branches to Delpha, "We're almost there." She squeezed his ankle.

☙

Edward Anderson's heart did not leave his throat for the three hours since the *Fingal* dropped anchor. None of the crew spoke while they waited for the first fan of sunlight to paint the horizon orange. Once the ruffles of the ocean became visible, Anderson told Bulloch, "Apparently, they don't know we're here."

No sooner had Anderson uttered those words than a cock in the chicken coop below started crowing, splitting the early morning calm. Bulloch darted below. A minute later Anderson heard a chorus of clucking, then solitude. Bulloch reappeared, wiping his hands on his trousers. "We won't be hearing from him again."

Anderson scanned the ocean with his field glass. "Lieutenant, we're about two miles south of Tybee Island. There's a Yankee warship about three miles to the northeast, and several others beyond it. It looks like they have control of the entire coast."

"Should we try to get in through Wassaw Sound?"

"No. With a good start, we can beat the closest ship to the entrance of the river, where we'll get cover from the fort. But we have to go in right now before they spot us. Don't raise our colors yet."

Before Bulloch could answer, another cock crowed. He snarled through clenched teeth and returned below. He soon reappeared with three crewmen, two each holding the handles of the cage filled with vocal birds. They hauled it to the side of the ship, and flung it overboard. It hit the water with a splash, and in seconds the crowing stopped. The men wouldn't be eating again on the ship in any case. Their next meal would be as heroes in Savannah, prisoners of the Union navy, or residents in heaven.

Anderson gave the order to build steam. The engine roared and the ship chugged for the south channel of the Savannah River. He alternated his field glass between the Union warship and Tybee Island, bending and straightening his knees as if riding a horse, trying to help the ship go faster. He said, "Lieutenant Bulloch, I don't see the range beacon on the Tybee tower or any sign of life. And that warship is getting up. The Yankees might have taken Tybee. This could be a trap!" As the *Fingal* reached top speed and rounded Tybee, Fort Pulaski came into view.

With the number of Union ships outside the mouth of the river increasing daily, Joseph manned his post at the first ray of daylight. In the early morning of November 13, he stood on the ramparts and gripped his field glass. He ordered a private standing nearby, "Get Colonel Olmstead—quickly!"

Moments later Charles Olmstead—who'd been elected to the new rank that month—appeared, buttoning his shirt. He asked, "What is it, Lieutenant?"

Without taking the glass from his eye, Joseph pointed to the southeast. "There's a ship rounding Tybee, steaming towards us. She's not flying any colors. There's a Union warship a mile to the north, also coming this way. Should we give cover to the first one?"

Olmstead hoisted his field glass and studied the ships. "Not yet. Let's make sure she's not the enemy." He then called out, "Artillery units Alexandra and Julia, prepare to fire on that ship heading towards us from the south."

The tide carried the rowboat down the river. Isaac stuck his head through the branches, peered over the side of the boat, and saw that they had cleared Cockspur Island and were in the mouth of the river. He looked to the north and saw a ship about a mile away, coming towards them. He felt goose bumps all over his body. "Delpha, we're almost at the ocean. I see a ship! I'm getting rid of these branches. Pick up that fishing pole and cast it in the water. If anyone sees us we're just two niggers fishing."

Delpha gasped, "Isaac, please pray for us."

"We're in His hands. He will deliver us."

Anderson decided to make the *Fingal*'s identity known before the fort mistook her for the enemy. "Lieutenant Bulloch, raise the Confederate flag at the main!"

Isaac grabbed the oars, and set them in the oarlocks. Delpha fumbled with the fishing pole, which got snagged under the rower's bench. Isaac turned to gauge his position and point the boat to the north. He froze as he saw another ship from the south, only twenty-five yards away, under steam, heading right at him. He started to row, looked up again, and realized that he could not get out of the ship's path. He turned towards his wife, who was still pulling at the fishing pole. He started to tell her that he loved her.

✺

As the men raised the flag on the *Fingal*, the lookout on the bow shouted, "Large tree floating twenty yards ahead! Jesus! It's a rowboat with people in it!"

Anderson looked to the fore, but couldn't see anything, and said to himself, "Too late now!" He heard a thud and fell forward onto the deck.

✺

Joseph pressed the field glass against his eye. "Colonel, the first ship just hoisted the Confederate flag. Don't fire!"

Olmstead hollered, "Artillery units, hold your fire!"

Joseph saw a patch of tree debris in the path of the incoming steamer. Then he saw branches fly off, exposing a small rowboat. A man sat up and started rowing. The first oar had hardly touched the water when the ship smashed into it, shattering the skiff into pieces and sending the rower flying. Joseph returned his focus to the ship.

✺

The *Fingal* entered the south channel and promptly grounded near Fort Pulaski trying to avoid one of the recently sunk pilings meant to deter Yankee boats. They were sitting ducks for the Union warship which had just reached the mouth of the river. But as if God had been looking over them, a fog bank rolled in and blocked the view of the *Fingal* from the ocean. The warship floated in place, while the crew waited for the fog to lift. Realizing the ship had entered the range of the fort's guns, the Yankees turned back.

Anderson took a lifeboat to the fort, where he received salutes and handshakes from the fort's officers. He sent a telegraph to the commander of the forces in Savannah, advising him of his arrival. When the tide came in and raised the ship, Anderson continued the *Fingal*'s journey to Savannah harbor, where practically every man, woman, and child lined River Street, waving Confederate flags and cheering the crew.

Joseph had to remain at his post and could not personally welcome Anderson. As he scanned the area, he noticed debris washing up on Kings Landing, the closest point on Tybee Island to the fort, and thought he saw a body floating amongst it. He ordered four privates to row to Tybee and investigate. Two hours later the soldiers laid two bodies on the south wharf, where Joseph met them. One private said, "We found these two darkies, Lieutenant. Must have drowned fishing."

Joseph stared at the bodies to make sure, but the man's hair and beard were unmistakable. He dropped his crutch and eased to one knee between the corpses. He gently moved Isaac's head so it would look up, but it rolled back, the neck broken. Joseph had to steady himself. He whispered, "Why, Isaac? Why? You were part of our family." The privates stared at each other, puzzled by Lieutenant McBain's fascination with two dead slaves. Joseph pulled down Delpha's brown dress from around her waist to cover her legs so she could sleep in dignity. He touched her face with his fingertips and whispered, "My poor, dear Delpha."

A tiny crab crawled towards Delpha's head. Joseph swatted it. He stood and said to the privates, "I'll have the doctor dress the bodies and prepare them for shipment this afternoon. Place them in the shade of the fort walls and guard them against buzzards or any other vermin until the doctor gets here. I don't want as much as a fly touching them. I have to send a telegram." The privates saluted Joseph as he walked away.

⚜

Savannah harbor grew larger as the *Ida* approached later that afternoon. The crowds that greeted the *Fingal* had long since disappeared. Joseph spotted his father standing on the wharf and was relieved to see that he had received his message. After docking, the two men stood aside for Hercules and Jefferson to carry the bodies from the *Ida* to McBain's flatboat. Hercules froze at the sight of his long-time friends. He looked at McBain, who merely shook his head. The two blacks carried away the bodies.

James whispered to Joseph, "Of all people, why Isaac? Along with Hercules, he was my most loyal man. I knew him my entire life. We grew up together. I had always taken care of him."

Joseph put his arm around the shoulders of his shaken father. He thought about an argument he had with his wife Emily when she lived in Savannah. She had maintained that slaves detested their bondage, no matter how appreciative they appeared to their white masters. She claimed that blacks developed two personalities, a false one to deal with whites and the true one for other blacks. Whites saw only the mask and never learned the real feelings of their slaves; she insisted that was even the case with Joseph's best friend Andrew. Joseph challenged Emily, but like all their conversations about slavery, he got nowhere. Now, standing on the wharf after delivering the bodies of Isaac and Delpha, he had to acknowledge that there must be some truth in what she said, as much as it pained him. "It's as big a riddle to me, Father. Are you going to allow a funeral, knowing that Isaac and Delpha tried to escape?"

James sighed as he considered the question. "Isaac made a mistake. After a lifetime of faithful service, he and Delpha deserve a proper negro funeral. I can't deny their sons that. Maybe it will be a lesson that running away has fatal consequences."

"What's next, father? Will others try to run? Is our peculiar institution so fragile that when Yankees are within earshot, our negroes will risk their lives to reach them?"

James lowered his head and spoke softly to his son, hiding his words from Hercules and Jehova. "We are in the middle of a war, Joseph, a very costly and bloody war with no end in sight. We must protect our assets and our way of life. I will send as many negroes as possible up the river to our pine forests, far from the Yankees. I will hire a new overseer—a white man—as soon as I can. And I will count the days until you return to run things." James placed his hand on his son's shoulder. "I need you here, Joseph. I'm tired."

Hercules called out, "All set, Massa." James shook his son's hand and walked to the flatboat. Joseph watched as they pushed away from the wharf and thought about how all the people that he loved, white and black, kept leaving him.

The three sons stared in shock at their parents lying on the Heritage wharf. They kneeled, rested their heads on the bodies, and sobbed. McBain stepped back to let the men grieve. He guessed that they knew of the escape attempt, but couldn't punish them after their loss. He gave them a few minutes before explaining, "Your parents tried to run away in one of the rowboats. At the mouth of the river a steamer crashed into them. They died instantly. Joseph was on guard duty at Fort Pulaski at the time and had the bodies recovered. I'll have them taken to the hospital where you can sit with them. You may have a funeral tomorrow night."

The boys embraced each other and James left.

James McBain stood on the small wooden platform at the front of the plantation chapel that Isaac had built and looked out at a sea of black faces, his extended family. Despite the cool November temperature, most of the slaves who packed the chapel held handkerchiefs to wipe the sweat from their brows. He heard muffled sobs, but no talking. Funerals for plantation slaves were normally held at night so the negroes wouldn't miss a day's work. And while slaves wanted to have the massa or a white minister present at their weddings, they preferred to bury their dead by themselves.

James started the ceremony by reading the Lord's Prayer above the wailing of several women. He told Isaac's family how much he appreciated the years of service that Isaac had given him, not only as a master brick maker and overseer, but also as the plantation minister. He recounted how Amy and Joseph as children rushed through supper so they could visit Delpha, who would fry apples for them in her cabin. He spoke of the many times the overseer taught Joseph and Andrew how to make and lay bricks. He felt relieved that Isaac's son, Solomon, had heard God's calling and would take over the plantation ministry. He concluded by saying, "Isaac and Delpha were good people who made a tragic mistake. They are now in the merciful hands of the Lord. We will miss them, even though they are in a better place. I want all of you to know that you are safe here. I have always provided for you and always will. I will never let the Yankees steal and abuse you."

McBain closed his Bible, stepped over to the two pine caskets at the side of the platform, laid a hand on each one, and said, "Isaac and Delpha, may you rest in peace." He turned to Solomon sitting on the front bench and said, "You may continue the service now." McBain then walked down the narrow aisle, out the door, and to the big house.

McBain stood on the end of the piazza and watched his plantation servants, almost one hundred seventy of them, walk in procession from the chapel to the negro cemetery, holding lanterns to light their way. In the distance, they looked like a giant, glowing snake. He thought of what lay ahead—hiring an overseer; moving Sarah and Danny to Roswell; sending workers to his pine forests up the river; and supporting the war effort. A sudden wave of exhaustion flowed over him and he leaned against a column for support. In the distance he heard the negroes singing.

> *O Lord, O Lord, what shall I do? Trouble done bore me down*
> *O Lord, O Lord, what shall I do? Trouble done bore me down*
> *He's gone on high to prepare a place. Trouble done bore me down*
> *For to prepare a place for me and you. Trouble done bore me down*
> *O Lord, O Lord, have mercy on me. Trouble done bore me down*
> *O Lord, O Lord, have mercy on me. Trouble done bore me down*

James wondered if they might also be singing for him. ⌘

CHAPTER NINE

"Dis Chile Will Receeb Him Lubingly"
November 1861 – January 1862

James McBain ground his teeth as he read in the *Savannah Morning News* that Lincoln's navy had arrested two Confederate diplomats on November 8 as they sailed to England on a British mail steamer. He thought about tossing the paper on the coach seat when an item caught his eye.

$500 Reward – Rund away from me on de 7th of dis month, my massa Julian Rhett. Massa Rhett am five feet 'leben inches big, big shoulders, brack har, curly shaggy whiskers, low forehead, an' dark face. He make big fuss, when he go 'mong gemmen, he talk var big, and use de name ob de Lawd all de time. Calls heself "Suddun gemmen," but I suppose will try now to pass heself off as mulatto. Massa Rhett hab a deep scar on his right shoulder from a fight, scratch 'cross de lef eye, made by my Dinah when he try to whip her. I 'speck he will make track for Bergen kounty in de furrin land ob Jersey whar I 'magin he hab a few friends.
I will gib four hundred dollars for him alibe, an fi' hundred if any body show him dead. If he cum back to his kind niggers without much trouble, dis chile will receeb him lubingly.
    —Sambo Rhett Beaufort, S. C., Nov. 9, 1861.

The newspaper had reprinted a northern satire of the advertisements run by Southerners for runaway slaves. McBain felt the heat rising in his face. The high-handed Northerners who had profited so much from the products grown by slaves and the illegal slave trade had a grand time mocking the planters. He crumpled the paper and threw it against the cab wall. He took a deep breath and tried to calm down for his meeting.

The coach pulled up to the Savannah, Albany and Gulf Railroad depot on the east side of town. McBain exited the cab before Hercules had a chance to open the door and coughed from the smell of the thick smoke from a wood-burning locomotive. He saw a wiry man in his forties in a baggy suit with stringy black hair parted in the middle and a drooping moustache which looked like a piece of black rope glued to his upper lip. McBain approached him. "Mr. Donnelly?"

The stranger turned around and faced the chin of a man wearing a top hat with silver hair flowing to his shoulders. He looked up. "Mr. McBain?"

James shook his hand and thought he was gripping a piece of iron. "Yes. I'm glad you could make it on such short notice." He pointed to the negro in a coach-man's outfit holding the door to the shiny black coach with yellow spoke wheels. "You had a good trip, I trust?"

Robert Donnelly climbed into the cab with beige, cloth-lined walls, and sat on the soft, dark-brown leather seats. "Yes, sir. I wonder how we got along before the railroad."

McBain sat across from him. As the coach bucked forward, he got down to business. "I understand you worked for Mr. Prince on St. Simons Island?"

"Yes, for five years. He moved to his plantation near Thomasville after the Yankees took Hilton Head. He already had an overseer there. I since moved back to Macon, my hometown."

McBain nodded. "Let me tell you something about the Heritage. I make bricks—probably more than any operation in the entire state. I also have a lum-ber mill and an iron forge. Between these operations, the supporting functions, the house servants, and those too old or too young to work, I have one hundred seventy negroes. I took a risk about twenty years ago by making my best man the overseer. It worked well until the Yankees came and he betrayed me—ran away and drowned in the process." James gazed out the window and thought of Isaac lying lifeless on the wharf and wondered why.

Donnelly twirled one end of his moustache. He sensed McBain's disappoint-ment in his overseer. After an uneasy pause, he said, "That's a good size planta-tion, sir. How many drivers do you have?" Drivers—usually slaves—supervised gangs of workers for the overseer and received extra rations for the increased responsibility.

"One for each operation, three in all, but as there's so little iron available, I'll be shutting down the forge. I have good men who keep things moving along. They work hard and know their jobs. Some do have the negro tendency to be lazy, but only need to be told to speed up." McBain leaned closer to Donnelly and spoke softly. "With few exceptions, I've known my negroes for their entire lives. I grew up with the older ones. I presided over their marriages. My wife named many of their children and personally tended to their sick babies. I treat them well. I use the task system. Daily work allotments are assigned, and once they're completed, the men are free to pursue other interests for the rest of the day. They can trap, fish, or tend to their vegetable gardens. They can sell the produce they grow at the market in town. They work until one o'clock on Saturday and are free on the Sabbath. They have Christmas week off. I provide generous rations and furnish clothing twice a year. I sign passes so they can visit friends on nearby plantations. Nothing works better for control than granting these privileges."

Donnelly nodded. "I understand, sir, but I imagine there are times when you have to use some form of punishment."

McBain knew a good overseer would raise that issue. "On a plantation this size, a few will manage to find trouble. I use several methods of discipline. As a first measure I take away one of their privileges—I refuse to give them passes. If that doesn't work, I don't let them sell their produce. These usually solve the problem. However, if their behavior is particularly objectionable—like fighting or refusing to follow instructions—harsher measures are necessary. You are authorized to apply up to twelve lashes, but you mustn't cut the skin. If the problem persists, I will sell him or her, even at a loss. If he's married and has a family, I'll sell the whole family. I haven't had to do that in ten or fifteen years, but bad attitudes can be infectious."

Donnelly nodded again. "I agree, sir."

The men chatted about common acquaintances on St. Simons Island and in Macon and Mr. Donnelly proudly talked about his wife and three girls, ages six-, five-, and four-years, who were living in Macon with his wife's family while he tried to find work. Before McBain knew it, the coach turned from the Augusta Road onto the Heritage's avenue of oaks, the shady, oak-tree-lined drive that cut through the plantation. The coach bumped past the wheat and corn fields at the front part of the plantation, and Donnelly gazed at turbaned women in plain black dresses bent over, clearing the field of dead corn stalks. Next, they rode through the Quarter where the slaves lived in white-washed brick cabins laid out in squares, three to a side, with a large, shared backyard. McBain said in a low voice, "These are troubled times. The Yankees are on our doorstep, and the negroes know it. I don't want them to get false notions of freedom. It's for their own good."

They passed between the two-story brick overseer's house and the plantation hospital. Four white-haired men sat and chatted in front of the hospital, while two others caned chair seats. Several grey-haired women held babies in their laps, while young children laughed and kicked up dirt during a game of tag. McBain explained, "Those too old to work mind the young children of the others."

They approached the big house, an elevated, two-story, white-stucco Greek Revival mansion with dual elliptical front stairs, sitting in the middle of a one-acre, landscaped lot, and surrounded by a white wooden fence. They bore left on the road that split, encircled the house, and joined again at the back side. The coach followed the road in the direction of the river and McBain identified for Donnelly the out-buildings flanking both sides: the brick, white-washed kitchen, dairy house, ice house, and laundry, and the wooden smokehouse and granary. The stables and corral could be reached by taking a feeder road on the right for one hundred yards.

Hercules turned left on a road that led to the brick-making operation and stopped at the molding tables. The men exited and McBain said hello to the twenty workers. With a wave of his hand, he explained the process to Donnelly. He told a story about how he and the men had overcome the 1854 hurricane and yellow fever epidemic to produce a record number of bricks. He grinned, slapped the back of one of the negroes standing nearby, and said, "Isn't that right, Sammy?"

The bald, slightly hunchbacked negro with a stubbled beard, nodded. "Yas-suh, Massa. Ah sholy 'member dat!" Donnelly couldn't help but smile at McBain's pride in his plantation.

Donnelly volunteered to make a raw brick. He handed McBain his jacket, rolled up his sleeves, and stepped to the nearest table. Two men moved aside. Donnelly said to the man on his left, "What's your name?"

"Roman, Massa."

McBain broke in. "Roman is one of our best molders. He's been at it for thirty years and can do it with his eyes closed."

Donnelly laughed. "All right, Roman, go ahead, slowly, and I'll follow you."

Roman grabbed a single mold, wet it in a nearby barrel of water, and then sprinkled it with sand. He took two large handfuls of clay from a wheelbarrow, rolled them together in sand spread on the table, and pressed the resulting lump into the mold. He paused to glance at Mr. Donnelly, who had duplicated all the moves. Roman took his strike, a six-inch long, flat piece of wood, and ran it over the top of the mold, removing excess clay and flicking it back into the wheelbar-row. He handed the strike to Donnelly, who copied the step. A negro boy about twelve years old ran over and carried the molds, weighing close to fifteen pounds each, to a covered, drying area, where another man removed the raw bricks and stacked them onto a pallet in a herringbone pattern. The boy brought the molds back to the table.

McBain applauded Mr. Donnelly's effort, and the direct yet reasonable man-ner in which he dealt with the workers. He felt confident he had his man.

The slaves nodded at each other as Donnelly rinsed his hands in the water barrel, dried them with a rag, and took his jacket from Mr. McBain. The two men next visited the lumber mill and iron forge. McBain noticed the workers stealing peeks at Mr. Donnelly and knew that they would have a lively discussion later in the Quarter, guessing whether the overseer would be kind or mean.

Next, McBain gave Donnelly a tour of the stables and, lastly, the overseer's house. When they settled in the coach, McBain said, "If you want it, the job is yours. The pay is one hundred dollars a month plus full rations." Mr. Donnelly ac-cepted the position and said he would be able to start in a week, early December, after he returned to Macon to gather his family and belongings. The men shook hands. McBain leaned back and exhaled as if he had been holding his breath for three hours. He could finally relax.

Joseph heard Colonel Olmstead and Captain Sims running up behind him, having climbed the thirty steps to the ramparts to answer his summons. Joseph pointed toward the western tip of Tybee across the south channel, about one mile away. "Three Yankees are standing on the beach at Kings Landing. They turned around, dropped their trousers, and bent over. Now they're jumping up and down, playing leapfrog."

The seven weeks since the *Fingal* incident tested Joseph's tolerance of the Confederate leadership. General Lee had started out well enough by sinking ships and pilings at strategic points in the Savannah River and its tributaries around the fort to keep out the Union navy. He also reinforced the small garrison on Tybee Island, knowing that the Yankees would attack it before the fort. But after Lee toured the rebel defenses along the South Atlantic coast, he decided to concentrate his forces at the vital water approaches to the Cumberland Sound, Brunswick, Savannah, and Charleston, and pulled soldiers from all other locations, including Tybee Island. Joseph thought that abandoning Tybee invited the enemy to construct a base there to attack Fort Pulaski. Lee, however, rationalized that the Union artillery couldn't dent the fort's thick brick walls, and he didn't want to waste manpower holding territory that he couldn't adequately defend.

Just days after the rebels burned the Tybee lighthouse and evacuated the island, the Yankees landed. The chief engineer of the expeditionary force, Captain Quincy A. Gilmore, advised the Union commander, Brigadier General Thomas W. Sherman, that strategically placed batteries of rifled guns and mortars, which delivered their shells with much greater force and accuracy, could indeed obliterate the fort's walls. Sherman agreed and obtained approval for the attack from Washington. While Sherman requisitioned the needed guns and supplies, a regiment started building batteries behind sand dunes and out of sight of the fort.

Since then, Joseph had seen supply ships make constant runs to the island without hindrance. The Yankees became more brazen each day, until, in January 1862, three of them felt they could expose their backsides without consequence.

Sims grabbed Joseph's field glass and squinted. "Those arrogant bastards!"

Colonel Olmstead said, "Let's send a greeting to our new neighbors." He called out, "Sergeant Hammond, prepare to fire Julia at those rascals on Kings Landing." The artillery units at the fort gave women's names to their heavy guns and painted them in white on the shiny, black breeches. "Julia" hurled thirty-two-pound cannon balls up to two thousand yards.

Under the command of their sergeant, the six-man crew scrambled into action, pushing the cloth-covered charge into the barrel, hoisting up and loading the cannon ball, and cramming in the contents with a rammer. The gunner called out the coordinates to his men, who adjusted the angle of the weapon. A corporal shouted, "Piece is ready."

Olmstead used his field glass and said, "They're standing together, waving at the fort. Hopefully, this will land close enough to end the merriment."

The gunner shouted, "Fire!"

BAMMM! Joseph and the other officers flinched at the ear-piercing sound. Seconds later, the middle soldier disappeared. The two men flanking him gaped at each other, looked back over their shoulders, stared at each other again, and then ran away like scared rabbits. After twenty yards, they stopped and each picked up a clump—remains of their comrade—and carried it over a sand hill.

Joseph dropped his cane. Olmstead gasped, "Holy mother of God, Hammond! What a shot! You blew him in half!"

The crew stood on the ramparts, frozen in amazement. After a moment of silence, they broke into cheers and pumped their fists in the air.

Sergeant Hammond replied, "Colonel, shall we send another greeting?"

As Olmstead headed downstairs, he said, "Not necessary. I don't suspect they'll return. Let's get back to work."

The garrison spoke of nothing but the miracle shot for the rest of the day. Captain Sims told the other officers what many of them were already thinking; "Now the Yankees know what awaits them. They'll deliberate long and hard about attacking us."

That night, Joseph wrote a letter to Danny but did not mention the incident. Instead, he promised to take him horseback riding at the Heritage as soon as he returned in September. Joseph fell asleep, relieved that his son lived in safety in Savannah.

"You ready?" Danny yelled, as he gripped the rubber ball and held it by his ear.

Truvy McBain said, "Sure am!"

Danny said, "All right, who was the third president of the United States?" and threw the ball in the air.

Truvy looked up at the ball and glanced at the water pump in the middle of Pulaski Square to make sure he wouldn't run into it. "Thomas Jefferson, started his first term in 1801." He took three steps to the right and two steps backwards before the ball landed in his hands and his fingers wrapped around it like a possum trap.

Danny yelled, "I only asked who he was, you show-off."

Truvy took a bow. "Two points for me." Truvy held the ball by his shoulder. "When did General Oglethorpe discover Georgia?" He hurled the ball in the air.

The boys were playing "Catch History," a game invented by James McBain. After Danny finished school, Mr. McBain occasionally went to the square to have a segar and watch the boys play. He decided to make the time more educational. He had them sit at his feet and gave them a short lesson—usually about early Georgia and U.S. history. He then threw the ball high in the air to each of them, asking a question based on his lesson, and awarding a point for a correct answer and one for a successful catch. McBain was amazed at how well they remembered the lessons. Truvy won as often as he lost.

Vitruvius James McBain was born in October 1855, hours after Daniel Joseph McBain, just as their fathers had been born on the same day in 1820. Truvy's mother Patience made certain that he received an education, though it was illegal to teach any person of color in Georgia to read or write. She and Andrew, while he was alive, had read to him and taught him the alphabet at night. At age five, Truvy started attending Sunday School at the First African Baptist Church and learned to read the Bible. A year later, his mother sent him to a secret school for blacks. The proprietor, a free woman of color, held classes in her house on Bay Lane near Warren Square. The students concealed their books under clothing or in bags, and entered and left one at a time so as not to arouse the suspicion of white neighbors. Now, at six years of age, Truvy could read and write simple texts and perform basic addition and subtraction, and he spoke more like an educated white boy than a slave. And, like Danny, he was fascinated with history. When he joined his friend in the afternoons in Pulaski Square, they always played "Catch History.

The ball sailed over Danny's head and he gave chase while hollering, "1733." The ball landed on the brick walkway, and bounced over the wood-railed fence that enclosed the square. "Two points for me."

Truvy, with jet-black skin, short, perfectly trimmed hair, and round white eyes, stood as tall as Danny, but had broader shoulders. He shouted, "You have to catch the ball, too, to get a point."

Danny yelled back, "You have to throw it so I have a chance to catch it!" He climbed over the fence to the ball that rested in the sandy street and spotted a wagon parked by the curb just ten yards away. The driver, who wore a floppy-brimmed leather hat, grinned at him. Danny felt goose bumps all over. He picked up the ball and ran back to Truvy. "Do you see that creepy man in the wagon?"

Truvy whispered, "Yes. He's ridden around the square twice since we got here."

Danny replied, "Maybe I should get Jefferson or Dante." Before Truvy could answer, the wagon rolled away. Danny said, "Oh well, he's gone now. I'm going to tell Dante anyway." The boys ran to the house and found Dante in the servant's room on the ground floor. He was being measured by Chloe, who was tailoring his only suit for the negro ball that would be held in two weeks. Danny decided not to bother him.

CHAPTER TEN

The Negro Ball

January 1862

Hercules tied the horse to the post, brushed off his white shirt and black pants with his hands, walked to the front door, and knocked. He heard the patter of little feet and adult footsteps. The door opened. "Hercules! What a pleasant surprise. Come in."

Hercules half-bowed. "Thank you, Patience." He stepped inside, picked up two-year-old Gully, and carried him to the couch.

Patience said, "Have a seat. You'll need to rest after carrying that load."

Hercules laughed, sat with a whoosh, and placed the child next to him. "He's not that heavy. How are you doing, Patience?"

She sat on the other side of Gully and put her arm around the boy. "Just fine. I'm still cooking for Master Hartridge. The family is very nice and they allow me to bring Gully. He plays with their children and sleeps."

Hercules said, "I see Truvy all the time playing with Danny when I'm in town. They're just like Master Joseph and Andrew when they were young."

Patience nodded slowly. "Truvy tells me whenever he sees you. I can't thank you enough for spending time with him. I couldn't ask for a better boy. When he comes home after playing with Danny, he pulls out his father's book on architecture and looks at it until supper. He always asks me how to pronounce a word in it and tell him the meaning. Andrew would be so proud." Her voice began to crack. She looked up at Hercules. "How are you getting on?"

"Good. I guess you heard about Isaac and Delpha?"

"Yes. Chloe told me. How sad. At first I couldn't understand why they'd try it. Then I thought, what if I had a chance to run away, would I do it? I must tell you, Hercules, I'd consider it. As nice as Master Joseph is to me, I want my children to have the same opportunities as the whites, and they'll never get them here. Truvy is so smart. He could do so much. I think Gully, too. Do you understand?"

Hercules felt like holding Patience to comfort her. He admired her strength, despite the pain she suffered. "Yes, but running away is still dangerous, especially for a woman and two children."

"I know, but I'd still consider it." Patience looked up and held Hercules's stare. "What would you do if you had the chance?"

Hercules scratched his head. "I can't say. I know I'm a slave, but Massa treats me fair. I want to be free as much as anyone, but I'd still like to work for him. There's a good chance we'll all be free if the Yankees win. It's safest to wait. I want to be alive to see the day." Hercules paused to pat Gully's belly. "There's a negro ball Saturday night. Have you heard about it?"

Patience swiped at a crumb on Gully's lower lip. "You mean the one to benefit the soldiers who are fighting to keep us enslaved."

Hercules smiled. "That's the one. The whites probably wouldn't let us have a big party for any other reason. I'm going. Would you like to join me?"

Patience frowned. "Thank you for thinking of me, but the Hartridges are having a party and I have to cook." She squeezed his hand. "You must go and tell me about it."

Hercules tickled Gully's armpit. The child giggled. "I will." He stood and said, "I've got to get back to Pulaski Square. I'll see you later."

Patience walked him to the door and asked him to come back when he had time. He got on his horse and rode off. She waved goodbye even though he wasn't looking.

⁂

On a cold night in mid-January 1862, Dante strode into the foyer of the building and immediately felt the vibrations of the music run through his body and pull him along like a magnetic force. A wall of noise hit him as he stepped into the large hall. About two hundred black people dressed like white folks at a wedding—the men in black and white, the women in every color of the rainbow—talked, laughed, and danced. Dante walked around the large room for a few minutes, greeting acquaintances until he spied her standing alone on the edge of the dance floor. Summoning up the courage as he fiddled with his tie, he crept up and said over the music, "How do, Miss Ahsettuh."

Isetta looked at Dante, who smiled and held his hat in his hands. She turned back to the dance floor.

Dante persisted, "Ah tole you ah comin' back."

She stared straight ahead. "You sholy tek yuh time, mistuh chep."

He stepped to her side. She looked beautiful wearing a green day dress, yellow bodice with a lace trim at the neckline and cuffs, gold-colored drop earrings, and white gloves—all handed down from Mrs. Lamar. A matching green turban completed the elegant outfit. He pressed his hat to his chest. "Ah been lookin', Miss Ahsettuh, been walkin' all 'bout town fuh you."

She shrugged and rocked back and forth, moving her shoulders from side to side while watching Ross's Brass Band, their cheeks expanding and contracting like bullfrogs, blowing the bugle, cornet, clarinet, tuba, and trombone. Two others played the bass drum and fiddle. Dante spoke over the music. "Wanna dance?"

With a forced smile that flashed white teeth, she said, "All right." He put on his hat, took her hand, and led her onto the dance floor.

The colored population of Savannah had anticipated this night for months. Several free black men had approached the city council for permission to hold a party for the benefit of the sick and wounded soldiers of Georgia. The mayor and aldermen approved, elated that their negroes supported the war effort. The mayor appointed a committee of five white men to monitor the party, and they sat at a table on the side of the dance floor, tapping their feet to the music. With tickets priced at one dollar and fifty cents, the organizers expected to make a donation, after expenses, of about seventy dollars.

The war didn't enter Dante's mind as he tried to win Isetta's heart to the music of the black musicians, who had traveled all the way from Macon for the event. The pair joined ten other couples dancing the Cakewalk. The partners formed two lines, male and female, with an aisle between them, and shuffled in place. Couples then cakewalked through the gauntlet. The dance had its roots in the plantation, rumored to have been started by slaves mimicking white folks doing the minuet, but with their own unique swinging and swaying. Whites so enjoyed watching the negroes dance that they often attended the Saturday night parties in the Quarter and awarded a cake to the best dancers.

When Dante and Isetta's turn came, they took one step towards each other and bowed. Dante grinned as he held his top hat in the air with his right hand and offered his left hand, which she took in her right. They faced up the aisle, raised their chins in the air, and took five high steps, shuffled their feet, and stopped. Dante pulled her towards him, then twirled her away. They bowed to each other again, and repeated the steps. When they reached the end of the line, Isetta lifted her dress slightly with her left hand and high-kicked to the left and to the right, as Dante, balanced on the balls of his feet and bent at the knees, swiveled his legs in and out. They bowed to each other, Dante replaced his hat, and they stepped and shuffled in place opposite each other while the next couple cakewalked up the aisle.

The dancing had the couple laughing and looking into each other's eyes. Dante's heart beat like the bass drum. After an hour he led Isetta off the floor to the punch bowl. He poured two glasses and handed one to her. They clinked and drank. Dante smacked his lips and graciously praised her dancing. "Dat's some pair ub feets you got!" The music blared so loudly that she leaned closer to hear better. The aroma of her peach-scented perfume made his body temperature rise.

"Hello, Dante. Who is this pretty lady?" Dante turned and faced Hercules, who was smiling at Isetta. She coyly dipped her head, feigning embarrassment.

A shock of jealousy ran through Dante's body, but he composed himself and made the introduction. "Ahsettuh, dis muh fren' Huhclees, best hawseman in all Sabannah."

Hercules bowed and said, "Nice to meet you, Isetta." He turned to a man standing at his side. "Isetta and Dante, meet March Haynes, a local river pilot."

A man about Dante's height but solidly built, with short salt-and-pepper hair and a Van Dyke beard stepped forward. John Rowland of Savannah owned him and rented out his services. March lived on Wilmington Island and knew the cuts, streams, creeks, and rivers around Savannah and the coast better than any man alive. He lived with his wife and three children on March's earnings, after his owner took a twenty per cent commission. March looked at the table of white men, and, seeing their eyes fixed on the dancers, removed a small bottle from his jacket and poured a shot of the copper-colored liquid into Isetta's and Dante's glasses. Isetta thanked March and sipped.

Never having tasted alcohol, but not wanting to seem backward, Dante took a gulp. His throat felt as if it had been set on fire. He tried to blink away the tears that welled up in his eyes, bent forward, and started coughing, while Isetta turned away, trying to conceal her laughter.

March said to Isetta, "Wanna Breakdown?"

Isetta handed her glass to Dante, who stared at it like a bomb with a lit fuse. She grasped March's arm and followed him onto the floor. Hercules said to Dante, "Close your mouth. March is married. He just likes to dance."

Dante scowled. He could see Isetta's face glow under the gas-lit chandelier as she and March did the Breakdown, bending at the knees, swaying their hips, hopping up in the air, coming down with one leg bent, gyrating their hips. "Den let he fine he own gu'l!" he muttered.

People approached the punch bowl and the two men moved to the side. Hercules changed the subject. He had spent the past few days at the Heritage and hadn't seen Dante in a while. "You still looking for Andrew's killers?" Dante, whose eyes were fixed on Isetta, didn't respond. "Dante, you listening to me?"

"Huh? Oh, ah only looks in town. Ah nebuh see 'em. Ah got tuh go back tuh dey house. Dat's de only way. But dey see me 'round, dey kill me. Ah cain' do it alone."

Hercules grabbed Dante's shoulder and squeezed. "Master Joseph said not to do anything stupid."

Dante removed Hercules's hand. "He tell me dat two, t'ree munts ago. Ah don' 'membuh by now. When ah gits de chance, ah gwine tuh kill 'em. Don' care 'bout Massa Joesup. You kin he'p by dribin' me in de coach. Dey don' know you."

A voice interrupted them. "May ah return dis fine, lubly lady?" A smiling Isetta took back her glass from Dante and drank. Dante glared at March, who ignored him.

Hercules and March bid adieu and moved on. With steam rising up to his face, Dante led Isetta back onto the floor. As they danced, she whispered to Dante, "Dat man dance good, but ah radduh dance wid you." Dante's heart nearly popped out of his chest. He pulled back and saw her smile at him. They danced until eleven o'clock, closing time as mandated by the city council. All the partygoers had passes from their masters or guardians, allowing them to be on the streets past dark. Even Hercules carried a pass, although all the policemen knew him and never bothered him.

Dante insisted on escorting Isetta home. They walked from Bay to Broughton Street, and then east to Habersham. Isetta asked, "Who you massa?"

"Massa McBain. He own de Huhtage plantation, an' de house on Plaski Squaw. Ah lib dey." Before Dante could ask Isetta about her massa and missus, she stopped in front of a three-story house on the northeast corner. Dante glanced at the mansion and asked, "Kin ah see you aftuh chu'ch dis Sunday?"

"Don' know. Can you 'member bettuh dis time?"

"Yessum. Ah promise."

A white man rode up on a horse and said, "Isetta, open the gate, will you?"

She replied, "Yes, Massa," and did as she was told. Dante shivered as he felt the man's eyes drill into him. Isetta broke the tension. "He open, Massa."

The man turned to Isetta and said, "Did you enjoy the dance?"

"Yes, Massa. Sholy did."

Charles Lamar rode through the gate and to the coach house. Isetta said to Dante, "Ah bettuh go. See you at chu'ch."

CHAPTER ELEVEN

General Lee's Mistake

January - April 1862

The officers' heads popped up from their plates when they heard the distant explosions. Joseph, whose leg had improved enough so that he could walk mostly with a cane, limped from the mess behind the others, taking one step at a time up the stairs to the top of the gorge wall. They joined Lieutenant Blair, who was watching the *Ida* chug towards the fort in the south channel. Another report bounced off the heavens and a huge geyser of water rose in the air twenty yards from the ship's bow. Joseph looked at the South Carolina side of the river and spotted for the first time a Yankee battery on Venus Island.

Over the previous weeks Joseph had had a clear view of the Union navy removing timber pilings and other obstructions that General Lee's men had sunk in the creeks and streams to seal off all waterways leading from Hilton Head to the Savannah River below the fort. By late January federal gunboats had anchored in those waterways and started firing at ships trying to reach the fort from Savannah, but they were too far away to do any damage. However, this new battery, built at night over several weeks, changed everything. Venus Island was closer to Savannah than the fort by two miles and the Yankee guns could now reach the south channel—and Confederate vessels like the *Ida*.

Joseph urged on the steam tug by slapping the top of the ramparts and calling, "Come on, Captain! Move it, move it!" A direct hit would blow the *Ida* to splinters. Several more fountains of water spurted into the air near the ship, but the tug finally made it to the south wharf and out of range of the federal gun. Blair turned to Joseph and said, "What's next from those devils?"

They soon learned. Two days later, after the *Ida* returned to the city via the circuitous St. Augustine Creek to the south of the south channel and beyond the range of the Venus Island guns, the federals built a new battery on Bird Island, in the middle of the river, and much closer to the Georgia mainland. St. Augustine Creek was now within range. Then the Yankees cut the telegraph lines from the fort to the city. By February 22, 1862, Fort Pulaski was completely isolated. No rebel ship could reach it, and no communications could be sent or received, other than by couriers who carried letters at night in small boats over ribbon-like creeks. But almost always, the Union patrols captured them, with one exception—March Haynes.

Despite all this, the garrison's spirits remained high, as the men knew that the Union guns could not harm their fort. They had one year's supply of provisions with unlimited oysters and fish in the river. Also, the summer was only four months away and an outbreak of yellow fever would surely send the Yankees packing.

Joseph had his doubts. At night he heard the enemy building batteries behind sand dunes on Tybee Island. He felt like a fly trapped in a spider's web. He had recently seen Union ships arriving off Tybee with heavy guns and other ordnance. Since then, at night, he heard even more hammering, sawing, and digging directly across the south channel at Kings Landing, just one mile away. He reported this to Olmstead and suggested bombarding the area, but the colonel didn't want to waste precious ammunition on targets he couldn't see. Joseph saw the spider moving closer and wondered if anyone in Savannah had any intention of helping them.

Gazaway Lamar pumped his right arm as if he were hammering a nail into a board as he shouted to the businessmen gathered in the long room of the City Exchange building. "We cannot allow the Yankees to sail any deeper into our river and bomb us into submission. We need a ship that will send them back to hell! With your generosity, gentlemen, we can have it—in just months."

Inspired by a group of women from South Carolina, several Georgia ladies began a fund-raising drive to build an iron-clad floating battery to add to Commodore Josiah Tattnall's Mosquito Fleet to protect the Savannah River from deeper incursions. Aided by publicity from newspapers around the state, money began to flow into the Ladies Gunboat Fund. Lamar was appointed treasurer of the fund, along with two other local businessmen. He used his contacts in Georgia to purchase scarce materials such as iron to build the craft.

James McBain waited for the other men to hand donations to Lamar before approaching him with a check for two hundred dollars. Lamar looked at the amount and patted James on the back. "Thank you, my friend." He slipped the check into his jacket pocket. "At this rate, we'll have enough in a few weeks."

The men left the building together and walked onto the Bay, as locals referred to Bay Street. McBain asked, "Do you know if Mr. Molyneaux is heading north soon? I need to send a letter to New York." Edmund Molyneaux, the British consul in Savannah, often traveled to Washington City to meet with British officials.

"Yes, he is. But I must warn you, he carried a letter for me to Washington and mailed it to my associate in New York. Union spies got hold of it against all rules of civility. I used some strong words about the Yankees and Lincoln's barbarians accused my associate of being a southern sympathizer. He had to escape to Canada to avoid arrest. You might be placing this person at the same risk."

Southerners faced many obstacles in sending letters to the North after formal postal services between the two sections were terminated, but they still had their ways. British consuls like Molyneaux carried the letters of friends in their diplomatic bags and posted them in northern cities. Businessmen sent letters on blockade runners to the Bahamas or Bermuda, where they were mailed to the north on British ships. Union prisoners of war, upon their release, were paid by their southern captors to mail letters when they returned home. Some enterprising men living in southern border towns, for a fee, sneaked across Union lines to post letters.

McBain shook his head. "I don't think so. The authorities here are trying to take my daughter's house on Madison Square under the new sequestration law. They claim she's an alien enemy living in New York." In August 1861 the United States passed the First Confiscation Act, which gave authority to seize southern property used for insurrectionary purposes. The Confederate Congress responded by passing an act to seize all property located in the seceded states owned by alien enemies.

"The thieves!" Gazaway shouted. "It's bad enough that we have to fight the Yankees, no less our own government."

McBain watched as Hercules pulled up in the coach. He said, "I want to notify Amy, though there is little she can do, short of returning and fighting it in court. And that would be impossible."

Lamar laughed loudly. "Of all women, Amy McBain just might. I'll see what I can do to get that letter to her."

James said, "Thank you. May I give you a ride? I'm off to the Heritage."

Lamar patted his jacket pocket. "No. I need to take these funds to the bank. Speaking of the Heritage, how is the new overseer working out?"

McBain shrugged in despair. "He's excellent, and now I may lose him. I tell you, Gaz, this war is killing me."

The plantation ran smoothly under Mr. Donnelly. He learned the operations quickly and the slaves worked almost as hard as they had under Isaac. McBain felt comfortable enough to spend most nights in town. However, a few weeks earlier Donnelly had approached him at the plantation without his characteristic smile. "Sir, Governor Brown says that President Davis has requisitioned Georgia for twelve more regiments. Chatham County has a quota of more than two hundred. If they don't get enough volunteers, they'll draft the rest into state service to make up the difference. I could get taken."

McBain knew about the governor's proclamation but he never thought it would affect Mr. Donnelly. He asked, "How old are you, Mr. Donnelly?"

"Forty-five, sir. The paper says that every able-bodied white male between the ages of eighteen and forty-five years not already in service must report. The governor made some exemptions, but none for overseers."

James kicked at a broken piece of brick at his feet. Mr. Donnelly had made his life so much easier and he could not afford to lose him. He said, "Surely enough men will volunteer. I hear that the government is offering an enlistment bonus of fifty dollars. Don't underestimate the patriotism of our boys. Savannahians will answer the call!"

Donnelly crossed himself and said, "I pray so, sir."

☙

A few weeks later, on March 4, 1862, several hundred men drifted slowly onto the parade ground at the south end of Forsythe Place as if they were headed for their own executions. A colonel and several non-commissioned officers waved their arms and called out, "Chatham County enrollment over here!"

Donnelly walked onto the ground prepared to present his case: he was a resident of Bibb County, having been born and raised in Macon and owning land there. He had found temporary employment at the Heritage in Chatham County. He knew that Bibb County had a smaller quota and would certainly fill it. Of course, he hoped enough men would volunteer that day to fill the requirement, negating any need for a challenge. About two hundred somber faces lined up double-file in a large "U" formation on the grass, shoulder to shoulder, around Colonel J. F. Pelot. Six corporals walked along the lines, pulling the men by their shirts to get them to squeeze closer together, and yelling at them to stand straight. Pelot groaned as he surveyed the rabble and thought how differently they appeared from the proud boys who had volunteered after Fort Sumter.

The colonel called for quiet and read Governor Brown's proclamation. He then announced that two new companies comprising one hundred sixteen men had just tendered their services to the state, leaving a local quota of just one hundred. Donnelly heard someone near him mutter, "Hallelujah." Pelot then announced he would call the roll of all eligible men, and if a draft were necessary, absentees would be taken first, then unmarried men and bachelors; and lastly married men and widowers. Donnelly kept tabs during the roll call and counted ninety-eight absentees. He relaxed, confident that he would avoid the draft if just a handful from this group volunteered.

Pelot shouted, "All men wishing to volunteer for service in defense of their liberties, families, and homes, and to illustrate the glory and patriotism of the great state of Georgia, take two steps forward now." Six did.

The officer blinked several times in disbelief and scanned the field. He put his arms to his side, raised his chin to the heavens, and hollered. "I repeat! All men wishing to volunteer for service in defense of their liberties, families, and state, take two steps forward!" A few black birds flew from the branches of a nearby tree, but no additional men advanced. The officer shook his head and spat, "You call yourselves Georgians? You're more like parasites. One last time!" Pelot repeated the offer, with no response. "Lord have mercy on our Confederacy." He asked the six volunteers to follow one of the corporals to a table to register.

Pelot then shouted, "Those applying for an exemption for medical or other reasons, step forward." All the remaining men took the step in perfect unison. Pelot put his hands on his hips and glared. "Deplorable! Go line up at the other table and give your cowardly alibis." The colonel almost got trampled in the dash. Two hours later, Donnelly spoke to a corporal, who recorded his request for exemption in a register and told him to report to the Oglethorpe Barracks in two weeks, when he would be advised of his status.

Despite being married and in the last group to be tapped for draftees, Donnelly left the park in a dark mood. Georgia boys, at least those not already in the army, weren't answering the call. It didn't bode well for him.

☙

Hercules leaned into the cab and said to Dante, "You just speak through the little sliding window, and keep low in the coach so no one sees you." He had declined Dante's previous requests to drive by the house of Andrew's killers because Master Joseph had told them to wait for his return. Nor did Hercules want to be near Dante when he had that gun. But Dante feared walking to the house alone and kept pressing Hercules to take him in the coach. One day, when Massa took the train to Charleston on business, Hercules succumbed to Dante's pestering on the condition that he not bring his revolver. Just in case, Hercules searched Dante before he climbed into the cab.

As they turned onto Anderson Street, Dante spoke through the window, "Dat house tuh de right, wid de big fence." He slouched low in the seat.

Hercules, who had planned to drive slowly by the house, parked in front. Dante felt the coach stop. He peeked out and felt his heart sink. Part of the fence had been pulled down, the stable roof had a huge hole in it, and the front door had a board nailed across it. He heard Hercules ask a passerby, "Pardon me, sir, but I have a message to deliver to Sam, Harold, or Willie, the men who live in this house. It looks deserted."

The man replied, "No one has lived there for a month or two. Left the place in a mess, too. Don't know where they went. Good riddance, I say."

They returned to Pulaski Square and Hercules told Dante, "I don't suspect we'll ever see those men again."

Dante leaned against the coach and shoved his hands into his pockets. "Ah 'magine not." He felt like he had let down Andrew. Only a white man like Master Joseph could conduct a real search and question other white men. He wondered when Joseph would be coming home.

The officers sat around the long wooden table in Colonel Olmstead's quarters. A few days earlier, on March 31, a Confederate scouting party had captured a Union guard boat off Wilmington Island with seventeen soldiers. One of the privates confessed that the Union had two regiments of seventeen hundred men, two companies of engineers, and two companies of artillery on Tybee and planned to attack the fort in ten days. Olmstead examined Joseph's hand-drawn map of Tybee Island, with the seven suspected locations of the Yankee batteries along the northern shore, and four question marks on nearby Kings Landing, where Joseph had heard so much nighttime activity. Olmstead reiterated, "Even at a mile, their guns can't damage the walls of this fort. You heard General Lee."

Joseph countered, "We know we're going to be attacked, and soon. Those prisoners told us as much. Why allow them the freedom to build batteries? A few shells will send them scampering. They think they can do anything without reprisals."

Olmstead admired Joseph, sixteen years his senior, as a successful businessman, loyal Georgian, and hero of Manassas who would not speak without considering the impact of his words. But he disagreed. "Lieutenant, we don't know their exact positions. Firing would be guesswork. We can't waste the gunpowder."

"Colonel, they are dictating the entire action. We need to send a message that we know what they're up to and we'll take steps to stop it." Joseph looked around the room. He knew a few of the other officers shared his views, but none spoke up.

The young commander responded, "We're better off waiting for them to make a move. Then we'll know their exact locations. It will come soon enough."

A knock on the door interrupted the meeting. A guard entered the room, stood at attention, and saluted. "Excuse me, Colonel. You wanted me to inform you the moment March arrived with mail. He's here." The men stood and cheered.

"Bring him in, Private!" Olmstead yelled. Although the federals had tried to block all approaches to the fort, March Haynes, whose owner, John Rowland, was one of the garrison, knew every passage through the marsh. After the Yankees surrounded the fort, Rowland's wife arranged for March to deliver letters from town at night. The negro, in coveralls, flannel shirt, and rubber boots stepped into the room and the officers crowded around him. He handed a leather satchel to Olmstead, who distributed the mail.

Joseph read a letter from Danny about losing a front tooth and longed to see his son. But he knew that first he would have to endure a bombardment from the largest guns in the Yankee arsenal.

Over the next ten days the defenders continued preparing for an attack. They built traverses behind the guns on the casemate and barbette levels, and then piled dirt against the wooden shields to protect the men from shots from the rear. The surgeon sharpened his saw for the inevitable amputations. The artillery units in the casemates spread sand on the brick floors to soak up blood and prevent slippery footing.

On the morning of April 10, Joseph and Lieutenant Blair stood on the barbette level and chatted about the plump oysters they had enjoyed the previous night as they scanned the horizon with their field glasses. Joseph hushed for a few seconds and said, "Jesus, look at Kings Landing. The deep brush and bushes covering the dunes are gone. I see several large guns."

Blair raised his field glass and gasped, "I'll be damned! There's a rowboat with a white flag of truce leaving the island. That can mean only one thing. I'll get the colonel."

Olmstead, his staff officers, and the company captains appeared in minutes. They observed the approaching skiff as it flopped up and down against the white-caps. When the ship came within one hundred yards, Olmstead told Captain Sims to receive the visitors. Joseph watched as two privates from the fort helped secure the rowboat to the south wharf. They stood to the side, ramrod straight, as the rowers helped the lone officer alight. The Union lieutenant saluted Captain Sims and handed him an envelope. Sims returned to Olmstead as the Yankee officer stepped back and scanned the fort walls.

Olmstead removed the sheet of paper and read silently. He looked up at the officers. "It's a demand to surrender the fort. If I refuse, they'll attack upon the lieutenant's return." He told Sims, "Have the lieutenant inform his commander that I am here to defend the fort, not surrender it." He turned to the others. "Call your men to their stations."

Amid the stomping of boots all about him, Joseph remained at the southeastern corner of the barbette level and watched the boat return to Kings Landing. He had the responsibility of locating the enemy positions on Tybee and relaying that information to the captains. He looked at the men on the ramparts and felt a shiver of pride. Six soldiers stood at attention by each of the twenty-four rampart guns, staring towards the enemy, ready to execute the orders of the gunner, and ready to die for their fledgling country.

Before long, a familiar but unwelcome sound—the high-pitched buzz like a giant bee—screamed through the air. Joseph looked up just as the shell exploded in front of the fort, sending a torrent of earth raining down on the ramparts. Joseph used his cap to brush off the dirt and sod from his body. Another shell zoomed above, then another, and another. BAMMM! The wall of the fort shook, knocking Joseph to one knee and sending his cane flying. He heard the gunners shouting commands and the Confederate cannons began firing in retaliation.

The vibrations ran through his body.

Joseph crawled on his hands and knees to the parapet and saw smoke from the big Union guns puffing into the air, looking like passing locomotives. He counted eleven batteries, but the four at Kings Landing were doing the most damage. BAMMM! A shell hit the wall below him and sent him sprawling. Joseph shook his head to clear his mind. He struggled to his feet, grabbed his cane, and hobbled to the artillery units on the southern face, urging them to take out the guns at Kings Landing. He had a nauseous feeling in the pit of his stomach and sensed that those batteries would make a fool of General Lee.

Joseph knelt behind the parapet and watched his comrades perform their jobs at the guns. They wormed out and sponged the barrels, loaded the charge and the shell, rammed down the contents, inserted the fuse, aimed, and bent at the waist while covering their ears at the command of "Fire!"

WHAMMM! A shell hit the parapet near the thirty-two-pounder closest to him, about twenty yards away, blowing brick and dirt everywhere. He heard a scream. One of the men lay face down, writhing and holding his bloody shoulder. Joseph recognized him as a boy of just nineteen who routinely had caught the largest catfish from the north wharf. Two men from his team carried him to the far side of the traverse while the others picked up the shattered bricks and debris around the gun, which fortunately stayed on its platform rails. Sergeant Hammond hollered down to the parade, "Ambulance!" Moments later two men ran up the stairs. They laid a stretcher on the ground, pulled the injured man onto it, and carried him to the hospital in one of the storerooms below.

Joseph, who had basic instruction in artillery, limped to Sergeant Hammond and offered to replace the wounded private. Hammond assigned him to position number 1, sponging the cannon barrel after firing. He served for several hours, even as his leg ached so badly that he didn't think he could stand anymore. He fought through the pain and concentrated on the job as sweat poured down his face. He coughed incessantly at inhaling so much smoke and brick dust. Several times, as he turned away from the gun before firing, his leg gave way and he fell off the platform onto the ground. Each time he pulled himself up, cursing, and went back to work as the Yankee fire smashed again and again into the fort.

At seven o'clock, as darkness descended, Olmstead shouted "The enemy has stopped! Cease fire!"

Sergeant Hammond called to his men, "Clean Julia. Prepare her for tomorrow."

Joseph sponged the gun and sat on the platform to rest his cramping leg. He saw at least one hundred soldiers lying on the ground or sitting with their heads between their knees, exhausted by twelve hours of non-stop fighting. Not one of them had ever faced hostile fire before, yet they had done their jobs without flinching. They slowly gained their feet and trudged like sleepwalkers to the mess. Two privates had to help Joseph down the stairs as he couldn't put any weight on his left leg.

Before supper, in the faint glow of sunset, the officers accompanied Colonel Olmstead for an inspection of the exterior fort walls. The men froze, stunned at the sight of so many holes in the south face. One captain murmured, "It looks like a honeycomb." The sight reminded Joseph of a painting of a mountainside in the Holy Land full of caves where religious men lived. Half the guns on the southeast wall facing Kings Landing were disabled. Though no one said it, everyone realized the same thing—General Lee had been terribly mistaken. They had no defense against the rifled guns. Except for a miracle, only time stood between them and kingdom come.

They returned to the fort and ate. Olmstead came over to Joseph and patted his back. "Thank you for filling in, Lieutenant. I'm able to reassign men from destroyed guns to functioning ones. You can return to your guard duties tomorrow."

Joseph said, "Yes, sir," but wondered if the colonel believed that they had the slightest chance of holding onto the fort.

After supper the men went to their bunks. Union shells exploded around them at fifteen-minute intervals throughout the night, but the exhausted soldiers slept through them.

Reveille at 5:30 introduced the new day. Joseph could barely walk and had to use a crutch instead of a cane. The men ate breakfast without conversation and returned to their guns, knowing they couldn't hold out for long. The Yankees resumed the non-stop onslaught promptly at six o'clock.

Joseph gimped around with Colonel Olmstead, who shouted encouragement to the men as enemy shells drilled into the fort. By one o'clock most of the rebel stations had been put out of commission and the holes in the fort walls kept widening until cannon balls flew cleanly through them and skidded across the parade ground. Fortunately, they were stopped from doing more damage by the man-made ravines. The gunners stood their ground despite the unrelenting fire. The rebels had all sworn to fight to the last extremity, and now they were fulfilling their promises.

An incoming shell shattered the top of the traverse on the casement level shielding the magazine, and set the wood on fire. Soldiers dashed with pails of water to douse the conflagration. If the flames spread to the gunpowder, the fort would be destroyed from within, killing many of its defenders. Olmstead knew that the tide of battle could not be turned. It was senseless to sacrifice his men for a lost cause. He ordered a ceasefire and told Blair to raise the white flag over the fort, while it still stood. The battle for Fort Pulaski had ended, thirty hours after it had begun.

The soldiers, their bodies filthy with gunpowder, dirt, and sweat, and their spirits as pierced as the fort walls, watched the flag of surrender ascend in silence. The Union guns stopped. The men sat on the parade ground, many with their heads in their hands. Joseph went to the ramparts, pulled out his field glass, and called down to Olmstead, "Colonel, a skiff just left Kings Landing."

Olmstead went to his room, brushed off his uniform, donned his sword, and walked to the south wharf to receive the conquerors. He soon returned, leading three Union officers to his quarters. Thirty minutes later, Olmstead escorted the Union men back to their boat. He then gathered his officers along the gorge. "Under the circumstances," he announced, "I had very little leverage in negotiating with the Yankees. I believe the terms are as fair as can be expected. The fort, armament, and garrison have been surrendered to the forces of the United States. In a few days we will be moved to a military prison somewhere up north. You may take all private effects, including your servants, but not your weapons. Fortunately, we suffered only a handful of casualties. The sick and wounded will be sent under a flag of truce back to Confederate lines in Savannah. At the same time, you may send any letters, subject to inspection by a federal officer. God willing, we will soon be exchanged. That is the best I could do." Olmstead paused and looked over his defeated officers. "It was my honor to lead you in battle, and it is my deepest regret to surrender. They will be sending a company here in an hour to take command. Gather your belongings, stay out of their way, and be ready to depart at any moment. Please inform your men."

Later that day, after the Union company had arrived, each Confederate officer lined up to surrender his sword to a Yankee major sitting at Olmstead's desk. When Joseph stepped into the room on his crutch, Olmstead said to the officer, "Lieutenant McBain suffered a serious injury at Manassas and has a medical furlough for the remainder of the war. He volunteered for duty at this fort as an officer of the guard, and is not physically capable of serving in a fighting role. I request that he be sent back to Savannah with the other sick and wounded."

The Yankee looked up at Joseph, who removed his sword from his belt and placed it on the desk. Joseph said to Olmstead, "Thank you, Colonel, but I'm still in the service of the Confederacy, and I choose to be treated as the others are." He gave his name, rank, and company, and hobbled from the room with his head hung in humiliation. He was a prisoner of war. ❧

~

CHAPTER TWELVE

The Reunion
April 1862

On April 12, 1862, the day after the fall of Fort Pulaski, the federals started transferring their captives to Hilton Head Island and from there to Union prisons in the North. On April 14 the officers of the Oglethorpe Light Infantry and the Montgomery Guards sailed from South Carolina for New York. Before their departure, the Yankees told them that the sixteen slaves who had been taken at the fort would be given the choice of remaining on Hilton Head as free men or sailing with their masters. Eight opted to go north.

The officers had their own cabin and received rations of bacon, salt beef, hard bread, and coffee. However, they had to sleep on the floor, which caused Joseph's leg to throb throughout the night. But the Union guards treated them well and their original melancholy at being captured soon gave way to hopes of a speedy prisoner exchange. After all, the Confederates held far more prisoners than did the U.S. Joseph felt good for another reason—the possibility of seeing his wife, daughter, and sister.

The *Oriental* steamed into New York harbor on the morning of April 18. Joseph felt a pang of nostalgia at the sight of so many white masts rocking gently in the water. Still other ships glided back and forth in the harbor. The long piers looked like the spokes of a giant wagon wheel sticking out from the tip of Manhattan Island. He had always wanted to return to the city where he took his marriage vows in 1853—though under better circumstances.

He thought of the serendipitous way that he had met Emily Hulett—by accidentally knocking her over on the street as she raced to catch a ship home after teaching in Savannah for two years. The mishap caused her to miss her departure. During the two days that she waited for the next boat to New York, Joseph spent all his time with her and the forces of nature took over. By the time she sailed, romance had blossomed.

Over the ensuing year the two wrote each other almost daily, and Emily finally invited Joseph to visit, despite her parents' concern that his family owned slaves. For three weeks they toured the city, tasted the food, talked endlessly, and fell in love. With only a few days left in his vacation, and not wanting to miss the opportunity, Joseph asked Mr. Hulett for his daughter's hand in marriage. Seeing how Emily gazed at Joseph when they were together, and how she talked about him constantly when they were apart, he consented. The next day the couple decided to marry before Joseph sailed to Georgia, and Mr. Hulett, having already approved the engagement, had little choice but to agree.

The steamer docked at pier four and the Southerners, in their company uniforms, transferred under guard to another ship. Joseph could feel the burning stares of rushing merchants in suits and top hats and waterfront workers in blue jeans, and he bowed his head. They boarded a steam tug for the half-mile trip to Governors Island between Manhattan Island and Brooklyn. The men grabbed onto the bench seats and railings as the boat rocked like an empty bottle on the choppy waters. Their heads swiveled back and forth to take in the sights. Joseph laughed at the reaction of his fellow officers, most of whom had never left Georgia. He heard one say, "Look at that, would ya!" and pointed to a warship under construction in a shipyard along the Brooklyn shore. About thirty men stood on the stern twelve feet above the waterline, their arms stretched out, as a crane hoisted a cannon the size of a small rowboat in their direction. Joseph wondered if the Confederate navy had anything to match it.

As the tug bounced along, Joseph thought about how his marriage had crumbled. Emily joined him in Savannah a year after their wedding. They lived with his parents until Andrew built their new Italianate house on Monterey Square. They had two beautiful children. Emily tried to be a perfect housewife, but she never could accept the institution of slavery, despite her affection for the McBain servants and the way blacks and whites seemed to integrate without problem in daily life. Then in 1859, unbeknownst to Joseph, she accepted the offer of a local shoe-store owner from Massachusetts to teach slaves to read at night. Local vigilantes learned of the illegal, secret sessions and the shopkeeper received a suit of tar and cotton for his efforts. Emily got off light with a warning never to try it again from a masked man who knew her name. When Joseph found out, he raged that his wife would attempt such a thing. Emily countered that Joseph had spent his childhood educating Andrew, which was just as illegal. The incident opened a wound that never healed.

Joseph almost fell off his seat when the tug hit the wharf. He grabbed his valise and got in line behind the other men. As they exited the boat they heard children's voices singing nearby.

I wish I was in the land of cotton,
Old times there are not forgotten,
Look away, look away, look away, Dixie Land!

A group of six little street Arabs—dirty, scruffy boys, in torn, ill-fitting clothes—stood on a neighboring pier, laughing and pointing at the prisoners.

"Get lost, you stinking brats!" Captain Sims yelled, causing the ragamuffins to squeal louder. One of them had a rock, but before he could throw it, a Union guard yelled at him, and the taunting urchins scampered away, howling in hysterics.

The prisoners marched to the head of the wharf, where a slim, grey-haired Union officer with bony shoulders held his arms in the air. They gathered around him, and he announced in a croaky voice, "I am Colonel Loomis, the commandant of Governors Island. I will determine what you can and can't do, and when you can and can't do it. I do not know how long you will be here, or where you will be going afterwards, so don't ask. I will tell you as soon as I learn. You will be staying in the officers' barracks of Fort Columbus. The enlisted men and non-commissioned officers will be held in Castle Williams on this same island. Now, follow me." The aging officer turned, walked, and whistled, as if strolling in Central Park on a Sunday afternoon.

The men entered through the single door of the barracks. The long wooden room reminded Joseph of a cotton warehouse, about one hundred feet long and fifty feet wide, with four rows of double-bunk beds. Someone said, "I've slept in worse."

A group of men in a far corner of the room, standing by their bunks, stared at them. Loomis explained, "These men are your fellow officers from North Carolina, captured at New Bern. You can get acquainted after I leave." He continued, sounding more like a welcoming hotel keeper, "Claim a bed, men. You have access to the grounds between reveille and retreat. You must be in the barracks at all other times. You will receive rations twice daily and can use the garrison kitchen after the federal officers have finished. For a small charge, the wives of the enlisted men here will be more than willing to cook your food and wash your clothes. You may write letters but they will likely be read by our agents. The mail going south will be taken to Fortress Monroe in Virginia, where it will be transferred under a flag of truce. Inform your families that their letters should be addressed to you, "prisoner of war," care of me, Colonel Loomis, at Fort Columbus. You may purchase extra food or writing supplies from the camp sutler. I will come by a few times each day, if you should have any other questions. That will be all." Joseph laughed at the idea that by becoming a prisoner, he could legally send letters across Union lines.

The officers settled in, met their comrades from North Carolina, and by evening stood together along the sea wall, gazing at the orange glow of the sunset framing the buildings of lower Manhattan Island, looking like black cut-outs in a painting. Joseph inhaled the coal-scented harbor air, closed his eyes, and relaxed. He felt quite fortunate. He had survived another battle, received gentlemanly treatment by the enemy, and, he hoped, would soon see his family.

The next day Joseph wrote letters to Emily, Danny, Amy, and his parents. The one to his wife took several hours, though it ultimately comprised just three lines.

He was still angry with her for not returning with their daughter to Savannah from a visit to New York in January 1861. She had said that she couldn't expose her daughter to the horrors of slavery or a possible war. He didn't know if he could ever forgive her for abandoning him. He couldn't deny, however, that he felt empty inside and longed to see their eighteen-month-old daughter Charlotte again.

Like most of the Confederate officers, Joseph carried gold coins and paid the freckle-faced mess cook two dollars to deliver the letters to Amy and Emily. She first went to Twenty-fifth Street and Third Avenue, but when no one answered, she slipped Amy's letter under the door. She then visited Sixteenth Street between Fifth and Sixth avenues. Emily Hulett McBain answered the door, thanked the girl, and took the letter to her room. She sat on the bed and stared at the envelope, addressed in her husband's hand but not stamped. She had not heard from him since the previous May, when mail delivery between the two sections ended. Her hands shook as she opened it and read.

Dearest Emily,   April 19, 1862
I'm a prisoner of the United States at Fort Columbus on Governors Island. Our garrison surrendered Fort Pulaski on April 11. Please visit me with our precious daughter.
Your loving husband, Joseph

Emily leaned back onto the bed and closed her eyes. She had begged Joseph to move to New York with Danny, but he refused to leave his beloved Savannah. He had claimed that his bones were made of Georgia clay. Though it broke her heart to think she might never see him again, she decided to start a new life, and perhaps, as her father and brother suggested more than once, find a new husband. However, she vowed to see her son again after this dreadful war ended. Now, Joseph slept a few miles away.

That evening over supper, Emily informed her parents. Mr. Hulett smirked as he bit into a boiled potato. "Prison will do him good—let him see what it's like to be confined like a slave." After a sleepless night, Emily decided to see the man she loved. She wanted to hold and comfort him.

On a late April morning, after two hours of fixing her hair and dressing Charlotte, Emily caught a hack to lower Manhattan and a boat to Governors Island. A corporal escorted her from the guard house to Colonel Gustavus Loomis's office. The officer invited her in, held a chair for her by his desk, and took his seat. He folded his hands on the desk and smiled. "How may I help you, Mrs. McBain?"

Charlotte, sitting in her mother's lap, reached forward and banged her hand on the colonel's desk. Emily gently pulled her back. "My husband," she said, "Lieutenant Joseph McBain, is a prisoner here. I'd like to see him if I may, Colonel." Loomis squinted in confusion. Emily explained, "I moved to Savannah, his home, after we married. I lived there for seven years and came back here to visit my parents just before the war began. I couldn't risk going back with my baby."

Loomis leaned back in his chair and watched the auburn-haired woman in her mid-thirties remove her and then the baby's bonnet. He thought about the many different kinds of casualties inflicted by this war, including innocent families. "I'll get your husband, madam. You will be allowed fifteen minutes together. He is a prisoner of war and cannot be left alone with an outsider. I must be present."

Emily nodded. She wanted to be alone with Joseph, to tell him private things, like how much she missed his touch. "If that's the rule, then I have no choice." The officer stood, pulled another chair next to Emily, and left. Emily put Charlotte on the chair, removed a small mirror from her purse, and examined herself.

Joseph leapt off his bunk when Loomis informed him of his visitor. He donned his jacket and combed his hair, thankful that he had bathed from a bucket and shaved that morning. He grabbed his cane and followed Loomis. His heart pounded as if he were about to charge into battle.

As he entered the door he saw Emily holding a squirming child in a pink dress. He caught his breath. His eyes darted between Emily and Charlotte. He laid his cane against the wall and limped to them as Emily put Charlotte on her chair. They embraced, ignoring Loomis's presence. She spoke through tears into his chest, "Oh, Joseph, I've missed you so much." He held her and buried his face in her fruit-scented hair.

Emily relaxed her arms and looked up into the same hazel eyes that she had fallen in love with ten years earlier. Lines radiated from their corners, and dark circles supported them. "Joseph, what has this war done to you?"

A child's cry interrupted his response. Emily let go of Joseph, picked up Charlotte, and presented her to him. "Charlotte, say hello to your father." Joseph's tired eyes twinkled as he stroked his daughter's straight blond hair. She looked at him, then at her mother, then back to her father. She reached a hand towards her mother. Joseph bent and kissed her forehead. The child waved her hands back and forth. He took Charlotte in his arms, laid his cheek on her head, closed his eyes, and savored the moment. Emily gave him a few seconds before asking, "How is Danny?"

Joseph kissed Charlotte again and then replied, "He's a splendid boy, a bundle of energy. He's an excellent student and loves history, just like his great grandfather, and talks about as much. He misses you."

Charlotte said something like "Dandy." Joseph grinned and said, "Yes, Danny! That's your older brother." He laughed and snuggled the girl.

Emily wiped a tear from the corner of her eye. "Please tell me what happened, Joseph? That cane. How did you get here?"

While rocking on the balls of his feet to comfort his daughter, Joseph explained Manassas, his injury, and the capture of Fort Pulaski. She turned her wedding ring as he spoke. She said, "You mean, you could have gotten out of the war after being released from the Richmond hospital, yet you volunteered? Why?"

Joseph sat while holding his daughter. He didn't want to continue with this potentially explosive issue. He looked around the office, searching for a calm response, and locked eyes with Colonel Loomis, who turned his ear towards Joseph, as interested in the answer as Emily. In measured tones he replied, "I'm fighting for my state, the Confederacy, and my family. I answered the call to duty. That shouldn't surprise you."

Emily shrugged. "I guess not. But it still doesn't make sense."

Charlotte tried to grab her father's chin. Joseph kissed his daughter's hand before responding. "Emily, please. Let's not go through this. You know how I feel. I'm fighting for the right of the people of Georgia to determine how they want to live."

Emily rolled her eyes. "The South is fighting for slavery, Joseph."

Joseph realized that it didn't take long for Emily to get on his nerves. "Georgia is much more than slavery." He paused to take a deep breath. "It's a beautiful state with hard-working and friendly people. You lived with them—and happily—for years. And you knew my beliefs before we married."

Emily pulled a kerchief from her sleeve. "Yes, Joseph, I guess I did know. But you once told me that you could live without slavery, that deep down inside you thought it was wrong. I believed you."

Joseph closed his eyes. "I told you that whether one thinks slavery is right or wrong, the negro is better off under the care of a benevolent master. Emily, I haven't seen you or Charlotte in fifteen months. Can't we have a discussion without an argument?"

Emily crumbled her kerchief in her hand. "Joseph, look where slavery has brought us. We're at war against each other, American against American. My husband is fighting my own brother. I can't bear the thought of it." Her voice began to crack.

Joseph froze. "Laurence?" He had never met Emily's older brother, who had been working as a seaman on a merchant ship when Joseph visited New York in 1853. Joseph never returned to New York, and her brother never visited Savannah. Joseph had the feeling that Laurence hated Southerners as much as Mr. Hulett did. "Where is he?"

"He's in the navy, the very one you're trying to destroy."

The point tongue-tied Joseph. He never thought of the northern soldiers in personal terms. The enemy was a multi-armed and -legged monster bearing the face of Abe Lincoln. He struggled for a response. "And the one that's trying to destroy us."

Loomis, who tried to act disinterested by looking out the window, made an effort to save the deteriorating conversation. He pulled out his watch. "Seven minutes left."

Emily leaned forward and placed a hand on her husband's leg. "Joseph, let's be a family again. Tell Colonel Loomis that you'll swear allegiance to the United States. I'll go to Savannah and bring back Danny. We can live here in peace and pick up where we left off. I can take care of you while you heal. We can have more children. You'll be near Amy. Please, Joseph, it's the best thing for your family. Think of us. We need you."

Emily and Loomis could hear Joseph's breathing. His eyes narrowed into glowering slits. "You . . . you want me to desert?"

Emily squeezed Joseph's leg and leaned closer. "You're not deserting, Joseph! You're saving your family. Anyone would understand."

The silence hung in the air like a cloud of segar smoke. Loomis shifted uncomfortably in his chair. Joseph looked down at Charlotte and touched her cheek before speaking. "Emily, you broke up our family. You took my daughter away. Now, you're asking me to leave my home, my heritage, to fix what you destroyed."

Charlotte started to cry. Joseph rocked from side to side and she stopped. He wanted to be left alone to hold his daughter. Emily leaned forward and kissed him, trying not to disturb the baby. "I'm sorry, Joseph. I didn't come to argue. I want you back. I want Danny back. I didn't realize how badly until I saw you. Please don't be angry with me." She leaned back, dabbing at her tear-filled eyes. "I want to ask you so many things. How are your parents?"

"They're fine. Mother is spending her time raising donations, sewing uniforms, and volunteering at the hospital. Father wants me to run the plantation, but he's hired a good overseer and that takes a huge weight off his shoulders— and mine." Joseph had to tell her about Isaac, but didn't want to reveal the cause. "Isaac died."

"Oh, I'm so sorry. And poor Andrew? Did you catch his killers?"

Joseph coughed before answering, trying not to get emotional. "No. Dante claims he found their house and saw two of them. We were going there the day the Yankees attacked Hilton Head and I got called to duty. I'll get them as soon as I return. Patience and the boys are doing well. She's a strong woman."

"What about Dante? I'll never forget the time he cooked Country Captain when I first had supper at your parents' house." Emily teared up at the memory of that evening.

Charlotte giggled as Joseph flapped her lower lip up and down with a finger. "He's a cook at the City Hotel. Still lives at Pulaski Square and talks of owning a restaurant one day. He misses you and Amy. Speaking of Amy, I sent her a letter but haven't heard back. Do you know how she is?"

Emily looked away. She had wanted to maintain a friendship with her sister-in-law but Amy always had an excuse when declining the invitations to join her family for Sunday supper. The two women had met a few times in a park to see each other's babies, but Amy always had to run after an hour, and Emily became convinced that Amy didn't like her. "I haven't seen her in a while. I'll stop by her place and see if she's in town."

Loomis interrupted, "Your time is up. You'll have to leave, Mrs. McBain. You may return next week." The colonel stepped to the door and held it open.

Emily and Joseph stood. He noisily smooched his daughter's cheek and said, "Be a good girl. Your brother Danny sends his love."

Charlotte laughed and said, "Dandy. Love Dandy."

Joseph handed her to Emily, who put her free hand on his shoulder. "I still love you, Joseph. I always will. Please think about us." She gave him one last kiss.

Loomis escorted Emily and Joseph from the building. He told Joseph, "Return to your area now, Lieutenant." Joseph watched his wife walk away. His mind spun like a top. He thought he still loved her, although he didn't see how they could live together again. He also knew that when the war ended, he would stop at nothing to gain possession of his daughter. ❧

PART 2

Penny the Pretender
April 1862 – September 1862

CHAPTER THIRTEEN

⁓

Sam Bannister

March – July 1862

James McBain looked up from his desk on a mid-July afternoon and saw Dante standing behind William at the doorway to his study. McBain said, "Thank you for getting him, William. Dante, come in." The cook stepped to the front of the desk. McBain put down his pen and spoke. "Dante, I just heard from Mr. Bonaud. Business at the City Hotel, like most restaurants in town, is way off. He has to cut back and no longer requires your services." He saw Dante gulp. He knew that the servant was proud of his cooking and would take the news hard. "At the moment I have no need for you here or at the Heritage, but the Irish Jasper Greens are camped outside of town and their officers need a cook for their mess. You will join them next week. Until then, stay here and help Lilly in the kitchen. Jinny isn't feeling well."

The negro stared at the rug. McBain tried to lift his spirits. "Don't worry, Dante. Life will soon be back to normal and Jinny is getting old. I'll probably have you replace her soon. That will be all." McBain picked up his pen and resumed writing.

Dante stood still, looking at Massa. He didn't want to leave the relative comfort of his life in Savannah, nor did he want to be separated from Isetta. He had been seeing her after church on Sundays for almost six months and planned to ask her to marry him, with Mr. McBain's permission, of course.

McBain looked up. "I said that will be all."

Dante said, "Yassuh, Massa," and left.

McBain felt badly for Dante, but he had other problems. When Mr. Donnelly had reported to the Oglethorpe Barracks in late March to learn of his draft status, he was told by a sergeant that a residence of ten days in Chatham County qualified a man for conscription in the district and he would soon be notified where and when to report. Donnelly immediately informed McBain, who asked his lawyer if there was any way his overseer could avoid being drafted. The lawyer responded that, according to the law, the order to hold the March 4 draft had to come from the governor. But in this case it came from the adjutant general. In addition, Colonel Pelot, the officer who supervised the affair, had no authority to subdivide the men into separate groups and prioritize them.

McBain encouraged Donnelly to go to the state military authorities in Macon and make the case that the draft had been conducted illegally, and even if it were legal, as a married man, he should never have been selected so highly. Two days later McBain was wishing Donnelly good luck as the overseer boarded the cars of the Central of Georgia Railroad. A few days afterwards McBain read in the newspaper that the train had derailed, causing many casualties. He soon received a letter from Mr. Donnelly.

March 22, 1862
Deer Sir, I am sorry to say my trane to Macon rounded a curv too fast and fell off the rails. 4 peeple were killed and many more hert. I waked up hours later in a hospital with a real bad head acke, cuts all over my face and body, a fracktured collar bone and two badly spraned nees. I am still in the hospital but hope to go to my parents house soon to heel. The doc-ters say it will be many months before I can walk agane without kruches and for my collar bone to heel. I am writing my wife to come here to help me. I hope you will take me back when I am better. —R. Donnelly

The news devastated McBain. He had to return to the Heritage while he looked for another overseer. Finding a good one presented a challenge as most qualified men were either employed or in the army. While he ran the plantation, McBain placed advertisements in several Georgia newspapers, but he found no acceptable candidates and became increasingly depressed.

Finally, in early July, after a three-month search, he interviewed a forty-eight-year-old man who was not as bright or conscientious as Mr. Donnelly, but had experience running a small cotton plantation in western Georgia. The man was crude, cursing and spitting constantly, but seemed capable of managing things for a week at a time without McBain's presence.

As James deliberated whether to hire the man, he received two bits of good news. First, the Confederate Congress passed an act which gave the responsibil-ity for conscripting men into the army to the central government, and took it away from the state governors. The new law drafted all men between the ages of eighteen and thirty-five and excluded men over thirty-five who were not already in the service. Thus, Donnelly could return to work when he recovered from his injuries. Then he received a letter from Mr. Donnelly saying that he thought he could return to work by September. Since McBain would only need an overseer for two or three months, and felt he wouldn't find anyone better than the cur-rent candidate, he made a month-to-month offer of employment to the applicant, who accepted.

McBain had just invested five days training the temporary overseer and prayed that he could spend some time at home with his wife and grandson without any more problems at the plantation.

⁂

Sam Bannister dreaded taking a real job, even temporarily. It was against his nature. He simply didn't think in honest terms, just like his partners Willie Sloan and Harold Leyland. He had met Willie and Harold in 1858 at the Milledgeville state prison, where they were all serving time for theft. A strong bond formed amongst men with so much in common, and they agreed to pool their skills upon their return to society. Willie assured Sam and Harold that great riches awaited them in Savannah, with its wealthy populace and small police force. One year later they all lived in a house with a small stable on the east side of town. They stole items like bridles, saddles, harnesses, and buggies and tried to sell them through their "fence" in Savannah, stable-owner Johnny Tanner. If he couldn't liquidate the goods, the men traveled to their agents in Augusta and Macon.

The trio quickly made contacts in Savannah's criminal class, several of whom were involved in the Southern Rights Vigilance Association, which was founded to keep abolitionists and their literature out of the South. Though not politically motivated, the three men generally supported the organization's goal. They helped beat up a suspected northern journalist, who subsequently left town. A few months later, in May 1861, one of the association learned that a British sea captain had invited a local black man to dine with him on his ship in the harbor to the exclusion of whites. The captain needed to be taught a lesson, and when he ferried the negro and his wife back to the wharf after supper, ten local boys were waiting. Seven of them took the captain away to apply a coat of tar and cotton while Willie, Harold, and Sam detained the black couple until the deed was done. Then a white aristocratic fancy boy came to the pier and tried to free the darkey. In an ensuing fight, Willie shot the black man dead. To the trio's surprise, the people of Savannah rose up in outrage at the incident. The city council offered a five hundred dollar reward for information leading to the arrest of the attackers. The British consul added another one thousand dollars. A private individual offered two thousand dollars! Feeling the heat, the three left town, but returned four months later, and, with the war raging, no one seemed to be the wiser.

The war, however, made earning a living more difficult, even for thieves. The rumored presence of Union spies frightened the city council so much that it formed citizen ward patrols, which increased the police presence. The military posted guards at the entrances to the city and enforced a system of passports, making it more difficult to smuggle hot items out of the city. In addition, many residents left town, taking their most valuable belongings, and those who stayed watched their possessions more closely. Never ones to plan for a rainy day, the three needed money fast to survive.

In an attempt at a big payday, they stole an expensive, four-wheel, leather-upholstered, two-horse carriage. Greasing the way with a fifty-dollar bribe to a sentry at a guard post at night, they drove it to their Augusta fence. The man told them he would first have to paint the vehicle a new color and then take it to Aiken, South Carolina, away from snooping Georgia lawmen, before trying to sell it. Also, because of the poor economy, it might take some time to find a buyer for such an expensive item. Willie told him that they were desperate. As the sale amount could be three thousand dollars or more, the dealer promised to deliver the funds, less his commission of twenty-five percent, as soon as he sold the coach. The three returned to Savannah still needing cash.

Conditions didn't improve and towards the end of 1861, a few months after Harold and Sam had their run-in with Dante, the men decided to go their separate ways temporarily. Willie, at forty-two, returned to Atlanta to see if his parents or two older sisters had any jewelry or other items that he could borrow until he got back on his feet, and also to investigate opportunities for a man in his trade.

Harold, age forty-six, went to Columbus, Georgia to ply his craft. He eked out a living, but got creative in the spring of 1862. He learned that the new Confederate conscription law allowed men to hire substitutes who were not otherwise eligible to serve in their place. He traveled to Blakely in western Georgia and found in the Early County court records the name of a man who had died long ago at age thirty-five. Taking that identity Harold answered an advertisement for a substitute in the local newspaper. For a fee of three hundred dollars, he signed a contract with a banker and enlisted in a local militia company, certain that no one in the company had known the dead man. The next day Harold deserted, traveled west to Abbeville, Alabama and repeated the scheme. Six hundred dollars richer, he rode back through Georgia to Bryan County, directly southwest of Savannah, and hid in a cabin in the woods, where he fished, whittled, drank, and waited until he guessed that the authorities had given up looking for him.

Sam, the oldest of the group at forty-seven, went to Macon and for months stole anything he could from stores and individuals—men's jackets, top hats, shaving equipment—to pay for food and the shabby boarding house where he resided. Dejected at his lack of success, he moved back to Savannah at the end of June 1862, and faced the harsh reality that he had to take a real job until conditions improved. He answered an advertisement in the paper for an overseer at a brick plantation where he could live rent-free and get a salary and food ration. The owner's name was McBain. Sam rode to the plantation for an interview, making sure he arrived on time.

Mr. McBain told him that his previous overseer had been injured badly in a train accident and his only son had been captured at Fort Pulaski. He explained that he treated his negroes kindly and allowed his overseers to use the whip only as a last resort. Of course, Sam knew slaves understood but one language—that of the lash. Even though the old man seemed like an easy touch, Sam had doubts about taking a job that involved working with and living near so many blacks.

Sam's attitude changed when McBain gave him a tour of the plantation and showed him the coach house, stable, and barn. His eyes lit up like a forest fire. He had never seen so much bounty. The saddles, bridles, and harnesses were made of the finest leather, with shiny brass studs and perfect stitching. The buggy, coach, and wagons gleamed like new. And he could have access to them all! He put on his best behavior, trying not to belch in McBain's presence. McBain offered him the job on a monthly basis and even agreed to advance him fifteen dollars to pay his boarding house bill. Sam accepted and said he would move to the plantation the next day.

After getting the job, Sam went back to Savannah to pack his belongings. He bumped into Willie, who had just returned from Atlanta. Sam explained his employment at a plantation three miles west of town owned by James McBain and the treasure that awaited them. He said he needed a week to get trained and see how freely he could operate. Then he would contact Willie with his plan to pilfer McBain's property. Willie doubted that Sam could hold a job for a day, no less a week, but as he had just twenty dollars to his name, he told Sam that he'd wait to hear from him.

During the first week, Sam worked by McBain's side, listening to every word and asking many questions. His performance must have been acceptable as McBain left the plantation in his hands and returned home to Savannah. Sam hardly slept that first night on his own, thinking of the riches that would soon be his. He decided to steal McBain's most valuable saddle—probably worth three hundred dollars—first.

During a supply-purchasing trip to Savannah a few days later, he went to Willie's boarding house to inform him of the plan. Willie wasn't there, but Sam ran into the dealer from Augusta, who said he had sold the carriage, and although it was for only two thousand dollars, they were recently issued Yankee notes, or greenbacks, much more desirable than Confederate greybacks. The dealer gave Sam fifteen hundred dollars after his cut, made Sam sign a receipt, and left a note for Willie informing him of the payment to Sam. Sam also wrote a note to Willie, telling him that he would deliver a saddle on Saturday, at a location near town on the Augusta Road. Sam said he would give Willie his and Harold's share from the sale of the coach at that time, and assured Willie that the cash would be safely hidden in the overseer's house at the Heritage until then.

March Haynes walked up the West Broad Street wharf as Hercules, Jefferson, Jehova, and the rowers loaded supplies for the Heritage onto a flat-bottom boat. Since March's owner had been taken prisoner at Fort Pulaski, he piloted tugs to rebel batteries along the waterways closer to town. "Got a minute, Huhcles?" he asked.

Hercules called to Jefferson that he'd soon rejoin them. He and March walked down the pier, out of earshot. The river pilot asked, "You hear 'bout St. Simons Island?"

Hercules said years earlier he had once driven Massa and the Missus to a plantation on the island, fifty miles south of Savannah, but that was all.

March shook his head. "Ahm talkin' 'bout now. Ain' no white folk libin' dey. De plantuhs run like dogs when de Yankees tek Hilton Haid. De Yankees now sendin' runways tuh St. Simons. Dey grow crops an' git rations from de Yankees till de hahvest."

Hercules stepped back in disbelief. "Why're the Yankees doin' that?"

March shrugged. "Cain' say. Probly 'cause dey don' wan tuh lib wid us nig-guhs." He grabbed Hercules's arm. "T'ink 'bout it! Us kin lib widout whites."

Jehova called out, "Us done, Huhclees."

The coachman called back, "I'll be right over. Hold on a minute." He turned back to March, "What're you saying?"

"Ah hide muh boat in St. Augustine Crick. Ah kin git tuh St. Catrin's Island in de night widout no one knowin'. You git nigguhs tuh me an' ah kin git 'em tuh de Yankees. Dey ship 'em tuh St. Simons. Ah all now took eight!"

The thought of the risk involved made Hercules's voice climb to a near squeal. "You want me to help people run away from Massa?"

March spoke in a whisper, "Ah don' trus' no one else. All whites 'roun Saban-nah know you. De police an' soljuhs don' nebuh stop you."

Hercules looked at the boat and saw Jehova and Jefferson lying on the bench-es, enjoying a little rest. "I'll have to go through the guard posts to get to your boat. How do I explain a wagon full of niggers? We're going on a picnic to Tybee beach? Why don't you bring your boat closer to town?"

"'Cause dey kin see me on de ribuh. Ah kin hide bettuh in de cricks."

"You know what happens if we get caught?" Hercules placed his hand on his neck and gave a slight squeeze.

"You wan' tuh be uh slabe till you die? Dis chance mightn nebuh come agin."

Hercules blew out air through his flapping lips. "Gimme some time. I'm go-ing to the plantation in a few days and then I got to take Dante to a soldiers' camp the day after. I'll get back to you." He headed to the flatboat with his mind spin-ning. He yearned to be free. He wanted all blacks to be free. But he didn't want to die trying to achieve that, as Isaac did.

When Hercules first heard of Dante's new job, he wished him luck and told him to get that revolver out of their room. If Massa discovered it after Dante left, Hercules would be blamed. Dante couldn't think of a safe place to hide it in any of the outbuildings, and as his departure date neared, he started to panic. Two days before he was supposed to leave for the military camp, Hercules mentioned that he was picking up some bridles for Massa at the Heritage the next day.

A light flashed in Dante's mind. There must be hundreds of secure spots at the plantation to hide a gun. He asked, "Kin ah come?"

Hercules said, "If it's all right with Massa. Just be ready by noon." Dante promised. He waited until Hercules went to the main house. Then he carried the gun box to the coach house and crammed it in the shelf under the back side of the bench seat on the wagon, where it was barely visible. Dante slept better that night.

They left the next day at noon. Fifteen minutes later they approached the military guards on the Louisville Road. Dante had forgotten about them. His mouth went dry at the prospect of the wagon being searched. He closed his eyes and prayed. Fortunately, the guards knew Hercules and waved them through.

After Dante relaxed, he asked Hercules, "You meet de new obuhsuh?"

"Once at the plantation and once in town this week. I hardly spoke to him. He looks mean. I hear he never gets off his fat arse. He just sits around and drinks and has a temper. He already whipped Roman, Prince, and Kitt. I don't think Massa knows. Isaac didn't whip that many in fifteen years."

Dante nodded. He wondered why Massa would hire a man like that.

⬤

That same Saturday morning, Sam sat on a tree stump and watched the slaves at the molding tables. He whistled tunelessly and flipped a coin in the air, waiting for one o'clock so he could load McBain's saddle in one of the plantation wagons and deliver it and the cash to Willie. With his five-hundred-dollar share from the sale of the coach, Sam no longer had to sit around and watch a bunch of darkies make bricks. The Heritage, however, was too full of riches and too easy a mark to ignore, so Sam decided to work for two more weeks, take everything he could, and quit after receiving his pay. If McBain discovered that property was missing before he resigned, Sam would blame it on the slaves. Everyone knew they stole anything not nailed down. Besides, he would be leaving and didn't care what McBain might think.

Sam checked his pocket watch. Only noon—a full hour before shut down. He bristled at how the slaves worked like machines, keeping their heads down, performing their tasks, and occasionally breaking out in song. He thanked God he wasn't one of them. A crash jolted Sam from his thoughts. He saw Jehova at the stacking area, kneeling next to an overturned pallet of freshly molded bricks, scattered and squished on the ground. Sam didn't like the boy, who always wore a dumb grin as if he was enjoying himself. He walked over, took the whip off his belt, and lashed Jehova's back. The negro screamed and bolted upright. Every man within earshot turned and saw Sam strike Jehova again on the shoulder. The slave stepped back, tripped over the pallet, and landed on his rump on the ruined bricks. His face stretched in pain.

Sam pointed the whip handle at him. "Clean up that mess in thirty minutes. You don't, I'll beat you till you're white!"

Jehova nodded frantically as he got to his knees. "Yassuh, Massa, yassuh!"

Sam looked at the other slaves, coiled the whip, slapped it against his hip, and returned to the stump. The slaves continued working, exchanging glances. At one o'clock, Sam left for the stables without saying a word.

As Hercules and Dante drove up the avenue of oaks and around the big house, they saw about thirty men returning from the clay pits, their work done for the day. Hercules put fingers at the corners of his lips and whistled like a bob-white, but only a few folks looked his way. Hercules thought their reaction was odd. Usually on a Saturday afternoon at one o'clock the men practically danced back to the Quarter. He continued to the stables.

The road ended at a big circular turnaround, with the stables and coach house on the left and a barn and the blacksmith's shop on the right. A grassy field twenty yards wide separated the far side of the stables from a heavily wooded area. Dante looked around, sizing up the buildings.

Hercules parked, jumped down, and wondered aloud why he didn't see any of his men. He entered the stables and quickly reemerged. "No one in there." They heard a noise from the back of the coach house. Hercules said, "I'll be right back," and walked along the path between the two structures. Dante immediately removed the gun box from under the seat, ran into the stables, and looked for a place to hide it.

Hercules reached the grassy area behind the buildings and saw one of the plantation wagons parked at the far end of the coach house. Wagons were always loaded from the front of the building on the turnaround. As Hercules approached the vehicle, the overseer emerged from the back door lugging a saddle in both hands.

Sam saw Hercules coming towards him and cursed. He had been caught stealing, but he had no time to deal with McBain's coachman. He was already late getting to his meeting with Willie, and he still had to stop by the house to get the cash. He threw the saddle into the bed and shouted, "I told all you boys to stay away from here today. That includes you."

Hercules immediately understood the absence of workers, and he recognized the saddle as Master McBain's most valuable. He knew that if Massa wanted it in town, he would have asked him to bring it. "You didn't tell me 'cause I wasn't here. I've run these stables for thirty years and never saw a wagon loaded from this side. I was curious."

Sam scowled. "Well, you don't have to be curious no more. Now, get the hell out of here."

Hercules pointed to the bed of the wagon. "That's Massa's saddle, sir. I'm driving back to town soon. If he needs that, I can take it to him."

Sam felt the heat rising in his face. No nigger had a right to question him about anything. "I'll ask for your help when I want it. Now leave! Don't make me tell you again." Hercules didn't move. Sam took the whip off his belt and snapped it inches from Hercules's ear.

Hercules flinched but stood his ground. Usually, serious consequences await-ed any black who struck a white, but he felt certain that Massa would take his side if he defended himself while protecting Massa's property. Sam cracked the whip again, this time ripping the front of Hercules's white shirt. The negro glared at his tormentor. "Don't," he said slowly, "do that again, sir."

But Sam struck again, hitting Hercules's neck and buckling his knees. The coachman straightened and felt something trickle down his shoulder. He touched the wound and saw blood on his fingers. Like a snake, he sprang at Sam, who jumped to the side, snapped the whip low around Hercules's ankle, and pulled, flipping him on his backside. Sam screamed, "You damned nigger!"

Hercules tried to struggle to his feet, but Sam delivered another lash across the shoulder and sent him flat onto the ground. The negro held his arm up for protec-tion and tried to rise, but Sam hit him again. Hercules's bicep felt like it was on fire. He rolled over and tried to crawl under the wagon, out of the overseer's range, but Sam coiled the whip around his leg and held him on the open ground. Sam reared back, yelled like an Indian warrior, and swung so hard at Hercules's arse that his hat fell off. As Sam gritted his teeth and cocked his arm for another blow, an explosion boomed through the plantation like a summer thunderclap, splintering a hole in the top edge of the wagon's side panel, and causing the horses to rear up.

Sam spun around and saw a black man five feet away, holding a gun with two hands. Sam's eyes strained as if he recognized him. Then quicker than a frog's tongue, he flicked the whip around Dante's left wrist and tugged, yanking Dante off his feet and flat on his stomach. As Sam set himself to lash the negro, Dante rolled onto his back and fired with his right hand. Sam dropped the whip and hunched over as if he had a bad stomach ache. He tried to walk but couldn't.

Dante scrambled to his feet. Sam reached out a hand. Dante aimed and fired again, from three feet, and blew a hole in Sam's forehead. The overseer collapsed backwards like a felled tree. Dante lowered the revolver. His shoulders heaved with each breath as he stared at the body spread-eagled on the ground.

Hercules pulled himself up using the side of the wagon and clutched his shoulder. "Dante," he gasped, "you killed him."

Dante replied, "Lawd hab mussy." ✑

CHAPTER FOURTEEN

"Looks Like You've Lost Your Balls, Sir"

July 1862

"Dat's one ub 'em," Dante said in a shaky voice, pointing the gun at the corpse's belt buckle of an eagle. "One ub de men dat kill Andrew."

Hercules froze. "WHAT?"

Dante wiped his sweaty face with a kerchief. "He lib at de house wid de wagon."

Hercules toed Sam in the side to make certain he was dead. "You sure?"

"Ahm all time suhtin."

The men stared at the body. Hercules finally spoke. "Holy Jesus! Massa hired one of Andrew's killers and didn't know it." He then squeezed Dante's arm until the cook grimaced. "You brought that gun here through the guard post without telling me?"

"Din' know wut else tuh do."

Hercules released his grip. "I guess I'm glad you did. You saved me. But now we got to get rid of him. Massa can't protect us from killing a white man, even if he did murder Andrew, which we could never prove."

Dante's legs wobbled at the thought of the possible consequences of killing Sam. He held onto the side of the wagon for support. "H . . . how?"

"Bury him somewhere, but not here." Hercules looked up at the sky, as if seeking advice from the heavens. He told Dante. "Hide that gun someplace good. We'll get rid of it later. We need to load him in the Savannah wagon. Hurry! Everyone here heard them shots and wants to know what happened."

Dante dashed to the stables, put the gun in the box, found a ladder, and hid the weapon in the rafters.

Hercules rinsed his wounds at the water pump and rolled his blood-stained shirt in a ball, knowing he had to avoid suspicion of anyone he might meet on the way back to town. He took an old, soiled blanket from the coach house and met Dante. "Put his body on this to keep the blood off the wagon." Hercules spread the blanket on the ground next to Sam. The coachman grabbed the legs and Dante the arms. As they raised Sam, his head drooped back and a stream of blood and saliva ran out of his mouth and onto Dante's hand. Dante dropped his end, fell to his knees, and vomited on Sam. Hercules shouted, "No time for that. Get up and lift." Dante dragged his hand on the ground and tried again.

After they lay Sam in the bed, Hercules splashed the bloody ground with a bucket of water. He put away the plantation wagon and horses, got a shovel from the stables, and said, "Let's go! I need another shirt." Hercules often slept at the Heritage when Massa stayed overnight. He shared a cabin with three unmarried men and kept clothes there.

On their way to the Quarter they waved to the house servants, who were standing on the rear stairs of the big house, looking for an explanation for the gun shots. As Hercules drove past the overseer's house, he realized that they also had to dispose of Sam's belongings. They stopped, ran into the house, and stuffed Sam's possessions into his carpetbag. Fortunately, Sam traveled light.

When they reached Hercules's cabin a sea of people swarmed around them like a black tide. The closest ones stared into the bed at the body. A few pulled away at the sight, but most smiled before moving to let others look. Hercules stood on the wagon bench so everyone could see his welts and gashes. He called out, "We just caught Sam tryin' to steal Massa's best saddle. We stopped him. I don't think he's going to whip any more niggers. But we have to be quiet, all of us!" The crowd nodded in unison. They hated Sam. "Dante and I just cleaned out the overseer's house of his belongings. We can't leave a trace of him here."

One man called out, "Don' fuhgit he hoss."

Hercules said, "Holy Jesus! That's right. Someone go to the stables right now and bring her. His saddle, too." One of the stable boys dashed off.

Hercules jumped down and ran into his cabin. The folks focused on Dante, wanting more details, but he still felt nauseous and lowered his head.

Hercules reappeared in a few minutes wearing a dark shirt to hide any trace of oozing blood and watched the stable boy tie Sam's horse to the wagon. He stood on the driver's seat again and shouted, "I been looking for Sam the overseer. He tried to steal Massa's saddle and I caught him. I think he ran away. Anybody see him?"

A man replied, "Ah seed he ride out on he hoss. Habunt seed he since."

Hercules yelled, "All of you here see Sam ride out and never come back?"

A chorus of "Yassuhs" rose from the crowd.

"Good, 'cause if Massa or any other white man come lookin' for him, that's what you tell 'em." Hercules spoke to a man standing by the wagon. "Roman, let the folks in the big house know." Hercules handed Sam's carpetbag to Jehova and said, "Burn this to ashes, you understand?" Jehova nodded and ran off.

Hercules sat, cracked the whip, and the horses trotted up the avenue of oaks onto the Augusta Road. He took a trail that branched to the south midway between town and the plantation. After a quarter-mile he turned into an open field and drove behind a clump of bushes and palmetto trees fifty yards off. The two men took turns with the shovel and buried Sam in a three-foot-deep grave behind the foliage. They stamped down the ground, smoothed it with the shovel, and covered it with leaves and palm fronds. Dante asked, "Wut 'bout he hoss?"

The horse neighed, as if she knew they were talking about her. Hercules patted the blond mare's neck and inspected her hide with circular brown patches on her hind flanks. "Beautiful animal. Probably stolen. We can't take her into town—no place to hide her. We got to set her loose. There's a militia camp at the Ten Broeck Race Track. I'll send her in that direction. The soldiers will take her." Hercules removed the saddle and bridle and put them in the wagon. Then he gave the horse a hard slap on the backside and she raced away.

A mile closer to town, Willie sat on his wagon, smoked his twentieth cigarette since he arrived, and awaited Sam, the cash, and the saddle. He needed the money bad. He laughed when Sam had told him he had found an overseer's job, but reconsidered when his partner said that the plantation had enough bounty to support them for years. Willie saw a small cloud of dust in the distance and knew it was Sam, two hours late. Typical. If the saddle really had value and Sam had the cash from the sale of the coach, Willie would forgive his tardiness. Ten minutes later, the wagon came into view, driven by two darkies. As they passed, the men smiled and called out, "Ebnin', Massa." Willie gave a slight nod and flicked away the cigarette butt.

After passing the man, Hercules said to Dante, "Wonder what he's waitin' for?"

"Dunno. Wut you gwine tell Massa 'bout Sam?"

"The truth—sort of. I caught him stealing a saddle, he whipped me, and ran away. First, I have to hide this saddle and bridle in the coach house without Jefferson seeing. We'll sell them later."

⚜

Sarah McBain placed her tea cup on the white china plate bordered in a gold garland design, and pushed it away. "I am not leaving, dear husband, with all the uncertainty at the Heritage. I'm too involved in the hospital and the relief committee to even think of it. Who does General Pemberton think he is, asking the city council to remove all the women and children to camps outside of town? He makes me miss General Lee."

James said, "Dear, General Pemberton is the new commanding officer of the Department of the South. He's thinking of your safety, should the worst come to pass. But you needn't worry. The city council refused his request. Still, I'm concerned, and I'd like you and Danny to go your sister's house in Roswell. You'll be safer there and you can serve the soldiers by helping her and her husband run their shoe factory."

Sarah shook her head. "My place is with you and Danny, right here. And I want to be home when Joseph returns."

William knocked and McBain asked him in. "Master, Hercules is back and wants to have a word with you, if it's convenient. He says it's important."

James looked at his watch. "Send him in." Sarah decided she had said all she needed to and left the room.

McBain tapped his finger on the ink blotter. He looked at the daguerreotypes of Amy and Joseph in a gold-plated, dual picture frame on his desk and wished that they were with him. Hercules stood before him, having just described the confrontation with Sam. The coachman had even removed his shirt to show his wounds. McBain believed Hercules, but he thought it unusual that a white man would run off and not remain to challenge a black man's side of the story and collect his pay. Clearly, hiring Sam was a mistake and McBain hoped that he wouldn't come back. Still, he dreaded the thought of looking for another overseer. He finally spoke. "Hercules, tomorrow's Sunday. I'll be attending church and spending the day with Mrs. McBain and Danny. I'll ride to the Heritage on Monday. I want you to go there now and watch things. If Sam returns, tell him to come here at once and see me."

Hercules nodded. "Yes, Massa." He cleared his throat. "One other thing, sir. Dante was with me today at the Heritage. He says Sam was one of Andrew's killers, but he told me after Sam rode off."

McBain's jaw dropped and he stammered, "How . . . how does Dante know that?"

"You know he saw a wagon with three men racing from town the night Andrew got shot. He saw the wagon again a while back and followed it to a house. Sam was there with another man. Dante told Master Joseph, but that was the same day he got called to Fort Pulaski and couldn't search for Sam. He told us not to do anything until he returned."

McBain rested his elbows on the desk, held his head in his hands, and groaned. He mumbled out loud, "So I hired Andrew's killer." He looked up at Hercules. "If Sam returns, apprehend him and bring him to me. I'll take him to the police."

Hercules said, "Massa, I'm taking Dante to the army camp tomorrow."

"Oh, I nearly forgot. Have Jefferson take him. You go to the Heritage now. I need you there most of all."

After Hercules left, James stood and stared out the window at Danny and Truvy playing in the square. He wondered how many other mistakes he would make, and then informed Sarah of the turn of events.

Willie went to Fowler's Bar after giving up on Sam. He figured that an emergency must have prevented his partner from leaving the plantation. Now, nursing a glass of whiskey, and in need of funds, he concluded that he couldn't wait for Sam to contact him. He had to go to the Heritage to collect his money. By noon the next day he was riding up the avenue of oaks and admiring the white mansion with green shutters in the distance, framed by the green, arching branches of live oak trees. He knew why Sam took the job. The place oozed wealth.

He approached the Quarter and saw about one hundred blacks in front of their cabins, weaving baskets, mending clothes, and chatting with each other. They fell silent the moment they spotted him. Willie asked a man crossing the road, "I'm looking for Sam, the overseer of this place."

The negro replied, "Jes' uh momen'" and ran to Hercules's cabin.

Hercules emerged and recognized the man as the one sitting in the wagon on the Louisville Road the previous day. He figured that the visitor must have been waiting for Sam and the saddle. Hercules tensed up in anticipation of trouble. "I understand you're looking for Mr. Sam."

"Yeah. Where is he?"

The intruder wore a holstered gun on his right hip, a sheathed knife further back on his belt, and had a coiled whip strapped on the rear of his saddle. Hercules couldn't let him get hold of any of them and stepped to a few feet from the man. He looked up and spoke politely. "He's gone, sir. Left yesterday and hasn't returned. That's all I know."

Willie scratched his chin whiskers. Sam wouldn't leave for good without telling him. He doubted that Sam would take all the money and the saddle for himself, especially after arranging a meeting with him. Willie looked Hercules in the eye, trying to detect if the Sambo was lying. "He just left? Did he pack his belongings? Did he tell McBain?"

Hercules watched the man's hands out of the corner of his eye as he replied, "He packed his things and left, sir, but didn't say where to. He didn't tell Massa, who's in Savannah, but Massa knows he's gone."

Willie looked around the area, as if Sam might be hiding behind one of the cabins. He said to Hercules, "Who are you?"

"Massa's coachman."

"If you're his coachman, and he's in town, what are you doing here?"

"He asked me to come out and look after things when he heard about Sam."

Willie realized that he wouldn't get any truthful information from the coachman. If Sam left on his own, he would have taken the cash. However, if something bad happened to him, as Willie suspected, then the money was where Sam said he had hid it—in the house. "I need to look in Sam's place. He left something for me."

Hercules's eyes didn't leave the stranger. "I'm sorry, sir. Massa don't want no one on his land without his permission."

"I'll only be a few minutes, and then I'll leave. Where's the house?"

"I can't let you do that, sir. You need Massa's permission."

Willie's lips tightened at the coachman's insolence. He was done being nice. "Who's gonna stop me?"

Hercules saw the veins in the man's neck start to bulge and inched closer to him. "I will, sir, if it comes to that. I hope it don't, but Massa gave me instructions, and I mean to follow them. That's all I got to say. You want to know more, speak to Massa."

Every pair of eyes in the Quarter focused on the two men. Not only did Willie have to search that house, he had to teach this darkey a lesson in front of his fellow niggers. He reached for his revolver but Hercules expected that move and grabbed the man's wrist. Willie tried to pull away but Hercules held his grip and yanked the stranger off his horse. Willie hit the ground on his side with a thud, and the revolver skidded across the road. Hercules stepped over and picked it up.

Willie got to his feet, rubbed his shoulder, and held out his hand. "Boy, give me that gun—NOW."

Hercules, who had been taught to handle a gun years ago by Massa in case he ever needed to protect the man, held the revolver at his side, pointed at the ground. "I can't do that, sir, because I don't trust you. You just tried to pull it on me."

Willie took two steps towards Hercules, who raised the gun and pointed it at the stranger's chest just ten feet away. Willie froze, stepped back, and bumped into his horse. He turned and saw all the blacks to his rear clearing away.

Hercules wanted the man to leave, but he also wondered if he could be one of Andrew's killers, in which case he would bring him to Massa. Dante had said that Sam's partner's names were Willie and Harold. Hercules pulled back the hammer with his thumb.

Willie held up his hands at shoulder height. "Hold on, boy. I'll speak to McBain."

"What's your name, so I can tell him to expect you?"

Willie slowly lowered his arms. "You don't need to know my name. I'm a friend of Sam, that's all."

Hercules asked, "You Willie or Harold?" The man didn't reply. Hercules wanted to tie him up and bring him to town, but if the intruder wasn't either one, Hercules would probably go to jail. "Which is it, sir, Willie or Harold?"

"I don't know who you're talking about."

Hercules kept the gun pointed at the man's chest and said, "Turn around and put your hands on your horse." Willie took a few seconds, but did as he was ordered. Hercules stuck the barrel in the man's back, pulled the knife from its sheath, took the whip from the saddle, and stepped back. He put the gun in his belt and sliced the whip in half. He said, "You can turn around now." Willie faced Hercules, who tossed the two pieces at him. Willie glared at Hercules and his eyebrow started to twitch. Hercules pulled the gun from his belt and threw the knife to the side of the road. He told the man to stand by the horse's head.

Hercules then stepped to the saddle bag and pulled out a powder flask and a cloth bag. He turned over the flask, depressed the lever, poured the gun powder onto the ground, and kicked dirt over it. He loosened the cord on the pouch with his teeth and slung the round bullets down the road. Hercules said loud enough for all to hear, "Looks like you've lost your balls, sir." The slaves erupted in laughter.

Willie's face turned beet red. He seethed, "You black son of a bitch."

Hercules replaced the empty flask and cloth bag in the saddle bag and said, "I'll give your gun to Massa. You can get it from him. You can leave now."

Willie had been completely emasculated by a nigger in front of a hundred of his fellow tribesmen. He wanted to kill the coachman so badly he could taste it. He mounted his horse, pointed a finger at Hercules, and said, "You haven't seen the last of me. I'm gonna kill you, if it's the last thing I do. I hope you know that."

Hercules didn't reply. He waited until the man rode away and wondered why he wanted to search the overseer's house. Hercules made a point to make a thorough inspection. Something was in there and the stranger would return for it—and soon.

The Heritage slaves returned to their business, congratulating each other on Hercules's performance. Kitt, the youngest son of Isaac, walked over to Hercules and said, "You get a chance to kill a white man, you oughta do it."

Hercules studied the twenty-four year-old for a moment. "You actin' very big, Kitt. Your pa wouldn't want you to talk like that." Kitt walked away, muttering.

By the time Willie reached the Augusta Road, he had considered five different ways to torture the coachman, but he thought he might need help and decided to wait for Harold to return from hiding. Willie had another pressing concern—getting money for lodging, food, whiskey, and a new gun. When he arrived in town he rode up and down the streets, looking for an unattended horse or an open coach-house door for something to steal, but no such opportunity arose. He was desperate. He decided to go to the Marshall House Hotel bar to rob a drunk.

Four hours later, he lay on his boarding-house bed, inspecting the watch he had just taken from the hotel maid who he called Penny Savannah. He would be able to trade the timepiece the next day for at least fifty dollars, and he didn't have to beat up anyone to get it. Willie was disappointed that Penny didn't want to be his partner, but he knew where she worked. If an opportunity presented itself, he wouldn't hesitate to find her. He closed his eyes and thought of the girl. She sure was pretty.

⁂

James McBain looked at the revolver on his desk and then at Hercules. For the second time in as many days his coachman reported odd happenings at the Heritage. Hercules said, "I tried to get his name. Might've been one of Andrew's killers, but he didn't bite. I didn't want to tie him up and bring him here if I wasn't certain."

McBain mused, "You did the right thing. There would have been hell to pay if you had apprehended an innocent man, even if you did it on my property." McBain examined the gun. He was convinced that Sam was stealing, or about to, but he still thought his sudden disappearance puzzling, and the fact that someone came looking for him the next day and wanted to search the overseer's house made it more so. He continued, "That man, whoever he is, will return to the Heritage. He wants something, as well as his gun and revenge on you. I'll have to stay there until I hire another overseer. Let me speak to Mrs. McBain and I'll be ready to go. We can't leave the place unguarded for a minute."

"Yes, Massa." Hercules left to prepare to return to the Heritage. ⚮

CHAPTER FIFTEEN

Just Plain Dumb
April – June 1862

Life on Governors Island took a turn for the worse for Joseph soon after he saw Emily. The day before she was to make her second appearance, Colonel Loomis informed the prisoners that they were no longer allowed to have visitors, although they could still send and receive letters. So the couple wrote to each other almost daily. They concentrated on family news and avoided topics like slavery and the naval exploits of Emily's brother. Joseph enjoyed describing Danny's boyish pranks, like the time he brought a dead snake into the house, and cleared it of all the female servants. They didn't stop running until Joseph caught up to them at Chatham Square. Joseph and Emily's correspondence always ended with "All my love . . . ," although Joseph still wrestled with his feelings for the woman who had taken his daughter away.

Emily reported that she went to Amy's house twice but no one answered, and concluded that she must be out of town. She promised to keep trying.

Joseph and the other officers passed time playing chess and cribbage, writing letters, reading, and walking the grounds of Fort Columbus. The eating saloon overlooked lower Manhattan, Brooklyn, Staten Island, and the harbor. The men could not have chosen a better site to be incarcerated—at least in the spring, summer, and fall. And friends and relatives were allowed to send food, clothing, and money to the prisoners. Two Savannah men, one living in New York and the other sitting in a federal prison in Boston, each contributed five hundred dollars so the men could buy necessities from the camp sutler.

Their only major complaint, other than the prohibition of visitors, was the Yankee decision to release to the streets of New York the eight slaves who had chosen to accompany their masters from Hilton Head.

One day, as Joseph took an afternoon stroll in the warm May sunshine, he saw a pack of dogs roaming near the kitchen. A soldier opened the door and heaved scraps from a tin plate onto the grass. The canines converged on the food the way water rushes to a drain. Five of them hogged it all while a filthy white, curly-haired mutt not weighing more than six or seven pounds stood aside. When he attempted to snag a morsel, the others growled and snapped at him. As the others feasted, he sat a few feet away and whimpered.

Joseph hobbled towards the crowd of animals, waving his cane, and yelling "Scram." They scattered with strings of gristle hanging from their mouths. The pup retreated a few steps and, with a shivering tail, watched the rampaging human. Joseph picked up a small chunk of meat, tip-toed toward the outcast, knelt, and held out his hand. "Come on, little fella." The dog approached him as if walking on paper-thin ice, and when he got within two feet, Joseph placed the meat on the ground. The raggedy creature cocked his grime-caked head, snatched the brown lump in its teeth, swallowed it in one gulp, and yelped a thank you. Joseph slowly reached out to touch its head. The dog flinched, but closed his eyes and received his first taste of human affection with a soft moan. Joseph gathered a few more scraps, and watched the starving animal eat.

Satisfied by his good deed, Joseph headed to the barracks. Half way there he stopped and turned. The dog stood just a few steps away, staring up at him, his tongue hanging from the side of his mouth. Joseph knew he couldn't keep a pet when he might be exchanged at any time, so he half-heartedly told the animal, "Git!" The mutt sat on his haunches and cried. Joseph didn't have the heart to chase him away, so he continued to the building, hoping the animal would somehow understand his predicament and disappear. Before opening the door, he snuck another glance and saw the little fluff-ball lying on his belly on the grass, his stubby tail fluttering like the wings of a bee. Joseph shook his head and said, "You're in a lot worse shape than I am, little fella. I guess a few days of food and attention are better than none." Joseph fetched a sliver of soap and a stringy grey rag from the barracks, grabbed a pail with a rope tied to the handle from the side of the building, and limped to the sea wall with his new companion close behind.

Joseph gave the pup his first bath to a sonata of howls, which drew laughs from the other prisoners in the area. After drying the fur he picked up the boney dog, looked underneath, and said, "Yep, you are a little fella, and now you almost look like a real dog." The pooch barked and rolled on his back on the dirt path that lined the sea wall. Joseph shook his head. "You idiot—now you're dirty again. You're just plain dumb. But then, you are a Yankee." He brushed off the dog with his hand and they headed back to the barracks. Before entering, Joseph pointed to the dog and ordered "Sit!" The dog didn't move. Joseph shook his head and said, "Just plain dumb."

A few hours later, when the officers left for supper, they were greeted with a bark. As they headed to the mess, the dog walked beside Joseph, who explained his day's experience to the others. The dog waited patiently while the humans disappeared into the dining salon. The men saved leftovers and scattered them on the ground as they left. The mutt gobbled down the best meal of his young life. Later that night, as the dog slept outside, by the steps of the barracks, the prisoners debated a name, and settled on JD, for their beloved president, Jefferson Davis. Over the following weeks, JD shadowed Joseph, and when the men marched to and from their meals, JD led them, trotting like the lead horse in a military parade.

While the dog added a pleasant diversion from prison life, the captives still spent hours speculating about a prisoner exchange. They heard countless rumors of a pending release, only to be disappointed each time. Then, one evening in late-May, Colonel Loomis walked into the barracks and announced, "Gentlemen, I have just been advised that you will be transferring tomorrow morning to a new prison on Johnson's Island in Lake Erie. Have your things packed and ready to go. I prefer not to send you under guard. I only ask for your word that you won't try to escape and you can travel like gentlemen on a parole of honor with just one supervising officer."

Colonel Olmstead stepped forward and assured him, "You have our word, Colonel. Thank you for that accommodation."

As soon as Loomis exited, the cursing began. The men had counted on being exchanged, not transferred. Joseph stomped the floor at the thought of leaving the proximity of Emily, Charlotte, and Amy and wrote a letter to his wife explaining his situation. He told her that he loved her and hoped they would be a family again soon. The next morning he paid the cook to deliver it.

After breakfast the men grabbed their luggage and left the barracks for the last time to catch a steam tug for Jersey City and the Erie Railroad depot. The second exodus of the morning confused JD, but he again greeted the humans with his usual bark and tail wag. Joseph couldn't look the dog in the eye and hoped that the next lot of prisoners would care for him. Oblivious of the turn of events, JD led the men toward the mess, but stopped and howled when they took another path. He scampered alongside Joseph, who tried to ignore his little friend. When they reached the boat, JD accompanied Joseph up the gangway. A guard stepped over, picked up the dog by the neck, and tossed him back onto the wharf. Joseph bit down in anger, but walked on. JD yelped as he stood to the side and watched the remaining soldiers gain the vessel. He followed the last man but the same soldier kicked him aside. JD bared his teeth and growled at the guard, who stepped forward to deliver a final kick. The Confederates standing at the ship's railing yelled at him to leave the dog alone. The red-faced soldier turned and shouted, "Shut up, you damned rebels, before I come up there and kick you!" JD seized upon the diversion and bounded up the gangway to the cheers of the men. He found Joseph and sat at his feet. The guard yelled, "Keep the stinking mutt!" JD, now a prisoner of war, barked. Joseph picked him up and held him over his head in triumph.

The train trip took a little over one day and included several stops, where locals, both black and white, came out in the hundreds. They pressed their noses against the car windows to see the "secesh," as Northerners often referred to Southerners. Joseph held JD to the window to stare back at the gawkers.

They arrived at Sandusky Bay in Ohio at noon the next day. Joseph hid JD in his jacket as the men passed guards to board a steamboat for the two-mile trip to Johnson's Island. They rode in silence and watched the remote island and the brown, square stockade grow larger. Midway through the voyage, JD stuck out his head, looked around, licked Joseph's cheek, and retreated under the jacket. After docking, ten soldiers holding rifles with fixed bayonets stomped onto the boat, followed by a first lieutenant who ordered the captives to follow him. They marched from the wharf onto land, along the stockade wall of thick logs. Four men were needed to push open the heavy wooden gate. The prisoners stepped onto a dirt road that bisected the grounds. On either side of the road sat six two-story wooden barracks. Joseph thought a good gust of wind would topple them like dominoes. As he placed JD on the ground, he looked around and guessed the area to be about eight acres of hard-packed dirt, and the stockade walls to be twelve feet high. A blockhouse sat atop each corner, fitted with cannons that leered into the yard like fire-breathing iron vultures.

The Union officer ordered the Southerners to line up shoulder to shoulder in two rows and face him while he conducted a roll call. "I am First Lieutenant Drake," he began before a low growl stopped him. He saw JD sitting at Joseph's feet with teeth bared. "What is that?"

Joseph looked down and said, "Easy, JD." He then said to the officer, "A dog. He followed us from Governors Island. I'm taking care of him."

Drake spat in disgust at having to deal with a pet. "What does JD stand for?"

Joseph did not want to annoy the lieutenant, who could take the dog away if he wanted. "Just Plain Dumb. We dropped his middle name. Now he's Just Dumb, or JD."

"Well, keep him out of our way. If he bites anyone, or shits where he shouldn't, he's going for a long swim." The officer then ordered each man to step forward at the call of his name and give up all his money to the corporal, who would issue receipts. The prisoners grumbled at having to hand over their cash.

When roll call ended, another officer walked through the gates, and the Union soldiers snapped to attention. He faced the new arrivals. "Prisoners, my name is Colonel William Pierson, the commanding officer of this installation. There are about one thousand other rebel officers here, temporarily confined to their barracks. The only way to maintain order with so many men is to demand strict adherence to the rules, so listen carefully." Pierson pulled a piece of paper from his jacket pocket and read from it. "Once a day you will receive a soldier's ration, the same as my men. Each barracks has one cook pot, so you'll need to form messes and take turns. Some of my soldiers will cook for you for a small fee. We have taken your money so you can't attempt to bribe my men. You may buy articles from the camp sutler and he will draw against your funds. We will settle all accounts upon your release. You must be present for roll call at reveille and tattoo. In between you have access to the stockade grounds. Once a week you will be allowed to bathe in Sandusky Bay."

The colonel looked up to make certain he had everybody's attention. "The area within thirty feet of the stockade walls is a dead zone. The line is marked with stakes three feet high. If you cross that line, my guards have orders to shoot, no questions asked. This is no idle threat." Pierson then surveyed the line of men facing him. He did a double-take at Olmstead, walked to him, and held out his hand. "Your sword, Colonel."

Olmstead explained that the Union commander at Hilton Head allowed him to keep it. Pierson cut him off. "I said, your sword, Colonel! I don't answer to that general." Olmstead handed it over, never relaxing his glare. Pierson said, "It will be returned upon your release, Colonel. Did you really expect to keep a weapon in prison? Is there anything else you'd like—a shotgun perhaps?"

Olmstead, still fuming, said, "All we want from the North is to leave us alone to live in peace."

Pierson froze. He glared at Olmstead and inhaled deeply to calm himself. He stepped back and spoke loud enough for all to hear. "You know, I've heard several rebels use those very same words—'Leave us alone to live in peace.' Gentlemen, let me help you with some history. Our country recently held a presidential election according to our Constitution, and the candidate representing the North promised that he would not interfere with your sacred institution of human bondage. He won, and you insulted him and refused to recognize the results. Yet we left you alone. One of your states seceded from the Union six weeks after that election and sealed off a federal fort with a federal garrison on federal land, denying access to federal ships, and we still left you alone. We sent a merchant ship—the *Star of the West*—with supplies and some reinforcements, posing no danger to you, and you opened your cannons on her, forcing her to turn around. Yet still we left you alone. Then other states—Georgia being one of them, Colonel Olmstead—seized federal forts, federal custom houses, federal post offices, federal arsenals, and federal mints—WHILE THEY WERE STILL PART OF THE UNION! YET WE STILL LEFT YOU ALONE!"

Joseph could hear Colonel Pierson snorting like a bull between words. He knew there was more to come. "As those states seceded, they started purchasing large amounts of armaments from northern gun dealers and arsenals for no other reason than to use against the North, and we still left you alone. Then seven slave-holding states formed a separate Confederacy hostile to our great Union, and what did you do? You bombarded with all your might a tiny seventy-five-man garrison holed up in Fort Sumter who threatened nothing except your silly pride. Did you think for a second what we might do in the face of this intolerable insult? You had pushed us over the brink, UNTIL WE COULD NO LONGER LEAVE YOU ALONE!" Pierson hollered. "Officers of the Confederacy, hear me, and hear me well. This war, all the dead, all the wounded, all the pain, all the shattered lives, all the broken families, are on your leaders' hands. I implore you to think of that the next time you ask us to leave you alone to live in peace."

Pierson turned to Drake, said "Take over, Lieutenant," and walked to the gate as he inspected Olmstead's sword.

Joseph looked at Olmstead and rolled his eyes. Drake led the prisoners into Barracks Five. They walked up a staircase wide enough for one man, and which creaked like a Georgia pine in a windstorm. The top floor had four rows of twelve bunk beds, each with a sack of straw for a mattress and a thin blanket. Sunlight sliced through the spaces between the log walls. Joseph hoped he would be gone before winter. "Pick a bunk, gentlemen. The first floor is your eating room. Roll call is at dusk." Drake left.

Olmstead sat on a bed and said to the men around him, "Based on the colonel's twisted lecture, I have a feeling that prison life will be less than bearable."

Joseph selected a lower bunk, pushed his valise and knapsack under it, and sat. JD curled up at his feet. Joseph rubbed his furry head. "Looks like we'll be spending some more time together, little fella. Good for you, bad for me." JD rolled on his back and wagged his tail.

Amy McBain Carson stepped on the two letters that had been slipped under the front door when she returned to her townhouse from a six-week visit with her husband's aunt on Long Island. The hack driver placed her luggage in the foyer, and while Colleen Mullins, Amy's Irish servant, put seven-month-old James Joseph Carson to bed, Amy took a seat in the living room. She first opened the unstamped envelope addressed in her brother's handwriting and read that Joseph was imprisoned on Governors Island, having arrived two days after she left for Long Island. She slapped the letter on the table, angry that he had been seriously wounded at Manassas and had still volunteered to serve at Fort Pulaski, which resulted in his capture. She pledged to see him the next day.

The other letter was from her father and caused equal consternation. The Confederate government had sequestered her house on Harris Street, including all the furnishings, and all rent payments from her tenants, which her father had been collecting. She sighed as she considered her options, but wouldn't choose until she spoke with Bob.

Amy McBain, Joseph's older sister, was raised to be a southern lady, refined in manners and culture; marry a wealthy southern gentleman; and raise a large family. But she had a rebellious spirit and insisted on attending college. After she graduated from Wesleyan Woman's College in Macon, she toured Europe with friends. Upon her return, she decided to help less fortunate Georgians and found employment as an attendant at the state insane asylum in Milledgeville. She worked dedicatedly for years, but after a disastrous flirtation with a patient, she returned to Savannah and opened a restaurant.

Soon afterwards, Amy fell in love with and married Robert Carson, even after she discovered that he was an undercover reporter for a New York newspaper and not an artist as he had claimed. To prove his commitment to her, Bob quit his job and worked with Amy in the restaurant. But he fell under the suspicious eyes of local vigilantes, who ambushed him one night and beat him senseless. For his safety, the couple moved to New York City, where they lived in Bob's inherited four-story townhouse. Amy gave birth to James Joseph Carson five months later in October 1861. Bob found a job reporting on the war for the *New York Standard*. He didn't like being away from his wife and son for extended periods, but he had to support his family, and covering the battles provided the excitement and prestige that he craved.

Amy didn't like being alone for weeks at a time. She had few friends in New York and limited visits with her sister-in-law Emily, the witch who had abandoned Amy's brother. When Bob left on his most recent assignment to cover the war in Tennessee, she decided to stay with his aunt on Long Island. She returned to Manhattan at the end of May—the day of Bob's scheduled arrival. He walked through the door three hours later.

As they lay in bed that night, Bob told Amy about his trip—the Union victories in Tennessee and the bubbling animosity between the commander of the department, Major General Henry W. Halleck, and the man most responsible for the successes, Major General Ulysses S. Grant. Bob also talked about another general, William Tecumseh Sherman, who had been sent home on a twenty-day leave the previous December by Halleck because he believed Sherman was physically and mentally unable to perform his duties. Reporters wrote extensively about Sherman's insanity, but the officer returned to service and redeemed himself at Shiloh, where he helped secure a Yankee victory and earned a promotion. "Can you believe it?" asked Bob. "He went insane and now he's a major general, leading men into battle?"

Amy's eyelids began to flutter and Bob asked about her time on Long Island. Instead, she told him about Joseph's capture and her plan to visit him the next day. Bob explained that he had to report to his office in the morning, but would visit Joseph as soon as possible, perhaps the day after. Then Amy described her father's letter.

Bob rolled on his side to face her. "The bastards! Is that legal?"

"My father says that under the new Confederate law they'll try to prove that I'm an alien enemy. If I'm not there to contest it, they'll win."

"That's absurd. You were born and raised in the South and lived there your entire life. You're a wife and a mother, not a soldier."

Amy shrugged. "I'm living in New York with no indication that I'll move back. In their eyes, I'm a Northerner."

Bob traced his finger over his wife's belly. "What are you going to do?"

"I don't know yet. But I won't let them take my property without a fight. First, I'm going to visit Joseph."

He stretched to kiss her lips. She put her arm around his shoulder and pulled him on her. Thirty minutes later, as Bob snored, she made a decision.

The next day Amy went to Governors Island only to learn that Joseph had been transferred a few days earlier to a prison in Ohio.

In mid-June, one week before Bob departed for Tennessee to rejoin Halleck's army for its expected assault on Corinth, Mississippi, Amy told him that she wanted to go to Savannah to save her property. Bob refused to give his permission, saying it was too dangerous. Besides, she had to go to the secretary of state in Washington to get a passport to travel to the South, and he issued very few.

So Amy remained in New York—but only until Bob left for Tennessee. Then she packed for a train trip south. A few days later, Amy sat next to Colleen, who, though the same height as Amy, took up three-quarters of the two seat bench, in a Washington City building with little Jimmy in her arms, waiting for the secretary of state. Two hours later a man emerged and Amy approached him. "Excuse me, sir. I know you're busy, but I've been waiting for hours. I'd like to have a word with you if I may."

The slim man with reddish-grey hair, two chins and a long, slightly hooked nose, looked at his pocket watch and wondered what favor she wanted. "I'm in a hurry, madam. What is so pressing?"

Amy stepped closer to block his path to the stairs. The man looked at the child and couldn't help but touch his head. "Mr. Seward, I live in New York City with my husband. He's a reporter for the *New York Standard*. I moved there from Savannah when the war started. The Confederate authorities have sequestered all my assets, claiming that I'm an alien enemy. I want to defend my right to my property in court. I would also like my parents and brother to see my baby, who was born in New York. Would you please grant me a passport to cross Union lines? You have my word that I will return to New York as soon as I settle my business."

William H. Seward didn't like Southerners very much, even attractive ones, and he certainly didn't want to help them. "So you're an enemy in their eyes? They're even more insane than I thought."

The hair on Amy's arm bristled. She didn't like his condescending tone, although she agreed with him. "Sir, I've traveled all the way from New York in the hope that you would honor my request. Will you, please?"

"You say you have a brother. Is he fighting for the rebels?"

The question surprised Amy. She couldn't reveal that Joseph was a prisoner of war—an active enemy of the Union. "No . . . no longer. He suffered a severe wound at Manassas and has a medical furlough. He has a wife and child living in New York."

A man walked up the stairs and called, "Mr. Secretary, the president is waiting."

Seward stroked the baby's hair once more and said, "I'm sorry, but I must deny your request. If I grant it to you, then I must for all Southerners who live here now and are learning of the wickedness of the secessionist government and its God-forsaken rebellion. Nor is it my responsibility to see that secesh have happy family reunions. If you will excuse me, I must take my leave now." He walked around her.

Amy kissed Jimmy's forehead and handed the child to Colleen, who said, "Holy Jaysus, Misses. His Honor is no gintilman. Ye spoke to him most kindly, ye did. What might ye be doin' now?"

"I don't know, Colleen. But he won't stop me. Let's go back to the hotel." ❧

CHAPTER 16

"The Perfect Person for the Job"

July - September 1862

When James McBain arrived at the Heritage after Hercules informed him of the visit by Sam's friend, he spoke to several of the older slaves. They all gave an explanation similar to that of Hercules for Sam's disappearance. Some even used the same words, "Ah seed he ride out on he hoss. Habunt seed he since." One of them revealed that Sam had whipped Jehova that day and Kitt, Roman, and Prince previously, something McBain had not known and confirmed with each victim. The next day he searched the overseer's house for clues to explain Sam's disappearance or the stranger's interest, but found nothing.

McBain remained at the plantation for almost two months, only venturing into town on horseback on Wednesdays to take care of administrative matters and Sundays for church and dinner with Sarah and Danny. Other than that, he spent his days with Hercules supervising the operations, ordering supplies, and issuing rations. After supper alone in the big house, he walked to the Quarter and talked to the people about their families and answered questions about the health of the Missus, Joseph, Amy, and the gran' chillun. Still, he didn't know how much longer he could run things full-time. He thought of making Hercules the overseer, but McBain relied on his coachman too much for counsel and needed him by his side.

One day in early September McBain and Hercules stood alone on the wharf at the Heritage watching a steam tug with a cargo of bricks sail down the river to Fort Jackson, one mile below the city. A lingering morning mist swallowed the boat. McBain said, "Hercules, you've been with me for thirty-five years. It seems like yesterday when I first saw you handle horses on Mr. Dunston's rice plantation. Where does the time go?"

When McBain confided in Hercules about plantation matters, he always started by referring to the time the two had been together. Hercules replied, "It goes up to heaven, sir, where everything, or most everything, goes."

McBain laughed. "Yes, I guess that's true." He cleared his throat. "Hercules, what's the mood of the men? I sense something's different."

The coachman looked to Hog Island in the middle of the river, where McBain kept about two hundred pigs. Of course, all the slaves wondered what a Yankee victory would mean for them, but Hercules didn't think Massa would want to entertain that thought. "They're scared you're gaining in years, Massa. They don't know what happens to them if you sell the plantation or if Master Joseph don't come back. Most have been here all their lives. They're afraid of a new massa."

McBain watched the tug slowly reappear, as if the mist were giving birth to it. Hercules's answer made sense. The quality of a slave's life depended largely on the benevolence of his or her master. "Tell them they have nothing to worry about. I received a letter from Joseph from the prison in New York. He hopes to be ex-changed soon and wants to return to the Heritage." McBain removed his hat and wiped his brow in the suffocating August heat. "There's another thing," he went on. "I don't have enough orders to keep everyone busy. The Confederate States Engineer Office needs men to work on the fortifications protecting the city and has notified planters that it will pay for field hands. The men will receive food, clothing, quarters, and medical attendance. It's a perfect solution for me. To start, I'm going to hire out twenty men for three months to work at the army camp at Causton's Bluff. I have to decide who to send."

Hercules said, "I guess the unmarried men should go first, Massa."

"That's what I'm thinking, too. Let's prepare a list. I'll want you to tell them. Make sure they know they'll be treated well and that it's only for a short time. I'll pay them seven dollars a month."

"Yes, sir. They'll like that. Do you know when they'll be going?"

"In two or three weeks. The chief engineer said he'd give me a few days ad-vance notice. We should know soon. You can drive them to the camp." McBain slapped Hercules on the arm and walked to his horse.

Hercules followed, his mind a jumble of thoughts as he realized that this was an opportunity to carry men beyond the military guard posts and allow them to slip away to March Haynes's boat. His first inclination was not to do it. He saw no reason for black folks to risk their lives running away when they might soon be freed by the Yankees. Africans had been enslaved for hundreds of years—they could wait a while longer. He also felt guilty about betraying Massa, and feared the consequences from the authorities if he were caught. However, upon reflec-tion, he believed that if a man wanted to escape, and he could help, he had some responsibility to do so, as long as he didn't get caught. Whites had to learn that all people yearned to be free, no matter how well their owners treated them. Hercu-les decided to speak to Jehova and Kitt, as both had talked about running away after being whipped by Sam. Then he would inform March Haynes.

Several days later McBain received a letter from Mr. Donnelly, who said that he had almost recovered from his injuries and was well enough to return to work, if Mr. McBain still wanted him. James immediately wired back, asking Donnelly to come as soon as possible. The overseer responded, saying he'd be at the plantation in ten days, around mid-September. McBain thanked God for the good news.

"A whiskey for me and a beer for my friend here," Willie said to the bartender at Fowler's Saloon near the corner of Bay and East Broad. Before the war, seamen packed the barroom. Now, only a few white-haired, toothless men whose seafaring days were distant memories nursed drinks and sat silently, with no one to share stories.

Willie led Harold to a secluded table in the dark, smoky bar. "I'm glad you're back," he said. "Any agents on your tail?"

Harold had just returned from hiding in Bryan County after his draft substitution scam and found Willie at his boarding house. Willie suggested a visit to Fowler's, his favorite place to relax and reflect. "None. I don't think they even tried to find me. They're too busy with the war. I could have come back months ago."

"I wish you had. We got a problem." Willie proceeded to tell Harold about the sale of the coach, his and Sam's attempt to steal from the Heritage, Sam's sudden and puzzling disappearance, the missing cash, and his failed attempt to search Sam's house at the plantation. "That damned coachman humiliated me in front of all the other slaves before running me off. He made me look like a dern fool and I'm going to kill him for it. I waited for you before I did anything. First, we have to talk to the owner of the plantation, a man named James McBain. My guess is he knows what happened to Sam and our money. I found out where he lives in town. I've ridden by his house but haven't seen him or his coachman. I figure they're at the plantation. By the way, I need to borrow one of your revolvers. That coachman stole mine."

Harold sipped his beer. "Sam wouldn't leave without telling us." He paused. "Willie, you think he took the cash from the sale of the coach?"

Willie stuck a pinkie in his ear and scratched. "Nah. I thought about that, too. If that was his plan he'd have done it right after the dealer gave him the money. Something else happened and I bet McBain knows."

"McBain?" Harold repeated. He drained his beer and his cheeks bulged into small balloons as he stifled a belch. "Wait a minute! Remember the darkey who threw horse shit in my face? I whipped him but he escaped. A week later I saw him driving with a kid in a gig. He dropped the boy at Chatham Academy and then drove to a house on Pulaski Square. There were too many other boys around for me to get to him. I went back a few times to find him before I left town but he never showed. The house is owned by a guy named McBain."

Willie nodded. "Yeah, that's where he lives—Pulaski Square."

Deep in thought, Harold ran his finger over his scar. He reached into his vest pocket, pulled out a leather tobacco pouch, and rolled a cigarette. He leaned back, took a drag, and blew a stream of billowing smoke towards the ceiling.

"Holy Jesus!" Willie slapped the table hard with both hands, startling Harold and causing his cigarette to shoot from his lips. The bar patrons looked their way.

Harold retrieved his cigarette from the floor and put it back in his mouth. "Damn, Willie, you scared the crap out of me. What?"

Willie leaned towards Harold and whispered. "Remember the night I shot that nigger? The man who offered the two thousand dollar reward—his name was McBain." Harold was speechless, and he flapped his cigarette up and down in shock. Willie drained his drink and bared clenched, yellow teeth at the burning sensation in his throat. "Think about it. I shoot that boy, and a guy named McBain offers a big reward. We leave town, and when we return one of his other boys follows you to our house and sees Sam. McBain hires Sam and then Sam disappears. That's a lot of coincidences. I can't explain 'em all, but these things must be connected. McBain knows what happened to Sam, I'm more certain than ever, and he's after us, too—laying a trap of some kind. When I was at the plantation, the coachman stole my gun, pointed it at my chest, and asked me if I was Willie or Harold. I told him I didn't know what he was talking about. If he knew who I was, he woulda shot me on the spot, I swear."

Harold wondered out loud, "We're being hunted?" He held the remaining inch of his cigarette in the tips of his thumb and index finger and took one last drag. The ember glowed in the darkness and smoke tumbled from his mouth as he spoke. "That night. It's coming back to me. The darkey called for 'Master Joseph,' and the white man called him 'Andrew.' I wonder what Joseph's last name is?"

Willie said, "Let's go to the post office tomorrow and look in the city directory. If there's a Joseph McBain, it's probably the old man's son. He'd want to kill Sam for certain. Us, too, if he gets the chance."

The next day, as the two men emerged from the post office onto the Bay, Willie said, "Well, now we know there's a Joseph McBain, and he lives on Monterey Square. Let's have a look, and make sure he's the guy who was at the pier that night."

They sat on a bench with their hats pulled low over their foreheads and watched a house on the northeast side of the square. After several hours Harold said, "Willie, we're wasting our time."

"No, we're not. We have to know if Joseph McBain is the man from that night. It will explain why he's after us."

Harold poked Willie's arm. Two colored women emerged from the driveway. The men walked up to them. "Excuse me, auntie," Willie said, "we're old friends of the McBain family. Is Mr. Joseph McBain home?"

Nannie, one of James McBain's house slaves, answered, "No suh. Massa Joesup in de Yankee prison. Bin dere 'bout fi' munts. Us jes' come obuh tuh clean ebry week."

Willie faked a look of sadness. "Oh, I'm sorry to hear that. What about his father, Mr. James McBain? We've also been tryin' to find him."

"He bin libin at he plantation, but he comin' home tuhmorruh, now dat de obuhsuh comin' back."

Willie smiled and said, "Thank you, auntie. You've been a great help." The men walked up Bull Street, away from the women. Willie said, "If Joseph's been in prison for five months, he couldn't have nothin' to do with Sam. He disappeared two months ago. It's the old man. We gotta get to him before he gets to us. And I'm also going to take care of that coachman. Tomorrow, we'll go to Pulaski Square and wait for McBain to return from his plantation. We've got to know what he looks like."

The next day Willie and Harold sat on a bench in Pulaski Square, far away from the McBain house, and watched for the old man. They saw an older white woman leave and concluded that she was McBain's wife. They spotted a boy of about seven who Harold remembered as riding in the buggy with the darkey who had thrown horse crap in his face. They figured he was Joseph McBain's son, who was living with his grandparents while Joseph served in the army. A tall negro, accompanied by a shorter, younger black boy, walked in and out of the stables, but Willie said the bigger man wasn't the coachman. Finally, at about five o'clock, a coach pulled into the driveway and parked. The coachman jumped down and opened a door. Willie grabbed Harold's arm. "That's the nigger who made a fool of me." A tall man with shoulder-length silver hair in a top hat stepped out and headed for the back entrance to the house.

Willie said, "That must be our man. Now we got to figure out how to speak to him with no one around, especially his coachman. Come on. Let's go to Fowler's. We need a plan."

The men took their usual table. After several drinks, paid for by Harold, Willie got down to business. "We've got to strike now, while McBain's not expecting it. Going after him and the coachman together is too dangerous. That Sambo knows me and he's got my gun. We need to watch the house and wait for McBain to leave alone. We'll surprise him, take him to a deserted place, and persuade him to fess up about Sam and the cash. Then we get the coachman. We can't take out the coachman first, because then McBain would know we're wise to him and he'd send the police after us."

Harold rolled another cigarette and smoked in silence as he gave Willie's obsession with the coachman some thought. "Willie, I have an idea how to take care of the coachman first if we get the chance—if we catch him alone—without McBain suspecting us. Frame the darkey for a bad crime. He rots in jail for life and we can have our chat with McBain."

Willie slapped the table, causing Harold to lift off his seat. "Good thinking, Harold. Death is too good for the nigger. I want to see him squirm—you know, suffer."

Harold added, "The problem is, we can't be the ones to set him up if it involves going to the police, with our records. Besides, McBain would find out we're behind it. Someone else has to do it."

"Yeah," agreed Willie. "But who?" He folded his arms and closed his eyes, deep in thought. He stared at Harold. "How much cash do you have from your draft deals?"

"About four hunnerd dollars. Why?"

"I have the perfect person for the job—a real tough little gal. Beautiful, too. I met her a few months ago. It might cost a few dollars. We'll split it, but you'll have to put up my half until we get the cash from the sale of the coach. Come on. Let's go for a walk."

The men stood on Broughton Street, with Willie peering inside the windows of the Marshall House Hotel. He said to Harold, "Wait until you see her." Harold yawned. Thirty minutes later Willie pointed. "There she is. I'll be right back." He walked into the lobby and approached the girl, who was carrying an armful of towels. "Hello, Penny."

The girl recoiled when she saw him. "I'm working," she hissed through clenched teeth.

Willie smiled and said, "Can I see you for a minute? I have a deal for you that will be worth your while—a lot more money than last time, and you don't have to steal."

Willie made Penny's skin crawl, but she was two weeks behind in her rent and days away from the poor house. She had decided to try to find a second job, but until then her boarding-house debt kept mounting. She looked around to make sure no one could hear them and whispered, "You mean I don't have to do anything against the law?"

"Not really. You just need to have a fuzzy memory. Let me explain."

She said, "I'll see you on the sidewalk in a minute."

When she stepped outside Willie made the introduction. "Penny Savannah, meet my partner Harold."

She nodded at the man. He was taller than Willie and every bit as objectionable looking, with a long scar on his cheek. She already started to regret talking to the men. "Tell me about this new deal. I have to get back to work."

Willie explained the plan. Penny put her hands on her hips and cocked her head. She spoke in a low but exasperated voice. "Falsely accusing a man of rape isn't illegal?"

Willie reasoned, "You're not falsely doing anything. You're just trusting your memory. You can't get in trouble for that! Besides, it's tough to tell darkies apart, especially at night. Every white person knows that. And no judge is going to believe a black man over a white girl."

Penny nervously glanced at the hotel door. "When would I do this?"

Willie shrugged. "Whenever the opportunity arises. It might be tomorrow, or it may not be for weeks. You'll have to be available at a moment's notice. When the time is right, one of us will tell you where to stand and start screaming."

The girl adjusted her white work cap. This wasn't as simple as Willie had made it seem. "No, Willie. It's too risky." She turned to walk away.

Willie said, "You get twenty-five dollars now and fifty dollars once he's in jail."

Penny stopped and faced the men. Seventy-five dollars was a lot of money, and she was desperate. She asked, "Won't I have to testify at a trial?"

Willie glanced at Harold before responding. He hadn't thought of that. "Yeah, probably. If you do, that's another twenty-five."

A voice in her head was telling her to go back to the hotel, but she had to have money. She decided to negotiate and ask for an amount the men would surely refuse. "Here are my terms—fifty now, fifty when he's in jail, and fifty if I have to testify."

Harold finally spoke, knowing that he was going to have to put up the funds. "You're pretty greedy for someone who's broke."

Penny glared at Harold. "You're asking me to put an innocent man in jail. You're the greedy one for offering so little. I won't do it for a penny less."

Willie mumbled to Harold, "Pay her. It's only seventy-five each. It'll be worth it." Harold dug into his pocket and handed her fifty dollars. When she took it, Willie grabbed her arm and squeezed. "You'd better keep your word, or you'll wish you never met me."

She yanked her arm away. "I already wish I'd never met you." She returned to work, stunned that the men accepted her offer. She wondered if she could meet her end of the bargain.

As the men walked back to Fowler's, Willie said, "I told you she was tough—and real purdy, too!"

❦

Early the next morning, long before Willie and Harold woke, Hercules drove Massa to a meeting downtown. While waiting for him, Hercules went to the harbor and found March at Stoddard's Wharf. He explained Massa's plan to hire out men to work for the army. "I'm taking twenty to Causton's Bluff tomorrow. Two want to go with you."

March said he planned to take six other people that day and had room for a few more. He instructed Hercules to drive three miles past Fort Brown, the outer post on the Thunderbolt Road, till he saw an old deserted barn about a hundred paces to the left of the road. Directly opposite, a hundred paces to the right of the road, were two large magnolia trees on the edge of a marsh. The boys should head into the marsh grass beyond those trees and crawl on their hands and knees on a small path until they reached the creek. March would pick them up with the others at dark, about nine o'clock. He also told Hercules to tell the soldiers at Causton's Bluff that two boys had escaped just before he got there so they wouldn't search near the real rendezvous site.

Hercules nodded. "They'll be there."

Willie woke up at one o'clock, hung over. He shook Harold and said, "Let's move it. We have to watch McBain's house."

In an hour the men were sitting again in Pulaski Square. Willie said to Harold, "There's that black kid in the driveway. Go over and tell him you have a message for Mr. McBain. Find out if he's home."

Willie watched as Harold spoke to the negro boy. Harold returned and reported, "McBain just left for the plantation with his coachman, who's driving some boys to Causton's Bluff tomorrow. He thinks Massa is coming back tomorrow."

A wide smile blossomed on Willie's face. He laughed out loud, slapped Harold on the back, and said, "This is our lucky day."

"How do you figure?"

"We're gonna get both of them alone. You and Penny Savannah can take care of the coachman and I'll handle McBain. This is working to perfection. Come on. We're going to have an early night for once. Tomorrow is gonna be big. Very big."

Regrets

September 1862

Harold regretted that he suggested framing the coachman the moment he and Willie came to terms with the girl. He wanted to learn Sam's fate and find their cash as badly as Willie. He just didn't want to expend any extra effort putting the darkey away—that was Willie's issue—nor pay one hundred fifty dollars to some desperate girl to accomplish it. They could wait to get McBain alone. But he realized that Willie was obsessed with ruining the slave and wouldn't budge from his position.

They arose before sunrise the next morning—earlier than they had since prison—and arrived at the Louisville Road, a few hundred yards before the guard post, at seven o'clock to await their prey. Two hours later they saw a wagon coming their way. Willie looked through his field glass and said, "It's the coachman and the slaves. I don't see McBain. Follow him through the Thunderbolt guard posts and wait. It should take him all day. When you see him returning, hurry back to town, describe him to Penny, take her to Crawford Square, and tell her what to do. In the meantime, I'll hide until the wagon passes, wait for McBain, and find out what he did to Sam. By tonight, we'll have our answer and hopefully the cash, and that damned nigger will be in jail."

Harold mused, "I know the plan, Willie. All I want is the cash. Just the cash."

Hercules regretted participating in March's scheme as soon as he left the Heritage carrying twenty slaves to Causton's Bluff. There were just too many potential pitfalls that he hadn't considered. What would he do if other slaves followed Jehova and Kitt when they ran from the wagon, or if they started to shout to him when the boys started to run? Would Massa believe his prepared explanation for not chasing after them—that they were so quiet he never heard them leave the wagon? What would happen if the soldiers captured them? The night before he warned both boys that, if caught, they had to confess to acting alone, and not implicate him or March, or they would harm every slave in Chatham County. They swore to God, but Hercules knew that if Kitt or Jehova received lashes "well laid on," their spirits could be broken.

The coachman stopped at the first post a few minutes past ten and handed the guard the passes, one sheet for each slave. The soldier counted the men, handed back the papers, and waved them through. When they pulled up to the Fort Brown post, a corporal took the passes and climbed onto the seat next to Hercules, placing his musket between his legs. "Drive," he said. Hercules froze. He never expected a guard to ride with them. He closed his eyes and prayed that Jehova and Kitt wouldn't try to escape. The soldier shouted, "I said, drive! Are you deaf?"

Hercules snapped the reins and the vehicle rolled through the caked, dormant rice fields. The soldier didn't speak but turned around occasionally to look at the men. About three hours later Hercules spotted the old barn on the left and the magnolias on the right. His heart sounded as if it were in his ears. He wanted to signal to the boys not to run, but couldn't without being noticed. The soldier suddenly stood and aimed his weapon towards the wagon bed. Hercules yelled, "No!"

The soldier screamed at Hercules, "Stop!" He then shouted, "Sit down!" Hercules turned and saw one of the men standing. The guard said, "What in hell do you think you're doing?"

"Gottuh pee, Massa, got tuh pee baddee." Hercules closed his eyes and exhaled.

The soldier kept his musket aimed at the man and said, "All right, everyone who gotta piss, stand up now and do it over the side of the wagon. Jump out and you're dead." The guard turned to Hercules and asked, "Why did you call 'No'?"

Hercules saw the barrel pointed at his head. "I thought I felt the left wheel coming off. Guess I just hit a rut in the road."

"I didn't feel nothin'. You're a damned fool nigger. Keep quiet and drive when I tell you."

"Yes, sir." After the wagon restarted and passed the escape point without incident, Hercules's pulse returned to normal. One hour later they arrived at Causton's Bluff, which overlooked St. Augustine Creek. The guard jumped down and handed the papers to a sergeant, who looked at the laborers and said, "It's three o'clock. I'll take you to your camp and then you can get to work."

Hercules took a deep breath, relieved that the scheme had been aborted. The Yankees would liberate the slaves soon enough. The guard told him, "Go back now." Hercules turned the wagon around and got the horses to walk faster. He wanted to make town in daylight.

About an hour later, as he rested his elbows on his thighs, he was startled by a loud thump on the side of the wagon. He pulled on the reins. A sweating black man in coveralls ran up beside him and begged, "Please he'p us! Us need he'p."

"Help with what, nigger?"

The man pointed to a gully on the side of the road. A woman stood up and held the hands of two shirtless boys about five years old. "Us lookin' fuh Jones Crik."

"You catchin' a boat?"

The man blinked several times at Hercules's knowledge of his destination. "Yassuh. An' if Massa ketch us now, he whup us tuh det!"

The wife and two boys joined the man. Hercules noticed lash welts on the chest and shoulders of one of the boys. Hercules looked down the road and guessed that they were about one mile from the magnolia trees. He said, "Get in the back and lay flat." Hercules's heart started banging again at the risk he was taking. Fortunately, he didn't see any other wagons or men on horseback. When they reached the drop-off point, Hercules gave the man directions for finding the creek. "Run to those magnolias!"

Before the family moved they heard gun shots. Hercules grabbed the man's arm. "Hold it." He looked west and saw two figures in the distance running in their direction. "My guess is those two are heading to the same place as you, and it looks like they're bringing soldiers with them." Hercules couldn't let the family go. They'd probably be apprehended. He surveyed the area and saw across a field of tall weeds the old, two-story, wooden barn with one of the double doors dangling off its hinges. He turned to the family and saw four faces crinkled with fear. "I'm taking you behind that barn to hide." He drove to the far side of the structure, parked, and said to the man, "Stay here until the trouble with those other runaways passes. Then cross the field to the trees and meet the boat at the creek. This is the best I can do. I got to get out of here."

The family climbed down and the man, who was near tears, thanked Hercules. But before Hercules could drive off, he saw that the two runaways and their pursuers—two soldiers with rifles and three civilians holding onto leashed dogs—were closer than he thought. If the soldiers saw him coming from behind the barn, they would probably search there. He jumped off the wagon and patted the horses to calm them. Then he and the family sat and prayed.

The barking and shouts of the men got progressively louder and crawled inside Hercules's head until he could hear nothing else. He looked past the corner of the building and saw two black men on the other side of the road diving into the high marsh grass past the magnolia trees with the pursuers about two hundred yards behind. Hercules had trouble breathing the oven-like air. He leaned back and told the family, "Don't move!" They continued praying.

In a few minutes Hercules peered again. The two soldiers ran towards the marsh while the three civilians stopped on the road, their heads jerking in every direction. The dogs strained on their leashes towards the barn. The men gave in to the hounds and headed for them. Hercules cursed. They were finished.

Two gunshots rang out. Hercules peeked. The hunters had halted and were looking in the opposite direction, towards the magnolias, where the two black men emerged with their hands in the air, followed by the soldiers. The civilians yanked the hounds away from their focus on the barn and hurried to the captives. One of the whites pulled a whip from his belt and started to beat the runaways on their heads, shoulders, and arms as they fell to their knees and clasped their hands in front of their chests, pleading for mercy. A wagon rolled up and the group got in and headed back towards Fort Brown.

Hercules waited for them to disappear from sight. He drove the family to the magnolia trees and said, "Get going. The boat will be here in a few hours."

The husband said, "God bless you! Us nebuh fuhgit you." The family jumped down and disappeared into the marsh. Hercules finally headed home, close to two hours behind schedule, but relieved that he had survived another potential calamity.

The soldiers at Fort Brown and the inner guard post on the Thunderbolt Road waved him through shortly after nightfall without checking his pass. He reached East Broad Street on the edge of town and knew that, because of the hour, he would have to spend the night at Pulaski Square. As he drove slowly along East Broad to Liberty Street, he started to think of an excuse to tell Massa for the length of the trip. Then he heard, "You, boy! Halt!"

A policeman approached him at the corner of Drayton and Liberty streets. Hercules recognized him to be Officer Reilly. "Evnin', sir."

Reilly squinted in the dim light of the gas-fueled street lamp. "Oh, it's Hercules. I have orders to bring in every negro I see tonight driving a two-horse wagon." Hercules reached for his pass and held it out. "Nothing to do with passes," the officer said. He jumped on the wagon. "Drive to the police barracks. This shouldn't take long."

Hercules wondered what the problem might be. It couldn't be about the runaways, otherwise the military guards would have stopped him. He parked in front of the station and followed Reilly in the door.

A sergeant, another policeman, and a striking strawberry-blond young lady sat at a table. She jumped up and pointed at Hercules. "That's him. He's the one who attacked me!" Hercules's knees went weak.

Sergeant Hart asked, "Hercules, did you attack this lady tonight?"

The girl shouted at the officer, "Are you going to believe him before me? I told you, he's the one."

The sergeant said, "Miss, we need to ask questions. I know you're under stress, but please don't interfere." He told the policeman, "Take Miss Pender to the other room." The sergeant turned to Hercules and said, "I'll ask again, did you molest that girl?"

"No, sir. I've never molested any woman, and I've never seen her before. She must be mistaken."

Hart asked, "Can you tell me where you were for the past hour, and can a white person verify your whereabouts?"

Hercules rested his hands on the table and felt his insides turn to ice. "I drove twenty of Massa McBain's men to Causton's Bluff. I returned to town on the Thunderbolt Road. The guards at both posts waved me through. I guess I passed through the last one at about nine o'clock. It took about fifteen minutes to get from the inner post to town, and another fifteen or twenty minutes before I was stopped."

"Will the guard at the inner post vouch for you?"

Hercules pulled out his kerchief and wiped his forehead. "I hope so. As I said, he waved me through and didn't ask for my pass."

Hart studied Hercules's face. He knew him to be the loyal, well-behaved coachman of James McBain, but he couldn't set free a black man who had been identified by a white woman as an attacker. No act enraged white people more. "When did you leave Causton's Bluff?"

Hercules's throat tightened. He had to tell the truth since the soldiers at Causton's Bluff would be asked to confirm his answer. "A soldier said it was about three o'clock."

"It doesn't take six hours to drive from Causton's Bluff to here in a two-horse wagon. Four-and-a-half, five hours at the most. What else did you do?"

"I rested and watered the horses and fixed a wheel. That took an hour or two."

Sergeant Hart looked at his watch. "It's past ten—too late to disturb Mr. McBain. I'll send you to the cell for tonight and contact him tomorrow morning. We'll put your wagon and horses in our stable for the night."

Hercules pleaded, "Sir, I swear to you, I didn't touch that woman, or any other."

Hart shook his head. "Hercules, all my men know you. You've never been in any trouble. But the charge is too serious. We'll try to settle this in the morning." He took Hercules inside and told Miss Pender she could leave, but to be available at any time for a court hearing.

⊶⊷

Penny walked into Fowler's and crinkled her nose at the heavy smell of cigarette smoke. She spotted Willie and Harold at a table and went to them as the other patrons stared at her.

Willie looked up. "Penny Savannah! How did it go?"

"They locked him up."

Willie laughed, slapped the table, and pulled out a chair. "Very well done, young lady. Have a seat and join us for a drink."

Penny pushed in the chair. "I don't drink. I'll take my money now. I have to get back to work. I told them I had a family emergency."

Harold pulled out fifty dollars in a wad, obviously pre-counted, and handed it to her without smiling. She counted it before putting it in her purse.

Willie said, "Penny, I know we can count on you to do this well in the trial." She walked off without saying a word. The men watched her leave. Willie said, "I know a way she could make another fifty dollars real easy." He laughed, toasted himself, and said, "You see how easy that was, Harold? The nigger is behind bars and although McBain didn't come through the guard post today, the day after tomorrow is the launch of the new ironclad. Every important man in town will be there. We're finally gonna have a chat with the old man." Willie tapped his temple with his index finger. "Yeah, my plan took a little extra money, but it worked like a charm. I know how to do these things."

Harold lifted his glass to Willie, but had a feeling the adventure wasn't close to over. Sure, Willie had gotten his revenge on the coachman, but they still didn't know where Sam was, and they didn't have their cash.

⁂

Katherine Downes—Penny Pender to the few people who knew her in Savannah, except Willie and Harold, who called her Penny Savannah—sat in the dark on the side of the bed in the small room at Duffy's boarding house, with her head hanging down. Her twelve-year-old sister woke up and asked, "Is that you, Oldest Sister? Please come to bed."

Katherine whispered, "I will in a minute, Pauline. I need to sit for a while."

Pauline wiggled over and sat next to her. "Was someone at work mean to you?"

Katherine hugged her. "No, I was mean to someone, and I'm sorry." She kissed Pauline's cheek. "Guess what? Tomorrow I'm going to buy you and Mary pretty new hair ribbons."

"Really?" Pauline turned and looked at the lump underneath the covers on the other side of the bed. "Can I tell her? She'll be so happy!"

"You can in the morning. Now get some sleep." Pauline flopped back.

Katherine changed out of her dress and into her nightgown, washed in the basin, and lay next to Pauline. She stared at the ceiling and remembered the look of fear on the negro's face—eyes and mouth wide open, forehead furrowed—when she accused him of attacking her. She thought about how far she had fallen, and wondered if she could sink any lower.

She already regretted accusing him. In fact, she regretted every major decision she'd ever made in her seventeen years, and wondered if the day would come when she wouldn't hate herself for her bad choices. But there was one decision for which she would never forgive herself and would carry the rest of her life—the one that she regretted more than anything. That was when she didn't scream at the top of her lungs when her father Zebudiah first snuck into her bedroom in the middle of night when she was only ten years old, lay next to her, took her hand, and made her touch him.

As she shivered in fear, shut her eyes tight to hold back tears, and fought the urge to vomit, he made her swear to God never to tell her mother or anyone, or he'd send her to live with the clay-eaters in the far-away mountains of Georgia, where they lived in dark caves with spiders, bats, and snakes.

Over the ensuing years he never told her when to expect him—he didn't have to. She knew by the way he acted at supper, telling her how beautiful she looked, and the way he kissed her for too long on the cheek. She never ate a morsel on those nights. The visits occurred about once a month, after midnight while her mother was fast asleep, for four years, with her father guiding her through the same routine, even after Pauline left her parents' bedroom and started sharing Katherine's.

Then Pauline caught a fever and Zebudiah thought it safest to let Katherine sleep in another bedroom until her sister recovered. He continued his visits, and that's when he began touching her. From the very first time, she stiffened like a board despite his whispered assurances that he would never hurt his beautiful daughter. She always crawled under the covers and cried herself to sleep after he left. She came to despise her body because it attracted him. She hated when her breasts started to grow and her waist and buttocks developed curves. She wished she didn't have a chest or a "baby maker," as her mother called it. She wanted to die so she would never again see her father, or have any more nightmares about him. She started to think of ways that she could kill herself, though she knew she would offend God by doing so.

At her father's insistence, Katherine never returned to her old room with Pauline. One night, four months after turning sixteen, as she lay shaking in bed awaiting him, she heard the creaking of footsteps and opening of a door, but this time it wasn't the one to her room. She jerked up, realizing that her father was visiting eleven-year-old Pauline. Petrified and repulsed at the horror that her sister's life was about to become, Katherine jumped out of bed, tiptoed into her parents' bedroom, and shook her mother, Delores. "Ma, wake up. Please help! Please!"

Delores sat up, blinked the sleep from her eyes, and whispered, "Whatever is wrong, Angel? You're going to wake your father and little Mary."

Katherine tugged hard on her mother's nightshirt. "No! Pa's awake. He's in Pauline's room. He's going to hurt her."

Delores paused for a second, then jumped up, put on her robe, lit a lantern, and rushed into Pauline's room, with Katherine following. They saw Zebudiah lying next to the sobbing girl. He scrambled out of the bed, and his excited state caused his wife to scream, "Oh, God, NO! NO!" as Katherine turned away. "You evil fiend! What are you doing to my child?" Delores put down the lantern, rushed to the bed, pushed him away with both hands, and sat next to Pauline. "My poor, poor sweetheart." Katherine sat next to her mother, who put an arm around each girl.

Zebudiah whined, "I heard Pauline crying and I came in to calm her. That's all!"

Delores pointed at her husband's deflating private parts and hollered, "Is that how you calm a child?"

His tone changed quickly and he snarled at Delores. "Woman, you need to calm down this instant, or I'll take my belt to you!"

She leaned forward and looked Pauline in the eye in the dimly lit room, as the girl hugged her doll. "Did he touch you, dear, in sacred places?"

Tears streamed down Pauline's cheeks and dripped onto her doll. "He wanted me to touch him, and then you came in."

Delores closed her eyes and murmured, "Dear God." She turned to Katherine, held her shoulders, and looked her in the eye. "Tell me the truth, Angel, and don't be afraid. I won't let him hurt you. Has he done bad things to you?"

Katherine's body quaked as she nodded. She could barely whisper. "For years, Ma."

Delores raised her head and howled like a wounded bear. "AHHHHHHH! AHHHHHHH!"

Zebudiah stomped from the room yelling, "You're a fool, woman! I'm tired of listening to this nonsense! I'm going to bed. You best forget about this, or you're going to have a big problem." He slammed the door behind him.

The mother and two daughters cried in each other's arms. Moments later Delores gasped, "Oh, no!" and ran from the room. She returned in seconds, carrying four-year-old Mary, and placed the confused child on the bed. Delores sat and rocked back and forth, moaning, "I'm so sorry. I'm so sorry."

Mary's eyes darted from her sisters to her mother and then she squeaked in fear, "What'th wrong, Ma?" Katherine put a finger to her lips and Mary clamped her hands over her mouth.

The Downes females sat together, sniffling and holding each other. Eventually, Pauline and Mary lay back and fell asleep. Delores stared at her red, calloused hands in the flickering lamp light and told Katherine. "You girls are the only things that have any meaning to me, and I've failed you." She started to take short, rapid breaths, sounding like a chugging locomotive. Katherine rubbed her mother's back, thinking she was about to faint. Delores's breathing returned to normal and she continued. "This farm, our house, they gave me comfort and security through the years. But, I don't know—maybe there were signs." Delores growled, grabbed her dark red hair in her hands, and started to pull as if she were going to yank out two clumps. She finally relaxed, kissed Katherine's forehead, and told her to mind her sisters and get some sleep. Then she left the room. Katherine curled up on the foot of the bed and drifted off.

BOOMMMM! The girls bolted upright at the ear-splitting explosion. Katherine's sisters stared wide-eyed in fright at her. Mary started to bawl and hugged Pauline's doll. Pauline asked in a wavering voice that sounded like she was on a bumpy wagon ride, "Tha-at was-n't thund-der, wa-as it, Old-dest Sis-sis-ter?"

Katherine said, "No. I don't think it was." She got up from the bed, walked to the door, and told Pauline, "Wait here with Mary. Don't move."

Pauline pleaded, "Please be careful."

Katherine left the bedroom and walked on shaky legs to the closed door of her parents' bedroom. She was about to knock when a hair-raising scream and another blast made her knees buckle and fall backwards on the floor. She sat up, gasped for air, and placed a trembling hand on her chest to calm her heartbeat. Tears ran down her cheeks and her nightgown clung to her sweaty body. She took several deep breaths, looked to the side, and saw Pauline and Mary fast asleep in Mrs. Duffy's boarding house bed. Katherine shook her head to jog the horrid dream from her mind, lay back, and begged God not to let her relive that night ever again. ✎

CHAPTER EIGHTEEN

"They're Decent and Respectable Girls"

September 1862

The jangling of the keys on the metal hoop ring announced the arrival of the deputy jailer, a short man with a bulging belly that hid the front of his belt. He escorted Hercules into the ten-foot-square, brick-walled room with a scarred wooden table and four creaking chairs, two of which were occupied. The lawman stood in the corner, holding a shotgun at his side. Hercules sat and looked down in embarrassment. "Mornin', Massa."

The corners of McBain's lips sagged at seeing his coachman and most trusted servant in handcuffs. "Hello, Hercules. I'm sorry I'm late. I stayed at the Heritage last night and rode in this morning. A policeman came by and said you were arrested for attacking a young woman. I was shocked to hear it."

Hercules leaned forward and placed his cuffed hands on the table. "It's not true, Massa. As God watches over us, I never touched her—never even seen her before."

McBain looked into Hercules's sleep-deprived, bloodshot eyes. "I believe you. I know you'd never do such a thing." He turned and put a hand on the shoulder of the stout, partially bald man sitting next to him. "Hercules, this is Mr. Williams. He's an excellent lawyer and I'm hiring him for your defense." The man nodded at Hercules.

Hercules nodded back and said, "Pleased to meet you, sir," relieved that Massa was defending him. Still, he had a splitting headache at being accused of a crime he didn't commit, and not being able to explain himself without revealing his role in a crime he did commit.

McBain continued, "You must tell us everything that happened yesterday, from the time you left the Heritage to the time the policeman stopped you at night. This is a very serious accusation but I can get you out of here right now if you can describe your whereabouts, and they can be confirmed by a white person. The sergeant tells me that you left Causton's Bluff at three and no one can vouch for your movements until you were picked up after nine, except perhaps the sentries at the guard posts. He feels that it shouldn't have taken you over six hours to get back to town."

Hercules recounted the sequence of events, substituting saving the runaway family with fixing the wagon wheel and resting the horses. He paused and looked McBain in the eye. "That's the truth, Massa."

Mr. Williams, who had been taking notes, asked Hercules, "How long did it take you to tighten the wheel?"

Hercules had never spoken to a lawyer before. He thought the man was trying to catch him in a lie, not defend him. "Not long. I also checked the other wheels, and I rested the horses. I guess I stopped for an hour or two."

Williams picked at his lower lip while he thought. He said, "Did you see anyone during the ride from Causton's Bluff to the outer guard post, even in passing—anything to establish your presence in that area?"

"No, sir, just the guards at the posts."

Williams turned to McBain, "I'll interview the guards. I'll speak to families who live around Crawford Square, where that lady says Hercules attacked her. I'll also see what I can learn about her. That's all I have for now." He stood and tried to lift Hercules's spirits. "Just because a white person accuses you of a crime doesn't mean that you'll be convicted. A white woman here recently accused a slave of rape. The case was brought to trial and a jury acquitted the man. We have a few obstacles to overcome, but we do have a system of justice and I'll do my best to see that it works for you."

McBain also tried to comfort Hercules. "Chloe will bring your meals. I'll be back when we have some news. Meanwhile, try to remember if there's anything that can help us prove your story." He reached across the table and patted his coachman on the arm. "I'll do all I can to get you out of this."

After the two men left, the guard nudged Hercules on the back with the butt of the shotgun. The coachman rose and returned to his cell, wondering why that girl would lie about him.

When McBain and Williams got outside, James said, "I'll accompany you to the guard posts. I want to get this over with as soon as possible." They drove in Mr. Williams's gig to the first post and explained their purpose to the officer in charge. The sergeant located the guards who were on duty at the time Hercules said he passed through and ordered them to appear at the jailhouse the next morning. McBain and Williams received the same commitment from the sergeant at the outer post. The officer also added that during the time Hercules claimed he was on the road, there were several attempts by local slaves to run away. Two were caught by the owner and a couple of his soldiers, but a family of four was still unaccounted for. The sergeant said that anyone in the area at that time should have heard or seen the capture of the two men, as shots were fired.

It was almost four o'clock by the time the men returned to town. They went to Crawford Square and knocked on doors, asking residents if they had heard screams the previous night. Two women said they did, around nine o'clock, perhaps a little before, but saw nothing when they went outside to investigate.

They visited Mrs. Duffy next. She said Penny Pender had left for work but her two younger sisters were in their room. She explained that the girls were from out of town and had been living at her boarding house for about seven months. "They had some money when they arrived here but went through it and Penny got a job in the evenings at the Marshall House. They're decent and respectable girls and don't cause any trouble. They say they're Baptists, but I don't believe they go to church, although the middle one, Pauline, always carries a Bible. Penny claims she's eighteen. She's often late paying her bill, sometimes by a few weeks, but somehow manages to come up with the money. That's all I can tell you, except the youngest one, who can't be more than five or six, eats more food than a stevedore. I only charge them twenty dollars a week for room and board. I swear I lose money on them, but they're so sweet I'd hate to send them away."

They thanked the woman and left. Williams said, "It wouldn't be legal for us to question the girl outside the courtroom, but I'll speak to Mary Marshall tomorrow. Her employees at the hotel will be able to tell us something about Miss Pender."

James said, "I agree. The girl seems to be of good character, but why are three young girls living away from their parents in a boarding house, even an inexpensive one? And how can they afford it on a cleaning woman's pay? Something is strange. Tomorrow is an important day. I hope the guards can identify Hercules as driving through their posts at the times he claims. That won't clear him, but it will prove he was in town for a very short period of time when he supposedly attacked the girl."

The next morning the jailer led Hercules to the empty visitor's room. The slave sat and traced his finger over the word "Jesus" carved in the table. The door unlatched and McBain and Williams entered, followed by three soldiers. Hercules realized that these were guards trying to identify him.

One stepped forward and said, "Yes, I seen him driving through in mid-morning with a wagon full of boys. Can't say I remember him returning. A wagon came by after dark and I waved it through. I didn't notice the driver." Hercules cursed to himself.

Williams said, "Next."

The middle soldier said, "I was on duty at Fort Brown from eight o'clock on. Two or three wagons came by, but I didn't get a good look at the drivers. One mighta been him, but I wouldn't swear to it."

The third soldier, who Hercules recognized as the one who rode with him to Causton's Bluff, stepped forward. Hercules felt his hair stand on end. "Yeah, I drove with him and a gang of boys to Causton's. He acted kind of strange, nervous. At one point a slave stood up and I ordered him to sit down. Then this man here yelled 'No' for no good reason. I thought he was crazy. He dropped me off with the workers at about three o'clock. I didn't see him again. I stayed at the battery until nine."

Williams thanked and dismissed the men. He said to Hercules, "We can establish that you were at Causton's Bluff about three o'clock, but we still can't prove where you were until you were arrested after nine. I'm still working on that. We spoke to a few residents who live around Crawford Square who claimed that they heard a woman scream, but they didn't see anything."

McBain asked, "Hercules, what did that soldier mean when he said you were acting strange?"

The coachman cleared his throat. "I felt a vibration and thought the wheel was coming off. I got worried with so many men in the wagon. Turned out it was loose." McBain stared at his closest man for a few seconds. He never knew Hercules to worry or get excited over trivial matters, certainly not a loose wheel, which he could easily fix.

Williams said, "Another thing, Hercules. We heard that two slaves from Brewton Hill plantation ran away and were caught by their owner and some soldiers, just about the same time you said you were in the area. Do you know anything about that?"

"No, sir. I heard gunshots as I was fixing the wheel, but I didn't see nothing."

Williams leaned forward and placed his palms on the table. "We also learned that on that same evening, a family of four—a husband, wife, and two young boys—ran away from Deptford plantation. They haven't been seen since. Did you come across them?"

Hercules held the man's stare. "No sir. I didn't see no one until the guards." Williams kept his eyes on him. Hercules knew that the lawyer didn't believe him.

Williams said to McBain, "That's enough for now. We need to do some more searching. I'll leave you alone with Hercules and wait outside."

After the lawyer left, McBain asked, "Are you getting your meals? Patience knows you're here and insists on bringing them."

"Yes, Massa. Thank you."

McBain put his hand on Hercules's shoulder. "Mr. Williams is working very hard for you. You must help him as much as you can. Don't be afraid of him. I'll be back as soon as I have more news." He left and the guard kicked Hercules's chair. The negro stood, knowing that Massa didn't believe him either about seeing the runaways.

When McBain stepped from the jail onto Hall Street, Williams asked him, "Do you think he's telling the truth?"

James gazed north across the street at the spraying fountain in Forsyth Place. "Hercules would never attack a woman, white or colored. I'm certain of that."

"I mean, do you think he helped those runaways? He was in the area around that time. He had to have seen something."

McBain removed his top hat and massaged the ache developing in his fore-head. "I don't know. He said he doesn't know anything other than hearing gun-shots, and I believe him. He seems to be hiding something, though, but I can't believe he'd do something so illegal, so dangerous. It sounds like you do."

"It's possible. However, I do believe him about that girl. Her story makes no sense. He drives by Crawford Square, sees her, jumps off his wagon, attacks her, jumps back on the wagon? Then he drives slowly through town? Nothing fits. She's either mistaken about his identity, or she's lying. But why would she?"

Before McBain could respond, a lieutenant in a grey uniform with red trim on the jacket collar and at the cuffs rode up to them. "Excuse me, but are either of you Mr. James McBain?"

"I am, Lieutenant." McBain hoped the officer had good news about finding a witness who could verify Hercules's account.

"I apologize for bothering you, sir, but your wife said that I could find you here. A boy named Kitt did not answer roll call at Causton's Bluff this morning. We understand that he's yours. We searched all over but couldn't find him or his belongings. We believe he ran away."

So much air rushed out of McBain's lungs that Williams thought he might shrivel up. James groaned. "Yes, he's mine."

The officer continued, "Maybe it's a coincidence, but two privates also missed roll call. We don't think they escaped together. That would be highly unusual." Slaves weren't the only runaways. Soldiers, especially foreigners who had come to America for a better life and were drafted into a war in which they had no patriotic ties, thought twice about risking their hides, and deserted. "If your boy returns, please let us know. If we learn anything, we will inform you."

James said in a weak voice, "Thank you for reporting this to me."

The soldier left. McBain looked at the ground and guessed that Kitt ran away in reaction to the death of his parents. He pulled out his pocket watch. "Mr. Wil-liams, please do what you must to exonerate Hercules. I know he's innocent of this charge. He's been arrested for attacking a woman, not for helping slaves run away, so let's concentrate on that. I'm going to the river now to see the launch of the ironclad. I should be home in a few hours. Please come by and give me an update on your investigation." The two shook hands and Williams departed.

As McBain boarded the gig he felt slightly dizzy. He took a deep breath. Ev-erything seemed to be unraveling, but he had to stay strong and protect his family and property. Nothing was more important. He snapped the reins.

⁂

The day after Hercules dropped off McBain's men at Causton's Bluff, when soldiers and slaves finished work and rushed to their messes for supper, a corpo-ral ordered Kitt to bring in all the shovels along the outer earthen wall of the fortification facing St. Augustine Creek. As Kitt gathered the implements, he noticed two soldiers under the cover of foliage along the creek bank about fifty paces away tying a small rowboat to a branch of a drooping live oak tree. He could think of only one reason for their actions and thanked God for giving him another chance to escape. He considered telling Jehova, but figured that including an extra person would only complicate matters and limit his chances for success.

That night, after tattoo, Kitt snuck past two cigarette-smoking, chatting guards to the boat. The deserters arrived at midnight and jumped out of their skins when Kitt greeted them from inside the boat. "Ebnin', soljuh men."

One of the men pointed his musket and threatened to shoot Kitt if he didn't return to the camp. Kitt whispered that if they shot him, the noise would fetch every soldier in camp and they would be hanged on the spot for desertion.

The men talked to each other in a language that Kitt didn't understand and climbed into the boat. The soldier with the rifle spoke in hushed tones, "You make noise, I shoot you, verstehensie?" Each soldier took an oar and started to row slowly, trying not to make a sound. A cloud cover hid the moon and made the night pitch black. The coordinated movements and steering by the two men convinced Kitt that they had planned their route well.

They crossed St. Augustine Creek and entered another smaller stream. The men pulled in the oars and leaned back until they lay flat on the rower's and passenger's benches. One turned to Kitt, slapped his leg, and hissed, "Down!" In a few minutes they resumed rowing, going from creek to creek, and occasionally lying back and coasting. Kitt noticed a few campfires along the banks, but no sentries spotted them. They finally reached a wider channel and the men rowed more rapidly. Thirty minutes later they stopped and hugged each other. One said, "Vassaw Sound?" The other chirped, "Javohl!" He pulled out a watch, held it close to his face, and said, "Five o'clock."

They rowed in circles for an hour to avoid drifting back to shore. At first light they saw the outline of a ship and headed towards it. Three sailors appeared on the deck with their rifles aimed at the boat. The deserters pulled in the oars, stood up, waved their hats, and shouted, "Ve love Union. Ve love President Lincoln." Kitt remained seated, praying that the ship belonged to the Yankees.

The sailors lowered a rope ladder and the runaways climbed to the deck. Kitt ascended last and said to the first soldier he faced, "T'ank you, massa, t'ank you!"

"I ain't your massa, boy. Come with me."

A few hours later, after being questioned by two Union officers about his escape, the conditions in and about Savannah, and what he knew about the Confederate defenses, Kitt was transferred to another ship. He sat on the deck with six other negroes who nodded to him but otherwise didn't speak. Kitt thought that they, like he, were runaways overwhelmed at the prospect of what lay ahead. By evening, they sailed into a sound between two islands. Kitt stood at the railing as the ship dropped anchor. He and the other blacks, under a guard of four soldiers, boarded a lifeboat. Four oarsmen rowed along a creek on the landward side of the island to a wharf.

They marched along a path which led up a bluff to open land. Before them stood the back of a two-story, white plantation house with tall windows and wide piazzas on each floor. They walked along a brick pathway to a circular drive in front of the mansion. A string of white-washed outbuildings stood on the far side of the house. Kitt looked down the main road and saw in the distance a cluster of wooden, unpainted slave cabins. A smiling black man in coveralls, bare feet, and a five-inch long indentation on the top of his head emerged from the big house and approached them.

The soldiers stopped and one spoke. "This is St. Simons Island, your new home, and this man is Hope. He's in charge of this village and will assign you to your quarters. You will work in the fields five days a week. Saturday is cleaning day, and Sunday is the Sabbath. You will support yourselves through your own labor. Our government will help you until your crops are harvested. Once a week several of you will be allowed to go to Jekyl Island just south of here in one of our ships to kill cattle for your beef ration. If you neglect your work, you will not get your ration. If you continue to ignore your responsibilities, you will be placed in irons. There is another negro village on the south end of this island. In all, there are close to five hundred freed slaves. No whites live here, but some rebel soldiers have landed and are looking for trouble, so don't go wandering off at night. You have enough flintlock muskets to protect yourselves. We'll come by periodically to monitor your progress. Now, Hope will get you settled." The four soldiers marched back to the boat.

Hope addressed them. "Welcome to St. Simons. You are free men and women."

Kitt dropped to his knees and rested his forehead on the road. His tears splashed on the hard ground. "We're here, Ma and Pa. We made it! We're free!"

⚒

James McBain stood with Gazaway Lamar and several other men on the Exchange Building dock and stared at the river. They looked like pigeons, with their shoulders moving back and forth, as they urged the CSS *Georgia* upstream. McBain thought the ironclad looked like a floating, hundred-foot-long, side-gabled roof, with five evenly placed cannons poking out from dormers about six feet above the waterline. A railing on the top ridge enclosed a narrow walkway, and a smokestack spewed black clouds and sparks. McBain wondered what kept it afloat and thought that it must be hotter than a kiln in the vessel's belly. He prayed for the behemoth to gain speed.

The Ladies Gunboat Fund, co-managed by Lamar, had performed a minor miracle by raising about one hundred fifteen thousand dollars from citizens and organizations around the state. The colored people of Roswell even contributed five dollars. Construction began a few weeks after cash started flowing in. The gunboat had been launched the previous May to a cheering crowd seemingly unconcerned that several guns were missing, the engine and boiler needed adjustments, and it lacked a full coat of iron. Work resumed at full pace and on this day in late September 1862, the committee, naval officers, donors, workers, and hundreds of onlookers lined up to watch Savannah's terror of the seas negotiate the river which it was built to defend. But the incoming tide of four miles per hour kept the ship's engine grinding at full steam, and the vessel couldn't get out of its own wake. The captain finally decided to head back to the dock.

Lamar turned to McBain and the other committeemen and said, "Looks like she still needs some work." The men, at a loss for words, simply nodded. They were all disappointed, but none more so than Lamar, who had invested so much time and money in the vessel. He was depending on it to blast the Yankees to hell, and convince them to leave the South alone to live in peace.

McBain bade farewell to the others, returned to his gig on River Street, and went home, unaware that he was being followed. As he drove around Pulaski Square, two men on horseback approached him. One asked, "Excuse me, sir. Are you Mr. McBain?"

James stopped and appraised the men as they dismounted. One was short, wiry, with chin whiskers and wore a crumpled suit, a string tie, dirty boots, and a top hat half as high as the standard seven inches. The taller one, dressed in blue jeans, a black leather vest, and a floppy, brown leather hat, had a long scar on his cheek. McBain knew they meant trouble. He stepped off the gig to face them. "Yes, I am. How may I help you?"

The shorter one stepped forward and spoke politely. "Good afternoon, sir. We only want a minute of your time. We have a business partner named Sam Bannister. He was your overseer. We haven't heard from him in over two months—since you hired him. Do you know where we can find him? It's very important."

McBain tensed up. He knew who they must be. He asked, "Did one of you visit my plantation and threaten my coachman a few months ago?"

The shorter man said, "I did go there, sir, but I didn't threaten anyone. Just so you know the truth, your boy took my gun when I wasn't looking and threatened me with it. I only wanted information on Sam—to know he's safe. He owes me and my partner here money. We think you were the last person to see him. So I ask you again, sir, with all due respect, do you know where Sam is?"

"No, I don't. One of my men caught him stealing a saddle. Sam whipped him, packed his belongings, and rode off. That man was the last to see Sam, and I haven't heard from Sam since."

Willie glanced at Harold, surprised by this new information. He said to McBain, "Sir, that don't make sense. Sam wouldn't steal, but if he did, no nigger could stop him. Sam sure as hell would whip him, but he wouldn't run away. You must know that."

McBain laughed to himself at hearing that Sam wouldn't steal. "I'll admit that I'm also puzzled by Sam's sudden departure, and would like to learn more about it, but as he's never returned, I can't get his side of the story. There's nothing I can do. I wish I could be more helpful. If I should hear from him, I'll let him know his friends are looking for him. May I have your names?"

Willie ignored McBain's request. "Sir, do you mind if we speak to the boy who Sam whipped? I'm sure he'll remember better what happened if we question him."

McBain repeated, "And your names?"

Willie stepped closer and grabbed McBain's wrist. "Our names aren't important. Just let us speak to the boy who Sam whipped—the last man to see him."

McBain's face turned red and he spoke through clenched teeth. "Get your hand off me!"

Willie leaned back, surprised at the old man's fury, and lightened his grip. "Sir, we've asked you as gentlemen to help us find our friend. That's all we want. Please let us talk to your boy—alone."

James pulled his arm away, causing Willie to stumble forward a step. Harold jumped to Willie's side. "Let's take care of this old coot already."

McBain snarled, "For your information, the man who Sam whipped is in jail, so it's impossible for you to question him, unless you join him."

Willie's jaw dropped at the news. "You . . . you mean your coachman who stole my gun was the last man to see Sam?"

Alarm bells started clanging in McBain's head. He wondered how these men would know Hercules was in jail. He had to learn their names. "Tell me, which one of you is Willie, and who is Harold?"

A voice called out from the other side of the square, in front of McBain's house. "Is everything all right, Mr. McBain?"

The three turned towards the voice. James shouted, "Mr. Williams, can you find a policeman? He'll be interested in speaking to these two gentlemen."

Williams called back, "There's one right around the corner. I'll be right back."

Willie pointed a finger at McBain. "You haven't seen the last of us, sir." He and Harold jumped on their horses and rode off. When they got to Forsyth Place, Willie said, "Did you hear that? The coachman who we just put in jail is the last one to see Sam?"

"It sure sounds that way, Willie."

Willie spit. "I'll bet my right arm he knows where Sam and our money are. We have to talk to him, but we can never show our faces at the jailhouse. We got to get him out. Where's that girl? She has to take back her story."

Harold almost fell off his saddle. "Willie, are you insane? I've already given her one hundred dollars to lock him up."

"I don't care. We have much more at stake than that, and the coachman has it or knows where it is. Now find her, damn it!" ❧

CHAPTER NINETEEN

❦

Penny the Pretender
September 1862

James McBain thanked his lawyer for helping scare off Willie and Harold. Then he went to the city jail and warned police chief Lyde Goodwin that two men might show up and ask to speak to Hercules. If they did, he should arrest them for the murder of Andrew McBain. James also requested help in tracking down the criminals, who were living somewhere in town, but Goodwin said he didn't have the manpower to spare. In fact, he was so short handed that he had been forced to ask the military to help patrol the town at night. McBain left the jail thinking how he could apprehend the outlaws.

The last place that Willie or Harold would go on their own volition was a jail. Now that McBain suspected their identities, they had to lay low. Willie returned to Mrs. Benoist's boarding house on Elbert Square while Harold searched for Penny to get her to retract her accusation. He visited the Marshall House and, under the guise of being a relative, learned that Penny lived at Mrs. Duffy's on Washington Square. He found her sitting on a bench, watching two younger girls play nearby. He said, "Penny!"

Katherine looked up and blanched. "How did you find me here?"

Harold laughed. "Do you think you can hide from us?"

Her sisters ran up and stared at Harold. Katherine stood, put a hand on Pauline's back, and said, "You two go inside for now."

Pauline shivered at the sight of the man. She wondered what such a beastly looking character would want with her sister, but Katherine's narrowed eyes told her to leave immediately. She grabbed Mary's arm and pulled her away.

Katherine wanted to slap Harold for intruding on her privacy, even though she knew she had put herself in this position. In an icy tone she asked, "What do you want?"

"We need you to take back your charge against that coachman. He's got information we need. We have to speak to him face to face."

"WHAT?" Katherine realized that she had shouted and looked at her sisters, who were watching from the top of the stairs of the boarding house. She lowered her voice. "After you two tied yourselves in knots getting him locked up, and had me lie to the police? What could be so important?"

"You don't have to concern yourself with that."

It dawned on Katherine that Harold and Willie were bumbling fools. "Pay me the remaining fifty dollars you owe me and I'll do it. That's our deal."

Harold was in no mood to negotiate with the girl. He'd already wasted one hundred dollars on her. "Why? You won't have to testify now. That's what the last fifty is for. You don't get paid for work you don't do."

"No, but I have to tell a judge that I was mistaken. He'll know I lied. That's worse, and I don't know what he'll do to me. Give me the money and I'll go to the police tomorrow."

Harold seethed, "You're not getting another cent."

Katherine stepped closer to him. Lines formed at the corners of her eyes. "Look, you need to go. I've done everything you've asked of me. Give me twenty-five dollars now and you have my word I'll go to the police tomorrow morning. You can pay me the other twenty-five afterwards. I'll meet you at about ten o'clock on the east end of the Strand." Katherine was referring to the grassy park between Bay Street and the bluff overlooking the river.

Harold thought for a moment and then reached into his pocket. Katherine positioned herself to block the girls from seeing the stranger giving her money. He peeled off the greybacks and she stuffed them into her purse. He said, "If you don't go to the law first thing tomorrow, I'll find your sisters and tell them about your real life, how you steal and lie. Then I'll slap you around in front of them. Got me?" He walked away.

Katherine wondered if all men were pitiless bastards. She needed to make her sisters forget about Harold and called up to them, "Come, let's get some candy."

Mary, almost six years of age, with wavy red hair, green eyes, and freckles, ran to Katherine and jumped up and down while turning in circles, singing, "Candy, candy!"

Pauline, a few inches shorter than Katherine and five years younger, had pure white skin, green eyes, and light red hair. She asked, "Who was that scary man?"

Katherine scrambled for an explanation. "He owns a hotel and was going to give me a better job, but it's no longer available." She looked out the corner of her eye to see her sister's reaction.

Pauline made a sour face. "That man owns a hotel?" Katherine realized that Pauline was getting too smart to be fooled by her fibs.

The two older girls walked in silence to Whitaker Street, watching Mary twirl and skip all the way. They entered a grocery store and Katherine bought a few lumps of rock candy, the only kind available in the sugar-deprived South. They exited with Mary leaping at her side like a dog that hadn't been fed in a week. Katherine reached into the small bag and gave her a piece, which she popped in her mouth before trotting up Congress Street and into Johnson Square. Kather-ine called, "Don't go too far, Mary," as she and Pauline sat on a bench. She sai to Pauline, "Mary never stops moving until she sleeps. Ma said she has squirrels for feet."

They watched the girl hop along without a care in the world. Pauline held Katherine's arm and leaned against her. She asked, "Oldest Sister, do you miss Ma?"

Katherine pulled away to look the girl in the eye. "Of course I do! What kind of a question is that?"

Pauline rested her head on Katherine's shoulder and said, "Please don't be angry with me for asking, but do you think she knew what Pa was doing, you know, before that night?"

Katherine froze. She had tried to bury those memories, with little success. Apparently the mere mention of their mother affected Pauline. Katherine put her arm around her sister and held her tight. She closed her eyes and wondered how to answer a question that she had asked herself so many times. Reluctantly, she thought back to that night when her mother had caught her father with Pauline. She could still hear the explosions in her mind.

After the second blast from inside her parent's bedroom, sixteen-year-old Katherine Downes got up on shaky legs, put her ear to the door, and called, "Ma?" She heard rustling and footsteps from within and stepped back, fearing that her father would appear. Delores opened the door a sliver, squeezed out, and closed it. She pointed at the dining table and in a quivering voice said, "Sit and I'll explain everything." Eleven-year-old Pauline emerged from the bedroom, stiff as a sleepwalker, and joined them.

Delores sat and placed her hands on her lap. She asked Katherine to fetch the whiskey bottle and a cup and pour it half-full. Katherine and Pauline watched their mother use two shaking hands to lift the cup without spilling the contents, lower her head, and slurp the alcohol like hot coffee. She leaned back and swallowed. The woman took another gulp and started to cough. She put down the cup and wiped her mouth on her sleeve. "I don't want either of you going into that bedroom tonight for any reason. Your father is dead. He's the devil and had to pay for what he done to Katherine and was about to do to Pauline. It's that simple."

The girls stared at each other. Neither one shed a tear at the news. Still, they were speechless at their mother's confession. Delores stared at the bottle on the table. "We'll drive to town in the morning. I'll turn myself in to the sheriff. He'll have no choice but to arrest me."

Pauline screamed, "No, Ma," and started sobbing. Katherine moved her chair ⌐ her sister.

ᵒres reached across the table and squeezed Pauline's arm. "Stay with me, 'et me say what I got to say, while I'm able to say it. I thought this through before I shot the damned rascal the second time. A grand jury will determine if I should be charged with a crime, but I won't tell the sheriff about you—about tonight."

She then held Katherine's hand. "Angel, you'll have to testify about what you've been through. That will be painful, but you must do it. Your father had a lot of acquaintances in Thomasville, being a deacon at the church, but once the jurors hear of his deviltry, they won't charge me. Then we'll be a family again."

Katherine turned a light shade of crimson. "Ma, I can't tell anyone about what he did to me. I can't! I'll die of shame."

Delores teared up at the agony she was causing her daughter. "You must, Angel, or I'll never see the light of day again. My heart breaks to ask this of you, but you're my only hope."

Katherine stared at her mother, who wore the expression of someone drowning, her head barely above water, and grasping for someone's hand. She realized that she had no choice if she wanted her mother back, but after the trial she would never be able to show her face in Thomasville again. "I'll do what you ask, Ma."

Delores took another drink. "Angel, you're only sixteen and you've already been dragged through hell. But you're going to have to take care of Pauline and Mary while I'm in jail." She poured more whiskey, the neck of the bottle clinking against the rim of the cup. She plunked a leather pouch on the table. "Here are some gold and silver coins—over four hundred dollars worth. It's all I have. You'll need this to take care of yourselves, buy food, necessities, and such until I get out of jail. You'll have to find a lawyer for me. Your father, may he rot in hell, told me that Mr. Dillon is good. He drew up our wills. Try to convince him to take the case for free by claiming poverty. That won't be easy. Lawyers have no pity or scruples. There's still a note on our farm, and you'll have to pay the bank twenty-five dollars a month. Bankers are worse than lawyers, but that money should last until I come home." Delores patted the pouch. "Don't give this money to any man except to pay bills, no matter how good he claims his intentions are. If the authorities ask about relatives to send you to, say you don't got none. Don't mention your father's brother in Alabama. I don't trust him no more than your pa."

Fortunately, Zeb had taught Katherine farm basics, like how to milk cows, collect eggs, and slaughter and dress chickens. She could saddle, bridle, ride, feed, and otherwise care for horses. But she felt the responsibility descend upon her shoulders like a leather harness. "Don't worry, Ma. I'll take care of my sisters and the farm."

"I know you will, Angel. Now both of you—try to get some sleep." Delores stood, kissed both girls on the forehead, drained the cup of whiskey, and returned to her bedroom.

The two girls tossed and turned, while Mary snoozed through the night. The next morning Katherine drove the family buggy along the Boston Road to town with Mary sitting on Delores's lap and Pauline on the end of the bench. Oth than Mary asking periodically, "Where are we going?" no one said a word on the three-mile trip. The girls waited outside as Delores walked into the jailhouse.

The sheriff and his deputy doubted the Bible-toting Mrs. Downes when she told them that she had shot her husband, but they had to investigate her wild claim. As they followed the buggy back to the farm, the lawmen speculated that the woman had gone insane and was having devil- or alcohol-induced visions. However, one look at the partially headless body of Mr. Downes on the blood-soaked bed confirmed her story.

The two men loaded the blanket-wrapped body into their wagon, helped Delores onto the bench between them, and returned to town. The sisters followed in the buggy. After being booked at the jail and sent to a cell, Delores met her daughters in the small visitors' room. The moment Pauline saw her mother in handcuffs, she buried her face in Katherine's shoulder. Mary asked, "Ma, what are you doing in thith plathe?" Katherine told Pauline to take Mary outside and wait for her.

Mother and daughter sat across from each other at the sole table in the room. Katherine nervously pumped her leg up and down. She felt like crying but had to keep her composure for everyone's sake. Delores absentmindedly pulled at the cuffs of her sleeves and said, "Angel, I'm so proud of you for the way you're handling this. I'll make it up to you when I get out of here. Now go to Mr. Dillon's office—I think he's on Broad and Jackson—and tell him what I did. Have him come here as soon as he can. Then go to Pastor Lewis and ask him to see me, too. Go home after that. There are several bags of rice and flour and you have all the eggs and chickens and milk you need. You and the girls must clean the house every day. The stable and barn, too. I want you all to read the Bible after supper and say your prayers at bedtime."

"What about the farm, Ma—the corn and wheat crops?"

Delores clasped her hands together and rested her forehead on them as if she were praying. Katherine knew she had asked her mother about something that she had not considered. Delores raised her head. "Go to our neighbors—the Darnels and Shorts—and ask for help. They're good Christians. Promise them half the crop." Her lips quivered. "You'd best be on your way. There's a lot to do."

Katherine kissed her mother's cheek and assured her that they'd visit her every day. When the girls arrived at the lawyer's office, Katherine had Pauline and Mary wait in the buggy. A bell tinkled when she entered the small dark office. A man sat writing at a desk. He spotted the girl and stood. "May I help you?"

Katherine took a half-step forward. "Sir, my name is Katherine Downes. I . . ."

The man interrupted, "Oh, yes, Mr. Downes's daughter." He looked her up wn. He was only a few inches taller than the girl, had curly brown hair that his ears, and wore a necktie with the knot half-way under his shirt col- you in church occasionally. You certainly have grown into a beautiful young lady. How is your father?"

"He's not doing so well, sir. He's dead."

The lawyer recoiled. "I'm sorry, Miss Downes. This is so sudden. When did he pass?"

"Last night."

"His liver?"

"No, sir. His head. Ma shot him."

The man's jaw dropped. "Why in God's name would she do that?"

Katherine felt a jolt run through her body. She couldn't tell a stranger what her father had done to her. She hugged her small purse to her chest. "He was mean to me. Ma found out."

The lawyer arched his eyebrows. "Good Lord! He must have been very mean for Mrs. Downes to shoot him. Where is she now?"

"In jail. She wants to see you. She needs help." Katherine's voice cracked.

Dillon said, "Yes, of course. I have some paperwork I must take care of, but I'll go see her as soon as I'm finished, about an hour. Would you care to wait for me?"

"I can't, sir. My sisters are outside. We need to see Pastor Lewis."

Dillon stepped past her and held the door. "I understand. I'll see her as soon as I'm done here."

Katherine drove to the Second Baptist Church to inform Pastor Lewis. The man scared her because his sermons convinced her that she was going to hell. She again left her sisters outside and found him in a small office in the back. He was a foreboding figure at six feet tall, as thin as a flagpole, a head of white hair piled high, and an Adam's apple that stuck out like a tree knot. Although only two hours had passed since her mother's detention, he already knew about the killing. "I'm very sorry to hear about your father, Miss Downes. Zebudiah was a good man, much admired in the church and the community. We will miss him." Katherine gulped at the possibility that if her father was so admired, people wouldn't believe her. "Please sit and tell me what caused your mother to do what she did, against all the teachings of Christ, and take this good man from our midst, and leave you and your sisters fatherless? Was it liquor? We all know she liked to imbibe on occasion."

"My father, too!" Katherine offered without thinking. She sat and looked out the window at the church graveyard, and wished she were in it. "He was mean to me, Pastor Lewis. Very mean, and Ma learned of it."

"That's not the Zebudiah I know, er, knew. He often told me how much he loved his daughters. Sometimes fathers must exercise discipline. They don't like to, but it's all a part of raising obedient, God-fearing children. Did you tell your mother about your father, or did she see this so-called meanness for herself?"

Katherine felt dizzy and clutched the arms of the chair. It was clear that th pastor didn't believe her. "Ma said she'd explain it to you when you visit her."

Lewis nodded. "I know you're very upset. I'll drop in on your mother today. She will need the Lord's comfort. Are you and your sisters all alone?"

Unable to look the pastor in the eye, Katherine stared at the cross on the wall and answered, "Yes. But we're quite capable of taking care of ourselves."

The pastor paged through a small booklet on the desk. "We can't allow three young girls to live alone. I'll speak to some of our parishioners and find a family to take you in until your mother's problem is resolved. I'll also arrange your father's funeral here at the church and order a small headstone. I can accommodate you on Thursday at ten o'clock. Of course, I still expect to see you here on Sundays. You may go now. Remember, you are not alone." He held up his Bible. "The Lord is with you."

Katherine left as quickly as possible without running. The girls spoke little during the drive to the farm. Mary still didn't comprehend the situation. "Why ithn't Ma coming home with uth?" Katherine told her that Ma had to stay in town for a few days and that Pa wouldn't be home for a long time, and that she would be her ma for a little while. Mary clapped her hands, "Yeth, you can be my ma." The four-year-old's innocence lifted the spirits of her sisters.

The next day when they visited Delores, Mary sat on her lap. Pauline reported that they had done all their chores and read the Bible. She also described how she and Katherine had slaughtered, dressed, and cooked a chicken. Pauline then read a few passages from the Bible. Delores complimented the girls and said, "Now remember, when I'm not at home, always listen to your oldest sister."

Mary said, "I alwayth obey my oldetht thithter."

Delores laughed for the first time in days. She asked Pauline to take Mary outside so she could talk privately with Katherine.

Delores revealed that Mr. Dillon had agreed to represent her and thought that her chances for not being charged by a grand jury were very good. She also said that Pastor Lewis came by and admonished her for taking Zebudiah away from the community, but thought that God, in his mercy, would forgive her if she repented. She recounted how the pastor had lectured her on a fathers' duty to shield children from all the wickedness and sin in the world. Delores told the pastor that Zeb was the wicked one by taking liberties with her daughter. Lewis questioned if she knew that for a fact, or if Katherine was telling wild stories to get attention. Delores told Katherine it was all she could do to suppress a scream.

Katherine said, "He makes me feel so uncomfortable, Ma. Please say we'll never go to his church again once this is over."

Delores nodded. "I promise, but you must accept him until that day comes."

❦

sisters donned their church clothes the next day for the funeral. None
ional black mourning outfits. Katherine had two skirts and three bod-

ices. For the funeral she wore her emerald-green skirt and light-green bodice, thinking them the most somber. Pauline and Mary wore simple red, one-piece dresses, hand-me-downs from Katherine. About fifteen women parishioners attended the service. Pastor Lewis delivered a glowing eulogy to Zebudiah, recalling how faithfully the deceased deacon had served God and the community.

After the service, as everyone stepped outside for the burial, the mourners offered condolences to the sisters. One woman, who Katherine didn't recognize, introduced herself as Mrs. Wells and told her that she had spoken to Pastor Lewis and would move them into her house later that day. Mrs. Wells explained that she and her husband had moved to a farm on the other side of town three months earlier, and as their son was away, fighting in Virginia, she had plenty of room.

Katherine didn't want to leave her house and live with strangers, but she couldn't refuse an elder. "Thank you, Mrs. Wells."

The sisters stood by Pastor Lewis's side at the grave as he recited a prayer. Katherine kept still with her hands folded at her waist and head bowed, unable to block the vision of her father entering her room at night with ember-glowing, devil eyes. She ground her teeth, hoping for the burial to end. Four men lowered the casket into the ground and started covering it with dirt. The pastor wished Zeb a safe journey and ended with, "Rest in peace, dear friend and brother Zebudiah." Katherine exhaled, relieved that the ceremony was finally over.

Then the pastor said, "Miss Downes, please say a few kind words about your father."

Katherine glared at the pastor while the mourners stared at her, waiting for the heartfelt blessings of the distraught girl. She felt her insides squirm. She closed her eyes, took a deep breath, and spoke from the heart. "Pa, it's Katherine. I hope that you can hear me, because I can finally speak to you without fear. I'm so happy that you're dead and in the ground so you can never destroy my sisters' lives like you did mine. I hope there's a trap door beneath your coffin that will soon release and send you right to hell, where you belong with all the other evil men who poisoned this world."

Mourners started to gasp and whisper loudly among themselves. Pastor Lewis put his hand on Katherine's shoulder and whispered in her ear, "Miss Downes, you control yourself right now. Stop making a fool of yourself and dishonoring your father's memory."

Katherine said, "Yes, sir. I'm so sorry. I'm almost done." She delivered one last thought. "Pa, all I ask of you in death is to leave me alone in life. I hope God will erase you from my mind forever. Then you can burn eternally in hell."

One woman shrieked and fainted. Pastor Lewis grabbed Katherine's arm and pulled her across the graveyard and through the side door of the church as Pauline and Mary trotted after them. Within his office, Pastor Lewis yelled, "Miss Downes, how dare you insult your father and embarrass us all? I will suspend you and your sisters from the church if you ever act like this again. Now you apologize to me and the mourners of your poor father who came out today to wish him a safe journey home."

Katherine had never seen a face turn so red. She thought she saw rouge on the roots of his white hair. She looked him in the eye. "Sir, I'm not sorry and I won't apologize. You're the one who should apologize to my family for eulogizing such a terrible man. My mother tried to tell you and you wouldn't listen. Now I'm telling you."

The pastor clutched his stomach and sat. Katherine ushered her sisters to the buggy. As they drove to the jail, Pauline hugged Katherine and said, "I love you, Oldest Sister."

Katherine did not talk about the service to her mother, but did report that a parishioner, Mrs. Wells, wanted to take them in. Delores said the Wells family was new in town and that she vaguely knew Mrs. Wells and had never spoken to Mr. Wells. But she assumed that they were good Christians and told her to accept the invitation as it would put her mind at ease to know that they were safe and being cared for. Katherine accepted her suggestion without comment.

Later that day, Mrs. Wells arrived at the farm in a wagon driven by a smiling, grey-haired negro man wearing a stained, moth-eaten cloth hat. Katherine, broom in hand, left the house to greet her. "Good afternoon, Mrs. Wells."

The rotund, grey-haired woman with thin, almost invisible lips replied, "I hope you're feeling better than this morning. We women at the church talked afterwards and understand the grief and stress that you're under, which made you lose control. We forgive you. I've come to help you pack your things and move you to our place. You'll feel right at home."

Katherine leaned on the broomstick. "We're really doing quite well, ma'am. We don't want to be a bother. We only ask that you help us with the crops."

"Don't be silly, dear. Three young girls can't live alone on a farm. It's not safe with all the deserters, stragglers, and thieves roaming around. As I told you, my son is off, and Mr. Wells and I would love the company. It's best for you, it really is. We'll see to it that your farm is tended to." Two hours later, the Downes girls were packed and riding in their buggy, following Mrs. Wells to their new quarters.

The woman and negro helped the sisters move into a second-floor room. She then served them all slices of cherry pie with fresh cream poured on top. Katherine sat next to Mary to make sure she minded her manners. Mary grabbed her fork and didn't look up until she ate every morsel on her plate. Pauline told her to chew each bite twenty times with her mouth closed, and then swallow before opening her mouth again. Mary stopped to say, "Yeth, Pauline," and a chunk of cherry shot from her mouth and onto the table. She scooped it up and chomped it down. Pauline and Mrs. Wells laughed. Katherine thought that the arrangement might work out.

She changed her mind that night when they sat for supper with Mr. Wells, a man with a barrel chest, thinning but long brown hair, pink skin, and a red, bulbous, bumpy nose, his face's most prominent feature. He rested his elbows on the table for the entire meal, whether eating, talking, or, rarely, listening. He led them in prayer and then laid down some rules, banging his knife handle on the table while he spoke, as if hammering them in: work around the house from eight to one; dinner; school lessons and Bible reading until five; help Mrs. Wells prepare supper and eat at seven; clean up; in bed at nine; bathe on Saturday evening; and church on Sunday.

Katherine felt a headache coming. Although the rules weren't much different from the ones her parents made, she resented being ordered around by this stranger. "Mr. Wells, we must visit our mother each day."

A fat index finger pointed at her eyes. "A sixteen-year-old girl shouldn't be driving a buggy, or exposing herself and her sisters to the very lowest of our society."

Katherine sat as rigid as a tree and rested her fists on the table. "Sir, I've been driving on my own since I was ten. I can handle horses better than most boys. AND MY MOTHER ISN'T THE LOWEST OF ANYTHING!"

Mr. Wells's face turned pinker. "I didn't mean your mother. I meant the other prisoners. But she is in jail for murder, young lady." He speared a piece of pork with his fork and pointed it at Katherine. "Now, you listen to me. You are living in my house, and you will obey me, and that's that. I heard all about your performance at your father's funeral today. You ought to be ashamed. That fresh mouth of yours won't be tolerated here, I can assure you. Now be quiet and eat." He mouthed the food.

But Katherine had more to say. "Just so you're aware, sir, I also have to take time to see my mother's lawyer, Mr. Dillon."

Mr. Wells banged his fist on the table, rattling all the plates and silverware. "That no good thief? I wouldn't let him represent a copperhead after what he did to me when I bought this farm."

"That's your opinion. He's been very helpful to my mother. And you can't tell her what to do."

"Don't you talk back to me, young lady! I don't want you seeing him."

Mrs. Wells looked on as if she were watching her house burn down. She interrupted. "Mr. Wells, let's you and I talk this over after supper."

"Very well. If you're finished, you girls are excused. Go to your room, wash your faces, say your prayers, and go to bed. And don't raise your voices or I'll be up there with my strap!"

Katherine and Pauline were on their feet the instant the man finished his sentence, but Mary remained in her seat. "Can I have thum pie, Mithuth Wellth?"

Pauline grabbed Mary under her arms, lifted her, and said, "Not now, Mary." They climbed the stairs to their bedroom.

They changed into their nightgowns and crawled under the covers. Pauline whispered, "Oldest Sister, he's as mean as father. I hate him. I want to go home!"

Katherine held her sister. "We'll leave here as soon as possible. We're going to see Ma tomorrow. He'll have to shoot me to stop us. We'll ask her for advice, but I don't know what to do until she gets out of jail."

The next morning at breakfast Mrs. Wells tried to put on a cheerful appearance. "Hello, girls. How are you on this bright, sunny day?"

Katherine, happy to see that Mr. Wells was absent, forced an, "All right, I guess."

"I have good news! Mr. Wells will allow you to keep your lawyer and visit your mother on Monday, Wednesday, and Friday at noon and after church on Sundays. But you must return here afterwards for your lessons." The girls glanced at each other and ate without comment.

After cleaning up and taking a reading and writing lesson with Mrs. Wells, they drove to town. Katherine and Pauline spent most of the visit telling Delores about the first day at the Wells farm as Mary sat on her mother's lap and talked to her doll. Delores told them to be strong, that she soon would be free, and they would be living together again. Pauline read a few passages from the Bible. Then she took Mary outside, leaving Katherine and Delores alone.

Delores confided, "I spoke with Mr. Dillon. He said that my case will go to the grand jury next week. He's still confident the jurors will not find a true bill against me as long as they believe you. Angel, this is almost over, but you must be prepared to explain what your father did to you, from the time it started."

Katherine started to tear up. "Ma, what will people think of me? It makes me sick that Mr. Dillon and Pastor Lewis know."

"Angel, only your testimony will free me. I need you for this. We'll move away from here after it's over. But first I have to get out of jail." Delores clutched her daughter's hand. "I know how painful this is for you, but I don't regret what I did, saving you from that beast."

The girl hung her head. "I'll do what I have to, but it hurts." She paused to dry her eyes. "Ma, does the memory ever go away? Will I ever stop thinking about it? Or will it always be with me—haunt me—every day and night for the rest of my life?"

Delores dabbed at her eyes with a handkerchief. "Only time heals these wounds, Angel. But they will heal, and you'll be a stronger woman for it."

Katherine looked down at her chest. "I don't feel like a woman. I hate me as I am."

"You're a beautiful girl. Soon you'll have hordes of handsome young men courting you."

Katherine closed her eyes and shook her head. "Ma, I don't want a man. Father was a man, and I hate him so much! Mr. Wells and Pastor Lewis, too!" She started crying, "I feel so worthless. If I didn't have Pauline and Mary, I'd kill myself, I swear."

Delores lost her grip on her Bible and it slammed on the floor. She scolded her daughter. "Hush, young lady. Don't let me hear you talk like that again. All men aren't like your father or the others! You're going to marry a kind man and have lots of children!"

"I don't want children! I don't want a man touching me ever again! Never!"

The door opened. The jailer peeked in. "Time's up, Miss Downes."

Katherine called, "Just one more minute, sir." The door closed. "Ma, you look very pale. Are you feeling all right?" Delores nodded weakly. Katherine placed the back of her hand on her mother's forehead and said, "Ma, you're burning up. Please get some rest." She immediately regretted her words, as there was little to do in jail but rest.

Katherine kissed her goodbye and the girls returned to the Wells farm, dreading supper time. They ate an hour early, as Mr. Wells was rushing to a meeting in town, the purpose of which he shared at the table. "Those thieving German Jews—think they can sell their goods at those prices and cheat us, during a war no less. They aren't even faithful Southerners. We'll decide what to do with them tonight. I'll run every last one of them out of this town if I have to." Katherine peeked at Pauline, who rolled her eyes at the rant. Fortunately, he finished his meal and left.

Silence followed his departure. Mrs. Wells smiled and asked, "Who would like a piece of pie?" Mary raised both hands.

⁂

On the girls' next visit to Delores the jailer told them that she had a high fever, severe headache, and nose bleed, and couldn't see them. They returned two days later and met with her. She said she felt better but sat doubled over during the thirty-minute session. Katherine could hear her teeth chatter and demanded that the jailer get help.

Later that afternoon a doctor transferred Delores to the hospital for negroes and poor whites, where the jailer directed the girls when they next appeared. However, Dr. Bruce said that their mother could not see them because she was vomiting blood and showing signs of delirium. He took Katherine aside and told her that her mother had a bad case of yellow fever and he could not say if she would survive. He also said that the lawyer knew of her condition and had requested a postponement of the trial.

Four days later the girls were allowed to see their mother in her hospital bed. Delores's face was pale yellow with sunken cheeks. Her pallor and the dark circles under her eyes made her look like a ghost. Pauline read from the Bible, she and Mary gave their mother a kiss, and they left her and Katherine alone.

The woman took Katherine's hand and spoke in a whisper. "Angel, I don't think I'm going to make it. You must promise me to take care of Pauline and Mary."

"You'll be all right, Ma," Katherine lied, as her voice cracked.

Delores slowly raised a hand and tried to wipe away her daughter's tears.

"Don't cry, Angel. You and your sisters have your whole lives ahead of you. Rejoice in that."

"Ma, I can't rejoice in anything. We need you. I'm afraid of the future."

The dying woman managed a smile that only a happy memory can evoke. "Do you remember when you were little, whenever you were sad I told you the story of Penny, the lonely girl who spent her days playing a princess?"

"Yes, Ma. I remember Penny the Pretender."

Delores said, "And the poem Penny's mother recited to make her believe that brighter days lay ahead?" The girl nodded. "That's you, Angel. You are special and things will get better, even if you're sad today." Katherine was unable to speak. Delores asked, "Do you want to hear the poem? I want you to think of it whenever you or Pauline or Mary are unhappy."

Katherine knew that these would be some of the last words she'd ever hear from her mother. She said, "Please say it."

Delores held Katherine's hand and spoke barely above a whisper.

> *There's a place deep in the sky*
> *Known only to a few*
> *A special place by and by*
> *Where angels go when feeling blue.*
> *The tears they shed soak the earth*
> *Make flowers grow so high*
> *Beauty follows my oh my*
> *Where angels go to cry*

Delores weakly squeezed Katherine's hand. "I'm so tired, Angel. Take care of your sisters. And please forgive me. Please don't let me go without it."

Katherine touched her mother's cheek. "Forgive you for what, Ma? If there's anything, of course I forgive you."

Delores's face strained as she lifted her arms to hug her daughter. She only managed to place a hand on her shoulder. "Your father. I'm so very sorry."

Katherine's tears dropped onto her mother's nightshirt. "Ma, you don't. . . ." Delores's arms dropped onto the hard straw mattress and her mouth and eyes remained open. Katherine held her lifeless mother until a nurse came by and helped her sit up. The nurse handed the girl her mother's pocket watch and Bible, and then pulled the sheet over Delores's head.

❧

Mary's laughter while chasing a pigeon around the Nathanael Greene monument brought Katherine back to Johnson Square. Katherine rubbed her eyes and said, "I don't know, Pauline. Ma apologized to me before she passed, but I don't know if she did it because she knew or thought she should have known. I'd be very hurt if she had known and didn't stop him, but I don't want to hate her memory. I hate our father's. That's enough for us to bear. It's in the past now, and as hard as it is, we have to try to leave it there. Our parents are gone and we only have each other. We need to survive. That's all that matters." She stood. "I have some business to take care of tomorrow morning. When I return, we're going find a school for you and Mary."

Pauline's eyes lit up as she rose from the bench. "No fooling? That's wonderful news, but how can we afford it?"

"I'll manage. Here, finish the candy."

Pauline called, "Mary, there's another piece of candy! Do you want it?"

Mary ran towards them, her doll cradled in one arm and her red hair bouncing up and down. "Candy for me? Yeth!" ∾

CHAPTER TWENTY

❧

Escaping Thomasville
September 1862

Willie and Harold stood at the iron railing that ran along the edge of the Strand and overlooked the warehouses lining the harbor. They watched a gang of about fifty black men dig up the cantaloupe-sized stones that paved the ramp from the Bay to River Street below. The stones, which had been ballast on so many incoming ships over the years and were dumped to take on cotton, were being removed to weigh down vessels that the Confederates were sinking in the river to keep out the Union navy. A voice behind them said, "It's done." The men turned around and faced Katherine. "I withdrew my charge."

Willie looked her up and down and grinned. "What happened, beautiful?"

Katherine shivered at the remark. "I told the judge that after much thought, I didn't think the negro I accused was the one who attacked me. I apologized to him and the negro, though he wasn't there. The judge berated me for taking up the time of the justice system and putting an innocent man in jail. He said he had a good mind to lock me up. It wasn't pleasant. I'll take my twenty-five dollars now and we can part ways. For good."

Willie started towards the Bay. "Come on, Harold, let's have a drink. We need to figure out how to deal with that coachman, now that he's out."

Katherine grabbed Willie's sleeve. "I said twenty-five dollars."

He pulled away his arm and snapped, "We've already paid you one hunnerd twenty-five dollars and didn't get a damned thing for it. We're not any closer to finding our partner or our money."

Katherine put her hands on her hips. "That's not my fault. I did what you asked. A deal's a deal. Now give me my money."

Willie tried to pat her shoulder in mock sympathy, but she stepped back. He said, "Penny, why don't you see that judge friend of yours and tell him that we cheated you? I'm sure he'll throw us in jail." The men laughed and left her.

Katherine sat on a bench and waited for them to disappear before she left the Strand. Although angry that they had cheated her out of the money, she had anticipated it, and was relieved that she wouldn't have to deal with them again, nor testify in court against the innocent negro.

She had looked through the newspaper at the Marshall House the previous evening and saw a notice for seamstresses and decided to apply, fully aware of how exhausting two jobs would be. However, she could cover most of her expenses and use the last twenty-five dollars from Harold to send her sisters to a real school, if only for one term. She pulled the newspaper from her purse, checked the address, and headed to Lippman's Dry Goods store on Congress Street.

When she entered the shop a thin man of about fifty years with straight black hair, a trimmed beard, wearing spectacles and a black suit greeted her with a smile from behind the counter. "Good morning. I'm Mr. Lippman. How may I help you today?"

The warm greeting gave Katherine confidence. "Good morning, sir. My name is Penny Pender. I saw you advertised for seamstresses."

"I did. Have you done much sewing, Miss Pender? You look quite young."

Katherine replied, "I've made clothing for me and my sisters. I learned to sew by hand from my mother. I've also sewn with a treadle."

Mr. Lippman nodded his approval. "Did you do this sewing in Savannah?"

"In Thomasville, sir." Mr. Lippman winced at the mention of the town. She asked, "Is something wrong?"

Lippman said, "Some men in Thomasville recently maligned my people, the German Jews, accused them of profiteering, and threatened to expel them from town." The memory of Mr. Wells ranting at the dining table jumped into Katherine's mind.

Mr. Lippman changed subjects. "I'm the chairman of the Committee on Manufacturing Cloth. We collect donations of cotton and wool from people around the state and weave the material on our looms for soldiers' uniforms. We need seamstresses. The pay is one dollar and fifty cents a day—from eight to four o'clock. The work is done in the back of this store. You must be able to perform your duties well. We need to get the clothing to our boys and can't afford to employ laggards."

"I'd like the job, sir. I need the money. But I work from three o'clock to eleven at the Marshall House. Could I adjust my hours here so I can keep that job?"

"You must work two jobs?"

"Yes, sir. It's just me and my two sisters. They're too young to work and I'm trying to send them to school. We're living at a boarding house and I need two jobs to pay the bills."

"If you don't mind me asking, Miss Pender, where are your parents?"

Katherine lowered her eyes and said softly, "They're deceased, sir."

Lippman stared at the beautiful girl—so young and burdened like so many war-time families. "If you can be here at seven-thirty tomorrow morning and do good work, you may leave a few minutes before three to get to your other job."

Katherine smiled. "Thank you so much, Mr. Lippman. You won't be disappointed." Katherine said goodbye and stepped out on the sidewalk, relieved to have more money coming in. She walked to the boarding house to deliver the good news.

About the same time that Willie and Harold left Katherine standing empty-handed on the bluff, Hercules followed Massa McBain out of the jail house. They climbed onto the gig and James said, "You're out of there, Hercules. Thank God."

Hercules took the reins and replied, "Thank you, Massa. I don't ever want to come back." He drove off and after a few moments of silence, asked, "Massa, do you know who that girl is?"

McBain said, "No. Mr. Williams and I investigated her, and she seems like a good girl—never been in any trouble that we could learn, but her circumstances are puzzling." He patted Hercules on the shoulder. "It's over with, that's all that's important. Forget about her. I have you and Mr. Donnelly back. Now I want to send those two men, Willie and Harold, to the gallows."

Hercules wanted to get those men, too, but he also thought about his accuser. He had to find out why she did it. He wasn't willing to forget.

Katherine approached Duffy's and saw Pauline and Mary in Washington Square watching a company of black firemen working the bars of a hand-pumping fire engine. The girls ran to her. Pauline said, "Oldest Sister, the firemen are filling the cistern. They pump the water from the river from one engine to another to reach all the way here. The men are so nice. Can we watch some more?"

"Of course. I'll sit right here."

The girls ran back to the fire engine. Mary spoke to one of the firemen. The negro lifted her from the waist, and she grabbed onto the pumping bar. Then he lifted her up and down so she could pump with the other men. The negroes and Pauline laughed, as did Katherine. She closed her eyes and thanked God that they were in Savannah and had escaped forever the unbearable Mr. Wells.

The sisters had lived in misery with the Wells family for almost six months after their mother's death. Katherine pitied Mrs. Wells because she was afraid of her husband. Their daily routine had followed the plan Mr. Wells had laid out that first night. When Katherine had some free time in the late afternoon she patched her sisters' clothes. Fortunately, Mrs. Wells owned a treadle—a foot-powered sewing machine that allowed a seamstress to use both hands to handle the material. If Pauline finished her chores early, she practiced drawing, for which she had a natural talent and which Mrs. Wells praised. The woman even bought her paper and sketching pencils, upon a promise that she wouldn't tell Mr. Wells.

During supper they often had to listen to Mr. Wells lecture them on his favorite topic—his son Jonas, who had only lived with his parents in Thomasville for a week before going off to war in Virginia, and never gave him a stitch of trouble. Katherine thought the boy must be a real rascal if his father was so proud of him.

The sisters never spoke to Mr. Wells unless he addressed them. They all went to church together on Sundays, where the other parishioners stared at the girls. On Katherine's behalf Mrs. Wells convinced Mr. Wells to let them go to town on their own on Wednesday afternoons to visit their mother's grave, which, after a heated argument with Pastor Lewis, and with the support of Mr. Dillon, was placed in a corner of the yard, far from Zebudiah. Other than that one liberty, life with the Wells family had been strict and humorless.

One night at supper Mary whispered something to Pauline, who laughed out loud. Mr. Wells told Pauline that joviality was not allowed during meals and ordered her to her room. Pauline thrust her head forward and declared, "No!" Mr. Wells leaned across the table and slapped her face. Pauline held her hand to her cheek as tears welled up in her eyes. She said, "I hate you!" and ran upstairs.

Katherine stood to follow her as Mary darted around the table and started beating her little fists like pistons on Mr. Wells's arm, screaming, "You leave my thithter alone!"

Mr. Wells pushed her away with one hand. She fell on her rump and started to wail. Katherine rushed to pick her up. She yelled at the man, "Don't you ever lay a hand on my sisters again!"

The man stood, hiked up his pants, and pointed a stubby finger at Katherine. "Shut that fresh mouth, young lady, or you'll feel the back of my hand! And it won't be a slap! My boy never gave me this much sass in his entire life!"

Mrs. Wells clutched her head in her hands and screamed, "Stop! Please!"

Katherine lugged Mary up the stairs as Mr. Wells hollered, "You selfish brats better get back down here and clean up, after all I've spent taking care of you and your farm." She slammed the door behind her and the girls crawled under the bed covers.

Pauline tugged on Katherine's arm. "Please, Oldest Sister. I can't stand another day. I beg you to get us out of here."

Katherine put an arm around each sister. "I will. I swear on Ma's grave."

Mary bawled, "You promith?"

"Yes, if it's the last thing I do."

Mr. Wells did not come after them and the younger girls eventually drifted off to sleep. Katherine spent hours staring into darkness, trying to think of a way to escape from their living nightmare. She considered fleeing in the buggy, but they had no place to go, and three young girls traveling overland alone would raise eyebrows in lawmen and busybodies, not to mention bandits. If they were stopped and returned to Thomasville, there would be hell to pay with Mr. Wells. She fell asleep depressed and with a headache.

Fortunately, during harvest time, Mr. Wells left the house at sunup and wasn't present when the sisters appeared at breakfast the next morning. A red-eyed Mrs. Wells said, "Good morning, girls." The girls replied in kind, and that ended the conversation.

Things did not improve over the following days and Katherine was desperate for a solution. The next time the girls visited their mother's grave, she stopped to see Mr. Dillon, who Delores had appointed executor of her estate, and who Katherine had come to like as she had no other adult with whom to talk. He was the only one who was pleasant to her. He greeted her. "Miss Downes, how are you?"

She explained that Mr. Wells had hit her sisters and they couldn't tolerate living with him another day. "Can you help us, sir?" Dillon said that they couldn't move out until she turned eighteen—over a year away. He explained that a judge wouldn't consider her complaint as they were orphans and the Wells family sheltered and fed them during a time when everyone had to sacrifice. Katherine defiantly raised her chin. "Then we'll run away. I'm almost seventeen, and I know I can pass for eighteen anywhere but here, where people know me. We have to get away from him! Don't you understand?"

Dillon said, "Believe me, Miss Downes, I do understand. I've had my own problems with Mr. Wells. You wouldn't call us friends."

Katherine said, "He wasn't happy when I told him that you were our lawyer."

Dillon laughed. "I had some dealings with him shortly after he moved here. He's a nasty and vindictive man. When I heard that he and Mrs. Wells were taking you in, I was going to advise your mother against it, but, of course, she was having problems of her own, and I didn't. Now, I wish I had said something."

Katherine groaned and said, "Me, too."

Dillon studied the girl and felt partly responsible for the ugly situation she and her sisters were in. He decided to help, but he had to be careful or he might put the girls in harm's way. "You've been through a lot. I might be able to do something, but you must swear on the Bible never to tell anyone."

"Oh, sir, could you? Oh, please! I won't tell a soul. You have my word. I'll do anything to escape that man."

"Miss Downes, you must understand that running away won't be easy. You can't be seen leaving and you must find a place to live where you can't be traced by Mr. Wells. And you must be able to support yourselves. Have you thought about these things?"

Katherine put her face in her hands and shook her head. She looked up and said, "No, but I'm thinking about them now. Can you help me?"

Dillon leaned back in his chair and stared at the ceiling, deep in thought. "If it were me, I'd go to Savannah, where you can hide among many people. You can catch the early morning train, but you mustn't leave from Thomasville. No one from here can see you board or they'll tell Mr. Wells. Can you leave the farm without him or Mrs. Wells knowing?"

Katherine chewed on her lower lip. "Mrs. Wells visits a neighbor very early on Fridays to collect lint and make bandages for the soldiers. Mr. Wells leaves for the fields at sunup. That's the only time we're alone. As soon as Mrs. Wells leaves, we could drive to the next station—Boston."

Dillon said, "When she returns and can't find you, I imagine she'll come to town looking for you and will certainly pay me a visit. I'll tell her that we spoke about estate matters today, but that I haven't seen you since, which will be true. Someone will report finding your horse and buggy at Boston Station and Mr. Wells will know that you took the train somewhere. If he searches, he'll have trouble finding you in Savannah. But he probably won't even bother as it's harvest time. It sounds like he'll be thankful that you're gone." The lawyer saw Katherine's frown transform into a smile. He continued. "Do you have any money?"

She remembered her mother's warning and hesitated to reveal that she had over four hundred dollars, but the man was trying to help her and decided to be half truthful. "About two hundred dollars."

"That's good. There's a female orphanage in Savannah where you can stay for free. Two hundred dollars should keep you for a good while, but at some point— probably when you turn eighteen—you'll have to get a job."

Katherine felt like hugging the man. They had a way to flee Mr. Wells forever! "Thank you so much, sir. I'll never forget this. Never!"

Dillon reminded Katherine that her family owed him thirty dollars for his work on her mother's legal defense and ten dollars for her mother's headstone. "I'm trying to sell the assets of your mother's estate. With the war, that has become more difficult. But the farm and your horse and buggy have good value and will pay the outstanding debts, including my bill, with something left over, which will be distributed to you."

The more Mr. Dillon came up with solutions, the more Katherine glowed. "Sir, your kindness is overwhelming. This is the nicest anyone has ever been to us. I wish there was some way I could repay you."

"Don't worry about it, Miss Downes. For now, you must make a successful escape, or life for you and your sisters will be even worse. When can you leave?"

"This Friday, I guess. That's our first opportunity."

Dillon couldn't remember when he had made anyone so happy. He stood and said, "Good luck, Miss Downes. If you need anything else, write to me." He led her to the front door. She squeezed his hand, thanked him again, and ran to the buggy.

She took the reins and Pauline asked, "Why are you so happy?"

Katherine whispered, "I'll explain later." When they arrived at the farm, Katherine took Pauline aside and said, "Mr. Dillon told me how we can escape.

We're going to Savannah on Friday."

Pauline grabbed Katherine's arm. "Oldest Sister, are you serious?"

Katherine smiled, nodded, and kissed Pauline's cheek.

❧

Two days later, after Mr. and Mrs. Wells left the house, the sisters packed their carpetbags and drove seven miles to Boston Station. Katherine patted her horse's neck and left a note on the seat asking the finder to contact Mr. Dillon of Thomasville. The girls boarded the cars and arrived in Savannah that evening. They found a boarding house across from the depot. Katherine's hands shook as she had to do things she had never done before, like asking for a room for the night, while trying to act as if she had. The desk clerk's eyes darted from one girl to the next, but he pushed the hotel register in front of Katherine, which she signed as Katherine Downes.

The next day the innkeeper gave them directions to the Savannah Female Orphan Asylum on Madison Square. As they walked, their heads swiveled like birds on a branch at all the sights. Pauline was particularly excited and pointed out the sights. "What a beautiful house!" and "Look, another park! I can't wait to sketch them."

Katherine patted down her sisters' hair and adjusted her bonnet before knocking on the asylum door. A woman answered and surveyed the three girls. The older two held carpetbags. She said, "I'm Mrs. Cohen. May I help you?"

Katherine said, "Yes, ma'am. I'm Katherine Downes and these are my sisters Pauline and Mary. We're orphans and need a place to live."

Mrs. Cohen invited them into a small room with a desk and three wooden, straight-back chairs. Katherine sat Mary in the middle and explained that their parents had recently died from the fever. Having no other family, they came to Savannah.

The woman asked, "Miss Downes, please tell me your ages."

"I'll turn seventeen next month, Pauline is twelve, and Mary is five."

Mrs. Cohen said that the girls in the home were sent by their parents, relatives, a church, or other guardian who was unable to care for them. The relative or guardian had to sign an indenture of apprenticeship agreement which allowed the asylum to bind the girls to a family to work and learn a useful trade from which they could support themselves once they turned eighteen. The asylum provided schooling for children who were not bound out. "Miss Downes, as you are not an adult, you can't sign the agreement for yourself or your sisters. I suggest that you ask the Savannah minister of your denomination to write to your minister in your hometown for approval to sign an indenture agreement on your behalf. I will allow you to stay here until that is done." Katherine's moan was audible. She could never let Pastor Lewis know where they were. She also realized that she should not use their real names if they didn't want to be found.

Mrs. Cohen continued. "If you meet the requirements and live here, you will have to leave when you turn eighteen, but your sisters will have to fulfill their indentures. Perhaps you could get guardianship of your sisters at that time, but it is not certain that the court would grant it if you can't support them."

Stunned by the news, Katherine stammered, "I . . . I could never be separated from my sisters. We must be together always."

Mrs. Cohen sympathized with Katherine but said she had to abide by the rules, which, she believed, were the same as the other orphanages in town. She stressed that they could stay there until they heard from their pastor.

Katherine gazed at the floor. Her plans were already crumbling. She decided not to stay at the asylum, even temporarily, as she feared the authorities might try to separate her from her sisters. She told Mrs. Cohen that she had some money and asked her for the name of a nearby boarding house. The woman recommended Mrs. Duffy's on Washington Square, but urged Katherine to stay at the orphanage for the time being.

Katherine said she needed to think about it. The girls left and headed directly to Mrs. Duffy's, which looked to be clean and comfortable, and served breakfast and supper. Katherine negotiated a price of twenty dollars a week for the three of them on the basis that they only needed one room with one bed and didn't eat much. Mrs. Duffy asked Katherine to register, and the girl racked her brain for a fake name to avoid being traced. She thought of the fairy tale about Penny the Pretender and signed "Penny Pender." When they got to the room, she told her sisters that she had changed their last name to Pender so Mr. Wells couldn't find them. She changed her own first name to Penny but they should continue to call her "Oldest Sister," as they always had. She made them repeat their new names ten times and promise to always use them from now on.

Soon after they moved in, Pauline insisted on going to church. They attended the First Baptist Church on Chippewa Square and sat in the back row. The appearance of three young girls without parents caught the eye of several parishioners. After the service one woman met them out front and introduced herself. She asked Katherine where they were from and about their parents. Once again, she had to scramble for answers. "We're orphans, ma'am. Our parents died of the fever and we moved to Savannah where I could find work. I am sorry, but we do have to leave. We look forward to next Sunday." Katherine took each sister by the hand and walked away. As they headed home, she told Pauline, "You're going to have to read your Bible with Mary for a while, until we find a different church to attend." When Pauline complained, Katherine asked her if she wanted to live with Mr. Wells again and the discussion ended.

The next six weeks—into January 1862—were the happiest of the girls' short lives. They had no chores other than cleaning the room and sewing and washing clothes. There were no mean adults, just a city with countless parks, called squares by the locals, stately mansions, and a beautiful harbor, which Pauline sketched in her notebook.

Most of the other boarders were older men, who were generally very polite to them. One evening a man with ears that stuck out like Katherine's father joined the guests for supper. Katherine couldn't look at him. She rushed her sisters through the meal and they left the table early. That night Katherine dreamed that Zebudiah was entering their room. Pauline had to shake her awake and hug her until she calmed down. Fortunately, the boarder left the next day.

Still, Christmas with the Duffys and four other boarders, virtual strangers, was the best they could remember, with a turkey supper followed by Christmas carols.

In January, with rapidly diminishing funds, Katherine decided to find a job. She felt remotely qualified to be a seamstress, but saw no advertisements for them in the newspapers. However, she did see an advertisement for a night job for a white cleaning woman at the Marshall House Hotel. It wasn't ideal, but working at night would allow her to be with her sisters during the day and leave them to read at night, when they would be confined to their room. She applied and was hired.

The salary of one dollar fifty cents per day for six days a week wasn't nearly enough to pay the boarding house bill, so Katherine continued to use the money that her mother had left her to cover the shortfall. By June it was gone and she fell behind in payments to Mrs. Duffy. She was broke, facing eviction, and realizing that she may have no choice but to return to the orphanage. Somehow, she needed to get more money. Then she saw a hotel resident drop some valuables on the floor outside of his room. Reluctantly, she picked up the money and a watch and kept them. The cash saved her from eviction, but at the price of meeting Willie.

⁜

"That wath tho much fun, Oldetht Thithter. Can I be a fireman one day?" Katherine looked up and saw Mary and Pauline grinning down at her.

Katherine stood and took Mary's hand. "Maybe, but first, we're going to enroll you and Pauline in a school for girls. You'll make lots of friends."

Mary jumped up and down. "Yeth! Thcool!"

The sisters walked from the square and passed the firemen hauling the engine by its pull ropes back to their firehouse. Mary and Pauline waved and the men waved back.

They reached Whitaker and Broughton and entered J. S. F. Lancaster's School for Young Ladies and Misses. With money she had set aside from Harold and the security of a second job with Mr. Lippman, Katherine negotiated with Mr. Lancaster an installment plan for the fall semester of ten dollars for each girl, with another ten dollars each payable in a month and the final five dollars each payable when the term ended in January. She handed the man the twenty dollars and promised that the girls would appear for classes the next morning.

Katherine walked with her sisters back to Mrs. Duffy's and then went to work at the Marshall House. She slept well that night for all she had accomplished, and thanked God once again for allowing them to escape Thomasville.

⌘

Pastor Lewis counseled, "Calm down, Mr. Wells. Christians don't talk of revenge. Frankly, you should be grateful the older one is gone from under your roof."

Mr. Wells had not taken the disappearance of the sisters well. Initially, he felt like celebrating when his wife told him that she couldn't find the girls anywhere and their buggy was gone. When he and his wife inspected the girls' bedroom, Mr. Wells picked up a sheet of paper from one of the pillows. It was a drawing of the backside of a donkey, which had a human face with big ears, long stringy hair hanging from the sides, and a bulbous nose, just like his. The man hissed, "The little bitch."

That night he fumed at supper. "I supported those little devils for six months, took care of their farm, taught them manners, gave them a secure family life, and this is the thanks I get? They owe me hundreds of dollars and, mark my words, one day I'm going to take it out of the older one's hide."

Mr. Wells's humiliation was just beginning. Word of the girls' departure spread around town, and it was considered a black eye to any family to have children run away from home, even if one of those children was Katherine Downes. The parishioners at church were now talking about him. Rumors started to circulate that Mr. Wells had tried to molest the oldest one, which caused the girls to run away. The women at church began to shun Mrs. Wells, who couldn't stand the isolation, and begged her husband to address the congregation and deny the rumors. He, in turn, asked Pastor Lewis to speak on his behalf before he went searching for the girls and beat them within an inch of their lives. The pastor agreed to address the parish if Mr. Wells promised not to seek revenge.

Wells gave his word, as he figured out ways to track down the sisters. ⌘

PART 3

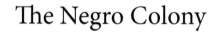

The Negro Colony
September 1862 - November 1862

CHAPTER TWENTY-ONE

"Trying to Get to Savannah"
June - September 1862

Joseph lay in the lower bunk, his hands clasped behind his head, unable to sleep. He felt JD's weight against his leg but didn't want to disturb him. Johnson's Island had been better than expected. The men spent their days playing base ball, card games, and quoits, eating, sleeping, and discussing the latest rumors of a prisoner exchange. Some men carved trinkets such as pipes, rings, and chess pieces from wood and meat bones. A few enterprising officers started laundry, tailoring, and watch-repair businesses. Prisoners were allowed to send and receive mail, and Joseph heard from Emily, Danny, his parents, and Amy. Each letter made him increasingly homesick. Danny said Hercules was teaching him and Truvy how to ride a horse. Amy explained her absence from New York, and confided that she had tried to travel to Savannah to save her property but failed to get a passport from Washington. She said she didn't know what to do about it. Emily still confessed her love for him and her desire to reunite.

The pain in Joseph's leg diminished slightly, and though he still walked with a limp, he only used his cane when he had to be on his feet for more than five or ten minutes. He hoped that if the improvement continued, he could rejoin his company in an active status. Such a move would upset his father, but Joseph couldn't return to the Heritage as long as the war raged.

Joseph especially looked forward to the weekly swim in Lake Erie, which occurred at the same time that a scheduled excursion boat from the mainland sailed by. The boat, painted red, white, and blue, had a brass band that always blasted "Yankee Doodle" for the rebels. Yet the passengers waved to their former countrymen, and the prisoners returned the greeting.

But nothing created more excitement in the prison than news of Confederate victories as reported by newly arriving prisoners. The men learned of the great triumph by the rebels over the federals at Secessionville, near Charleston, in mid-June; of General Robert E. Lee's successes over General George B. McClellan around Richmond in late June and early July; of General Nathan Bedford Forrest capturing the nine-hundred-man brigade of General Thomas T. Crittenden at Murfreesboro in mid-July; and now, in mid-August, of General Thomas J Jackson, nicknamed "Stonewall" after Manassas, defeating General Nathaniel P. Banks at Culpeper, Virginia.

Word of this latest triumph spread around the camp in minutes, and, overcome with joy, the officers started to sing "Dixie." The singing spread like a forest fire, and soon all fourteen hundred captives joined in. Many of the men marched in place and waved their arms like orchestra conductors as they bellowed out the words. Red-faced guards screamed from the blockhouses for the prisoners to quiet down, but their orders couldn't be heard above the celebration. The impromptu concert finally ended, and the officers continued their back-slapping in the barracks. The next morning during roll call, Colonel Pierson explained to the rebels that he barely prevented his sentinels from shooting them the previous day, but the men ignored the scare tactics.

That same day, rumors swirled again that the North and South had signed a treaty covering prisoner exchanges. Lying in bed that night, Joseph prayed that the grapevine was correct for once. The Confederates must have taken thousands of prisoners during the last few months. Surely each side would want their men back. Someone banged against his bunk. Joseph whispered, "Who's there?"

A voice answered, "It's Lieutenant Madson. I'm sorry. It's so dark in here and I'm not feeling well. I have to get to the privy."

Joseph remembered Madson as a soft-spoken, thin, bushy-haired man from a Mississippi regiment who looked more like a priest than an officer. "Don't worry, Lieutenant, I'm awake anyway."

Moments later Joseph felt JD jump off the bed, and heard his paws tap on the wooden floor towards the door to await the return of the officer. He closed his eyes and thought about being in Savannah with Danny, fishing from the wharf at the Heritage in the evening, just as he did as a child.

Joseph started to doze when he heard a rifle shot, a loud thud on the barrack's floor, and the squealing of an animal, which could only be JD. He sat up, pulled on his pants, and felt his way to the door. He arrived at the same time as Colonel Olmstead, who was holding a lantern. In the dim light they both looked down. Joseph gasped, "My Lord, they shot him!" He knelt beside the face-down body and saw a hole with burn marks around the edges in the middle of his nightshirt. He rolled the body over and the left arm flopped on the floor like a dead fish. Madson stared blankly at the ceiling.

Olmstead knelt next to Joseph and touched Madson's forehead. "The bastards murdered him—shot him in the back. I'm going to see Pierson." The colonel marched from the barracks with Joseph and the other officers following.

They got twenty yards before a voice called out, "Halt where you are! Don't take another step, you damned rebels, or I'll shoot every last one of you!"

Olmstead stopped and held his arms up, causing many followers to bump into the backs of others. "This is Colonel Olmstead. I demand to see Colonel Pierson."

An explosion ripped through the night and kicked up dirt ten feet in front of Olmstead, causing him to jump back. The sentinel screamed, "Who are you to give me orders? Return to your quarters or the next shot will be a lot closer."

Olmstead called out, "Cowards. We're walking to the dead line to call for the colonel. Go ahead and shoot if you must." The men marched on, chanting "Cowards," emboldened by their growing numbers.

The sentry shouted, "Don't take another step! There are twenty guards up here itching for target practice."

The stockade gates creaked open, stopping the procession. In the moonlight a swarm of soldiers ran into the yard, carrying their rifles with fixed bayonets, and stopped a few yards from the rebels. The guards stepped aside and Pierson appeared. He approached Olmstead. "What's the problem, Colonel?"

"Your guards shot one of our men in the back in the doorway of our barracks. He's dead. That's the problem."

Pierson looked past Olmstead at the mass of lanterns in the yard and said, "If what you say is true, I'm certain that the guard had just cause for his actions."

Olmstead stepped closer, ready to confront Pierson nose-to-nose, but the guards aimed their rifles at his head and he froze. "Shot in the back in the doorway is just cause? You have a grotesque view of war, if I may say so, Colonel."

Pierson ignored the insult. He had but one objective—to quell this protest before it turned bloodier. He spoke over his shoulder to one of his aides. "Lieutenant Drake, have your men recover the body, and find out who fired the shot. Have him and the officer of the guard report to me." He then shouted skywards, "Prisoners of Fort Johnson, you have my word that I will investigate this incident and deal with the findings appropriately. You have no reason to be out here now. Return to your barracks or I'll have no alternative but to deal with you as rioters. I prefer not to do that."

Olmstead growled, "Your secretary of war will hear about this outrage, Colonel."

Pierson shrugged and walked back to the stockade gate, followed by his guards, who retreated backwards, their guns trained on the prisoners. The men returned to their barracks. Few, however, could get back to sleep. If their captors could shoot Madson, they could kill any of them. The rebel officers sat on their beds, talking about the cowardice of the Yankees and vowing revenge when they returned to the battlefield.

The captives eventually blew out the candles. Joseph heard a whimper and remembered JD. He reached under his bunk and felt the mutt hunched down. He pulled out the dog by the scruff of his neck, and put him on the bed. He said, "Don't worry, little fella. I have a feeling that we'll be out of here soon."

Joseph went about his daily routine for the next few weeks, but the angry mood in camp remained. They never heard a word about Colonel Pierson's investigation. Also, the rumors of an exchange died on the prison grapevine. Then another incident inflamed the passions of the men. One day, as Joseph sat in his bunk writing to Danny, he heard shouting, cursing, and jeering. He hurried out-side and saw three Confederate prisoners surrounded by ten bluecoats holding their rifles at the ready, walking towards the main gate. Rebels threw handfuls of dirt at the formation, and a few spat. Captain Sims walked by Joseph and said, "The bastards took the Yankee offer of freedom by signing their oath of alle-giance. It's best that they turn now, instead of in battle." Joseph shook his head and wondered what would make men walk away from their families, friends, and heritage.

A few days later, near the end of August, Colonel Pierson gathered the pris-oners in the yard and announced that a prisoner exchange had been negotiated, and that they would be sent to Vicksburg as soon as they settled their sutler ac-counts. This turned out to be a monumental task, as each of the thousand-plus prisoners challenged at least some of their charges. Five days later, with the bal-ance of his money returned to him, Joseph started packing for his departure. JD sat on the floor, with his tail wagging furiously. Olmstead walked by and asked, "What are you doing with the dog?"

JD barked as if demanding an answer. "I've become attached to the little guy. He'll make a nice gift for my son." JD barked again and Joseph rubbed his head.

On September 1 over twelve hundred Confederate officers filed out of the fort, luggage in hand, and, in Joseph's case, a dog inside his jacket. Olmstead tried to reclaim his sword as Pierson had said he could, but the colonel was unavailable that day, so he left without it. The prisoners boarded steamers to Sandusky; took three trains over three days to reach Cairo, Illinois, at the juncture of the Mis-sissippi and Ohio rivers; and boarded the steamboat *Henry Chouteau*. However, they had to wait four days for prisoners from other camps to arrive. They received rations of hard bread, coffee, sugar, and bacon. As no cooking facilities were pro-vided, they ate the bacon raw. No one minded too much. They were going home. Nor did they mind JD, who provided a source of amusement for the prisoners on the long trip home. Many of the men took turns playing with the animal and tried to teach him tricks. However, it was Joseph's job to clean up after the dog after the mutt pooped and peed at the foot of a railing at the stern of the ship.

On September 8, with over five thousand men stuffed into eight two-deck paddle-wheel boats, and escorted by one lonely gunboat, the prisoners began their voyage. With the ships under steam, the prisoners were able to cook their rations on the rounded shoulders of the smokestacks.

A week later they stopped in Memphis, which had been occupied by Union forces since early June, to take on coal. Thousands of locals—aware of the im-pending arrival of the prisoners—lined the riverfront, and greeted the flotilla by waving Confederate flags. The boats dropped anchor near the wharf. Joseph squeezed up to the railing, with JD in his left arm, and waved to the well-wishers. Federal troops lined the wharf to prevent residents from getting too close to the ships, and prisoners from exiting them.

A Union officer stood on a portable platform and hollered to the crowd, "By order of the commanding officer of the military district of Memphis, Major General William T. Sherman, you are ordered to disperse." No one paid attention. The crowd surged forward and the soldiers gave way, but they slung their rifles over their backs, linked arms, and pushed back. The residents screamed at the guards. Women held up baskets in the soldiers' faces but the guards shook their heads. The prisoners booed the Yankees.

One lady grabbed a parcel from her basket, took a few steps back, and flung it over the heads of the guards about thirty feet to the top deck of the *Henry Chouteau*. A prisoner near Joseph caught an apple and held it over his head for all to see. Another woman threw an article to the adjacent boat. The recipient waved a fried chicken leg and shouted, "Thank you!" Soon, thousands of pieces of food—chicken, pork, fruits, cakes—flew through the air like flocks of starlings at sunset. At first the Yankees held up their arms in an attempt to block the items but soon relented and laughed at the spectacle instead. Joseph caught a pork chop and gave a chunk to JD. He also snared a chicken leg and gave it to a nearby, empty-handed soldier. One prisoner leaned too far over the railing to catch a morsel, lost his balance, and tumbled over the side into the river, drawing laughter from the Yankees and rebels alike.

An hour later, with the airborne food transfer completed, the women waved their empty baskets over their heads and slowly returned to their homes. Despite the Stars and Stripes flying over the harbor, the prisoners knew they were in the South again.

The flotilla departed the next day for Vicksburg. For a week the prisoners did little but stare at the river bank and talk about home, families, and returning to the war. The ships anchored at night, unable to navigate in the dark. Joseph and JD slept on the top deck, side-by-side with the other men.

Joseph awoke the first morning to the glowing golden dawn piercing through leafy tree branches and the whistle of a whippoorwill. He also heard a creaking noise and the voices of men from below. He went to the railing, careful not to step on any of the sleeping soldiers, and saw six Confederate officers boarding one of the lifeboats, followed by two guards. Four prisoners on the first deck lowered a large parcel that looked like a rolled-up carpet, though two feet stuck out of one end, to the outstretched hands of the six prisoners in the boat. They lay the body down and rowed to shore as a white mist lifted off the river. With shovels provided by the guards, the prisoners dug a shallow, muddy grave near the river bank and laid their comrade to rest. One of the men found two branches and, using a vine, tied them together in the form of a cross. He hammered the marker into the ground with the back side of the shovel, the banging sound reverberating through the morning solitude. The rebel officers stood by the grave and lowered their heads as one read from a Bible. The two guards stood near the boat, smoking cigarettes and chatting to themselves. The hammering became a sad refrain each morning for the rest of the trip, as soldiers succumbed to sickness and were buried in nameless, forgotten plots along the river.

Six days later the prisoners heard the booms of nearby cannons and, thinking they were being fired upon, fell flat on the deck for protection. The men slowly crept to the railing and one yelled, "Look, they're ours!" Joseph jumped to his feet and saw a battery downriver with soldiers standing atop earthen walls waving the Confederate flag. He and the other men waved their caps in the air. The ships soon rounded a bend and they saw a glorious sight: piers penetrating the river, scores of wooden warehouses lining the bank, three-story brick, front-gabled buildings covering the bluff, and soaring church spires dominating the crest. They had reached Vicksburg. More cannons boomed, sending vibrations of freedom through their bodies.

The ships docked and the men lined up, smiling and laughing, anxious to step foot onto southern soil. Instead, they waited for hours as three Confederate and three Union officers sat on opposite sides of a table atop the gangway, reviewing papers and checking off the names of each prisoner. When Joseph's turn came, JD stuck out his head from his master's jacket and growled at the Union officers. Joseph pushed him back in.

The men eventually gained their release and Joseph and the other Oglethorpe officers convened on the wharf. With the help of a local lieutenant, they rented a deserted house in town with no furniture and a hole in the roof caused by a Union naval bombardment. They pooled their dwindling funds and hired a negro cook, who made JD sit on his hind haunches and wave his front paws for scraps. Joseph used the floor of the library for his bed and slept better than he had in months. The men spent the following days writing letters and walking around the city of pock-marked buildings, often stopping to chat with other recently freed officers, while the quartermaster's staff worked feverishly to arrange transportation home for several thousand soldiers.

Four days later, near the end of September 1862, the men from Savannah boarded a train for Mobile on a slow, circuitous journey home. Joseph spent most of his time staring at his daguerreotypes of Danny and Charlotte. He couldn't wait to see his son again. He was grateful that his parents were able to look after him, but knew the boy needed his father. He also realized that Danny, like every child, needed a mother.

Joseph also removed from his wallet the daguerreotype of his sister Amy and realized how much he missed her. He wondered if he would ever see her again.

❧

"I'm trying to get to Savannah," Amy McBain Carson told the female stranger. They leaned against the railing of a boat with one hundred other passengers on their way to Memphis. While Amy's servant Colleen Mullins sat on a deck chair holding Amy's son Jimmy, Amy pointed to a clearing on the Tennessee side of the Mississippi River and said, "Look!" Large columns of grey smoke billowed up from about fifteen different pads where houses used to stand. Tall, baking-hot chimneys, looking like tall grim reapers, served as macabre reminders of the village that once existed. A wooden church remained amidst the destruction, as if spared by God. A group of women and children congregated at the edge of the bluff, hypnotized by the sight of their smoldering hamlet.

Amy asked a crewman if he knew the cause of the fires. He shrugged and said, "Don't know, ma'am. Probably rebel guerrillas. They burn down everything, even houses of their own kin." Amy turned back to the railing and thought how typical for a Yankee to blame Southerners without knowing what happened.

After Amy had returned in late June from her failed attempt to get a passport in Washington City, she wrote letters to her congressmen for help. But they told her to apply to the secretary of state, who had just rejected her request. She grew increasingly depressed and angry over the thought of losing her property, but couldn't think of a way to travel to Savannah legally to defend herself.

Amy's husband Bob came home again in late August for two weeks after following General Grant's army. She endured all his stories about the war and the generals, especially General Grant, who he proclaimed a military genius. However, he said that there was increasing talk among the other reporters that Grant drank heavily and presented a danger to his command. Bob had never witnessed such behavior, but wouldn't deny that it might be true, as drinking was common among military men.

Amy found one story particularly interesting. It involved General Sherman, the officer who suffered a mental breakdown in late 1861 but recovered to become a major general. Grant's army had captured Memphis, Tennessee on June 6 and a month later Grant put Sherman in command of the area. The city sat on the eastern side of the river across from Arkansas and on the northern border of Mississippi, two states also in rebellion. Sherman's military authorities found it impossible to prevent people from entering and leaving the city, as Memphis residents and farmers in the surrounding countryside depended on trading with each other. So the Yankees stopped trying, especially since the Union desperately needed the South's cotton to make tents. Sherman issued an order opening Memphis to trade and travel with the environs, regardless of loyalty, with cargoes subject to search. Amy realized that she could cross into the South from Memphis to get to Savannah. It wouldn't be an easy trip—Memphis was a thousand miles from New York and Amy would have sixteen-month-old Jimmy with her. But she had no other option.

In mid-September, ten days after Bob had left to cover the Iuka – Corinth, Mississippi campaign, Amy, Jimmy, and Colleen began their long journey with a railroad trip to Cairo, Illinois and a boat trip to Memphis. On September 24, they were witnessing the destruction of Randolph, Tennessee.

Upon arriving in Memphis the next day, ten days after Joseph had depart-ed the place, Amy checked into a hotel, made a few inquiries, and hired a hack which took them to Fort Pickering, three miles from the city. She told a guard that she wanted to see the commanding general, and the soldier escorted them to a half-acre grassy area bordered by eight tents. He placed two wooden chairs for Amy and Colleen under the shade of a tree, took Amy's name, and left. Three men in business suits standing nearby tipped their hats to them and returned to their conversation. The women sat for an hour as Jimmy walked uncertainly on the grass in a dress that reached his shoes. They watched as an officer called the men individually into the largest tent, and heard each one muttering as he left.

Finally, the officer poked his head from the front flap and called, "Mrs. Car-son?"

Amy left Jimmy with Colleen, and walked into the dark, hot, canvas cave. It smelled moldy and stuffy. She sat in a chair by a wobbly table that served as a desk. The officer in the blue uniform on the opposite side leaned back in his chair and glanced at a piece of paper on top of a pile. "Good afternoon, Miss . . . Mrs. Robert Carson. I am Major General Sherman. What may I do for you?"

Amy studied the man. His short, reddish-brown hair lay flat on the sides but spiked in several directions on the top of his head. Lines covered the parts of his face not concealed by a short, neatly trimmed beard, and radiated from his sad brown eyes. Amy thought him handsome, but wondered when he had last smiled. She sensed she couldn't engage in light, flirtatious talk with the man and got right to the point. "I would like a pass for me, my child, and my Irish girl to return to the Union from Savannah, sir."

The general studied Amy for a few seconds before responding, making her squirm in her seat. "Ma'am, you don't need a pass to travel out of Memphis, or to return, as long as you take one of five designated roads and do so during day-light."

"I understand, sir, but that's how things currently stand. I plan to be in Sa-vannah for a few weeks, and it takes time to travel there and back. Things could change—new orders could be issued making border crossings impossible. I'd like to be assured that I can return to my husband and home in New York. A pass from you will do that."

Sherman looked at his aide-de-camp standing by the front of the tent. He wanted to be fighting the enemy, not listening to women who wanted special passes or men asking him to track down their runaway slaves. "What business do you have in Savannah that is so important that you'd travel there, with a child no less, in time of war?"

She explained how she left Savannah for New York and how the Confeder-ate authorities had confiscated her property. "That property is my life savings. I earned most of it, inherited some. I'm not letting anyone take it from me without a fight."

The general nodded sympathetically. "Why doesn't your husband accompany you on such an arduous trip?"

"My husband is a newspaper reporter and is with General Grant's army. Besides, he's from New York and couldn't go into the South safely even if he were free to do so."

Sherman picked up a rock that served as a paperweight and rolled it in his hands. "As you may have heard, I'm not fond of newspaper reporters. Who does he work for, if you don't mind me asking?"

Amy wanted to kick herself. She had avoided revealing that her brother was a Confederate soldier, but dug a deeper hole by disclosing Bob's occupation. Now, she had to crawl out of it. "The *New York Standard*. His name is Robert Carson. He has written many favorable articles about General Grant. He also praised you at Shiloh."

The general looked skyward, trying to recall the articles, and shrugged. He no longer seemed interested in the subject. "You are aware that the surrounding territory is dangerous for travel, with all the rebel guerrilla bands about?"

"Yes, sir. On the trip down from Cairo, I saw a village on the Tennessee side burned to the ground, except for one church. Did the guerrillas do that?"

The general smiled for the first time. "In a sense, they did. A few days ago a ship of ours with women and children, food, and merchandise for the locals—secesh families—came down the river and guerrillas fired at it from that village. I decided to set an example. My men burned to the ground every building but one in the town to serve as a reminder to all that any such acts will be similarly punished."

Amy gulped upon hearing of Sherman's wanton action. Those were houses of women and children, not factories of war or soldier's barracks. Sherman saw her reaction and continued. "To make sure there is no confusion, madam, I am issuing an order today, that if such a cowardly act should happen again, I will expel from Memphis ten families who are known rebel sympathizers for every boat fired upon. I hope, for the sake of the locals, that no one tests me."

Amy shuddered. She had no doubt that the man meant business. "General, may I have that pass?"

Sherman pulled out a blank piece of paper and wrote, "Allow Mrs. Robert Carson, child, and servant girl to cross from Confederate lines into Union territory at any point within these United States until December 1, 1862. Major-General, Commanding, W. T. Sherman, Memphis." He pushed it across the table.

Amy took it, stood, and said, "Thank you, General. I appreciate your help."

The officer rose and said, "I wish you luck in reclaiming your property. I hope you aren't appealing to the rebel sense of fairness." As Amy exited the tent she thanked God that she wouldn't have to see General Sherman again.

With Jimmy giggling in her massive arms, Colleen approached Amy and asked, "Did ye spake to the general, Misses?"

"I did, and I got passes for us to return to the North. I also learned that he ordered the burning of the town we saw on the boat."

"Holy Jaysus. Sounds like the man soold his soul to the divil to win this war."

Amy laughed. "It sure sounds like it." When they returned to the hotel, Amy booked a hack the next morning to the closest, Confederate-held railroad depot in Mississippi. They went to bed early in preparation for a six o'clock start. But Amy had trouble falling asleep at the excitement of the ever-nearing prospect of seeing her family again. She hated the war, thought it could have been avoided, and anguished over the huge toll it was taking on the South. However, she drew comfort knowing that her parents and Danny were safe in Savannah. ✑

CHAPTER TWENTY-TWO

∽

Honoring Sam

September 1862

Willie felt lucky after he and Harold left Penny Savannah fuming on the bluff. On their way back to the boarding house, they drove their wagon up and down the lanes of Savannah for several hours until they passed a coach house with open doors and no one inside. Willie moved like a bobcat after a rabbit. He jumped off his seat, ran inside, grabbed a saddle, and threw it in the bed. They charged off laughing. Willie shouted, "Just like the good old days, huh, Harold?"

They went to Johnny Tanner's stables, where they kept their wagon, mules, and horses. Willie told Johnny they had some business for him and held up the saddle like a prize fish. Tanner studied it and said he had several potential customers in Macon and believed he could get at least two hundred dollars for it, less his commission.

The two proud thieves bought a bottle of whiskey and went to their room to plan their next-day's visit to McBain's coachman. It took a few hours, but they devised a solid strategy. They would check out of the boarding house in the morning; find the coachman—either at Pulaski Square or the plantation; torture him into explaining Sam's disappearance and the location of the money; get the cash at the Heritage; take one of McBain's wagons and load it with all the saddles and bridles that would fit; travel back to town; pick up their wagon and mules at Tanner's; and hide out in Bryan County where they would never be found. With the few remaining drops of alcohol, they toasted their brilliance and soon passed out.

Willie opened his eyes the next day with a throbbing headache and squinted, as sunlight flooded the room. He thought he was in a lumber mill. With difficulty, he lifted his head. Harold was snoring with his mouth wide open. Willie sat up, reached over, and shook his partner's leg. Harold didn't budge. Willie went to the basin, scooped up a cup of water, stood over Harold, and poured the contents into his mouth. Harold bolted upright, coughing and sputtering, as Willie howled with laughter. He said, "Come on, Harold. Move it, fer Chrissake. It's past two o'clock. We got work to do."

Harold muttered, "Jesus, Willie. Next time, try shaking me."

The two men packed their bags, paid Mrs. Benoist, and walked to the stables. They found Johnny Tanner in the barn, brushing a horse.

Tanner, who wore his black hair to his neck to hide a missing ear that had been cut off in a barroom fight, said, "I've been waiting for you all day. This morning I sent one of my men to deliver two horses to the company camped at the Ten Broeck Race Track. About a mile before the track he saw a group of soldiers standing in a field. Turns out they had found a body—mostly old clothes and bones—in a shallow grave that vultures had uncovered. There was a hole in the skull. They brought the remains to the marshal. My man said that the most noticeable piece of clothing was a silver belt buckle with an eagle design. I know only one man who wore one like that."

Willie's eyes almost popped out as he said, "Holy shit!"

Johnny went on. "When my man delivered the horses at the camp, he saw a blond mare with circular brown patches on her hind flanks. He asked the captain where he got her. The officer said the horse roamed into their camp a few months ago with no bridle or saddle. They ran an advertisement in the newspaper. No one ever claimed her. Sounds like your friend Sam's horse."

Harold said, "Jesus! What are we going to do now, Willie?"

Willie said to stable owner, "Thanks, Johnny. Give us a minute." Willie led Harold aside and whispered, "Sam's dead. The only thing that's important now is getting our money. There's no guarantee that we'll find it at the plantation, and I don't feel like fighting a hundred niggers for some saddles. Sam was killed on or near McBain's land. He's responsible, and he's plenty rich. We'll get a lot more cash from him than what's in that house, and much quicker. It'll be our way of honoring Sam. I'll take care of the coachman another time. Let's squeeze the money out of McBain, tie him up, and dump him some place where he can't be found until we're long gone."

Harold said, "The sooner we get the cash, Willie, the better."

They walked back to Johnny. Willie said, "We're leaving town for a long while. Hook up the mules and tie the horses to the wagon. We need to settle up."

James McBain sat in the deserted square as Danny and Truvy played Catch History. Danny darted about like a water spider since learning that his father was coming home the next day. James was celebrating the release of Hercules, who was busy driving Sarah and her friends to the hospital, and his son's upcoming return with an afternoon segar. He closed his eyes and felt the warm, late-September sun on his face and listened to the laughter of the boys. He heard Danny shout, "Race you to Orleans Square," and heard their staccato footsteps stomping off. He smiled, knowing that Truvy, with the speed of a colt, would soon overtake Danny.

Then he heard a man say, "We're back, sir." James opened his eyes and held up his hand to block the sun's rays. Two men stood over him. One said, "It's time to pay up for Sam, McBain."

The familiarity of the voice caused his heart to race. He dropped his segar and tried to stand, but a hand on his chest pushed him back. James said, "I can't see you. Let me up." He tried to rise again, but a hand clamped onto his arm.

One of the men said, "Don't play coy, McBain. You know who we are. We know Sam's dead, and you killed him."

"What are you talking about?" McBain replied.

"I'm tired of your lies, old man. We lost a friend and fifteen hundred dollars in greenbacks because of you. But I'm gonna give you a chance to save your life. Pay us ten thousand dollars right now and we'll call it even. If not, you're joining Sam."

McBain again tried to rise, but another hand clutched his other arm, pinning him down. "You're insane. I won't give you one cent. The police will hear about this."

A face moved closer to James until a nose almost touched his. A blast of stale breath that smelled like the inside of a stable hissed, "And if they do, they'll learn that Sam was working for you when he disappeared and was found dead in a field near your plantation. Who else would have killed him but you or one of your niggers? You're not so important in this town that you can get away with murder."

James looked around the square for help, but saw no one. "I said I'm not giving you anything." A hand clasped his neck and slowly tightened until James had trouble breathing. He tried to pull it away but was overpowered. He twisted his head to break free and get some air.

The voice said, calmly, "Think I'm fooling?"

The grip tightened. James tried to scream but could only gag. He kicked his legs towards his attackers without effect. The hand on his neck relaxed just enough to let him breathe. He inhaled loudly as his chest heaved up and down. He croaked, "I don't have cash in the house. I'll have to go to the bank."

"Grandpa, what's wrong?" James heard footsteps running towards him.

The boys' voices diverted the men's attention. As Willie and Harold turned, they loosened their grips. James pulled away, jumped up, grabbed a derringer from his jacket, and shouted, "Stop right there!" The men faced McBain and stared at the small, double-barrel pistol. James called to the boys, who were on the other side of the outlaws, "Danny and Truvy, run to the house, now!"

Willie lunged, grabbed Danny, locked his arm around the boy's neck, and Harold snared Truvy around the chest. Willie pulled his gun and stuck the barrel against the boy's temple. Danny yelled "Hey, that hurts!"

McBain's hands trembled at seeing his grandson being roughed up and thought the devil never grinned more malevolently than Willie, whose long chin whiskers looked like needles. "Drop that gun, McBain, I'm warning you." Willie ran the tip of the barrel along Danny's face.

McBain placed the derringer on the bench. "Release the boys. I'll get the money."

Danny wiggled like a worm on a hook, trying to break free. Willie shook him like a dust mop. James yelled, "Danny, don't fight and they won't hurt you."

The boy relaxed. Willie snarled, "Good advice from Grandpa." Then he told McBain, "Listen to me. You go to the bank, get the money, and come back here—ALONE—in a half-hour. We'll take these boys, and we'll be watching you. No tricks or you'll never see them again." He turned to Harold, "Pick up that derringer and let's go."

James held up his hands in surrender. "Let the boys go now and I'll order them not to say a word to anyone. You can take me to the bank and I'll get the money. You have my word."

Willie looked around the square, mulling the offer. But he knew he could never trust the man who had been trying to kill him and his partners. "No! You got thirty minutes. Get moving! You tell the police and the boys die. That's a promise."

The men holstered their guns, pushed Danny and Truvy to the fence, hoisted them over the turnstiles and lifted them into the wagon bed. Willie whispered to Harold to drive to Tanner's. Then he jumped in after the youngsters and hissed, "Lie face down and don't make a peep, or I'm going to kill your grandpa and then you. You hear me?"

The boys nodded, their teeth clicking in fear. Willie covered them with a blanket. He told Harold, "Go!"

Minutes later they arrived at Tanner's, drove past Johnny as he hoisted a bale of hay from a wagon, and went straight into the barn. Willie told the boys not to move or talk and left the barn with Harold, closing the doors behind them. Johnny dropped the hay and asked, "What in hell are you doing? You just told me you were leaving town."

Willie nervously looked up and down the street. "Our plans changed. We need to hide for a bit. This guy McBain owes us big money. We took his grandson and a picaninny as security while he goes to a bank for the cash. We're meeting him in thirty minutes to collect it. Then we're leaving."

Johnny pointed to the barn. "The McBain boy is in there?"

Harold said, "Don't worry, Johnny. They're scared to death and they don't know where they are. They won't budge."

Johnny kicked the hay in anger. "Don't worry?! Sorry, men. I don't mind selling your stolen goods, but kidnapping gets twenty years of hard labor. I've done work for McBain over the years. He's always treated me good and pays on time. Take those boys out of my barn now. I'll bet McBain's already gone to the police."

"Aw, Johnny," Willie whined. "The old man won't take a chance as long as we got the boys. If anything comes back to you, I'll swear you had no part in it."

Johnny laughed without humor. "Willie, somehow I don't think your word will impress a judge much. Besides, your plan is full of holes. Stick to stealing saddles. Now, blindfold those boys and get them out of here."

Willie looked at the barn. "Johnny, what're we going to do for half an hour? You can't let us hang in the wind after all the business we've done together."

Johnny turned away and spat. "You're insane to stick around for one minute. The police are probably already looking for you and will be waiting at the square. You'd best leave town right now."

"Then how do we get our money from McBain?"

"That's your problem. You swiped them kids, you figure out how to collect."

Harold broke in. "Willie, we could take the kids out of town, send a ransom letter, and have McBain deliver the money to us. That would be safer than going back to the square. The cabin in Bryan County where I hid from the agents is perfect, and I'm certain it's empty. We just have to figure out how to sneak the boys past the guard posts."

"I'll tell you what," Johnny said. "I got four big, empty rice barrels. Stick the boys in one each and use the other two as decoys. If those boys aren't too big, they can sit or kneel. I'll drill holes around the top for air. But they better not come to no harm, whether you get the cash or not. If they do, you'll have a big problem."

Willie looked at Harold, who nodded. Willie said, "All right."

Johnny walked towards the barn. "Let's go. I don't want to be seen with you."

Fifteen minutes later Willie and Harold drove off, carrying two frightened boys sitting in rice barrels, knees to their chests, hands tied in front of them, and kerchiefs tied tightly around their mouths.

◦◈◦

An hour after the designated meeting time, McBain gave up and walked into the house. He met Sarah as she returned from the hospital. She looked at her husband's pale face and said, "James, darling, what in the world is wrong?"

"Please come into my study. I have very troubling news." He explained the events of the day. "I immediately went to the bank, withdrew the money, and waited in the square." He lifted a black cloth sack. "I didn't tell anyone. I just wanted Danny and Truvy back. But the men never returned."

Sarah held her husband's hand while she fought back tears. She feared for Danny and Truvy and worried for her husband, whose face was whiter and more drawn than she had seen since his sun stroke three years earlier. "James, we have to go to the police. These men are kidnappers and murderers. And I have to tell Patience about Truvy."

McBain went to the door and called into the hall, "William, please send Hercules here." He said to Sarah. "I'll speak to Chief Goodwin now, although he's already told me that he's shorthanded. Maybe a kidnapping will motivate him to help. Thank God Joseph comes home tomorrow."

Hercules arrived and James briefed him. "They have Danny and Truvy and we've got to find them." The coachman looked away. He knew his and Dante's actions led to this, even if they had acted in self-defense. He felt especially responsible for Truvy, and dreaded telling Patience, who would be devastated by the news. McBain continued. "The man—Willie, I believe—said Sam's body was found in a field near the Heritage. Who would have killed him?"

Hercules coughed into his hand as he searched for an answer. He realized that he had to find out if Sam's grave really had been uncovered. If it were, McBain would surely suspect him. Who else would kill Sam except the man he had just whipped? "I don't know, Massa. Maybe Mr. Sam isn't dead and Willie's just saying that to get money from you."

McBain pondered those words. "Hmmm, that's a possibility. I'll try to find out more about Sam another time. Prepare the gig for me. I'm going to the police. I want you to take Mrs. McBain in the coach to see Patience."

Three hours later, after seeing Chief Goodwin and driving around the west side of town for the boys, James dragged himself into his study. Sarah sprang up from her chair as he entered. "What did the chief say?"

James looked into her bloodshot eyes. "That he'd try to help, but couldn't promise anything. What about Patience?"

"She's very upset. I told her we're doing everything possible and that we'll find them. Sarah lay her head against his chest. "Oh, James, what are we going to do?"

James held her tight. "Everything we can, dear. Everything we can."

⚬⚬⚬

Joseph stepped off the train the moment it stopped and limped down the boarding path, holding his cane but not using it. He dropped his bag and hugged his mother. She held on longer than he expected. When they separated, Sarah leaned back and stared at her son. She thought she could fit two fingers between his buttoned shirt collar and neck. JD popped his head out of Joseph's jacket and barked. Sarah leaned back. "A dog?"

Joseph pulled out JD and held him in one hand. With a big smile, he explained, "A gift for Danny. Where is he?"

James stepped up and shook hands with his son. "Thank God you're home, son. I have some terrible news. Danny's been kidnapped."

Joseph dropped the dog, which whimpered and looked up at his owner. "What do you mean? When? By whom?"

"Yesterday afternoon, by two of the men who killed Andrew—Willie and Harold. They took Truvy, too." Joseph's jaw slowly lowered as James explained the circumstances. "I've spent all my waking hours looking for him. The police know but they don't have enough men to help."

Just hearing those names again made Joseph's hair stand on end. "Mother of God! Those bastards. Let's go. We still have several hours of daylight!" Joseph picked up his bag, cane, and JD and limped to the street. His parents walked double-time to keep up.

Hercules greeted him at the coach and took his things. "Welcome back, Master Joseph." Joseph thanked him and waited for his parents. On the short ride home, James told his son about his recent experiences with Sam, Harold, and Willie. "I spoke with the marshal, who has the remains of the body—bones, basically. They can't identify him, but Willie and Harold are convinced it's Sam."

Joseph shook his head in disbelief. He hoped the body was Sam. These vermin had made the lives of the McBains a living hell. Joseph couldn't wait to take care of Willie and Harold—after he found his son.

The servants greeted Joseph with forced smiles, as the pall of the kidnapping took a toll on them as well. William picked up his bag and Chloe carried away the dog as the McBains removed to James's study. Joseph sat and rubbed his temples as he pondered his next move. When he looked up he noticed the dark circles under his father's eyes, his sunken cheeks, and deeply lined forehead. He realized that he had to find Danny to save his father, too. "Where's Dante?"

"Hired out. He's cooking for the Jasper Greens at their camp outside of town."

"Can you bring him back to help us? He's seen the one named Harold."

"Son, I can't just pull him out. The contract only has six days left. Until then, Hercules can identify Willie, the ringleader. I can recognize both of them. And you saw all three the night they killed Andrew."

The hall clock chimed seven times. Joseph said, "That was a year and a half ago, and at night. But let's start searching. Those men are either hiding in town or they've left. If they're still here, someone knows it. Let's first concentrate on this area. Have Hercules drive you to every house. These streets don't have much traffic. Someone must have seen two men and two boys in a wagon. I'll meet you back here."

Two hours later, father and son were sitting at James's desk. Joseph said, "I went to a few saloons on the Bay. The bartender at Fowler's knows Willie and Harold but hasn't seen them in a few weeks. He said they were staying at Mrs. Benoist's boarding house. She told me that they left yesterday, but didn't know where they were headed, or the stable they used here. But it has to be in this area. We'll find out tomorrow."

James said, "I went to every house on Barnard Street between Liberty and Gaston. No one saw the boys."

Joseph took out writing paper and pulled his chair next to James. He wrote in large letters at the top, "REWARD - $2,500.00." He followed that with "For information leading to the return of Daniel McBain and Vitruvius McBain, both seven years old, and the capture of Willie and Harold—last names unknown— who abducted the boys." He added descriptions of Danny and Truvy, and, with

James's help, Willie and Harold.

Joseph then asked his father, "Would you have Mother go to Mr. Purse first thing in the morning and have him print three hundred copies. Pay extra for immediate handling. We'll post it all over town—all over Georgia, if necessary. Someone will come forward. Tomorrow morning I'm going to all the guard posts on the Savannah roads. If any one of them saw a wagon with two men and two boys passing through, we can concentrate on the countryside. Meanwhile, continue your search in town. First, you and Hercules go to the stables in this area— there are only a few—then to all the coach houses large enough to hide a big wagon."

James stood and said he would start by himself as Hercules had asked for permission to go to the Heritage in the morning for a few hours. "He wants to give a thorough search of the overseer's house for any clues that Sam might have left behind. He said that when Willie showed up at the Heritage, he was itching to get in Sam's house. There might be something there that could lead us to Willie. I looked once, but didn't find anything."

Joseph said, "What would he uncover that you or Mr. Donnelly or his wife haven't already found?" He paused for a moment, as if trying to answer his own question, but then continued, "I guess we can't leave any stone unturned. Maybe Sam did hide something. Make sure Hercules gets back here no later than noon."

The men embraced. "I'm glad you're home, son." James closed his eyes, bowed his head, and started to sob on his son's shoulder. He then turned away and grabbed the back of his chair. Joseph had never before seen his father cry and thought back to when he was five years old. He had fallen, skinned his knee, and bawled. His father wagged his finger at him and explained that southern boys bear pain. They may be hurt, but they never cry! Now, Joseph watched his father break down, with his heart skinned raw.

He put his hand on James's back. "Father, you're not responsible. We're dealing with hardened criminals. We'll find the boys, and then I'll take care of those two."

James shook his head. "I am responsible, son. I've done everything wrong. I hired Sam. I should have been better prepared to protect Danny. He and Truvy are gone because of me, and I can't stand it." James started to breathe heavily. Joseph eased his father into the chair, stepped to the cabinet, and poured a glass of brandy. James took several sips, closed his eyes, and leaned back. He said, "I'm better now. I felt dizzy."

Joseph took the glass. "Get some sleep and see how you feel in the morning. Maybe you should see Dr. Arnold." James nodded, stood, and trudged upstairs.

Exhaustion covered Joseph like a fog, but he knew he wouldn't be able to sleep. Someone had stolen his son, and he was losing his father. He looked at the portraits of his great grandfather and grandfather hanging on the wall over the fireplace and thought of all the challenges they had faced and overcome to build the McBain legacy. Joseph shook off his depression, finished his father's snifter of brandy, and wrote twenty more copies of the reward notice to hand out at the guard posts the next day while the others were being printed. ☙

CHAPTER TWENTY-THREE

"I'm Doing Your Grandfather a Favor"

September – October 1862

The next morning, when Joseph walked into the dining room, JD ran from Sarah to him and rolled on his back. Joseph knelt without his cane and rubbed the dog's belly. He said to his mother, "I see you two have gotten acquainted."

Sarah said, "He's adorable. Please tell me how you two met." Joseph explained, which provided a little lightness into the depressed household. She added, "Danny will be delighted when he gets home, but I don't want JD running around the house when you're not here. Chloe will keep him in the servants' room and her room."

"Whatever you wish, Mother. My focus is on getting Danny back. Did Father ask you to get the posters printed?"

Sarah said he had as James entered the room. He assured Joseph that he was feeling better and was ready to get to work.

After breakfast they started on their missions. Though he had only dozed for a few hours during the night, Joseph felt a bolt of energy run through his body. First, he went to the Oglethorpe Light Infantry headquarters to report in and was welcomed as a hero. The officer in charge gave him time off to look for his son. Then he rode to the guard post on the Thunderbolt Road on the east side of town and explained to a sergeant that his seven-year-old son and a negro friend had been kidnapped two days earlier by two white men, whom he described. The sergeant questioned the soldiers on duty that day, but none recalled seeing the wagon or the men or boys. Joseph left a reward notice and rode to the outer post in case the guards from the inner post missed the men. He next went to the posts on the White Bluff Road and got the same response, but still left reward notices.

A sentry at the inner guard post on the Ogeechee Road, south of town, recalled that a wagon had come by at about four o'clock on the day in question with two men matching the descriptions, but he didn't see any boys. Two horses were tied to the wagon and a few carpetbags and four rice barrels were in the bed. The only barrel he checked was empty. The guard looked at their passports and thought the names were Semmes and Jackson, but he didn't ask their destination.

The sentries at the outer post confirmed the sighting of the wagon and said they didn't inspect the passports or rice barrels.

Joseph wanted to follow the road south to Bryan and Liberty counties but wasn't packed for a search that would likely last weeks. Instead, he rode to the Louisville Road posts and left reward notices in case the outlaws tried to return to Savannah by that route.

Confident that the men could not return to town without being spotted, Joseph charged home. He saw Hercules in the driveway and told him to water and feed his horse as he would be leaving in an hour and be gone for several days. Joseph then asked, "Did you find anything at the overseer's house?"

Hercules shook his head and said, "No sir, not a thing."

Hercules didn't feel guilty about lying to Joseph. The coachman needed to know if Sam's body had been found and took advantage of the search for Danny and Truvy to learn. Once he had passed beyond sight of the guards on the Louisville Road, he raced to the gravesite. It had been dug up and there was no trace of Sam's remains. Hercules knew that Massa would suspect him, if he didn't already. Still, Hercules had no choice but to deny any involvement.

Hercules then rode to the Heritage. He regretted not giving a more thorough search of the house when he had been living at the plantation after Sam disappeared. Now he felt compelled to find whatever was hidden there—undoubtedly money—before anyone else did. As Sam had probably stolen the cash, Hercules wouldn't be stealing from Massa if he found and kept it. In a sense, it would be the ultimate revenge on Sam, after being whipped by him. Also, if he did gain his freedom as a result of this war, he would need money to get by.

He located Mr. Donnelly and told him about Danny's abduction, and his desire, with Massa's approval, to inspect his house for clues Sam left behind that might explain Willie's whereabouts. Donnelly knew that Mr. McBain trusted Hercules completely and took him to the house. Mrs. Donnelly was sitting at a table in the main room, giving reading lessons to their three daughters, when the two men entered. The little girls waved to their father, who said, "Don't mind us. We'll only be a few minutes."

With Donnelly following him, Hercules started on the main floor. He looked behind the two paintings on the wall, tapped on the brick work around the fireplace, knocked on the woodwork and the floors, peered under all the furniture, and pressed down on cushions. They went upstairs and Hercules searched the four bedrooms. He lastly tapped the bricks around the fireplace in the overseer's bedroom and froze when a brick on the right side of the mantel moved. So did two bricks on the row below. All the other surrounding bricks held firm. He glanced at Donnelly, who leaned against the doorway with his arms folded, staring out the window. Hercules couldn't look behind the brick without drawing his attention. He would have to come back another time, and soon, when no one was home. "Nothing here. I'll go back to town now and tell Massa."

Donnelly said, "Assure him that the operations here are running smoothly."

Hercules said he would and returned to the Heritage, where he ran into Joseph.

❧

"No, Master Joseph," Hercules replied. "Sam didn't leave nothing that I saw."

Joseph then asked, "Hercules, my father told me that a young lady accused you of accosting her and that you spent several days in jail until she changed her mind. Do you have any idea why she did that?"

"No, sir. I never saw her before. Maybe someone put her up to it."

"Sure sounds like it, and I think I know who. Once we find Danny and Truvy, I'll learn more about her." Joseph went into the house.

James was sitting at his desk in the library studying a map when Joseph entered. "Hello, Father. A wagon with two men fitting Willie and Harold's descriptions drove through the Ogeechee Road guard posts two days ago at about four o'clock. The sentries didn't see the boys, but they did notice four barrels in the bed. My guess is that Danny and Truvy were hidden in two of them."

James nodded. "Very likely. I saw Johnny Tanner this morning. He told me the men had stabled their horses, mules, and wagon with him, but left in a rush two days ago."

Joseph headed for the door. "I'm packing. I'm going to follow the Ogeechee Road. I won't be back until I find them."

James jumped up. "Hold on, Joseph. I think you're better off staying here for now. You know the road they took, but not where they're headed. It goes all the way to Darien and has many branches. That's a lot of territory. They could be anywhere. And I might remind you that although you're on a medical furlough, you're still in the Confederate service and need approval to take a leave."

Joseph whacked his cane into the palm of his hand. "Then I'll get it if that's what it takes to find my boy! I'll post reward notices on every tree and in every saloon in every town. Twenty-five hundred dollars is a fortune to most people. Someone will respond."

"Son, these thieves want money. I'm certain that we'll receive a ransom demand soon. Let's wait a few days. Paying it will be faster than searching all over Georgia. Besides, those reward notices won't be ready until tomorrow. Mr. Purse is printing something for the military. They have priority."

Joseph closed his eyes and sighed. "Perhaps you're right. It's so difficult, knowing that Danny's out there, helpless. I'll wait two days for a ransom demand, but that's all." Joseph left to tell Hercules that he wouldn't be leaving after all.

Danny and Truvy sat cramped in the rice barrels for two hours as the wagon passed through two guard posts. They heard men's voices at each stop, but were too scared to scream. At dusk the wagon stopped and Willie lifted them out, removed the kerchiefs from their heads, and untied them, to their great relief. He told them to sit in the wagon bed and not say a word. They traveled in darkness over bumpy roads for four more hours until they reached a small cabin in the woods. Harold entered first, lit some lamps, and Willie led the boys in.

Danny examined the room of exposed log walls, one table with four wooden boxes for chairs, one bed against the back wall, and a fireplace with a rod across it to hold skillets, pots, and kettles. There were two windows on either side of the front door. The flickering shadows created by the lamp light convinced Danny that ghosts lived there.

While Willie unharnessed the mules and brought in their possessions, Harold told the boys to lie at the foot of the bed so he could tie them to it. Danny begged, "Mister, can I go to the privy, please, please." Danny held his crotch with both hands and jumped up and down.

Harold looked at Truvy. "You, too?" The boy nodded. Harold said, "All right, follow me." He picked up a lamp and walked out the front door and around the house to a lopsided wooden structure in the back. Truvy and Danny, still grasping his privates and hopping like a kangaroo, followed. Harold pulled open the creaky door and said, "Go on, and be quick about it. I'll keep the door open and hold this light up for you."

Danny dashed in, dropped his trousers, and let out one continuous, "Ahhhh-hhhh," as he urinated into the hole in the wooden bench.

Harold said, "Quiet, damn it. I don't need to hear a symphony while you pee."

Just then, a long-legged cellar spider descended on a strand of web onto Danny's head. He let out a shriek that could make a stone flinch and ran out of the privy, still squirting like a little fountain, and swiping madly at his hair. He took two steps before tripping over the pants around his ankles, spinning to the ground.

Harold yelled, "You little son of a bitch! You pissed on my leg."

Truvy was unable to muffle his laughter at the sight of Danny lying face down on the ground, his butt exposed, and slapping wildly at his head. He then rushed into the privy to take his turn.

Willie came running in the darkness, his gun drawn, and saw Danny writhing on the ground, half-naked. "What the hell?"

Danny rolled over, his face scrunched up in fear. "A giant spider attacked me!"

Willie holstered his gun. "You coward, afraid of a little spider. I'd be embarrassed to say you was my kid. Now pull up your trousers and get back in the house."

Harold said, "Willie, the little rat peed all over me."

Willie looked at the wet stain on Harold's blue jeans and laughed. "You finally got those jeans washed."

Truvy emerged from the privy and they returned to the cabin. Willie tied their hands together in front of them, and then tied a foot of each boy to opposite legs of the bed. "Get to sleep, and don't try any tricks."

Danny's stomach growled, but he thought better of asking for cornbread and jam. Exhausted from the day and happy to be alive, the boys fell asleep on the wooden floor.

The next morning Willie untied their hands and feet. "Both of you, get up and sit over there against that wall." They groaned as they moved their stiff, aching bodies. Willie stood in front of them and bent forward, his hands on his knees. He studied the white boy, knowing that he was the son of the "Joseph" he had confronted on the pier, and grinned for getting the last laugh over that nigger lover. "You two pests, listen to me. I don't want to hear a word out of either of you, understand?"

Truvy nodded. Danny said, "Yes, sir."

Willie flattened his hand and held it at his chest, ready to backhand Danny. "You see! I tell you not to say a word, and you say two."

Danny shook his head, his hair swirling back and forth. "But mister, how can I answer a question without saying a word?"

Willie relaxed his hand. "Like your colored friend here. He nodded." Willie exaggerated a slow nod. "That's yes." Then he shook his head. "That's no. Now do you understand?"

"Yes. Ooops, I mean. . . ." Danny nodded.

"Jesus, you are stupid! I'm probably doing your grandpa a favor by taking you."

Harold bellowed and slapped his thigh as he sat at the table. "Willie, I can tell you never raised no boys."

Willie turned to Harold. "Oh? And you're an expert?"

"I had two boys." Harold looked towards a window in a state of reverie. "Both died of the fever with my wife six years ago. I tell you, they were a pile of trouble, but I never had so much fun."

"Well, if they're so much dern fun, you watch 'em. Just keep 'em quiet, especially this white one." Willie returned his attention to the boys. "I never wanted nothing to do with you. Now that you're here, I have to put up with you. Just don't get on my nerves. As soon as your family pays us our money, you'll be out of our hair. Until then, sit and be quiet." The boys nodded so fast they looked like tuning forks.

Willie went to his bag, produced a pen, bottle of ink, and piece of paper, and sat at the table. "All right, Harold, let's write the ransom letter to McBain and take it to the post office so he gets it tomorrow. We need supplies, too. I'm starving."

Willie wrote as Harold looked over his shoulder. When he finished, he told Danny, "Come here, kid, I want you to write something to your grandpa. Tell him you're safe and if he pays us our money you won't come to no harm." Danny stood at the table and wrote Willie's demand in two sentences.

Harold put the letter in his vest pocket and said to Willie, "I'll be back in a few hours." He rode his horse to Eden, a small town five miles away.

Willie stood in the doorway and watched his partner disappear. He knew that their plan was well thought out, but it had become more complicated once they left Savannah. Still, they would soon have ten thousand dollars and be on their way to Mexico. He turned around and saw the boys looking at him. "Harold just left for provisions, so don't pester me for food."

Danny asked, "Mister, can we go outside and play?"

Willie shook his head. "I don't want you running around and screaming. And I don't remember giving you permission to talk."

Danny placed his hand over his heart. "We won't scream, I promise."

Willie sat on a box and yawned. "What's your name, kid?"

"Danny. Daniel McBain. I'm named for my great grandpa."

"Did your great grandpa talk all the time like you?"

"I don't know—I never met him. He died before I was born. My grandma says I ask a lot of questions, which means I'm very smart, just like my great grandpa. He fought against the British in our War of Independence. He was a hero. He escaped when the British attacked Savannah and fought with great patriots like Andrew Pickens and Elijah Clarke and drove the British from the South."

Willie closed his eyes and took a deep breath. Before he could tell Danny to stop talking, the boy went on. "And my great, great grandpa sailed from the highlands of Scotland to Georgia in 1736, just after the colony was founded. On the ship he made friends with Chief Tomochichi. . . ."

Willie slapped the table. "Shut up, fer Chrissake! You're giving me a headache."

Danny scolded, "If you said that word in front of my grandma, she'd send you to your room without dessert."

"QUIET!" Willie stood and motioned as if he were stepping towards Danny, who clamped a hand over his mouth. Satisfied that he would not hear again from the white boy, Willie eyed the black boy with the neatly trimmed hair and red shirt and black pants of a quality worn by whites. "What's your name?"

"Truvy. It's short for Vitruvius. My pa named me after the great Roman architect."

Willie shrugged. "You darkies sure come up with some strange names. How come you speak so good—like a white kid?"

"My ma teaches me to read and write. She's real smart. I also go to a school." He paused, wondering if he should mention that schools for blacks were illegal.

"And Danny lends me his school books."

Willie drummed his fingers on the table. "Where's your pa?"

Truvy looked down. "He's dead. Someone shot him."

Willie realized the boy's father had to be the man that he shot that night on the pier. He felt a touch uneasy facing the dead man's son. "Let's go outside. But keep your mouths shut, and if you scream or try to escape, you'll wish you were never born."

Both boys said, "Yes, sir!" trying to muffle their excitement.

Willie sat on a tree stump and watched them throw pine cones against the tree from fifteen paces. The black boy possessed uncanny accuracy. The boys played until Harold returned three hours later with bread, coffee, eggs, bacon, and rice. Willie ordered the boys into the house and then helped carry in the provisions. Once inside, Willie sniffed the air and asked Harold, "Have you been drinking?"

Harold breathed on the back of his hand, inhaled the rebounding fumes, and said, "If you call one drink 'drinking.' I ran into Rudy Thorn at the saloon." Rudy was a fellow thief who frequently came into Savannah to sell his bounty, usually jewelry and silver. "He owed me twenty dollars from when I was here last. He paid me ten, so we have some more money. Times are real tough, he says. He was leaving for Bloomingdale for a pick-up. I told him I'd cut a dollar from his debt if he mailed our letter from there today. McBain will have it tomorrow afternoon, and he can't trace it to Eden."

Willie slapped Harold's back. "Good thinking. Did you tell him about the boys?"

Harold pulled out a box of matches and lit kindling in the fireplace. "Course not. I told him that we was resting here for a few days before moving on."

"Good. Now let's eat. I'm starved. I'll go pump some water." Willie went outside with a pot, praying that the letter would reach Savannah in a day or two.

"I'm not waiting any longer, Father," Joseph declared as they sat in the coach on the way to the post office. "If there's no letter in today's mail, I'm leaving. I'll hunt them down, even if it takes ten years." It had been two days, and two mail deliveries, since James convinced Joseph to wait for a ransom note. Joseph had lost patience. While he went to company headquarters each day, his father had spent his time with Jefferson and Hercules, posting the reward notices on every street in town. James also placed an advertisement in the *Savannah Republican* and *Savannah Morning News*. But no one came forward with information and Joseph spent his nights with his father studying a map and speculating where Willie and Harold might be hiding.

James looked out the coach window and said, "It's your decision, son. I'll do whatever you suggest."

Hercules parked at the corner of Bay and Bull streets. The McBain men entered the post office on the ground floor of the Custom House to await the four o'clock mail. It arrived on time and the postmaster handed James a stack of letters. He fanned through them and stopped at one in the middle. They stared at an envelope addressed in child-like handwriting. Joseph snatched it and the two men moved to the back of the room.

Joseph opened the envelope and read to himself, occasionally pulling the page closer to his face to decipher the words while James stretched his neck to read over his son's shoulder. Joseph whispered to his father, "They want you— alone—to put the money in a cloth satchel, pack it in a wooden box, and deliver it to a cotton field in Bryan County at four o'clock tomorrow afternoon. They describe the location. They'll leave instructions telling us where we can find the boys. You're to return to Savannah the way you came. They claim they have lookouts and can see for miles around the area and will know if you're playing any tricks. Danny wrote that he and Truvy are unharmed."

Joseph pocketed the letter and walked to the door. He finally was making progress in getting the boys back. ∞

CHAPTER TWENTY-FOUR

A Nice Young Man

October 1862

At seven o'clock the next morning James McBain boarded his gig with the ten thousand dollar ransom in a wooden box. Joseph and Hercules followed on horseback, planning to camp after they passed through the second guard post in case James didn't return on time.

About the same hour that the McBains left Savannah, Willie rode from the cabin to the road that divided two large, weed-covered, abandoned cotton fields. He dug a hole at the base of a palmetto and deposited a letter telling McBain where and when to expect the boys. He then went to his observation spot—a thicket by the Savannah-Darien Stage Coach Road—a mile away. He tied his horse to a tree, stood on its back, grabbed the lowest branch, and pulled himself up. He climbed ten feet to a limb that provided a clear view for miles and took out a field glass. Only a few wagons drove along the road during the day, and none stopped. The war had reduced commerce between the countryside and the city and people preferred to take the train. Still, Willie only put down the field glass to roll cigarettes.

In the mid-afternoon he saw dust kicking up in the distance and trained his glass on the object. Ten minutes later he recognized McBain in a buggy and smiled at being so close to all that cash. McBain turned onto the side road that divided the fields and drove to the middle of three palmetto trees. He removed the letter from the hole, deposited the box, and left the way he came. Willie whispered to himself, "That's right, old man. Go back to your rich friends and tell them that you met your match."

Willie checked his watch. Four o'clock—just as planned. He'd survey the area until Harold arrived at five o'clock and pick up the ransom. Then they'd drop off the boys at Ways Station on the Savannah, Albany and Gulf line to catch the next day's train. By the time the boys reached Savannah, he and Harold would be long gone. He pulled the tobacco pouch from his vest.

Harold woke the boys late and fed them two-day-old bread and bacon. He let them play in the yard. Twice he had to tell them to quiet down. He whittled a piece of wood and thought of having five thousand dollars in Mexico, being waited upon by beautiful, dark-skinned women, and not worrying about his next heist. The time crawled, but four o'clock finally arrived. He called to the boys, "Clasp your hands together."

"Why?" Danny demanded.

Harold reached into his back pocket and pulled out two leather straps. "I got good news for you—you're going home. But first I have to tie your hands because you're going back into the barrels."

Danny stamped his foot. "No! I don't want to."

Whack! Harold cuffed Danny across the ear. "Don't argue with me, kid. You should know to respect your elders." Danny rubbed his ear and kept quiet, though he wanted to tell Harold that he'd be in big trouble when his father finds him. Harold bound the boys' hands, marched them to the wagon, and hoisted them into the barrels. He stopped and pulled his gun when he heard the clippedy-clop of a galloping horse, but he lowered the weapon when he recognized his friend. "Something wrong, Rudy?"

Thorn did a double-take at the heads of two boys sticking out of the barrels. "There's a gaggle of army agents in town looking for deserters and draft evaders. They came into the saloon and had a sketch of you. The bartender directed 'em here. My guess is they'll be coming this way soon. You'd best leave, but be careful. I hear there are more agents to the south and west and they have all the roads covered."

"Damn! I'm going to meet Willie now."

"Think real hard about that. You'll be riding into those agents. Word is soldiers are deserting in large numbers and the army wants to set an example."

Harold kicked a wagon wheel and cursed. Danny glanced at Truvy and wondered what this news meant to them.

☙

From his perch in the tree, Willie watched Harold snapping the reins, pushing the mules into a fast walk. When the wagon reached him, he called, "What's the hurry?"

Harold jumped down and yelled. "Rudy Thorn came by the cabin. He said the town is crawling with agents looking for deserters. They have names and a drawing of me. That damned bartender in Eden told them where we was. We got to get going! They're guarding all the roads around here."

Willie eased down the tree, grabbed onto the bottom branch with both hands, swung back and forth like an ape, and dropped to the ground with a thud.

Harold paced back and forth. "What're we gonna do, Willie? Where do we go?"

Willie mounted his horse. "The old man left the cash. Cover me and I'll get it. If you see trouble, fire your gun in the air." Willie dashed to the palmetto trees, retrieved the box, and charged back. He dismounted, knelt, and started counting the notes on the ground. He handed a stack to Harold. "I think that's five thousand. Check it!"

Harold counted out loud. "Two hunnerd ten, two twenty, two thirty . . . ."

Willie hollered, "Talk to yourself, dern it! You're making me lose my place."

Both men started over. Harold called first, "Five thousand." He stuffed his bills in his carpetbag. Willie paid Harold the money he owed him.

Harold pressed his partner. "So where're we gonna go?"

Willie inhaled the musty scent of the wad of money before putting it in his saddle bag. "Harold, I can't take a chance being with you if you're gonna bring the law down on us, with my prison record and made-up age and passport. If they catch you, they'll search us and be suspicious about all the money we have. And if we still have these kids, we'll be doing hard labor for twenty years. You need a place to hide for a few days, but you can't go back to the cabin—probably not any cabin in the county." Willie kicked at the dirt. Then he snapped his fingers and whispered so the boys wouldn't hear. "Savannah! You can hide there easy with so many people around. Go to the sailor's home or the hospital for the poor and tell them you have the fever. The agents won't go near that place. It's the only chance you got, but you should take the train and avoid the guard posts in case McBain notified them. I'll drive you to Ways Station right now. We have less than an hour. I'll keep your horse. When it's safe in a week or two, take the train to Thomasville. I'll wait there for you."

"What about the boys? We were gonna drop them off at Ways later tonight to catch tomorrow's train to Savannah. You can't let us out together."

Willie looked at the ground and then looked up with a sparkle in his eyes. "I'll take them to Fleming Station further west after I drop you off. They can catch tomorrow's train to Savannah. Come on, let's get going!"

Forty-five minutes later they arrived at Ways Station as the train pulled in. Harold grabbed his carpetbag, jumped down, and ran.

Willie waited until Harold boarded and then headed southwest. He stopped thirty minutes later and removed the lids from the barrels. The boys popped up like corks released from under water. Danny said, "Are you letting us go?"

"Shut up, kid. I'm taking you to a railroad station. You can sleep there tonight and get on the train to Savannah tomorrow." Willie drew his revolver and aimed it at the boys' heads. "You two have behaved so far. If we stop again and you hear voices, don't say a word or I'll shoot both of you. Do you understand me?" The boys nodded. "Good. Now sit so I can put these lids back. You'll be home before you know it."

James McBain handed the letter to his son as soon as he reached the guard post. Joseph read out loud, "McBain—Go bak to yur house in Savannah. If you left the cash and you dont play no tricks, the boys will be in town toomurro evening. You have my word, tho you dont diserve it, after killing Sam. That Danny sure talks up a storm."

The last comment gave Joseph faith that the boys were unharmed. He looked at his father. "Why go back? They obviously want time to distance themselves from us. They're going to leave the boys out here somewhere and take off. Their letter was sent from Bloomingdale. I'd bet that they're leaving them at a station on the Central Georgia line. Let's go to the Pooler and Bloomingdale stations."

James replied, "What if the boys aren't there? What if Willie and Harold see us snooping about? Let's do as they ask. They have their money and don't want to deal with two boys any longer than they have to. I'm certain they'll keep their word."

Joseph looked westward at the open country. The waiting tore him up, but his father made sense. He had been right about the ransom note. Joseph hoped he would be right about this, too. They rode home in silence.

⚬❧⚬

Willie spotted the two men riding towards him on the stage road, but continued as if he had nothing to hide. They stopped him, identified themselves as Confederate agents, and demanded papers. Willie produced his Savannah passport, which listed his age at forty-eight and his name as George Semmes. One agent read twelve names and asked him if he had seen or knew them. They even produced a sketch of Harold, scar and all. Willie said that he didn't know any of them and that he was delivering barrels to the railroad depot before going home. The agents looked in the wagon and, seeing nothing suspicious, let him pass.

Two hours later, Willie freed the boys from their wooden cells. "This is Fleming depot. Go to the loading platform and sleep there. You'll be safe. No one is going to bother two kids. Here, take this bread. It'll keep you till tomorrow. The train to Savannah comes by in the afternoon. Tell the railroad man your grandpa will pay your fares when you get to town."

In the moonlight, Danny and Truvy saw the raised wooden platform about thirty yards long with a wood bin and water tank on stilts at the far end. They hopped off the wagon and looked up at Willie, not believing that he was letting them go. He said, "Go on, now!" The boys dashed to the platform as Willie cracked his whip and drove away. They jumped up and down like bouncing balls at their newly found freedom.

Danny said, "I'm tired and hungry." He squinted in the darkness, walked to the wood bin, and sat against it. Truvy followed and they ate the bread.

Danny looked up at the stars. "The first thing I'm gonna do when we get home is have hot cornbread with butter. Oh, my pa is home! I'm going to show him how good I can ride a horse now. What about you?"

"I'm going to see Ma. She'll make pancakes. Then I'm going to church to thank God for saving us, like I prayed for him to do."

"WHOO, WHOO, WHOO."

Danny stiffened. Truvy laughed. "It's only an owl, Master Danny." Danny hunched over and shivered in the balmy, early autumn night air. Truvy asked, "Were you scared when we were with those bad men, Master Danny?"

"I'm not scared of anything." The boys heard rustling nearby and Danny grabbed Truvy's arm. "What's that?"

"Just squirrels chasing each other."

Danny peered into the darkness looking for ghosts. He confessed, "I guess I do get scared sometimes. A few weeks ago I was walking home from school with Elizabeth Hargrove and she said she wanted to kiss me. I ran home before she could do it."

Truvy slapped his cheek. "That is scary. I'll never let a girl kiss me, I know that for a fact. Now, I'm scared of barrels."

They heard more noise from nearby brush. Danny yelled, "Shut up, you stupid squirrels!" Truvy giggled. The area fell silent. Danny said, "See, they're afraid of us." Then they heard footsteps creaking up the stairs to the platform. Danny froze and could hardly breathe, no less talk. He swiveled on his butt to Truvy's side. In the moonlight, they saw three black men with machetes walking towards them. Danny screamed.

＊＊＊

During the one-hour train trip Harold showed his passport, which gave his name as Darly Jackson and age as forty-nine, to a soldier, who returned it without question. He spent the ride biting his nails, smoking, and wondering where to go once he arrived. He decided on the Sailors' Home on Washington Square, a ten-minute walk from the depot on the east side of Savannah and far away from the two McBain houses. Since commerce from the Atlantic had died with the Union blockade, few sailors used it. Harold hoped that Confederate agents would be less likely to search there, but he knew he would have to keep moving to avoid capture.

He gained admittance to the nearly empty facility by claiming that he was an unemployed sailor. The moment he entered the tiny room, he collapsed on the bed.

＊＊＊

Katherine Downes left Mr. Lippman's store for the Marshall House and stopped to read the poster tied to a street lamp. It announced "REWARD" and promised two thousand five hundred dollars for information leading to the rescue of two kidnapped boys, Danny and Truvy McBain, and the capture of their kidnappers, Willie and Harold. James McBain of Pulaski Square offered the reward. She shook her head in disgust at the actions of Willie and Harold, though she wished she knew where they had gone. Twenty-five hundred dollars would solve many problems.

Matters had worked out fairly well for Katherine over the past few weeks. By working two jobs she was able to keep current on her boarding house bill. Her sisters loved attending J. S. F. Lancaster's School for Misses and Young Ladies—learning so many things and meeting other girls, although a few of them made fun of Mary's lisp. Katherine felt proud for being able to provide a formal education for her sisters, something she never had, though she couldn't afford to send them for another term. As she was about to enter the hotel, she heard someone say, "Excuse me, Miss. I'm from out-of-town. Can you direct me to the City Hotel?"

Katherine turned and saw a smiling young man with long brown hair and dark brown eyes who she judged to be about five years her elder. "Yes, it's on Bay Street." She gave him directions.

He said, "Thank you, Miss. My name's Peyton Smith. I'm here for a few days on business. Can you recommend any entertainment in town?"

Katherine thought for a moment. "I've only lived here a short while and I never go out. There may be a play or concert at the Savannah Theatre on Chippewa Square. I'm sorry I can't be of more help."

Peyton looked at the hotel entrance and asked, "Do you live here?"

"Oh, no, Mr. Smith, I could never afford it. I clean here in the evenings."

Peyton removed his cap and held it over his heart. "You're much too pretty to be cleaning hotels, Miss, if you don't mind me saying."

Katherine blushed. "It's not so bad. These are difficult times. I'm thankful to have work. It's been nice meeting you, Mr. Smith. I must go in now."

Peyton said, "It was a pleasure meeting you, Miss, Miss . . . ?"

"Pender."

"Miss Pender, thank you for your help." He tipped his cap and left.

Katherine went to work, thinking that Mr. Smith was quite handsome and a nice young man. Only three months shy of her eighteenth birthday, she had never been courted—not that she minded. She was wary of men. But she did want people to like her, including men, and regretted that she met so many unlikable males. She was content to raise her sisters. Having a male friend was the furthest thing from her mind.

When she left the hotel after work that night for home, she heard, "Good evening, Miss Pender."

Peyton Smith was standing on the corner of Broughton and Abercorn with his cap in his hands. She stopped and smiled. "Mr. Smith! Did you find the City

Hotel?"

He staggered back a step and said, "I did. It was pretty quiet."

Her smile disappeared. She suspected that he might be intoxicated, and she despised drunkenness. "Sir, are you all right?"

"Yes. I did have a drink or two. I got lonely and wanted someone to talk to."

Katherine used a suggestion that she had often heard her mother tell her father. "I think you should get a good night's sleep. You'll feel much better in the morning. Good night, Mr. Smith." Katherine resumed walking.

Peyton matched her stride. "I hope you don't mind if I walk with you, Miss Pender. Savannah is a beautiful place. How long did you say you've lived here?"

The young man sounded respectful, but Katherine didn't want to share personal information with him. "Not very long, Mr. Smith."

He laughed. "I'd guess that you're a country girl with that accent. I like it."

Katherine didn't reply. Peyton kept up with her. "Do you have family here—parents, brothers, or sisters?"

Katherine started to get nervous and picked up her pace. "I'm very tired, Mr. Smith. I think you should be on your way."

Peyton laughed again. "Don't mind me. I just like keeping you company."

Katherine's heart began to pound. He wouldn't leave and she didn't want him to find out where she lived. They were blocks from Mrs. Duffy's and the streets were deserted. She turned around and headed back to the hotel. He followed.

After a few minutes of silence, he spoke, and his friendly tone changed. "What's the matter? You think you're too good to talk to me?"

Katherine looked straight ahead. "I have nothing more to say. Please leave me alone." She turned onto Broughton Street and saw the Marshall House one-half block away. She heard his footsteps beside her. "Leave me alone or I'll call for a policeman."

He grabbed her arm. "Don't you dare. You have no reason to do that. I'm being nice to you."

She pulled her arm away. "If you want to be nice to me, you'll leave. Otherwise, I'll scream."

"I'm warning you not to do that." He clutched her shoulder and squeezed.

She couldn't wrestle away and cried out, "POLICE! HELP!"

Peyton panicked, released his grasp, and backhanded her with full force in the face, catching her flush with his knuckles. Her left eye exploded in pain and she felt herself falling. Then everything went dark.

When she opened her eyes she saw the blurry vision of a man staring down at her. She raised her hand over her head and cried, "No! Don't hit me again. Please."

The man said, "You have nothing to fear, young lady. I'm a doctor."

Katherine rolled her head to the side and saw the night manager kneeling next to her. He said, "You're safe, Miss Pender. We heard you holler and found you on the sidewalk. We carried you into the lobby and sent for a doctor. What happened?"

Katherine took a deep breath to summon the strength to answer. "A man hit me."

The manager jumped up and said, "That's outrageous! I'll notify the police. We'll find the coward. He'll pay for this."

Although the left side of Katherine's face throbbed, she said, "No, don't get the police. Please. I'll be all right."

The doctor said, "Be still while I hold this wet towel against you to keep the swelling down. Ice is scarce since the war. What little we get goes to treat the soldiers."

She hissed through her teeth in agony when the towel touched her skin. A few minutes later the doctor said, "I'm going to help you up so you can drink some laudanum." He slid his hand under her back, pushed her up, held a glass to her lips, and said, "It's mixed with water and tastes bitter. But drink it all."

She sipped and thought someone pushed a spike into her face. "Oh, God, that hurts." She took a deep breath to build her courage and consumed the liquid in four gulps.

The doctor said, "You'll feel better in a few minutes. Lie here and keep the towel on your face. You have a nasty bruise but no broken bones. You can go home when you feel up to it, but you must get plenty of rest. It will take a few weeks for the pain, swelling, and discoloration to subside." Katherine nodded and grimaced. She grew very tired and drifted off.

Katherine woke up an hour later, past midnight, and saw the manager sitting on a chair beside her. She sat up and felt nauseous, and grabbed the side of the sofa until the dizziness passed. He asked. "How are you feeling? Can I get you anything?"

She closed her eyes and said to the manager, "I'm so tired. I'd like to go home."

He said, "I'll have the hotel coachman drive you." He helped her up, held her arm, and slowly guided her through the door. "I'll tell the day manager about this. Don't worry about work tomorrow. If you need anything, let me know."

As they passed through the lobby Katherine glanced at a mirror hanging on the wall and stopped. At first she thought she was looking at a grotesque painting of the devil with a lopsided, dual-colored face, but the image moved when she did. She stepped closer. Her eye was swollen shut, her cheek puffed up, and the whole thing was tinted purplish-black. She whispered, "Oh, my God!" and turned to the manager, who shook his head in sympathy.

The coachman helped her up the front stairs to Mrs. Duffy's and departed. Katherine approached the door of her room and prayed that her sisters were asleep. She slid the key in the lock and turned the knob. The lamp was lit. Mary was sleeping under the covers. Pauline looked up from the book she was reading. Her expression changed from a smile to wide-eyed fright. She climbed off the bed and tiptoed to Katherine. "Oldest Sister?"

Katherine held her sister tight. Tears trickled from her eyes, making the purplish skin glisten like an eggplant. She released Pauline, who looked at her and screamed, "NO! NO!"

Mary appeared from under the covers, rubbed the sleep from her eyes, looked at Katherine, and buried her head in the pillow.

Katherine sat on the bed next to Mary and stroked her back. She said, "My dear sisters, I'll be all right. Please don't cry." Mary didn't budge. "Mary, sit up." The little girl shook her head in the pillow. "Mary, please?" She finally rolled over, stared at the wound, and wrapped her arms around Katherine, who stroked her hair. "A man hit me on the street in front of the hotel. It's just a bad bruise. I'll be better soon. But I'm very tired and I'd like to go to sleep."

Katherine put on her nightgown and joined Pauline and Mary in bed. The sisters, all alone in the world, lay in each other's arms.

Harold awoke after a restless night at the Sailor's Home. He decided that staying in Savannah was too risky, but he couldn't take the train to Thomasville with agents still patrolling the area. Then an idea flashed in his mind. He packed his bag and left for the Central of Georgia Railroad depot and the train to Macon, far away from the agents. From there he would catch a train to Atlanta and then to Thomasville. As he walked he noticed posters on the side of almost every building, fence, and lamp post. He stopped to read one and dropped his bag. Old man McBain was offering a huge reward for him and Willie. The notice included a detailed description of him. Everyone in town must have seen it. He pulled the brim of his hat low on his forehead, looked down, and resumed walking.

When he got within a block of the depot, he saw several men in suits checking passengers' papers. They were agents, not soldiers. He turned around and cursed. He was trapped in the city with no way out. Then he remembered Willie's other suggestion. It was his only chance. He started to walk across town.

CHAPTER TWENTY-FIVE

The Poor House and Hospital
October 1862

Katherine stared at the ceiling for most of the night, with her face pounding and the image of Peyton's angry sneer in her mind. Daylight finally arrived. She ached, felt weak, and wanted to avoid the stares of others, but couldn't afford to miss a day of work. She crawled from bed, looked in the mirror, and gasped at her image. She stepped backwards, found the bed with her hands, and sank back. Her sisters woke up and sat next to her. She told them, "Please wash, get dressed, and have breakfast while I get ready for work." Katherine dreaded explaining her injury to Mrs. Duffy or the other boarders. Nor did she think she could chew.

Pauline said, "You can't go to work. Please stay here and rest."

"I must, Pauline. We need the money, and once I get there, the sewing will take my mind off the pain."

Pauline rested her head on Katherine's shoulder. "Mary and I can get jobs and help out."

Mary shouted, "I can be a fireman!"

Katherine managed a laugh. "I hope that won't be necessary. But I do want you to walk with me to work on your way to school. Now go to breakfast."

Katherine lay in bed with a wet towel on her face. When the girls returned she dressed and tried to wear her bonnet askew on her face, but she couldn't find a way to conceal her injury. They walked to Mr. Lippman's store, about fifteen minutes away. Pauline held Katherine's arm with one hand and her school books in the other while Mary skipped ahead. Katherine kept her head bowed. When they entered the store, Mr. Lippman came from behind the counter. "Good heavens, Miss Pender. What happened?"

Katherine turned her head to the side to try to hide the injury. "A drunken man attacked me last night outside the hotel. The manager called for a doctor. He said there are no broken bones. Just a bad bruise."

Mr. Lippman winced. "That's more than bad. You can't work with an injury like that."

Katherine finally looked him in the eye and pleaded, "Please, sir, I need the money. I'll be able to sew, I promise."

The man placed a hand on her shoulder. "You listen to me, young lady. Go back to your boarding house and rest. I'll arrange it so you can make up for your lost pay. And I'll speak to Mrs. Marshall at the hotel. If you're not feeling better by tomorrow, I want you to see the doctor again. And don't worry, I'll pay for it."

She forced a smile. "Thank you, sir. That's very kind of you." Katherine turned to the girls. "Mr. Lippman, these are my sisters, Pauline and Mary."

The girls curtsied and Lippman smiled. He said, "It's nice to meet both of you. Where are you off to now?"

Pauline said, "To school, sir."

Mr. Lippman said, "Before you do, please walk your sister back to the boarding house. I'm certain your teacher will understand if you're a little late." They didn't question him. He then took Katherine's hand. "The most important thing is for you to get better."

Katherine thanked him again and the three girls headed back to Mrs. Duffy's, with Pauline taking an arm. Halfway back, while crossing Lincoln Street, Katherine stopped and lowered her head. Pauline asked, "Katherine, are you all right?"

Katherine took a few deep breaths. "I need a minute to gather my strength. I'm feeling a little. . . ." Her eyes rolled back in her head and she collapsed, falling onto the sandy street and sending her purse flying. Pauline and Mary screamed.

Pauline knelt and rubbed Katherine's hand. "Oldest Sister! Say something! Please talk to me!" Mary sat on the sidewalk and began to weep. Katherine's one good eye peered blankly at the sky. Pauline looked around and spotted a one-horse wagon turning onto Lincoln. She ran alongside it and grabbed the negro driver's pant leg. "Mister, my sister just fainted. Please help. We need a doctor!"

The bald, white-bearded man pulled on the brake and trotted to Katherine. He looked at the prone body and said to Pauline, "Don' hab no doctuh, mistess. Ah kin tek she tuh de po' folk hospital."

Pauline said, "Yes! They must have a doctor there."

The man bent at the knees, slid his arms underneath Katherine, and stood. Sand drifted off her body and through his fingers. Her head drooped back; Pauline supported it with her hand. The man carried Katherine to his wagon and lay her gently on the hay in the bed. Pauline fetched Katherine's purse and the girls climbed next to her. Pauline waved her hand back and forth over Katherine's face as the vehicle moved forward.

When they arrived at the Savannah Poor House and Hospital on the east side of Forsyth Place, Pauline thanked the negro, jumped down, and grabbed the arm of a man in a suit walking in the front door. "Sir, my sister fainted and she's still not awake. Please help her into the hospital. She's in that wagon."

The man ran to Katherine, looked at her eye, and felt her wrist. He carried her across the sidewalk, through the door, and to a bed in the woman's wing on the first floor. Pauline and Mary followed. The man asked a nurse for a towel and a basin of water.

The nurse said, "Yes, Dr. Arnold," and ran off.

Dr. Arnold asked Pauline, "How did she get this terrible bruise?"

"A man hit her last night."

Dr. Arnold grimaced at the thought. "What's her name?"

Pauline said, "Kather . . . I mean Penny. Penny Pender. She's my sister. I'm Pauline and this is Mary."

The nurse returned and placed the items on a small table next to the bed. Dr. Arnold wrung out a rag and placed it gently on Katherine's eye. He asked Pauline, "Where are your parents?"

"They're dead, sir." She put her arm around Mary's shoulder. "Our oldest sister takes care of us." Pauline's voice began to crack.

Arnold said, "I'm sorry to hear that. How old is Penny?"

"Seventeen, sir. I just turned thirteen and Mary is six."

The doctor nodded at what he assumed was another tragedy of the war. "For now, we'll keep cool compresses on the injury. I'll keep coming by until she regains consciousness. So will the nurse, Mr. Nichols."

Ten minutes later, with Pauline and Mary kneeling by her side, Katherine opened her good eye. Her head felt as if it were made of stone. She tried to touch her wound and felt the damp rag. She slowly raised up on her elbows, looked to the left and right, and saw a long room with about fifteen occupied beds lining each wall. Pauline stroked her arm. "It's all right. You fainted on the street. We took you to this hospital. They put you in a nightgown and a doctor examined you."

Katherine moaned and lay back. She heard the woman in the next bed vomiting into a bucket and another one further away coughing incessantly. Katherine said, "I don't like it here. I'm leaving."

Dr. Arnold stepped past Mary to her side. "Not so fast, Miss Pender. I want you to stay put, off your feet, and in my care." The man squatted by the bed and touched her pulse. "I'm Dr. Arnold, a director of this hospital. I want you to rest. I'll give you some laudanum for the pain and keep a damp towel on your eye to reduce the swelling. If that doesn't work, I'll try leeches. Once I think you're out of danger, you may leave."

Katherine would never disobey a doctor—to his face. "Yes, sir," she said meekly.

Dr. Arnold removed the towel. He prepared a glass of water with laudanum, helped her sit up, and let her drink. He eased her down and replaced the towel. "I'll keep checking on you. If you need anything, ask your nurse, Mr. Nichols. We want you to get well." He hurried to another patient.

Katherine told her sisters, "I guess I'm safe here and I am tired. Go to school now but come back afterwards."

Pauline asked if she were sure and Katherine nodded. The sisters kissed her goodbye on her uninjured cheek and left. Katherine closed her eyes. The next time she looked up, her sisters were staring down at her. She felt the towel on her head and said, "I thought I told you to go to school."

Pauline laughed. "We did. It's six o'clock. We got here at four, but you were still sleeping. The nurse said that you had slept the whole time, so we went to Forsyth Place. It's such a pretty park."

Mary chirped, "We played by the fountain. I thaw a turtle!"

Katherine took a deep breath and tried to judge how she felt. Her eye still ached and she wanted more sleep. She wondered if she had the strength to sit up.

Pauline said, "You'll never guess who we saw coming back from the fountain."

Katherine said, "I can't guess—tell me."

"We saw the man who came looking for you in Washington Square—the one with the leather hat and the long scar on his cheek. I'll never forget him. We were entering the hospital and he bumped into me to get in the door and didn't even excuse himself. The ugly brute has no manners. He was trying to hide a bottle under his vest."

Katherine groaned and thought, "Just my luck—the last person I want to see." Then she bolted up to a sitting position, propelling the towel off her face. "Are you sure it's him?"

"Positive. He looked right at me because I was in his way."

Dr. Arnold came by and told Katherine to lie back. He examined the bruise and replaced the towel on her eye. "You need some more rest. Please do as I say."

When the doctor left, she took off the towel and sat up. Pauline said, "What are you doing? You heard the doctor."

"Where's my dress?"

"Under the bed, but you can't leave."

Katherine looked up and down the aisle to make sure Dr. Arnold or Mr. Nichols wasn't near. She donned her dress and bonnet and stood on shaky knees. She led the girls to the stairwell and asked a nurse for the location of the men's ward. He replied that it was on the second floor, but women weren't allowed there. When he walked away the girls snuck up the stairs. They stood in the stairwell and opened the door just enough to stick their heads through. Katherine asked Pauline, "Do you see him?"

Pauline scanned the rows of beds. She whispered, "On the left, three beds down, reading the newspaper and drinking from a glass."

Katherine squinted through her good eye and said, "That is him!" She closed the door and led her sisters down the stairs and onto the street. She told them, "Go to the boarding house right now. I have important business to attend to. I'll be home soon."

Pauline pleaded, "But you heard Dr. Arnold. You should be resting in bed."

Katherine hugged her sisters. "I'll rest when I get back. Now, go to Mrs. Duffy's before it gets dark. You know the way, don't you?" Katherine watched her sisters leave. Then she headed to her destination.

Joseph and James waited at the Central of Georgia Railroad depot as the last train of the day, the six o'clock from Macon, pulled into the station and the passengers disembarked. The boys never emerged. The men walked through the cars, but didn't see Danny or Truvy. When they returned to the coach, Joseph said, "We've been had. I'm leaving with Hercules now. I won't be back until I find the boys." James said he would join them, but Joseph asked him to remain in Savannah in case they received mail from Willie and Harold or any other leads.

Fifteen minutes after the men returned home, Joseph limped into his father's study with a Colt revolver holstered on his belt and a hunting knife strapped to his leg. "I'm ready, Mother, Father. I had Lilly pack food. I want to reach Blooming-dale tonight. I'll write when I'm near a post office or a telegraph."

A knock on the front door stopped the conversation. They stood still, hoping someone had brought good news about the boys. Moments later William tapped on the family parlor door. James said, "Yes?"

The butler entered. "A young lady wants to speak to you, Master."

The McBains looked at each other, wondering who the visitor could possibly be. They walked into the hall. Sarah gasped at the sight of a girl with a purple, swollen eye the size of a large egg. She stepped forward and took the girl's arm. "Please come in. My poor dear, what happened to you?"

Katherine entered the hallway and stared in awe at everything around her: the silver-plated wall lamps, the two matching jade-green vases as tall as her, and the wide carpeted staircase framed by two white, fluted columns with gold-gilded capitals. She had never seen such opulence and felt dirty in the presence of such rich, important people. "Excuse me, ma'am. A man hit me. The doctor said I'll get better in time."

James said, "I'm Mr. McBain. I'm very sorry to hear about your injury. Please come in and sit down."

"I'm afraid there's no time, sir. I saw your poster. I know where you can find one of the kidnappers."

Joseph stepped up to Katherine and placed his hands on her shoulders. "Where?"

"At the Savannah Poor House and Hospital—the men's ward on the second floor. His name is Harold."

James asked, "How do you know it's him?"

Katherine hesitated. She wasn't prepared to explain her relationship with Harold, but she couldn't think of any way to get around the truth. "He paid me to accuse your coachman of molesting me, for which I'm very sorry and I apologize. I needed the money to survive."

James asked, "You're Miss Pender?"

Put on the spot again, Katherine decided not to reveal her true name. "Yes, sir."

Joseph said to James, "We can discuss that later. Let's go." They asked William to tell Hercules to find the police chief and bring him to the Poor House. They ran off.

Left alone, Sarah and Katherine looked at each other for a few uneasy seconds. At first, Katherine thought Mrs. McBain looked like many of the grandmothers at church in Thomasville, in her bonnet with grey-streaked hair. Then the woman held her hand and looked her in the eye. The grip was firm yet warm and the smile focused and sincere. Katherine felt that Mrs. McBain really cared about her.

Sarah said, "Please come in and have a seat, Miss Pender. May I offer you something to eat or drink?" She couldn't help feeling sympathy for the girl. Other than the eye and her common clothing, Miss Pender was beautiful, poised, and well-spoken, the opposite of what she had imagined of Hercules's accuser. Most importantly, she had come forward with critical information.

Katherine wanted to wait to see if the McBain men found the two boys so she could collect the reward, but she felt uncomfortable in the presence of a woman whom she had hurt so deeply with her actions. She decided to return later. "I really must be going. I have two younger sisters to care for. There's just the three of us."

Sarah raised her eyebrows. "But you're so young yourself."

"Our parents are deceased, ma'am. It's my duty."

Sarah wanted to comfort the girl, but sensed her desire to leave. "Thank you so much for coming forward, Miss Pender. I pray that it will lead to the recovery of my grandson and his friend. Please wait a moment. I'll have Jefferson take you home."

"That's not necessary, Mrs. McBain. I can walk."

"Nonsense. I won't hear of you walking with that injury." She left the room and told William to have Jefferson bring the gig to the front of the house. Sarah then escorted Katherine outside. She thanked the girl again and said that her husband would get in touch with her. Katherine told her where she was staying and climbed onto the soft leather seat, praying that the boys would be found.

Joseph and James entered the men's wing and walked along the aisle, excusing themselves as they bumped into hustling male nurses. James stopped, grabbed Joseph's arm, and nodded towards a patient who appeared to be sleeping. Joseph moved between the beds and saw the telltale scar. He pulled his hunting knife from the sheath and placed it an inch from Harold's nose.

A nurse ran over. "Sir, what are you doing?"

Without taking his eyes off Harold, Joseph said, "I'm apprehending a murderer and a kidnapper. The police will be here soon."

The outlaw opened his eyes, which crossed to focus on the point of the blade. His lips started to twitch, but he didn't speak. "Harold, don't you move. My name is Joseph McBain. We met once before, when you and your partners killed my friend on a wharf a few years ago. You recently kidnapped my son. I'm certain that you know who I am."

Harold indicated "no" by moving his eyes from side to side. Joseph stuck the tip of the knife into his nose. Harold screamed and pulled back his head into the hard, horse-hair mattress. A dot-sized bulb of blood formed. A group of nurses and patients gathered near the bed. Joseph eased up on the knife. "Where's my son?"

Harold kept his head still and gasped, "If you kill me, you'll never find out."

Joseph again poked the knife into Harold's nose.

Harold cried out and grabbed the sides of the bed. Blood ran from his nose and puddled on his upper lip. "Lemme go and I'll tell you."

"You want to negotiate? All right, here's my counter offer." Joseph jabbed Harold's nose again and Harold yelled louder. A nurse called for help. Joseph growled, "Answer me right now."

Harold, breathing in short gasps, spoke quickly. "My partner was gonna leave the boys at a station on the Savannah, Albany and Gulf line to catch today's train here."

Joseph kept the knife poised over Harold's face. "Did you harm them?"

"No, they were good when I left them."

Police Chief Lyde Goodwin arrived. Joseph sheathed his knife, stepped away from the bed, and stumbled over something. He saw a carpetbag sticking out from beneath Harold's bed and reached for it. Harold leaned over, grabbed it, and shouted, "That's mine!" Joseph yanked it back, nearly pulling Harold off the bed, but the man wouldn't ease his grip. Joseph pulled his revolver and pointed it at Harold's forehead.

Chief Goodwin put his hand on the gun and pushed it aside. He said to Harold, "You're under arrest. Let go of the bag." Harold hesitated, then released his grip. Joseph unhooked the bag and saw the ransom money.

He told the chief, "This is one of the men who murdered Andrew McBain and kidnapped my son. He tells me my boy is on a train to Savannah. I'm going to the Savannah-Albany depot now and I'm taking this ransom money—our money—with me. I trust you'll lock him up."

Goodwin said, "Joseph, you can be sure this one won't see daylight until a judge tells me otherwise."

"Thank you, Chief." He turned to his father. "Let's go. The train should be pulling in now."

CHAPTER TWENTY-SIX

"It Feels Like Another City"
October 1862

The train had just arrived as the McBain men ran into the depot. Joseph hobbled along the boarding path, sidestepping departing passengers, until he saw Truvy hop off the baggage car. He nearly knocked over a man to get to him, and then he picked up the boy. "Truvy! Thank God you're here. Where's Danny?"

Unable to look Joseph in the eye, Truvy looked at the man's chest. "Runaway slaves took him, Master."

"WHAT?! WHERE?"

"A man named Willie left us at Fleming Station last night to catch today's train. While we waited, three runaways came by and took Danny, saying they'd keep him until they got to the Yankees. They said they had no use for me. I waited and took this train. The conductor let me ride in the baggage car."

Joseph put Truvy down and yelled, "Damnation!"

James asked the boy, "Where did the two men take you?" Truvy explained how he and Danny were squeezed into barrels, driven to a cabin somewhere in the woods, and kept there for four days.

Joseph took Truvy's hand. "Let's get you to your mother. She can't wait to see you." When they reached the street, he hoisted the boy in the front of Hercules's saddle. Joseph told the coachman to take Truvy home, and then be ready to leave at six o'clock in the morning to begin searching for Danny.

When James and Joseph walked into the family parlor without her grandson Sarah dropped onto the couch. James sat next to her and described Danny's second abduction. She covered her face in her hands for a few seconds. Then she looked up and reached for a telegram. "Here, a messenger delivered this while you were gone."

James read aloud, "Arr Tues at 7 on Cent Georgia with Jimmy and girl. Amy."

Joseph, who was pacing the floor, stopped short. "Amy? Mother, did you know she was coming?"

Sarah shook her head. "This is the first I've heard. I'm shocked, but happily so."

Joseph stabbed his cane at the floor. "I'm leaving in the morning with Hercules to find Danny. Please tell Amy why I couldn't be here, but that I'll be back soon." He kissed her cheek and told his father, "I'm taking one thousand of the five thousand dollars with me. I may need it. I'm going to try to get some sleep."

⁂

Patience opened the front door and sang, "Truvyyyyy!" She stooped to hug and kiss her son. "I've been worried sick about you, but the Lord has answered my prayers." She hugged him again and sat him at the table in the front room. "You look so thin." She left the room and returned with a plate of cornbread and jar of peach jam.

She sat next to her son, rested her chin on her hands, and watched him eat. Hercules retired to the sofa and smiled at the happy reunion. Truvy alternated between chewing, yawning, and describing his ordeal. His voice wavered when he talked about Danny's kidnapping. Patience kissed his cheek and said, "Don't talk about it now. Finish your food and get some sleep. You can tell me more in the morning."

Truvy picked up the plate and licked the crumbs. When Patience put him to bed, he insisted that they kneel and pray for Danny.

She returned to the family room, sat next to Hercules, and rested her head on his shoulder. "Thank you so much. I didn't think I'd ever see my boy again."

Hercules stroked her back. "Thank Master Joseph. He went after the boys like a hound after a fox. But you'll have to wait to do it. We're leaving at daybreak to search for Danny. I'm sure we won't come back until we find him." Hercules discussed the evening's events. "Master Joseph said a girl came to the house earlier tonight. She knew where one of the kidnappers was hiding—at the Poor House." Hercules didn't mention that the man was also one of Andrew's killers.

Patience looked up at Hercules. "Please be careful. We need you here. You know that, don't you?"

He rubbed her shoulder. "We won't be in any danger. And I'd never leave you or Truvy or Gully. You have my word." Patience looked up at him for a few seconds and kissed his lips. He pulled away and stared at her. She held his gaze until he returned the kiss. She got up, closed the door to the boys' bedroom, curled up on the sofa, and snuggled against him.

⁂

Joseph and Hercules departed the next morning on horseback with a pack mule in tow. Joseph told him, "First stop is Fort McAllister. My guess is that the runaways went to Ossabaw Sound to get to a Union ship and passed near the fort." Joseph didn't speak again until they passed the second guard post on the

Ogeechee Road. "Hercules, I heard the stable doors open quite late last night. Is Patience all right?"

Hercules's head was spinning, as he wondered if he had betrayed his friend Andrew. "Yes, Master Joseph. She needed someone to talk to. She wants to thank you for rescuing Truvy, but she's still sad about Danny."

Joseph glanced at the coachman, who stared straight ahead. They rode in silence along the Ogeechee Road, across the Kings Bridge over the Great Ogeechee River, and onto the Bryan Neck Road. At noon they reached the partially completed earthen-walled fort sitting on a bend of the Great Ogeechee, twelve miles from the Ossabaw Sound. Construction had begun in June 1861 to prevent the Yankees from gaining a land approach to Savannah and destroying the Savannah, Albany and Gulf Railroad, so critical to transporting troops and supplies around southwestern Georgia. Since the fall of Fort Pulaski, its strategic importance had become even more crucial.

A private escorted Joseph into the officers' quarters, the lone building in the fort. Lieutenant George A. Nicoll of the Republican Blues, one of two companies manning the battery, walked around a desk and glanced at the insignia on Joseph's uniform. "Captain McBain, you're back. The last I heard, you were being exchanged."

Joseph shook Nicoll's hand. "I returned about a week ago, although it seems like a year. I just got brevetted to captain for my service at Fort Pulaski." Joseph described Danny's abduction. "I have to find him and would appreciate your help." Joseph unrolled a map on the desk.

A black cat with white paws jumped up and lay on the map. Nicoll picked up the fort mascot and scolded, "Not now, Tom. Go outside and catch a marsh rat." He placed the feline on the floor, but he jumped onto Nicoll's chair and curled up.

Joseph held down the map with his fingertips. "I assume the runaways are heading for the Union navy in Ossabaw Sound."

Nicoll replied, "Your timing is fortunate. Mr. Watson of Bryan County has obtained an order from General Mercer for us to take him to the Union fleet under a flag of truce so he can request the return of his runaway slaves. We're leaving in a few minutes. You can join us. If the runaways who took your son made it to the coast, the Yankees should know about it."

Joseph told Hercules to wait in the negro campground. Then he boarded a skiff with Nicoll, Mr. Watson, and four oarsmen. As they left the pier, Nicoll noticed that Joseph was looking at a side-wheel steamer at anchor further up the river. "That's the Nashville," he said, "a blockade runner. The Yankees chased her up here last July and we've been protecting her ever since. The Union gunboats never leave the river. They have her trapped."

Two hours later they reached Ossabaw Sound and hoisted a flag of truce to a Union ship cruising a mile away. A rowboat descended and headed towards them. When it got within ten yards, a Yankee petty officer stood and called, "State your business."

Nicoll stood. "I'm Lieutenant Nicoll, officer of the day at Fort McAllister. Two gentlemen wish to speak to the commanding officer of your gunship. One is aware that several of his slaves have reached the Union fleet. They are noncombatants and he wants them returned."

The Union officer replied without hesitation, "I must deny your request. It's my government's policy to give refuge to anyone seeking it, regardless of color. We take no measures to entice parties to us, and they are free to leave us whenever they wish. Apparently, the people you seek have chosen to stay."

Mr. Watson shot up and almost fell over in the rocking boat. Joseph grabbed the man's arm to steady him. Watson called to the Yankee, "Those are my slaves, paid for out of my own pocket. You have no right to confiscate private property."

"Sir, your so-called property has legs, and they have used them to reach us. They can just as easily use them to return to you. I have nothing more to say."

Nicoll pulled on Watson's sleeve and the grumbling man sat. He then asked the petty officer, "One more thing. Some runaways kidnapped Captain McBain's son two days ago. He believes they escaped to your ships. Have you seen or heard of the boy?"

The petty officer eyed Joseph's uniform. "I have not, but I will alert all of our ships in the area. If we recover him, what is his name and where shall we send him?"

Joseph stood and held onto an oarsman's shoulder. "My boy's name is Daniel McBain. He's seven years old. Please return him to me, Captain McBain, in Savannah, if at all possible, or to Fort McAllister."

"We'll do all we can, Captain. You should know that we have established a colony of freed slaves on St. Simons Island. Our ships have been taking runaways and abandoned slaves there. I'll see to it that our men ask after your boy."

Joseph thanked the officer and they returned to the fort. The Yankee's pledge to help lifted Joseph's mood, but he couldn't wait for word from the Union ships. He and Hercules immediately left for St. Simons Island by way of Darien—a two-day trip.

Sarah and James took turns embracing Amy and then holding and kissing Jimmy. As the family walked from the depot to the street, and with James carrying the child, Amy introduced Colleen to her parents. Colleen said, "It's a noble playsur to meet you, Misses, and your Riverince." Sarah and James laughed at her accent, being so familiar with it in heavily-Irish-populated Savannah. Jefferson greeted Amy with a smile and bowed to her as she entered the cab.

The female house servants, wearing grey dresses with white collars and white work caps, stood by the iron fence in the front yard and waved as soon as the coach came into sight. Goose bumps covered Amy's arms. She hadn't felt so happy since she first saw her newborn son, nor had she seen so many smiling faces at one time since she left the South. Jefferson opened the door and Amy stepped out with Jimmy in her arms, followed by Colleen and the McBains. Amy walked across the brick sidewalk and Nannie took the child as if he were the baby Jesus. The five other female servants took turns hugging Amy. Chloe said, "Mistess, you still pretty as a Jawjuh sunset."

Amy introduced the servants to Colleen and headed to the house. She stepped into the foyer and the familiarity of home engulfed her like a warm blanket. Her parents asked her to get settled and then meet them later in the family parlor. Amy went upstairs to her old bedroom, sat on the edge of the four-poster bed, lay back, and stared up at the floral-print canopy. The sweet scent of freshly washed linens brought back memories of living in Savannah. A knock on the door caused her to sit up. "Come in," she called.

Chloe entered. "Mistess Amy, you wan' me tuh fix uh bat?"

The thought sounded delightful. "Yes, thank you, Chloe. And please unpack my bag. Also, could you give Colleen a tour of the house and grounds and settle her in the room next to me."

"Yessum, Mistess."

After bathing, Amy went to see her parents in the family parlor and passed the female servants in the hall, who were busy tickling Jimmy. Lilly said, "He look jes' lahk ole Massa Bob." Amy kissed her son on the head. She loved the boy more than anything, but after three weeks of being together day and night, even with Colleen, who loved the boy like her own, Amy looked forward to surrendering some of his care to the servants.

She entered the parlor and looked twice when a little white dog barked at her. "Who's this?"

James scooped up the mutt in one hand. "This is JD, short for Jefferson Davis. Joseph found him in the New York prison and brought him home for Danny."

Amy's eyes darted around the room. "Where is Danny—and Joseph?"

James put down the dog and took Amy's hand. "We have some bad news. Danny has been kidnapped by runaways. Joseph and Hercules are searching for him."

Amy stepped back and shouted, "NO! How did that happen?"

James said, "It's a long story. I'll tell you over supper."

As her father explained the saga, Amy fiddled with her food. She pushed away her plate. "I feel terrible, Mother and Father. You've suffered through all this and I wasn't here to help."

Sarah said, "You couldn't have done anything to prevent these things. You're home now, and we're thankful for that, though I would never have asked you to come during these times, especially with Jimmy. Why don't you get a good night's sleep? Joseph and Danny will be home soon. I just know it." Amy kissed her parents goodnight.

The next day the family took a ride through town. Amy could hardly speak. Before she left Savannah the streets on Saturdays were jammed with farmers' wagons stocked with fruits, vegetables, smoked meats, and hides flowing in from the countryside. But now the area was almost deserted. Soldiers patrolled the streets, which were lined with shops with "CLOSED" signs pasted on their windows. Jefferson parked the coach and the McBains strolled along the Strand. They saw ships floating peacefully in the harbor instead of being loaded with cotton and other produce. No stacks puffed, no horns bleated.

With Colleen carrying Jimmy, they walked the few blocks to the City Market. Slaves still sat on the sidewalk around it, hawking their baskets, home-grown produce, and home-made trinkets, but they were subdued by the lack of shoppers. The family toured the building, a quadrangular brick structure encircling all of Market Square with an open center for the fish mongers. Only about half of the vendor stalls were occupied.

When Amy asked about the vacant booths, James sighed and said, "Business is way off. Some merchants are renting multiple stalls to keep out competitors, which enables them to charge exorbitant prices for their goods. I tell you, the behavior of some of our citizens in these times is despicable."

When they returned to the street, Amy observed, "The color, gaiety, crowds, and calls of the negro women tending the stalls, they're all gone. It feels like another city."

James explained. "The war has changed things. Most people are impoverished. Men go to war for pitiful pay, not enough to support a wife and children. If they're killed, their families become paupers. The city council just appropriated two thousand dollars for provisions to be distributed to the poor and one thousand dollars for the relief of orphans. But it's a drop in the bucket. They need tens of thousands of dollars."

On the drive home, the McBains saw four soldiers escorting another, his hands tied behind his back and blood streaming from his nose, in the direction of the military barracks at Bull and Liberty. James read Amy's mind. "We're having a problem with the soldiers coming into town from their camps, getting drunk, and starting fights. General Mercer just issued an order banning soldiers from the city after eight in the evening. I doubt it will help. They'll still start trouble, only earlier." McBain looked out the window for a few minutes. He felt motivated to defend his hometown. "It's just a few bad people, Amy, but they have a visible impact. Far more people are donating their time and money to the soldiers and their families. It's still a good town with good people."

Amy's spirits improved on Sunday. She gave Colleen the day off to relax and roam around Savannah on her own. After church, the family drove to the Heritage. They stopped in the Quarter and in moments a throng of servants surrounded Amy, smiling, touching her, and calling her name. It took two hours to greet them all and let the women hold Jimmy. One said, "When you comin' back home, Mistess Amy? Us bin missin' you. Li'l Jimmy need rearin' by he own people." Amy's childhood memories flooded back—playing "princess" with the negro girls; taking classes at the plantation schoolhouse with her neighbors and brother; and listening to the men tell ghost stories while she, Joseph, and Andrew ate Delpha's fried apples in the Quarter after supper.

Jefferson drove them to the family cemetery. Amy laid a flower on Grandfather McBain's grave and they all lowered their heads in prayer. Amy touched her fingers to her lips and blew a kiss to her grandpa, who had always spoiled her and made her laugh.

They walked fifty yards to the negro cemetery. Amy stood by Andrew's grave and wiped away a tear as she read the carved headstone:

ANDREW McBAIN
Loving Husband, Father and Friend
March 20, 1820 - May 6, 1861
HE BUILDS WITH THE ANCIENTS

James then led them to the graves of Isaac and Delpha. Amy clasped her hands together at her waist and closed her eyes. Solomon, Noah, and their families came by. Amy told them how much she loved and missed their parents. They thanked her and lined up around the graves. Amy wondered about Kitt but decided to ask her father later.

They visited the stables so Amy could see her horse, Dilly. As she petted the mare and fed her carrots, James strolled around the area. He stopped by one of the plantation wagons and stuck his finger in a damaged area on the top edge of the side panel. He summoned Jefferson and asked, "Doesn't this look like it's from a gunshot?"

Jefferson lowered his head to a foot from the board. "It sholy looks so, Massa."

"Fetch Mr. Donnelly. He'll have an explanation."

Ten minutes later the overseer stood alongside McBain. "I have no idea, sir. No one has fired a gun since I returned, except me, at blackbirds." Although it was against the law for persons of color to possess or handle firearms, some planters, far from the eye of the law, allowed their most trusted slaves to use guns to hunt small game or plantation pests. "Ask the drivers if they know of anyone firing a gun."

The McBains then left for the big house and a late-afternoon dinner of oyster stew, recently a staple as the shellfish was plentiful. The Heritage house servants fussed over Amy and Jimmy. The child, wearing a blue dress, with his silky brown hair ending in curls at his neck, giggled as the servants passed him around. During the meal, Amy talked about her trip to Savannah and the Union officer who gave her a pass. "General Sherman was courteous, very official, but he has the coldest eyes. He burned down an entire village with only women and children inhabitants to set an example. Be thankful he's not down here."

Sarah waited for a servant to place a dish on the table and leave the room before saying, "At least he issued you a pass to return to the North. I must admit, I'm quite surprised that Bob allowed you and Jimmy to make the trip."

Amy rolled the stem of her wine glass in her fingers. "He didn't, Mother. He doesn't know I'm here."

James and Sarah stopped chewing. Sarah asked, "Amy, why would you do such a thing? He's your husband."

Amy sipped her wine. "Because he wouldn't have approved. And I wasn't about to lose my house to the thieves who are running this Confederacy. I left Bob a letter, should he return home early from his assignment. He'll forgive me. He loves me."

James finally swallowed his food. "Amy, do you know where Bob is now?"

"Yes, he's following General Grant's army. I'll probably get home before him, even if I stay for six weeks. I'll tell him that I came here." She patted her lips before finishing her sentence. "Eventually." The family continued their meal listening to Jimmy's squeals and laughter.

As the McBains walked to the coach to return to the city, Mr. Donnelly rode up and told James that no one had heard gunshots recently.

On the ride back to town, Amy questioned James about Danny's abduction. "The girl who sent Hercules to jail and told you where to find one of Danny's kidnappers, what do you know about her?"

James replied, "Not much. She lives with two younger sisters at Mrs. Duffy's and works in the evenings at the Marshall House Hotel. Mrs. Duffy says they're good tenants although the girl, Penny, occasionally falls behind in payments. The hotel manager says she's a good worker. That's as far as we got before she retracted the charges. I was shocked when I met her. She can't be more than eighteen, is very polite, well-spoken, and, other than the blackened eye, quite attractive. I appreciated that she apologized for her behavior towards Hercules, although I can never forgive her. I didn't get a chance to speak to her as Joseph and I left for the hospital right away."

Sarah bounced Jimmy on her knee. "I talked with her for a few minutes after you left. I asked her to stay, but she said she had to return to her sisters, who she supports. It sounds very sad. I had Jefferson drive her home."

Amy said, "Mrs. Duffy's is a nice, clean place, isn't it? The girl must have some funds for three of them to live there." Amy reached over to smooth down Jimmy's hair and asked, "Father, if . . . I mean when Joseph and Danny return, are you going to give her the reward money?"

James rubbed his eyes, looking forward to sleep. "No. She's caused us all so much grief. It would be a betrayal of Hercules to give her the money."

Sarah said, "Dear, the reward was for information leading to the return of

Danny and Truvy and the capture of Willie and Harold. She led you to Harold. That's worth something. You can't go back on your word. Harold helped accost you, kidnap the boys, and murder Andrew. Have you forgotten how badly you wanted him? Willie and Harold tried to destroy Hercules and paid Penny to do it. She was just a pawn."

McBain gazed out the window. "If we get Danny back and she's the only one to come forward, I'll consider it. But I won't be happy about it."

Amy said, "Mother, I'm a little suspicious about her. She gets paid by those scoundrels for putting Hercules in jail, and now she's hoping to get paid for turning in one of them. It sounds like she's playing both hands in a poker game."

James nodded in agreement but Sarah countered, "Amy, she got us one of the men. I don't care about her motives."

Amy sighed. "So many strange things have happened since I left and none of them good. Things have to get better." She squeezed her mother's hand. ✦

CHAPTER TWENTY-SEVEN

∽

The Negro Colony
October 1862

Darien had a small population of about five hundred when the war began, and was a major port for lumber shipments. As with other coastal areas, the locals fled to the interior after the Yankees took control of the southern Atlantic, leaving behind a ghost town. Although Joseph knew this, he still scanned the street as he and Hercules rode through, hoping to see some sign of life in the buildings and shops. They arrived at the waterfront to find a few abandoned fishing boats. A mangy dog ran across a lot bordering the wharf. Joseph said to Hercules, "I guess we'll have to row ourselves to St. Simons."

After they dismounted, Joseph stood at the foot of a wooden pier and looked for a seaworthy skiff. He heard a creaking noise and watched a man ascend a ladder from a boat onto the pier. He was little more than five feet tall with thin white hair on the sides of his otherwise bald, tanned head, and wore a pair of dirt-smudged beige pants supported by red suspenders. He said, "Welcome to the port of Darien. My name is Earl."

Joseph nodded towards the harbor. "We need to get to St. Simons. Can you help?"

The man hooked his thumbs under his suspenders, stretched them out, and let them snap back against his body. "This may not be any of my business, but why in God's great kingdom do you want to go there? You got five hundred darkies on the one hand, and about twenty southern boys on the other, both trying to kill each other. Ain't a healthy place for a man of your complexion."

"Runaways took my seven-year-old son. I think he may be there."

The man snapped his suspenders again. "Here's the deal. For twenty-five dollars, payable in advance, I'll take you to Hazzard's wharf on St. Simons. There's an old slave there named Henry, who's loyal to his master, Mr. Hazzard. He's keeping an eye on the plantation while Hazzard is in the army. The runaways know Henry and leave him alone, at least for now. If there's a white boy on the island, he'll know. I'll wait near the wharf until two hours before dark, about half past four. Then I leave. If you miss me, I'll return tomorrow. But that'll be an extra twenty-five."

Joseph pulled out a wad of greybacks and peeled off a few bills. "I'm Captain McBain. This is Hercules. Where can we keep our horses? We're in a hurry."

"There's a barn behind these warehouses. I'll take you over and we'll get going."

Fifteen minutes later, armed with a revolver and an Enfield rifle, Joseph sat in the front of the boat as Hercules and Earl took the oars. He busied himself by loading powder and ball into his rifle as he considered how to negotiate for Danny's release should he find him. Two hours later they pulled up to a pier on the landward side of the island and Earl tied a line to it. "This is Hazzard's wharf. If Henry can't help you, I'd advise you to come back here. Pronto. Them boys are in no mood to entertain their former masters."

Earl lit a segar and lay back on the rower's bench. Joseph left the rifle in the boat as it was too cumbersome to carry and followed Hercules down the pier. They walked along a wide dirt road shielded by the arching branches of live oak trees. Joseph stopped at a small clearing enclosed by an iron fence and studied the tombstones of past generations of Hazzards.

"Kin ah he'ps you, Massa?" Joseph crouched and reached for his gun. A thin black man wearing coveralls that reached his calf stepped from behind a tree. "Ah seed Massa Uhl tek you tuh de wha'af."

Joseph asked, "Are you Henry?" The man nodded and Joseph introduced himself and Hercules. He told Henry about Danny.

"Ah bin tole dat some nigguhs come yistuhday wid a boy. He at Gas-co-knees Bluff. Dat twenny minute hoss ride. Ah kin saddle up two fuh twenny dollah. Ah cain' tek you all de way, 'cause dem nigguhs don' truss me none."

Joseph pulled his watch. "It's already one o'clock. Let's go."

Henry drove them in a wagon to the stable. He saddled three horses and they departed. Ten minutes later, they pulled up. Henry said, "Tek dis road fuh fibe mile an' you at Gas-co-knees. 'Member, dey don' lahk no sudden white folk. If dey come aftuh you, git back tuh de wha'af. Leab dem hosses. Ah gits 'em laytuh."

Joseph and Hercules rode to a clearing with fifteen rickety, wooden cabins on either side of the road, raised on bricks with a single door and one shuttered, glassless window. A few women holding brooms and rakes stopped work to stare at them. One ran into a cabin and another towards the big house one hundred yards up the road. About twenty black men with old flintlock muskets materialized and blocked their path. The man in the middle, who wore coveralls and had a long groove in his bald scalp, stepped forward. "Wut you wan'?"

Joseph's body tensed into a giant knot. He glanced over his shoulder and saw that no one prevented their escape. He faced the man. "Runaways on the mainland took my son and came here. I want him back."

The leader flashed a two-toothed grin at the men by his side before replying. "You keep us nigguhs fuh two hunned yuh and nebuh free us. Now you wan' you boy aftuh jes' two day. Come back in twenny-fibe yuh. Us kin use he pickin' cotton, maybe whup he when he don' behabe aw don' wu'k ha'ad."

Another man broke through the crowd and spoke to the man in coveralls, "Hope, wut's . . . ." The man saw Joseph and put his hands to his face in mock surprise. "Massa Joesup! Huhclees, too! Good Lawdy! Ah din' 'spect you so soon. Welcome tuh St. Simons an' us colony ub free nigguhs." His face turned into a scowl. "Us alibe, unlike muh ma an' pa." Kitt turned to Hope and nodded at Joseph. "Dis ole Massa's chile."

Joseph's horse neighed and snorted, sensing trouble. Joseph patted its neck. "Kitt, my family loved your parents."

Kitt sneered, "Dat why you keep 'em as slabes? Dey lub ole Massa so much dey die runnin' 'way." Kitt whispered to another man standing next to him. The man snaked through the crowd and ran towards the big house.

Joseph knew he couldn't convince Kitt of his affection for Isaac and Delpha. "I understand that Danny's here. I want him back. I'll pay you one thousand dollars. That's all the money I have on me."

Kitt grabbed the musket of the man next to him and held it at his waist. "You wan' Danny? Bring muh brudduhs and dey famblies tuh me. Den maybe you kin hab he."

Joseph glanced at the other blacks. None had their muskets at the ready. He believed he could pull his revolver and beat Kitt to the trigger if he had to. He didn't want a fight—he wanted Danny—but he had to be able to defend himself. He felt beads of sweat running down his cheek. "You have my word that I'll deliver them, but I ask that you give me Danny now."

Kitt shook the musket in rage. "You don' tell me wut tuh do now, Joesup."

Joseph saw a black man and a white boy, who had to be Danny, walking towards them from the plantation house. He kept one eye on his son as he spoke to Kitt. "I'm not telling you what to do. I'm asking you to accept my word."

Hercules spoke. "Kitt, you know you can trust Master Joseph."

"Huhclees, ah see you still McBain's top nigguh."

Hercules glared at Kitt. "One day we'll meet when you don't have that musket, and I'll fix that loose mouth of yours."

Joseph barked, "Hercules, let me handle this!"

Danny and his escort finally reached the crowd and pushed their way next to Kitt. Danny yelled, "Pa!" and tried to run to his father, but the guard grabbed his shirt and pulled him back.

Joseph said, "Danny, be still and don't say a thing!" He had finally found his son, but was helpless to touch him. He told Kitt, "You have my word. Let Danny go and I'll give you one thousand dollars and have your brothers and their families here in a few days. I'm not leaving without Danny."

Kitt pulled the hammer to full-cock. "Den you ain' leabin'. Git down de hoss!"

Hercules disobeyed Joseph. "Kitt, don't be a fool. Release Danny and you'll get your family. That's what you want."

Kitt laughed. "Huhclees, who de fool? You ride dat hoss obuh tuh me an' you free an' libin' wid jes' nigguhs. Joesup cain' stop you."

BAM, BAM. The sound of gunfire distracted Kitt. He said to Hercules, "De Yankees let us hunt us ole massas. Ain' nuttin' bettuh den shootin' 'em. You kin join us."

Hercules looked at Joseph but didn't say a word. More gunfire exploded. Hope said to Kitt, "Dems gittin' close. Us need tuh git tuh de udduhs."

Kitt's eyes shifted from Hercules to Joseph. He said, "Go on, Hope. Ah be dere soon." Hope rode away and Kitt turned to Hercules. "How 'bout it—free aw slabe?"

Hercules's heart began thumping. He looked at Danny, who was staring up at him with huge eyes. The coachman took a deep breath, turned to Joseph, and said, "Sorry, Massa." He nudged his horse forward and the men next to Danny parted to make room for him. Hercules turned his horse around and stared at a pale-faced Joseph.

Kitt slapped Hercules's leg and laughed. Danny, who stood on the other side of Hercules's horse, looked up and squeaked, "Hercules, what are you doing?" Joseph felt as if someone had slammed him in the chest. He would be leaving St. Simons without Danny or the family's most loyal man.

More shots exploded nearby. Kitt said, "Joesup, delibuh Solomon an' Noah an' dey fambles in uh week an' you git Danny. You don' an' de boy dies."

Hercules glared at Kitt. A black soldier rode up. "Kitt, Hope say tuh git obuh tuh he now! Dem rubbles jes' kill two ub us an' dey gittin' away!"

As the people turned their attention to Kitt, Hercules leaned down, grabbed Danny by his pants, and pulled him up belly first onto the front of his saddle. He kicked his horse and charged past Joseph. "LET'S GO!"

The startled blacks turned back and saw the backsides of two horses that were kicking up dirt and sand. Kitt aimed his musket and fired. Hercules slumped forward, pinning down Danny. Kitt cursed and pushed through the crowd to a one-horse wagon. Three others joined him.

Joseph trailed Hercules by thirty yards and saw the coachman bent over, seemingly protecting Danny from gunfire. He leaned forward as well, making himself a smaller target, though he had a lead of several hundred yards over Kitt and his men. The moment he reached the pier, Joseph jumped off his horse and ran to Hercules but the negro remained crouched over Danny. He pulled the boy from under the coachman and put him on the ground. His son's shirt was soaked in blood. "Danny, are you all right?"

Tears poured from the boy's eyes. "Pa, Hercules got shot!"

Hercules's head rested on the horse's mane and his right hand clutched his left shoulder. Joseph shouted, "Danny, run to the boat!"

Joseph laid a hand on Hercules's back. "Can you get off the horse?" Hercules opened his eyes, but didn't speak. Joseph said, "I'll help you down. We've got to get to the boat!" He pulled on the back of Hercules's shirt and the negro slid off the saddle. Joseph's bad leg buckled under the weight and they both sprawled on the ground. Joseph struggled to his feet, lifted the coachman, put his head underneath Hercules's right armpit. He dragged him down the pier, moving like a drunken sailor as every vein in his arms, legs, and neck bulged. He heard a wagon rumbling closer and cried out in pain as he strained to move faster. But his injured leg gave out and he dropped to his knees, bringing Hercules on top of him. Joseph regained his feet but had no strength to lift the negro.

Earl ran to them, grabbed Hercules around the waist, and screamed, "Let's go! There's a bunch of niggers at the pier with guns and they don't look happy!" He and Joseph carried Hercules the final ten yards to the rowboat. As they laid him down a musket ball splintered the post to which the boat was tied, causing Joseph to slip into the boat and land head-first on the rower's bench. Earl untied the line and pushed off.

Joseph got to his knees as his pursuers approached. He grabbed his rifle, pulled the hammer to full-cock, aimed, and fired. The man to the left of Kitt fell, flopped off the wooden deck, and splashed into the water. Joseph pulled his revolver and fired two shots, dropping the man on the other side of Kitt, who, with his remaining partner, scampered back to the protection of the trees at the base of the pier. Joseph told Danny to lie next to Hercules. He and Earl grabbed oars and rowed as if their arms were steam-powered.

Kitt resumed his advance. He knelt on the pier and fired his flintlock. The ball smacked against the side of the boat and ricocheted into the water, causing Joseph and Earl to duck. Kitt started to reload. As he fumbled with the ramrod, Joseph could see that he was inexperienced. When he finally fired, the ball splashed in the water ten yards short of them. Kitt shook his fist and yelled, "You ain' seed de las' ub me, Joesup!"

Joseph handed his oar to Earl and kneeled next to Hercules. "Can you hear me?" The coachman blinked. "Can you speak?" Hercules weakly shook his head.

Danny, who had been lying next to Hercules, hugged the negro around the waist. "Please get better, Hercules. It's me, Danny!"

Joseph held Danny's arm and said, "Sit on the bow, son. Let me give him water." Joseph gently lifted Hercules's head and placed a canteen to his mouth. The water streamed over the negro's lips and cheeks. Joseph knew that the man would soon be dead—for saving his son. He looked at Danny. Tears streamed down the boy's face. Joseph couldn't tell him not to cry.

Earl shook his head. "We won't be in Darien for two hours, and there ain't a doctor within fifty miles. He don't have a chance in hell. Sorry. I can tell that darkey means a lot to you."

Joseph took off his jacket and laid it over Hercules's torso. He bowed his head, held Hercules's limp hand, and prayed.

Dr. William Daniell held the chair for Amy and then sat at his desk on the second floor of the Custom House. "How time flies, Miss McBain. Or should I say Mrs. Carson? You're a married woman with a son. It seems like just yesterday when. . . ."

Amy, in no mood for light banter, interrupted, "Yes, Dr. Daniell, it does."

William Coffee Daniell had practiced medicine in Savannah for years, served as its mayor, and represented Chatham County in the Georgia House of Representatives. After retiring from the medical profession and civic life, he became a planter and by 1862 owned the Oglethorpe plantation on the South Carolina side of the river, growing wheat and rice. After the government passed the Sequestration Act in August 1861, Georgia District Judge Edward J. Harden appointed the seventy-year-old Daniell as the receiver, responsible for taking control of the sequestered properties of his friends and neighbors. It was a thankless job. "I imagine you're here regarding your house on Harris Street?"

"Doctor, I've traveled all the way from New York to contest your decision."

Dr. Daniell coughed into his fist. Amy McBain had always had a reputation for speaking her mind, and he sensed that after a journey through a war zone, she hadn't softened. "I'm sorry for the inconvenience, but our government enacted the law and I was appointed to enforce it, despite my personal feelings for some of the violators. You own a building in town and are living in New York. As such, you're considered an alien enemy. I had to sequester your property."

Amy slapped her palms on the desk, scattering Daniell's papers. "Doctor, that's outrageous and you know it."

"Mrs. Carson, you'll have an opportunity to present your case to Judge Harden. I will schedule a hearing for you in two weeks. That's the best I can do. Will you have representation?"

"No, sir. I will speak to the judge directly." Amy turned and left, slamming the door behind her.

Dr. Daniell shook his head, arranged his papers into a neat pile, and headed to the City Hotel barroom.

⁂

Dante stopped in his tracks as he approached Pulaski Square. He dropped his carpetbag and called, "Mistess Amy?"

Amy looked up. "Dante!"

The negro charged across the street, through the turnstile, and to within two feet of her. He panted, "Mistess Amy, you movin' back home?"

Amy thought Dante had aged well, despite a head of hair that hadn't been cut in months and an expanded belly. He still had that sleepy, eyes-half-closed look, even when excited. "Dante, it's so good to see you. I'm only here for a visit. I want you to meet someone." Sarah walked over with Jimmy in hand.

Dante said, "Hello, Missus."

Sarah smiled. "Hello, Dante. Welcome back. Say hello to Jimmy." The child tugged on Dante's trousers.

Dante squatted. "Hello, Jimmy. You hab de mos' bes' momma in de wuld." Dante liked Amy more than any white person—almost more than any black—he had ever known, for making him a cook at her restaurant. Other than the night that Andrew was murdered, the saddest days in Dante's adult life were when Miss Amy sold the restaurant and moved from Savannah with Massa Bob.

Jimmy laughed and waddled away on short, stubby legs. Sarah followed, waiting for the inevitable fall. Amy said, "Dante, I heard you're cooking at an army camp."

"Yessum. But dat obuh. Ah wan' tuh cook in uh restran' agin."

"I'll see what plans my father has for you. If he approves, I'll speak to some friends, but so many people have left town, and there are fewer restaurants." Then Amy smiled and said, "I also hear you have a special girl. Is that true?"

Dante flashed a full-toothed grin. "Ah sholy do, Mistess Amy. Ahsettuh. Massa Lamah own her."

Amy patted Dante's arm. "I hope it all turns out well for you." Dante thanked Amy, picked up his bag, and went to the house. Patty and Chloe greeted him as he entered the servants' door at the back. He assured them that he was in good health after his stint in the camp, and then went to his room next to the stables. He sat on his bed, lay back, and prayed that Miss Amy could help him. Two hours later, William shook him awake and told him to see Massa right away.

McBain's eyes followed Dante as he walked into the room. He didn't flash the bright smile that Dante had expected after his long absence. "Welcome back, Dante. How did you enjoy cooking for the officers?"

"Ah don' lahk it, Massa. No suh."

McBain leaned back in his chair. "How would you like to go back to the camp—tomorrow?"

Dante's eyebrows arched, horrified at the suggestion. "No suh, Massa. No."

McBain drummed his fingers on the desk. "Very well. I have some questions for you, and based on your answers, I'll decide where you'll work next."

Dante held his breath. "Yassuh."

"Good. You remember Sam the overseer?" Dante blinked twice at the sound of the name. "He disappeared from the Heritage the day before you left for the Jasper Greens. In fact, he whipped Hercules that day and you apparently saw it. Soldiers found him buried near the Heritage." Dante gulped. "It must have been done on the plantation or soon after he left, about the time you were there. Now, do you know who killed Sam?"

"No, Massa."

McBain stared at Dante for a full minute. Dante met his eyes, but his insides rumbled. "I visited the Heritage a few days ago. I found a small round hole in the side of one of the wagons. Mr. Donnelly said that no one has fired a gun there since he returned, other than him—at birds. Do you know how that hole got there?"

"No, Massa."

"Frankly, Dante, I'm not unhappy that Sam's dead. He was one of Andrew's murderers. But if there was a killing on my plantation, I must know about it. Someone from the Heritage knows what happened, and I believe you and Hercules do. You'd better fess up, or you're going to be in trouble. For the time being I've hired you out to cook for General Mercer's officers here in Savannah. You start tomorrow and can live here. Be thankful I'm not sending you to a camp outside of town. I can always change my mind."

Dante hung his head in disappointment at not getting restaurant work, but he was happy that he would be living at home and near Isetta. "Yassuh, Massa."

The study door flew open, banging into the wall. Amy bounced in the room with the look of a child on Christmas morning. "Father, Joseph and Danny are here!"

James stood, dashed around the desk, and escorted Dante out. He said, "You think real hard about Sam," and followed Amy. ❦

CHAPTER TWENTY-EIGHT

Danny's Prayer

October 1862

Joseph limped into the family parlor holding a sleepy Danny against his chest. James, Sarah, and Amy followed. Joseph handed Danny to his mother and embraced Amy. He said, "You must be mad coming here in the middle of a war."

Amy held him tight. "No, dear brother. I refuse to let this government of lunatics steal my property." She released him and announced, "I want to see my nephew." She took Danny from Sarah and kissed his forehead. "How you've grown, my precious boy."

Danny rubbed the sleep from his eyes and hugged her. "Aunt Amy!"

"Where's Jimmy?" Joseph demanded.

Amy smooched Danny on the cheek. "He's asleep. You can see him tomorrow."

James poured four glasses of port and they all sat. Danny curled up like a cat next to Amy on the sofa. The adults raised their glasses and James toasted, "To the family, together again." After everyone sipped, he asked, "Don't keep us in suspense, Joseph. How did you find Danny?"

Joseph stepped into the hallway and asked Chloe to put Danny to bed. After they left, Joseph closed the door, sat, took a deep breath, and explained, "Saving Danny is the good news." He looked around at his family. "There's some bad news, too. Hercules was shot—injured real bad—and I had to leave him. I don't know if he's still alive."

Joseph saw three sets of eyes focused on him. James clutched the arms of the chair. "My God, what do you mean?"

⁂

As Hercules lay dying, Joseph and Earl rowed towards Darien. Joseph felt helpless and weak. With all his money there was nothing he could do for his life-long coachman. Danny whispered over and over, "Please, God, please."

"LOOK!" Earl shouted, pointing to a three-masted, wooden-screw steamer chugging past the northern end of St. Simons Island. "Yankees! Let's get out of here!"

Joseph screamed, "No!" He handed his oar to Earl, stood, took off his shirt, and tied it to the barrel of his rifle, which he waved it back and forth over his head. He pulled his revolver and fired it in the air. "Earl, row to it! It's worth another twenty-five dollars."

The vessel changed course and sailed towards them. Joseph slipped back into his shirt and retook the oar. The ship pulled alongside and an officer in a blue uniform and cap shouted over the railing, "State your business."

Joseph called up to him, "Do you have a surgeon on board? I have a wounded man here. He needs immediate attention. I'll pay whatever you ask!"

The officer barked commands to his crew. Seconds later a sailor threw a line to Earl while others unrolled a rope ladder over the side. Still others lowered a stretcher attached to four ropes. Joseph and Earl strained to lift Hercules onto it, tucked his arms to his sides, and watched him ascend, as if he were rising to heaven.

Joseph lifted Danny onto the ladder. "Climb up, son. I'll be behind you." He turned to Earl. "Stay here. I'll let you know my plans in a minute."

When Joseph gained the deck the officer approached him. "I'm Acting Master Long. The negro has been taken to our surgeon. I'm no doctor, but he's in bad shape."

Danny shouted, "You have to save him, sir. You must!"

The officer stared at Danny's blood-soaked shirt. "Is this boy wounded?"

Joseph placed a hand on his son's shoulder. "The blood is from our negro."

Long asked, "Is it now rebel policy to bring their children to war?"

Joseph bit down and didn't respond to the insult. He introduced himself and Danny and explained their presence in the area, how Hercules had been shot, and their escape. "I didn't think we had a prayer of finding a doctor—then we saw your ship. You're our only hope."

Long said, "Our surgeon will report to me as soon as he's ministered to your man. In the meantime, I'll have a basin of water and a clean shirt sent to my quarters so your son can clean up. Petty Officer Irwin here will take you."

Joseph thanked the officer and he and Danny followed the sailor. Fifteen minutes later, with Danny wearing a Union navy shirt that fit like a full-length dress, they returned to Acting Master Long, who was in conversation with another officer.

Long smiled at the boy. "You look like you'll make a fine sailor, Danny."

Danny thanked him, not wanting to salute a Yankee. Long then introduced Joseph to the other officer. "Captain McBain, this is Dr. Braunstein."

The doctor reported, "Your negro was hit in the upper arm. The ball smashed a bone and then passed through his breast. The arm must be amputated. He's lost a lot of blood and is barely breathing. I'm not sure he'll survive, but we'll do all we can. I must get back to him now." Braunstein hurried off.

Joseph turned to Long. "Can we wait here? If he revives, he should see a familiar face. If he dies, I'd like to preside over his burial. I've known him my entire life. He's part of my family."

Long studied Joseph and tried to understand why a white man who kept a negro in bondage would think of him as a family member. "I'm sorry, but you can't stay. We're heading to St. Marys now. You have my word that we'll care for him. If he dies, we'll give him a proper burial at sea. If he lives, he'll need weeks to recover under proper medical care, which he can receive at our hospital on Hilton Head."

They heard Earl shout, "Captain McBain, we've got to leave now!"

Joseph walked to the side of the boat and replied, "Hold on, Earl. We'll be there in a few minutes." He returned to Long. "I have a small favor or two to ask. When you reach Hilton Head, would you write to me in Savannah about Hercules's fate? Also, I'd like to write a letter to him now and, if he lives, I ask that you read it to him. If he should die at sea, I'd like you to say a short prayer that my son will write now."

Long nodded. "Come to my quarters." He sat Danny at the small desk, handed him a pen and some paper, and said to Joseph, "I'll give you a couple of minutes."

With Joseph's help, Danny wrote, "Dear Lord, please take extra special care of Hercules. He was a good friend who showed me how to ride a horse. He saved my life and I never got to thank him. Please thank him for me and tell him that I miss him. Amen. Danny McBain." Joseph wrote his note to Hercules and left the papers and five gold coins on the desk.

They went to the top deck. Long said, "Captain, I hope that the next time we meet will be under more agreeable circumstances."

Joseph shook Long's hand and Danny, having warmed to the officer, saluted. Then they descended the ladder.

❧

Joseph refreshed his drink. "Hercules was in critical shape when I left, and many soldiers don't survive amputations. I believe the officer will keep his word and inform me. All we can do is pray for him."

James slumped in his chair as if he had been de-boned. He had lost his most trusted servant to either God or the Yankees. "The last year hasn't been kind to Hercules. He deserved better."

Joseph reasoned, "We can never recover from his loss, but we have Danny and Truvy back. And one of Andrew's murderers is dead and one is in jail, hopefully to be hanged. Now I'm going after the last one and I won't rest until I find him. Harold said he went to Florida, but I don't trust him."

Sarah said, "Maybe that girl, Miss Pender, knows something. I'll try to speak to her. James, now that we have the boys back, are you inclined to give her the reward? She gave you Harold. If you refuse she isn't likely to give us any more information."

Amy looked sideways at Sarah. "Mother, you seem very trusting of her."

Sarah held her daughter's hand. "Perhaps I am. She earned the reward, you can't dispute that. From what I know, she's quite young, orphaned, and somehow supports herself and her two sisters in a strange town with no family. She admitted that what she did to Hercules was wrong and apologized for it. And she was beaten senseless by a stranger. If all that doesn't merit some compassion and trust, I don't know what does."

James told Sarah, "I'm still reluctant to give her money, especially now with Hercules's fate so uncertain. Talk to her if you wish and see what she knows. If she gives us Willie I might change my mind. In the meantime, the servants will want to know where Hercules is. I'll have to tell them that he got shot while saving Danny and Joseph and we had to leave him with a Yankee doctor to save his life."

A howl from upstairs grabbed their attention. Joseph hobbled up the stairs to Danny's room. He saw Chloe standing by the bed, laughing at the boy, who was on his hands and knees, barking at JD, who was lying on his back, paws up, and tail thumping. Danny saw his father, hopped off the bed, and hugged him. "Chloe told me you got me JD." The dog barked. "This is the best present ever. I can't wait to show Truvy!"

"You're welcome, Danny." Joseph hugged his boy, relieved that he was home, and that he had made him so happy. But as he lay in bed that night, he couldn't shake the thought of finding Willie—the murderer of Andrew, assaulter of his father, and kidnapper of his son. He needed some idea of where to look. He anxiously awaited his mother's visit with the mystery girl.

⚬✿⚬

Katherine's luck turned even worse after her day in the hospital. She returned to work two days later, and although Mr. Lippman welcomed her back and paid her for the missed days, the hotel manager informed her that they didn't need a night-shift cleaning girl anymore and sent her home. She was down to one salary again. The next day Mrs. Duffy told her that she had to increase the weekly charge by ten dollars a week due to the soaring costs of food and wood for fuel. In mid October, with only one job and little savings, Katherine and her sisters moved to a cheaper place in a poor section of town.

The room featured one single bed, frayed furniture, creaky floors, no meals, and unshaven men in dirty clothing all about the streets. The sisters shared the kitchen with other boarders and ate rice, the one inexpensive food item in Savannah, and an occasional egg. Katherine had to find another job soon or they would have to move to the Poor House. She could never go back to the orphanage and risk being separated from Pauline and Mary. Paying for school for her sisters after the current term was impossible.

She considered asking twelve-year-old Pauline to find a job, which wouldn't be easy with so many adults looking for work, and slaveholders willing to hire out their girls at very cheap rates. Her only other option was to try to collect the reward money for turning in Harold, but she didn't know if the boys had been found or if Willie and Harold were in jail. Nor did she know her rights to the reward and assumed that she would have no way of forcing payment from a man as powerful and influential as Mr. McBain, who surely hated her for her actions against his coachman. Still, she was desperate and had to find the courage to visit Mrs. McBain and ask for half the reward.

Depressed at her situation, Katherine took her sisters to the Strand on the first Sunday after moving and watched them play tag. She sat on a bench, closed her eyes, listened to the girls' laughter, and tried to shut out her problems, if only for a few hours. She started to doze when she heard a voice. "Good afternoon, Miss Pender." Katherine looked up and saw an older woman smiling at her. "I'm Mrs. McBain. You came to my house a few weeks ago with information for my husband."

Katherine stood, surprised that the woman had sought her out. "Yes, of course, Mrs. McBain. Good afternoon."

Sarah stepped aside and said, "Miss Pender, please meet my daughter, Mrs. Carson. She's visiting from New York."

Katherine smiled at the beautiful woman with light-brown hair, hazel eyes, and full lips. "It's nice to meet you, Mrs. Carson." Amy returned the salutation, but couldn't help but stare at the black eye.

Sarah said, "We went to find you at Mrs. Duffy's. She told us you moved out five days ago but thought we might find you here." Sarah motioned to the bench. "Do you mind if we talk for a little bit?" Katherine sat on one end, Sarah in the middle, and Amy at the other end. "I wanted to tell you that the boys are back, safe and healthy. Thank you so much for telling us where to find Harold. My son is intent on finding his partner, Willie, but he has no idea where to look. Do you know where he might have gone?"

Katherine's heart sank when Mrs. McBain didn't mention the reward. "Thank God the boys are safe, ma'am, but I don't know anything about Willie or where he might be. And I want to apologize again for the pain I caused your coachman and family. I'm ashamed of my behavior."

Amy leaned forward and spoke past Sarah. "Miss Pender, my mother told me that your parents are deceased and you're taking care of your sisters. Do you mind if I ask your age and how long you've been here?"

Katherine took a deep breath. "I'll turn eighteen in two months, Mrs. Carson. We moved here from Thomasville one year ago."

Sarah said, "You poor girl. It sounds so sad. Your parents must have been very young. How did they pass?"

Katherine's lower lip trembled. She wished to keep her past a secret, but she also wanted Mrs. McBain to understand her behavior and not hold her in contempt. She watched little Mary try to catch Pauline, almost a foot taller and running backwards, as she spoke. "My father was an evil man. When my mother found out, she shot him dead. The marshal arrested her. While she was in jail awaiting trial, she caught yellow jack and died. We became orphans. We have no other family."

WHAP! Amy lost her grip on her purse and it smacked on the brick path. She picked it up and said, "I've never heard of anything so terrible."

Sarah said, "I'm so sorry. Did you come to Savannah after your parents died?"

"Not right away. A family from our church took us in. We didn't know them. The man was very mean and we ran away last November—to here."

Amy clutched her purse with both hands, preparing for another horror story. "Could that man have been worse than your father?"

Katherine gazed at her folded hands on her lap. "Nothing could have been worse than my father. But life with the other man was still a nightmare. When we escaped, I changed our names so he couldn't find us. My real name is Katherine Downes, not Penny Pender."

The women stared at each other, at a loss for words. Amy finally asked, "How have you survived this long?"

"I had my mother's savings—a few hundred dollars. I got a job at the Marshall House. Between those two sources we were able to live at a boarding house. But the savings didn't last and the pay wasn't enough. We were on the verge of eviction when I met Willie at the Marshall House." Katherine decided to pass over the incident with the drunk. "He said he'd pay me to frame a negro—your coachman—for trying to rape me. That bought us some time, and I got a day job as a seamstress. I just lost my job at the Marshall House and we had to move to a cheaper room in Yamacraw."

Sarah felt so badly for the girl that she held her hand. "Miss Pender—I mean Miss Downes, my heart weeps for you, it truly does."

Pauline and Mary ran up to Katherine, stopped a few yards from the bench, and stared at the strangers. Pauline asked, "Oldest Sister, can we go play in Johnson Square?"

Katherine said, "Pauline and Mary, please say hello to Mrs. McBain and Mrs. Carson." The girls curtsied to the smiling women. "Yes, you may go, but come back in fifteen minutes." The giggling girls ran off.

Sarah watched them for a few seconds and said, "They're adorable!" Amy nodded in agreement. Sarah turned to Katherine. "I admire your devotion to your sisters and your honesty with us. You've been a great help. The matter of the reward is up to my husband, but I wield some influence, and I will use it." She opened her purse and pulled out some bills. "I want you to have this now, to help in these hard times." She put the money in the girl's hand.

Katherine accepted the cash. "Thank you so much, Mrs. McBain. You don't know how much I appreciate it."

"You're welcome, my dear. And you have my word that we'll get back to you regarding the reward. Where can we find you?"

"At Mr. Lippman's on Congress Street. I'm not certain how much longer we'll be at our room in Yamacraw."

The women stood. Sarah said, "Thank you again. I'm so glad we had this chat." Sarah and Amy walked to their coach.

Katherine sat, exhausted, but relieved that someone seemed to understand her actions. When the coach pulled away she counted the money. Forty dollars! It would certainly help for a month or two, maybe even let her buy some bacon one day for supper. But she knew that soon she would be broke again.

That night after supper, while Danny was playing outside with JD, Sarah told James and Joseph of their talk with Katherine. "It's so sad. They've lived through unspeakable hardships. We have to give the girl the reward."

Amy had changed her attitude. "I'm convinced that she didn't put Hercules in jail—those men did. If Miss Downes didn't do it, they would have found another girl."

James asked, "She said her father did evil things. Did she say what?"

Sarah replied, "No. It was obviously too personal. It must have been horrible."

Amy said, "Horrible enough for a woman to shoot her own husband."

Joseph sliced a piece of chicken breast and pasted rice on it with his knife. "She doesn't know where Willie went, and that's what's important to me now. But she gave us Harold. In my mind, Father, she's worth the money."

Sarah replied, "I agree."

James said, "Frankly, I'm tired of Miss Pender—or should I now say Miss Downes? I have other things on my mind besides giving her money, like finding out about Hercules and getting him back." James put down his wine glass with a thump, adding an exclamation point to his statement.

Sarah said, "Dear, you always said that a man is as good as his word. I hope your emotions don't let you forget that."

James pushed away his plate and looked at his family. "I need to get some sleep. I'll be better in the morning." He walked from the room. His family could hear his sigh.

CHAPTER TWENTY-NINE

Mitchelville

October – November 1862

Hercules awoke and saw a man in a blue jacket staring down at him. He moved his head from side to side, but didn't recognize his surroundings. The man spoke. "Hercules, my name is Dr. Braunstein. You're under my care on a United States Navy ship." Hercules closed his eyes and vaguely remembered his ride with Danny. "You were shot and badly wounded on St. Simons Island. During your escape, Captain McBain of Savannah signaled us for help and we picked you up. You were minutes away from bleeding to death. I couldn't save your arm and had to amputate four inches below the shoulder."

Hercules tried to move his left arm but the scorching pain caused him to arch his back and moan. His head started to spin and he thought he might vomit. He gasped, "Sir, my shoulder's on fire."

The doctor sat in a chair next to the bed, helped him sit up, and said, "Drink this. It will take the pain away for awhile. Your recovery will take some time." Hercules held the doctor's wrist and gulped down the bitter liquid.

Hercules asked, "Can I see Master Joseph?"

"If you mean Captain McBain, he isn't here. We were on a run to St. Marys when he hailed us. You needed immediate treatment and we couldn't delay our mission. He and his son had to leave. He left some coins and a letter for you. Would you like me to read it now?" Hercules nodded. Braunstein took a piece of paper from a nearby table.

Hercules, the Yankee captain said I can't wait on the ship, so I have no choice but to leave you. I will be forever grateful to you for saving our lives. Captain Long says that when the ship reaches Hilton Head, you can choose between staying with them or returning to Savannah. I urge you to come home, where we will take care of you. If you decide to stay on Hilton Head, remember that you are always welcome back here. I left one hundred dollars in gold coins for you. We will hold your belongings and pray for you. Captain Joseph McBain.

Hercules closed his eyes. The laudanum took hold and he drifted asleep.

Over the following days Hercules remained in bed, where he was tended to by the doctor and an orderly and visited by Captain Long. When food was brought to him, mashed and cut into bite-size morsels, he was able to push himself up with his right hand into a sitting position, and eat with a fork. On the third day, during supper, he laid his fork on his plate while he propped himself up into a more comfortable position. The fork fell off the left side of the plate. Hercules instinctively reached for it with his missing left hand and lost his balance. He knocked the plate off the bed, scattering the food over the floor. He cursed out loud and swore revenge on Kitt.

On the fifth day, the doctor suggested that Hercules get dressed and walk around the deck for exercise. A crewman brought him a sailor's outfit. It took him twenty curse-filled minutes to dress and button the shirt and pants, but he was able to do it successfully. For the most part the crew made him feel welcome.

When the ship docked at Hilton Head the captain came to his room. "Hercules, I informed Captain McBain that you can remain here as a free man or return to him as a slave. If you choose to stay, you will live in the camp hospital until your wound heals. Then you will transfer to the negro barracks while you and others build a cabin in a new village set aside for freed slaves. You must work to support yourself. And let me repeat—you will be a free man."

Hercules had thought of little else during the past week. He missed Patience—their night of intimacy still fresh in his mind—and remembered his promise not to leave her and the boys. He also considered where he would be better off with only one arm. He knew that Massa would treat him well, but he had the same worry as all the other Heritage slaves—what happens when Massa dies or sells the plantation? Also, he felt fate had put him with the Yankees. He turned down a chance at freedom on St. Simons Island, got shot, and wound up with another opportunity. God seemed to be telling him to stay on Hilton Head. And if the North won the war, he would be reunited with Patience without fear of separation. "I'll stay here, sir."

The captain shook his hand. "Hercules, you've made the right choice. I'll write to Captain McBain about your decision. I'll take you to the hospital now."

Hercules followed the officer down the gangway. He stumbled on a wooden strip and reached for the railing with his left hand to balance himself. He fell to the floor. Captain Long knelt by his side, pulled out his kerchief, and dabbed at Hercules's eyebrow. Hercules saw his blood on it. Long said, "It doesn't look too bad. The doctor will bandage it at the hospital." Hercules felt his face steam in embarrassment. It seemed he couldn't do anything without someone else's help, and would spend the rest of his life dependent on others, a fate he considered worse than death. He knew he had to overcome his disability if he were to live with any dignity.

He and Long continued down the pier and across the military campgrounds.

Hercules had stopped at Hilton Head with Master McBain four years earlier on a trip to Charleston. At that time the landing had just one old wooden house. Now, the house had been renovated and repainted and there were three four-hundred-foot-long storehouses, ordnance buildings, barracks, a mansion—probably for the commanding general, and a hospital. In the distance, beyond the village, he saw a large fenced-in structure which he guessed was the prison.

The surgeon put Hercules in a bed at the far end of the first floor of the hospital. During the next three weeks a doctor cleaned and dressed his wound every morning and evening. Each day, with slowly decreasing degrees of difficulty, Hercules shaved and dressed himself. He walked to the camp corral and stables and got to know the sergeant in charge, who took a liking to him and promised to hire him after his release from the hospital. Hercules, despite all the frustrations, gradually adjusted to life with one arm.

Three weeks after Hercules arrived on Hilton Head, the doctor told him that his wound had healed to the point where he could start working and building his cabin. An hour later an officer and a black man came to his bed. The officer said, "Hercules, I'm Captain Putnam and this is Lafayette. He's going to show you Mitchelville, where you, he, and another man will build a cabin for your permanent residence and live with the other contrabands. Despite your injury, you will still be expected to find work and support yourself."

Hercules said, "I already have work at the government corral, sir."

"Very good. You will live in the negro barracks until your cabin is completed. I'll leave you now with Lafayette. I'm glad you're with us."

Hercules and Lafayette walked to Mitchelville. Lafayette explained that the Yankees referred to the black folk on Hilton Head as "contrabands" because they were deemed property taken from the enemy in war. When they reached Mitchelville, Hercules surveyed the streets lined with newly built, simple, one-story cabins, and others in various stages of construction. He asked Lafayette, "How did this all come about—a separate town for us?"

Lafayette, who had been enslaved on Hilton Head when it fell to the Yankees, explained the history. When Brigadier General Ormsby Mitchel arrived on the island in the late summer of 1862 to take over the command of the Department of the South, he was appalled at the filthy, crowded barracks of the thousand freed negroes who had lived on the island when the Union military took control, and the hundreds of others who had escaped to Hilton Head from nearby islands. He allocated a twenty-acre plot of land one-and-a-half miles from the Union camp and told the freed slaves that they had to build their own living quarters and work to support their families. As a contest, General Mitchel asked the army engineers and a group of contrabands each to design and build a model cabin for the village. Mitchel selected the freedmen's version, which looked similar to a typical plantation slave structure. He provided the blacks with lumber, nails, and tools, and they went to work. Each house had a garden in back for raising vegetables and chickens, which the families could consume or sell to the white soldiers. Unfortunately, General Mitchel never saw the community develop. A few weeks before Hercules arrived, he succumbed to yellow fever and died.

Hercules was elated at the idea of a community of black folks who would live by their own labor and run their own affairs. He hoped it would work out better for him than the negro colony on St. Simons Island.

Hercules moved into the negro barracks while he, Lafayette, and King, also unmarried, built their cabin with help from other contrabands. Hercules could not hold a nail in place to hammer, but he did carry lumber and other materials to the site and held boards in place with one hand while the others hammered. He was also able to rest a plank on a bench, secure it with a knee, and saw with his right hand. Occasionally he dropped things and had to ask for help with tasks he easily could have done by himself before his injury, like tying a knot in a rope, but these incidents occurred with diminishing frequency. He rarely felt sorry for himself, but each time his missing limb caused an inconvenience, he swore vengeance on Kitt.

The sergeant kept his word and gave Hercules a job at the stables watering, feeding, and exercising horses for forty cents a day, better than the pay for a cotton-field worker, who received twenty-five cents. The sergeant also let him try bridling, saddling, and riding a horse. As with building the cabin, in the beginning Hercules dropped many items and had difficulty figuring out how to perform certain tasks, like saddling a horse and buckling the strap with one hand. The sergeant once witnessed Hercules kicking a bucket in frustration. He patted him on the back and said, "You're doing fine. It's going to take time, but you'll get it. I know you will." Several weeks later Hercules, using his right hand, teeth, and chin, could saddle and ride horses on his own.

Through these trials, Hercules's mind often wandered back to Savannah, Patience, and the McBains. He knew that he would return one day.

⸎

A few weeks after Hercules arrived at Hilton Head, a soldier delivered a letter to Joseph at home. He brought it into his father's study and read aloud. "Captain McBain, in keeping with my promise to inform you about Hercules, I am able to report that he survived the amputation without infection and is slowly regaining his strength. He has informed the military authorities here that he wishes to remain on Hilton Head as a free man. He thanks you and your father for taking care of him all these years and looks forward to seeing you after the war." The two men sat in silence for a minute. Then, shaking his head, James went upstairs to lie down.

The McBains had to explain to their servants why Hercules would not be coming back, but they couldn't admit that he chose to stay with the Yankees.

Instead, they told them that the Yankee doctors were keeping him until he recovered fully from his injury and learned to adapt to life with one arm, which would take many months. Sarah told Patience, who broke down in tears and fell into the white woman's arms. Joseph told Dante and the other Pulaski Square servants, who were stunned and wondered amongst themselves if Hercules would ever return.

⌘

Amy spent from mid October to mid November with her family, touring Savannah, visiting friends, and showing off Jimmy. Her enjoyment was marred in late October by a notice from Dr. Daniell the day before her sequestration hearing that Judge Harden had taken ill and the case had to be delayed by several weeks. Amy protested to Daniell that she had to leave by the end of November, but the doctor responded that there was nothing he could do about it.

Sarah spent as much time as possible with Amy, but still spent several hours a day volunteering at the Poor House and Hospital and collecting clothes and food for the Georgia Relief and Hospital Association. Danny returned to school a hero and never tired of describing his kidnapping ordeal to his friends. With each retelling, Willie and Harold got meaner, and the spider grew bigger. He spent his afternoons playing in Pulaski Square with Truvy and a new neighbor, Parker Lee Tyler, whose father had recently moved to town to take the position of head postmaster for Savannah. They boys were usually joined by Jimmy and JD.

Joseph went to the Oglethorpe Light Infantry headquarters each day, recruiting, raising donations of food and clothing, getting medical reports on injured soldiers, and receiving shipments from the front of Oglethorpe Company bodies, all of whom he knew. Too often Joseph attended funeral services of acquaintances and consoled mourning families. James ran the business and, because of the slowdown in activity, hired out more of his men to the army, which eliminated some of the financial burden of supporting so many slaves, and gained the gratitude of General Mercer.

One night over supper, Amy said to her father, "I'm visiting Mary Marshall in the morning. Dante has told me he wants to cook in a restaurant. Can I offer him?"

James shook his head. "No. He's hired out to General Mercer for six months. The officers enjoy his cooking, and I'm not inclined to do anything special for him. I'm certain he knows something about Sam's death, though he denies any knowledge of it."

"As far as I'm concerned," Joseph said, "if he had anything to do with killing Sam, I'd give him a reward."

James exhaled and closed his eyes. He didn't want to argue with his family. "Today he asked for permission to marry one of Charlie Lamar's girls. I haven't given it. Does anyone object?"

Sarah said, "James! Of course I don't object. It's about time he got married. You tell him he has our permission."

Amy said, "I want to attend the ceremony. Ask the Lamars to hold it as soon as possible. I don't have much time left."

Joseph raised his glass. "Here's to Dante, Father. I'll arrange a visit with Charlie and Caro to seek their approval."

Amy became increasingly agitated during the days leading up to the sequestration case, which had been rescheduled for November 17. On the morning of the hearing, she joined her parents after breakfast in the family parlor and plopped into a chair. "I can't wait for this to be over. I walk by MY house each day and can't even knock on MY door and speak to MY tenants. The government is even collecting MY rents! The Confederacy says it's fighting a war to free itself from an oppressive central government that doesn't respect individual property rights. In its place it has set up an oppressive central government that doesn't respect individual property rights."

James laughed. "Do you plan to express that to Judge Harden?"

"I don't want to annoy him. I hear that few people win sequestration appeals."

James said, "We can only hope for the best. I still think you should have hired a lawyer to represent you, but it's too late now. We should leave for the court house."

With her father and mother watching from the spectators' section at the back of the courtroom, Amy sat in front of Judge Harden, who hunched forward in his chair, his folded arms resting on the elevated desk. He studied the papers in front of him, twice looking at his pocket watch, indicating that he would rather be anywhere but listening to these matters. He finally looked up and smiled at Amy, the daughter of his good friend James McBain. Harden had seen her grow from a spoiled child into a beautiful, sophisticated woman. He was fond of her, but the law was the law, and he administered it judiciously, which earned him great respect from most folks in town.

First, the judge had Daniell present the government's case, which the doctor did in a monotone voice that had everyone in the room yawning. Even Amy felt drowsy.

After Dr. Daniell finished, Judge Harden asked Amy, "Mrs. Carson, I understand that you wish to represent yourself. Is that true?"

"Yes, sir."

"Then please proceed."

Amy stood and addressed the judge. "First, your honor, I would like to ex-
plain the issue of my current residence. As you and Dr. Daniell know, until recently I've resided in Georgia my entire life. I married a New Yorker who I met in
Savannah and we lived in my house on Harris Street with no thought of moving.
He quit his job as a reporter and worked with me in my restaurant. We were very
happy here. Then, one day"—she paused before shouting—"LOCAL VIGILAN-
TES BEAT HIM SENSELESS!" Judge Harden straightened at her raised voice.
Amy stared at Dr. Daniell. "We had no choice but to leave here." She turned back
to the judge. "I was run out of my own hometown by a bunch of criminals, and
for that, my property is confiscated? In what society is that considered justice?"

Amy paused while the judge cleaned his eyeglasses on the sleeve of his robe.
She removed a newspaper clipping from her purse and held it up. "Even the Confederate Congress agrees with me. This year's amendment to the sequestration
act exonerates me from being a so-called alien enemy. It states ever so clearly
that married women who are natives of Confederate states and didn't voluntarily
contribute to the cause of the enemy are not deemed alien enemies. What more,
your honor, do you need?"

Dr. Daniell stood and said, "Your honor, I'm aware of that amendment. At
first glance, it does clear Mrs. Carson. But she is the wife of a northern newspaper
reporter who helps the cause of the enemy by writing lies about the Confederacy."

Amy took a step towards Dr. Daniell, as if she were about to charge at him,
but stopped. She pointed a finger at the man. "That is not true, sir. My husband
reports honestly about his observations and experiences. Otherwise he wouldn't
have taken the position!" Amy then turned to Judge Harden. "Your honor, Dr.
Daniell claims that my husband aids the enemy by writing lies about the Confederacy. Let him show you proof of it. Just one article."

Judge Harden shifted his eyes to Daniell.

The receiver looked down and slowly shook his head. Judge Harden shuffled the papers on his desk and pretended to read something. He took one last
glimpse of Amy and announced, "I rule that by the amendment of February 15,
1862, to the original Sequestration Act, Mrs. Carson is not an alien enemy of
these Confederate States and that she is entitled to retain the title to all her property, including her house on Harris Street, as well as the accumulated rents." He
banged down his gavel. "That is all."

Amy stood and said, "Thank you, your honor." She marched from the courtroom without looking at Dr. Daniell, who stood with his hands in his pockets,
examining his notes. He, too, was happy that the affair was over. James and Sarah
McBain approached him, bid farewell to their friend, and followed Amy from the
courtroom.

On the ride home from the hearing, Amy took a deep breath and said, "I can
finally relax and enjoy my last few weeks here. Father, tomorrow I'm transferring

the title of my house to you for one dollar. Then I won't have to worry about it again."

James replied, somewhat meekly, "Whatever you say, Amy."

That night, the McBains celebrated Amy's victory over supper. James raised his wine glass and said, "Amy, you would make a great lawyer, if women were allowed in that profession. I think you frightened Judge Harden and Dr. Daniell half to death."

Amy laughed. "That was my plan. But it helps when the other side has a weak case. Now, tomorrow, I'm taking my son, nephew, and mother on a picnic."

The next morning, Amy sat in the family parlor with her father, reading the morning newspaper, when her mother walked in. Sarah said, "Amy, I'm going to the hospital for a few hours. We'll go on our picnic when Danny comes home from school."

Amy said, "That sounds good," and went back to the paper.

Sarah bid them goodbye and made it to the hall when she heard her daughter scream, "I don't believe it!" Sarah returned to the room.

Amy looked up from the newspaper, her face as white as a cotton ball. "Listen to this article! 'The Yankees and Freedom of the Press. Major General Ulysses S. Grant had a reporter arrested for writing an article under an alias about his heavy drinking while on duty. Robert Carson of the *New York Standard* has been shipped to Alton Prison in Illinois for exercising his right of freedom of speech, though he denies he wrote the article. This outrage is in accordance with the Lincolnites' concept of other freedoms guaranteed by the Constitution. Will our friends in the north ever see the right of habeas corpus restored?'" Amy nearly choked on her words. "They arrested Bob!"

Sarah said, "Good heavens! What are you going to do?"

"I have no choice! I'll go home and then take the cars to Illinois. Bob must have written to me from jail and is awaiting an answer. Father, I've got to get to Hilton Head. From there I'll catch a ship to New York."

James reached over for the newspaper and said, "That will take some work. General Mercer must allow you to go on the boat that exchanges official communications between us and the Yankees, and there are only a few of those each week. Then the Yankees have to accept your pass from this General Sherman."

Amy said, "I'll handle the Yankees. Please speak to General Mercer. Remind him of all the men you've hired out to his army. He'll have a boat for me." She slapped the arm of the sofa. "I hate this war. Both sides are run by idiots."

❧

Two days later, Amy stood on a pier hugging her family goodbye. They all knew that they probably wouldn't be able to communicate again until after the war. Amy took Jimmy from Colleen and presented him to Sarah, James, Joseph, and Danny for last kisses. Danny asked Aunt Amy to kiss his ma and sister for him. Joseph handed Amy a letter for Emily.

A sailor called, "We're leaving, Mrs. Carson." Amy, Colleen, and Jimmy squeezed onto a bench at the stern of the skiff manned by six sailors and an officer and pushed off. As they passed over the pilings at the western tip of Elba Island, one of the sailors hoisted a flag of truce. A Union patrol boat steamed from the South Carolina side of the river and pulled alongside. The Confederate officer shouted, "I have correspondence from General Mercer for General Hunter. We also have a passenger who has a passport signed by U.S. Major General William T. Sherman to cross into Union lines. Will you take Mrs. Carson, her child, and servant to Hilton Head Island so they can catch a ship to New York?" The officer held out Amy's pass.

The Yankee captain read it, glanced at the three passengers, and returned it. He said, "We'll take care of Mrs. Carson." Amy, Jimmy, and Colleen boarded the Yankee ship. Five days later Amy was in her New York City townhouse, preparing to leave for Illinois. She missed her family and Savannah more than ever.

◠◡◠

Amy's early departure left a pall over the McBain household. Joseph loved his sister and hated to see her go. He now became easily irritated. The day after she left, over supper, Joseph saw Danny sneak a piece of bread off his plate and lower it to his side. He leaned back in his chair, looked under the table, and saw JD sitting on his haunches snatching the food into his mouth. "Son, I've told you at least ten times that the dog is not allowed in the dining room. Take him away. You can play later."

Danny got up and whistled. JD followed him from the room. When he returned to his seat, Danny said, "Pa, I miss Aunt Amy and Jimmy. Can we go to New York and see them and Ma and Charlotte?"

"Son, you know we can't travel to New York while the war is going on. Now, please eat your soup."

The seven-year-old held the dripping soup spoon to his lips, slurped in the liquid with as much noise as possible, and said, "Ahhhhhhhh!"

Joseph reached over and held Danny's wrist. "If you continue to misbehave, I'll send JD to the Heritage to live with the rattlesnakes until you learn some manners."

Danny's lips turned down. "I'm sorry, Pa."

Sarah and James looked at each other and smiled, thinking how much Danny acted like his father when Joseph was the same age.

The City Exchange bell halted their conversation. The adults looked towards the window and listened. The ringing stopped, followed by a moment of silence, in turn followed by three gongs. James said, "Beat three."

Danny banged the spoon against the bowl three times. Joseph glared at his son and the boy stopped. "What do three bells mean, Pa?"

"It means that there's a fire in beat three, the northwest side of town. That tells the fire companies where to pull their engines."

The McBains ate quietly, concentrating on the far-off shouts of the firemen on the street. Soon, the bells of the Independent Presbyterian Church and the guard house joined in. James mused, "This is a big one."

The servants cleared the soup bowls and put down clean dishes. William carried in a domed silver serving tray. Lilly removed the cover and William served the pork chops. Halfway through the meal someone knocked on the front door. William entered the dining room and said, "Mrs. McBain, Mrs. Anderson said the fire has burned down several buildings and they're taking the displaced people to the Poor House. She's gathering all the volunteers and says they could use your help."

Sarah told William to have Jefferson get the coach ready. James asked, "Is there anything Joseph and I can do?"

"I don't know. If they need more help, I'll send Jefferson for you." She kissed everyone on the cheek and left.

When the men finished supper, Joseph said to Danny, "You can go to your room and play with JD now. I want to talk to Grandpa."

The boy leaped from his chair, his white napkin still hanging from the neck of his shirt, and ran from the room. The men then discussed affairs at the Heritage—the hiring out of more men to the army, trying to sell bricks and lumber to the military at inland fortifications, and supplying proper rations to the slaves. The long conversation had them refilling their wine glasses several times. Before they knew it, they heard voices at the front door. James looked at his pocket watch. "Ten o'clock already. That must be Sarah. Let's greet her."

They walked into the hallway and saw Sarah and William helping three girls with their carpetbags. Sarah looked at James and Joseph. "Their boarding house burned down. The Poor House is full and they have no place to go. I'm letting them stay here for a few nights."

Katherine Downes looked at the men and said, "Sirs, we can't thank you enough." ⚮

PART 4

∾

"Jutht Two"
November 1862 – December 1863

CHAPTER THIRTY

"Jutht Two"

November - December 1862

Sarah felt the bed shake about every thirty seconds. She finally said, softly, "I know you're awake, dear. What's wrong?"

James whispered, though no one other than Sarah could hear him, "I'll find a clean, safe place for them in the morning."

Sarah rolled on her side and faced her husband. She could barely make out his silver hair in the darkness. "Why don't we let them stay here for a little while, with all they've been through? It's our Christian duty to help."

James thought he deserved a few weeks of peace and quiet after all he'd been through. He doubted he would get either with three young female strangers in the house. "Sarah, you know we don't have room."

"Of course we do with Amy gone." Sarah sat up and rested against the headboard. "It will be nice to have some life in the house. It's so quiet now. And just think, Danny will have playmates. He's surrounded by adults."

James guessed that the last thing Danny wanted was a couple of girls for playmates, but he heard Sarah's voice rise in excitement at having more children around. She had always wanted a bigger family and now she would have one, if only temporarily. "We certainly can't have the older one in the house when Hercules returns."

"I agree, but Hercules isn't coming back. For better or worse, he's staying with the Yankees. However, we can't let the servants know that Katherine put Hercules in jail. Only Joseph, you, and I know that, and we must keep it a secret. For now, those girls are homeless and we have to do something."

James sighed. "All right, but just for a few days. And I mean just a few."

Sarah rubbed her husband's arm. "James, if you had given Miss Downes the reward, which she earned, then the sisters wouldn't have been living in the building that burned down, and they wouldn't be with us now. In a sense, I'm glad that you didn't, because I'm happy to have them here, but I want you to give her the money tomorrow. That's the right thing to do. Please stop putting it off."

James considered going downstairs to his study and the whiskey cabinet. "I will, and then they'll have enough money to get their own place. Good night, dear." James rolled over. Sarah smiled, eased down, and went to sleep.

Katherine got up when she heard the knock on the door. She put on her wrapper—a morning dress she had managed to pack before leaving the burning building—and answered it, while Pauline and Mary pulled the covers up to their necks. A black woman the same height as Katherine, but much wider, walked in. She wore a grey dress, white apron, and white cap, and held a white ceramic basin of water with several towels draped over her arm. Her toothy smile lit up the room. "Mawnin', l'il angels. Call me Chloe. Time fuh breakfus." Katherine stepped aside as Chloe placed the big bowl on the marble-top washstand. Chloe said to her, "If you Mistess Katrin, Massa Joesup want tuh see you in de fambly polluh." Chloe waved to Pauline and Mary and left.

Katherine washed her face, brushed her teeth, combed her hair, and pulled it back into a single bun. Then she donned her shimmy, petticoat, blue dress, and blue and white bodice, the clothing she was wearing when they escaped the fire. She didn't know what the man wanted, but she had to try to look her best. After one last peek in the mirror she told her sisters, "Wash up, get dressed, and come downstairs. And be on your best behavior. Do you hear me, Mary?"

"Yeth, Oldestht Thithter."

William greeted Katherine at the bottom of the stairs. "Good morning, Miss Katherine. Please come with me. Captain McBain wants to speak with you."

She entered the family parlor and Joseph, dressed in his uniform, put down a book, and stood by the sofa. "Good morning, Miss Downes. Please have a seat. You all slept well, I hope?"

Katherine looked at Joseph—the hazel eyes, dirty-blond hair parted in the middle, straight nose, and dimpled cheeks and thought him the handsomest man she had ever seen. She knew right away that he was Mrs. Carson's brother. She sat and folded her hands on her lap. "Yes, sir. Thank you again for your kindness."

Joseph pulled a chair next to the sofa. "We're glad we could help. I want to thank you for telling us about Harold. He's in jail, where he belongs, but I must find his partner, Willie. He's caused us great pain. My mother said that you don't know where he is. I implore you to search your memory."

Katherine smelled a hint of cologne on the man. "I only met him a few times, Captain. He's very mean and owes me money. Believe me, if I knew his where-abouts, I'd tell you. I'd like to see him in jail, too."

"Do you know anything about him—where he's from, if he has family? Some-one else who might know him?"

Katherine shook her head. "I'm sorry, sir, but I never wanted to learn any-thing about him. He made me feel so uncomfortable. After we conducted our business, I couldn't wait to get away from him."

There was no hesitation in her voice and Joseph concluded that she was telling the truth. He decided not to press her any further. He leaned to within a few feet of her face and stared into her green eyes. Her heart started to beat faster as she held his gaze. He said, "I'm glad to see your injury is healing nicely." He leaned back in his chair.

She lightly touched the bruise. "I'm glad it's almost gone. That's all people noticed about me."

Joseph laughed. "Miss Downes, believe me, there's plenty to notice about you. Did the police ever find the man who attacked you?"

Katherine felt at ease with Joseph's pleasant manner. "No, sir. I never heard from them."

"They're overworked and undermanned," he explained. "Do you know anything about him? Maybe I can convince them to do something."

"He told me his name was Peyton Smith and he was in town for business. But I'd rather forget about him, and I'd like to avoid the police after lying to them about your coachman. I'm so sorry."

Joseph said, "Believe me, we forgive you. My mother feels that Harold and Willie put Hercules in jail and I agree. They simply used you to achieve their goals."

"Thank you, Captain, but I'll carry the guilt for the rest of my life. I don't know what I'll say if I see him."

Joseph stood. "You should know that Hercules was shot and is being cared for by the Yankees on Hilton Head. It's a long story, but you don't have to worry about crossing paths with him for the time being. And only my parents and I know about your involvement in his arrest." With a sweep of his arm he motioned to the door. "Come, let's have breakfast." She followed him into the empty dining room. Joseph walked to the far side of the table and said, "I believe Mother wants you to sit here." Katherine stepped over to him. For the first time in her life, a man held a chair for her.

She smiled and said, "Thank you, sir." The chair slid gently behind her knees.

Danny stopped in his tracks outside his bedroom door. He asked, "Who are you?"

The shorter of the two girls knelt and held out her hand to JD at Danny's feet, and tried to entice the dog. The taller one said, "I'm Pauline and this is my sister, Mary. We slept here last night. Did your boarding house burn down, too?"

The boy's eyes shifted from one girl to the other. "Boarding house? I'm Danny McBain. I live here with my pa and grandparents."

Unable to get JD to do more than sniff her hand, Mary stood and said, "We almotht died."

Danny's eyes opened as wide as silver dollars. He thought he was having a bad dream. Sarah emerged from her bedroom and spoke to the gathering across the stairwell. "Danny, I see you've met two of our house guests. Their residence was destroyed in last night's fire and they're going to stay with us until they find another home."

Danny finally blinked. "Oh."

Mary asked Danny, "Do you want to play after thcool?"

Sarah said, "You can talk about playing later. Breakfast is ready."

Danny raced down the stairs and JD bounded after him, but the dog stopped at the dining room door. The girls followed Mrs. McBain and saw Katherine sitting with the McBain men at the ten-foot-long, black walnut table under a glittering chandelier. Sarah placed the girls on one side of the table with Katherine in the middle, Joseph and Danny on the other side, and she and James at the ends.

The girls stared at the shining silver utensils, sparkling glasses, snow-white plates with green scrolls around the edges and a red "M" in the middle. Pauline thought that this must be what rich people's weddings were like, but they were only having breakfast.

Sarah said, "Katherine, Pauline, and Mary, last night you met my husband, Mr. McBain, and my son, Captain McBain. Pauline and Mary just met Danny upstairs. Katherine, this is my grandson, Danny."

Katherine said, "It's a pleasure to meet you, Danny. You are a very handsome young man."

Mary raised her hand and said, "I think tho, too!" Katherine gently lowered the little girl's arm.

Danny blushed and looked down as the adults laughed. He said, "Pleased to meet you, Miss Katherine."

Mary pointed at her plate. "Look, the 'M' ith made of little brickth!"

Katherine said, "Mary, it's 'bricks. Brick-suh.'" She explained to the McBains, "Mary has a lisp. We used to think it was cute and let it go. Now we're trying to fix it."

James explained, "We have a plantation, Mary. We make bricks there."

Joseph studied the three girls. Katherine was truly beautiful and composed beyond her years. Whatever she was doing—eating, talking, listening—she always kept an eye on her sisters. He imagined that every bachelor in town would pursue her once the war ended. He thought Pauline would grow to be just as attractive as Katherine. She was almost as tall as her older sister, had white skin and green eyes. She pulled her light red hair straight back and let it hang to her shoulders. Mary, who he guessed to be a little younger than seven-year-old Danny, had wavy red hair, white skin dotted with freckles, green eyes, and a stubby nose. She wouldn't be as beautiful as her older sisters, but her constant smile revealed an innocent, internal happiness. He was interested to see how Danny would react to her.

William, Lilly, and Patty walked in, each holding a domed silver serving tray, which they placed on a side table. Sarah introduced the sisters to the servants, who smiled and half bowed. Katherine said "Nice to meet you," while Pauline and Mary, who had never before been formally introduced to negroes, stood and curtsied.

William served pancakes and bacon to the boarders. Mary's eyes followed his hand as it moved from the tray to her plate and back. Danny thought she might hypnotize herself. The girls had been taught by their mother to wait for everyone to be served before eating, but Katherine had to hold down Mary's hand to remind her. William placed a sauce boat in front of Mary. Sarah said, "Because of the blockade, we have no maple syrup, but we do have peach preserves for your pancakes."

Pauline announced, "I'll say the prayer."

Katherine put a hand on her shoulder. "Pauline, we're guests. We don't decide to say a prayer. Please be quiet and eat."

Pauline looked at the McBains, lowered her head, and said, "Sorry."

Sarah didn't want Pauline to feel uncomfortable. "We don't usually say a prayer at breakfast, Pauline, but I think it would be appropriate on this occasion, after the Lord saved so many lives from last night's fire. Please, go ahead."

Danny peeked at his father, who slowly shook his head, as if to say, "Ssssshhh."

Pauline closed her eyes. "Dear Lord, thank you for this meal and the many blessings that you have bestowed upon us. And thank you for letting us meet the McBain family, the nicest people in the world. Please give them extra special blessings. Amen."

Everyone said, "Amen." Sarah glowed at Pauline's respect. James said, "That was very nice, Pauline. Thank you. Do you go to a church in Savannah?"

Katherine put down her cup of chicory, a bitter substitute for coffee and tea, other casualties of the blockade, but made more palatable with enough milk, and answered, "We're Baptists, sir, but we've only been to the church in Savannah once. We don't want the pastor here to contact the church in Thomasville and reveal our location."

James, who had learned of the girls' plight from Sarah, nodded slowly. "Yes, I understand."

Mary lathered her pancakes with preserves as a bricklayer would spread mortar on a brick, sliced into them, took a big bite, and started to hum as she chewed, a habit she had adopted to block out the voice of Mr. Wells, and continued at Mrs. Duffy's to drown out the slurping of the other residents. "Hmmmm, hmm, hmmmmm, hmm, hmm."

Katherine gasped, "Marrrreeee! No humming!"

The girl raised her eyes without moving her head and saw the others looking at her. "Oooopth. Thorry." James, Sarah, and Joseph smiled at the antics of the youngster.

Danny chewed on his first bite of pancake and noticed that Mary already had finished half her portion. He wondered when she had last eaten. "Mary, where are your parents?"

The young girl gulped down her food, but Katherine answered for her. "Our parents died when we were very young, Danny. They're no longer with us."

Danny frowned. "I'm sorry. I didn't know."

"You don't have to apologize. You asked a sensible question. Sometimes the answers aren't happy, but you don't know until you ask."

Joseph saw his mother nod at how deftly the girl handled Danny.

William reappeared and saw Mary's empty plate. "Would you like more pancakes, Miss Mary?"

Mary looked up at Katherine, who arched her eyebrows and silently mouthed, "No!"

Mary turned to William, clasped her hands under her chin, and said, "Juth two."

The McBains, including Danny, and William laughed out loud. Katherine closed her eyes and shook her head. Pauline said, "Dear Lord." William lay two pancakes and two strips of bacon on the girl's plate.

As Mary reached for the preserves, Sarah explained the rules of the house. "Until you find other suitable accommodations, you may stay here. We have breakfast every morning at seven, like today, and at eight on Sundays. During the week you'll have dinner here after school. On weekends we have dinner at one o'clock. We sit for supper every night at seven, and I expect you to be clean, dressed, and punctual at the dining table. You may walk to and from school, but on rainy days our coachman Jefferson will drive you. You must perform your school lessons when you get home, after milk and cornbread." James and Joseph glanced at each other. Clearly, Sarah had spent some time formulating these rules. "You may study and read in the family parlor, but you mustn't go into Mr. McBain's study or the formal parlor unless invited. If there's still daylight after you finish, or on the weekends, you may play in the square or sit in our garden. You must be in the house before dark. Always be polite to our servants and remember to say 'please' and 'thank you.' I will arrange a bathing schedule for you."

Katherine answered, "Yes, Mrs. McBain. We'll do anything you ask."

Sarah continued, "I know you lost some of your possessions in the fire. After breakfast I want Nannie to measure you. She, Chloe, and Dolly are excellent seamstresses and I have some homespun material that will make pretty dresses and petticoats. Then we'll drive to town and buy you other necessities."

Katherine thanked the woman. Although they had saved some of their old clothes from the fire, Katherine felt they wouldn't fit in with their new surroundings. Mary and Pauline's dresses had once been hers and had been patched many times over the years. She considered her own clothes rags compared to Mrs. McBain's.

Joseph told Sarah, "Have Jefferson drive by the school and Mr. Lippman's store. Katherine can inform them about the fire and that they'll be a little late. I must leave now. I'll see you at supper." Katherine realized that this would be a good time to tell Mr. Lippman and Mr. Lancaster their real names, something she had longed to do.

The girls excused themselves to get ready and went upstairs. Pauline closed the bedroom door and grabbed Katherine's sleeve. "Oldest Sister, is this really happening—living in a mansion with nice people and servants, with milk and cornbread after school?"

Katherine gathered the girls on the bed, which had already been made. "We're guests of the McBains. They are very nice to take us in, but it's only for a few days until we find other arrangements, so don't get too comfortable. We must always be on our best behavior. Let's go. We don't want to leave Mrs. McBain waiting."

⁂

When Katherine returned to the house that evening, Mr. McBain asked her into his study. He sat her on a chair by the desk and said, "Miss Downes, my wife and daughter explained to me why you falsely accused our coachman. You were destitute and needed money to survive. I forgive you. I only ask that you understand why I was angry with you for doing it. Hercules has been with me for thirty-five years and is very important to the whole family." Katherine nodded. "That's why I initially hesitated giving you the reward money for turning in Harold. That being said, I am now fulfilling my commitment. The twenty-five hundred dollars is yours. However, because you are not yet eighteen and living in my house, I am going to hold the funds and will release portions to you when you make specific requests. This is for your own good—so you don't squander the money or have it stolen. After you find new quarters, which I urge you to do as quickly as possible, I'll give you the balance."

Katherine had no choice but to accept Mr. McBain's terms. He had been so generous by taking them in that she didn't dare protest. "I'll do whatever you suggest, sir. And thank you again for all you've done for us. I promise that we won't be a bother. And I'll start looking for a new place immediately."

"You're most welcome, Miss Downes. I'm certain you know that it was Mrs. McBain who insisted on taking you in. Your thanks belong to her."

"Yes, sir. We'll forever be in her debt."

James stood, escorted her to the door, and said, "I'll see you at supper."

Katherine couldn't blame Mr. McBain for wanting them out. They were strangers intruding in his house and family. But with twenty-five hundred dollars, she figured they could live comfortably independent for two years.

⁂

The following night at supper, Mrs. McBain asked Danny, Pauline, and Mary about their day in school. Danny mumbled about how much he hated Latin.

With no coaxing, Mary took over. "We learned how a lady mutht uthe a fan."

Pauline lightly elbowed Mary. "Use, not uthe. U-suh. Say it with your tongue stuck to the bottom of your mouth."

"U-tha." Mary waved her hands in front of her mouth, as if it were on fire. "Let me try again. U-suh!"

Sarah, James, and Joseph applauded. Sarah had Lilly bring a fan to the girl and said, "Please show us, Mary."

Mary opened the fan, which covered her face. She peered over the top at Pauline and said, "If I carry it in my right hand, in front of my fathe, it meanth, follow me."

Pauline threw up her hands at Mary's lisp. "I give up!"

Mary looked at Mrs. McBain and demonstrated as she spoke. "If I let it retht on my right cheek, it meanth 'Yeth.' If I let it retht on my left cheek, it meanth 'No.'"

Sarah smiled. "Very good, Mary! Show us more."

The girl then stared at Danny, who was about to take a bite of pork chop. She bounced her eyebrows up and down and said, "If I carry it in my left hand, it meanth 'I am dethirouth of your acquaintanth'". Danny froze with his mouth open. He looked at his father, as if to say, "Save me!"

The girl grinned at Danny. "If I plathe the handle to my lipth, it meanth, 'KITH ME.'"

Danny's fork dropped to his plate, clanked, and bounced onto the tablecloth. Katherine shouted, "Marrrrreeee!" as Danny recovered his food and utensil.

Sarah, James, and Joseph had to wipe tears from their eyes. James, seeing his grandson's face flush red, composed himself and asked, "Pauline, what did you learn?"

"Well, I learned the language of the fan, too. And the teacher let me practice drawing. She says I have a natural talent. My ma taught me years ago, and I sketch every chance I get when I have paper and a pencil or charcoal. And if you'll let me, I'd like to sketch the McBain family after supper as a gift for being so nice to us."

James looked at Sarah, who nodded her approval. Joseph said, "We'd be honored. As soon as we're finished eating, we'll go to the family parlor."

James, Sarah, and Joseph settled on the couch and Danny climbed onto his father's lap. Pauline and Katherine sat on the two-seat sofa across from them. Pauline, with a piece of paper resting on a large book furnished by Mrs. McBain, said, "This will take about thirty minutes. People look so serious in daguerreotypes or portraits. But I think smiles are nicer, and I'm going to sketch you looking happy. You can help by smiling. Danny, you can hold JD if you want."

Joseph said, "You're the artist. Let Mary talk and I assure you we'll smile."

As Pauline sketched, Mary sat on the floor in front of her, practicing her fan language. She asked the McBains, "What doeth thith mean?" and drew the fan across her cheek. Before anyone could answer, she whispered, "I love you." The adults beamed as Danny looked to the door and pondered escaping.

After forty minutes, Katherine, who had been fixated on her sister's effort, kissed Pauline on the cheek. Pauline stood and handed the sketch to Mr. McBain. James gawked. There was his family, or most of it, together, happy, with remarkable individual likenesses. He had commissioned individual portraits before, but nothing with all of them together. He handed it to Joseph, who said, "Pauline, this is excellent. Thank you so much. I'm going to have it framed and put on my desk."

Sarah took it and said, "Wonderful, Pauline. You're so gifted." Danny held it in both hands and said, "It looks just like us. Even JD looks like JD!"

James said, "Pauline, do you ever use pastels?"

"Oh, no, sir. They're much too expensive."

Sarah said, "I'll see what I can do about finding some for you. In any event, this is a special way to end the evening. Thank you again. It's late and we all have busy days tomorrow. We'll see you at breakfast."

Everyone went upstairs to bed. In the darkness, Sarah said to James, "Katherine asked Mr. Lippman for permission to take off Saturday morning to look for an apartment to rent. She asked me to help her find one."

James waited a few seconds and said, "Well, there's no hurry. As long as Hercules isn't here, I believe we have enough room."

Sarah wiggled over and kissed her husband's cheek.

⁂

On the first Saturday of living with the McBains, after breakfast, Pauline and Mary walked to Pulaski Square. They saw Danny playing catch with two boys, one white and the other black, and approached them. Pauline asked, "Hi, can we play?"

Danny shrugged. "All right, I guess." He introduced Truvy and Parker to the girls. The five stood in a circle and threw the ball around, laughing at JD, who dashed from person to person, hoping to snare it. Danny was impressed with Pauline's ability to throw and catch, but Mary couldn't do either. After a while, Danny took a few steps back, called, "Here, catch." He threw the ball high in the air to Pauline and shouted, "Who was the fourth president of the United States?"

Pauline stepped back, looked at Danny for a second, and asked "What?" Then she cried "Ouch," as the rubber ball bounced off her forehead. The boys bent over in hysterics while JD fetched the ball. Pauline shouted, "Very funny. You distracted me." She pried the ball from JD's jaws and asked, "Why did you ask that?"

Truvy said, "It's a game we play." He explained the rules.

Pauline said, "James Madison. I get a point."

Danny squealed, "No you don't. Truvy just said that you have to answer the question before you catch the ball."

Pauline threw the ball in the air towards Danny and called out, "Which was the first state to ratify the U.S. Constitution?"

Danny caught the ball, but didn't answer the question.

Pauline laughed. "Delaware. You lose."

Danny said, "How do you know that?" He threw the ball to Mary without asking a question, but it flew over her head and rolled under the fence. JD chased after it.

Mary yelled, "Throw it thtraight, why don't you!" and ran through the turnstile to get the ball. Danny, Truvy, and Parker took a shortcut and climbed over the fence.

When Mary and Pauline arrived, Danny stood with one hand on his hip and tossed the ball in the air with the other. "Beat you!"

Pauline snatched the ball in mid-air. "You cheated. Wanna race? I bet I'm faster than you." She put a hand on her hip and tossed the ball with the other, mimicking Danny.

Danny shook his head. "I can't bet, my pa won't let me gamble. But we can still race—from here to Orleans Square. How about a head start?"

Pauline flipped the ball to Truvy. "If you think you need one."

Danny stomped his foot, creating a small cloud of sand dust. "Not for me—for you!"

Pauline shrugged. "Very well. We'll start even. Truvy can give the signal."

Truvy drew a line in the sand with the toe of his shoe, and he, Parker, and Mary stood to the side. JD barked. Mary picked him up and told him to hush. Danny and Pauline, five inches taller and six years older than the boy, lined up and leaned forward, with fists clenched. Truvy raised an arm in the air and called, "Readyyyy . . . GO!" Pauline, in her new black dress made by Nannie, which reached just above the top of her boots, and white collar and bonnet, looked like a salt shaker that had been shot from a cannon. She flew down Barnard Street, the movement of her feet barely visible.

Mary yelled, "Go, Pauline!" She dropped the dog and followed the runners.

Danny ran through the street, kicking up sand behind him, struggling to stay a respectable distance behind Pauline. When he got to Orleans Square, Pauline was leaning against the fence with her arms folded. "Beat you!"

Danny bent from the waist and put his hands on his knees, gasping for air. The others trotted up. Truvy asked, "Miss Pauline, how did you get so fast?"

She smiled. "From God. Who else? I used to catch chickens in our yard."

An embarrassed Danny sought redemption. "I bet you can't beat Truvy."

Pauline straightened her bonnet. "I'm done racing for the day. Let's throw the ball some more."

They went into the square and played Catch History. Whenever Parker got the ball, he tossed it gently to Mary so she could sometimes catch it, and always asked her an easy question, like, "Who was the first president?" After Mary answered, whether correctly or not, she always thanked Parker for being so nice.

After an hour Pauline said to Mary, "Katherine only works a half-day today. Let's wait for her at the house." She turned to the boys and said, "We can play more tomorrow." The girls waved goodbye and departed.

The boys watched them skip away in the sandy street. Truvy said, "They're funny. I like them."

Parker said, "Me, too."

"Yeah, I guess," muttered Danny as he dusted the sand off his pants.

Pauline and Mary arrived at Pulaski Square at the same time as Katherine, who greeted them with a hug. They entered the quiet house and Katherine said, "I guess the McBains are still at City Market. We'll wait for them for dinner. They have such a lovely garden and it's mild. Why don't we sit outside? I know you have reading for school."

Pauline said, "I'll get our books," and bounded up the stairs. Katherine called after her to walk quietly, then studied the painting on the wall of a man wearing a blue jacket with gold buttons, white pantaloons, and a three-pointed Continental Army hat. Mary walked along the hall towards the back, stopped at a door, looked it up and down, and wondered where it led. She opened it just as Chloe stepped out. Mary screamed. Katherine ran to her sister who stood frozen, with her shoulders up to her ears.

Chloe laughed and said, "You seed uh ghos', li'l missie?"

Mary put her hands over her face with her fingers spread apart. "I opened the door to thee what wath behind it, and you walked out."

Chloe bellowed another laugh. "Deese de stuhs fuh us nigguhs."

Pauline called from above, "What happened? I heard a scream."

Katherine said, "Mary stuck her nose where it didn't belong, as usual."

Chloe smiled. "Kin ah gits you some cawnbreads?"

Katherine said, "Not now, Chloe. Thank you. We're going to sit in the garden."

The girls exited the back door, followed the stairs into the back yard, which was bordered on three sides by a six-foot-high brick wall covered in ivy. The garden was divided in half by a four-foot-wide brick path, which led from the back of the house to an iron gate in the middle of the far wall. Mary wanted to know if this was what paradise looked like. Katherine smiled and said, "Maybe it is." Pauline and Mary sat on one of the benches along the path and opened their books while Katherine went to investigate.

She stepped through the gate onto the sand driveway. A string of attractive buildings, including the stables and coach house, lined the other side. A black man exited one of the doors and froze when he saw Katherine. She said, "Hello, my name is Katherine. My sisters and I are staying here for a while. I wanted to look around. I worked with horses on my family's farm."

Dante had heard from the other servants that Missus had taken in three girls and was very fond of them. He approached the young woman. "Ah show you 'round, Mistess Katrin. Call me Dante."

"Hello, Dante." Katherine pointed at the building with four sets of double doors on the left. "Is that the coach house?"

"Yessum." Dante led her through the far left set of doors. She examined the side wall with a spotless worktable and tools and bridles hanging on hooks. The rest of the area was empty except for a four-wheeled wagon. "Massa Joesup tek de gig an' Jeffuhson dribin' Massa an' Missus in de coach. Huhclees keep dis place clean as de kitchun, but he wid de Yankees. Jeffuhson runnin' it now." Katherine felt even worse at witnessing Hercules's pride in his work.

Dante led her along the driveway through the last set of double doors. There were eight stalls. Three held horses, two had mules. One of the horses neighed. Katherine walked over and patted his neck. Dante pulled carrots from a bin and handed them to her. She broke one in half and held it up in her flat palm. The horse snatched it in his teeth and chomped it down. She fed the other horses and said, "These are beautiful animals."

Dante stood straight with pride. "Only de bes' fuh Massa, mussy boo coo."

They left the stables and were greeted by Pauline and Mary. Pauline said, "We're tired of reading. Can we go to the square?"

"First say hello to Dante. Dante, these are my sisters, Pauline and Mary." Both girls curtsied.

Dante said, "Hello, li'l missies," before they ran down the driveway.

Dante pointed to the other structure, a two-story brick building with two pairs of single doors on the ground level and four windows on each level, spread equally over the face. "Dat's fuh us slabes. Willum an' he wife Dolly, an' Jeffuhson an' Nannie lib in de big house, 'case Massa aw Missus need 'em quick. Us res' lib in deese."

Katherine studied the building and thought they looked much nicer than the slave cabins around Thomasville. She said, "Thank you for the tour, Dante. I heard Mr. McBain talking about one of his men wanting to get married. Is that you?"

"Yessum, Mistess. Massa gwine tuh ask Massa Lamah fuh puhmishin."

"I'm sure he'll approve, Dante."

Dante smiled. "Ah sholy pray so, Mistess."

Katherine bid Dante goodbye and walked to the square to join her sisters, feeling better than ever. Mrs. McBain told her the night before that Mr. McBain consented to let her and her sisters live at Pulaski Square for the foreseeable future, and there was no need for her to search for an apartment or get a night job.

Mrs. McBain appeared to be as happy in giving that news as she was in hearing it. Katherine thought of her mother and the poem about the crying angels. Maybe there really were brighter days ahead. ∾

CHAPTER THIRTY-ONE

Dante's Wedding Day
December 1862

Dante, in his black suit, white shirt, and black tie, chatted nervously with Jefferson on the driver's bench. Inside the cab, James and Joseph prepared to meet with Charlie Lamar to seek approval for the marriage of their servant to Isetta. Slave marriages weren't legal unions in the eyes of the state. However, most owners recognized and encouraged them as they created stability in the lives of their negroes and also produced more slaves.

James and Joseph went inside first. Lamar welcomed them and after a glass of port and a discussion of the progress of the war, James brought up Dante's proposal. He presented his servant's case, explaining that the man had been with him his entire forty years and was currently hired out as a cook to General Mercer's staff officers. James stressed that he had no doubt Dante would be a responsible husband.

Lamar remarked that the name sounded familiar, but he didn't know why. He only wanted assurances from James that Dante didn't drink, gamble, or cause trouble, activities in which Charles Lamar participated with reckless abandon. James assured him. They agreed that Dante would continue living with McBain, Isetta with Lamar, and the couple could spend Saturday nights and Sundays together at Dante's room.

Charlie called for his wife, Caro, while Joseph fetched Dante. The negro entered the parlor and the Lamars appraised him. The sight of Massa Lamar's dark eyes, framed by a close-cropped but full-face, reddish-brown beard, made Dante's knees knock. Mrs. Lamar, who had a natural smile, started asking questions. "Dante, do you promise to take good care of Isetta? We're fond of her and we don't want to hear her ever complain."

"Missus, ah tek good care ub Ahsettuh, you kin be all time suhtin."

"Do you promise to have a big family? Isetta wants lots of children." As the Lamars would still own Isetta, they would also own her children.

"Yessum, Missus. Dey be li'l nigguhs runnin' all obuh de place."

The whites laughed. Caro continued, "That's good to hear, Dante. With Mr. McBain's permission, we'll have a ceremony here the Saturday before Christmas."

James said, "That's fine with me, and I'm sure with Mrs. McBain. I'd like to bring the house servants from our place in town, and Patience, Andrew's widow, and her two boys. Also, we've taken in three orphaned sisters. May we bring them?"

"Of course, Mr. McBain. Our daughters will love to meet them. We'll let the servants have a small party in the back yard after the ceremony. Please wait just a minute. Let me fetch Isetta and tell her the news." Caro Lamar soon reappeared with a grinning Isetta at her side. Caro said, "Isetta, please say hello to Mr. and Captain McBain."

Isetta bowed and said, "So nice tuh meet you," as she had rehearsed all that day. She and Dante smiled at each other.

Caro said, "Master McBain has asked for our permission to allow their boy, Dante, to marry you, and we approve, if you do."

Isetta coyly lowered her chin and eyes and replied, "Missus, ah sholy do."

Caro put her arm around the girl's shoulders, gave her a squeeze, and said, "I thought you might. You'll be married here two weeks from today and have a party afterwards."

Isetta hugged Caro and said, "T'ank you, Missus and Massa Lamah, Massa an' Cap'n McBain." She waved to Dante and departed.

The McBains said goodbye and left with Dante, the happiest man in all Savannah.

That night after the table had been cleared of dishes, the house servants marched into the dining room behind William, who held a cake with red-and-white icing and shouted, "Happy Birthday, Miss Katherine." William placed the cake on the table. The servants applauded for Katherine and left. Katherine asked Mrs. McBain how she knew. Sarah looked at Pauline, who raised her hand and said, "Guilty." Katherine thanked everyone as William sliced the cake. She was now eighteen and eligible to become her sisters' legal guardian. No one would ever be able to take them from her.

Excitement pervaded the McBain household on the afternoon of Dante's wedding day. The Downes sisters barricaded themselves in their room, preparing for their first-ever social function other than church. Pauline, at thirteen, and Mary, six, dressed as children, which annoyed Pauline to no end. Both donned split white, cotton drawers, which reached mid-calf, followed by a white cotton chemise, a loose-fitting, nightgown-like garment that hung from the shoulders to just below the knees. Mary's crimson-colored dress with black corded trim at

the hemline and black buttons from the waist to the neckline, and topped with
a white lace collar, reached slightly below her knees, indicating her young age.

Pauline's indigo dress with a beige corded trim at the hemline and beige buttons from the waist to the neck line, and topped with a beige lace collar, reached a
few inches above her boot tops, signaling that she was nearing womanhood. She
wore a belt with a small purse attached to it.

Both girls wore white socks to the knees and their old but polished leather
lace-up boots, the most difficult and expensive item to acquire for a woman's
wardrobe during the war. Their hair was brushed back and clipped in place, so it
cascaded to their shoulders.

Katherine's fitting routine was a more complicated affair. After she put on
drawers and a chemise, Chloe laced up her corset, which was lined with curved
whale bones. The garment was designed to give women a fashionable bell-shaped
silhouette and to lend back support, and reached from the hips to mid-breast.
Next came a camisole or corset cover, followed by a cage crinoline, to further ac-
centuate her figure. Then she put on a cantaloupe-colored dress, with black buttons running from the waist to her neck, and a black, bunched-up strip of fabric,
stretching in a semi-circle from one shoulder to another across her chest. She
sat on the edge of the bed while Chloe put on a pair of Amy's black leather lace-
up boots. Katherine stood and Chloe said, "Mistess Katrin', dey ain' uh greatuh
beauty in all Jawjuh."

Katherine blushed. She stood before the mirror and smiled. "Thank you,
Chloe." Then she brushed her teeth with Oriental toothpaste for the second time
in an hour.

When the girls walked down the stairs to leave, Sarah McBain beamed like
a proud grandmother, while the McBain men, all three generations, stood slack-
jawed, and the servants applauded. The girls and the McBains stepped outside
and met Dante in his top hat and black suit. This time he sat in the cab.

When the family arrived at the Lamar house, they were escorted by a servant
to the first-floor piazza in the back, where they were met by the Lamar family
and Isetta. The bride-to-be wore a red skirt and hoop, a white bodice with red
buttons, and a string of pearls loaned by Mrs. Lamar. The bride and groom stood
next to each other, looking into each other's eyes. The adult McBains and Katherine could see how much Dante loved Isetta.

Charlie Lamar faced them holding a Bible. Slaves wanted a white person to
preside over their weddings because it validated their union. And while Charlie
was a slave trader, he considered most of his servants as part of his family.

The McBains and Downes sisters stood on Dante's side. The Lamars—Caro
and three of her four daughters, and Charlie's father Gazaway and two of his
five young children—stood on Isetta's side. Nine McBain and eight Lamar house
servants, as well as Patience, Truvy, and Gully, listened in the yard one-half floor
below.

Charlie read a prayer, led the couple through the wedding vows, and pronounced them man and wife. Then he slammed shut the Bible and shouted, "Let's dance." The McBains shook Dante's hand while the Lamars took turns embracing Isetta. The whites walked down the stairs first and the bride and groom followed. The blacks crowded around Isetta and Dante, hugging and cheering them.

The pleasant late afternoon weather had allowed Caro to set up tables on the grass on either side of the brick patio in the middle of the back yard. The servants sat at a group of four tables on one side. The whites occupied two tables on the other, one for the adults, including Katherine, and one for the children, including Pauline and Mary. Servants brought out six large, flat cakes covered in red, yellow, and white icing, and placed one on each table. Pauline had to restrain Mary from scraping off the icing with her finger.

While the blockade made it nearly impossible to purchase imported luxuries, Gazaway Lamar, with business contacts around the South, had been able to procure tea, and the servants brought out several pitchers of it, though without ice. Charlie produced two bottles of whiskey for the white, adult table.

Caro had hired a band of three negroes, with a fiddle, banjo, and mandolin. When they started to play, Charlie motioned to the newlyweds with a sweep of his hand that the dance floor was theirs. The servants flooded the patio, formed two lines, and cakewalked, the first dance that Dante and Isetta had shared together. The whites watched, tapping their feet and clapping their hands. Pauline and Mary and four of the Lamar girls stood on the lawn, formed two lines and tried to copy the negroes. Danny remained seated, waiting for the right moment to join Truvy across the yard.

After thirty minutes and two glasses of whiskey, Charlie stood, stuck two fingers in his mouth, and whistled. The music and dancing stopped. He walked to the musicians. "Can you play a galop?"

The fiddler replied, "You wanna galop, Massa, put on you galopin' boots."

The servants retreated to their tables, wanting to dance more, but they knew that they couldn't be on the same floor while the whites occupied it. They would have to wait and watch the whites dance, always a source of amusement to them.

Charlie approached Sarah, bowed, and offered his hand. She took it and followed him to the floor. James stood and took Caro's hand. Gazaway escorted his daughter Lottie. Joseph, in his military uniform, limped around the table to Katherine. "I do have a bothersome leg injury, which I ask you to overlook. I will make up for it with energy."

She said, "Captain, I'm not much of a dancer. I've only had one lesson, and that from my mother."

"That's all right. Just hold on to me and follow my lead. I'll go slowly." He led her onto the patio.

The four couples stood equally apart in a circle and the band began to play. The men bowed to the women, who curtsied in return. Joseph placed his right hand on Katherine's waist, took her right hand in his left, and smiled at her.

The music began to play. Joseph performed the basic galop step—a combination skip and slide—to the center, and back. Katherine caught on quickly. They galoped in a circle three times, the men twirling the women as they glided over the floor. They returned to their original positions, slide-stepped to the left, and then back to the right. Joseph was slow with his steps to the left, but Katherine didn't mind—she felt comfortable in his hands. They and Charlie and Sarah, opposite each other, galoped to the center and back. Then James and Caro and Gazaway and Lottie did the same. They all galoped in a circle, gliding and twirling, repeating the steps over and over, and switching partners often to allow everyone to dance with each other.

Mary snuck up on Danny, grabbed his arm, and pulled him to the edge of the patio, to the cheers of the other children and the servants. Danny tried to escape, but Mary clutched his arm. He gave in and they tried to follow the adults. He held Mary as far away as possible and spun her around in place until she tripped and fell onto the grass. Danny ran to Truvy's side while Pauline pulled Mary back to the table.

The whites eventually gave up the floor to the servants. Joseph finished with Katherine as his partner and escorted her back to the table. As she sat, he said, "You dance very well, Miss Downes. Thank you. I haven't had this much fun in a long time."

Katherine glowed and couldn't hide her smile. "You're welcome, Captain. I enjoyed it, too. You are such a good teacher."

Patience, who kept her eye on Joseph the entire time, said to Chloe, "Did you see that look in Miss Katherine's eyes when she danced with Master Joseph?"

Chloe nodded. "Yessum, ah sholy did. An' ah see uh storm headin' dis way."

Patience glanced at Katherine across the yard. "I believe it could be a big one."

After two hours of dancing and alternating the dance floor with the negroes, the McBains departed. The Lamars went into the house, leaving the servants a few hours to celebrate on their own.

Katherine turned off the gas lamp and crawled into bed with her sisters. Mary said, "That wath tho much fun. I think Danny lovth me."

Katherine said, "I'm sure he likes you, Mary. Danny is a very sweet boy, and he likes everybody."

Pauline sang, "I know who Katherine likes."

Mary laughed. "Me, too. Me, too."

Katherine hissed, "Sssshhh! Whatever are you two talking about?"

Pauline said, "Oldest Sister, Captain McBain danced with you more than anyone. I saw you look at him."

Katherine lightly slapped Pauline's arm. "Don't be silly. He was only being polite. He's more than twice my age."

Mary started to sing, "Katherine lovth Captain McBain, Katherine lovth, lov-ssssuh, Captain McBain."

"Hush, the two of you, and go to sleep. Remember, we're guests here and they've been very nice to us. Don't cause problems with your wild imaginations."

Mary and Pauline giggled themselves to sleep, but Katherine lay awake. She stared into the darkness and wondered if Captain McBain liked her. She recognized that a gentleman so rich and gallant would never be interested romantically in a much younger, poor country girl. Besides, he was married, though he or his parents never mentioned his wife. She couldn't deny, however, that she held a special feeling for him—not love, she didn't even know what that was, but a deep admiration. Most men scared her, thanks to her father, Mr. Wells, and Pastor Lewis, not to mention Harold and Willie. But Captain McBain was different, and not just because he was so handsome or asked her to dance. He held chairs and doors for her. He smiled at her in the morning and evening, making her feel welcome in his home. He enquired about her day at work and tried to include her in dinner table conversations. He told Pauline and Mary how pretty they looked and asked about their classes at school. He showed kindness to her and her sisters that no man ever had. Katherine simply felt comfortable and safe in his presence.

Katherine closed her eyes and relived the best night of her young life. She soon drifted off and dreamed that she and Captain McBain were dancing alone in a grand ballroom, she in an evening gown, and he in his uniform. They looked into each other's eyes as he held and twirled her. He complimented her dancing, and she thanked him. Then she saw a door open. Her father stepped into the room, grinning like the devil. She screamed and started to run away, but tripped and couldn't regain her feet. She crawled on her hands and knees but they felt like lead. She called for Joseph, but he was gone. She rolled onto her back and realized that she was in a bed. Zebudiah stood over her in his underdrawers, ready to join her. Katherine attempted to scream but no sound emerged. He sat on the edge of the bed, took her hand, and pulled it towards him.

She woke up in tears, with Pauline holding her wrist. "Oldest Sister, you're having a nightmare." Katherine sat up and muffled her sobs in the blanket.

When she calmed down, she kissed Pauline and said, "I'm all right now."

Pauline whispered, "Is it Pa? Is he back?" Katherine nodded. Pauline started to cry for her tortured sister. Katherine held the girl in her arms and patted her back. Pauline eventually fell asleep, but Katherine couldn't. She realized that she was still a prisoner of the past, and wondered if she would ever escape it.

∽≈∾

Joseph walked into the room behind the assistant jailer and sat at the small table as the lawman stepped to the side. He stared at the man seated across from him and tried to remain composed. "Hello, Harold." Harold's blank expression displayed his disinterest in the visitor. Joseph got right to the point. "Can you help me find Willie?"

"Why should I tell you anything?"

"It might help you."

The prisoner folded his arms across his chest. "How?"

"I can't say, but you have nothing working in your favor now. It might be worth the gamble to do something good."

Harold leaned forward and rested his elbows on the table. "Who told you I was in that hospital? Tell me his name and I might consider it."

Joseph smiled. He derived pleasure from knowing that this was eating up Harold. "Some observant gentleman. I put up posters all over town describing you. You must have seen one. You were a twenty-five-hundred-dollar prize. Look, Harold, I'm not trying to fool you. I have no use for you except how you can help me find Willie. He's the one who shot my black friend and I'd bet it was his idea to kidnap my son. You'll never see him again, so you shouldn't feel any loyalty towards him."

"Tell me who squealed on me."

Joseph drummed his fingers on the table as he formed a response. "You don't know him. For the money I offered, Willie would have turned you in."

Harold stood, said, "Jailer, take me back to the cell," and walked to the door.

Joseph called after him, "Think about it, Harold. If you change your mind, tell a guard." He then found Chief Goodwin and said, "Whenever Harold mails a letter, get me the address. Whenever he receives a letter, I want the return address." Goodwin nodded.

⁂

The McBains and the sisters sat in the family parlor at the Heritage and sang Christmas songs as Sarah played the piano. It was the girls' first visit to the plantation. When they arrived, Mary and Pauline pressed their noses against the coach window to see the massive live oak trees. As they passed through the Quarter, Mary shouted, "Pauline, it'th a village of negroeth and they're all waving at uth." Mary waved back.

After Jefferson dropped James, Sarah, and Joseph at the house, Danny gave the girls a tour of the grounds, including the outbuildings, brick area, lumber mill, iron forge, and stables, all quiet on Christmas day. At the brick wharf Danny explained, "This is where our men fish on their time off. Pa says Grandpa took him fishing here, too, and he took me a few times before the war."

The sisters were overwhelmed by the enormity of the place. On their return to the big house they saw a long line of slaves snaking from the back door, through the back yard, and onto the back side of the avenue of oaks. Danny explained, "At Christmas my grandpa gives the winter clothes ration to the men and women. He also gives them three hogs to cook for Christmas supper and a week off from work."

After the slaves received their gifts, the McBains enjoyed a Christmas supper of oyster stew, roasted pig, and a dessert of rice pudding. Though it was much less elaborate than before the war, it still impressed the girls. Then they all retired to the parlor. Sarah took her place at the piano as the sisters sat on the couch, Joseph and Danny shared a leather chair, and James stood by the piano.

Katherine closed her eyes and thanked God for the good fortune he had bestowed upon her and her sisters. When they escaped from Thomasville in the autumn of 1861, miserable, alone, and afraid, she never would have guessed they'd spend the Christmas of 1862 in comfort with people who made them feel like part of a real family. She didn't know what the future held, but it had to be better than the past. She opened her eyes and stole a glimpse of Captain McBain sitting across the room. He had his arm around Danny as they sang "One Horse Open Sleigh." She thought of the night she and the captain danced together, and wondered if they would ever do it again. She still admired him, as well as his parents, for the kindness they showed her and her sisters.

Joseph couldn't help thinking about the coming year. He would face monumental challenges. Somehow, he had to rejoin his unit and help the Confederacy win this war, despite his injury, which was slowly but steadily improving. He had to regain custody of his daughter, with Emily or without. And he had to find Willie. He looked across the room at the sisters, holding hands and singing along, looking as happy as any girls he had ever seen. Katherine looked at him and their eyes met. They exchanged smiles.

James McBain, wearing a red ribbon in his hair that Danny had tied, stood next to the piano and led the singing in his baritone voice. James gave thanks for many things, like having Danny home, safe and secure; having Joseph out of prison and in Savannah, even though he wasn't yet committed to the plantation; having a competent and trustworthy overseer to run the Heritage; and seeing his wife so happy since the three orphans had found their way into her life. But still his insides churned at the prospects for 1863. Demand for his products was way down, with the only construction taking place being military related. He worried about his other slaves running away, after having lost Isaac and Hercules. But most troubling of all was the fact that the war was dragging on with no end in sight. He concluded that the longer it lasted, the less likely the South could defeat the North, with its greater population, larger army and navy, and manufacturing capabilities. The British and French, although desperate for good southern cotton, showed no signs of throwing their support behind the rebels. The Confederacy's only hope depended on the Yankees tiring of war and negotiating a settlement. James felt that this was unlikely. He knew that life was to get much more difficult for Savannah and its people. He hated to admit it, but he had to start planning to protect his family and property in case of defeat. He looked at the sisters, singing and giggling, and knew he had to care for them, too. He didn't mind at all. ❧

CHAPTER THIRTY-TWO

A Cake for Harold

January - June 1863

Music blared from the band. People danced. Women hugged strangers. Men shook hands, patted each other on the back, and shouted to the heavens, "T'ank you, Massa Lincum!" White officers and ministers gave long, mind-numbing speeches filled with words like "freedom" and "the glorious Union" to loud applause. It was January 1, 1863, on Hilton Head Island. Hercules and several thousand other blacks, some of whom were transported from Beaufort on U.S. Navy boats, celebrated President Abraham Lincoln's Emancipation Proclamation, which freed all slaves in the states in rebellion effective that day. The festivities, organized by the new military commander of the district, were held in the Yankee camp.

Hercules cheered with the others. For the first time, he was able to attend a party with more than seven fellow blacks in a public place without having to obtain permission from whites. He smelled wood burning and the rich, fatty aroma of pigs roasting, odors he had inhaled many times before, but now they smelled better. It was the greatest day of his life. Later that afternoon, exhilarated and exhausted, he returned to his cabin in Mitchelville, thinking how much Patience and the boys would enjoy being there, tasting freedom with him. He wondered how they were faring, although he knew Master Joseph would take good care of them until he returned to Savannah.

"Huhclees!"

Hercules looked up and saw a young man staring at him. "Jehova?"

Jehova rushed over to him. "Huhclees ah habunt . . . ." He stopped in mid-sentence when he saw one sleeve of Hercules's shirt tucked into the waistline of his trousers. "Wut happen?"

Hercules explained his experience at St. Simons Island and journey to Hilton Head, though he did not mention Kitt's name. He asked Jehova, "How did you get here?"

Jehova, who had traveled to Causton's Bluff with Kitt, told of his escape from the rebel camp, just the week before, with four other slaves. They had waited two days in the marsh for March Haynes, who took them to a Union ship in Ossabaw

Sound, which then brought them to Hilton Head two days earlier. He was sent to the negro barracks to live until he and three others built a cabin in Mitchelville. Hercules told Jehova that he had an extra bed in his cabin and invited the boy to move in with him. Jehova jumped at the invitation. Hercules now had a friend who he could trust and could help him as he adapted to life with one arm.

⤜⤛

JD raised his head and barked to the heavens in front of the stables. He hopped back several steps, looked up at Danny, and resumed howling. Danny asked Mary, "Where did you get it?"

Mary picked up the grey cat with white paws and a white patch on top of the head and petted him. "I found him in the thquare. He followed me here. He'th, I mean hez-suh very friendly."

When she put the cat down, he sat on his haunches, licked a paw, and rubbed it over his ear. JD took two steps toward the cat, which arched his back and hissed. JD jumped back and whimpered. Danny asked, "What are you going to do with it?"

Mary stroked the feline, which purred loud enough for both of them to hear. "I want to keep him—or her, I can't tell which. Do you think Miss-sez McBain would mind?"

Danny picked up the cat, looked at it from behind, and said, "Him. I don't know what Grandma will say, Mary. What about JD?"

"Oh, they'll be friend-suh—wait and thee."

Danny knelt and petted the cat, which arched his back, this time in affection. "I'll ask Grandma when she gets home." Danny stood and eyed the animal as he rubbed against his leg. "You know what we could call him, being all grey with a white cap?"

"What?"

"General Lee!"

"Who-suh he?"

"Are you kidding? He's the great general leading our troops in Virginia, and that's what he looks like in his grey uniform and white hair. I know—I met him."

"I don't know much about the war. As-suh long as-suh I can keep him."

⤜⤛

As James McBain had predicted, life in Savannah worsened for almost everyone. A sense of gloom still blanketed the town. Goods, especially clothing, food, and salt, remained scarce and expensive while speculators profited. Local charities tried to feed soldiers' wives and children, and the city council opened a store to sell food to the poor at cost. Most depressing of all were the mounting casualties. So many boys didn't return from the front. Others did, but with limbs missing. By April 1863 the hospitals in town overflowed, straining volunteers and other resources.

The McBains, with their plantation and wealth, fared well. They raised hogs, chickens, and cattle; had a dairy; and grew wheat, corn, and sweet potatoes. But they also had one hundred twenty plantation workers to feed, even after hiring out fifty men to the army. As a result, James had to purchase huge quantities of rice, the one product available in abundance, as the Savannah River rice plantations started to thrive again.

Life at the McBain household in Savannah changed dramatically with the addition of the Downes girls. Sarah loved having them to fuss after. She even consented to let Mary keep General Lee, though the cat had to stay on the ground floor with the servants or outside, and not on the first and second floors.

Danny proved to be a decent surrogate brother, and teased Mary only on occasion. He, Truvy, and Parker usually welcomed Pauline and Mary to join them in the square to play. Danny, however, refused invitations by Mary to play Prince and Princess.

Katherine continued to work as a seamstress for Mr. Lippman, but eliminated Saturdays so she could volunteer with Mrs. McBain at the Poor House and Hospital, tending to sick and homeless women and children. In the evenings, after supper, she helped Pauline and Mary with their school work. The sisters started attending the Independent Presbyterian Church with the McBains and using their real names. Katherine asked Mr. McBain twice for money to pay for tuition at Lancaster's school, and he gave it without hesitation. She consented to allow Mr. McBain to convert her Confederate dollars into gold, as he was doing for himself.

The girls liked Sundays the best. After church, the family drove out to the Heritage, where the girls rode horses with Captain McBain and Danny before eating an early supper at the big house. After the meal Pauline and Mary accompanied Danny to the Quarter to visit the slaves, most of whom greeted them with smiles. Katherine stayed with the adult McBains, who talked mostly of plantation matters. She was grateful that Joseph called her "Miss Downes," treating her as a woman and not a child.

Joseph continued to spend his days at the Oglethorpe Light Infantry barracks on Liberty Street and his nights after supper talking with his father about business, the war, and the plantation. They were stunned to learn of Jehova's escape from the camp at Causton's Bluff, and blamed it on Sam, who had whipped him as well as Kitt.

They also discussed the possible whereabouts of Willie and the upcoming trial of Harold. They wanted Harold tried for the murder of Andrew, but they had more evidence against him for the charge of kidnapping Danny and Truvy. Their efforts, however, were being thwarted by the Confederate government, which wanted to try Harold first for draft evasion, desertion, and fraud. While the attorney general tried to sort out the legal mess, Harold sat in the Savannah jail.

One evening before supper in late April, Joseph asked William to bring Katherine to the family parlor. He stood to greet her and motioned to the sofa. They both sat and he handed her an envelope. "I was at the post office today. They keep a list of undelivered letters and I saw your name."

She studied the handwriting addressed to "Miss Katherine Downes, Savannah, Georgia." It looked familiar, but it couldn't be from a friend or relative as she had none, other than her sisters. It could only mean trouble. Her heart rose to her throat.

Joseph said, "I can leave while you read it, or you can read it later."

She stared at the envelope and concluded that if it contained bad news, he might be able to help. "I'd like to read it now. Please stay." He took a letter opener from the desk. She sliced the top, took out the single sheet, and read in silence. She then explained, "It's from the lawyer in Thomasville who administered my parents' estate. He says he finally sold the farm, horses, other equipment, and paid all the debts. There's five hundred forty dollars left over for me and my sisters. I have to sign papers for the court before he can release the funds."

Joseph said, "That's fabulous! When can you go?"

Katherine reread the letter and held it in her lap. "I really don't know. I never want to go back to Thomasville. I have too many bad memories."

"You can't give up the money. It's yours. Perhaps Mrs. McBain will consent to accompany you. The process should only take a day if planned properly. The train takes about thirteen hours—a day—each way. That's only three days. Mr. Lippman will understand."

Katherine liked Joseph's solution. "If Mrs. McBain joins me, I'd feel much more comfortable, but she's so busy. I don't want to inconvenience her."

"I think that she'd be delighted to help you. I'll ask her later. It might take her a while to arrange her schedule, but you have time." Joseph stood and held out his hand to help her up. "It's time for supper."

She took it and stood. "Captain, I know you want to get that man Willie. I might be able to help."

Joseph froze while still holding her hand. "How, Miss Downes?"

"I could visit Harold at the jail, offer to help him in some way, and see if I can get him to tell me where Willie is. I don't know if he'll see me, or if he even has any useful information, but it's worth a try."

Joseph's eyes grew into small moons. He gently squeezed her hand and said, "That's an excellent idea. We'll go tomorrow after work. I'll drive you there and wait outside. I'll have Jinny and Lilly bake something to sweeten him up."

Harold did a double take as he entered the visitor's room and saw Penny Savannah sitting at the table and a guard leaning against the wall. He didn't smile, although she was his only guest, other than Joseph McBain, since his incarceration. Not one of his supposed friends or associates had bothered. He had run out of money and had to eat the gruel the jailer served the penniless prisoners. He sat. "Well, look who's here. I ain't got your twenty-five dollars, if that's what you want."

Katherine lifted a package wrapped in paper from her lap onto the table. "I didn't think you did."

He eyed the item. "So why'd you come?"

"I can tell you're not a Christian, Harold. You have no faith in the goodness of mankind. People can be kind to each other simply as an act of fellowship and love of Jesus. It is its own reward. Strangers have been nice to me. I have a job and a good family took us in. I help others because the Lord helped me when I had lost all hope."

Harold rolled his eyes. Katherine tore open the package, revealing a pre-sliced cake with yellow icing that seemed to glow like gold. Harold gaped. With the serving knife she had brought, she handed a slice on a piece of newspaper to him and another to the guard and listened to them chomp and suck the icing from their fingers. The jailer said, "Thank you, ma'am. That's the best thing I ever et," and returned to the corner.

Harold smacked his lips and said, "I must be getting some religion because that cake tastes like it came from heaven."

"It's all yours, Harold." She paused as he stifled a belch. "Is there anything I can do for you? Unfortunately, though all my needs are taken care of, I have no money."

Harold replied, "Nothing can help me now. I have a wheelbarrow full of charges against me and I face a judge soon. I'll be going to the Milledgeville Pen for a long time."

Katherine leaned closer and whispered, "What about Willie? Can't he help?"

Harold spoke in a normal tone, unconcerned about the deputy. "He's as bad as my other so-called friends. He's in as much trouble as me, only they haven't caught him."

"Can't he lend you money? Is he here in Savannah?"

"No. He went to Thomasville after we collected a debt from this family in Savannah. I was supposed to meet him there, but someone squealed on me and I got locked up. That was about five or six months ago. He don't write to me. Who knows if he's still there, though I doubt it."

She wanted to run to Joseph with that information, but stayed calm. "No family, either?" Harold shook his head. She stood and said, "I'll try to visit you again, Harold. I wish you luck with your trials. Tell the judge that you know what you did was wrong, that you apologize to everyone you hurt, and that you want to spend the rest of your life spreading Christian fellowship. It's your only hope. Enjoy the rest of the cake."

Katherine left Harold on his chair and walked outside. She hurried to Joseph, who helped her onto the gig and drove off. She explained the crux of the meeting. "After Harold came to Savannah, Willie went to Thomasville to wait for him. But that was five or six months ago. He doesn't know where he is now."

Joseph's beamed. "Thank you, Miss Downes. It's a start, a clue, which I hope will lead to another, and another, until I find him." He looked at her and added, "I think I'll accompany you and mother to Thomasville." Katherine didn't object.

Jehova sat at the table with his head in his hands. Hercules sat across from him, waiting for his friend to gather himself. Jehova finally looked up and whined, "Huhclees, ah didn' run 'way tuh git killed!"

Hercules shook his head. "You got no say. You either serve, go to a Yankee prison, or return to Savannah. Just remember, the only way colored folks are gonna be free is if the North wins this war, and they're askin' us to help. You can't blame 'em."

Jehova groaned. Things had been going well for him since he moved in with Hercules. He had gotten a job with a shopkeeper by the harbor and started living the life of a free man. Now it was all falling apart.

As soon as General David Hunter replaced General Thomas W. Sherman as the commanding officer of the Department of the South, he made a splash, one heard by the entire nation. In early May 1862 he issued a general order freeing all slaves in his department—South Carolina, Georgia, and Florida. President Abraham Lincoln immediately rescinded it, as Hunter had no authority to issue it, but the notion of freedom excited the slaves and enraged white Southerners.

Hunter next organized hundreds of abandoned male slaves from Beaufort, Hilton Head, and other nearby islands into a military brigade called the First South Carolina Volunteers, causing an uproar in the North as well as the South. The U.S. government had not defined a policy for handling freed slaves, leaving the issue to the individual commanding officers. Hunter seized the opportunity, believing he could raise a fighting force of forty to fifty thousand black troops. But others were not sold on the idea, especially folks from the four slave-holding border states that remained in the Union, who didn't want their slaves thinking they could take up arms against their masters. A Kentucky congressman demanded an inquiry into the matter and Secretary of War Edward Stanton asked Hunter to explain his action. Hunter replied that when he received his command he had been authorized to employ all loyal persons offering their services in defense of the Union, whether civil or military, without any express restriction as to the character or color of the persons. That, he concluded, included fugitive slaves.

Stanton didn't object and Hunter pursued the experiment. He pressured male contrabands by telling them that they had to enlist in the army in order to get their certificates of freedom. When recruits for the first regiment reached eight hundred, Hunter set up a camp on the plantation next to Mitchelville, about two miles from the Union army camp, and assigned white officers to drill them.

Some Yankee soldiers resented the presence of black troops, openly insulted them, and complained that the negroes were issued arms and equipment superior to theirs. One general from Massachusetts declared that he would rather be defeated by the rebels than fight alongside negroes. General Hunter immediately had the general arrested.

Despite the resistance, Hunter never lost faith in the black soldiers. Between November 1862 and February 1863, he sent companies from the First South Carolina Volunteers, under the command of white officers, on three missions along the Florida and Georgia coasts. They recruited more slaves from abandoned plantations, burned towns, and destroyed salt works and other rebel facilities. The black soldiers fought the rebels so fiercely that their commanding officer reported, "No officer in this regiment now doubts that the key to the successful prosecution of this war lies in the unlimited employment of black troops. . . . They know the country . . . and, moreover, they have peculiarities of temperament, position and motive which belong to them alone. Instead of leaving their homes and families to fight, they are fighting for their homes and families. . . . It would have been madness to attempt with the bravest white troops what I have successfully accomplished with black ones."

By March 1863 the volunteers had formed three regiments with close to three thousand men, and soon helped capture Jacksonville, Florida. Hunter instituted a draft, targeting all able-bodied male negroes between the ages of eighteen and fifty years within the military lines of the Department of the South who were not already employed by the Quartermaster and Commissary Departments. One of those black males was Jehova.

"I know udda nigguhs dat ain' goin'," Jehova claimed.

Hercules didn't want Jehova to go into the army. He relied on him for help, and liked his company. But he also wanted his unconditional trust and was going to use this situation to ensure it. "The sergeant at the corral listens to me. Perhaps I can get you a job there. It's under the quartermaster. That would get you out of the draft."

Jehova grabbed Hercules's arm. "Huh? You kin do dat?"

"No promises, but I'll try."

Jehova sank to his knees and begged, "Please. Ah do anyting fuh you, Huhclees."

Two days later, Jehova had a job at the corral holding sick horses, and was exempted from the draft.

On June 1, 1863, a few nights before Joseph, Sarah, and Katherine left for Thomasville, Gazaway Lamar visited James. Over the past few months Lamar had run ships with cargoes of cotton through the Union blockade from Georgetown, South Carolina, and Wilmington, North Carolina to England. All attempts failed for one reason or another. Despite this poor performance, Gazaway knew that a fleet of fast blockade runners was vital to the South's war effort. He told James that he was going to form the Importing and Exporting Company of the State of Georgia, raise two million dollars in capital, and purchase six fast steamers. Since no such ships existed in the South, Lamar wanted to send his son Charlie and several other men to England to purchase them. Gazaway implored James to invest in the company, for the sake of the Confederacy and the hefty profits to be made.

James knew that action had to be taken. However, he didn't trust Charlie Lamar to purchase the ships or to do most anything else. He told Gazaway that he'd think about it. After Lamar left, James told Joseph about Lamar's proposition and that he was prepared to invest ten thousand dollars in the venture, but wanted Joseph to make the trip to Europe to represent his interests. Joseph didn't want to leave Danny to watch after Charlie Lamar for three months, although he understood the importance of the project. "Father, I'll need permission to leave the Oglethorpes for three months."

"Son, nothing could be more important to the South than having these ships. A lot of people know about the trip, including Governor Brown. I'll speak to General Mercer. I'm certain he'll grant it."

Joseph groaned. "If he approves, I'll go."

The next day James told Lamar that he would invest in the company provided that Joseph accompanied Charlie. Lamar agreed and explained that the men would be leaving Wilmington at the end of June. James told Joseph about his meeting with Lamar, saying, "That's less than a month away. Enjoy your trip to Thomasville."

CHAPTER THIRTY-THREE

"I Believe You've Met My Son"

June 1863

Katherine wrote to Mr. Dillon that she would arrive on the Savannah, Albany and Gulf Railroad with Captain Joseph McBain and Mrs. James McBain on the night of June 10. She asked him to arrange two rooms for two nights at a hotel in town and a horse for Captain McBain for the next day. She also asked the lawyer to have all papers ready to review and sign so that she could satisfy the court and collect her funds in a day.

The night before they left, Katherine consoled her weeping sisters in their bedroom. "I'll be back in a few days. You're safe here—more than any place we've ever lived. You can play with Danny and Truvy to your hearts' content. Chloe and the other servants will take good care of you."

The girls had taken a special liking to Chloe, and she to them. She washed and patched their clothes, prepared their baths, brushed and fixed their hair, helped them dress for school, welcomed them home afterwards, and called them little angels.

Pauline pleaded, "Please be careful. I'm worried that you'll see Mr. Wells."

Katherine assured her sister, "Believe me, I'm not going near his farm."

Mary crawled on her hands and knees across the bed to Katherine. "You promith you're not running away with Captain McBain to get married?"

Pauline laughed as Katherine administered a light slap on Mary's rump. "Mary, will you ever hush up? The captain is our friend, almost family, and he's married. How many times do I have to tell you?"

"But you love him. I know it. Yeth, I do, yeth, I do."

Katherine gently shook Mary's shoulders. "You don't know any such thing. And it's 'Yessss, I do,' not 'Yeth, I do.'"

"Yes-suh, I do, yes-suh, I do."

"I want you to behave while I'm gone and don't ever talk such foolishness in front of the McBains. If anyone hears you, I'll be very embarrassed. Now go to bed."

The next morning Sarah, Joseph, and Katherine caught the seven o'clock cars for Thomasville. The bumpy ride and the smell of the smoke from the wood-burning engine brought back happy memories to Katherine—when she and her sisters had escaped from Thomasville nineteen months earlier. She was excited to be in Joseph's company for so long. He talked about many things, including his first train journey twenty years earlier, when the family visited Amy at her job at a lunatic asylum in Milledgeville. He described the slowness of the train, which could only reach speeds of twenty miles an hour. He didn't tell a story without mentioning his friend Andrew, Truvy's father, and she realized how close they had been and better understood his obsession with finding Willie. At one point Sarah mentioned Joseph's wife and child, and Katherine finally learned that they lived in New York, and had since before the start of the war.

They arrived at Thomasville at eight o'clock that night. A coachman drove them to the Planters Hotel, where Sarah and Katherine shared a room.

The next morning, as they waited for Mr. Dillon in the large, open, dark-wood-paneled lobby, Joseph asked Katherine, "You're certain that you won't run into your previous . . . family?"

"Yes. Mr. Wells never comes into town except on Sundays, or at night if there's a meeting. He keeps to his farm."

"Very well," he said. "But be careful."

Mr. Dillon strode into the lobby. "Miss Downes, how good to see you again. My, how you've grown in just—what—less than two years?" Katherine had initially been angry with Mr. Dillon for the faulty information that he had given her about the orphanage, but she never would have escaped Thomasville without him. Besides, he couldn't have known the asylum's rules. And if they had been admitted to the home, they would never have met the McBains.

She said, "It's good to see you, Mr. Dillon. Thank you for making the arrangements. I'd like to introduce you to Mrs. McBain and Captain McBain."

The lawyer half-bowed towards Sarah and shook Joseph's hand. He said, "I have all the papers ready at my office. I'll review them with you, then we can visit the judge, and you can sign them. If there are no unforeseen problems everything will be settled today." Dillon turned to Joseph. "Will you be joining us, Captain?"

Joseph replied, "No, I need to take care of other matters. I'll meet the women back here this afternoon." He said goodbye and left to get his horse.

Dillon drove the women to his office and explained all the receipts, expenditures, and other papers related to the settling of the estate. Katherine reviewed each item and thought everything was in order. She looked at Sarah, who nodded her approval. Dillon said to her, "I should tell you that Mr. Wells tried to get the proceeds from the estate, claiming that he had taken care of you and your sisters for six months. The judge told him that that was his choice and unless he had a written document from your mother or a court stipulating reimbursement or compensation, he had no valid claim. As this had no effect on you, I chose not to tell you about it." Katherine agreed with his decision.

They parted for the court house at noon and had to wait two hours for the judge. He finally called them into his office and said, "So you're the Downes girl." Katherine introduced Sarah and signed the papers. The judge issued letters dismissory and Dillon handed her a bank check for five hundred forty-two dollars. As they left the court, Katherine asked Dillon if she could borrow his buggy for an hour or two to run some errands. She promised to have it back by five o'clock. Dillon consented.

Katherine dropped off the lawyer at his office and cashed her check at the bank. She said to Sarah, "If you don't mind, as I'm here, I'd like to visit my mother."

Sarah replied, "Of course not. I'll enjoy the ride. This is such a pretty town."

They drove to the Second Baptist Church. Katherine parked and said, "I'll only be a few minutes. I want to avoid the pastor. You're welcome to join me."

Sarah followed Katherine as she walked through the side gate, along a path to the cemetery, and down another path to the end of a row of graves. She stopped in front of a plain tombstone that read, "Delores Acton Downes / November 11, 1824 – October 25, 1861." Sarah stood a few feet off to the side. The girl bowed her head, closed her eyes, and prayed silently. Then she buried her face in her hands. Sarah stepped over and stroked her back. Katherine pulled a kerchief from her sleeve and held it to her eyes. "I'm sorry. Her last days were awful. She was so filled with guilt. She asked for forgiveness and I gave it, but it wasn't enough. There was nothing I could say. She died in misery."

Sarah held Katherine's arm. "Even if she passed that way, God accepted her with love. He forgave her and she would have rejoiced in that. You must believe that she's in the Lord's care and looks down and sees what wonderful young ladies you are."

Katherine hugged Sarah and said, "Thank you so much, Mrs. McBain, for everything you've done for us. We'd better go before the pastor comes out." As the women walked along the path to leave the cemetery, Katherine looked up and thought she saw someone within the church. She lowered her head and kept walking.

When they reached the buggy, Katherine said, "It's half past three. If you don't mind, I'd like to go to a store and buy my sisters some small presents."

Sarah laughed and said, "That's a splendid idea. They'll forget that they were ever mad at you for leaving them for three days."

Joseph spent the morning visiting stables and asking about Willie. The owner of the fourth one said a man with that name and who fit the description kept his wagon, two horses, and two mules there. He arrived in November, paid his bill promptly, and left in March without mentioning a destination. The owner believed that Willie stayed in a boarding house in town, so Joseph next visited all he could find. The proprietor of the fifth one remembered Willie Sloan as a quiet man who kept his account current and spent a lot of money in local saloons, although he showed no signs of having a job. It wasn't much information, but at least Joseph had a last name.

After lunch at the hotel, Joseph spent the afternoon hitting the barrooms. Three bartenders offered no information, but the fourth flinched when Joseph mentioned Willie Sloan. He told Joseph that Willie sounded like thousands of men he had served. Joseph reached into his pocket and placed a ten dollar Confederate note on the counter. The old man eyed it and said, "Those greybacks are losing value every day." Joseph peeled off another ten.

The bartender pocketed the two bills. "I seem to remember a man like the one you describe. He was here for about four months, waiting on a friend. The friend never showed and this fella left. Said he was going to western Georgia to wait out the war."

Joseph leaned closer to the man. "Did he say where in western Georgia?"

"No. I told you all I know. He didn't talk much."

Joseph sat on a barstool. As badly as he wanted, he couldn't go to western Georgia until after the war. He looked at his watch—half past four o'clock. He could do nothing more in Thomasville. He decided to return to the hotel and meet the women.

Katherine and Sarah walked into Mr. Dillon's dark office, where the lawyer sat hunched over his desk, reading through a stack of papers by lamplight. Katherine said, "Five o'clock, sir. Right on time."

Dillon stood and greeted them. "I'm just completing my work. Please sit and I'll drive you back to the hotel." He pulled up two chairs by his desk. Ten minutes later he announced, "That should do it," placed the papers in the desk drawer, and locked it. They all stood as the front door opened. Two men walked in, their eyes on Katherine.

The older man said, "We meet again, you ungrateful wretch."

Katherine blanched. "Mr. Wells! How did you know I was here?"

"Word travels fast." He nodded at the younger man, who removed his cap. "I believe you've met my son, Jonas."

Katherine's jaw dropped. The long brown hair and dark brown eyes were branded on her mind. "Peyton Smith!" She heard Sarah gasp.

Jonas grinned. "I'm really Jonas Wells. I didn't mean to hit you so hard, but I guess I had a little too much to drink and then you screamed for the police. I had no choice. Besides, you deserved it, the way you humiliated my ma and pa."

Katherine repressed the urge to spit at the boy. She looked at Wells. "You evil snake! How did you find me in Savannah?"

Mr. Wells laughed. "The train conductors remembered you. One recalled three girls going all the way to Savannah from Boston station. Pastor Lewis wrote to the Savannah pastor and learned that three red-haired girls attended services one Sunday. When Jonas wrote that he was coming home from Virginia on furlough, I wrote back, described you all, and told him to stop in Savannah on the way and try to find you."

Jonas said, "It only took me two days. Pa said you'd probably go to an orphanage. Changing your name didn't fool me none."

Sarah said, "Mr. Wells, you approve of your son hitting a girl?"

Mr. Wells tipped his hat to Sarah. "Pleased to meet you, old lady. I had to teach this fresh one a lesson for making me look like a complete fool, even a criminal, in front of the entire town—my friends, neighbors, and fellow parishioners. I hope she's learned it. And this is her lucky day. She happened to return when my son is back. Now, if you'll excuse me, Miss Downes and I have a business matter to attend to." He said to Katherine, "You lived in my house and ate my food for almost six months, and I tended to your farm until it was sold. That wasn't for free."

Katherine hissed, "And my sisters and I cleaned your house, yard, and stables, and helped prepare your meals and then cleaned up, and did every other chore you could think of. And we had to put up with you. THAT wasn't for free."

Wells laughed, something he never did the entire time the sisters had lived with him. "I see you haven't lost that sassy mouth. A little bird told me that you just received some money from your mother's estate and have the cash on you. I originally thought of taking you home and making you work off your debt to me. But since I can't stand the sight of you, I'll take the cash and call us even. It's a fair deal."

Dillon spoke. "Mr. Wells, you have no claim on that money. The judge told you so. The matter is closed. Now please leave my office. Your behavior is revolting."

Wells sneered, "Shut up, you little thief." He stepped over to Dillon, who he dominated by about six inches and one hundred pounds, pushed him onto the desk, and pinned him down by his shoulders. He said, "Jonas, get sassy mouth's purse and let's go." Dillon wiggled and kicked to get up, but the bigger man raised a knee into the lawyer's crotch and stopped all resistance.

Jonas turned to the women and grabbed Katherine's purse. She pulled it away, the strap snapped, and the purse fell to the floor. Sarah grabbed it, sat in a chair, and bent forward, clutching Katherine's and her purse to her belly. Jonas tried to pull the sixty-seven year-old woman's arms away, but couldn't. He snarled, "Let go, you old cow," but Sarah remained folded over, as tight as a knot. Jonas said, "Don't say I didn't warn you." He started to slap her on the cheeks with his open hands, lightly at first and then harder. Sarah tucked in her chin and turned away from the blows.

Katherine screamed, "LEAVE HER ALONE!" and grabbed Jonas by his shirt. He swung his arm backwards and hit her in the forehead with the heel of his hand, knocking her against a chair.

Jonas returned to Sarah. "One last time, granny, before I hurt you bad!"

Katherine looked around and spotted the reading lamp on the desk. She snatched it and with both hands swung it against the back of Jonas's head. The glass shattered and the whale oil splattered over his head and neck. He screamed and turned towards Katherine with bared teeth. He clutched the top of her dress and was about to deliver a punch when a flame rose from behind him, making him look like a grotesque, human-faced candle. He shrieked, let go of Katherine, and tried to rub away the fire, but in doing so he pushed shards of glass deeper into his scalp. He hollered, "Pa, help me!"

Mr. Wells got off Mr. Dillon and leaped to his son. He shouted at the women, "Quick, get me a glass of water!" No one moved. Wells took off his jacket and wrapped it around Jonas's head, trying to smother the flame. Then he led the screeching lad to the street, placed him on the ground, and threw dirt on the burning flesh.

Mr. Dillon gathered himself and yelled at the women, "Let's go!" They ran out the door, boarded the buggy, and drove to the hotel, where they found Joseph waiting out front. He walked up to them and froze. "Mother, you have red welts on your face! Miss Downes, too. Someone hit you!"

Sarah said, "I'm all right, Joseph. I'll explain everything. I just need to sit and relax. A glass of wine will help."

"I'll buy you a whole case, but you must tell me what happened." Joseph helped her down and Mr. Dillon aided Katherine. They all retired to a sofa in the hotel lobby.

Sarah explained the encounter with Mr. Wells and Jonas. Joseph said to Katherine, "You know where they live. Take me there now."

Katherine said, "Captain, Peyton . . . Jonas is injured very badly. I suspect his father took him to the hospital."

Joseph thought for a moment and said, "Please take my mother to your room, have her lie down, and put a wet towel on her face. Mr. Dillon, take me to the hospital, if you don't mind. Then I'll want you to fetch the law to arrest those men."

Ten minutes later Joseph and Mr. Dillon pulled up to the hospital run by Doctors Bruce and Reed. As they were about to enter the front door, a man wearing a badge walked out. He eyed Joseph before saying, "Good evening, Mr. Dillon. What brings you here this evening?"

Dillon tipped his hat and said, "Good evening, Sheriff Johnson. I'm looking for Mr. Wells and his son. I think they may be here."

"They are, and the boy is in bad shape. Mr. Wells told me that he paid you a visit at your office and in an argument over a debt, the Downes girl smashed a lamp against his boy's head when he wasn't looking. Is that true?"

Before Mr. Dillon could reply, Joseph shouted, "That's a lie. Those men accosted my mother and Miss Downes acted in self-defense. They must be arrested."

Sheriff Johnson asked, "Who are you, Captain?"

"I'm Captain Joseph McBain of the Oglethorpe Light Infantry. My mother and I accompanied Miss Downes here while she settled her parents' estate with Mr. Dillon."

The sheriff looked at Dillon, who explained the incident in detail. Joseph said, "I'm going inside now to have a word with Mr. Wells. I want to see if he's as brave with men as with women."

Johnson said, "If you do, Captain, I'll have you arrested. I suggest you come with me now to your hotel and I'll take statements from your mother, Miss Downes, and Mr. Dillon. Then I'll arrest Mr. Wells and his son, although the boy won't be leaving the hospital for a long time. You may return for the trial."

Joseph exhaled. "I guess you're right. But one day I'll see them burn in hell."

The day after the group returned from Thomasville, Joseph sat in Pulaski Square with his father and watched the children play hide and seek. Joseph told James that it would be fruitless to seek revenge on Jonas. "The boy is in terrible pain. Infection is sure to set in. If he survives, he and his father will stand trial for attacking Mother and Katherine. We'll go then. If a local jury won't convict them, we'll decide what to do."

James tapped his foot on the walkway. No man could allow such an outrage on his wife to go unanswered, but he knew that Joseph was right. "I'm thankful for Katherine. I know that Sarah wouldn't have been there in the first place if it weren't for the girl, but it sounds like she fought like a lioness protecting her."

James watched Mary tip-toe towards a bush which shielded Danny. As she slinked around it, Danny leaped at her, waving his hands and hollering, "YAAH-HH!" Mary screamed and jumped backwards, falling into another bush. All James could see of her were two black shoes and white stockings sticking out from the bush, pumping up and down. Danny doubled over in laughter.

Parker ran to Mary and pulled her up. Mary picked leaves off her dress and wagged a finger at Danny. "You wait, Danny McBain. I will not forget thith inthivility."

"Incivility," Danny chimed, still humored by his action.

James returned to Joseph. "The day you left, our so-called mosquito fleet suffered another humiliation. The ironclad *Atlanta* sailed out to Wassaw Sound to take on the Yankee monitors. She opened fire and promptly grounded. The Yankees blasted away until the commander hoisted the white flag. She's now part of the U.S. Navy."

Joseph groaned. "How many men did we lose?"

"One dead, several injured, and about one hundred twenty-five taken prisoner." James examined the veins on the back of his hand. "The war is going badly, Son. Our troops are doing all they can, but we're losing territory—Georgia's coastal islands, much of Tennessee, New Orleans. Grant has Vicksburg under siege. If we lose this war the Yankees won't treat us kindly. They'll take our property and our Confederate notes will be worthless. They're losing value daily as it is. I have to prepare for the worst. You know I've been accumulating gold since the war started, although at progressively higher premiums."

Joseph interrupted his father, "Are you insane? Most of our leaders consider bailing out of our currency an act of treason. The vigilance committees are on the lookout for people doing it." Vigilance committees were unofficial policing organizations formed by local citizens in cities throughout the South before and during the war to look for any acts that they considered to be disloyal to the Confederacy. The committees usually operated with the consent of the city government and the police. Any individual called upon by the committee had better have a good explanation for the activity being investigated, or face the pain of punishment as the law may decree.

James said, "I'll do what I must to protect my family. Besides, I've always owned gold and northern bank notes. They can't prove when I acquired them. And I'm still heavily invested in Georgia, more so than anyone who would accuse me. On your trip to Europe I want you to take one hundred thousand Confederate dollars and exchange them for New York bank notes at whatever exchange rate you can get. There's a risk that I could lose much of my investment if there's a peace agreement and we remain independent, but if that occurs, the South will prosper like never before and I'll be able to earn back the losses in no time."

Joseph pulled out a segar but didn't light it. "I understand, and I agree with your strategy, although I still think we can force the Yankees to negotiate, if Lee could just get one big victory in Pennsylvania."

James sighed. "I wish I shared your optimism. But we must have fast blockade runners. If we can't import arms, medicines, and other necessities, we'll lose. Governor Brown knows about your trip, and we're all counting on you and Charlie Lamar."

James paused as he watched Pauline stand behind Danny and hold her hands over his eyes while Mary, Truvy, and Parker found hiding spots. Mary scooped up something and hid behind a tree. Pauline removed her hands from Danny's eyes and said, "You have two minutes. Go! One, two, three . . . . He crept up to the tree next to Mary.

James said, "Be prepared to hear Danny scream." Joseph looked towards the children and saw Danny tip-toeing to a tree. When the boy poked his head around it, Mary jumped out, grabbed his shirt, and shoved something down it. Danny started to race in circles, hollering. He stopped, unbuttoned his shirt, and a frog hopped out. James admitted, "Little Mary can dish it out pretty well."

The men heard someone calling for Parker and saw Mr. Tyler, the Savannah postmaster, driving a two-horse wagon with his wife, who was holding a baby. "Parker, get over here now!"

Parker said, "But Pa, I'm playing."

Mr. Tyler shouted, "Get over here now. I mean it!"

Parker ran to his father. James stood and walked to the wagon to greet Mr. Tyler, but Parker climbed into the bed and Mr. Tyler drove off without even looking at James. McBain returned to Joseph and said, "That was odd."

Joseph rubbed his chin. "It sure was. He must be in a big hurry to act so ungentlemanly." The men walked back to the house, leaving the children to their games.

That evening Gazaway Lamar dropped by the house to give Joseph last-minute instructions for his upcoming trip. As he was leaving, he asked James, "Did you hear about Mr. Tyler, our postmaster?"

James said, "No. But we were sitting in the square this afternoon and Mr. Tyler came by in his wagon to pick up his son. He rode off without saying a word to us."

Lamar explained, "The local vigilance committee heard that he had visited a northern state last year without getting permission from the committee, or even reporting the trip to them, which he was required to do. He was summoned to explain himself at the next meeting. Mr. Tyler promptly gathered his family, packed his bags, and left town. No one has seen or heard from him since."

Joseph said, "Well, that explains his rudeness today at the square. Do you think he's a Union spy?"

James said, "Why else would he have run off? We better not tell Danny. He'll be heartbroken."

Lamar stood, patted Joseph on the shoulder, told him that all Georgia was depending on him and Charlie, and disappeared into the warm June night.

⁂

The next morning Joseph said goodbye to the servants in the dining room and the sisters in the foyer. Pauline clutched her Bible to her chest and promised that they would say a prayer for him everyday. Mary hugged him around the waist. Katherine said, "Please be careful, Captain."

Joseph donned his jacket and said, "I'm not going into battle. I'll be eating at some of the finest restaurants in the world and seeing some of the most historic sites. There's no need to worry. Just keep an eye on Danny while I'm gone."

Mary pulled away from Joseph and said, "Don't worry, Captain McBain, I'll protect Danny from giant frogth."

PART 5

❧

"We'll Be Back
Before You Know It"
December 1863 – December 1864

CHAPTER THIRTY-FOUR

A Little Dark Cloud

December 1863

The train from Charleston pulled in at ten o'clock at night. Overjoyed to be home from his six-month trip to Europe, Joseph walked in darkness from the Central Georgia Railroad depot to Pulaski Square. He stepped through the front door expecting everyone to be in bed, but saw that the family parlor was well lit. His mother stepped from the room, gasped, "Joseph!" and embraced him in the hall. Danny ran out and jumped into his arms. Then Pauline and Mary emerged. Joseph gave each girl a hug. He said, "It's great to see you all again."

Joseph carried Danny into the parlor and sat with him on the couch next to Sarah as Pauline and Mary retreated to the sofa across from them. He mussed Danny's hair and said, "You've become more handsome and Pauline and Mary are even more beautiful." Danny hugged his father but the girls sat stone faced. Joseph asked, "Why are you children up so late? And where's Father and Katherine?"

Sarah said, "Katherine was late coming back from her nursing duties at the hospital. We got worried. Jefferson took Mr. McBain to look for her."

"A nurse? She was helping you at the Poor House. Women can't be nurses, can they?"

"Oh, Joseph," she exclaimed. "So much has happened since you left."

❧

The medical profession had always been a male domain. When the war broke out, women nurses were practically unheard of, both in the South and North. Southern women played a vital role in the early war effort by raising donations of money, food, clothing, blankets, and other necessities. They brought edibles to soldiers in camps, knitted socks, sewed uniforms, made bandages, and assembled rifle cartridges. If they were allowed in a hospital at all, it was to bring food to wounded and sick soldiers and provide comfort by reading to them.

Sarah McBain performed most of these roles, especially raising donations for the Savannah Relief Committee, an arm of the Georgia Relief and Hospital Association, which was organized to aid Georgia soldiers in the field. And she volunteered at the Savannah Poor House and Hospital, caring for destitute wives and children of soldiers.

As casualties mounted, additional capable hands were needed in hospitals. In September 1862 the Confederate Congress passed an act which, among other things, allowed army hospitals to hire women as matrons, responsible for the domestic economy of the facility. This included preparation and apportionment of food, running the laundry operation, preparing beds and bedding in wards, and dispensing medicines.

Despite this act, many doctors and nurses still resented the presence of females in their wards. They questioned their competence and the propriety of exposing them to partially or fully naked male bodies. It was left to the surgeon-in-charge of each hospital to define a woman's role, if any.

But the numbers of sick and wounded continued to rise, creating a severe shortage of caregivers. Hospitals attached to Confederate armies were constantly on the move, having to retreat and relocate in the face of advancing federal troops, and were always in need of volunteers at the new locations. Doctors had little choice but to expand the role of women to include nursing duties.

By mid-1863 the deficit of medical personnel reached Savannah. While wounded soldiers from battles as far away as North Georgia and Charleston were sometimes sent to the city, most of the patients in the hospitals came from the military installations near the town, victims of the debilitating sicknesses so common to camp life.

The Confederate medical department established three hospitals in town. In addition, the women of St. John's Episcopal Church opened a hospital for sick soldiers, and the Georgia Relief and Hospital Association set up a wayside home— an overnight resting place for soldiers going on or returning from furloughs—in the abandoned Pavilion Hotel on Bull Street and South Broad.

Initially, Katherine volunteered with Sarah on Saturdays, bringing food and beverages to sick soldiers. Upon seeing how hard the older woman worked, Katherine added two additional evenings to her schedule. She proved so adept that the head nurse expanded her responsibilities, allowing her to provide clean bedding, wash soldiers' hands and face, serve special diets as directed by the surgeon-in-charge, read to them, and write letters. She received high praise from the managers for her ability to make soldiers feel comfortable.

Near the end of 1863, the surgeon-in-chief of the military medical facilities in Savannah transferred several women, including Katherine, to the Confederate hospital at Broughton and Jefferson streets. She started in the sick ward, but after a week was sent to help the male nurses in the wounded ward. While most of the doctors accepted her, the male nurses usually ignored her other than to order her around. Katherine overlooked their slights. She was more concerned with the soldiers.

However, a fifty-year-old nurse named Mr. Hughes took a liking to her and she assisted him as much as possible, with the approval of the ward nurse, Mr. Ball. Hughes showed Katherine how to clean and dress wounds and soon let her attend to soldiers under his supervision. He also taught her how to mix and apply a poultice to reduce swelling and inflammation.

One night two volunteers carried a soldier to an open bed. Katherine brought him a tin cup of coffee and wiped his face with a damp rag. She cringed at the site of a white, red-stained towel wrapped around his mid-section. Because the wound looked far more serious than the ones she had treated, she didn't dare examine it. The boy opened his eyes. She said, "The doctor will be here shortly. You're going to be all right, soldier."

The boy moved his cracked, parched lips. "I pray so, but I don't think I'll be right ever again. My belly is on fire." He squeezed shut his eyes and bared his teeth.

Katherine stroked his hand. "Have faith. These surgeons work miracles."

The boy cried out and clutched the sides of the bed. "Oh, God, that hurts. Please get a doctor quick. I'm scared. I wish I would die so I won't be so scared no more."

"What do we have here, Miss Downes" a doctor said, walking up behind her.

He untied the shirt and the boy groaned, "Oh, God, please, God." Katherine saw the long gash in the boy's mid-section and pink matter sticking out.

The doctor quickly re-tied the bloody shirt around the boy. He then reached for his satchel, took out a bottle with white powder, sprinkled some in the cup of water, and helped the boy drink. He picked up his satchel, looked at Katherine, and nodded towards the end of the room. She followed him. He whispered, "The poor lad doesn't have much time. I wonder why they sent him here in the first place, unless his wound reopened during the ride. The morphine should keep him comfortable until he passes. Inform the nurse when he returns. Do what you can to keep the boy at peace."

Katherine returned to the soldier, determined that he should not die alone. She knelt beside him. "What's your name, Private?"

The boy's eyelids fluttered open and he looked straight up at the ceiling. "Brantley, Miss. Private Edward Brantley." His eyes shifted to her. "I know I'm going to die. I could tell by the doctor's face."

She held his hand. "Have faith in the Lord, Edward. You're going to make it."

Edward swallowed and whispered, "Miss, I have a favor to ask. Please—I beg you."

Katherine couldn't refuse a dying soldier. She had to consent and decide later what to do. "Of course, I'll do you a favor."

"My . . . my watch. It's the only thing I own that I care about. He grimaced as he reached into his pocket, pulled it out, and held it loosely in his hand. I bought it with my army pay, a year's worth. I want my ma to have it to remember me by. Bring it to her and tell her I was thinking about her at the end. Mrs. Edith Brantley of Milledgeville. Please. Then I can go in peace."

Katherine ran her hand through the boy's hair. "I promise, Private. But you'll be able to do it yourself in a few days. You have beautiful blue eyes, did anyone ever tell you that? Private? Edward?"

The sightless eyes looked up. She touched his cheek and whispered, "Have a safe journey. The Lord loves you." Katherine took the watch. She called for a doctor who officially pronounced Edward dead and asked two volunteers to remove the body.

Katherine went to Mr. Ball's desk at the head of the ward to ask his advice about the watch, but he wasn't there. She found a pen and paper, wrote "Mrs. Edith Brantley, Milledgeville, mother of Private Edward," and put it and the watch in her apron pocket. She fetched clean sheets and made the bed just before two volunteers deposited a soldier with a nasty gash over his eye. A mound of black and purple scab covered it. She said, "Lie back and relax. A doctor will be with you soon. You're going to be all right."

The soldier said, "I'm fine, Miss. I just blacked out a few times. Don't know why. The last time I hit my head against a brick ledge and I got this cut."

Katherine brought him coffee and wiped his face, neck, and hands with a damp towel. He smiled and thanked her. "I didn't expect to be looked after by a pretty girl. I just might bang my head more often." Katherine laughed and patted his hand. He took a gulp of coffee. Then he started to cough, sporadically at first, then more frequently and violently. Coffee and saliva shot from his mouth. He stood up, screamed "NO!" and then collapsed on the floor next to his bed. Katherine knelt by his side. She touched his wrist to check for a pulse, as Mr. Hughes had showed her. The soldier's arms and legs started to twitch at first, and then shook uncontrollably.

Katherine had never encountered anything like this. She stood and saw several male nurses in the ward, but all appeared busy with other patients. She called, "HELP! I NEED A DOCTOR NOW! PLEASE!"

The soldier arched his back, tilted back his head, and started to gag as his eyes bugged out of his head. Katherine grabbed a wet towel, knelt, and tried to place it on his forehead, hoping that it would calm him. The boy swung an arm at her and knocked her against the next bed. He got up and started to walk down the aisle, screaming. Katherine ran after him, grabbed his wrist, and fell to her knees to stop him. He tried to run and dragged her along the floor. She pulled on his arm and tried to wrestle him down, but he was too strong. Two nurses ran over and tackled him at the head of the ward. She continued to hold onto his arm until two more nurses appeared and bound his ankles and hands. The men carried away the boy as he squirmed like a snake.

Katherine slowly regained her feet. A doctor came over and helped her to a chair by the ward nurse's desk. She explained the incident. He said, "Sounds like he had an epileptic fit. You did very well under the circumstances. Thank you."

The doctor left and Katherine sat for a while longer to catch her breath. The clock chimed and she realized that it was ten o'clock, an hour past her quitting time. Saddled with a banging headache, she took off her work cap and put on her bonnet and shawl. As she left, she said good night to Mr. Ball, who barely acknowledged her. She was anxious to discuss the incident with Mrs. McBain and see if there were any books on the condition that the soldier suffered.

She walked a few paces on Barnard Street when Mr. Ball and Mr. Marsh, another nurse, stopped her. The ward nurse said, "Excuse me, Miss Downes."

Katherine replied, "Yes, Mr. Ball?"

"Mr. Marsh here just told me that he saw you take a watch off a dead soldier and put it in your pocket. Is that true?"

Katherine froze. She had to think back to Private Brantley. Her experience with him seemed so long ago. "No, of course it's not! The boy asked me with his last words to give the watch to his mother. I didn't know what to do. I wanted to help him. I looked for you, but you weren't at your desk or in the ward. I held on to it and then that other soldier had an epileptic fit. I had completely forgotten about the watch."

Marsh stepped toward Katherine. "Liar. We have a place to store the valuables of dead soldiers so they may be properly distributed. Nurses don't take that responsibility on themselves—unless they want to steal something."

Katherine's eyes narrowed to glowering slits. "I don't know anything about the storage area. I was granting a dying soldier his last request. And don't you call me a liar!"

Mr. Ball said to Marsh, "Let me handle this." He turned to Katherine, "Mr. Marsh is right about the procedure. Do you have the watch with you?"

Katherine reached into her apron pocket and pulled out the timepiece. Ball said, "Please, come back with me. The surgeon-in-charge will determine whether to simply ban you from the hospital or report you to the police."

Katherine said, "What on earth do you mean? I haven't done anything."

"Miss Downes, you were seen taking something from a dead soldier. It's on your person outside the hospital. I have no choice. Let's go."

Minutes later the three were at Mr. Ball's desk. He said, "I'll be right back," and walked away. Katherine glared at Mr. Marsh, who smirked and turned his head.

Mr. Ball returned with the surgeon-in-charge, Dr. W. B. Waring, who said, "All right. What's the problem?"

Mr. Ball said, "Doctor Waring, Mr. Marsh saw Miss Downes take a watch from a dead soldier and leave the hospital with it."

Marsh said, "Doctor, she should be punished for such an outrage."

Katherine shouted, "Dr. Waring, this is all a big lie!" She explained her actions.

Waring asked Mr. Ball, "I've heard only good things about Miss Downes from the other doctors. Several soldiers have told me how much they appreciated her attentions. Tell me why you doubt her. . . ."

Waring froze when he saw James McBain walk into the ward. He said, "Mr. McBain, how are you?" The doctor knew the McBains well and was aware that they were among the most generous supporters of the Georgia Relief and Hospital Association.

James shook the doctor's hand and said, "It's good to see you, Doctor Waring." Then, to Waring's astonishment, he hugged Katherine and said, "Thank God you're all right. It's past ten and we were worried about you. Have you been here all this time?"

Katherine glanced at Dr. Waring. "Yes. I've just been accused of stealing a watch from a dead soldier by this man here." She pointed to Marsh.

The doctor's eyebrows arched to his hairline. "Mr. McBain, are you and Miss Downes related?"

"In a sense, sir. We took in Miss Downes and her two sisters last year. They've lived with us ever since." McBain asked Katherine, "My dear girl, can you explain to me what's going on?"

Katherine recounted the incident to James and Waring. She ended her story by nodding at Marsh and saying, "Then this loathsome scoundrel accused me of stealing it."

McBain said to Waring, "Doctor, you were going to punish an unpaid volunteer for granting a soldier's last wish?"

Waring said, "I wasn't going to do anything, sir. I'm just learning the facts myself." He asked Katherine, "What's the mother's name?"

Katherine pulled out the slip of paper from her apron pocket and read, "Mrs. Edith Brantley of Milledgeville."

Dr. Waring said, "You wrote down her name?"

"Yes, when I couldn't find Mr. Ball. I didn't want to forget it."

Waring asked Ball, "Isn't this proof beyond a doubt that Miss Downes intended to contact the mother?" Mr. Ball turned as red as the old Georgia state flag. The doctor said, "Sir, if you value your job, you will apologize to this young lady right now."

Ball turned to Katherine. "I sincerely apologize, Miss Downes. You were obviously trying to help the soldier."

Waring said to Marsh, "You are now reassigned to the contagious disease ward. Apologize and never harass this woman again, do you understand?"

Marsh lowered his head like a naughty schoolboy. "Yes, Doctor. I'm sorry, Miss Downes."

Waring said, "Miss Downes, I know that you will send the watch to the soldier's mother." He said to James, "I'm very sorry for the confusion, sir. I have heard nothing but compliments about Miss Downes. She needs to be commended for her service. You should be very proud of her."

McBain said, "I certainly am." He tipped his hat and Katherine took his arm as they marched from the hospital. Katherine wondered what might have happened to her if she hadn't had Mr. McBain's support.

❦

When they entered the front door, Pauline and Mary ran from the parlor into Katherine's arms. She asked, "What are you two doing up so late?"

Pauline said, "We were so worried. Mr. McBain went looking for you and then Captain McBain came home."

Sarah, Danny, and Joseph joined them. Katherine said, "Captain, you're back!"

Joseph stepped up, shook his father's hand, and embraced Katherine. After she explained the incident for the fourth time that evening, he joked, "You couldn't stay out of trouble while I was gone, could you?"

Katherine's face flushed. She said, "I'm so sorry. I embarrassed you all."

"You didn't embarrass anyone, Miss Downes," Joseph said. "You made us all proud the way you handled yourself. It just seems like you have a little dark cloud that follows you wherever you go."

Sarah laughed. "Bad luck seems to befall her, but good luck always follows."

James went to the cabinet, poured three glasses of port, and said, "Son, I know it's late, but you must tell us a little about your trip."

Sarah said, "I agree. Danny, Mary, and Pauline, it's time for bed."

Danny defiantly folded his arms. "Pa, promise you'll tell me about it tomorrow?"

Joseph hugged his boy again. "I promise, Danny." The children kissed the adults goodnight and went upstairs. Joseph took a sip of his port and said, "The effort took a lot longer than we thought. Europe is full of representatives from various governments looking for ships. Prices seemed to increase daily. But we purchased three steamers, all capable of carrying up to eight hundred bales of cotton, making seventeen knots, and drafting in nine feet of water. They'll be delivered here over the next three months."

James raised his glass and said, "Congratulations! That's excellent news. The generals, President Davis, and Governor Brown will be delighted."

Joseph raised his glass but didn't drink. He said, "They won't be happy for long. We were in England just a few days when we learned of the fall of Vicksburg and the defeat at Gettysburg. The British and French don't think we have a chance of winning and won't back us, as we've been hoping since the war started."

James said, "Our government knows that. The blockade runners are more important than ever to our survival."

Joseph explained, "I agree, but they'll be having a more difficult time reaching our shores. England, Bermuda, and the Bahamas are crawling with Union spies. They alert their navy whenever one of our ships leaves port. We almost got intercepted coming into Wilmington. We grounded and had to take the lifeboats up the Cape Fear River. We lost the ship. The Yankees have it now." James's face turned glum. An uncomfortable silence passed.

Katherine spoke. "Captain, tell us about all the historic places you visited. That must have been so exciting. Did you think about how people lived hundreds of years ago, without so many of our modern conveniences?"

Joseph smiled at her. He thought Katherine had become more beautiful and womanly than when he left. He wanted to tell her all about his trip. "Yes, I had those very thoughts, but we'll talk about them another day. I'm exhausted." The family retired for the night. Katherine went to bed, glad that Joseph was back, and happier than ever to be with the McBains. ⌒

CHAPTER THIRTY-FIVE

"We'll Be Back Before You Know It"
April – June 1864

James McBain sat on his horse on the avenue of oaks behind the big house and looked to his son for suggestions. "Well, any ideas?"

Joseph replied, "Father, I think you're worrying needlessly. The Yankees haven't made a move yet into Georgia, and if they do, we'll beat them back to Tennessee. They won't get near Atlanta, no less Savannah."

James said, "I hope you're right son, but you'll be leaving soon and if anything should happen to your mother or me in your absence, I want you to know where our gold and Yankee dollars are hidden."

Joseph reached over and patted his father on the shoulder. "If it will give you comfort, then let's do it."

James said, "I just want to identify the places so you'll know. I won't hide it until they're at our door." He surveyed the area. "The house is out. They'll tear it apart if they get this far." He twisted around in his saddle so he could see more of the property he had worked so hard to build into an economic force. "What about the stables or the coach house?"

Joseph said, "The stables make sense. Let's take a look."

It was April 1864 and James McBain's fear of defeat was creeping towards reality. In November 1863 the Yankees had repulsed the Confederate attempt to retake Chattanooga, known as the "Gateway to the South." Since then the Union had started amassing a huge army on the Tennessee-Georgia border, leaving no doubt that they planned to march on the state. The rebels, with vastly smaller numbers, had to drive the invaders from their land or Georgia would crumble and their revolution smolder in ashes.

McBain was one of the wealthiest men in Savannah because he always planned for eventualities. He realized from the start of the war that if the Union won, the Confederate currency would be worthless. By April 1864 he had accumulated a small fortune of forty thousand dollars in gold and eighty thousand dollars in greenbacks and northern bank notes. However, he still stood to lose most of his assets if the Yankees prevailed, as there was no way he could protect his investment in his one hundred eighty slaves, worth about two hundred thousand dollars, other than by selling them. This he was loathe to do, as he felt responsible for them. Besides, few men in the South had the funds or the backbone to make such a large investment in the current state of affairs. James had to shield what he could and decided to identify four hiding places, two in Savannah and two at the Heritage. If the Yankees found one or even two, he would still have enough to survive.

When Joseph returned from Europe, he informed his father that his leg had improved to the point where he could get around without a cane or crutch, although he still limped a bit and couldn't run full bore. But he felt he could ride a horse and shoot a rifle as well as any man and was anxious to defend Georgia.

James used his connections to get Joseph into active service and paid a visit to General Hugh Weedon Mercer, who commanded the Savannah defenses. Mercer had spent much of his time trying to convince Georgia planters, often unsuccessfully, to hire out their slaves to the military to build earthworks around the city. The general appreciated James McBain for sending so many of his men and gladly accommodated his friend. By April Joseph had been transferred to the staff of General Mercer's brigade, enabling him to go to northern Georgia, but not in a regiment of infantry, which always suffered the most casualties.

James and Joseph entered the building and walked its length. There wasn't much to the interior—twenty stalls on the ground and rafters above. Joseph pointed up. "We could hide a box somewhere on those beams. No one goes there."

"A box would get destroyed in a fire."

Joseph kicked at the dirt. "How about burying a box in a stall?"

James said, "Hmmm. I think that would work. I'll have to dig the hole without the servants seeing me. But I like that idea. Now, we need one more spot on the plantation."

Joseph rubbed his growling belly. He was getting hungry. "How about the dairy house? It's all brick. I'll prepare a place in the wall before I leave for North Georgia."

James said, "Yes, I like that, too."

Joseph replied, "Good. Let's eat." As they returned to the house, they saw Pauline sitting on the front lawn of the big house, sketch book and pencil in hand, with Mary and Danny sitting on either side of her. Joseph called, "Time for dinner."

During the meal, Joseph asked fourteen-year-old Pauline about her drawing.

She explained that Truvy wanted to make a collection of sketches of some of the mansions and churches in Savannah, in memory of his father. "I said I'd do some for him. I'm also going to teach him how to draw. He's real excited to learn."

Joseph nearly choked up at Truvy's effort. He said, "Truvy is a remarkable boy. Thank you for helping him." James and Sarah echoed him.

James asked Pauline about her work at the Savannah Wayside Home. The girl had asked Katherine and Mrs. McBain for permission to volunteer. Sarah was thrilled at the request and convinced Mr. Isaac Cohen of the Georgia Relief and Hospital Association to let the girl perform cleaning duties for a few hours one afternoon a week after school. Pauline assured everyone that the effort was not interfering with her studies and she would prove it at next month's school examinations, which were open to the public.

Joseph said, "I'd love to be there, Pauline, but unfortunately I'll be gone."

Danny asked, "Pa, when are you leaving?"

"In a few days, Danny. General Johnston is already camped in northern Georgia and has ordered all his regiments to report to Dalton."

Danny looked down at his plate. "I don't want you to go, Pa. You're always leaving."

Mary said, "Me either. I want you to ssstay, too." Katherine sat quietly, unhappy as well at Joseph's departure.

Joseph smiled. "Mary, your lisp is improving." Mary grinned at the compliment. He then said to Danny, "I have a duty, son. It will be over soon."

"I hope so. Everyday at school some boy says he lost his father or uncle or brother in a battle. I want things to be like they used to. I want you here all the time. I miss Dante. And I wish Hercules would come home. I hope he's all right."

Joseph missed Hercules, too, and wondered how the coachman was faring.

⚬━⚬

Hercules had gained the trust of all the soldiers who worked at the Union corral on Hilton Head. The ten dollars a month pay was enough to survive, but the value of his new-found freedom couldn't be expressed in dollars and cents. Still, returning to Savannah and Patience was never far from his mind.

Hercules adjusted to life with one arm as best he could, and had Jehova to assist. Hercules asked little of the boy, but made it clear that he was to find him immediately if he ever saw Kitt on the island. Hercules believed that Kitt would jump at the chance to become a soldier, and if he did, he was bound to pass through Hilton Head. So Hercules was not shocked when Jehova sprinted up to him one day in April as he was feeding horses. "Ah see Kitt, Huhclees. He at de soljuh camp at Drayton plantation."

Hercules dropped the bucket he was holding and checked the position of the sun. He said, "It's almost quitting time, Jehova. Bring Kitt to Fish Haul Creek at the eastern end of Mitchelville in an hour. Tell him we need to talk and put our problems behind us."

Jehova said, "Wut problems?"

"Just get him. And don't say nothin' about my arm. Hear?" Jehova ran off.

The final hour passed quickly and Hercules headed to Mitchelville village, past the cabins, to an empty lot bordering Fish Haul Creek. He could hear himself breathing at the prospect of seeing Kitt face to face, but he wasn't certain how to handle the encounter. He had daydreamed of getting even, but he reasoned that he should first hear Kitt's explanation about the incident. Perhaps Kitt would apologize. Then what? Hercules stopped for a moment to calm himself. He would need all his wits about him. Kitt, in his mid-twenties, was strong and mean.

As Hercules neared the creek he spotted Kitt, wearing a blue uniform and cap, and Jehova sitting on the ground overlooking the creek and chatting. They heard his footsteps and stood. As hard as he tried to relax, Hercules could feel steam lifting off his face. He walked up to the pair and said, "Welcome to Mitchelville, Kitt."

Kitt smiled and appeared happy to see Hercules. "Hello, Huhclees. Ah see you finely come obuh tuh us free nigguhs. Ahm gladee you do." Then his eyes bulged when he noticed the empty left sleeve. "Wu . . . wut happen?"

The question angered Hercules. "What do you think happened? Don't you remember shooting me?"

Kitt glanced at Jehova to see if he were taking sides, but the boy stood still with his mouth hanging open. Kitt replied, "Ah jes' shoot de gun tuh warn you. Not at you."

"You have damned good aim for someone who ain't aiming."

Kitt poked his finger into Hercules's chest. "Den why you fool wid me? You come obuh tuh us, snatch up Danny, an' run."

Hercules slapped the finger away. Kitt obviously wasn't about to apologize. "You said that you'd kill Danny if you didn't get your family in a week. I believed you. I couldn't let that happen."

Kitt stepped closer to Hercules their noses almost touched. "Why you worry so fuh dat white boy? One day he own me an' you. And when us hab chillun, he own dem, too. Ah need Danny tuh git muh brudduhs."

Hercules shouted and a dot of saliva flew from his mouth onto Kitt's cheek. "Master Joseph promised—Danny for your family. You know he keeps his word. There was no need to threaten his boy."

Kitt put his hands on his hips and wagged his head in defiance. "Ah don' belieb no white man fuh nuttin'. Ah wanna shoot dem all."

"Well, you wound up shooting me. And I ain't white."

"You jes' as bad." Kitt spit in Hercules's face.

Hercules wiped his face with his hand and said, "You no good nigger!" He put his hand on Kitt's chest and pushed with all his might, throwing him to the ground. Kitt scrambled to his feet, charged low, and tackled Hercules around the legs. They both hit the ground but Hercules regained his feet first, grabbed Kitt by the arm, and dragged him towards the creek. Kitt managed to get to his feet but had no balance. Hercules swung him as hard as he could, sending Kitt rolling down the steep embankment into the water. Kitt went under but surfaced, clutched a piece of marsh grass, and pulled himself half-way onto the bank. Hercules side-stepped down the bank to the waterline. He placed his right palm on the ground for support and kicked Kitt in the face. Kitt screamed but managed to grab Hercules's ankle. Hercules tried to shake Kitt's grasp but couldn't, and started to slide into the water, too. He shifted his weight onto his butt and kicked Kitt in the face with his other foot, causing Kitt to lose his grip. Hercules panted as he watched Kitt reach in vain for something to grab and drift to the middle of the stream. Kitt waved his hands frantically over his head. He went under and rose to the surface, coughing out a blast of water and crying, "He'p me, Huhclees. Ah cain' swim."

Hercules grunted a laugh, wiped his hand on his pants, and said, "I know that."

Jehova shouted, "Huhclees, Kitt gwine tuh drown!" He slid down the embankment, knelt at the water's edge, and extended his hand towards Kitt, who stretched for it.

Hercules grabbed Jehova by the pants and pulled him back. He said, "Get up the bank before I throw you in!" Jehova gaped at Kitt, who slapped at the water, trying to stay afloat. Then he did as he was ordered.

Hercules stood and watched Kitt disappear. This time he didn't come back up. Hercules waited until bubbles started to explode on the surface. He side-stepped up the embankment, clutched Jehova's shirt, and pulled him face to face. "Now you know how I lost my arm. Kitt tried to kill me. I'm going to tell the sergeant that we were here talking and he slipped and fell in the creek. You and I can't swim and couldn't save him. That's our story. You understand?"

Jehova shook like a leaf in a wind storm.

Hercules shook Jehova. "Do you understand?" Jehova finally nodded. Hercules turned and stomped away.

⁂

Joseph told Danny, "I'm sure Hercules is doing fine, son, and can't wait to return here after the war."

"I hope so, Pa."

Katherine wondered about that. If the coachman did return, he would never accept her. Knowing the McBains' fondness for him, she and her sisters would have to leave. That saddened her, but she'd deal with it at the appropriate time. She had learned the future held too many surprises to plan for every possibility.

Joseph left for North Georgia one week later, in mid-April, leaving behind several heavy hearts.

⚜

Sarah waited until they were lying in bed for a few minutes, when James would be too tired to argue. In the warm, early June night she asked, "Dear, are you awake?"

James opened one eye, aware that his wife was about to ask for something by calling his name just as he was about to fall sleep. "Barely."

"The situation in northern Georgia is dire. General Johnston is retreating in the face of the Union army and taking heavy casualties. There's no question that the Yankees are headed to Atlanta, and we can't let it fall. At some point Johnston is going to have to stop and face General Sherman. Things will get worse."

"I agree," James said, "We must pray to God that our boys will be victorious."

"I feel the need to do more than pray. The hospitals of the Army of Tennessee have been moved to Marietta. I want to go to there with the Savannah Relief Committee and help."

James sat up. "Marietta?"

Sarah remained prone. "I received a letter from Isaac Cohen of the committee. He's there now. He and the other committeemen delivered the supplies collected in Savannah over the past few months. He says the town is overrun with sick and wounded soldiers and they're desperate for volunteers. He'd like Katherine and me to help at the hospitals and Pauline, if she's available, at one of the wayside homes. I also received a letter from my sister Rebecca today. Her husband is very sick and she wants me to help her close their shoe factory in Roswell and bring them back to Savannah. Marietta and Roswell are nearby. We can spend a month in Marietta with the relief committee, pick up Rebecca and Francis, and return here. We'll be back in two months. We won't be exposed to any danger."

James lit the lamp and faced his wife. "Absolutely not, dear. It's too dangerous. The way Johnston's been fighting, the Yankees will be in Marietta by July. That's one month away. The medical director will have to move the hospitals before then."

Sarah rolled onto her side and looked her husband in the eye. "As soon as he gives that order, we'll pick up Rebecca and Francis, drive to Atlanta, and be on the train back here. Besides, I'll get a chance to see Joseph."

"It's still not a good idea."

Sarah patted James's arm. "Are you saying that our sons can go to war and risk their lives but women can't take chances caring for them? We can let them suffer alone on a battlefield or in some dirty tent because there's no one there to comfort and treat them? What if Joseph is wounded again? Will you be consoled knowing that he won't get help because volunteers are worried about the danger?"

James took a deep breath and turned out the lamp. He knew the discussion was over. "When are you going?"

"In a few days. Katherine and Pauline have to prepare and pack. Please don't mention this to anyone. We want to keep it a secret from Danny and Mary until the last moment. They won't be happy."

"Isn't Pauline too young for this?"

"At first, I thought so, but Katherine wants her to come. Pauline's almost fifteen and has been helping at the wayside home here for two months. She works hard and knows her responsibilities. The soldiers and other women adore her." James didn't comment. Sarah thought he may have dozed off. She said softly, "We've been living under the threat of an attack on Savannah by the Union fleet for three years now, and it's still real. We're not much safer here than in Marietta."

James looked at the slivers of moonlight slicing into the room from between the curtains. The war that was supposed to be over in a few months was entering its fourth year and causing more harm to the South than he had ever imagined. He couldn't wait for it to end. "Promise to return as soon as the hospitals are evacuated from Marietta. There's no telling what those Yankee vandals will do."

Sarah leaned over and kissed her husband's cheek. "I promise, dear. Thank you. And don't worry. We'll be back here before you know it. I'll need to take two servants with me. Chloe loves the girls, and they love her."

James yawned and said, "Take Dante, too. He's out of work since the last of General Mercer's officers have left for North Georgia. He can carry bags and do all the physical things that you'll need, and you'll have a good cook."

"I understand his wife is pregnant."

"If you return in two months, he'll be back in plenty of time for the birth."

With her mission accomplished, Sarah closed her eyes and waited for sleep. Then James said, "Dear, please take Joseph's mail to him. He got a letter from Andersonville prison of all places. It had no return name, just the post mark."

"Andersonville? Who could it be from?"

"I'm sure he'll tell you when he opens it. I'm curious, too."

James McBain looked up but didn't stand when Katherine walked into his study. She said, "You asked to see me, sir?"

"Yes. Please forgive me for not getting up." General Lee peered over the desk, looked at Katherine, sniffed the air, and went back to sleep on McBain's lap. Within days of Sarah telling Mary that she could keep the cat as long as he stayed out of the first and second floors, General Lee had snuck upstairs and chose his favorite daytime sleeping spot—a human lap. James found the warm, purring animal soothing and didn't chase him away, although every time he went out he had to swipe cat hairs from his suit.

Katherine laughed at Mr. McBain's predicament. "Yes, sir."

"You're leaving for Marietta tomorrow. I want you to know how proud I am of you and Pauline for volunteering—although I still think Pauline is too young."

"She is young," Katherine acknowledged, "but I understand that women of all ages, from all over the state, are converging on Marietta to help. Pauline can be of great service. And Mrs. McBain says that we'll return here long before the Yankees get to Marietta, if in fact they ever do. It will be difficult enough for me to be separated from Mary. I couldn't bear to be apart from both of them for two months. I'm happy Mary will have Danny and Truvy while we're away."

"I understand. Have you told Mary yet?"

"No, I'll do that today when Mrs. McBain tells Danny. It won't be easy."

"Remember, I'm still holding your gold. If the Yankees make it this far, I'm going to hide my funds. What would you like me to do with yours?"

"Please hide mine, too. I won't need it in Marietta."

McBain placed General Lee on the desk, stood, and embraced Katherine. "I'm going to miss you. Please take care of yourselves."

Katherine held him tight. "Don't worry about us, sir. We'll be perfectly safe." ✑

◦⁓◦

CHAPTER THIRTY-SIX

The Loveliest Town in North Georgia

June 1864

Mary wept when she learned that she would be separated from her sisters for two months. Danny stomped around the family library, insisting that he could help fight the Yankees. Dante shrugged when he learned of his assignment. He wanted to be a chef for the McBains or at a restaurant and near his pregnant wife, but anything would be better than cooking in a hot, bug-infested camp for a bunch of officers, which Massa offered as his only alternative. Chloe looked forward to traveling, taking care of the two sisters, and a change in her lifetime routine.

On the morning of June 10, 1864, Sarah McBain and her group boarded the Central of Georgia Railroad for Macon. They stayed overnight in a hotel and early the next day took the Macon & Western Railroad to Atlanta. After another night's lodging they walked one block to the depot for the last leg of their journey. They stopped on the curb across the street from the Western & Atlantic depot and wondered how they were going to negotiate their way through the throng to get to the train. About a hundred wagons clogged the street. Countless workmen carried boxes of ammunition, burlap sacks with rice and potatoes, and packages of edibles, medicines, clothing, and other supplies from the wagons to the fifteen boxcars, screaming, "Coming through," and "Watch behind you! Watch! Watch!" More men stood inside the boxcars and stacked the items. Hundreds of soldiers returning from furloughs crammed the boarding path in front of the eight passenger cars.

The group walked around the wagons to the other side of the street. Dante staggered under the weight of Sarah's two valises and his own carpetbag, but Chloe easily handled the girls' two carpetbags and her own. They reached the back of the line of soldiers, who stood silently, shoulder to shoulder; their eyes were fixed straight ahead as if they were in a trance. Two privates turned and saw them, stepped aside, and tapped the shoulders of the men in front of them, who also moved away. They created a chain reaction that caused the others to part like the Red Sea. Sarah and the sisters walked through, thanking the men and boys as they passed, and boarded. Because there were so many passengers, Chloe and

Dante had to sit in the baggage car.

The ride to Marietta was subdued, with Sarah, Katherine, and Pauline as quiet as the soldiers, most of whom continually snuck glances at the females. However, there were a few outbursts of laughter from four privates sitting in the front of the car who acted as if they were going to a party. The twenty-mile, stop-and-go trip took three hours. When the train arrived in Marietta the women watched from inside the car as workers converged on the boxcars like ants, unloading the supplies and carrying them to a long line of covered and open wagons on an adjoining street.

The soldiers let the women exit first. As they stepped onto the boarding path, Sarah's sister, Rebecca Toll, appeared and embraced Sarah. Grey-haired Rebecca was two inches shorter than Sarah, squat, and walked with a slight limp. But she was a bundle of energy, constantly talking and waving her hands.

A nearby officer raised a hand in the air and shouted, "Soldiers and other passengers, move away from the cars now! This train has to return to Atlanta as soon as possible. All soldiers, report immediately to the officer of direction in the city hall building on the public square straight ahead of you. He will arrange transportation to your regiment. If a wagon is not available today, he will find you a place to sleep for the night. Move away now so we can unload and get the seriously wounded soldiers in the cars."

The women walked across the twelve-foot-wide boarding path to the front of the three-story, brick Kennesaw House Hotel. As soon as the area cleared, volunteers carried soldiers wrapped in bandages and rags on stretchers from the hotel to the box cars. Other men, mostly amputees on crutches, boarded the passenger cars on their own.

Isaac Cohen appeared and tipped his hat. "Mrs. McBain, girls, I'm so glad you made it. Here are your badges identifying you as Savannah Relief Committee volunteers. Wear them at all times."

Sarah introduced Cohen to Rebecca and said, "Sir, there's so much activity."

Cohen replied, "Sherman's moving closer and the battles are getting bloodier. Almost every resident has left town. The only people here, other than the sick and wounded, are soldiers, army medical staff, and volunteers from the relief associations. All buildings and houses have been converted into hospitals, headquarters for the officers, wayside homes, storage areas, or quarters for the volunteers. The Yankees control the rail line north of here to Chattanooga. We only operate it to Atlanta. All our supplies come from there. As soon as the train arrives, the sacks, crates, and containers are loaded onto wagons and taken to the front or to storerooms in town. Then we load the train with the badly wounded for treatment in Atlanta hospitals. It continues all day—ambulances, wagons, soldiers, and trains coming and going, and the job gets done."

The women grimaced. Finally, the whistle blew and the train lurched ahead, returning to Atlanta. When it cleared the station, Katherine pointed to a procession of about fifty wagons grinding along a street running parallel to the railroad tracks. Cohen explained, "That's Kennesaw Avenue, which connects Marietta with the battlefields. Those are ambulances coming from the front. They arrive all day long. Keep in mind that the soldiers were wounded long before they get here—perhaps a day or more—and although a field surgeon has already dressed their wounds, their condition is often deplorable. And it's made worse by the ride over these bumpy roads. Surgeons here examine each soldier to determine where he should be treated. The most serious cases remain at this hotel, but we also have six other hospitals in the area—fifteen hundred beds in all, and we're still woefully short. There's always a wait for a surgeon. Once a soldier has his operation, he is taken to a bed to convalesce. We volunteers and nurses help heal their wounds, feed them, and make them comfortable until they're sent home or back to the front. Of course, some don't survive and we must bury them."

Pauline pointed to a field jammed with tents on the other side of the tracks and asked, "What's over there?"

"That's a convalescing area for the sick and less seriously wounded, and soldiers waiting for transport to the front."

Sarah said, "Mr. Cohen, as I wrote you, I have to go to Roswell now with my sister for a few days. But the girls are staying here. Please take good care of them."

Cohen said, "I'll treat them like my own daughters. When you return, look for me in this hotel. It serves as our headquarters. Have a good trip." He lifted the girls' carpetbags and walked inside the building. Katherine and Pauline stared wide-eyed at each other, waved goodbye to Sarah and the others, and followed the man.

Cohen spoke over his shoulder to the girls. "This hotel is used as a receiving and distributing hospital, a surgery hospital, a recovery area for the more seriously wounded men, and quarters for medical staff and volunteers." He walked into the lobby and stopped to let pass two men carrying a soldier on a stretcher. He explained, "All the larger rooms—banquet rooms and storerooms—off the lobby are used for surgeries and soldiers recovering from surgery." He climbed one flight of stairs and, after knocking on a door, entered a room crammed with four beds. He put the bags on the floor and said, "The first floor is for women volunteers and these are your quarters, along with Mrs. McBain and Mrs. Branch, who's taken the bed against the far wall. Chose any other. We Savannah committeemen are staying in apartments upstairs."

Pauline dropped onto the closest bed, exhausted by three days of travel and Mr. Cohen's non-stop explanations. He said, "Don't get comfortable. We have work to do."

Pauline bounced back up. Cohen continued, "If it weren't for the Georgia Relief and Hospital Association and the relief committees, our boys wouldn't receive this care. All men who are able are fighting in the war. We must do our part. I'm taking you both to a wayside home. It operates just like the one in Savannah.

We try to work shifts of three hours on and two off, but because of a shortage of help, we can't always meet that goal. You must be prepared to assist anywhere at any time."

The girls followed Mr. Cohen out the back door of the hotel and up the street to a large park about three times the size of Johnson Square in Savannah. The area, once a spot to relax and mingle, was filled with tents. The activity in and around the square was no less frenetic than at the depot. Cavalrymen in grey uniforms galloped about on horseback; volunteers in jeans, work shirts, and caps, their arms laden with boxes and sacks, ran to emergencies; and soldiers wrapped in bandages hobbled on gnarly canes and crutches. The place smacked of desperation. Cohen said, "This used to be the loveliest town in North Georgia. Now it's the biggest hospital."

They walked along Church Street, past three houses of worship used as hospitals. Cohen said he hoped to get Mrs. McBain and Katherine working in one as soon as Mrs. McBain returned. They arrived at the wayside home farther down the street and Cohen introduced the girls to Charlotte Branch of Savannah, the supervisor of the day. Cohen said he would check on them later and left. Mrs. Branch showed them around and explained their duties. Within an hour they were welcoming soldiers, serving them food and coffee, and writing letters for them.

During a break, Katherine told Mrs. Branch that she, Pauline, and their younger sister had been taken in by the McBains eighteen months earlier. Charlotte said, "Mrs. McBain is one of the most dedicated women in all Georgia. She has so much energy for a woman her age. You're fortunate to be living with that family." She explained that her oldest son John had been killed at the first battle of Manassas, fighting alongside Joseph McBain. Her second oldest son, Sanford, was captured at that battle. He was eventually exchanged and then seriously wounded and captured at Gettysburg. He was currently recuperating in a Delaware prison.

Katherine said, "Ma'am, I'm sorry for your loss."

"Thank you, dear girl. I have another boy, my youngest, Hamilton— we call him Hammie. He fought at Manassas with his brothers, all members of the Oglethorpe Light Infantry. He returned to Savannah and became a lieutenant with the Savannah Cadets, part of Mercer's brigade. He's at the front now, but I hear he's coming to Marietta tomorrow. You must meet him. He's very handsome and bright. And I'm not saying that just because I'm his mother."

Katherine laughed. "I'd be honored to meet one so brave. Captain McBain is with the First Georgia on General Mercer's staff."

Charlotte folded a towel with stringy edges and fluffed it in her hands. "Ah, yes, Joseph McBain. When he was a bachelor every eligible girl in town wanted to make his acquaintance." She sighed. "Then he married a Yankee girl." Five soldiers, each carrying tattered haversacks, walked in the front door. Charlotte said, "Back to work. I'll check their papers and register them. Get them coffee with lots of milk and sugar."

The next day Mrs. Branch had Katherine come to the front room to meet her son. He was as tall as Joseph, almost as handsome, and, she guessed, a few years older than she. He combed his shiny brown hair straight back and parted it on the side. Mrs. Branch said, "Miss Downes, this is my son Hamilton. Hamilton, please meet Miss Downes."

Hamilton's face turned into one giant, tooth-filled smile. "Hello, Miss Downes. It is my pleasure to meet you." Hamilton tugged at his crumpled grey jacket to improve its appearance, and then smoothed his hair with his hand.

Katherine smiled back and said, "It's nice to meet you, Lieutenant. I've heard so much about you from Mrs. Branch."

"You can call me Hammie, Miss Downes. All my friends do."

"I'd be glad to, Hammie. What were you doing in Savannah before you became a soldier?"

Hamilton was relieved the girl asked him a question, as he didn't know what to say next. "I worked in the counting house of a commission merchant on the Bay. I'm real good with numbers. I can add them in my head." Katherine laughed. She found the young man friendly and engaging. He asked her, "What about you, Miss Downes? What kind of work did you do back home?"

"I worked for Mr. Lippman, sewing uniforms for the soldiers. I also volunteered at the hospitals. I kept quite busy."

Hammie fiddled with the brim of his cap as he spoke. "What do you like doing with your leisure time?"

Katherine said, "We go out to Mr. McBain's plantations on Sundays and ride horses. Other times I sit in the squares with my younger sisters and watch them play."

Hamilton smiled and asked her, "What's your favorite square in Savannah?"

Katherine put her index finger on her chin in thought. She admitted, "I don't know that I have just one. They're all so beautiful."

The couple chatted for a few more minutes about the squares. Then Hamilton said, "I have to catch my ride back to the front, but I'd like to visit you next time I'm here, when I have more time."

Katherine replied, "I'll look forward to that, Lieuten . . . I mean Hammie."

Hamilton bowed and left. Katherine said to Charlotte, "He's very charming." Charlotte's face glowed. She said, "I told you so."

Katherine laughed and returned to work. Pauline, who witnessed the meeting from the kitchen doorway, sang, "I think someone likes my sister." Katherine gently tugged her hair.

⁂

The sisters were up sixteen hours a day for the next four days. Their youth and beauty made them popular with the soldiers. While Katherine was used to attention from men, Pauline, at fourteen, was not. She had met soldiers at the Savannah wayside home, but not this many. At first she shied away from them, but in a few days she learned that a smile was as good as any food she could offer. After a while, she befriended lonely looking boys, sketched their portraits, and mailed them to their families.

Sarah returned from Roswell with Chloe and Dante in one of Rebecca's wagons pulled by two mules, which Sarah arranged to keep at a stable near the hotel. She found Mr. Cohen, who got her settled, and then took her to the wayside home to see the sisters. Katherine embraced her and inquired about Mr. Toll's health.

"He's too sick to travel. My sister will contact me when he recovers and we'll immediately return to Savannah, where he can get better care."

Mr. Cohen told Katherine and Sarah that he had arranged with Dr. Dudley Dunn Saunders, the chief surgeon in Marietta for the Army of Tennessee, for Sarah to work as a nurse at the Presbyterian church and Katherine at the Methodist church. Katherine was excited to be serving in a hospital, but unhappy to be apart from her sister during the day. She promised to visit Pauline on breaks.

Cohen found jobs for Dante as a cook and Chloe as a washerwoman in the hotel. Dante slept in Mrs. Toll's wagon. Chloe stayed in a slave cabin with five other washerwomen at a house in town.

Sarah, Katherine, and Pauline spent the following week working from morning till night as mangled soldiers flowed into Marietta. They had breakfast and supper together in the small dining room in the hotel set aside for volunteers.

Pauline behaved far beyond her years and was soon trusted by her supervisors to perform almost every task in the home, including checking in soldiers. One day an emergency call went out from the operating room in the Kennesaw House for clean rags and towels. Mrs. Branch sent Pauline with an armful to the hotel. With her chin resting on the top of the pile to keep it secure, Pauline weaved through the streets and into the hotel. As no one was guarding the door to the operating room, she walked in, unaware that females were not usually allowed entry. Severely injured soldiers lay against two facing walls on makeshift pillows of straw and cotton, leaving an aisle in the middle. Not knowing where to put the rags, Pauline walked to the head of the room, a few feet from a four-by-six-foot wooden board, four inches thick, resting on three evenly placed stacks of wooden crates. A surgeon wearing a white shirt splattered with blood bent from his waist on the far side of the table. He was fixated on a prone soldier wearing only dirt-stained underdrawers and with boney ribs that looked as if they were about to break through the skin. An assistant surgeon sat by the patient's head, dripping chloroform onto the pointed top of a rag wrapped into the shape of a cone and positioned over the soldier's nose and mouth. Without looking up, the surgeon said, "Put those towels on that table. Then pick up that fan and wave it to keep these flies off the soldier's leg."

Pauline deposited the rags, stood opposite the surgeon, and fanned for dear life, moving only her wrist and hand. She looked down to check for flies and saw just above the patient's kneecap a wound the size of a fist exposing the leg muscles and other tissue. She stared at the ceiling. She was no stranger to knives and blood, having helped Katherine behead and dress chickens, but this was a human. Curiosity made her glance down again. The surgeon lifted the leg, took a long knife, and made a deep cut completely around the thigh above the wound. He then flayed two inches of skin from the meat of the leg above the incision. Pauline looked up again and felt her stomach begin to churn. She started taking deep breaths.

"Fan faster!" the doctor yelled. "More to the left! Get those flies off of him!"

She wagged her wrist and silently prayed, "Oh, God, please don't let me get sick. Please." As she peeked again to see if the flies were gone, the doctor cut deeper into the quivering flesh, muscles, and tendons, until the bone was exposed. He grasped an artery with a pincer and tied a thread tightly around it. Pauline looked up and began counting the beams in the ceiling. Then she heard the grinding of a saw. The voices sounded distant, as if they were coming from another room. She tried to swallow and raised her free hand to wipe away the flashing lights in her eyes. Then she collapsed, banging her head on the floor and sending the fan flying.

The surgeon glanced at her and shouted to the assistant, "Pay her no mind! We've got to finish this amputation. Damn those flies!"

A private sitting on the floor nearby with a bloody white rag tied around his shoeless foot inched off his seat onto his backside. He grabbed Pauline under her arms and dragged her toward his place. He picked up his tin cup, poured water on his fingers, and patted her forehead. He said, "Tweren't for this dern war, she'd have every boy in Georgia bringing her flowers. And I'd be first on line."

The soldier sitting next to him said, "Sure is purdy. Don't 'spect she'll be nursin' again anytime soon."

The surgeon finished sewing together the flayed skin over the leg stump, tossed the amputated leg on top of a nearby pile of limbs, and called out, "Take this soldier away. Make sure he gets morphine when he comes to. And get this girl out of here. She shouldn't have been here in the first place. Next man!"

Two committeemen entered the room and hurried to the table, stepping around Pauline. They placed the new amputee onto a stretcher and left for a convalescing room. As they departed, two male nurses ran in and helped the next soldier onto the table. One apologized to the surgeon for being late. He looked at Pauline, who had just opened her eyes and was blinking rapidly. The nurses pulled her up, but her legs wobbled and she dropped onto her backside. They lifted her again and held her. She shook away the cobwebs and said, "Thank you. I'm all right, I think." When the men removed their hands, she kept her balance. She noticed the surgeon staring at her while the assistant surgeon administered chloroform to the next patient. She placed a hand over her mouth and said, "Oh, sir, I'm so sorry. Please forgive me."

As she spoke, the doctor realized Pauline's youth. "There's no need to apologize, young lady. I should never have asked you to stay. You did your best, and I thank you. It's time for you to leave."

Tears ran down Pauline's face. "I failed you and the soldier." She ran from the room, ashamed of her performance. She wanted to pray for forgiveness in private, but every church was occupied. She walked up Church Street, past the wayside home, sobbing, and looking for a place to hide forever.

Katherine had just finished giving a patient medicine when a messenger handed her a note from Sarah asking her to come to the square on her next break to meet Joseph. Katherine told the ward nurse that she had a personal emergency and would return in an hour. She walked at a quickened pace and couldn't suppress a smile when she saw Joseph sitting on a bench next to Sarah. "What a pleasant surprise, Captain."

Joseph stood and took her hand. "You've brightened my day, Miss Downes."

Katherine glowed like a Savannah sunrise. She and Joseph sat and Sarah described her visit with Aunt Rebecca, the drive back from Roswell with Dante and Chloe, and their subsequent work in Marietta.

Joseph talked about his upcoming trip, escorting four hundred prisoners to Andersonville and the many rumors about the prison there. A number of the stories, he assured them, were just Yankee lies and exaggerations. Sarah said, "That reminds me, I have your mail from home." She reached into her purse and pulled out a two-inch-thick stack. "One is from Andersonville."

As Joseph started to thumb through the letters, a grinning Hamilton Branch strolled up the path with his left hand behind his back. Joseph slipped the letters into his jacket pocket. He liked Hammie and admired Mrs. Branch's sacrifice of her three sons. They all stood and greeted him. He returned the salutations and said to Katherine, "I told you I'd be back. Did you receive my letters?"

Katherine said, "I did. It was nice of you to remember me."

Hamilton revealed his left hand, which held a freshly picked bunch of pansies, each having three purple and two yellow petals.

Katherine's mouth opened in shock. "Johnny Jump-Ups! They're beautiful. Thank you so much, Lieutenant." She showed the flowers to Joseph, who appraised them with narrowed eyes, and wondered if she had detected a trace of jealousy. She said to Hamilton, "I will treasure these, Lieutenant."

Hamilton said to Katherine, "I'm glad you like them." He then told Joseph, "It looks like General Johnston is finally going to give Sherman the beating he deserves."

"I agree, Hammie. Have you heard from your brother Santy?"

"Yes, Captain. He's in a prison in Delaware, waiting for his parole. The wound to his lung is a little better, but not much."

Joseph said, "Let's pray he come home soon."

Hamilton agreed, and then half-bowed to Sarah and Katherine. "Please pardon my intrusion on your time. I only had a few minutes and I must be leaving."

Katherine said, "Thank you again, and please be careful."

Hamilton replied, "I'll write again soon." He bid goodbye and left.

Joseph watched him leave before asking, "Where's Pauline? I was hoping to see her." Katherine twirled the flowers in her fingertips and explained that Pauline worked at a wayside home and she would take him there. They all walked the short distance to Church Street where Sarah left them to return to her hospital.

Mrs. Branch greeted Katherine and Joseph and said that Pauline had left for the hotel at noon but hadn't returned. She assumed that Mr. Cohen had sent her on errands. Katherine checked her watch. It was four o'clock. Pauline would never go away for so long without leaving word for her. She and Joseph decided to search for her. They found Mr. Cohen at the hotel, but he hadn't seen Pauline all day. They inquired at the church hospitals and spoke to the workers in the buildings surrounding the square, but no one had seen a fourteen-year-old girl with light red hair in a blue dress and white apron. They walked the clogged streets of Marietta, but without success. Katherine was near tears.

Joseph suggested, "Mother has Aunt Rebecca's wagon at a stable nearby. Let's get it. Pauline can't have gone far on foot." They drove back to the wayside home but Pauline still hadn't returned. However, one soldier overheard them and said he had seen a girl walking on Church Street earlier in the afternoon. "She was cryin' somethin' awful."

Katherine grabbed Joseph's arm and pleaded, "My God, Captain! Let's go!"

The sky was darkening and thunder rumbled in the distance. Joseph told Mrs. Branch that he and Katherine were going to drive down Church Street. Fifteen minutes later they reached the outskirts of the village, but hadn't seen a soul. They continued on the desolate tree-lined road.

Several ear-splitting blasts of thunder shook the ground. Despite the danger of being out in the storm, Joseph drove on. He said, "Don't worry, we'll find her." He cupped his hands around his mouth and yelled "PAULINE!" but they heard only an echo.

Minutes later a soldier on horseback sprinted to them. "Captain McBain?"

"Yes, Private?"

"Mrs. Branch wants you to know that the girl Pauline is back safely at the wayside home."

Katherine clasped her hands together and gasped, "Oh, thank God!"

The soldier said, "Better get back, sir. This is one big storm acomin'," and left.

Joseph turned around the wagon and drove a half-mile before the heavens opened. He pulled off the road into a heavily wooded area that provided some protection from the rain. He parked on a large mound and told Katherine, "Quick, get underneath."

He took a tarp from the bed and spread it on the ground under the wagon. They sat two feet apart. Joseph had to slump over to avoid hitting his head on the undercarriage. They watched little rivers of rainwater flow by their sides. Katherine felt like she was shipwrecked on an island. Joseph looked at her. "Feel better about Pauline?"

Katherine hugged her knees to her chest. "I'm so relieved. I'm going to scold her, but I can't wait to hug her." She looked at Joseph and acknowledged, "I'll hug her first."

CRACK! A huge flash of lightning lit the sky. It lifted a terrified Katherine into the air and nearly on Joseph. He put his arm around her and held her to his side. "That was close, but we're safe here." He stroked her shoulder. "You're shivering. Don't be afraid." He looked at her, his face only inches from hers.

Katherine held Joseph's gaze, although she trembled inside. She said, "I'm not afraid, Captain. I feel very safe."

Joseph moved an inch closer and she closed her eyes. He kissed her, lightly at first, and, when she didn't protest, more firmly. His heart beat as fast as hers. He pulled away and they stared at each other, both breathing a bit heavier. He kissed her again and she put her hand on his shoulder. He bent forward and she leaned back, pulling him onto her. She wondered if he could tell that this was the first time she had ever kissed a man. Their lips met again. She felt a wave of heat flow through her body and whispered in his ear, "Oh, Joseph."

Joseph had one degree of self-control left. Yet he thought he was about to burst with desire. Katherine was beautiful and he wanted to be with her. He kissed her again, longer and deeper, and then held her tight. He felt her warm breath on his neck. He pulled away. When she opened her eyes he touched a finger to her lips and said, "I think it's stopped raining. We'd better get back to Pauline."

Katherine was speechless. She was aroused and wanted to continue. Joseph seemed to be enjoying the moment, too. She wanted to ask him why he stopped—if there was something she did wrong. But she didn't dare question him, afraid of his answer.

On the drive back they speculated where Pauline might have gone. During periods of silence, she kept thinking about the tenderness they had just shared.

Joseph wondered if he was losing his mind. He was treading on dangerous territory—with many potentially disastrous consequences, such as jeopardizing his marriage, damaging his relationship with his parents, and embarrassing himself in front of his son. He vowed never to allow himself to be so weak again.

As soon as the pair entered the wayside home, Pauline ran to her sister and held her. "I'm sorry, Katherine. Please don't be angry with me." Pauline released her and announced, "You're soaked!" She turned to Joseph, "I apologize, Captain. I caused you trouble as well. I'm nothing but a problem to everyone." She started to cry again.

Katherine said, "No, you're not, Pauline. Now please tell us what happened."

Pauline recounted the day, right up to the time when she hid behind a church, asked God for forgiveness, and heard a voice in the thunder telling her to return to the wayside home.

Joseph said, "You're back safe, that's all we care about." He looked at Katherine. "I have to return to my men to prepare for our trip tomorrow. Take care of yourselves."

Katherine squeezed Joseph's hand and said, "Please be careful, Captain. And thank you again for today. I'll never forget it." Joseph smiled and left.

Katherine returned to the hospital and apologized to the ward nurse for her absence, explaining that her sister had gone missing, but had since been found. Over supper at the hotel later that night, Katherine retold most of the day's events to Sarah as Pauline stared at her plate, still ashamed of her behavior. Sarah held Pauline's hand and said the surgeon must not have noticed that she was so young. She added that Pauline was being forced to grow up much quicker than normal, but that she'd be a better woman for it.

In bed that night, Katherine thought of Joseph. Her body tingled. She had to admit that she felt much more than admiration for him. But she knew that she'd made a big mistake. Their intimacy, if revealed, would ruin her relationship with the McBains and force her and her sisters to move, something she could never let happen. Also, she had kissed a married man—an immoral act which could stain her reputation forever. As much as she yearned to be with Joseph, she could never let it happen again.

Pauline whispered, "Katherine, are you awake?"

"Yes."

"The bombs sound like they're getting closer. I'm scared."

"Captain McBain said that our troops are dug in on Kennesaw Mountain. The Yankees have to get past them to reach Marietta. General Johnston will make a stand and beat them back. Get some sleep and don't worry. We'll be going home soon."

Katherine lay back and closed her eyes. She dreamed that she and Joseph were lying in a meadow. He kissed her again and again. He whispered in her ear that he loved her. He gently ran his hand over her body, from her most private place to her breast. She groaned and arched her hips. She heard a voice say, "Do you like that, Katherine?" She opened her eyes and saw her father sitting on the edge of a bed, grinning at her. She screamed and tried to roll away, but he grabbed her shoulder. She started to cry, "No, please don't," when she heard Pauline say,

"Oldest Sister, you're having a nightmare."

Katherine sat up, took a deep breath, wiped the tears from her eyes, and looked around the room. Thankfully, she didn't wake Mrs. McBain or Mrs. Branch. She whispered, "I'll be all right, Pauline. Go back to bed."

Pauline hugged her sister for several minutes before going back to sleep. Katherine stared into the dark, trying to purge the dream from her mind. Zebudiah didn't appear often, but when he did, it was with the power of a lightning bolt. She felt battered and defenseless and wondered if she could ever have a romantic moment with a man without her father appearing. Eventually, she drifted off. Fortunately, Zebudiah had slithered back into a dark, remote cave in her mind, content to rest and plan his next visit.

Joseph lay in his tent, thinking of Katherine and her warm, stirring kisses. Although he felt a responsibility to reunite with Emily for the sake of his children, he couldn't shake his anger at her for deserting him and Danny. And he wanted Katherine more. But he had to put these thoughts aside and deal with the present—the war. Joseph pulled from his jacket the letters that his mother had given him that afternoon and fanned through them until he saw the one with the postmark from Andersonville. He opened it and read.

> Lieutenant Joseph McBain:
> Sir, my name is Laurence Hulett, brother of Emily, and your brother-in-law. I am one of the crew of the Water Witch, captured by rebels off the coast of Georgia in early June, and sent to Andersonville prison. If you are in any position to do so, I beg that you help us get out of this hell-hole. Time is of the essence. If you could see this place, you would understand.

Joseph's head spun. He wondered what he would say to Laurence, and how he could possibly help him. Though they'd never met, Joseph knew from Emily that her brother had no love for any Southerner. Joseph closed his eyes and his thoughts returned to that afternoon, and the way Katherine had whispered in his ear, "Oh, Joseph."

CHAPTER THIRTY-SEVEN

"Protect Those Girls With Your Life"

July 1864

Over the next few days Katherine often thought of her romantic interlude with Joseph, even though she regretted it. Her daydreaming ended with a huge flow of soldiers from the fighting around Kennesaw Mountain. She worked all day on the wounded, washing and dressing wounds, bandaging them, and administering medicines. Fortunately, Dr. Saunders, the surgeon-in-charge of Marietta's hospitals, appreciated female nurses.

Dr. Saunders, age twenty-nine, was introduced to Katherine on her third day at the Methodist church during his daily review of the hospitals. He was impressed by her speed and efficiency and ability to put soldiers at ease with consoling words. The next day he observed her standing over a new patient and calling to a male nurse for a mustard plaster for his wound. "Please mix the poultice," she said. "I'll apply it." Dr. Saunders walked over, looked at the inflamed injury, and nodded to the nurse.

Later that morning on her break, Katherine sat on a bench in the shade of a tree outside the church, trying to ignore the stifling June heat while reading a book. She was mentally exhausted at seeing so many injured boys. She heard someone say, "Good morning, Miss Downes. Taking a much-needed rest, I see."

Katherine said, "Hello, Dr. Saunders!" and rose.

Saunders removed his top hat and pointed to the bench. As they sat, he said, "I've been very impressed with your work. Have you been nursing long?"

"For about a year, in Savannah. I mostly tended to the sick. We had so many from the camps around the city. But I also cared for some of the wounded. A nurse there showed me how to wash and dress wounds, and mix poultices. Since I came here with the Savannah Relief Committee, I've been working with the wounded."

"You've learned quite well. We're fortunate to have such dedicated volunteers." He looked at the book in her hands. "What's that you're reading?"

"It's a medical manual I found lying on the desk in the surgeons' and nurses' room. I read it on my breaks. It's a little advanced, but I understand a good deal of it."

Saunders took the book and looked at the title page. It read, A Manual of Military Surgery, 1863. Saunders said, "This is my copy. I left it for the surgeons as reference material. I'm gratified that you'd want to read it."

"It's very instructive. The section on gunshot wounds helped me with several patients. It also allows me to communicate better with the doctors."

Saunders said, "Miss Downes, you've lifted my mood immeasurably. Please keep up the good work." He thanked her again and left.

Katherine floated back to her ward. During supper that night, she told Sarah and Pauline about the doctor's compliments. Both of them hugged her.

The next morning Katherine first attended to her most seriously wounded patient. The nurse on the night shift told her that the boy was near death. This was the worst part of her work, seeing a soldier's life fade away. She knelt by his bed and held his hand. "Good morning, Private Walker. It's me, Miss Downes."

The boy opened one eye and uttered. "Who?"

"Miss Downes, your nurse."

The boy gasped, "Don't remember no Miss Downes. I want to go home."

"You will soon. First, you need to get better. I'm going to get you some water."

She went to the water bucket, dipped in a white, chipped cup, and started back to the boy. The head nurse stepped in her way. "Miss Downes," he said, "please stop wasting your time on that soldier. We have other men here who will live if given the proper attention."

Katherine froze. "You're saying I can't take a few minutes to give a soldier who sacrificed his life for the South one last drink?"

"He's almost gone. That water won't help him one bit. Do as I say."

She looked at the cup. "Sir, I'm taking this to the soldier, and I'll hold his head up to help him drink. I'll ask him if there's anything he wants me to tell his mother. I think he's earned that. Then I'll see the other soldiers."

As she walked past him, he said, "I'm reporting you to the surgeon-in-charge of this hospital for insubordination."

Katherine tended to the soldier, who died shortly after his last drink of water. She wrote a letter to the boy's mother on her break, telling her of his bravery and how he thought about her till the end. Katherine knew that she would have to answer for her actions, but she followed her conscience and was ready to defend herself. Still, she breathed a sigh of relief when she learned that the surgeon-in-charge of the hospital had gone to Atlanta with Dr. Saunders for the day.

Katherine didn't share the confrontation with Sarah or Pauline. These were incidents that women in hospitals had to endure. That night, as she lay in bed, Katherine rehearsed her side of the story for the hospital surgeon. The next morning she entered the church with her stomach in a knot. While she had stood her ground, she didn't want to be relieved of her duties. The surgeon-in-charge of the hospital immediately called all doctors, employees, and volunteers to the front of the ward. Katherine feared that she was going to be fired in front of the entire staff and stood at the back of the crowd. The doctor announced, "Please, everyone, Dr. Saunders wants to address us."

Dr. Saunders and an army officer stepped forward. The officer announced, "The commanding general has ordered the immediate evacuation of Marietta. We must move all the hospitals, patients, and equipment to Atlanta, Newnan, Macon, and beyond. Dr. Saunders will now explain how this is to be accomplished."

Saunders moved his glasses to the tip of his nose and spoke. "Those patients who can walk on their own or with crutches will board wagons as they become available for the twenty-mile ride to Atlanta, where they will be transported to a new facility. Those who can't walk will be taken by wagon to the depot for the trip to Atlanta and then will be transported to a new hospital. The surgeon-in-charge of each hospital will determine the order of departing patients and the nurses who will accompany them. Nurses who do not travel with the wounded, committeemen, and other volunteers will help the patients evacuate. Once that is completed, they will help move the beds and other equipment and supplies to wagons designated for that purpose. They will then proceed to the depot to await transportation to Atlanta. Once there, you will be informed of the name and location of the facility to which you have been assigned. Obviously, this effort is massive and will take several days. I thank all of you for your service." He and the officer left.

Katherine walked from the church, crossed the street, and found Sarah, who said, "I just heard the news. We'll help with the evacuation and then go to Roswell, get my sister and Mr. Toll, and return home. I'll inform Mr. Cohen of our plans. Please tell Pauline." Katherine hurried off.

Four days later, on July 1, Sarah, the girls, Chloe, and Dante began the thirteen mile drive to Roswell. Chloe and Dante couldn't have been happier. They had hardly seen Mrs. McBain or the girls during their time in Marietta. Chloe wanted to fuss over the sisters again. Dante couldn't wait to return to Savannah to see his pregnant wife.

They arrived in Roswell at seven o'clock. When Rebecca answered the front door Sarah gasped at the dark circles under her sister's eyes. Rebecca led them all to the family parlor. She fidgeted with a small silver cross as she spoke. "Francis is passing blood and is in great pain. There's no doctor in town to treat him. I've been giving him morphine. He's too weak to travel and I won't leave him. Sarah, you and the girls must leave tomorrow. We'll be safe. The Yankees won't harm a sick old man and his wife."

Sarah said, "I can't leave you, dear sister. Hopefully, Francis will be able to travel soon. We'll decide what to do when we know the Yankees are near."

Rebecca explained the local situation. "The cotton and woolen mills are still running at full capacity. All the workers are women and a few children who have no money or place to go. Barrington King, the owner of the two cotton mills, moved to Atlanta. He convinced his superintendent to remain, keep the mills running, and protect his property. Barrington's son James, who owns the woolen mill, is captain of the Roswell Battalion, which is guarding the town. Captain King transferred an interest in his mill to his French supervisor, Mr. Roche, on the condition that Roche stay behind and fly the French flag over all the mills. He hopes the Yankees will honor a foreigner's property rights. I think he's insane, but I'll admit that he is creative."

Mr. Toll groaned in the other room and Rebecca rushed to him. Sarah followed. Rebecca's servant Tilda served the sisters supper and then showed them to an upstairs bedroom. After long days helping in the evacuation, they could hardly keep their eyes open. As Katherine washed in the basin, Pauline asked her, "Are you scared of the Yankees capturing us?"

Katherine patted a towel against her face. "No, I trust Mrs. McBain's judgment. She'll get us out of here in time. Right now, I'm looking forward to a good night's sleep."

The next morning Sarah told the sisters that she didn't need help looking after Mr. Toll, and they should spend the day on their own. The girls looked forward to some relaxation and walked along Mimosa Street to town. They passed a church, schoolhouse, and several stately homes, but didn't see another soul. They reached a grassy, rectangular park roughly an acre in size and bordered on all sides by streets. Katherine pointed to the far side. "There's a shop. Maybe it's open."

They entered the store and waited for their eyes to adjust to the darkness. The shelves against the walls were bare except for a few boxes and cans. A woman behind the counter looked up from a newspaper. "May I help you?"

Katherine said, "We're new in town. We were taking a walk. I didn't think any place was open."

The woman explained, "This is the company store. The workers still got to eat."

Pauline asked, "What's a company store?"

The clerk laughed. "The mill workers get paid in company scrip. It's like money but it's good only in this store. Most don't got no real money of their own. They used to complain about it, but now, with Confederate money worth next to nothing, the folks would rather have company scrip. At least you can buy things here with it."

Katherine looked at the near-empty shelves and wondered what anyone could buy, even with a bag of gold. She asked, "Where are the mills?"

The woman gave the girls directions. They walked down the hill, stood on the bank of Vickery Creek, and peered up at the four-story brick cotton mill, which emitted a loud humming sound. Katherine pointed upstream and shouted above the din, "Look, a waterfall and waterwheel. It must power the machinery. Let's walk to where it's quieter."

The girls followed a dirt path around the mill and along the creek for a half-mile. Katherine stopped and observed, "This place is so beautiful—the trees, the clear water, the solitude, and the coolness in summer. I understand why people settled here." They sat on a flat rock by the thirty-foot-wide stream.

Pauline took off her shoes and eased her feet into the cool water. "This feels so good. Can we go for a swim?"

Katherine stared questioningly at Pauline. "In what?"

"In that pool over there where the current isn't so strong."

"No, silly! I meant, in what clothing?"

"In my shimmy. There's no one here to see. Please! I haven't been swimming since Thomasville. You know I love the water."

Katherine surveyed the area and heard only the rush of the waterfall. "All right, go ahead. I'll sit here and watch, but you must come out when I say so."

"I promise!" Pauline stood, pulled off her bonnet and dress, and removed her hair clip. She stepped into the water on submerged rocks that formed a natural staircase. As she descended, her chemise billowed up around her like the blooming flower of a magnolia tree, but she held it down until she disappeared. After a few seconds the girl surfaced and swam to the natural pool. "Katherine, this is so refreshing. You must come in!"

Katherine shook her head and said, "You enjoy yourself." Pauline spent twenty minutes swimming back and forth, diving under the surface, and floating on her back spitting fountains of water in the air. Katherine thought she heard someone stepping on a branch and stood, but saw nothing. She said, "Pauline, it's time to come out."

"Just another minute."

"No, that's enough for today. It's getting late. We'll come back tomorrow."

Pauline got out and stood with the wet garment clinging against her body. "That was so much fun!"

Katherine looked at Pauline's chest, almost as developed as her own, and knew that she would soon be attracting hordes of boys. She said, "Dry off in the sunshine." They sat and listened to the distant roar of the waterfall. Katherine lay back and closed her eyes. She thought of Joseph and wondered if he ever thought of her.

Pauline broke the silence. "Katherine, do you miss Captain McBain?"

Katherine catapulted up. "Of course! I miss all the McBains. Just what do you mean?"

Pauline stood and pulled on her dress. "You know what I mean."

Katherine also rose. "No, I don't know. Why don't you tell me?"

Pauline bunched her hair and squeezed out a few drops of water. "Well, the day I ran away, when you and he got back to the wayside home, the way you looked at him. . . . You know."

Katherine folded her arms across her chest. "When we heard that you were missing, he was so concerned that he helped me look for you, even though he was in command of a detail of soldiers. I would have been lost without his help. I was grateful to him. Is that so hard to understand? And how many times must I remind you that he's married and much older than me?"

Katherine stopped when she heard footsteps in the brush. She looked at the ground and picked up a rock the size of a small cannon ball. A man stepped from the trees. Katherine yelled, "Dante! You scared the daylights out of us."

Dante looked at the rock in her hand, which she dropped. "Missus bin missin' you gu'ls. Tole me tuh fine you. Ah got de wagon at de mill."

The girls followed Dante back and climbed up on the driver's bench, happy that they didn't have to walk up the hill. On the way back, Katherine asked Dante if he was excited about returning to Savannah. Dante liked Katherine because she spoke to him almost like a friend. "Yessum, Mistess, ah miss Ahsettuh."

"I understand, Dante. We want to get back, too. I think it'll be soon."

When they walked into the house, Chloe said to Pauline, "Lawdy, Mistess Pauline, you looks lahk uh drown dog. Come set out back so ah kin brush dem knots." One hour later Pauline had shiny hair which hung past her shoulders. Chloe gave a single, pronounced nod of the head and said, "Dat mo' lahk it."

The sisters did most of the talking at supper. Katherine told her favorite stories about Mary. Pauline talked about their day exploring the town and the creek. Sarah smiled at the girl's descriptions of the singing winds, bird choruses, and dancing leaves, happy for the diversion from watching Mr. Toll slowly die. Rebecca pushed her uneaten food around her plate.

The following morning Katherine asked Sarah if she and Pauline could help with Mr. Toll, but Sarah whispered that there was nothing anybody could do for him except pray. So for the next two days the sisters took long walks, exploring the town. They stayed out as long as possible. Sorrow covered Mrs. Toll like a shroud and the girls' excitement from the day turned to sadness the moment they entered the house.

On their fourth night in Roswell, during supper, when the only noise was the clinking of silverware, Rebecca answered a knock on the front door. She returned with a man in a grey uniform holding a military cap in his hands. She introduced Captain King, who explained, "The Yankees are in Marietta and our scouts say a regiment is camped about two miles from here. I just gave instructions to Mr. Roche to raise the French flag over the mills and at Bulloch Hall, where he's been staying. I'm leaving with my men tomorrow morning to the other side of the Chattahoochee. We'll burn the bridge after we cross and the Yankees will be stuck on this side. Roswell will be defenseless. You should leave, too, and follow us across the river. I've informed Reverend and Mrs. Pratt of the situation. As you might imagine, he won't leave until God personally writes him a letter."

Rebecca collapsed into her chair. "Captain, my husband is too sick and weak. Moving will kill him."

King glanced at Sarah and the girls. "I'm truly sorry about Mr. Toll, ma'am.

He's a kind man and a good Christian, but you'll be putting yourselves in danger. There's nothing more I can do for you. I wish you the best." King replaced his cap and left.

Rebecca pleaded, "Sarah, I know he's almost gone, but I have to stay with him until the end. You and the girls go home. My servants will be with me. I'll survive."

Sarah took Rebecca's hand and said to Katherine, "I'm staying here with my sister. First thing tomorrow, we'll pack the covered wagon with your things and Mrs. Toll's valuables. I want you, Pauline, Chloe, and Dante to go to Macon and wait for us. We'll prepare plenty of food and pack other necessities. It may take us a week or more but we'll reach you. I'll give you money and I'll write a letter of introduction to my good friend there, Mrs. Pope. She'll find you a place to stay and get you work in the hospitals. Don't worry, the Yankees won't harm us. As soon as they leave Roswell, we'll come to you. This isn't how I planned it, but we have to adjust to the circumstances."

Katherine understood. She would never leave Pauline or Mary in a time of need. "We'll do whatever you say, Mrs. McBain."

The next morning Dante and Rebecca's two male slaves, Samuel and Primses, packed the wagon with Rebecca's most prized and transportable possessions—china, silverware, jewelry, family heirlooms, and family portraits, all carefully wrapped in towels. In addition, they loaded the girls' luggage, blankets, towels, a mattress, food, canteens with water, and cooking gear.

Sarah took Katherine aside and handed her a leather pouch. "Here's two hundred dollars in gold coins. It should keep you until we get to Macon. Hide it in your dress and don't let anyone know you have it. But don't put yourselves in any danger for this or Mrs. Toll's possessions. The most important thing is your safety. I will inform Dante and Chloe that they are in your charge. They will do as you request. And one other thing, have you ever fired a gun?" Katherine shook her head. "I didn't think so. I'm giving one to Dante just in case. If the army or police stop you and find the gun, say it's yours—that I gave it to you." She paused to let those instructions sink in. "Do you understand all you're to do?"

Katherine nodded. The two women embraced and Katherine joined Pauline by the wagon. Sarah asked Dante to step inside the house. They stood in the foyer and Mrs. Toll joined them. "Dante, you've been with us your entire life. You're a part of our family. We've always taken care of you, and we let you marry Isetta."

Dante looked at Mrs. Toll and the object wrapped in a towel in her hands. "Yessum. Dat de troot, Missus. Ah sholy am t'ankful tuh dis day."

"I now have a very serious request of you. You protect those girls with your life. Do you understand me?"

Dante had never seen Mrs. McBain's lips so tight. "Yessum. Ah sholy do."

Sarah took the object from Mrs. Toll and placed it on a table. "Dante, have you ever fired a gun?"

Dante didn't know what to say. He couldn't admit he had fired a gun, as it was forbidden, yet he needed it for the trip. He lied, "Wid Isaac. Ah hole one, aim she, pull de trigguh, but ain' no powduh an' ball."

Mrs. Toll unwrapped the towel, displaying a revolver much like the one he had used to shoot Sam. It was a huge gamble to give a slave a loaded gun, but Sarah had no choice. If they were attacked by bandits, they had to be able to defend themselves. And she trusted Dante. "That will have to do. Use this if you must."

Rebecca, who had handled guns, said, "All the chambers are loaded with percussion caps on the nipples." Mrs. Toll aimed the gun with both hands at the wall. "Pull back the hammer to full-cock with your thumb. The cylinder will move one position. Get as close as possible to your target and pull the trigger." Dante nodded. She wrapped the gun in the towel. "Hide this on the shelf under the driver's bench."

Sarah said, "If those girls are in any danger, you must do what's necessary."

"Yessum, Missus."

The two women led him from the house and he stowed the gun.

Sarah hugged Katherine and Pauline, and kissed the younger girl's forehead. "I love you, Pauline. You need to be strong for Katherine and me." Pauline promised. They all climbed aboard the wagon and waved goodbye. Dante snapped the reins.

Twenty minutes later, at the sight of a group of soldiers, they stopped at the entrance to the bridge over the Chattahoochee. An officer stepped up and said to Katherine, "Weren't you at Mrs. Toll's last night?"

"Yes, sir. We're with Mrs. McBain, Mrs. Toll's sister. She decided to stay with the Tolls. We're headed to Macon."

Captain King shook his head in disapproval and said, "That's her decision. Listen closely. The roads are full of stragglers and bandits, so be on guard. Most of the people in these parts will let travelers stay with them for the night, though it may be in the barn. If other wagons are headed in your direction, ride along with them. Good luck."

Reverend Nathaniel Pratt came by later in the day to tell Rebecca that the Yankees had appeared at the bridge that afternoon. As it had been destroyed, they visited the woolen mill. Pratt heard about it and rode to the building, which was flying the French flag. He found Mr. Roche, the supervisor, explaining to a Union officer that he owned the mill and demanded that, as a citizen of France, a neutral in the war, his property rights be respected. The officer said he would return to his camp to inform his commanding officer of the situation. Rebecca felt better about the factory being spared, and hoped the others would be, as well.

Early the next morning Pratt came by and told Mrs. Toll that the Yankees had returned to the woolen mill. Tilda sat with Mr. Toll while Samuel drove Mrs. Toll, Sarah, and Reverend Pratt to the creek. As they descended the hill they saw heavy black smoke drifting above the tree line to the right. Pratt said, "They're burning the woolen mill, those bas . . . . I'm sorry. Please excuse my choice of words."

When they reached the creek, they saw Union soldiers carrying rolls of cloth from the cotton mill and loading them onto wagons. Pratt and the women climbed down and approached a Yankee colonel. Pratt asked, "Sir, why are you burning the mills?"

The officer eyed the reverend and two women. "A Frenchman claims he owns them and is neutral in the war, yet he's weaving 'CSA' into the fabric." The officer held up a swath of the cloth to their faces. "This material is being used by the rebels in their unholy rebellion against the United States. It's just as important to a soldier as a rifle. I have orders to burn every building in the area after we remove the finished product and all the books and papers."

Rebecca said, "You can't burn these buildings. They employ hundreds of poor, hard-working people who pose no harm to you." She pointed to her shoe manufactory. "We closed that building weeks ago. It's my husband's. It doesn't make anything now."

The colonel barked, "It no doubt is capable of making shoes and boots for rebel soldiers trying to kill my men. It's going up with all the rest."

"No! I won't allow it!"

The officer laughed. "Ma'am, you have no say in the matter. Leave the area now."

Reverend Pratt and the women returned to the wagon. They heard shouts from within the cotton mill. A parade of gaunt, pale women in their teens, twenties, and thirties, wearing faded brown and black work dresses and white work bonnets, and a smattering of boys in their teens and younger, walked out the door. A soldier led them to the creek bank fifty yards away. The spinning machines fell silent, leaving only the crashing sound of the waterfall. The colonel called to his soldiers, "Let's heat things up."

The soldiers charged into the building with tin cans, large clumps of cotton, and a few lamps. Sarah saw flashes of light through the windows. The glow grew as the soldiers ran out the door. In minutes they heard the crackling of the wooden floors and beam ceilings. Flames shattered the windows and licked the outer walls. The Union soldiers cheered, whistled, and waved their hats in the air. The celebration drowned out the cries of the workers as they witnessed the destruction of the source of their meager livelihoods. An officer approached them and ordered, "Go to your homes and stay there. You'll hear from us tomorrow about our plans for you."

The women moved up the hill en masse, slump-shouldered, looking like a large, low-lying, dark cloud, as the soldiers ran to the other buildings. Minutes later Sarah, Rebecca, and Pratt watched the destruction of the shoe factory. Rebecca leaned against Sarah. "This isn't happening. It's a bad dream." Sarah put her arm around her sister.

The colonel mounted his horse and rode to them. He scowled, "I told you to leave the area."

Sarah said, "Everything we heard about you Yankees is true. If I peeled off your skin, Satan would jump out."

The colonel leaned forward in his saddle. "Ma'am, you and your kind wanted a war. It was your choice. Well, now you have one. Not pretty, is it?"

⸎

Early the next morning Sarah stood in the corner of the dark bedroom as Rebecca sat on the bed, staring at her dead husband. Rebecca pulled the covers over his head, pressed her hands together in front of her face, and murmured a prayer. She stood and said, "I'll have Samuel and Primses make a casket and dig a grave at the cemetery. Reverend Pratt can conduct a service. It's best we do it now."

Later that afternoon Rebecca, Sarah, and Mrs. Pratt stood by the freshly dug hole as Samuel and Primses lugged the simple pine-board casket from the wagon to the graveside. The pungent smell of burnt wood filled the air as the cemetery was only a few hundred yards from the mills. The slaves stood ten feet behind the whites and removed their hats. The women bowed their heads as Reverend Pratt looked skyward and spoke. "Good Lord, we ask that you take our friend and neighbor Francis Toll, devoted husband of Mrs. Toll, loving father of Zachariah and Gerald Toll, into your Kingdom of eternal peace. We also ask. . . ." Reverend Pratt stopped at the sound of jangling spurs.

Two Union soldiers walked up to the gathering. One of them said, "Sorry to intrude upon you at this time. By the order of the commanding general, Major General William T. Sherman, you two women are under arrest for the crime of treason against the United States of America. Pack your belongings, no more than you can carry by yourselves, and be at the public square tomorrow morning at eight. You're going on a little trip." The soldiers turned and walked away.

Rebecca ran after them. "You have the rudeness to interfere with the funeral of my husband of forty-nine years? Well, I'm not going anywhere. I need time to mourn and then we have families to go to."

The one soldier said, "I'm sorry for delivering the order at this moment, ma'am, but we have no time to waste. Anyone who had anything to do with those mills is under arrest, including you and that other woman. There are no exceptions. Please do as I say." The soldiers left. Rebecca stood frozen in shock.

Reverend Pratt stepped over and took her arm. "Please, Mrs. Toll, we must finish sending off Mr. Toll."

Rebecca returned to the grave and sniffled as Pratt completed the ceremony and the slaves lowered Mr. Toll in the ground. Rebecca sank to her knees as they shoveled dirt on the casket. The reverend helped the woman to her feet. "For now, do as the soldier asks. I will have a word with the officer in charge. We can only hope he's a Christian."

When they arrived back at the house. Rebecca addressed her three servants in the dining room. "We've been arrested by the Yankees and they're sending us away. We have no idea where, or when we'll be back." Samuel and Primses stared blankly at her, but Tilda started to cry. "I want you to continue to live here and take care of the house and property, raise the cows, hogs, and chickens and tend to the fields and gardens. Of course, slaughter and harvest what you need to live. Tilda, I want you to visit Mr. Toll's grave every day and leave fresh flowers. You know how he loved them."

Tilda sniffled. "Yessum, Missus."

Rebecca and Sarah spent the rest of the day packing their carpetbags and organizing the house for their departure. They spoke little. On four occasions, when going through her husband's belongings, Rebecca sat and wept for minutes at a time. Sarah could only hug her and stroke her back. They went to bed right after supper.

The next morning Samuel carried their bags to the wagon and drove them to town. As they approached the square, Rebecca said, "Dear Lord, it looks like everyone in Roswell is here." The park and the surrounding streets were packed with hundreds of women, children, and a few old men. The women were dressed in the same faded, raggedy work dresses and bonnets that they wore to work. They stood quietly, waiting for orders. The Yankee guards held their rifles across their chests. Twenty military wagons, each with two soldiers on the driver's bench, lined Atlanta Street.

The street was too clogged for Samuel to go further. He helped down Sarah and Rebecca and handed over their carpetbags. The soldiers yelled at him and he left. The women pushed through the crowd and spotted a red-faced Reverend Pratt in a black top hat and suit at the head of the park, talking to a Union officer. They jostled their way to him and heard him say, "These women are not mill workers. One owns the shoe manufactory and the other is her sister from Savannah!"

The officer replied, "They're both guilty of supplying the rebels. That will be all, Reverend, unless you and your wife would like to join them."

Pratt turned and saw the women standing behind him. "Mrs. Toll, I will protest this outrage to the highest authorities, and I will pray for you every day. Do take care of yourselves and if you get the opportunity to write, please keep me updated on your whereabouts. I will not rest until you're safely back here." He patted her hand, tipped his hat to Sarah, and disappeared into the crowd.

Sarah said, "So much for Christian fellowship."

The officer mounted a wooden box, waved his hands in the air, and called for quiet. "People of Roswell, you are all under arrest for treason. There will be no hearing or trial. We're taking you to Marietta. From there you will be sent north in railroad cars, where you can find meaningful employment. This is the final decision of Major General Sherman. Start boarding these wagons in an orderly fashion now."

A chorus of murmurs lifted from the crowd. Sarah said, "Treason? No trial? Are they mad?" A tide of humanity pushed them towards the street. Sarah clutched Rebecca's arm and in minutes they were climbing into the bed of an army wagon. They sat on the floor and looked at the faces of the fourteen other women. Three were holding babies in their arms and three others had frightened young boys sitting on their laps. One looked to be Danny's age and made Sarah more homesick than ever.

The driver snapped the reins, shouted, "Heyahhhh," and the wagon lurched forward. Rebecca said, "Sarah, this can't get any worse, can it?"

Sarah didn't answer. She squeezed her sister's hand. ✎

CHAPTER THIRTY-EIGHT

❦

"Hell Would Be an Improvement"
July 1864

On July 2, 1864, after a week of delays and slow trains, Joseph jumped onto the boarding path at Andersonville, while guards climbed down ladders from the top of the boxcars holding the prisoners. He rubbed his old leg wound, trying to quell the dull pain, as he surveyed the surroundings. The only visible structures were a small, wooden white church with a pointed steeple, an unpainted, one-story house, a country store, and the depot building. The prison could not have been located in a more desolate place.

Lieutenant Theodorus Chapman of the Fifty-fifth Georgia, one of two regiments guarding the Andersonville facility, introduced himself to Joseph while a company of soldiers dispersed to the box cars with rifles at the ready. The lieutenant explained that his men would escort the prisoners to the stockade and Joseph's detail should follow.

Joseph handed papers with the prisoners' names, ranks, and regiments to Chapman and said, "Lieutenant, some of my men took ill on the trip down—dysentery, I believe. Could you have them taken to the camp hospital? They're in the last car." Chapman immediately ordered two privates to escort the sick men.

The boxcar doors slid open and the prisoners jumped off. The camp guards lined them up four abreast and marched them the quarter-mile to their new residence.

Lieutenant Graybill Harvey, Joseph's second in command, retrieved their horses from the stock car and said, "God almighty, Captain, what smells so bad? Did everyone in Georgia just crap in their pants?"

Joseph's nose crinkled as they brought up the rear of the prisoners. "I think we're about to find out."

The guards stopped on a grassy spot fifty feet from the north entrance to the stockade. Joseph and Harvey rode to the front of the group and dismounted. A sergeant shouted to the prisoners, "When I call your name, step to the area to your left, where you will be searched. Answer all questions and obey all orders and we'll have you inside in three to four hours."

Chapman said to Joseph, "After the prisoners are in the yard, I'll take your men to the guards' camp and you and Lieutenant Harvey to the officers' quarters."

Joseph thanked him. He looked up at the towering stockade wall of freshly hewed pine logs and commented, "This place is huge."

⁂

The main Confederate prison had been on Belle Isle in the middle of the James River in Richmond, but it could no longer accommodate the thousands of Union prisoners within its walls. Also, Confederate leaders feared that a successful Yankee raid would set loose a horde of the enemy in the middle of their capital. Prisoner exchanges, the most desirable way to reduce the prison population, had virtually ceased by late 1863, primarily over the issue of black Union prisoners. The South declared that they were property and had to be returned to their masters while the North insisted that they be treated like white soldiers and exchanged on a one-for-one basis. With the sides unable to reach a compromise, General Robert E. Lee and C.S.A. Secretary of War James A. Seddon agreed to construct a new prison in the South, where the weather was more agreeable, food and water more plentiful, and trees to build the facility more abundant. The location had to be remote, but close to a railroad depot.

Confederate representatives selected Anderson, in southwest Georgia. The government leased the land and construction began in early January 1864.

The structure was built on adjoining sides of two gently sloping hills, which had a fresh-water creek at their convergence. The trees on the hills provided the main source of timber. The work moved slowly and local slaves and free men of color had to be impressed to meet the deadline. In late February, before the stockade, cookhouse, and hospitals were completed, the first prisoners from Belle Isle arrived by train. They were placed within the unfinished walls of the "bullpen," as the stockade yard became known, under heavy guard from soldiers sitting atop sentry posts, or "pigeon roosts," surrounding the outsides of the prison walls.

The creek flowed from west to east and the prisoners drew water from the western end for drinking and cooking. They bathed further east, and relieved themselves on the eastern end as the water flowed from the stockade.

The camp encompassed sixteen acres. However, an uninhabitable marshy area on either side of Stockade Creek reduced the available space for the prisoners to erect shelters to twelve acres. The first prisoners used the few remaining uncut trees and wood debris to build their huts, often referred to as "shebangs."

Escape was difficult. The stockade walls, when finished, soared seventeen feet, and the logs were sunk five feet into the ground. A continuous row of three-foot-high stakes placed about twenty feet from the interior wall marked the dead line. Any prisoner crossing into the area between the dead line and the stockade wall, called the dead run, would be shot without warning and no questions asked, just as at the Johnson's Island prison, where Joseph had been incarcerated.

The campgrounds for the guards, Confederate hospital, prisoners' hospital, jailhouse, officers' housing, and a cookhouse were located outside the stockade.

❦

Chapman explained, "The camp was built to hold ten thousand prisoners. We passed that number on May 1, a little more than two months after it opened. We started expanding it three weeks ago, and we're just completing it. The prison ground now covers twenty-six acres, though only twenty-two are available for shelters. I guess the authorities didn't think we'd capture so many Yankees."

A loud roar thundered from inside the walls. Joseph and Harvey looked skyward and then at each other, though Chapman never flinched. Joseph asked, "What's that?"

"Come, I'll show you while my men take care of the prisoners."

Joseph and Lieutenant Harvey followed Chapman up a ladder to a sentry platform, several feet higher than the stockade wall, which gave them a full view of the prison grounds. Joseph cringed. The area below was packed with shirtless men, gathered around huts made of sticks and branches with blankets or other materials draped over the tops. Three streets provided the only order to the layout. Otherwise, it looked like a giant can of worms. Joseph asked, "How many men are here?"

"About twenty-seven thousand," replied Chapman, "and more are coming. We could reach thirty thousand in a few weeks. The new space will help." Joseph eyed the barren, uninhabited pen. The old northern wall, which separated the existing stockade from the new area, still stood. "After we transfer prisoners to the addition, we'll tear down that wall. It will be one big yard, separated by the creek and marsh."

Joseph calculated out loud, "If you originally had twelve acres for ten thousand men, that's about eight hundred men per acre. If you provide twenty-two acres for thirty thousand, that's almost fourteen hundred per acre. That's pretty tight."

Another roar exploded from the yard. Chapman pointed to a group of about twenty prisoners pulling a man squirming like a snake from a shebang. They bound his hands behind his back and dragged him towards the north gate. Other prisoners lining the roughly laid-out street applauded. Yet another cheer erupted as a different group of prisoners caught and wrestled down a man by his long hair and tied his hands. Onlookers threw handfuls of dirt at the captive as he limped past. Joseph asked, "Lieutenant, what in the world is going on?"

Chapman explained, "A group of about two hundred prisoners started terrorizing the other inmates with make-shift knives and clubs, stealing their rations and what little money or possessions they had. If the victims didn't yield, the bandits—they're called the Raiders—beat them, sometimes to death. A few days ago the Raiders got brazen and robbed the rations wagon. The prison commander, Captain Wirz, let it be known that until the other prisoners apprehended the culprits, he wouldn't issue any more rations. The Yankees banded together and formed a guard to arrest the Raiders. That's what you see now. It's been going on all day. The prisoners are taking them to the jail outside the stockade. Wirz has promised to hold a trial with prisoners as judge advocate, jurors, and attorneys. If convicted, they may hang."

Joseph said, "Incredible." He coughed and asked, "What's that horrid smell?"

The lieutenant pointed to the eastern end of Stockade Creek. "The prisoners relieve themselves at the far end of the creek. Then it passes out of the stockade. With close to thirty thousand men, well, that's a lot of crap. There are so many felled trees in the creek outside the wall that the waste gets trapped. This time of year, with the wind blowing this way, the stink is overpowering. One of the many joys of this assignment."

Joseph hacked and spit over the side of the platform. "I was in a Yankee prison for officers in the beginning of the war. I didn't much like it, but it was paradise compared to this. Those men down there are skin and bone."

Chapman shrugged. "We have no choice, Captain. There's no other facility and the generals can't agree on a prisoner exchange. Until they do, we have to put these fellows somewhere, and this is apparently better than Belle Isle. We're having trouble feeding our own soldiers, no less tens of thousands of Yankees. I'll admit, the rations are meager, even for us guards."

Joseph was about to spit again when he stopped and squinted. "Are those negroes I see in the yard?"

"Yes. They were captured in Olustee, Florida. They keep to themselves and don't cause any trouble."

Joseph smiled and said, "We could use a few more victories like that." In mid-February, five thousand Union troops, including a negro regiment, left Hilton Head for Jacksonville to establish strongholds west of the St. Johns River. Five thousand Confederates were waiting at Olustee Station and cut the Yankees to pieces in three hours, inflicting nineteen hundred casualties. Five hundred prisoners, some black, were taken to Andersonville.

The men climbed down the sentry-box ladder. The guards were still processing the prisoners. Chapman said to Joseph and Harvey, "I'll take you to your quarters now. It's a cabin near Captain Wirz's house. He'll want you to join him for supper."

The three men rode off and passed the south gate just as two prisoners under guard exited it, carrying a body by the arms and legs. They tossed the corpse into a three-sided lean-to. Chapman explained, "That's the dead house. With the increase in the population, we lose about twenty to forty each day. The bodies are carried by wagon from here to the Union cemetery and buried by other prisoners."

Joseph stared at the pile of dead men, dumped like trash, and treated with no more care than fish heads thrown aside by the mongers at City Market. He said, "I never thought I'd feel sorry for Yankee soldiers, but I do now."

Chapman defended the situation. "If it tweren't for that damned Lincoln and his position on an exchange, these prisoners wouldn't be here in the first place." The men continued on without further comment.

That night Joseph and Lieutenant Harvey had supper with Captain Wirz. The prison commander was a short man of medium build, about forty years old, with a full head of black hair and a full but neatly trimmed beard. In his Swiss accent, he dominated the supper conversation, complaining of the lack of support from authorities in running the prison—the shortage of space, food, wood, and medicines, to name a few, and assured Joseph and Lieutenant Harvey that the problems would only grow with the population. He promised to give them a tour of the grounds the next day.

Joseph told Wirz that his brother-in-law was in the prison and requested permission to speak with him. Wirz asked, "How did you get a Yankee brother-in-law?"

"I married his sister." Wirz frowned, and then told Joseph that he would arrange a meeting within the stockade walls after their tour.

The next morning, at the north gate, Joseph and Harvey met Captain Wirz, who was wearing a white linen shirt and white duck trousers with a revolver in a holster hooked to his belt, and a grey Confederate cap. He was accompanied by twenty soldiers. Four guards removed the huge plank securing the outer door and pulled it open. The group entered a holding pen. The guards closed the door behind them and replaced the plank. Four guards on the opposite side opened the inside door, revealing the stockade grounds. Joseph could feel thousands of eyes on him.

Wirz led them along Market Street, which bisected the bullpen. Joseph was overcome by the stench, a mixture of human excrement, burning wood, and cooked food. He breathed through his mouth, but it didn't help much.

They passed five Confederate soldiers talking to three prisoners, with a crowd looking on. Wirz said, "We're always trying to recruit Yankees into our army. With the Union unwilling to do an exchange, it's the one way they can get out of this place, other than escaping, which is very unlikely—and dangerous."

Joseph thought back to Johnson's Island and the Yankees trying to recruit Southerners. He said, "They can't be very loyal if they'll switch sides that easily."

Wirz replied, "Food is a powerful motivator. Many are foreigners—Irish and Germans—who had no real loyalty when they arrived in this country. Their allegiance has more to do with where they landed."

Joseph examined the prisoners' self-made shelters. Most consisted of three or four poles stuck in the ground with a blanket stretched over the top. But other men dug holes in the ground about three feet deep with niches at the end where

they could crawl for protection from the sun. Rain made these refuges temporary. Others dug up clay from the swampy area around the creek, hand-molded
it in the shape of bricks, dried them in the sun, and piled them up in three walls,
inclined to the middle to create a miniature, teepee-like structure. The crude hovels were jumbled about the grounds in no order. Regardless of the type of shelter,
the men looked the same—shirtless, skinny with their ribs showing, long, scrag-
gly hair, beards, and sour, joyless faces. Most seemed no thicker than the poles in
their shebangs.

Wirz stopped on the south side of the street in front of a crudely built stand
with a counter. "This is the sutler's stall. He sells goods to the prisoners who have
money or personal possessions to trade. They can buy flour, tobacco, beans, peas,
salt, rice, potatoes, and the like." He pointed to the north side of the street and
several poles sticking out of the ground with a few shirts, blankets, and other
items hanging from them. "The more clever Yankees trade and otherwise acquire
goods and sell them to their fellow inmates. One prisoner exchanges a Yankee
dollar for fifty Confederate greybacks. There's a brisk business going on all day."

They continued to walk along Market Street with Wirz nodding to the prisoners, but stopped short when two men ran across the road in front of them,
chasing a mouse. One dove and in an explosion of dirt caught the rodent. He
screamed, "Yahoo!" The other said, "I saw it first. We share!"

They heard screaming from the direction of the north gate and saw five soldiers surrounding two men carrying a body. Wirz trotted towards the commotion, and Joseph and Harvey followed. The soldiers told the two prisoners to drop
the body on the ground. One of the soldiers stuck the tip of his bayonet into the
corpse's backside. The body screamed, jumped up, and ran into the ghetto of
shelters with two soldiers giving chase, while the other guards remained with the
carriers.

Wirz laughed and said, "One of the more common ruses used to escape.
That's a fitting end to our tour. I know this isn't a pleasant place. I hope you have
some idea how difficult it is to manage. Let's eat before you meet your relative."
Joseph followed Wirz and wondered if he were in the middle of a bad dream.

After lunch, Joseph met Lieutenant Chapman at the north gate, where they
were joined by the same twenty guards from the morning tour. Chapman said,
"Your brother-in-law is waiting inside." They went through the outer and inner
gates. Chapman pointed to the north, "There's Seaman First Class Hulett in the
dead run. Have your chat. My men and the sentries in the pigeon roosts will be
watching. You have nothing to fear."

Joseph walked to the shirtless, sunburned, stocky man about five feet six
inches tall, with brown hair and a brown bushy beard. He said, "Laurence, we finally meet." He offered his hand and Laurence waited a few seconds before giving
his. It felt like a dead fish. Joseph got the message. There would be no friendship,
even pretended, in this meeting. Still, as family, Joseph felt compelled to help

him. "I'm sorry that it has to be here. I understand from your letter that you were captured on the Water Witch."

Laurence sneered, "Yes, and now I'm in this hell-hole you rebels call a prison. How my sister lived down here is something I'll never understand."

"She didn't live in a prison, Laurence. Prison camps are nasty places, even in the North. I know that first-hand."

Laurence turned away and spat. "Nothing in the North compares to this— sleeping on the ground with no shelter, packed in like rats, measly rations that a dog wouldn't eat, and if he did he'd die of food poisoning, medical care that's meant to kill and not cure, and water from the same stream where we shit. I can't take another day here."

Joseph believed that Laurence was right—Andersonville was a disgrace—but he couldn't admit that to him. "How can I help you?"

His brother-in-law spoke in a friendlier tone. "Joseph, if you can get me and a few of my shipmates out of here, I'd be forever in your debt."

Joseph stopped to think about what Laurence was asking of him. He replied, "You mean get you released? I can't do that." Laurence didn't respond. "Look, this is what I can do. I can give you money to buy food from the sutler. I can try, with no guarantees, to get you on hospital or cookhouse detail, where you'll get full rations and work outside of the stockade during the day. It's not ideal, but it's better than what you've got."

Laurence clutched Joseph's arm. "The money will help. You can't imagine what it's like in here. Hell would be an improvement. Get me on one of those work details. Otherwise, I'll go insane."

Joseph said, "I'll do my best. Now, people are watching us, so I'm going to shake your hand and give you thirty U.S. dollars. That's all I can spare. It should keep you fed for some time." He reached in his pocket, palmed the six coins, and the two shook hands.

Laurence shoved the gold pieces in his pocket and begged, "See if you can't find some way to get me released." He turned to walk away.

Joseph said, "Hold on, Laurence. I want to ask you about Emily and Charlotte."

Laurence faced Joseph. He hesitated as if searching for an appropriate response. "I haven't seen them in a year, but we write. They're both doing well. The last time I saw Emily she was more beautiful than ever. Charlotte, too. That's all I know."

Joseph suspected that Laurence knew more but was not going to be forthcoming. He said, "I'll see about getting you some work. I'm leaving tomorrow but I'll make certain someone contacts you."

As he left the prison, Joseph thanked God that he was returning to Mercer's brigade the next day. He spotted Lieutenant Chapman by the gate and asked him who he could see about getting his brother-in-law assigned to hospital or kitchen details. Chapman suggested the surgeon-in-charge of the hospital and the quartermaster, but those positions were highly coveted and difficult to get.

The surgeon-in-charge told Joseph that unless his brother-in-law had nursing experience, there were no openings at the time, but that he would keep the prisoner in mind when a more general position came up. The quartermaster gave Joseph a similar story, but promised to assign Laurence to the next available job, though it might take several weeks. Joseph returned to his quarters and wrote a note to Laurence explaining the situation and telling him to be patient, but knowing that his brother-in-law would not be happy. He then asked Lieutenant Chapman to have the letter delivered.

Joseph returned to his quarters and found a sergeant awaiting him. "Sir, Captain Wirz was just informed that there are negotiations taking place between General Sherman and General Johnston regarding an exchange of prisoners. General Mercer wants you to stay here in case you have to escort Yankees back to Atlanta."

Joseph closed his eyes and murmured, "Good Lord."

⸙

Joseph and Lieutenant Harvey spent the next two days visiting the sick men from their company at the Confederate hospital. Joseph thought the time dragged more slowly than when he was in prison in Ohio. The second night over supper he told Harvey, "Tomorrow, let's get away from here. We'll swim and fish in Sweetwater Creek, cook our catch, smoke segars, and drink whiskey."

Lieutenant Harvey smiled. "Sure sounds good to me, Captain."

The next morning as the two men were saddling up for a day of relaxation, Lieutenant Chapman galloped over. "Captain, there's been an escape. We took roll call this morning and six men are unaccounted for. One is your brother-in-law. We checked their shelters. One had a tunnel dug under it that led beyond the stockade wall. We're getting a search party together now. Care to join us?"

Joseph thought that his inability to get Laurence a job outside the stockade had caused this. He looked at Harvey and said, "Yes, we both will. We'll follow you."

Five minutes later Joseph and Harvey waited with ten other mounted soldiers by the south gate of the stockade. Joseph asked Chapman, "What's the hold up?"

"We're waiting for Corporal Turner. He's in charge of the dogs. Here he comes now." A soldier on a horse, holding the long leashes of six mongrel dogs, joined them. Chapman handed a shirt to Turner and said, "One of the prisoners left this behind."

Turner got off his horse, held out the garment to each dog's nose, unhooked the leashes as the hounds yelped, and shouted, "Go!"

The dogs charged into the woods behind the prisoner hospital. The men followed, but slowly as their horses had to negotiate around the trees. Chapman said to Joseph, "We don't know when they escaped, but it could have been as much as eight hours ago. Based on where these dogs are headed, I think they made for Sweetwater Creek to get to the Flint River. If they get to water, the dogs might have trouble tracking them."

Joseph said, "They're the ugliest dogs I've ever seen."

Chapman chomped down with his teeth exposed. "And the meanest, believe me."

The dogs ran for an hour, pausing occasionally by a tree, bush, or patch of ground. They stopped at a small footpath in the middle of the woods and howled. Then one dog darted to the north and the others followed, leaving the horses far behind. After ten minutes the barking grew louder. The search party cleared a small ridge and saw in the distance a bare-chested man holding onto the lowest branch of a tree, his feet about three feet off the ground, trying to pull himself up. One of the dogs leaped and clamped down on the man's thigh. He screamed and tried to shake off the canine. Another dog leaped and bit the man's other thigh, bringing him down. All the mongrels converged on him and started tearing at his flesh. Joseph saw nothing but wriggling animal bodies and teeth. The prisoner's shrieks cut through the forest. Turner got to the hounds and called them off, but to little effect. He dismounted and pulled them off one by one.

Joseph and the other men ran to the escapee, who lay moaning, covered in blood and holding his left thigh in one hand and the side of his head with the other. Joseph turned away, ready to vomit, and saw one of the dogs chomping on an ear. The man's face was barely recognizable, but he had a long full beard. Joseph knew it was Laurence. He got his canteen, poured water on his handkerchief and washed the blood from the wounds, despite the man's cries. He said, "Laurence, it's me, Joseph McBain. I'm taking you to the hospital now. They'll fix you up." Laurence bawled and babbled incoherently.

With Chapman's approval, Joseph and Harvey placed the escapee's bloody and torn body across a mule's back, and the three headed back to Andersonville. Joseph rode next to Laurence to ensure he didn't slip off. Laurence moaned and whimpered but he never spoke. Three hours later they arrived at the prisoners' hospital, a series of tents outside the stockade walls. Joseph explained the attack to the surgeon-in-charge, who grimaced when he saw two attendants lay Laurence on a board propped up on wooden boxes. "I'll see what I can do, Captain. We're short of medicines and this man is ripped up pretty badly. Let me clean him up first."

Joseph rode to Captain Wirz's headquarters, explained the situation, and requested that a doctor take special care of him. Wirz said, "This is the in-law who escaped last night? And you want me to give him the best possible care? I don't grant special treatment to runaways, even if they're relatives of Confederate officers. You may visit him whenever you want, and personally do for him as you wish, but that's as far as I'll go. He's lucky I don't put him in the stocks."

Joseph returned to the hospital tent and walked past several men lying on blankets on the ground barely breathing, with swarms of flies buzzing about them, to Laurence's make-shift table. The man's head, throat, arms, and legs were covered with rag bandages, with splotches of blood seeping through. A Yankee attendant was standing next to him. Joseph asked the young soldier, "What's his condition?"

The boy replied, "He's torn up something awful, sir. The surgeon says he doesn't know if infection will set in. He's missing an ear and the bite on his throat may have penetrated his windpipe."

"Can he eat or drink?"

"I don't know, sir. I asked him if he wanted some water, but he just moans. I've seen those tracking dogs. It hurts to look at them."

Joseph asked, "What's your name?"

"Private William H. Smith, of the Fourth Michigan Volunteers, sir."

"Where were you captured, son?"

"At Mine Run, on November 27, 1863. I was sent to Belle Isle, and then here. I arrived on February 26, 1864—one of the first."

"You look pretty healthy for someone who's been here four months."

"I've been on hospital detail most of the time. We get full rations and the doctor gives us passes to go to the woods and pick berries and swim in the creek. It's the boys in the bullpen who are really suffering."

Joseph reached into his pocket and pulled out three one-dollar Yankee coins. "Private Smith, I want you to keep an eye on this man. If he wants food or water, please get it for him. If there's medicine available, like opium, give it to him. Anything to make him comfortable. If you need more money, let me know."

The private looked at Laurence and shook his head in pity. "I'll do my best, sir."

Joseph bent down and spoke in Laurence's remaining ear. "Laurence, it's Joseph. You're in the hospital. They're going to fix you up. Have faith."

Joseph thanked the soldier and went back to his quarters. He spent the next four days checking up on his men and visiting Laurence at the prison hospital. The doctor had sewed Laurence's wounds and Private Smith made sure that a nurse washed and dressed them, but he wouldn't eat and hardly drank. On the fourth day the doctor told Joseph that infection had set in and the prisoner wouldn't live.

The next morning Joseph walked into the prison hospital and found Private Smith standing over Laurence. "How is he, Private?

Smith shook his head. "He's gone, sir. Died overnight. The doctor said there was nothing he could do. I'm sorry."

Joseph looked down at his brother-in-law. While he had no feelings for the man, he didn't want him to die, especially in this place. He knew Emily would be shattered by the news and he could never tell her the truth. "Private, when does the next dead wagon leave for the burial ground?"

"About noontime, sir."

Joseph thanked Private Smith for his help and left. He returned a little before noon, just in time to see some attendants heave Laurence's body into the dead wagon. His arm dangled over the side. Joseph followed the vehicle for a half mile to the cemetery. About twenty Yankees were digging a trench. At the very ends of the trench the men dug one more foot deeper and inserted wooden posts in each. Joseph walked to the Confederate sergeant guarding the work gang and asked, "What are they doing?"

The sergeant replied, "There isn't enough wood for coffins, and the prisoners don't want to throw dirt directly on their mates. So they lay a platform made of slabs of rough split pine over them and shovel the dirt on top of that."

Joseph watched as two prisoners lay the dead in the grave, face up and shoulder to shoulder. Another two men rested the wood slabs on the two posts and over the bodies. Yet another man hammered a wooden marker at the head of each body. A team of four men started shoveling in the dirt. Joseph yelled, "STOP!"

The prisoners looked up in surprise at Joseph, who said to the sergeant, I want to say a prayer over one of the bodies before they cover him. He's a relative. I'll be quick."

The sergeant stiffened. "Sorry, Captain, I didn't know. Go right ahead."

Joseph stood over Laurence's place as the prisoners lowered their shovels and bowed their heads. He recited The Lord's Prayer and then told the workers to start shoveling in the dirt. As they did he read from a copy of the Book of Common Prayer that he had borrowed from the prison chaplain:

In sure and certain hope of the resurrection to eternal life Through our Lord Jesus Christ, we commend to Almighty God our brother Laurence Hulett; and we commit his body to the ground; earth to earth, ashes to ashes, dust to dust. The Lord bless him and keep him, the Lord to make his face to shine upon him and be gracious unto him, the Lord lift up his countenance upon him and give him peace. Amen.

The prisoners said "Amen." Two crossed themselves. Joseph closed the book and thanked them. He returned to his quarters, exhausted and depressed. He looked forward to lying down and trying to erase the horrors of Andersonville from his mind.

Lieutenant Harvey greeted him at the door to their quarters. "You know those Raiders who were tried by their own men? The jury reached a verdict. Six of them will hang today at five o'clock. And Captain Wirz says there will be no prisoner exchange. We leave tomorrow."

"Thank God," Joseph muttered.

Joseph stood in the pigeon roost with Lieutenants Chapman and Harvey, looking down on a group of prisoners building scaffolds on the far end of South Street, one of the few areas where sufficient space existed. Almost thirty thousand other prisoners watched the construction. Six reinforced poles spaced evenly apart rose five feet over the wooden platform, each having three-foot-long wooden arms extending from the top. Nooses were affixed to them by a series of hooks, and positioned above trap doors. They swayed gently in the breeze. Men on the ground tested the spring release of the doors.

"WHAM, WHAM, WHAM, WHAM, WHAM, WHAM." The immense crowd of prisoners cheered. A worker called out, "They're ready!"

Lieutenant Harvey rubbed his neck as if trying to soothe a sun burn and said, "I have to compliment those Yankees. They're damn good carpenters." Ten minutes later the prison gates opened.

As Wirz promised, a trial had been held. About one hundred sixty Yankees were tried by twelve of their fellow prisoners. Eleven were found guilty, and six of them were sentenced to hang. At five o'clock on July 11, 1864, the condemned, their hands bound behind their backs, were led by Captain Wirz and his guards from the jail outside the stockade walls into the bullpen to the jeers and hisses of the prison population. Wirz handed them over to the Yankee chief of the prison police and departed with his guards, leaving only prisoners in the stockade. The chief led the six to the scaffold. Joseph had never seen a man hanged before and he doubted that such a ritual had ever been held before so many people in the United States.

The six, dressed in their torn and dirty uniforms, walked up the ten steps to the platform. Six executioners stepped forward and guided each of the men onto a trap door. A priest stepped forward and asked the chief to have mercy and spare the condemned. The chief said that the decision of the court was final and he was there to carry it out. Suddenly, the leader of the Raiders bolted down the stairs and ran towards the south gate. He was apprehended by the crowd and returned, kicking and screaming, to the platform. The executioners stepped forward and placed the nooses around the necks. The priest faced the men, said a prayer, made the sign of the cross in front of each man, and stepped to the side of the scaffold. Joseph could hear sobbing and pleas for mercy. He saw a pool of liquid forming at one of the men's feet. Nothing happened for a full minute. The crowd started to look around, wondering what was causing the delay.

SLAM! The trap doors swung open together, the men dropped, and their necks snapped. They dangled lifelessly except for the quivering of their feet. A few men in the audience clapped, but soon stopped. There were many ways for soldiers to become casualties of war, and the thousands of prisoners had just witnessed one of the most gruesome. There was no longer mood for applause.

Joseph descended from the roost with a headache. He was heading back to General Mercer's brigade the next day. He couldn't get away too fast. ∞

CHAPTER THIRTY-NINE

The Great Turkey Hunter

July 1864

The twenty-mile ride to Atlanta, over a rocky road, and powered by two mules with no sense of urgency, took two-and-one-half days. The few houses that the travelers passed in the evenings looked deserted and Katherine opted to camp by creeks near the road. Chloe fetched water, laid a blanket on the ground, and set dining places for Katherine and Pauline while Dante built a fire and cooked supper. Chloe and Dante ate from tin dishes by the fire after the girls had finished.

After the meals, Pauline read aloud from the Bible while the others looked to the sky and listened to the booms of distant cannon fire. The girls slept on the mattress in the wagon and Dante and Chloe slept on blankets underneath. On the second night, Chloe heated some water, washed the girls' hair, dried and brushed it, singing to herself, "No prettiuh gu'ls in all Jawjuh, no suh." Afterwards, Pauline sketched portraits of the two servants. They both thanked her, and Chloe studied her own image by the fire for ten minutes, often looking up and smiling at Pauline.

When they reached a sentry post on the outskirts of Atlanta, Katherine showed the soldier her volunteer's badge and explained that they had been in Marietta with the Savannah Relief Committee and were on their way to the Macon hospitals. The guard said, "Most folks except the diehards have already evacuated Atlanta, but if you see other wagons going in your direction, ride with them. Head to Lovejoy's Station and follow the road paralleling the Macon and Western Railroad all the way to Macon. It's about a hundred miles."

Later that afternoon, they passed a white, two-story plantation house with a flat roof. Katherine said to Dante, "Take this driveway. Maybe these folks will let us camp on their property for the night." When they reached the building, Katherine climbed the five steps to the front porch and knocked on the door. A buxom white woman about forty years old with brunette hair, wearing a red dress that exposed her shoulders, and holding a glass of wine, answered. Katherine caught a whiff of heavy sweet perfume.

The woman surveyed Katherine up and down. She stepped onto the porch, looked north and south, and asked, "Is Sherman coming?"

"No, ma'am, not that I know of. We heard he's trying to cross the Chatta-hoochee, but that's all we know. We left Roswell just before the Yankees arrived. My sister and I and two servants are on our way to Macon and wonder if we could spend the night on your property. The country is full of stragglers and bandits, you know."

The woman raised her eyebrows as she appraised Katherine one more time. "Of course you can stay. I have plenty of room in the house. My husband is off fighting the Yankees. Have your servants bring in your luggage. We'll sit for supper in an hour."

"Ma'am, please don't go to any trouble."

The woman sipped her wine. "It's no trouble at all. I'd love some company. I've been eating alone for months—since those scoundrels invaded our sacred state. If you'd like, I'll have my girls prepare a bath for you. I know what traveling these roads is like. You'll be much more relaxed for supper."

Katherine was dying for a bath. "Thank you, ma'am, but that isn't necessary."

The woman turned to a negro in a black dress standing at the other end of the hall and shouted, "Lucille, have Albert prepare a bath for our guests." She told Katherine, "Come, I'll show you to your room. One of my boys will take your servants to the barn and bring them some food. My name is Mrs. Burns, wife of Colonel Hardaway Burns."

"I'm Katherine Downes. My sister is Pauline. Thank you so much for having us."

After the girls got settled in the bedroom and put on their wrappers, Lucille led them to the bathroom and pointed to the tub. "You got soap an' towels. Hol-luh if yuh needs sumtin." She smiled and left.

Katherine slowly turned the key in the door. The girls undressed, sank into the hot water, leaned against opposite ends of the tub, and moaned in pleasure. Katherine whispered, "This feels wonderful, but I don't want to linger. Let's wash and get to supper. I have a strange feeling about Mrs. Burns."

Pauline asked, "What kind of a strange feeling?" but Katherine didn't answer.

They started soaping themselves. A few minutes later the doorknob turned. They froze and watched it go part way and stop. Katherine said, "Who is it?"

Mrs. Burns said, "Would you girls like a glass of wine to go with your bath?"

"No, thank you, ma'am. We're finished. We'll be out in a minute."

"As you wish. Come to the dining room when you're ready."

The girls finished, toweled off, hurried upstairs, and dressed. When they appeared at the table, Mrs. Burns asked, "Would you like that glass of wine now?"

Katherine said, "We don't drink, ma'am."

That didn't stop Mrs. Burns, who gulped until the bottom of her glass was in front of her face, which magnified the woman's eyes and, in Pauline's view, made her look like a bullfrog. She placed her glass on the table and said, "Don't drink?

Maybe that's best for girls so young. They say it's bad for the liver, but I don't know. My liver feels fine. They also say it makes a woman lose her inhibitions. Now that's something I do know about." She threw her head back and laughed, "HAH! I could tell you stories. I remember when I lived in Mobile. Now those folks know how to throw a party."

Pauline started to blink rapidly. Katherine changed the subject. "Mrs. Burns, we've never been out of Georgia. We lived in Thomasville and most recently Savannah. We'd love to travel and see the country, but of course that's impossible with this war."

"This war, yes, this damned war, pardon my language." Mrs. Burns told them about her forty-five-year-old husband going off to fight and leaving her to run the plantation. "If you stop at every house from here to Macon, you'll meet hundreds of families in the same position—men gone, women running the homestead. Most of the slaves have run off. The few men left are too old to do anything useful, not even . . . well, you know." The girls stole looks at each other. "But it's what we have to endure for our fledgling country."

The servants Albert and Lucille served a supper of roasted chicken and potatoes. Mrs. Burns held out her glass and Albert rushed to fill it. She continued. "Believe me, our cause is just. But who knows how it will turn out. General Johnston keeps running like a scared rabbit and our governor has donkey balls for brains."

Pauline stopped chewing. Mrs. Burns held her hand over her mouth. "Oh, goodness, I'm sorry. This wine has got the better of my tongue. I'm not a fan of Governor Brown is what I was trying to say."

Mrs. Burns quieted at the sound of horses in the driveway and left to investigate. Moments later the girls heard stomping on the steps, followed by Mrs. Burns saying, "Thank God, it's our cavalry. You had me worried that you were Yankees. How may I help you, Captain?"

A man replied, "We need food, ma'am. My men are presently searching your storehouses. I'm going to look in here."

The girls heard defiance in Mrs. Burns's voice. "Pardon? You'll look in here only when I invite you! My husband is a colonel fighting Sherman right now and I've supported our army with wagonloads of provisions. All you have to do is show some manners and I'll have my servants collect food for you."

The man barked, "Ma'am, get out of my way. I don't have to ask you for anything when my men are risking their lives to protect you."

Mrs. Burns wouldn't back down. "Oh, is that so? You just put on a grey uniform and can act like thieves? Not in MY house, Captain."

The girls heard Mrs. Burns shriek. Seconds later an officer and four soldiers entered the dining room with the woman behind them. The captain stopped when he saw Katherine and Pauline. He tipped his hat and said politely, "Good evening." He then ordered his men to take all the food on the table, plus the silver serving platter, and walked out, kicking over Mrs. Burns's chair in the process.

Mrs. Burns yelled, "Take the food right off our plates? You bastards! You're worse than the Yankees. May the devil piss on your graves!" Then she said, "My God, they're going to the outbuildings," and hurried out the front door. The girls followed her, worried about Chloe and Dante. They saw three soldiers leaving the smokehouse with hams. Several others exited the chicken coop carrying a few squawking birds to a wagon parked at the front of the house.

The girls ran into the barn as two soldiers pushed past Chloe and Dante to inspect their two mules. One soldier said, "I've seen dead dogs with more life than these."

Katherine stood by the back of the wagon. The corporals started to leave the barn when one looked at her and said, "Is anything in that wagon?"

"Nothing. Just dresses and women's things. I don't think you'd be interested."

The soldier stepped over to her and grinned. "I'm sure interested in you."

The boy didn't yet shave, and if clean and in his church suit, would look like a choirboy. Katherine said, "I'm surprised that a southern boy would speak to a southern girl in that shameful manner." The soldier's face flushed. "Do you have a sister? Would you want some boy talking to her like that? And what would your mother do if she heard you say that to me?"

The captain walked into the barn. "What's taking you two so damned long? Are those mules worth taking?"

"No, sir. They're old and worn out."

"Then let's get the hell out of here."

The girls followed the soldiers to the wagons where the others were waiting. As they rode away, Mrs. Burns screamed from the front porch, "May you all rot in hell!"

Mrs. Burns led the girls back to the dining room table. She slumped in her chair and said, "Well, at least they left my glass of wine. How considerate." She drained it and asked, "Lucille, did they find the hidden stuff?"

"No, Missus. Din' git close."

"Good." Mrs. Burns turned to the girls. "We have plenty of food left. Are you still hungry? Some peach pie?"

Katherine said, "No, thank you, ma'am. Those soldiers stole our appetites."

"Unfortunately, our cavalry has a reputation for its rascality and we know to hide most of our food and valuables. It's best to leave some out for them so they don't tear the place apart." Mrs. Burns yawned and stretched her arms. "Too bad. That captain was quite handsome. I wouldn't mind riding with him."

The girls thanked her again and climbed the stairs to their room. As they lay in bed, Pauline said, "Katherine, I've never heard a woman talk like that."

Katherine said, "Some women have hard lives, Pauline, and they pick up those words. But she has a good heart. That's worth more than anything. Now go to sleep." Katherine lay awake, waiting for the door knob to turn, but she soon drifted off.

The next morning they awoke to sunshine, washed from the basin brought in by Lucille, and joined Mrs. Burns for a breakfast of cornbread, bacon, and eggs. The woman said, "I'm sorry our wonderful evening was ruined by those vandals, but it's a good lesson for you. Be careful! You can't trust anyone, not even our own soldiers. If you run into trouble, you can always come back here. There are worse places to wait out the war."

The girls thanked her, boarded the wagon, and drove away as Mrs. Burns stood on the front porch, waving with one hand, and holding a glass of wine in the other.

During the day they joined three other wagons carrying women, children, old men beyond draft age, and servants who were also escaping the advancing Union army. Over the ensuing days, other wagons continually joined and departed the caravan. On the fourth day, with their wagon in the lead, Dante suddenly stopped, pulled on the brake, jumped down, and ran into the field bordering the road. Katherine yelled, "Dante, where are you going?"

Over his shoulder Dante shouted, "Gittin' suppuh." He ran through the knee-high grass for twenty yards when a wild turkey fluttered over the grass tops. It landed and darted away with Dante in hot pursuit. The other travelers stopped, stood, and cheered for Dante. The clucking bird maintained a five-yard lead as Dante called out, "Slow down, Mistuh Tucky, see boo play."

FLOP! Dante tripped, fell, and rolled head over heels. The turkey did an about-face and charged him. Dante squealed and crawled away on his hands and knees, but the turkey caught him and started to peck like a woodpecker at his backside. Dante cried out as if he had sat on a thorny rose bush, scrambled to his feet, and ran.

The people on the wagons started to jeer Dante, who zigzagged through the field while looking over his shoulder every few seconds. An older man, known to the other travelers as Mr. Hoecakes, hollered, "Peck that darkey good, Mr. Turkey." Dante stumbled and fell again and the bird jabbed at his head as if it were a cob of corn. He rolled on his back and kicked his legs in the air, trying to ward off the predator. Mr. Hoecakes, who wore a black top hat, had white sideburns reaching his jaw, and one cloudy eye, laughed so hard he almost fell off his wagon.

Pauline jumped down and ran to Dante's aid. The turkey heard her footsteps, swiveled his head, gobbled, and ran off. Pauline sprinted after him, and the refugees started whistling and waving their hats for Pauline. Seconds later she had the turkey by the neck and bowed to the applause as she carried the bird to the wagon, where Chloe waited with a knife.

Some of the folks hooted and hissed at Dante as he walked back to the wagon, swiping dirt and weed seeds off his pants. He called to them, "Dat's one baddee buddie. Ah gits eben when ah cooks 'im, mussy boo coo."

Katherine announced to the other folks, "It's time to stop for the day. Let's have turkey for supper." They all forgave Dante when they tasted the roasted fowl.

The refugees continued their journey the next morning and fell in with three other wagons. That night, sitting around a campfire, Mr. Hoecakes asked Mr. Clay, a grey-haired, toothless, slump-shouldered man from one of the new wagons if he had heard any news about the war. He reported that Sherman's army had crossed the Chattahoochee and was encircling Atlanta. He also said that Governor Brown requested President Davis to send the cavalry from Virginia to Georgia to cut off Sherman's supply line and attack his rear. But Davis said he couldn't send any more men, so Brown widened the draft age to include boys of sixteen and men between fifty and fifty-five and ordered them to Atlanta. Mr. Clay laughed, "Most are younguns. Folks are callin' 'em 'Joe Brown's pets.'"

Mr. Hoecakes said, "Well, that's cheery news. Do you have anything else that will lift our spirits?"

Mr. Clay responded indignantly. "You wanted to know what I heard, and that's what I heard. Johnston is so outnumbered he can't possibly stop Sherman. My guess is that Georgians will be singing 'Yankee Doodle Dandy' in a few months."

Mr. Hoecakes said, "Not me. Not never. Someone pass that bottle of whiskey."

Mr. Clay worked his gums. "Brown is getting what he deserves. This state's full of a bunch of damned fools for seceding. Dumbest thing I ever heard of."

"Huh?" Mr. Hoecakes shouted. "What are you talking about?"

"You heard me, old man. We had a constitution—a damned good one—and we tore it up. Now we're at war and the entire South is about to burn down."

"Who are you calling an old man, you old goat? Are you a Yankee, talking like that, or a Yankee lover?"

"I'm a Georgian, just like you, old man! But I voted to stay in the Union in 1860, like anyone with an ounce of sense, because I knew a war would destroy us."

"ENOUGH, PLEASE!" Mrs. Hoecakes shouted. "We don't want to hear two ancient fossils arguing. Ain't we got enough problems?"

With that, the women and children went to bed. As they lay in the wagon Pauline said to Katherine, "I don't understand all this talk about the governor and the president. They're both on our side, yet they're always arguing with each other. And I don't know why our troops steal from our own people."

Katherine replied, "It's what war does to people. But we don't have to understand it. Our job is to help our soldiers."

The next morning a hard rain forced them to stop in a meadow. The deluge lasted through the night and the roads got so muddy that they had to wait two more days until the sunshine baked the ground enough to allow travel. All the while, the sound of cannon fire reminded them why they were running.

Over the next week they passed by the stations of the Macon and Western Line without incident, except that each night ended with Mr. Hoecakes and Mr. Clay arguing about politics and the war. When they were camping outside of

Barnesville, a soldier rode up. One of the women gave him the standard Confederate army meal of cornbread and bacon. Mr. Hoecakes asked where he was headed.

The soldier sprayed food as he spoke. "Atlanta. President Davis replaced General Johnston with General Hood. Davis wanted Johnston to take a stand and he didn't. The troops idolized Johnston and are demoralized, but Hood don't retreat from nothin'. They'll be some fierce fightin' soon, and those Yankees are in for a big surprise." The soldier thanked the people and departed.

The next morning they heard the distant, non-stop reports of artillery fire. Mr. Clay said, "Sounds like them Yankees is knockin' on Atlanta's door. Hood better not open it." The explosions ceased only at night.

Mr. Hoecakes started riding as a scout one mile ahead of the wagon train. The day before they reached Forsyth, he returned from his position and told the people in each wagon, "There are four men riding in this direction and I don't think they're soldiers. They might be bandits. If they stop us, just sit tight and don't move. I'll take care of everything." He then rode to his wagon, which was fourth in the procession of eight, just behind Katherine's, tied his horse to it, and crawled in the covered bed with Mr. Clay and two other men.

A half hour later the four mystery riders reached the train. One separated from the others, stopped in the middle of the road, and pulled a gun from his holster and held it in front of his face with the barrel pointed to the sky. The wagons stopped. The three other men proceeded to the field on the left side of the road and drew revolvers.

Katherine and Pauline leaned forward to see past Chloe and Dante. The strangers aimed their guns at the drivers of the middle three wagons. One of them shouted, "I want all of you to get down on this side and stand right out front where I can see you. That means everyone inside the wagons, too. Listen to me and no one gets hurt. Now!" As Mr. Hoecakes had instructed, no one moved. The man's face tightened into a scowl. "All right, someone's gonna get hurt."

The man rode up to Dante, grabbed his wrist, and dragged him back to his partners. He dropped the negro to the ground and aimed his gun at him. "First, I'll kill this nigger. Then I'll kill a white woman. If you don't follow orders by then, we'll kill every damned one of you."

Dante's wide eyes moved from wagon to wagon, looking for help. When he didn't see any, he jumped to his feet and ran towards the sisters. The bandits aimed their pistols. BAM BAM BAM. Dante hit the ground belly first with a thud.

The girls screamed, leaned back, and covered their heads with their arms. When the vibrations from the gun blasts faded, they peeked and saw the three robbers lying on the ground. Dante looked up and said, "Lawd hab mussy!"

Katherine stepped past Pauline and Chloe and jumped down to help Dante as Mr. Hoecakes, Mr. Clay, and the two other men emerged from the next wagon with rifles in hand. Mr. Hoecakes said, "Purdy dern good shootin' for a bunch a old goats."

The man who had blocked the caravan came charging from the head of the train and stopped at the sight of his three felled comrades. He aimed his gun towards Mr. Hoecakes and the others. Katherine shouted, "Men! Look out!"

The four men ducked just as the bandit fired, and the ball tore through the canvas bonnet of Mr. Hoecakes' wagon. The outlaw cursed, aimed his gun at Katherine, and then lowered it. "You! Penny!"

Katherine's knees gave out at the sight of Willie! He re-aimed at her, but before he could shoot Mr. Hoecakes drew his revolver and fired, and Willie rode off. Mr. Hoecakes stepped over, helped her up, and thanked her for the warning. Then he went to the men on the ground, two of whom were motionless. The other squirmed and moaned. Mr. Hoecakes aimed his gun at him. Katherine and Pauline turned away at the moment of the blast.

The wagon-train men relieved the bandits of their guns, money, boots, and horses. Mr. Hoecakes proclaimed, "The rest is for the buzzards."

Katherine hurried to Dante, who staggered to his feet and started wiping his face with his handkerchief as if he were shining Mr. McBain's coach. She asked if he was all right. He took a deep breath and nodded. The folks climbed onto their wagons and continued their journey. Katherine could hear Chloe mumbling a prayer. Pauline, whose hands were still shaking from witnessing a shoot-out and killings, whispered, "Katherine, that evil man called you by your made-up name. Do you know him?"

Katherine looked straight ahead, not wanting to meet Pauline's eye. "He looked like someone I met at the Marshall House, but I'm not sure." She regretted ever crossing paths with Willie, but realized that Joseph would want to know that he was in the area. Maybe the unfortunate encounter would turn out for the best.

On the evening of July 29, twenty-four days after leaving Roswell, they reached the outskirts of Macon. The rest of the folks decided to camp for the night and resume their journey to Savannah the next morning. The sisters said they planned to stay in Macon and parted ways. Mr. Hoecakes said he'd be forever thankful to Katherine for saving his life. And he'd never forget Dante, the great turkey hunter. ⁓

CHAPTER FORTY

❧

"I'll Wait for Francis"
July – August 1864

The women's bodies vibrated and bounced as the wagon rambled over the rocky road. They didn't speak except to comfort or scold a child. Rebecca, exhausted from all the sleepless nights tending to her husband, put her head on Sarah's shoulder and drifted off despite the bumpy ride. After a few hours a hard jolt woke her. She looked around and caught the eye of a skinny woman no older than Katherine, with sunken cheeks, dark brown hair tied tightly in a bun, a mole the size of a one-cent copper on her cheek, and a baby on her lap. The girl asked, "Ma'am, aren't you Mrs. Toll?" The other girls stared at Rebecca and Sarah, curious about the two grandmotherly-looking women wearing clean, homespun work dresses devoid of patchwork.

Rebecca propped up. "Yes, I am. Who are you?"

"I'm Doreen Stans. My husband worked for Mr. Toll in the shoe manufactory before he joined the army. He's in Virginia, last he wrote a month ago. If you don't mind me asking, ma'am, what are you doing here with us?"

"I've been arrested for treason, just like you."

"Where is Mr. Toll?"

Rebecca tried to answer, but couldn't without spilling tears. Sarah held her sister's hand and said, "Mr. Toll passed this morning."

The woman crossed herself. "I'm so sorry. And they still arrested you?" Sarah nodded. "If they'll do that to a widow of a few hours, they'd do it to the Virgin Mary."

The Yankee soldier sitting alongside the driver said to the women, "We're pulling over to water the horses. There's a creek if you're thirsty. You can go into the woods, one at a time and under guard, to do your private business. Be quick about it. When you return, you'll get a ration of hardtack and boiled beef."

The women climbed down and stretched the pins and needles from their numb legs. After the break, the caravan traveled for four more hours before parking by the road for the night. The women were allowed a privy break and given more hardtack and boiled beef for supper. They tried their best to sleep on the hard wagon floor.

They continued at seven o'clock the next morning and arrived in Marietta, exhausted from a lack of sleep, that afternoon, July 9. Sarah's mouth was so dry she could hardly open it. She noticed that the streets of the town were just as active as when she had left, except all the soldiers now wore blue. A mounted sergeant met the wagon train on the north side of the public square and led it to the three-story, brick Georgia Military Institute one mile outside of town. The prisoners were ushered into the bunkless student barracks, their quarters until further notice. They had supper in the dining room, which lacked tables and chairs, and were given a ration of pork and bread, which they had to eat with their hands, and a tin cup of water. Afterwards, they returned to their room, lay on the wooden floor, and slept in their clothes, using their carpetbags for pillows.

Sarah opened one eye and wondered if she were dreaming or had actually heard a voice. A minute of silence passed and she heard it again. "Francis, we can't stay here. It's too dangerous. We'll be much safer in Savannah." Sarah rose up on her elbow and saw Rebecca sitting with her back against the wall, appearing in silhouette against the moonlit classroom. "The servants will guard the house." Rebecca then slid down and slept, which was more than Sarah could do as her mind began to race. She had shared the same bedroom with her sister several times over the past week and had never heard her talk in her sleep. Clearly, the stress and misery that she bore had affected her subconscious.

Sarah couldn't fathom how matters had evolved to this point. She had always lived a life of comfort, coddled by parents, tended to by servants, loved by husband and children, and respected by neighbors. Now she was a prisoner in her own state, being treated as if she were a common criminal. She imagined Danny laughing in the square as he and JD chased Truvy and Mary, and finally dozed off. Sarah awoke the next morning with her chemise sticking to her body, her scalp itching, and her mouth tasting like bile. Children cried all around her. Rebecca was sitting up, staring into space. "Good morning, dear sister." Rebecca responded in kind, without a smile. Sarah let her mourn, knowing that eventually she would return to normal.

After a breakfast of bread and a meat of unknown origin, the sisters passed the hours walking around the grounds of the institute. Later that day more women from Roswell arrived, as did men and women from the mill town of Sweetwater, about ten miles from Roswell. One of the men told Sarah that the Yankees had also burned their mills and arrested them. She wondered if there were no depths to which this General Sherman wouldn't sink.

That night, as the sisters ate their ration of boiled beef and bread, sitting against a wall, Rebecca started to whisper. Sarah asked if she were speaking to her. Rebecca was startled by the question. "I didn't realize I was talking. I guess I was thinking out loud."

Sarah said, "Dear sister, if you want to talk about anything to relieve your mind, please tell me. I know that you're in pain and I want to help."

Rebecca teared up. "I'm heartbroken, Sarah. Poor Francis died in such agony, and I couldn't even mourn his passing in peace. I'll be better. I just need time."

The women finished their meal in silence. It happened again that night. Rebecca sat up and talked to Tilda, telling her to serve fried chicken to Francis while she was away, and to give him only a small piece of peach pie for dessert. Sarah went back to sleep and dreamed that she and James were attending a wedding at the First Presbyterian Church in Savannah. The reverend administered the vows to the couple, whose backs were turned to them. He pronounced them husband and wife, and they kissed for a minute. Sarah looked at her husband, who was smiling and applauding. The couple turned around to leave. It was Katherine and Joseph! Sarah jerked up. Sunshine was flooding the classroom.

Rebecca said, "You were groaning in your sleep."

Sarah shook away the cobwebs. "I had a strange dream." She decided not to share it. "Everyone's left the room. They must be doling out rations. Let's eat while we can."

Wagonloads of women from Roswell and Sweetwater continued to arrive for the next few days. On July 15, their sixth day in Marietta, Sarah and Rebecca and about two hundred other women and children were ordered to board wagons, which took them to the train depot. An officer in front of the Kennesaw House Hotel addressed them. "Prisoners, today you are beginning your journey north. Pass by this wagon and you'll be given nine days of cooked rations. Guards will show you to a car for the journey to Chattanooga, where you will transfer to Nashville. You will receive further orders there."

Sarah took Rebecca's arm. With carpetbags in hand, they stood in line for their paper-wrapped allotment of hard tack and cooked beef. A few hours later they were sitting on the wooden floor of a dark, creaky boxcar with thirty other women and twelve children. Sarah kept shifting her weight from one side to the other, trying to get comfortable, and wondered if she would ever sit on a cushion again. But she had one hundred dollars in gold coins and when the Yankees released them, she and Rebecca would go to a hotel, eat a hot meal, and sleep in real beds. Then she would send Amy a telegram and buy train tickets to New York. They just had to survive the next few weeks.

The snail-paced trip to Chattanooga took three days. There were refueling stops every ten miles where the prisoners could get water. Sarah took advantage of the opportunity to brush her teeth and wash her face, but Rebecca didn't bother. A hole in the floor in the corner of the car served as an emergency privy vault, used mostly by children. As the trip progressed, Rebecca became more withdrawn and only spoke to Sarah in response to questions. When they reached Chattanooga they learned that the connecting train to Nashville would leave the following day, and they slept overnight in the boxcar.

During the trip to Nashville, Rebecca dozed while Sarah read a Bible that she had borrowed from the woman sitting next to her. She found comfort in the words and offered to read to Rebecca, but her sister shook her head. The next morning a boy sitting across from the sisters pointed to Rebecca and said, "Ma'am, you talked in your sleep last night. I heard you." The boy's mother hushed him. Rebecca took no notice. Later that day the same boy leaned forward as if someone had grabbed his tongue and pulled it, and he threw up, hitting the floor in front of Sarah and Rebecca and splattering their dresses. The mother apologized. Sarah wiped her dress with her kerchief, but Rebecca sat still as a stone, staring straight ahead, so Sarah did it for her. The sour smell soon blended into the rancid, stuffy, stifling summer air in the car. Later that day a woman got a case of diarrhea and didn't make the hole in the floor in time. Sarah turned her head sideways to breathe the air coming in through the cracks between the wood sidings.

They reached Nashville at dusk and spent the night in the car. The next morning they transferred to a train to Louisville. This time they sat across from a mother and three young girls who reminded Sarah of younger, homelier versions of Katherine, Pauline, and Mary. Like so many of the women from the mills, they were gaunt and dark-haired, and wore faded, patched, work dresses in grays, browns, and blacks. The mother was so pale that her black eyebrows looked painted on. She rested her head on her eldest daughter's shoulder while the youngest girl, about six years old, sat on the middle girl's lap. Sarah asked the eldest daughter, who introduced herself as Lucinda Wood, if she could help with her mother. The girl replied, "Ma's been sick for days and I don't know what's wrong. She isn't eating and barely talks. Easter, my littlest sister, is sick, too, but not like Ma. I asked a soldier in Nashville if we could see a doctor but he told me to ask when we get to Louisville. I don't know what else to do."

Sarah learned that Lucinda, her mother, and the girl's next oldest sister, Molly, worked in one of the Roswell mills. A year before, their father had been killed at Gettysburg. After the Yankees arrested them, they slept in the square for two days, waiting for a wagon to Marietta. The second night the general in charge gave a ration of whiskey to the soldiers. A few got drunk and tried to rape Lucinda's sickly mother as the daughters screamed for help. Only the intervention of an officer saved the woman and probably Lucinda from being molested. Her voice cracked as she told the story. Sarah said that when they got to Louisville she'd help find a doctor for her mother and sister.

That night, when Rebecca again talked in her sleep, telling Francis to go to the doctor about the blood in his urine, Sarah decided to send Rebecca to the doctor as well.

The next morning Sarah awoke to the sound of three weeping girls. She saw Mrs. Wood's head dangling lifelessly over Lucinda's leg—her eyes and mouth half-open. Sarah thought her a victim of General Sherman as much as any soldier who was killed on the battlefield. At the next refueling stop she told a guard that a woman had died. The soldier peered into the car, shrugged, and said he couldn't do anything about it until they reached Louisville. When they re-boarded the train, Lucinda tugged her mother's body next to her and the girls rode the rest of the day with the corpse, whose arms, legs, and head bounced ghoulishly from the train's vibrations, as if she were a marionette.

That evening, over two weeks after they left Roswell, Sarah, Rebecca, and two hundred other women and children reached Louisville on the banks of the Ohio River, across from Indiana. They climbed down from the car and Sarah asked a guard to find an officer. He said, "I don't take orders from secesh women."

Sarah replied, "I'm not ordering you, young man. I'm asking you as a Christian."

The soldier started to say something, thought better of it, and disappeared down the boarding path. He returned in five minutes with a lieutenant. Sarah explained, "A woman in our car has died and must have a proper burial, and my sister and this young lady's sister are ill and need to see a doctor."

Rebecca straightened. "Me? I'm not ill."

The lieutenant looked into the car and quickly turned away. "Ma'am, you're prisoners. You must stay with the others."

"What do we do? You can't leave the body on the train."

The officer scratched his head. "Ma'am, all the prisoners on this train are being sent to a refugee house in town. You, too. It's late, but I'll try to find a mortician to remove the body and hold it. I'll contact you at the home tomorrow morning. You do realize that the mortician will want to be paid?"

Lucinda gasped, "Sir, I have no money."

Sarah patted the girl's hand and told the officer, "I have money for the casket and burial. But you must let the girls attend the service for their own mother."

"I'll do my best, ma'am, but it's not my decision to make. Please go to the wagons and I'll see you tomorrow morning. Your name?"

"Mrs. McBain. And this is Miss Wood."

The two-story brick refugee home could barely accommodate the prisoners. The women and children crammed together into the large rooms and slept in beds on thin, lumpy mattresses. Sarah held herself together by remembering that they were getting closer to Indiana, freedom, and a hotel.

Louisville in July and August was every bit as hot and muggy as Georgia and after her first night in the home, Sarah felt as if she had slept in a wet blanket. Her scalp itched so badly that she thought it would jump off and run away, yet her thoughts were on Rebecca and the Wood sisters. An officer stood in the doorway and slammed his hand on the wall to get the people's attention. "Prisoners, listen to me. We are trying to arrange boats to take you across the river to Indiana, where you will be released to earn your livelihoods without doing further harm to the Union. This will take some time. I understand you were given nine days' rations when you left Marietta and that time has passed. I have no authority to issue more. Until you are sent across the river, we will try to hire you out to do domestic work so you can earn money for food. The agent of the Louisville Refugee

Commission is advertising in the local newspapers, offering healthy men, women, and children for employment. Also, local citizens are trying to raise donations of food for all refugees—not just you but thousands of others who have fled the fighting. You are at the mercy of the very citizens against whom you rebelled. This morning, out of the generosity of the federal government, you will be given rice soup. Follow me to the dining hall."

Sarah muttered under her breath, "How kind of them." This time the dining hall had tables and chairs, but the soup was served in bowls without spoons. They drank the watery broth and fished out the rice on their fingertips.

A soldier walked in and called for Mrs. McBain and Miss Wood to follow him. The lieutenant from the previous night and a captain awaited them in the entry hall. The lieutenant said to Lucinda, "I found a mortician yesterday. He picked up your mother but won't put her in a casket or arrange to have her buried until he's paid. The cost of everything is thirty dollars—greenbacks or gold, nothing Confederate." He asked Sarah, "You said you have money?"

Sarah appreciated the soldier's efforts. "Thank you for your help, sir. Yes, I have the money. Can the girls attend the service?"

The lieutenant looked at the captain, who said, "Yes, under guard."

Sarah wanted to scream. Did he think these three frightened, orphaned girls would try to escape? She reached into her dress pocket, pulled out a leather pouch, removed three gold coins, and handed them to the lieutenant. He said, "Thank you. I'll pick up the girls later today for the service and bring them back afterwards."

The captain held out his hand. Sarah stared at it. "I just paid the lieutenant."

"Ma'am, you're a prisoner of the United States and are not allowed to have any money in your possession. You should have been searched when you were arrested. Hand over the money. You'll get it back when you're released."

Sarah turned beet red. "This is MY money. I need food and medical care for my sister and for this child's sister. It's all I have."

"HAND IT OVER NOW!" The captain's voice reverberated in the hallway.

"And who is going to take care of us?"

"Why don't you write to Jefferson Davis? He got you into this. I'm sure he'll be happy to get you out."

Lucinda hugged Sarah and wept. "I'm sorry, Mrs. McBain. This wouldn't have happened if you hadn't tried to help me."

Sarah could feel the girl's body tremble. "It's not your fault, dear. You weren't aware of Yankee compassion."

The captain said, "Ma'am, there are thousands of mothers and widows of dead Yankee boys who weren't aware of rebel compassion. Now, give me that pouch."

Sarah handed it over and watched the officers walk away. Lucinda cried, "Please forgive me, Mrs. McBain."

Sarah cupped Lucinda's face in her hands. "Dear, we have to survive, for the sake of our families. That's all that's important now. Do you understand?" The girl nodded. "You don't have to apologize again. We have to find work while we're confined here. Let's see the director of the home now before you go to your mother's funeral."

The director said that it would be difficult to find employment for them as so many refugees were looking for work. However, the next day he reported that he had found them jobs: Sarah as a seamstress for two Yankee dollars a day in a private home; and Lucinda and Molly as washerwomen for one dollar a day each. They agreed that Easter, who had improved from her illness, would remain at the refugee home and watch Rebecca, who did little but sit and talk to herself.

Sarah's hands shook as she walked to the new job the next morning. Other than volunteering, she had never worked for anyone else. And she had washed only her face from a basin the past few weeks and felt filthy. The mistress of the house, Mrs. Reed, a woman not much younger than Sarah's sixty-four years, answered the door. She looked Sarah up and down and said, "You must be from the refugee commission. Do come in. I'm sorry I can't spend more time with you. I'm running out now to visit relatives. I'll be back in three days. While I'm gone, Olivia will supervise your work." She called into the parlor, "Olivia, please meet your seamstress."

Sarah's jaw dropped when a pretty mulatto woman about forty years of age, with a Caucasian nose and straight black hair pulled into a bun, walked into the foyer. Mrs. Reed said, "Olivia, please meet Mrs. . . . ."

Sarah stammered "Mc . . . McBain."

Olivia smiled and said, "So nice to meet you, Mrs. McBain."

Sarah took a deep breath. Her husband owned one hundred eighty slaves, and servants had tended to her all her life. She spent much of her time running a household staff of negroes. Now, she was about to take orders from one. "It's nice to meet you, Olivia." She glanced at Mrs. Reed, whose eyes were shifting from her to Olivia.

Mrs. Reed cleared her throat and said, "Have you much experience as a seamstress, Mrs. McBain?"

Sarah replied. "I went to a finishing school many, many years ago. I've supervised my own girls over the years. More recently, I've sewed uniforms and other clothing for the soldiers."

Mrs. Reed tried to put Sarah at ease. "You'll do just fine, I'm sure. I'll be back in a few days." A black man appeared with a valise and opened the front door for her.

After Mrs. Reed left, Olivia said, "Come this way, Mrs. McBain, and I'll get you started." She led Sarah into a room to a large table, and asked, "Can you work a treadle?"

Sarah said, "I can." She looked at the patterns. "A bodice and skirt?"

Olivia replied, "Yes. There will be a lace trim and ruching on the bodice. Here are your materials—a nice muslin. Do you need to wash your hands before you get started?"

Sarah stiffened, stared at the material, and took a deep breath. She growled, "No, Olivia, my hands are clean, thank you."

Olivia took a small step back. Then she looked Sarah in the eye. "Mrs. McBain, I'm not suggesting that you have dirty hands. I'm letting you know that in case you need to wash, we have a basin in the bathroom. I'll leave you now."

It took Olivia one visit to realize that Sarah was an excellent seamstress and she didn't disturb her again. At one o'clock, Olivia showed her to a small room with a table and a single place setting. Sarah ate alone, served by a pretty, young mulatto girl, who smiled and said, "It's me, again," each time she entered the room. Sarah had to force herself to eat the delicious beef stew slowly. She wanted to take some back for Rebecca and the girls, but she didn't have the courage to ask Olivia for permission.

For three days Sarah and the girls made enough money to feed the five of them. On the fourth day, when Sarah returned to the refugee home, she didn't see any of the sisters. She asked Rebecca, "Where's Easter?"

Rebecca stared out the window. "Easter?" she said, trying to place the name.

Sarah went to the director of the home and inquired after the Wood girls. He said, "The Sisterhood of Nuns of Nazareth came today and said they had a family who would take them in. We got the two older girls from their jobs and they left immediately. The older one told me to tell you goodbye, and to thank you for everything. I asked her if she wanted to write you a note, but she said she couldn't write." Sarah returned to her bed and found Rebecca fast asleep. She lay down, feeling forlorn that she had missed her chance to say goodbye, but rejoiced that three orphaned girls had a family once again. It made her miss her own three orphans, and of course Danny, more than ever.

The next morning, before she left for work, Sarah recruited another woman at the home to keep an eye on Rebecca for the day for fifty cents. Mrs. Reed greeted Sarah at the door, led her into the family parlor, and asked her to sit. "I'm sorry that I wasn't able to spend more time with you before I left. Olivia tells me that you didn't need supervision. I gathered that the moment I saw you. Could I ask, where are you from?"

Sarah told the woman about her life in Savannah, volunteer work during the war, arrest at Roswell, and journey to Louisville, including Rebecca's mental state. Mrs. Reed closed the door. She explained that she and her husband were devoted to the rebel cause, but their lives were attached to Kentucky, a slave state that never seceded, and they couldn't leave. "I heard about the arrest of the mill workers. I think it's disgusting." She took a deep breath and asked, "I hope you got along with Olivia."

Sarah exhaled and relaxed. "It was difficult at first. But she was respectful and let me be. She thanked me at the end of each day when she paid me. As I walked home that first day, I even laughed at the reversal of roles. Wait until I tell my husband. But I have to be honest with myself, the entire South might soon be going through a dramatic change. Our negroes may soon be set free. How we and they will adapt, I can't say. I love our servants—well, most of them—but I don't think we can live side by side on an equal basis. For generations we've been raised to believe that they're inferior beings and can only exist as productive members of society by serving under the care and direction of whites. That belief will be hard to change. It will be even more difficult if the Yankees force equality of the races down our throats."

Mrs. Reed admitted that she hated to see the Confederacy in such trouble and the slaves emancipated. "We had eleven house servants. My husband's man-servant Tim, his wife Olivia, and their daughter remained with us. I pay them and they continue to reside here. It's working well so far. But the other eight left as soon as they could. They're at a federal camp outside of town, lazing about at taxpayer expense. I can't imagine four million of them living on their own, trying to survive without our help." Mrs. Reed leaned forward in her chair. "Mrs. McBain, is there anything I can do for you in your current circumstances?"

Sarah closed her eyes in thought. "Yes, if you don't mind, there are a few things. I will reimburse you as soon as I can. I'd like to write a letter to my daughter in New York, if you could kindly supply me with paper, pen, and ink, and post it. I need to inform her of my situation and have her prepare to send funds to me once I arrive in Indiana. Also, could you loan me thirty dollars? I will need money to send her a telegram once I get to Indiana, and my sister and I will need to stay in a hotel until I receive the funds."

Mrs. Reed said, "I'll loan you one hundred dollars so you can take the train to New York as soon as you arrive in Indiana and won't have to wait for a wire. I'll give you the money just before you leave so the soldiers won't seize it. While you write your letter I'll have Tim prepare a bath. You must be dying for one. Then I insist you join me for dinner. I won't have you sew for me, but you can come here each day and get out of that refugee home if you wish. You must bring your sister as well, poor woman."

When Sarah returned to the refugee home that evening, Rebecca was curled up in a ball, sleeping in her bed. Sarah shook her awake. "Rebecca, look what I have for supper. Fresh baked bread, roasted chicken, and sweet potatoes."

Rebecca sat up and, although she had stayed in bed all day, had dark circles around her eyes. "I'm not hungry, Sarah."

"Dear sister, you must eat. You're losing too much weight."

Rebecca picked at the food. Sarah finally offered it to another woman.

Sarah and Rebecca spent the days of the following week with Mrs. Reed and talked about the South's future. With Mrs. Reed's generosity, they took Rebecca, who hardly spoke, to a doctor. He concluded that the woman needed rest and steady doses of laudanum. One week later, in early August, the director of the refugee home told Sarah that they were leaving the next morning for Indiana. Sarah went to Mrs. Reed's alone with the news. Mrs. Reed gave her one hundred dollars in greenbacks. The women embraced, and Sarah promised repayment as soon as she got to New York.

Sarah returned to the home and found her sister. "Rebecca, we're finally leaving. Tomorrow night we'll be in a nice hotel and sleep in a real bed. And we'll be with Amy in a week. Isn't that wonderful?" Rebecca stared at her sister and then lowered her head. Sarah helped Rebecca lie in her bunk, and prayed that the prospect of freedom would return her sanity.

Sarah awoke the next morning to the shouts of the director. "Wake up, everyone. Get dressed and pack. We're taking you to the pier."

Sarah shook her sister. "Come, Rebecca! We're leaving for Indiana."

Rebecca opened her eyes. "Where are we going?"

"To Indiana, and then New York. We're almost free."

"I don't want to go to Indiana or New York. I'll wait for Francis."

"Rebecca, you can't stay. Francis isn't coming. Don't you want to see Amy?"

She stared at her sister blankly. "Who's Amy?"

Tears streamed down Sarah's face. She had lost her sister. "Rebecca, please. Get dressed and come with me."

A soldier walked by and shouted, "Let's go, ladies. The wagon's leaving in a few minutes and you have to be on it."

Sarah said to him, "My sister isn't feeling well. Please give me some time."

"That's not my problem, ma'am. Go to that wagon right now." ❧

CHAPTER FORTY-ONE

❧

"De Lawd Bin Lisnin'"

July – October 1864

K atherine, Pauline, Chloe, and Dante entered Macon on the evening of July 29. They had to stop at the Macon and Western Railroad Depot as the streets were crammed with people and ambulances. They learned from a passerby that battles were raging around Atlanta and a train with hundreds of wounded soldiers had just arrived. Volunteers carried the injured from the train to ambulances and other vehicles, which took them to one of the seven hospitals in town. Katherine thought the effort was as well coordinated as in Marietta. After an hour waiting, and getting directions from another passerby, the sisters knocked on the door of Mrs. Pope's Italianate house on Mulberry Street.

A tall, thin woman with salt-and-pepper hair about Mrs. McBain's age opened the door and appraised the young ladies. Katherine said, "Mrs. Pope?"

The woman peered over her spectacles. "Yes? Who are you?"

"I'm Katherine Downes and this is my sister, Pauline. We live with Mr. and Mrs. McBain in Savannah and are returning from. . . ."

The woman's face lit up. "Oh, yes, Mrs. McBain wrote me several times about the three sisters." She stepped aside and said, "Please come in. How is she?"

The girls entered the foyer and Katherine explained that they had left Mrs. McBain in Roswell and traveled to Macon with two servants. "She said that you may be able to help us find a place to stay and volunteer work in a hospital until she joins us. She wrote this letter of introduction."

Mrs. Pope took the letter and read in silence. "Of course I can find you shelter—right here in my home. I'll have my servants bring in your luggage." The woman moved the girls into a bedroom on the second floor, across the stairwell from her own room. Then she supervised one of her servants and Dante as they moved Mrs. Toll's valuables into a locked room on the main floor. She put Dante in a room over the coach house and Chloe in a cabin with one of her female servants.

During supper the sisters described their time in Marietta and Roswell. Mrs. Pope replied, "It's not easy getting around the country now and there's no mail service from northern Georgia. If the bridge at Roswell was destroyed, they'll need to go upriver to cross, and when they do, the roads may not be open to travel. My guess is that she's in some small town, waiting for the right opportunity to come here. I wouldn't be concerned about her. She's a very resourceful woman."

Katherine nodded, "Yes, I know she is. But we can't help but worry."

Mrs. Pope patted Katherine's hand and said, "I understand." She then described the local situation. General Hood replaced General Johnston and immediately took the offensive against the Yankees. Three major battles had just taken place around Atlanta, resulting in thousands of Confederate casualties, many of whom were sent to Macon. There was an urgent need for volunteers, nurses, and surgeons. In addition, in the weeks before the girls arrived, a huge influx of refugees, including wives and children of soldiers, had flowed in from Atlanta and North Georgia. They packed the town and further strained resources.

Mrs. Pope explained that her husband had died of a heart attack in 1860. After Fort Sumter, their two sons joined the military. One was killed at Second Manassas and the other was currently serving in Virginia. She spent her time supporting the Ladies Relief Society by cooking food, collecting clothing and other necessities, and knitting socks for the troops. Katherine offered Dante to help with the cooking and Chloe with knitting and sewing. Mrs. Pope gladly accepted the offer.

Katherine asked about volunteer opportunities in Macon. Mrs. Pope said that she knew every important person in town and could get them work in the Macon Wayside Home, but a hospital would be impossible. "I and other women of the Ladies Relief Society visit the hospitals daily, bringing the soldiers food and helping out as best we can. But there is some resentment to our presence by the surgeons, even though the surgeon-in-chief of Macon hospitals claims that we are welcome. I'm not aware of one female performing nursing duties in any of the hospitals. However, the Macon Wayside Home does admit sick soldiers as well as those in transit, and most of the volunteers are women." Mrs. Pope offered to take them to the wayside home the next day, an easy walk.

After supper Mrs. Pope supplied the girls with writing materials and showed them to a desk in the family parlor. Katherine wrote to Mr. McBain, telling him of their experiences. After she read it to Pauline, she added a postscript:

P.S. If you should hear from Captain McBain, please send him our best wishes. We saw him in Marietta before he was about to escort hundreds of Yankees to the Andersonville prison. He looked well. Please tell Mary we are expecting a letter from her as soon as her little fingers can write one.

The next morning Mrs. Pope took the sisters to the wayside home on Mulberry and Fourth streets. Dr. J. P. Cannon accepted them with open arms. The girls agreed to work six days a week from seven thirty in the morning to three thirty in the afternoon. Their spirits rose. After spending twenty-four days on the road, they were helping soldiers again.

※

Two days after their arrival in Macon, as they walked to work, the girls heard rifle fire to the east. Pauline said, "That's close."

Katherine replied, "If there's any danger, I'm sure Dr. Cannon will warn us."

The gunfire crackled all morning. The sisters learned from other volunteers that the Yankees were across the Ocmulgee River to the east of town and the Georgia militia was trying to prevent their advance into Macon. Pauline told Katherine, "I'm scared. I thought the Yankees were at Atlanta."

Katherine said, "Me, too. They seem to be everywhere."

The gunfire was still raging when they left work. Pauline said, "Let's walk faster." One ear-splitting explosion caused Pauline to scream and start to run. Katherine followed. When they reached the gate to Mrs. Pope's house, they heard a loud buzzing noise. The girls looked skyward and saw a projectile heading towards them. Before they could react, a geyser of sand about two stories high erupted from the dirt sidewalk just twenty-five yards away, followed by a crashing sound like a tree breaking in half. Pauline shouted, "Look!" and pointed to the neighbor's house. One of the columns had been cut in half and a hole had been blown through the second floor wall.

Katherine said, "My God, they're firing cannons into the town."

They ran into Mrs. Pope's house and lay face down on the parlor floor with their hands covering their heads. They didn't move for an hour as explosions boomed all around them. When the attack stopped, Mrs. Pope entered the room. "My goodness. The Yankees have no qualms about killing civilians. You can get up now. I think our boys have chased them away. I'm going to check on the rest of the house."

The sisters followed her and found Dante and Chloe in the basement, both shivering in fear. Dante said, "Ah belieb de Lawd he tellin' us sometin.'"

That night at supper Mrs. Pope explained what she had learned of the incident. "Five thousand Yankee cavalrymen came down from Atlanta to free the prisoners held at Camp Oglethorpe in Macon. Our boys blocked their advance, so they burned the railroad bridge and bombarded the town. Our artillery drove them off. The Georgia militia has set out after them."

Pauline's hand shook as she lifted a glass of water. "Mrs. Pope, I'm terrified." She glanced at Katherine to see if her sister shared her anxiety.

Mrs. Pope replied, "I don't blame you, but I don't think the Yankees will return."

Katherine wanted to be in Macon when Mrs. McBain arrived, and to help at the hospital, but she couldn't bear for her sister to live in fear. "Pauline, I don't think the surgeon-in-charge would put his medical staff in any danger, but if we're attacked again, we'll leave." Pauline nodded, but was only partly relieved.

All of Macon breathed a sigh of relief two days later when the Georgia militia caught up with the Yankees at Sunshine Church, twenty miles outside of Macon, and captured the general and five hundred of his men. That night, in view of thousands of cheering locals, the prisoners, with heads held high, were marched through town under Confederate guard to Camp Oglethorpe. Pauline said to Katherine and Mrs. Pope, "Except for the uniforms, they look just like our boys."

That evening, when they returned to the house, Mrs. Pope handed Katherine a letter. She read it to Pauline in their bedroom.

August 2, 1864
Dearest Katherine and Pauline:
I am relieved to know that you're safe. I haven't had a word from Mrs. McBain since she left Marietta. If you should hear from her, please inform me immediately. Captain McBain has returned to General Mercer's brigade, which, with the rest of our army, retreated across the Chattahoochee. We are praying that our army can hold Atlanta.
Please make sure that you are sitting down before you read further. Before I begin, I want you to know that Mary is doing well. Several weeks ago she, Danny, and Truvy walked to the river. On the way Mary befriended two poor sisters playing in a vacant lot. While Danny and Truvy went to the river, Mary stayed with the girls and they ate some of the poisonous Jamestown weed that was growing wild in the lot. Mary became quite ill and lost consciousness for two days. I had to put her in the hospital. Danny and Truvy spent every free moment at her bedside. She recovered but didn't eat for two more days, if you can imagine that. She's much better now and is eating more waffles and pancakes than a regiment of soldiers. I am enclosing a note from her. Sadly, one of the other girls, a three-year-old who also ate the weed, died—another unfortunate casualty of this terrible war.
We have just received news that our troops repelled a Yankee raid on Macon. You may stay there and wait for Mrs. McBain as long as you feel it's safe. But if there's a chance of another attack, or if the hospitals are moved, I want you to come home at once, by train if necessary.
Please give my best wishes to Mrs. Pope and thank her for me for showing you such gracious hospitality.
Warmest regards, J. J. McBain

Katherine commented, "Eating a weed? What could have gotten into her mind?"

Pauline said, "Thank God she's all right. Even under Mr. McBain's care she still finds trouble and she can't blame it on Danny this time. Katherine, I must see her. We've been gone two months. I can't bear to think that she was ill and we weren't by her side."

Katherine sat on the arm of Pauline's chair. "I feel the same way, but we must be patient and wait for Mrs. McBain." She then unfolded Mary's letter.

My Dear Sisters:

When are you coming home? I miss you. Mr. McBain asked me to call him Grandpa. I like doing it. He told you I ate a bad plant and got very sick. I'm sorry. I was making beleeve I was eating cake with two girls who were very poor and didn't eat all day. I'm better now and go to school and play with Danny and Troovy in the afternoon. Danny was very wurried when I got sick and prayed for me. I know he loves me, even tho he won't say so. Grandpa and the servants take very good care of me, but I wish you were here. JD and General Lee are very good friends now. General Lee caut a big rat for Grandpa.

Love and kisses, Mary

Katherine hugged Pauline. "We'll go home soon, I promise."

The first weeks of August passed quickly. The sisters had a daily routine of sitting for breakfast at six-thirty with Mrs. Pope and going to work. Afterwards, Katherine often joined Mrs. Pope and the Ladies Relief Society on their visits to the soldiers in the other hospitals and Pauline sketched houses in town for Truvy. On Sundays the girls went to church with Mrs. Pope. Dante and Chloe joined them and sat in the negro gallery. After services, the sisters, usually accompanied by Dante and Chloe, walked around Macon on their own. Pauline often stopped to sketch. Her favorite house was a grand Italianate villa on Georgia Avenue, near Mrs. Pope's house. It was two stories over a ground floor, with a large tower sitting like a mushroom on the roof. Pauline said that there was nothing like it in Savannah. It took her three Sundays to finish it to her liking.

One night Mrs. Pope invited several guests for supper, including Dr. E. J. Roach, the surgeon-in-charge of the Floyd Hospital. After hearing of the girls' experiences, the doctor claimed that they were examples of what made the South great—women as dedicated to the cause as men. Katherine thanked him. She wanted to tell him that she could be of more service as a nurse in a hospital, and that she was just as worthy as most male nurses she had met, but she didn't want to embarrass Mrs. Pope.

The flow of injured soldiers slowed by mid-August, but the sisters continued their daily routine. Dante impressed Mrs. Pope with his cooking for the soldiers and she let him, along with her own cook, help prepare supper for her and the sisters. Katherine wrote a letter to Mrs. Lamar in Savannah, asking her to tell Isetta that Dante was fine and to write back about her pregnancy. Subsequently, Katherine received weekly letters from Caro Lamar with reports on Isetta, who was feeling well and getting bigger every day.

Along with her sewing duties, Chloe attended to the sisters every morning, helping them dress and brush their hair, and every night, helping them undress. She often reminded Pauline, "You a young lady now and need uh cawset," and "You soon be as priddy as Miss Katrin. Dem soljuhs see you two gu'ls, dey run tuh de hospital, holdin' dey gizzahds, cryin' dat dey need nussin."

The lull in casualties from Atlanta proved to be temporary as the heaviest artillery fire they had yet heard erupted at the end of August at Jonesboro, southeast of Atlanta. It continued for two days. Trains filled with injured soldiers began arriving in town and medical staffs worked non-stop. A few days later, on the night of September 1, General Hood's army evacuated Atlanta and the next morning the Union troops, at the invitation of the mayor, marched into the town unopposed. Word spread that nothing could stop the Yankees from going wherever they wanted in Georgia, including Macon.

When the girls walked home from work on September 2, the streets were crowded with people on wagons packed with household goods and baggage. At supper Mrs. Pope reported what the girls had already seen—that local residents were fleeing in droves. She heard it was almost impossible to get a ticket on the train, and the railroad was not allowing non-military passengers to ship any freight to Savannah.

That night in bed Pauline asked Katherine, "Do you really think it's safe to stay here? Won't the Yankees try to take Macon next?"

"It's possible, but we can't leave with all the soldiers in need of help. Atlanta is a hundred miles away. Surely we'll have some warning if they march in this direction."

Pauline said, "But if they do come here, it won't take them long. And from what Mrs. Pope said, we can't get tickets for the train. We must take the wagon. We won't have much of a head start."

Katherine still wanted to wait for Mrs. McBain, but Pauline's anxiety worried her and she had to consider sending her home alone. "I understand Dr. Stout, the medical director of the Army of Tennessee, is in Macon. He won't keep his hospitals here if he thinks they'd be in danger. Let's hear his plans and then I'll decide what to do."

The next morning during breakfast, a messenger from Dr. Roach delivered a note for Katherine. She read it aloud. "Dear Miss Downes: A Captain McBain from General Mercer's staff has just been admitted to the hospital with serious injury. Is he a member of the family with whom you live in Savannah? If so, you may want to visit him. Dr. E. J. Roach, Surgeon-in-Charge."

Katherine dropped the note on the table. "Oh, dear God! Pauline, let's go. We have to see him." The girls said goodbye to Mrs. Pope and rushed from the house. Katherine walked so fast that Pauline had to trot to keep up. Katherine said, "Go to the wayside home and tell Dr. Cannon I'll be there as soon as I can." Pauline wanted to go with Katherine but knew that her sister felt the need to see Captain McBain alone.

After fibbing to the ward nurse on the second floor of the hospital that she was kin of Captain McBain, Katherine was taken to his bed. His eyes were closed and his face was as white as an egg shell. The nurse said, "He was shot in the side and treated at a field hospital. He's lost a lot of blood. We don't know if he's sustained any internal injuries. A field surgeon sewed him up."

Katherine said, "As a family member, I would like to take care of him." She explained her nursing experiences. While many surgeons frowned upon women in their hospitals, either as nurses or visitors, they did allow relatives such as wives and mothers, and even slaves, to be personal caregivers.

"Of course. I'll inform Dr. Roach."

Katherine pulled up a chair and sat by Joseph for an hour and wiped his face with a wet rag every few minutes. She still thought him the handsomest man in the world, even with an unshaven face. She couldn't deny that she loved him, even though she knew she could never have him. She pulled back the cover and studied the large bandage on his side. His eyelashes began to flutter. She said, "Captain, can you hear me?"

He murmured, "Huh?" and opened his eyes to slits.

"Joseph, it's me, Katherine." His lips slowly curved upwards. "We're in Macon, in a hospital. You were wounded and I'm going to take care of you. I won't leave until you can walk out of here on your own." She held his hand and his smile widened.

When Joseph went back to sleep, Katherine walked the one block to the wayside home and found Pauline. They sat on a bench in the hallway. "I'm not going to leave him, Pauline, until he recovers. Mr. and Mrs. McBain would want that. I know you're nervous about being here. So I want you to take the train to Savannah as soon as a seat is available. You'll be safe and back with Mary. When Captain McBain recovers, I'll come home with Chloe and Dante."

Pauline protested, "I'm not leaving you. I can't."

Katherine took her sister's hand. "I want you to go to Savannah where I won't have to worry about you, especially if the Yankees come this way. Mrs. McBain never intended for us to be away for so long or near any fighting."

Pauline leaped to her feet. "No! I'm staying. I'm not afraid. I can still help here."

"All right, you may stay. But if I sense there's danger, I'll insist you go back, and you'll do as I say." Pauline nodded. "Good. Now I have to return to Captain McBain."

⟢

Despite the loss of blood and the size of the wound, Joseph apparently suffered no internal damage or infection. Her spirits grew as he slowly recovered over the next few weeks. She sat by his side for an hour in the morning, an hour around noon, and two hours in the late afternoon. She fed him, sponged his wound, changed the dressing, washed his face, combed his hair, and brushed his teeth. Once a day Dr. Roach checked on Joseph and assured him that he was getting better care than any other man in the hospital. Katherine spent the rest of her daytime hours at the wayside home and with the Ladies Relief Society.

When Joseph regained some strength, Katherine told him about his mother and that she hadn't heard from her since they left Roswell. She described the trip to Macon and how a wild turkey attacked Dante. Joseph laughed so hard that he had to grab his wound in pain. She also told him about the incident with Willie. He mumbled a curse.

As she sat by his side, Joseph opened up to her about his younger years—about growing up on the Heritage with his friend Andrew, making bricks, going on maroons, and learning history and architecture from his grandfather. It took him a full day to describe how in 1838, at age eighteen, he, Andrew, and Charlie Lamar had survived five days and nights drifting on wreckage at sea after the sinking of the SS *Pulaski*. One hundred thirty-six passengers and crew out of one hundred ninety-five had perished. He reminisced about Amy and how, after a childhood of spatting and hissing like two cats, they had come to love each other. He explained how Hercules had taught him to ride a horse. He recalled that Dante was a pest growing up, but had changed after he discovered his love of cooking. He revealed Dante's trip to Africa on Charlie Lamar's slave ship, the *Wanderer*. But mostly he talked about Andrew, and how Willie, Harold, and Sam murdered him the day before he was to sail to England to work as an apprentice architect. Katherine almost cried at hearing the story and wished she could hug poor Patience.

One week after Atlanta fell, Dr. Roach joined the Pope household for supper and said it appeared that Sherman was resting his army and would make no advance deeper into Georgia at the time. The doctor also heard that Sherman had informed General Hood he intended to remove all remaining residents from Atlanta. He promised to provide transportation to Rough and Ready Station for Atlantans who wished to go south. They could bring all their movable possessions, including slaves who gave their consent.

By the end of September, the Union army began transporting about fifteen hundred Atlantans in Union vehicles to Rough and Ready. From there, Confederate wagons waited to take them to Lovejoy's Station, where they would be on their own.

When the evacuation started, Joseph had improved enough to continue his recuperation outside the hospital. Katherine informed Mrs. Pope, who invited Joseph to move to another bedroom on the second floor of her house. Katherine and Pauline visited him every morning and evening and Chloe tended to him during the day. Soon Joseph was washing himself from the basin, getting dressed each morning, and taking walks.

On his first Sunday in the house, Katherine came home alone after church and was about to enter her room when she heard Joseph say, "You're home early."

Katherine turned and saw Joseph standing in the doorway to his room. She smiled and said, "Pauline wanted to sketch houses for Truvy and Mrs. Pope is still at church. How are you feeling?"

Joseph stepped up to her. "Much stronger. I walked to headquarters today. I'm leaving for Rough and Ready tomorrow to help in the relocation of Atlanta residents."

Katherine's brow furrowed. "I'm going to miss you. I like taking care of you."

Joseph said, "I'm glad you were here. You're the reason I recovered so quickly." He held out his hand and she took it.

He led her into his room, closed the door, put his hands on her shoulders, and kissed her. She moaned with pleasure. He said, "Lord, how I've missed you."

He went to kiss her again, but she turned her head away and said, "Please don't, Joseph. As badly as I want to, you're married. It's not right. I feel so guilty about Marietta. I couldn't help myself, but it was wrong then, and it's wrong now."

Joseph kept holding her. "At first, I regretted Marietta, too, but I've thought of you every day since. I want you to know that my marriage is over. My wife took my child from me and I realize I can never forgive her. I want to be with you."

Joseph's words shocked Katherine. They sounded like a proposal. She said, "I've thought about you too, Joseph. I haven't thought about much else. But I don't want to make another mistake. You're still married."

"I understand how you feel. But as soon as the war ends, so will my marriage. Then we can. . . ." Someone knocked on the door. Joseph released Katherine and retreated to the side of his bed. He called, "Who is it?"

"Chloe, Massa Joesup. Time fuh dinnuh."

Joseph looked at Katherine and nodded. She opened the door.

Chloe walked in holding a tray of food. She stopped in her tracks when she saw Katherine. "Oh, Mistess Katrin! Massa Joesup!"

Joseph said, "Miss Downes and I were chatting. You can put the tray on the table." Chloe did as she was told and left the room. Katherine, embarrassed that Chloe suspected something, said to Joseph, "I'd best be going. I'll see you at supper," and departed behind Chloe. She and Joseph didn't have another moment alone though, as he departed for Rough and Ready Station early the next morning.

Katherine longed to ask Joseph if he had proposed, but she realized he couldn't do such a thing while he was still married. She loved him, but was as confused as ever about his feelings for her. The next day, Katherine wrote to Mr. McBain, describing Joseph's improvement and his assignment at Rough and Ready.

⌘

In early October word spread that Sherman had given chase to General Hood, who was trying to retake the towns and fortifications that the Union army had captured on its march through northern Georgia. It became clear that Sherman wouldn't head south or east anytime soon. The sisters continued their daily routines, but with each passing day Sarah's arrival in Macon became more and more dubious, and Katherine considered returning to Savannah. She told Pauline that they'd wait another week or two, and if Mrs. McBain didn't reach them or somehow communicate, they would leave. Two weeks later Katherine received a letter from Mr. McBain.

> Oct. 27, 1864
> Dearest Katherine and Pauline,
>   All reports indicate that General Sherman and his army have thwarted Hood's attempts to retake fortifications in North Georgia and returned to Atlanta. He is undoubtedly preparing to press deeper into the South, although his destination is unclear. Based on the uncertainty of things, I want you to come home. You'll be safe here and can continue to work in the local hospitals. If you should encounter any danger on the journey home, I want you to abandon the wagon and take the train. You should be here by mid-November. I still have not heard from Mrs. McBain. Mary and Danny send their love.
> With warmest regards, J. J. McBain

Katherine said, "It looks like we're going home. I'll inform Dr. Cannon tomorrow. We'll be on our way in a few days."

Pauline hugged her sister. "I can't wait to get home and see Mary."

Katherine informed Mrs. Pope at supper and thanked her for her generosity and kindness. Mrs. Pope told the girls that she would miss them and treasure their three months together.

After supper Katherine informed Dante and Chloe that they would depart for Savannah in two days and to make sure the wagon was in good order and the mules were ready. Dante looked to the sky and said, "De Lawd bin lisnin." ⌘

CHAPTER FORTY-TWO

Mrs. Price

November – December 1864

On November 1 Katherine and Pauline finally waved goodbye to Mrs. Pope. Although heartbroken at not reuniting with Mrs. McBain, the sisters felt confident that she was safe somewhere. And they were excited to return to Mary, the McBains, and the safety of Savannah. No one looked forward more to going home than father-to-be Dante. He took roads that ran parallel to the Central of Georgia line but only made about eight to ten miles each day as the mules were not as lively as he had hoped. They spent most nights at houses or in barns along the way. Mrs. Burns was right—all men capable of fighting were absent. Only widows, wives, children, old men, and slaves remained.

On an evening in mid-November near Millen, Dante turned up the driveway of a large plantation mansion. Ten yards from the circular drive fronting the house, the wagon caved hard to the right, causing the riders to slide into each other. Chloe nearly fell to the ground. They got off and Katherine gasped, "Good Lord! The front wheel came off."

Dante knelt and examined the damage. "Don' look broke. Jes' need tuh git back on de spindle."

An old bald negro stepped from the house and ambled up to them. "Kin ah he'ps?"

Katherine pointed to the problem. "Our wagon has to be repaired. We also need a place to spend the night. Is the master of the plantation here?"

"Mistess, dey ain' no massa. He die fightin' Yankees. Missus Price inside, sick an' carryin' chile. C'mon in. Her see you."

Katherine and Pauline followed the man into the house, where they met two grey-haired, frail, black women in the hall. The man said, "Call me Henry. Dis am Minnie an' Holly."

The sisters introduced themselves and followed the servants up creaking stairs to a bedroom. Minnie knocked on the open door and walked in. The girls followed. The room was warm, stuffy, and dark. A woman was sleeping in a canopied bed with two pillows propping up her head. Minnie gently shook the woman's shoulder and whispered, "Missus, us got guests."

The woman opened her eyes and stared up at the canopy. She said in a barely audible voice, "What is it, Minnie?"

"Two gu'ls wantin' tuh see you, Missus." Minnie slid her hand underneath Mrs. Price's back, lifted her forward, and put another pillow behind her head. Minnie pointed to Katherine and Pauline at the foot of the bed.

The woman squinted. Holly opened the curtains a few inches to let in some light. Katherine said, "Good evening, Mrs. Price. I'm Katherine Downes and this is my sister Pauline. We're traveling to Savannah and our wagon lost a wheel in your driveway. We need a place to sleep, but we don't want to intrude. We didn't know that you were pregnant." Katherine guessed that Mrs. Price was in her thirties, but she had dark circles under her eyes and stringy brown hair that looked as if it hadn't been washed in weeks.

Mrs. Price lifted her hand from under the covers and held it in the air. She said, weakly, "Please stay. I'm all alone except for my negroes." She paused to take a deep breath. "My husband was killed near Atlanta in July. My son and daughter went to live with my sister in Pennsylvania at the start of the war. Most of my slaves, forty of them, ran off in my wagons a few weeks ago. It's just me, Minnie, Holly, and Henry. They're too old to run."

Minnie interrupted, "Us ain' runnin' cause us lub you, Missus."

Mrs. Price closed her eyes for a moment before replying, "I love you, too, all three of you. Miss Downes, they're taking care of me. I'm due to give birth any day now, and there are no doctors or midwives left. I'd be so grateful if you'd stay and help me through this. You may use any of the other bedrooms."

Pauline, her mouth open in shock, glanced at Katherine, who responded, "We'll do what we can, Mrs. Price. Do you know who might be able to fix our wagon? The wheel has to be put back on. We need a few strong men."

Mrs. Price paused to scratch her scalp. "Mr. Newton's plantation is the closest. I hear he and his wife ran off last week—scared of Sherman. If any of his negroes remained, they might be able to help. Henry will take you there tomorrow in my one remaining wagon." She took a deep breath. "He'll fetch your bags if they're not too heavy." Mrs. Price coughed uncontrollably for fifteen seconds while everyone looked on nervously. When she stopped, she said, "Minnie will cook your meals. You'll eat well. I still have chickens, pigs, hams in the smoke house, milk cows, and sweet potatoes."

Katherine thanked the woman and said, "We have two servants who can carry our bags. We do have valuables in the wagon. May we store them in the house?"

"Of course. Henry will show you where to put them. Your servants can have their choice of cabins." The woman hesitated and blinked her eyes. "I'm very tired. We can finish our conversation later. Please make yourself at home. I'm so happy you're here." Mrs. Price closed her eyes.

The sisters and slaves went downstairs. Minnie said, "Missus don' do nuttin' but sleep. Her don' ebuh git outta bed 'cep fuh privy mattuhs."

When the sisters stepped outside, Pauline tugged Katherine's arm. "Oldest Sister, we can't stay here! We're so close to home."

Katherine surveyed the front of the property. "I couldn't refuse her at that moment. First, we have to get the wagon fixed. Then I'll decide what to do."

The sisters took an upstairs bedroom. Chloe opted to sleep in the formal parlor on the ground floor. Then they inspected the slave cabins. Most were two-room hovels that hadn't been cleaned in months. Pauline muttered, "No wonder they ran away."

Dante said, "Bettuh den de soljuh camp." He chose the one closest to the house. He and Chloe spent thirty minutes cleaning it up. He hid the revolver under the bed. Then he and Henry moved Mrs. Toll's valuables into a room in the big house.

The next morning Katherine, Dante, and Henry took Mrs. Price's open wagon to Mr. Newton's plantation three miles away. They were greeted by a middle-aged black man named Leopold who acknowledged Henry with a two finger wave. Katherine explained their problem. Leopold told them that only he remained on the plantation. The rest had left to live with relatives on other farms. However, he expected a few men to return in a week and Leopold promised to bring them to Mrs. Price's. The three left and continued their search, but had no luck.

When they returned to Mrs. Price's house, the sisters retired to the family parlor. Katherine described her day to Pauline, who asked, "What are we going to do if we can't get the wheel fixed?"

Katherine slumped back in her chair. "We don't have many choices. Mrs. Price's wagon can't carry all of our things and it isn't covered. We'd be at the mercy of the weather. We could leave most of our baggage here and have Henry drive us to the train depot, but we may not be able to get passage for days. Mrs. McBain said we shouldn't put ourselves in any danger to save Mrs. Toll's valuables, but I'd hate to lose them after carrying them this far. Let's wait a few days to see if we can get the wagon repaired. We only need a few more men, with Dante. We should be able to find them."

Pauline whispered, "I spent the day with Mrs. Price. She only moves to use the chamber pot. She's frail and hardly eats. The baby can't be getting any nourishment."

Katherine leaned closer to Pauline. "I'm worried about her, too. I've never delivered a child. Minnie has, but at her age she says she needs help. We can't just leave the woman." Pauline bowed her head.

⟨❧⟩

Katherine, Dante, and Henry spent the next two days looking for able-bodied help at other nearby plantations, but all white men were off to war and all black men had left to taste freedom. Katherine asked Dante to stand by the main road during the day and ask passing wagons if they could help, but the few he waved down carried only old folks.

Pauline and Katherine watched Mrs. Price, who lay in bed all day and spoke little except to complain about pains in her belly and chest. Katherine insisted that Mrs. Price eat some scrambled eggs. "You're going to have a baby. You must feed it, too, even if you're not hungry. If I'm going to stay here and help you, you're going to eat."

Katherine opened the windows to get fresh air circulating in the house, and she refused to close the curtains even when Mrs. Price asked her to. Pauline and Holly forced Mrs. Price to take a bath and they changed her sheets, but it didn't seem to help. After a week Katherine told Pauline that the woman's life was in the hands of the Lord.

Ten excruciatingly long days after they arrived, Katherine decided to abandon their wagon and most possessions and catch the train to Savannah. She apologized to Mrs. Price, but said they simply couldn't wait any longer. Henry said he would drive them to the depot the next morning. But that afternoon, Leopold and three other men finally appeared. He examined the wheel and said, "Twenny dolluh tuh fix." Katherine thought the price was too high, but she felt desperate to get back on the road, so she accepted.

The men found a boulder about three feet high and moved it by the side of the wagon. Leopold retrieved an old pine pole from the barn, laid it over the rock and under the carriage, and three of the men pushed down on the pole to jack up the side of the wagon. Leopold took an old patch of leather, rubbed it in grease, wrapped it around the spindle to prevent the wheel from wobbling, and placed the wheel onto the spindle. He replaced the nut and the three men lowered the wagon. Katherine hardly breathed while Dante hooked up the mules, drove the wagon up and down the driveway two times, and said, "Her ride good." Katherine handed Leopold two ten-dollar gold pieces. He bowed and left with his men.

Katherine leaned against the wagon and said to Dante, "Thank God that's over with. Our luck is finally changing."

From the front door Holly shouted, "Mistess, come quick. Missus habbin' she chile." Katherine, Pauline, and Chloe ran to Mrs. Price's room.

Minnie was sitting on the bed with Mrs. Price, whose nightdress was pulled up to her chest and her buttocks was raised high. The pregnant woman's legs were bent and spread apart. Minnie said, "Push, Missus. Push. Push dat chile out."

Katherine went to Mrs. Price's side and stroked her arm. The woman's head rolled from side to side, her eyes shut tight and teeth clenched in pain, with tears running down her cheeks. Minnie repeated, "Push on de chile, Missus, please push. PUSH . . . PUSH! She comin', Missus, she comin. Push on out . . . PUSH!"

Pauline paced back and forth at the foot of the bed with her hands over her face.

"PUSH, MISSUS! PUSH! Chile's comin."

Suddenly, Mrs. Price's face turned a deep red. Her breathing turned to gasps as if she couldn't inhale any air. She grabbed at her chest and saliva started to bubble at her mouth. Katherine placed a damp towel on the woman's head. The woman arched her back, cried, "Oh, God! God, No!" and then her body went limp. Her face was frozen in a mask of horror, with her mouth and eyes stretched open, as if she had just seen the devil. After a few moments, Katherine felt for her pulse.

Minnie held the new born baby by her feet, administering light spanks, and pleading, "C'mon, chile! Cry fuh Minnie. Cry fuh dis ole nigguh." But the baby was as quiet and limp as her mother. Minnie finally placed the child at Mrs. Price's feet.

The group stood as still as statues—too terrified to move. Then Minnie and Holly kneeled by the side of the bed and began wailing, "Missus is gone. Her gone." Henry rocked back and forth on the balls of his feet and prayed.

Pauline shouted, "I hate this war! I hate it!" and sobbed on Chloe's shoulder.

Katherine stepped to her sister and held her arm. "We all hate it, Pauline. But now we have to bury Mrs. Price and her child before we leave for Savannah." She asked Minnie, "Is there a cemetery here?"

Minnie wiped away tears. "Not fuh white folk, Mistess. Dey only lib in de house ten yee'uh. No one die."

"Did Mrs. Price have a favorite place—a spot where she liked to sit?"

"Yessum. She lub tuh set by de gahdin in back."

Katherine told Henry to fetch a few shovels. She asked Dante and Chloe to wrap Mrs. Price in a blanket and the baby in a towel. They all followed Minnie and Holly to the back of the house. Katherine picked a grassy spot next to the garden and Dante, with sporadic help from Henry, dug a hole five feet long, three feet wide, and three feet deep. Two hours later Dante and Chloe lay Mrs. Price, still wrapped in a blanket, in the grave and placed her baby on her chest. The mourners stood with their heads bowed and hands folded at their waists. Henry recited the Lord's Prayer. Minnie thanked Mrs. Price for being so kind to them. Holly said that she would serve Missus on the other side.

The three negroes looked to Katherine, who realized that, as the white adult, she would have to say a few words. She took a half-step forward, closed her eyes, and said, "Mrs. Price, thank you for the hospitality that you showed us, even at the worst of times. This war has taken many fine, innocent people as casualties. But God watches over His flock, and He will take good care of you and your baby. For that, you may rejoice." Katherine opened her eyes, stepped back, and nodded to Dante.

Pauline turned away as the men shoveled dirt onto Mrs. Price. Then Dante planted a wooden cross consisting of two small tree branches made by Henry at the head of the grave. Holly, Minnie, and Henry kneeled and prayed some more.

They all returned to the house and collapsed on chairs in the family parlor. Katherine rubbed her eyes in exhaustion and said, "It's too late to leave today. We'll start in the morning. Chloe, cook as much food as you can now—for about ten days." She looked at Henry, "Do you all want to come to Savannah with us?"

Henry answered for the three of them. "Us stay here, Mistess. Dis us home."

"But it may not be safe here."

"De Lawd watch obuh us, Mistess. Don' you worry none."

The next morning Dante and Henry went to the stables to water and feed the mules and harness them to the wagon. Chloe remained in the house to pack the food and other necessities for the trip. Katherine, Pauline, Minnie, and Holly went to the laundry, the closest building to the house, to gather and fold their clothes, bedding, and towels.

The women hadn't been there five minutes when they heard horses coming up the driveway. Katherine looked out the door and her heart sank at the sight of about fifty soldiers in blue uniforms, half of whom were mounted and the other half seated in six wagons. She knew they were bummers, groups of soldiers who raided local plantations, farms, and houses every morning to feed their army. Katherine turned to the others, "Yankees! They're going to take anything they want. Let's finish with these clothes and get to the house."

As they worked they heard laughing soldiers entering the chicken coop, smoke house, dairy, and granary. Then Katherine heard a distant scream. "What's that?"

Minnie said, "Someone holluh in de house."

They all heard the next scream. Katherine said, "Who in the world. . . . Oh God! It's Chloe. The three of you stay here. Keep the door closed and don't dare leave."

Katherine left the laundry and ran past soldiers carrying hams, squawking chickens, and bags of corn. She also passed Dante and Henry, who were standing by the covered wagon talking to three soldiers. She entered the house and followed the hooting and laughing into the family parlor. Her knees went weak when she saw six soldiers standing in a semi-circle in front of the fireplace with their backs to her. One had his pants at his ankles. Chloe lay on the floor, naked and hunched up in a fetal position. Her face was stretched in a combination of terror and pain. A small pool of what appeared to be blood formed by her buttocks. Katherine stepped towards them and screamed "Stop!" She pushed two soldiers out of the way, knelt by the girl, and stroked her head. "Chloe, it's me, Katherine." Chloe's eyes were closed tight but tears still streamed from them. Her hands shook uncontrollably. Katherine hissed at the soldiers. "You animals! Your officers will hear about this."

A sergeant pulled her up by her arms and said, "You're next, rebel sow." She tried to wrestle away but he wrapped his arms around her from behind and dragged her to the side. He said, "Billy, it's your turn with the nigger. Get on with it."

Katherine shouted, "Leave her alone!" and squirmed, but couldn't free herself.

Billy dropped his underdrawers, got on his knees, and lay on top of Chloe. He tried to roll her on her back, but she scrunched up more, pleading, "Please don', mistuh soljuh. Please! Ahm huhtin' baddee."

Katherine yelled, "LEAVE HER ALONE! HELP! HELP!"

The sergeant clamped his hand over her mouth and said, "Shut up, or I'll break every bone in your body."

Another soldier called out, "Go on, Billy. Ride the darkey from behind."

Katherine stomped on the sergeant's boot. He yelped and she broke away, grabbed Billy by the collar, and pulled with all her might, toppling him off Chloe. The sergeant grabbed Katherine around her back, lifted her up, and started kissing her neck.

Katherine kicked her feet backwards, but couldn't hurt the man. He paused to drink from a bottle of whiskey being passed around.

Billy snuggled up to Chloe, spoon style, and tried to enter her, to the cheers of his mates, but she rolled tighter into a ball, thwarting his efforts. Two other soldiers grabbed her by the legs and shoulders and pinned her flat on her back. Billy tried to press himself into her but she lifted her hips off the floor and turned them to the side. She begged, "Please, mistuh Yankee. Ahm all tawn up."

Two more soldiers entered the room. One hollered, "Hey boys, look what we found." The soldiers turned and saw a beautiful young girl twisting in the grip of their two comrades. They dragged Pauline next to Chloe.

Katherine hollered, "PAULINE," and tried to wrestle free, but the sergeant squeezed her tighter until her arms and ribs hurt. He said to the others, "Forget the nigger. Let's screw these secesh."

The soldiers shouted their approval. Billy dragged Chloe aside while the two boys started ripping off Pauline's dress, leaving only her shimmy. Another soldier grabbed her by the ankles. She screamed, "KATHERINE! HELP ME! DON'T LET THEM HURT ME!" She wiggled and squirmed, but was helpless against the stronger boys. They lifted her shimmy as they held her up by the arms. She looked as if she was being crucified. The room quieted. A soldier said, "For the love of Jesus, look at that body."

Pauline's eyes flashed with horror, "KATHERINE, HELP ME!" Sobbing, she continued to struggle, but soon lost all her strength. Her captors pinned her on the floor.

Katherine yelled, "LEAVE HER ALONE! I'LL SEE THAT YOU HANG IF YOU TOUCH HER!"

The sergeant said, "We're going to touch her, and then you, and no one will ever know." The others laughed.

Another soldier walked into the room and said, "Sergeant, we're done here. We're going to the next plantation." He paused for a second. "What the hell is going on?"

The sergeant said, "Corporal, you and the rest go ahead. We'll catch up."

Katherine screamed, "HELP US! PLEASE!"

The sergeant held his hand over Katherine's mouth and said to the corporal, "We're having a little party with these rebel girls. We'll be with you soon."

The corporal left and the sergeant continued, "Billy, you lost your turn. Carl, you brought her here, you're first on the younger one."

Carl spread Pauline's legs with his feet and loosened his trousers. Pauline closed her eyes and pleaded, "No. Please, no."

Chloe, lying only a few feet away, her face glistening from tears and sweat, crawled over and lay on top of Pauline. The sergeant said, "How touching—a slave trying to save her whore mistress."

Billy pulled Chloe away by her feet, streaking her blood on the floor. The soldiers re-formed a semi-circle around Pauline and started to clap in time, as if it were a Saturday night dance. Carl kneeled between her legs and started stroking himself to get ready. He placed one palm on the floor by her head and started to descend.

The door slammed, shaking the room. Carl jumped up as the other soldiers turned around. Dante pulled back the hammer of the revolver, held it with both hands, and waved it slowly from left to right. He stepped to the sergeant and stuck the gun in his ear. "You touch dem gu'ls, ahm gwine tuh blow you tuh hell. An' dat de troot."

The sergeant, with his arms still wrapped around Katherine, moved only his eyes and said, "Keep calm, nigger. That's not a toy. You'll be dead in two seconds if you fire that gun. So will the girls."

Dante said, "An' you, too. Now let Mistess be." The sergeant didn't budge. Dante heard the whimpers of Pauline and Chloe and called across the room, "Missie Pauline an' Chloe, git 'way from dem soljuhs. Come obuh tuh me. Any ub you mens try tuh stop 'em, ah shoots dis man dead."

Pauline staggered to her feet, collected their clothes, and dragged Chloe to a chair behind Dante. She wrapped their dresses around them. The two girls cried in each other's arms.

The sergeant kept his grip on Katherine. He said, "Boys, I don't think the nigger has the balls to shoot. He knows what will happen to him and the girls."

Dante mimicked the man. "Boys, say bye tuh dis soljuh, cause he gwine tuh hell."

The sergeant reasoned, "I thought you darkies wanted freedom. That's why we're here—to free you." Dante pushed the barrel into the man's ear. He yelled,

"Ow!"

The front door of the house banged open and Dante heard footsteps come into the room. He didn't know which way to turn. He couldn't take his eyes off the Yankee holding Katherine, but he had to know who had just entered. All the soldiers in the room snapped to attention, including the one holding Katherine, who broke free, rushed to Pauline and Chloe, and helped them get dressed. The soldier who was about to rape Pauline pulled up his pants. Dante kept his gun lodged in the sergeant's ear and glanced at the parlor door. He saw three more soldiers in blue.

One of them said, "What in the world?"

The sergeant said, "Captain Bowen, this darkey is trying to kill us."

Katherine stepped towards the officer and almost spit in anger. "I'll tell you what's going on, Captain." She pointed to her sister and Chloe huddled together on the chair, shivering in fear. "Your gallant heroes just raped my girl and were about to rape my sister and me. My negro is trying to protect us."

The officer looked at Dante and then asked Katherine, "Miss, tell your negro to lay the gun on the floor. Nothing will happen to any of you. You have my word."

"Your word?" Katherine sneered. "First, remove these animals from the house. Then he'll give up the gun."

Captain Bowen said to the molesters, "You men are all under arrest." He turned to the two lieutenants who entered with him. "Take these men to a wagon outside and tie their hands." The sergeant slowly stepped away from Dante. The two officers, with guns in hand, herded the prisoners out the door. Dante stood alone, holding the gun at his side.

When Katherine heard the front door close, she said, "Dante, put the gun at your feet." Dante did as he was told. The captain stepped over, picked it up, released the hammer, and wedged the weapon under his belt.

He said to Katherine, "I'm Captain Patrick Bowen. I'm on the staff of Major General Davis, commanding the Fourteenth Army Corps. I happened to be riding by the plantations in this area, checking on the foraging parties. A soldier told me to come over here immediately, that some girls were being attacked by our men. You have my deepest apologies. You can be assured they will be dealt with."

Katherine replied, "I thank you, Captain, but your apology won't erase what my sister and girl just went through." She turned to Pauline, who was still shaking in fear, and said, "Take Chloe upstairs. I'll be there in a minute." Pauline helped Chloe from the room, as both clutched their torn dresses to their bodies.

Katherine then asked Dante to fetch Chloe's carpetbag and bring it and a basin of water to their room.

When left alone, Captain Bowen asked Katherine, "Do you live here?"

Katherine was wary of the man, but appreciated his respectful, non-threatening manner. She tried to be more civil. "No, we stopped here for shelter on our way to Savannah." She explained the situation, including the breakdown of their wagon, and the death and burial of Mrs. Price and her child.

"What are your plans now?"

Katherine gazed at the floor and shook her head. "I'm not sure. We didn't know your army was so close. I guess we'll continue to Savannah—to our family—if you'll let us."

"That will be very difficult, Miss. There are sixty thousand Union soldiers headed there right now. You're bound to run into them. There will probably be heavy fighting. You'll have to wait until the city falls into our hands, which it most assuredly will."

Katherine sighed and looked around the room. "Then maybe we'll stay here."

The officer said, "I don't think that's wise either, Miss. . . ."

Katherine thought no harm could come from telling him her name. "Downes. Katherine Downes. My sister is Pauline."

"Miss Downes, more foraging parties might come by, and there are stragglers about. May I suggest that you follow us? I'll. . . ."

Katherine turned red with rage. "After what your men did to us? For a minute I thought you were a gentleman, Captain."

The officer waited until the girl's face returned to its normal color. "Please, let me finish. To make up for the indignities you suffered at the hands of some of my men, I'll post two guards for you around the clock. You can ride at the rear with the freed slaves who are following us. You have my word no harm will come to you and you'll be going back home. You can't get there any faster, or more safely. Once Savannah falls, hopefully without a fight, you can return to your family."

Katherine took a deep breath. "I apologize, sir. Thank you for trying to help. Give us some time to clean up and pack. We have things stored in the house. Could you have a soldier help my man load it in our wagon? It's out front. At least it was."

Bowen said, "I believe my men have already started packing your wagon with provisions. I'll check."

Katherine followed him outside and saw soldiers loading sacks into the covered wagon. Katherine said, "That's our wagon. Your suggestion that we follow your army—did you mean on foot?" Captain Bowen approached one of the soldiers. Within seconds the bounty was being transferred to another wagon.

Bowen said to Katherine. "Please get ready. My men will help load your wagon."

Katherine sniffed the air and said, "Wait! I smell smoke." She descended the stairs, walked to the road that passed by the side of the house, and froze. Flames rose from several of the outbuildings. Mrs. Price's grave seemed to have been disturbed. She ran down the road and stopped short. The grave had been dug up. The tiny, doll-like baby and Mrs. Price glistened in the sunshine, splattered with dirt, the blanket and towel having been cast aside. Katherine gasped, stepped to the corpses, got on her knees, and pushed them back into the hole. Then, with cupped hands, she started shoveling the soil over the bodies. She looked up at the captain. "Digging up the dead and leaving them to the vultures? Rape isn't enough amusement for Yankees?"

Bowen's tanned face turned pale. "Believe it or not, many Southerners hide valuables in fake graves, so our boys search them. Please get up. I'll have my soldiers rebury them."

Katherine didn't respond. She remained on her knees and hung her head for a moment. Then she stood without looking at the officer and returned to her room. She found Chloe sitting slumped over on the edge of the bed. She sat next to the girl and said, "We're safe now. Those soldiers are going to jail and that officer is letting us follow them to Savannah with guards to protect us. We have to get ready."

Chloe leaned her head on Katherine's shoulder. "Ahm huhtin', Mistess."

Katherine said, "I'll clean you up and help you get dressed. We'll be back in Savannah soon and get you proper care. But we have to get there." Chloe nodded. "Please lay back on the bed."

Katherine got a piece of cloth, wet it in the basin, and started to clean the blood and sperm from Chloe, who hissed, curled up in a ball, and cried "Oh, Mistess!"

Katherine touched Chloe's cheek. "This will only take a few more seconds. I'll take good care of you." Chloe kissed Katherine's hand. Katherine finished cleaning her as best she could. She and Pauline helped her dress and finished packing.

They left the house and met Henry, Minnie, and Holly crying on the porch. Katherine asked, "Are you sure you want to stay?"

Henry dried his eyes in a kerchief and said, "Yessum, Mistess. Us got wu'k tuh do. Got tuh git dis place back tuhgedduh."

Katherine reached into her pouch, gave each one of them a five-dollar gold piece, and said, "May God bless you all."

Dante helped Chloe and Pauline climb in the back. Then he and Katherine got on the driver's seat. Bowen called out, "Ready?" Katherine nodded and they started their journey to join the Fourteenth Corps of Sherman's army.

As they exited the driveway, Katherine called to Major Bowen, "We aren't taking the road that runs along the railroad?"

Bowen replied, "That's right. Our orders are to ride north to the river and then follow it to Savannah. Don't worry, we'll get there just the same. Let me know if you need anything." Bowen rode back to the other officers.

Katherine touched Dante's arm. "Thank you for saving us from those soldiers. I'll never forget what you did."

Dante straightened. "Missus say tuh protect you an' ah done it. Ah do it anyway."

Katherine turned in her seat and watched Mrs. Price's house fade from view. Behind it, funnels of smoke drifted to the sky. ∽

CHAPTER FORTY-THREE

"Us Lookin' fuh de Rainbow"

Early December 1864

Later that day the sisters, Dante, and Chloe stopped in a field with hundreds of negroes huddled around campfires. Beyond them, a line of parked covered wagons stretched as far as the eye could see. Dante let the mules to graze. He asked a neighboring family where he could find water and a man who introduced himself as Cyrus directed him to a nearby creek. Dante grabbed the bucket while Katherine collected loose branches for a fire. Captain Bowen rode up to her and said, "Miss Downes, we're camping for the night. You can stay here with the negroes or by us. In either case you'll be perfectly safe."

Katherine knew the feelings of Pauline and Chloe, who were resting in the wagon. "We'll remain here."

"If that's your wish, I'll assign two guards. If you need anything, ask them and they'll get it for you. Do you want one of our surgeons to look at your girl?"

"I . . . don't know. Let me ask her." She walked to the back of the wagon. Pauline was sitting on the mattress next to Chloe, who seemed to be sleeping. Katherine whispered, "How is she?"

Pauline said, "Not well. She keeps apologizing for not protecting us."

Katherine touched Chloe's cheek. "Chloe, it's me, Katherine. The Yankee officer who saved us is offering to have one of his doctors see you. Would you like that?"

Chloe shook her head. "No, Mistess. Ah wan' you tuh look aftuh me."

Katherine returned to Bowen and said, "I'm a nurse. Give me a day with her. If she doesn't improve, I'll accept your offer."

Bowen said, "Just let the guards know. He tipped his cap and rode off.

Fifteen minutes later two soldiers came by, introduced themselves to Katherine as her guards, and helped gather wood. Afterwards, one said, "Miss, we're going to camp by that tree just twenty yards away. We'll be watching, so don't you worry about nothin'."

Katherine thanked them and started to lay down blankets for supper when ten soldiers rode into the area. They moved through the crowd, bellowing the same message:

"Attention, negroes. All men who can perform manual work like digging trenches and chopping trees, report to one of us immediately. All women, children, and men who can't perform heavy labor, go back to your homes. We are fighting a war and you're a bother to us. We can't slow down for you, we can't protect you, and we can't feed you. I repeat, go home and wait for the war to end. You'll be safer there."

A few of the younger, healthier men approached the soldiers, but no one else moved. They looked determined to cling to the army, their salvation.

Dante built a big fire for the chilly, early December night and Katherine, Pauline, and Dante ate together by it. Katherine brought a piece of chicken to Chloe, who was curled up on the mattress under two blankets. She said she wasn't hungry, but Katherine insisted and watched her eat.

After supper Cyrus and three other men introduced themselves. They all wore coveralls, tattered shirts, and ill-fitting cloth jackets. Cyrus had grey hair and eyebrows and chewed on a stubby, unlit segar. He approached Katherine and said, "Ahm Cyrus. Ah see Dante fine de crick. You need anytin'?"

Katherine said, "No, thank you, Cyrus. We're fine."

Cyrus said, "Hope you don' mind me askin', Mistess, but dey ain' no udduh white folk campin' wid us black folk."

Before she could answer, the two guards walked over with their rifles in their hands. The blacks stepped back. One private asked, "Miss, is everything all right?"

Katherine replied, "Yes. We're having a friendly talk."

The soldier took a long look at the negroes and said, "Holler if you need us." The Yankees returned to their fire.

Katherine said to Cyrus, "We're returning to Savannah. We feel safer back here with you. Why are you following them? The soldiers told you to go back to your plantations. It doesn't sound like they want you."

"Us followin' Massa Shummin' tuh freedom, Mistess. Make no mattuh what dem soljuhs say. Us lu'n dat Presdint Lincum say us free, an' sen' Shummin tuh Jawjuh tuh make it so. Us cain' go back now. Us lookin' fuh de rainbow. Might take munts, but us gwine tuh fine it." The other men spoke their concurrence.

Katherine glanced at Dante and wondered if he considered himself free. Chloe called from the wagon, "Mistess Katrin, Missie Pauline!" Pauline ran to her.

Katherine told the men, "Some of General Sherman's soldiers weren't so nice to us. They hurt my girl very badly."

Pauline came back to the campfire. "Katherine, Chloe's bleeding. I don't know what to do."

Cyrus said, "Muh missus kin he'p. She do nussin'. It maw bettuh dat a black puhsin see she."

Katherine said, "Please have her come now."

Five minutes later, under the light from lamps held by Katherine and Pauline, the man's wife, Venus, climbed into the wagon. Katherine said, "Chloe, Venus is an excellent nurse and is going to help you." Chloe opened her eyes, saw the woman, nodded her head, and showed a faint smile.

Venus inspected the injured area and said, "Ah need uh rag an' wattuh."

Pauline fetched the items and Venus got to work. She finished and said to Katherine, "Keep dat rag packed. Ah see she in de mawnin." Chloe reached up and squeezed Venus's hand. Katherine thanked her and they returned to the campfire.

Venus told the men, "Dem Yankees almost kill dat gu'l, but her git bettuh." The negroes bid the girls goodnight and left.

Katherine and Pauline slept on the floor of the wagon and gave Chloe the mattress. Dante curled up under covers next to the fire, which he kept feeding through the night. Katherine awoke at the sound of crying. When her eyes adjusted to the darkness, she saw Pauline sitting up with her face in her hands. Katherine slid over and held her. She realized that it was only hours earlier when soldiers had stripped and almost raped her younger sister, and it was all catching up to her. Katherine said, "It's all right, Pauline. We're safe now. No one will hurt you."

Pauline whimpered, "This is all so horrible. Please make it go away. Please. I can't stand it." Katherine felt Pauline's tears soak her neck and shoulder.

Katherine said, "We'll be in Savannah soon. I know you've been through hell. But we have to be strong and make it home—for Mary."

Then they heard Chloe say, "Missie Pauline, ah fail you. Please fuhgib me. You gu'ls muh angels." Pauline crawled next to Chloe and told her she didn't have to apologize for anything. The two fell asleep weeping in each other's arms. Katherine stared up at the wagon bonnet, praying to God to get them to Savannah.

The next morning they awoke to gunfire. Katherine got down and saw about two hundred mounted Yankees racing westward. One of her guards came over and explained, "General Wheeler's rebel cavalry is following us, trying to attack our rear. Don't worry, we'll take care of them. You best have your breakfast now. We'll be moving out soon."

Katherine noticed all the blacks crouched behind old, rickety, two-wheeled wagons. Cyrus and Venus walked over to her. Katherine asked them why they were hiding. "Cause dem rubble soljuhs don' like us leabin' us massas. Dey wan' tuh kill us."

Katherine hesitated as she realized that she, as well as the negroes, were being protected from Southerners by the Yankees. She finally said to Cyrus, "It looks like the soldiers are running them off."

"Ah pray so, Mistess, ah sholy do."

Venus then visited Chloe, who smiled upon seeing the black nurse. Katherine followed and watched her administer a liquid to her private area and re-dress the wound. Venus said, "Her bittie bettuh. Jes' need some time."

The Fourteenth Corps started moving at daybreak and camped again at two o'clock. Captain Bowen came by on a two-horse wagon. He removed his cap and Katherine got a good look at him. He had blue eyes and black, wavy hair, was about thirty years old and very handsome. "Good afternoon, Miss Downes. Major General Jeff Davis wants to have a word with you and your sister."

Bowen helped the sisters onto the bench seat. Katherine asked, "The president of our Confederacy is here?"

Bowen laughed. "That's Jefferson Davis, and we'd love to get our hands on him. No, the Union general goes by the name Jeff C. Davis." They rode past the negro camp and then a herd of cattle. The captain said, "We have fresh beef just about every day." Katherine thought, "Yes, from cows that you stole from the local farmers."

For the next three miles they passed hundreds of covered wagons. Katherine asked, "Captain, how long is this wagon train? It goes on forever."

"This one is about eight miles. Moving a corps of fifteen thousand men is a huge effort. We have a forward guard of mounted soldiers. Also up front is our engineering corps. They lay bridges over rivers and creeks and repair roads and bridges to allow the main army to march over them without holdup. It takes scores of wagons to carry all the pontoons, rails, ties, and other supplies. Next there's the main body of infantry—the foot soldiers. They're supported by wagons carrying rations, munitions, supplies, and tents. Believe me, fifteen thousand men can eat a lot of food and shoot a lot of bullets. We have an artillery corps and all their field guns, powder, and supplies. Then there are the field hospitals with surgeons, nurses, tents, medical supplies, and ambulances. Then there's the rear guard. Imagine moving a medium-sized city every day."

Katherine marveled at the enormity and organization of the procession. They turned off the road and proceeded a few hundred yards to a group of large tents. A corporal helped the sisters step off. The girls followed Bowen to the largest tent, about ten feet wide and fourteen feet long. Two guards saluted and pulled aside the flaps. They entered and Bowen introduced the girls to an officer sitting at a table. "Miss Katherine and Miss Pauline Downes, please meet Major General Davis, commanding the Fourteenth Corps of the Army of the Mississippi." The girls curtsied.

The full-bearded Davis neither stood nor smiled. He pointed to two wooden folding chairs and said, "Have a seat." Davis continued writing for a minute as his straight brown hair dangled over his forehead. He put the pen aside, applied a blotter to the paper, and looked up. "I hear that you two nurses had trouble with some of my boys and are now traveling to Savannah behind my corps."

Davis's moustache was so overgrown that Katherine couldn't see his lips move when he spoke. She thought a ventriloquist might be hiding in the tent, doing the talking. But there was no mistaking his official, cold tone. "Yes," Katherine said.

"We're trying to get back to our family in Savannah. After your soldiers raped my girl and tried to rape my sister and me, Captain Bowen, who rescued us, suggested that the safest way to get home would be to follow your men."

The general leaned back and clasped his hands behind his head. "That was very charitable of Captain Bowen. My men are very well-behaved, considering they're fighting a war started by your government. We're bound to have a few bad ones in an army this size and it's unfortunate that you crossed paths with them. They're now being held by the provost marshal and will pay for their actions." Davis scratched his beard as if he were trying to catch something. "The truth is, I don't really care a wit about two rebel girls, other than how their treatment reflects on my command. I'm probably going to hear something about what happened to you, and I don't want another incident like it. So I approved Captain Bowen's decision to provide protection for you."

Katherine knew that they were fortunate to be following the Yankees and didn't want to annoy General Davis, though he made her skin crawl. She tried her best to hold her tongue. "We're grateful for that, sir."

Davis paused for a few seconds before saying, "You know, once we get to Savannah, there's a good chance that we'll bombard the town and perhaps your family. I imagine you'll have difficulty watching, or even listening."

Katherine hadn't considered that. She glanced at Pauline, who sat frozen with her hands gripping the seat of her chair, overwhelmed by being in the presence of such a powerful, yet callous man. Katherine told Davis, "Of course it will be hard for us. But you're going to do it whether we're with you or not and the closer we are to home when it's over, the quicker we can see our family. We hate this war and pray that there'll be no casualties on either side."

The general stroked his beard. "The only way there won't be is if the rebels surrender. Any civilian blood that's shed will be on Confederate hands. They're the ones who are choosing to hide behind citizens in a city."

Katherine put her arm around her sister. "In that case, we'll pray for surrender. We want the killing to end. We've seen enough mangled bodies to last a lifetime."

Davis stared at Katherine. He didn't care for secesh women, but this one was feisty and had common sense. "I hear you'd prefer to camp with the niggers than us?"

"The negroes didn't attack us, sir."

The general glared at Katherine. "I hope I don't hear about you two again. Have I made myself clear?" Katherine nodded. He told Bowen, "Take them back now, Captain."

During the ride back, Katherine said to Bowen, "General Davis has all the warmth of a rattlesnake."

Bowen laughed. "He's not known for his joviality. A few years back he shot and killed his commanding officer, a general, who was unarmed. He was arrested but was never tried. And here he is today, commanding a corps of General Sherman's army."

Katherine gulped and said, "We'll stay clear of him."

"You should have no need to see him again. But keep in mind that he's a very proud man. He was in the garrison at Fort Sumter when the rebels bombarded it in 1861, which started this mess. He hasn't forgotten it."

They continued on in silence. Katherine was happy to get back to the negroes.

❧

The next week passed slowly, waking at six, moving out at seven, traveling during the daylight hours with breaks to eat and rest the horses and mules, and making camp in the late afternoon, usually about four o'clock. Chloe steadily improved under Venus's care and the two became friendly, chatting and laughing much of the time they spent together. Chloe seemed so comfortable with Venus that Katherine allowed her to ride in Cyrus's one-mule wagon during the day, although Chloe ate and camped with the sisters at night.

Captain Bowen checked on the girls every other day. One evening after supper he came by and sat on the blanket with them. He asked Katherine about growing up in Georgia. She and Pauline reminisced about farm life without revealing the horrors of their childhoods. Katherine told him they were orphaned at the beginning of the war and made their way to Savannah where they were taken in by the family to whom they were returning. After an hour he told the girls he enjoyed chatting with them and rode off. Pauline grinned and told her sister, "I think the captain likes you."

Katherine shook her head and said, "You think every man who talks to me likes me. First it was Captain McBain. Then Hamilton Branch. Now, it's Captain Bowen." Katherine winked at Chloe, who limped to the wagon. "He's looking after our welfare, and he's doing his job, that's all. You are the silliest girl in all Georgia, except for Mary."

Pauline said, "I am not silly! I may be young but I can tell these things."

"Yes, you are young, but not as young as yesterday." Katherine leaned over and hugged her. "Happy fifteenth birthday, Pauline."

Chloe emerged from the back of the wagon with a large square of cornbread covered in a white icing that she had made at Mrs. Price's house. "Special budday cawnbreads fuh priddy Missie—priddiest gu'l in all Jawjuh." She sat and placed the treat on the blanket and gave a full-tooth smile for the first time since that day at Mrs. Price's.

Pauline hugged Katherine, who said, "Chloe knew your birthday was coming and suggested at Mrs. Price's house that she make something special." Pauline swiveled next to Chloe and hugged her.

Katherine cut the cake and handed out the pieces. Dante said, "Happy budday, Missie Pauline. Dis de all time bes' cawnbreads."

After they finished eating, Chloe had Pauline turn her back to her, removed the pin from her hair, which fell past her shoulders, and started combing. She said with a smile, "Yessum, dat Yankee soljuh sho' is consunned 'bout Miss Katrin."

Pauline laughed. Katherine blushed and said, "You're both silly."

Chloe concentrated on Pauline's hair and said, "Yessum, de priddius' gu'ls in de whole Union."

⧼⧽

The next day the wagon train stopped at one o'clock. Katherine said to Pauline and Dante, "This is early. Are they making camp?"

Dante stood on the seat and cupped his hands around his eyes. "It don' look so, Mistess. De soljuhs, dey all standin' still."

Katherine surmised, "I guess they're waiting for a bridge or road to be repaired. Do you see Cyrus's wagon?"

Dante scanned the area again. "Don' see it. Dey mus' be up a way." He called Chloe's name several times, but got no reply.

They sat for four hours, moving just a few yards every now and then. In the late afternoon a soldier on horseback sprinted up to the guards, exchanged some words, and returned to the wagon train. One of the guards rode to them and said, "Miss, we have orders to take you up front to the general. Please follow us."

Katherine said, "Our girl isn't here. Let me find her."

"Sorry. My orders are to take you now. She can follow with the other darkies."

Katherine stood on the bench and looked for Chloe or Venus, but saw neither. "I guess we'll find her later."

Dante followed the guards. Thirty minutes later, after driving on the side of the road to get around the stalled negroes, they arrived at a single-lane, raised causeway that ran through a marsh. A company of soldiers stood at the entrance, preventing access to the negroes. One of the soldiers waved Dante and the girls through and the rest retreated behind them, walking backwards, with their rifles at the ready. The negroes funneled onto the road and followed them. The quarter-mile-long causeway led to a pontoon bridge that had been laid over Ebenezer Creek, itself about forty yards wide, and was guarded by more soldiers. As the wagon crossed the bridge, the sisters heard shouting from behind. They saw through the back of the wagon bonnet the engineers pulling up the wooden ties, rails, and pontoons, and the guards preventing access to the negroes. Katherine called to their two guards riding ahead, "Why are the soldiers pulling up the bridge and not letting the negroes cross?"

One said, "I don't know nothin' about that, Miss."

Katherine told Dante to stop after they crossed the bridge. She jumped down and trotted back to the officer in command, bumping into soldiers carrying away the materials. "Sir, what are you doing? The negroes need to cross. Our girl is with them!"

The officer replied, "Miss, I'm following orders. Now, get back in your wagon before you get hurt."

Katherine squinted into the settling darkness. The causeway and surrounding marsh were jammed with blacks waving their arms and screaming at the soldiers. She heard one holler, "Dem rubbles am comin'."

Katherine grabbed the engineer's sleeve. "Don't you see? They're frightened that they'll get killed. You can't leave them there!"

The man pulled away his arm. "Young lady, you heard me—I'm doing my job. Now, get off this bridge. That's an order. You're in the way."

She trotted back and stood on the creek bank. Pauline joined her. They tried to spot Chloe on the opposite side but had trouble picking her out in the dusk amongst all the people. Then Katherine pointed across the water. "There she is! Right at the edge of the causeway with Venus!" She started waving her arms and yelling, "Chloe! Venus! Stay there! We'll wait here and get you later!"

Suddenly, a few of the negroes jumped from the causeway into the creek. Then more and more followed. It looked as if Chloe had been pushed in the melee or lost her footing and fell into the creek. The sisters momentarily froze in horror as hundreds of fully clothed men, women, and children flailed at the water, attempting to stay afloat.

Katherine ran to a soldier standing nearby and pleaded, "Help us save them. They'll drown. Please get some men." The solder turned away without saying a word.

Katherine returned to Pauline, who undressed down to her chemise, took two steps, dove in, and swam towards Chloe. She started hollering, "CHLOE! SAY SOMETHING! LET ME HEAR YOUR VOICE!"

Katherine also stripped to her shimmy and joined Pauline. The water was bracing, but Katherine hardly noticed. In the growing darkness Pauline tread water and shouted, "CHLOE! SAY MY NAME!"

Amidst the screams of the drowning negroes, they heard, "MISSIE! MISSIE!"

The sisters swam to their right and Pauline yelled, "CHLOE! I'M COMING. SPEAK AGAIN."

"MISSIE! HE'P ME!" The voice sounded closer.

"I'M HERE, CHLOE!"

"MISS. . . ." The fading voice sounded only yards away.

Pauline and Katherine kept swimming. Pauline cried, "CHLOE, ONCE MORE! PLEASE!" She waited a few seconds. "CHLOE?"

The sisters dove under the surface and extended their arms as far as possible as they swam, trying to feel Chloe in the black water. They surfaced, panting, and heard fewer screams. Pauline tried again, "CHLOE, CAN YOU HEAR ME? PLEASE HEAR ME!" They got no answer.

Katherine, her chin at the waterline, said, "Pauline, I must go back. I'm too tired."

Pauline cried, "She's gone, Katherine. Chloe's gone."

"Let's pray that God saves her. But I have to get back. I have no strength."

Pauline sobbed as they swam towards the shore, which they could barely see in the darkness. They passed three men who were holding onto a large tree limb. One of the men lost his grip, let go of the branch, and grabbed Katherine's arm. He started to go under and pulled her with him. Katherine tried to free herself but couldn't. She kicked him away and they both surfaced. She yelled, "Don't grab me and I'll take you to the branch!" But the frightened man punched the water with his free hand and yanked her under again.

Katherine broke free once more, floated to the top, and called into the darkness, "Pauline, where are you? I don't think I can make it." The panicked man gripped her shoulder, causing her to swallow water. She thrashed about, felt the man's face, pushed him off, and surfaced just as she inhaled, gulping in air and trying to stay afloat.

Something bumped the back of her head. Pauline shouted, "Katherine, hold onto this tree limb!" Katherine clutched the floating object for dear life. Pauline dove and surfaced seconds later with her arm around the drowning man's neck. "Grab this branch and I'll help you!" She called to Katherine, "Paddle towards the shore. I know you're tired but it's not far."

With her arms feeling like iron bars, Katherine bit down and paddled with one hand. They reached shore just as she was overcome with exhaustion. She lay half in the water and half on the muddy shore, with her shimmy stuck to her body. Dante, who couldn't swim, dragged her from the creek, and wrapped her in a blanket. He carried her up the bank, and lay her on the ground. He took another blanket and ran back to Pauline, who had crawled out of the water on her hands and knees. He put the blanket over her, said, "Ah got you, Missie," and brought her next to Katherine. The two sisters lay together in the freezing December night, with their hair pasted to their heads and chests heaving up and down.

Pauline held her hands over her face and cried, "Chloe! Chloe! I'm so sorry."

In a few minutes Katherine was able to sit up. She saw a crowd of soldiers staring at them and said, "Not one of you could help us or those poor people?"

The engineer officer stepped forward. "We were only following orders. None of us wanted this." The soldiers walked away, knowing that their commanding officer never would have approved of his men helping the negroes.

The girls' teeth began to chatter. Dante fetched the wagon and lifted them on. He drove to the rear of the army camp and built a fire. The girls gathered the strength to dry off and put on fresh clothes. They sat in a trance by the campfire, and were soon joined by the negroes who had made it to land. Together, they prayed for their loved ones, who were most likely lying on the bottom of Ebenezer Creek.

The girls barely slept, the horror of the evening branded on their minds. At daylight, despite soreness in every muscle, Katherine had Dante drive back to the creek. As he turned the wagon around, their guards rode up and said to Katherine, "Miss, excuse us, but the army's leaving. We have to follow it."

Katherine replied, "You saw what happened last evening. We're going to look for our girl and bury her. We'll catch up later."

The guards whispered to each other. Then one said, "We'll stay with you, but please don't take too long."

Fifteen minutes later they parked at the creek and the sisters and Dante started their search. Bodies floated face down in the water by the shore, like human logs on the way to a lumber mill. Dozens more lay sprawled on the bank. They side-stepped corpses and turned over the females, trying to find Chloe. Pauline broke down at the sight of so many dead innocent people, who were alive just the previous evening. She sat on a nearby tree stump and hugged her arms around herself, unable to continue the macabre hunt. She couldn't bear the thought of finding Chloe's body. Katherine maintained her composure and forged ahead, but she soon stopped in her tracks. Venus lay on her side at the edge of the water as if she were asleep.

Katherine and Dante dragged Venus up the bank and lay her on high ground. Then they continued looking for Chloe. An hour later, unable to find her, they returned to Pauline. Dante and the two guards dug a shallow grave. The sisters and Dante buried Venus in her final resting place. Pauline started to read a prayer from her Bible but she couldn't make it through the first line. Dante, who had rarely shown any emotion during the trip, dropped to his knees and held his head in his hands. Katherine took the Bible from Pauline. She closed her eyes and said, "Thank you Venus for taking such good care of Chloe and making her last days happy ones. Please tell her we love her, and please look after her in heaven. We will always remember you and Cyrus in our prayers." Then, with the sound of the deadly creek gurgling in the background, the three trudged back to the wagon and followed the guards to the army.

They were getting closer to Savannah, but they were still in hell. ❧

PART 6

⁓

The Most Beautiful Sight
She Had Ever Seen

December 1864 - February 1865

CHAPTER FORTY-FOUR

The Foreign Battalion
December 1864

Captain Bowen got off his horse and walked towards the campfire, not expecting a warm reception. The news of General Davis's order to dismantle the bridge before the blacks could cross and the subsequent drownings spread quickly through the corps. Bowen heard about it the next day and went to find the sisters after the army made camp. Neither girl nor Dante looked up at him. "I heard about last night. The captain of the engineering corps told me how you tried to save your girl. I'm sorry."

Katherine stared at the campfire. "After a while, apologies have no meaning."

"I can't explain yesterday. Are you all right? Is there anything I can get you?"

Katherine picked up a branch and poked at the embers. "We could have used help this morning giving proper burials to those poor souls who drowned and are now rotting on the creek bank." She finally looked up. "Captain, I've never owned a slave, but I do know what this war is about and I'm just as happy to see slavery end. But the Yankees' boast that they care about the negro is just a big lie." She looked at the fire. "For now, I think we can get by on our own."

Dante figured that a Yankee victory in this war would result in freedom for the slaves, and he prayed for it, but he hated the Yankee soldiers for what they had done to Chloe and the other blacks. He was happy that Katherine had scolded the soldier. He looked at her, caught her eye, and nodded his approval.

Bowen knew that nothing he could say would change her mind. "I know how you feel and I won't intrude. If you need anything, please tell your guards." He galloped off.

The next day, December 11, they camped on a rice plantation on the Savannah River across from the Manigault plantation on Argyle Island, only eight miles from Savannah and five miles from the Heritage. They were almost home.

Bowen had them camp on the northwest end of the plantation, as far from the river as possible, as rebel gunboats might fire on Union positions. Katherine dropped some of her icy demeanor towards him, certain that he had nothing to do with the Ebenezer Creek incident, and asked him if they could drive to the Heritage. He wouldn't allow it, as they were in a war zone and could be targets of either side.

The sisters spent the next week huddled by the fire, reading the only book they had, the Bible, while Dante constantly combed the area for firewood and tended to their camp. They existed on the diminishing supply of food that Chloe had prepared at Mrs. Price's house and cooked rice that Captain Bowen brought them. Mostly, they tried to keep warm. Dante often spoke about Isetta and wondered if their baby was a boy or a girl. Katherine asked him if they had chosen a name. Dante said that if the baby were a girl, they would call her Neeka. They hadn't chosen a boy's name yet.

The first day the girls arrived at the plantation, Captain Bowen reported that all of Sherman's sixty-thousand-man army had arrived in the area and formed a giant semi-circle around Savannah, each end reaching the Savannah River above and below the city. The rebels could escape only by crossing the river into South Carolina and Sherman was in the process of sealing off that route. Bowen conceded that the rebels were solidly entrenched in two lines of artillery surrounding the town and an attack would be bloody.

Two days later Bowen told them that the Yankees had captured Fort McAllister on the Great Ogeechee River, about twenty miles south of Savannah, and Sherman had linked up with the Union navy on the coast, further tightening the noose on the town. A few days after that they learned Sherman had given an ultimatum to the commander of the Confederate forces in Savannah, General William Hardee, to surrender or subject the city to the harshest measures. Bowen assured them that Savannah would soon fall.

The sisters and Dante, in fear for their families in Savannah, prayed at each meal that General Hardee would wave the white flag and spare any bloodshed—especially the blood of their loved ones.

⊙≫

Captain Joseph McBain sat in a trench alongside the Augusta Road, not more than five miles from Katherine, on the night of December 17, waiting for an attack by the Yankees. After he left Macon to assist in the relocation of the displaced Atlanta families, he rejoined General Mercer, who had been transferred to Savannah under the command of General Hardee.

During his time in camp Joseph had several opportunities to see Danny, his father, and Mary in town. The visits were somber as James had not heard from Sarah since she had visited Roswell or the sisters since they left Macon. He blamed himself for letting them go to Marietta in the first place. Each time Joseph stepped into the house, Mary ran to him, hugged his waist, and asked if he had found Katherine and Pauline. Joseph told her not to worry as he knew they were safe, but he was just as anxious as she to learn their whereabouts.

Joseph knew that the rebel chances of holding Savannah with about fifteen thousand men against the overwhelming numbers of Sherman's army were slim. They would either have to fight to the death in Savannah or retreat to South Carolina. He soon learned which it would be. The day after Sherman issued his ultimatum, Hardee had his men confiscate all rice flat boats at the river plantations and bring them to the harbor to build a pontoon bridge from Savannah to South Carolina for a full retreat. Joseph would not see his family or Katherine for some time.

A lieutenant rode up to him as he stood outside his tent. "Captain, one hundred men from the Foreign Battalion tried to cross over to the Yankee lines. Our pickets saw them and called the First Georgia Militia, which apprehended them. Some of the officers are holding a court martial right now for the seven ringleaders. You had better come."

Joseph was not the least bit surprised. The Foreign Battalion consisted of about three hundred Europeans, mostly Irish and German, who had emigrated to the United States, joined the Union army, and were captured by the Confederates. To avoid starvation and the other horrors of prison life, they took an oath of allegiance to the Confederacy and joined the rebel army. The "Galvanized Yanks," as they became known, were sent to Savannah under General Mercer's command, not to fight but to dig trenches and build fortifications. However, when the Union cavalry made moves on Savannah, the Galvanized Yanks were issued arms to help defend the town, despite their unreliability.

Joseph replied, "Where are they?"

"By the Ten Broeck Race Track."

Joseph looked at his pocket watch. It was nine o'clock. He told his men to guard the camp and headed with the lieutenant for the race track. When they got within two miles they crossed paths with a large group of Galvanized Yanks under heavy guard. Joseph asked the sergeant in charge, "What's going on?"

"Sir, we just held a court martial for seven members of the Foreign Battalion, found them guilty, and sentenced them to death. The execution is about to take place."

Joseph said, "Who gave the authorization to. . . ."

BOOM! A volley of rifle fire exploded from the direction of the race track, followed by human screams. BOOM! Another volley, then a third, and all went quiet. Joseph charged towards the track. He reached a clearing in the woods and stopped in shock when he saw seven dangling bodies tied to trees. There was something about executions—the condemned having time to think about their impending demise—that horrified him. Joseph started to approach the officer in charge when he heard heavy gunfire from the direction of his camp. He turned around and raced to the campground, where he found thirty of his men standing in a circle with their hands raised above their heads. He also saw as many soldiers in bluecoats pointing their rifles at him.

Once again, Joseph McBain was a prisoner of war.

The day after Joseph's capture, General Hardee replied to General Sherman's demand for surrender. He said that the Union guns, four-and-a-half miles away, could not reach the city, and he refused to give up the town. Hardee, who had requested more troops from Confederate authorities, was merely stalling until he received word if he would get them. Sherman decided not to attack the town. Instead, he took a boat to Hilton Head Island to ask General John G. Foster, commander of the Union army in South Carolina and Georgia, for troops to block a Confederate escape across the Savannah River. While the two Union generals conferred, General Hardee learned that he would not receive significant troop reinforcements. With the pontoon bridge to South Carolina near completion, he ordered his men to evacuate on the night of December 20. The operation went flawlessly. The rebels opened fire on the Yankees to keep them at a distance, spiked their large guns, poured water on the gunpowder, set aflame and sank the ships in the river, and crossed the bridge under the cover of darkness. By three o'clock in the morning of December 21, with General Sherman still in Hilton Head, the rebel army reached South Carolina and destroyed the bridge behind it.

Ninety minutes later Mayor Richard Arnold and several city council members took buggies down the Louisville Road, surrendered the city to the first Union officer they met, and asked for protection of the property of the citizens. By six o'clock, Union soldiers marched up the Bay.

For Savannah, the war—but not the suffering—was over.

On the night of December 20 the sisters heard heavy artillery fire from the direction of town. Katherine, Pauline, and Dante held hands and prayed for the safety of their loved ones. None of them slept well.

The next morning Captain Bowen rode by to tell them that the Confederate army had escaped to South Carolina and the city was now in Union hands with no known civilian casualties. He said he would inform them when they could enter the town. The dark grey cloud that had hovered over them since leaving Macon began to lift.

CHAPTER FORTY-FIVE

"Ain' uh Slabe No Maw"

December 1864

At noon on December 23, two days after Union troops occupied Savannah, Captain Bowen appeared at the wagon and told the sisters that he was leading a squad into town and they could follow him. He laughed at the speed in which they and Dante extinguished the campfire, loaded the wagon, and climbed on. Fifteen minutes later they were riding behind Bowen and twenty mounted soldiers.

They passed the entrance to the Heritage on the Augusta Road and saw ten Yankee guards standing around and talking. Katherine didn't see any activity on the avenue of oaks but did spot hundreds of tents on the wheat field fronting the plantation. She wondered if Mr. McBain was there or in town.

The road to Savannah was crowded with soldiers lounging, joking, and smoking cigarettes. Many waved at the sisters as they passed by, but the girls ignored them. They entered the city and passed the Central of Georgia Railroad depot and maintenance yard, once one of the busiest spots in Savannah, with its repair shops, blast furnace, and towering smokestack, but now quieter than a graveyard. Dante continued across West Broad onto Liberty Street while Captain Bowen's squad turned south. Except for several groups of Union soldiers marching in various directions, the streets were eerily deserted of locals. Other than garbage strewn on the streets, the area looked the same as when they had left.

Bowen rode alongside the wagon and told the sisters, "I'll see you home." Pauline elbowed Katherine lightly in the arm.

Katherine said, "That's not necessary, Captain."

"I want to be sure of your safety, Miss Downes." Pauline elbowed her sister again.

Dante turned right on Barnard Street and as the wagon entered Pulaski Square the girls' eyes locked on the sandstone-colored, two-story Greek Revival house with its dual, elliptical front stairs and four Corinthian columns—still standing majestically. Pauline squeezed Katherine's arm and bounced excitedly in her seat. Katherine stared at the front windows, looking for any signs of life. Dante, who had been stoic during the ride into town, turned to the sisters and flashed a wide smile. He drove to the front gate and the sisters climbed down. Katherine asked him to take the wagon to the driveway and she would send out someone to help him move Mrs. Toll's possessions inside.

Captain Bowen dismounted and his eyes widened as he surveyed the mansion. "It's beautiful."

Katherine took Pauline's hand, anxious to go inside. "I thank you again, Captain, for everything. I can confidently say I met an honorable and gentlemanly Yankee."

Bowen removed his cap and held it to his chest. "There are many good Yankees, Miss Downes—a whole country full. I hope you'll see that after this war is over."

She smiled. "Perhaps." The sisters bid him goodbye, walked up the front stairs, and stood at the door. Katherine said, "It's been so long, I don't know whether to knock or just walk in." Pauline knocked. They heard footsteps running down the stairs.

Danny opened the door. His jaw dropped so far that Katherine could see his tonsils. He lunged and hugged her. After a few seconds, he switched to Pauline. Then he turned and shouted, "Mary! Come here!"

Mary stood at the top of the stairs and said, "What, Danny? No tricks."

"I promise! Come see for yourself."

Mary came down a few steps, saw her sisters, then scurried down and flew into Katherine's arms. Katherine kissed the top of her head. Then Mary pulled Danny away from Pauline and embraced her.

Katherine said, "Let's go inside." She turned to close the front door and saw Captain Bowen on his horse, watching them. He gave a final wave and rode off.

They stepped into the hall. JD trotted up and started barking as he circled them. Pauline knelt and scratched his ears. William, Jinny, Lilly, Patty, and Dolly heard the commotion and rushed into the hallway. Jinny hollered "Lawd hab mussy!" and they all hurried to greet the sisters.

Katherine fought back tears of joy and said, "It's so good to be home and see you all again. William, could you have Jefferson help Dante unload the wagon and put the packaged items in the storage room? Mr. McBain can decide later where he wants them."

The smiles disappeared from the servants. William said, "Mistess Katherine, Jefferson and Nannie are gone."

"Gone? Are they all right?"

"Yes. They left yesterday, when the Yankees said they could go. They live in a house in town with some other folks. I'll have Barney help Dante." Katherine glanced at Pauline, shocked at the news. She liked Jefferson and loved Nannie, and wondered what other surprises awaited them. William continued. "I'll bring your luggage to your room. I'm sure you'll want to get settled and relax." The servants gave the girls a final embrace and went back to work.

Katherine was about to call them back and tell them about Chloe, but decided that Mr. McBain would want to do it. She asked Danny, "Is your grandfather here?"

Danny frowned as if he had been sent to bed after supper without dessert. "He's upstairs resting. He's very sad. We haven't heard from Grandma in months. Grandpa's not allowed to go to the plantation and he doesn't know what's happening. Pa was captured by the Yankees and is in prison in town." Katherine made an audible gasp, but Danny kept talking. "We're not allowed to visit him yet. I'll get Grandpa. He'll want to see you. That will make him happy." Katherine told Danny to let him rest, but the boy shot upstairs anyway.

The girls went into the family parlor, with JD close behind. General Lee was sleeping on the desk chair. He opened one eye, rose up, stretched his body, yawned, and sat on his haunches, waiting for the humans to come to him. Katherine picked him up and he rubbed his head against her face. Pauline cradled him in her arms and listened to his purr, which sounded like a small steam engine. She kissed his white crown and put him back on the chair, where he curled up.

Katherine noticed that the pocket doors to the formal parlor were open and two long sofas had sheets and covers on them, neatly made up into beds. The sisters sat on the couch, with Mary in the middle. The girl said, "I missed you so much. I have so many stories for you." She lowered her voice, "Danny still won't admit he loves me, but. . . ."

They heard footsteps on the stairs and stood as James entered the room. He froze in his tracks. Katherine noticed that he had lost weight—too much weight— and his skin hung loosely on his face. She and Pauline embraced him, each taking a side. He held them tight. "My dear girls. I'm so glad you're home. When did you arrive?"

Katherine released him and said, "Minutes ago."

McBain asked, "Where are Dante and Chloe?"

Katherine looked at Pauline, who sat on the couch and lifted Mary on her lap. "Dante's outside with Barney, moving Mrs. Toll's property to the storage room." She took a deep breath. "Chloe didn't make it. She drowned in a creek on the way back."

James stepped away from the girls, slumped into a chair, and hung his head. Katherine sat on the arm and rubbed his back.

Danny walked in circles, saying, "No, no, no."

Mary started to cry and leaned against Pauline, who said, "Don't be sad. She's with the Lord. He's taking good care of her."

Mary said, "But she's not here with us. I'll never see her again."

McBain sat up straight, startling Katherine. "Good Lord, do the servants know?"

Katherine said, "I haven't told them. Dante might have, though he's been busy unloading the wagon."

They heard a scream followed by loud wailing. James bolted from his chair and ran downstairs to the servants' sitting room next to the kitchen. He saw Lilly, Patty, Dolly, and Jinny seated at the table, crying, and William leaning against the wall with his eyes closed. Dante stood nearby, stone-faced. James patted Dante on the shoulder, said, "Welcome back." He cleared his throat and addressed them. "This is a very sad day for us all. As you already seem to know, I have been informed by Miss Katherine that on their journey home, Chloe drowned in a creek."

Dante spoke up. "Dem Yankees kill her. Ah seed it. Didn' gib no nigguhs de chance tuh craws de ribuh."

McBain would have to wait to get the whole story from Katherine. He said, "We'll hold a memorial service for Chloe tomorrow morning in the garden. William, have Barney make a small cross. You all may take time now to pray." As James left the room, he said to Dante, "Thank you for bringing Miss Katherine and Miss Pauline home safely. I can't tell you how grateful I am."

Dante stood straight with pride. "Ah done wut Missus tell me tuh do. Massa, kin ah see Ahsettuh now?"

McBain said, "Of course. I'll want to speak to you tomorrow morning." Dante thanked him and ran from the house.

James returned to the family parlor and sat on the sofa next to Katherine. He held her hand and said, "The servants know. I've given them time to pray." He took a deep breath. "Please tell me about the last time you saw Mrs. McBain."

Katherine explained their stay in Roswell. "Mrs. McBain wouldn't leave Mrs. Toll. The poor woman suffered so much, watching her husband pass." Katherine looked at Danny and Mary. She didn't want to be too graphic in her description and upset them. Mr. McBain sensed Katherine's concern. Katherine continued, "Mrs. McBain's heart was breaking for her. She insisted that we go to Macon and wait for them."

James rubbed his eyes. "She loves her sister. Mrs. Toll is the only remaining member of her immediate family. I've since read that General Sherman ordered his men to arrest the mill workers in Roswell and Sweetwater and send them by train to Indiana. It's possible that they got caught up in that. If so, she'll need our prayers. I know that the Lord is watching over them." He then reported, "Joseph was captured by the Yankees a few nights before our troops escaped to South Carolina."

Katherine said, "Danny mentioned that. What happened? Is he all right?"

"I don't know much. We haven't seen him yet." James nodded towards the formal parlor and asked the girls, "Do you know that we have guests—two Union officers?"

Katherine said, "I see the bedding."

James looked at his pocket watch. "I'll invite them to supper tonight. They appear to be gentlemen of the highest order, and I think you'll enjoy their company, but we must be careful what we say." James yawned. He knew there was much more to learn, but he didn't want Danny and Mary to hear it. He stood and said, "I'm a bit tired and need to lie down. You can tell me more at supper. I'm so glad you're home." He kissed both girls on the cheek and went upstairs.

Danny sat on the couch next to Katherine. She ran her hand through the boy's hair and said, "You're so handsome, and you've grown. All the girls in Savannah must be chasing after you."

Still sitting on Pauline's lap, Mary shouted, "No they aren't!"

Katherine laughed and said, "Mary, you're turning into a young lady. I think it's time to let your hemline down a few inches."

Mary turned to Danny, and stuck out her tongue. "See, I am a young lady."

They heard a knock on the door. William answered it. "Good afternoon, General, Colonel. Please come in. Mr. McBain requests your presence at supper tonight."

A deep voice replied, "Yes, of course. We'd be honored."

Danny whispered to the sisters, "They're the Yankees who are staying here. They usually mess with the eight officers who are staying at our house on Monterey Square. All the Union officers who are stationed in town are living with local families. General Wilbin and Colonel Simmons are real nice—for Yankees. They're on General Geary's staff. He's the officer in charge of Savannah. Grandpa didn't like them the first day, but now he says that no soldiers will vandalize this house or my pa's with them around."

Two men in dark blue uniforms with gold buttons lining their jackets walked into the room. The girls and Danny stood. Danny said to the men, "Hello, General Wilbin, Colonel Simmons. Mary's sisters just got home and we were using your room to talk." Danny introduced the girls to the men.

Katherine said, "It's a pleasure to meet you."

Wilbin replied, "We've only been here for two days but we've heard a lot about you both from Mr. McBain. I look forward to chatting more, perhaps at supper." The general stepped to the desk to lay down some papers and said, "Oh, pardon me, General Lee. I don't wish to disturb you."

Katherine said, "We'll see you at supper then."

The sisters and Danny went into the hall. William came by and asked Katherine if she needed anything. She requested that someone prepare a bath for her and Pauline. Then she and Pauline went upstairs to their room. Pauline closed the door and said, "Oldest Sister, if Mr. McBain or those officers ask you about our trip, you can't tell them what those soldiers did to me."

Katherine thought about the time she made a similar request to her mother about exposing her father's abuse. "Don't worry, Pauline. I would never do that. But I must tell him you were attacked. We'll have to testify to that if there's a trial for those soldiers. And what they did to Chloe."

Pauline held Katherine's arm. "Just not everything that happened to me. Please."

The girls unpacked, put on their wrappers, and went to the bathroom. Mary joined them. As Katherine and Pauline relaxed in the tub, the usually talkative Mary sat on a stool and slowly waved her hand back and forth in the water, still saddened by the news of Chloe. She wanted to know Chloe's last words, and where she is in heaven. Katherine told her that they would talk about such things another time. After they returned to the bedroom, Mary became more animated and brushed her sisters' hair. She said, "This is for Chloe. If she were here, she'd be doing it."

The sisters dressed and went to supper. They found Mr. McBain sitting alone in the dining room. He rose quickly and held out their chairs. Danny bounded in and took the seat to the right of his grandpa and across from the sisters. General Wilbin and Colonel Simmons entered and sat alongside Danny. Mrs. McBain's seat at the other end of the table remained empty. The general turned out to be a lively conversationalist and Katherine thought that he seemed more like a grandfather than a soldier. Both officers were big men. The general had salt-and-pepper hair on the sides of his otherwise bald head, with big, bushy eyebrows that looked like untrimmed hedges. Colonel Simmons had curly red hair and a sandy moustache with the ends waxed into points that extended to his ears and moved like a conductor's baton when he talked and chewed.

McBain asked Pauline to say a prayer. Then William and Lilly served the meal. The conversation centered on life in Ohio, home of the two Yankees. Mary asked the officers to describe snow and if there really were faces of angels on each flake. Pauline apologized twice during the meal for yawning. After the plates were cleared, General Wilbin said, "Miss Downes, I understand that you and Pauline traveled all the way from northern Georgia to Savannah in the midst of the fighting. I know you're tired, but if you don't mind, would you please tell us a little about it? It seems incredible that you could make that trip on your own."

James said, "Pauline, I can see you're exhausted. You can go to bed now. Danny and Mary, too."

Pauline and Mary stood, but Danny said, "I want to stay!" However, one look at his grandfather's narrowed eyes had him on his feet and saying good night to everyone.

Katherine said, "General Wilbin, we didn't do it on our own. We had two servants with us, without whom we wouldn't be here. I'll tell you about our journey, but some terrible acts were committed by your soldiers. I don't want you to feel uncomfortable as guests in Mr. McBain's house. If I tell you, I must tell it all, not just pieces. Otherwise, it won't be an honest account."

The general replied, "I appreciate your concern, Miss Downes. I prefer to hear everything." Colonel Simmons nodded in agreement.

Katherine rested her hands on the table and chose her words carefully, often closing her eyes when recalling the events, trying to describe them precisely, while omitting any detail that would embarrass Pauline. McBain turned white at hearing the incidents at Mrs. Price's house and Ebenezer Creek. He reached over and clutched Katherine's hand. "My poor girls. I had no idea."

After she spoke about the rape of Chloe and the attack on Pauline, General Wilbin left the room and returned seconds later with several pieces of writing paper, a pen, and an inkwell. He placed the items in front of Colonel Simmons, who took notes. The general said, "Please continue, Miss Downes."

When Katherine finished, McBain, with trembling hands, poured port for the officers and himself. General Wilbin pledged to learn more about the status of the trial of the soldiers and the investigation, if any, of the Ebenezer Creek incident. Katherine thanked him without much confidence that anything would be done.

Colonel Simmons said, "I am truly sorry to hear of your experiences, Miss Downes. They're gut-wrenching. I have two young daughters myself. But I must tell you that many atrocities have been committed by the rebels. The stories that we hear about Andersonville and other Confederate prisons are quite unbelievable."

"Colonel, I can only tell you about what happened to us, and I did so because you asked. It's not pleasant to discuss."

The general dabbed his napkin to his mouth and said, "Mr. McBain, I thank you for supper and for introducing us to this brave and mature young woman. I look forward to more stimulating discussions of a less troubling nature in the future." Colonel Simmons echoed the sentiment and the officers excused themselves.

When McBain heard the door close across the hall, he again reached over and held Katherine's hand. "I'm sorry. I should have told you to take the train from Macon. If I had, these things wouldn't have happened, and Chloe would still be with us."

Katherine rubbed his hand and leaned closer to him. "Sir, you had nothing to do with it. If the wagon hadn't broken down at a house with a sick, pregnant woman, we would have missed the Yankees by weeks. It was simply bad luck."

McBain whispered to Katherine, "You mentioned the crimes committed by the Yankees during your trip home. Do you know what Sherman did to Atlanta?" She shook her head. "After the city fell, the Yankees lived in and around the town for over two months. They evacuated all the residents, and when the army left in mid-November, Sherman burned the place to the ground. I hear that practically nothing is left."

Katherine's face drained. "I had no idea."

"I think we're safe here. The rumor is that the Yankees are in Savannah to stay." McBain sighed. "Tomorrow morning we'll have a simple service for Chloe. Poor Chloe. She suffered so much. Mrs. McBain and Joseph will be crushed." McBain stood and hugged Katherine good night.

When Dante arrived at the Lamar house, he saw Isetta standing in the drive-way and called her name. She shouted and ran to greet her husband. He wrapped his arms around her and lifted her off her feet before kissing her. They went to her room in an outbuilding behind the main house. Dante froze at the sight of the two-month-old baby, curled up and sleeping on the bed. He picked up the tiny boy, who Isetta had named Azekiel, after her father, and sat in the lone chair in the room.

Isetta told Dante that all slaves now were free and could leave their masters if they wanted. Most of Colonel Lamar's negroes had departed. Isetta said that she loved the five Lamar daughters and didn't want to leave Mrs. Lamar alone to care for them with Colonel Lamar away in the army. Dante sat silently with his eyes closed, rocking his child. His mind was scrambled like an egg. He was seeing his son for the first time and beginning to understand the meaning of his freedom. He had trouble comprehending it all. Isetta said, "You gwine tuh say sumtin'?"

The new father lifted Azekiel and replied, "Ah don' know wut tuh say. Dis muh bes' day all time. Us kin leab Massa, but wut us gwine tuh do? Us need tuh wu'k fuh 'Zekiel. Ah needs tuh talk wid Massa." Dante put his son on the bed and the couple slept in each other's arms for the first time in six months.

The next morning McBain explained to Dante that Katherine had told him about the trip and how he had saved her and Pauline from Yankee soldiers and at Ebenezer Creek. He thanked Dante and handed him a ten-dollar gold coin as a reward. Dante stared at his hand as if he had caught a shooting star, and thanked McBain. Then McBain said, "Dante, everything is changing. You're now free and can find another job and place to live or you can stay with us. I've told this to all the other servants. Jefferson and Nannie left, but the rest are remaining. You've been with us your whole life. I will take care of you, as I always have. I can't say what job you'll have because I don't know what's happening with the Heritage. When things settle down I'll have you cook here. For now, I want you to be my coachman. I'll pay you forty cents a day, plus you can live here with Isetta. If you leave, be aware that Savannah is very poor now and will be for years to come. Getting a job in a restaurant will be difficult."

Dante didn't hesitate. He wanted the security of a job and a place to live. "Massa, ah wu'k fuh you." He thanked McBain and left to tell Isetta. McBain exhaled. He knew he was going to lose some of his negroes and needed to keep everyone he could.

The early morning sun shone brightly, and birds chirped loudly, as if to keep warm in the chilly air. Danny and the sisters stood on the backyard walkway on James McBain's right while the servants stood to his left. William hammered a two-foot-high, white wooden cross in a corner of the flower bed. McBain told the gathering that he would plant a flower in the spring so that Chloe would always be remembered. He praised her as a kind, generous, and loyal soul. He then read scripture from the Bible. He closed the book and asked everyone to sing "Rock of Ages."

General Wilbin and Colonel Simmons watched from behind a curtain. Wilbin said, "I guess they really loved that colored girl."

After the service the sisters and Danny walked to the harbor and observed the change in the town. Soldiers built small cabins in all the squares. Shops and businesses displayed "Closed" signs in their windows. Bluecoats jammed the Bay. Ships bobbed in the river as far as the eye could see. Danny explained, "General Wilbin said the Union navy is removing all the sunken vessels and pilings in the river so ships can get in and out again. It should be cleared in a few weeks."

The girls and Danny sat on a bench on the Strand and watched the people on the Bay. Most of the citizens were women with children, and almost all wore black. Pauline pointed out that they were going out of their way to avoid walking under the U.S. flag flying from the portico of the City Exchange building. Whenever a Yankee soldier approached a white woman, she crossed to the other side of the street. The scene was peaceful, but it was far from happy.

They returned home by a different route and spotted Jefferson towering above ten other men loitering on a street corner. Pauline and Katherine walked up to him while Mary and Danny stood back. Katherine said, "Hello, Jefferson."

He faced them without a smile. "Ah lu'n you come back. Ah lu'n Chloe don."

Katherine said, "No, sadly, she didn't. We loved her very much."

Jefferson glanced at his male companions and said, "You know ah ain' uh slabe no maw. Us free."

"Yes, we heard. We wish you the best." Jefferson said nothing. Katherine knew it was time to leave. She said, "Please say hello to Nannie for us. We miss her."

"You mean, you miss Nannie cleanin' up fuh you."

"No, Jefferson. I meant exactly what I said. We miss her." They walked off. Danny didn't speak for the rest of the way, feeling Jefferson's betrayal the most.

When they arrived at the house, Katherine saw Captain Bowen leaning against the railing enclosing Pulaski Square. She told the others to go into the house and that she'd be in shortly. Bowen walked up to her and removed his hat. "Good afternoon, Miss Downes. I was near this part of town and thought I'd come by and see how you and your sister are getting on."

"We're doing well, Captain, and happy to be home. Are you camped nearby?"

"No, we're outside the city, near the plantation of your adopted family. I trust you had a happy reunion."

"Yes, but Mr. McBain still hasn't heard from Mrs. McBain, and his son is in the local prison. He was upset to hear of our experiences and the death of his girl. But it's good to see everyone again and sleep in a real bed."

Bowen looked into the square and saw a bench. "Shall we sit?"

Katherine paused. She had observed that all the women in town were shunning the soldiers, but as the McBain family had two officers living with them, she saw nothing wrong with sitting with him. She said, "That would be nice, though I haven't much time." They entered the square and sat. Katherine adjusted her bonnet, wrapped her shawl tightly around her shoulders, and told him about their walk to the river and back.

He said, "I hear the businesses will be allowed to reopen soon. Savannah is so charming. I've never seen anything quite like it—all the squares and the mansions. You must enjoy living here."

"Yes, we all do. We're very fortunate that the McBains took us in."

Bowen looked at the house. "Fortunate is putting it mildly. This is one of the most elegant houses in a town full of elegant houses."

Katherine thought the captain was very handsome and charming, and was flattered by his attention. "Sir, I know so little about you. Where are you from? What did you do before the war?"

"I was teaching history at Oberlin College in Ohio when the war started, and I hope to return there. I was born and raised in Lancaster, Ohio, General Sherman's hometown. When the war started, I helped form a mounted cavalry company."

"What's Lancaster like? I've never seen a northern town."

Before he could answer Mary yelled from the front door for Katherine to come inside. Katherine told Captain Bowen that she enjoyed seeing him again, but she had to return to her sisters. Bowen walked her back to the house, told her that he enjoyed their chat, and left.

When Katherine walked through the front door, Mary grabbed her hand and said, "You promised you'd read to me. Who is that soldier?"

"He rescued Pauline and me from some very bad men. We're forever in his debt."

Katherine read to Mary and Danny and had them read back to her for an hour. Over supper, Mr. McBain told Danny and the sisters that General Wilbin had obtained a pass for all of them to go to the Heritage the next day—Christmas—and one for Danny and him to visit Joseph in prison the day after. Danny clapped his hands.

Lying in bed that night, Pauline said, "Katherine, I'm so happy to be back. I only wish Mrs. and Captain McBain would come home. Then everything will be perfect. Promise me we'll never leave here again."

Katherine thought of her time with Joseph in Marietta. She said, "I promise." ⁊

CHAPTER FORTY-SIX

Colonel Allen's Proposal

Late December 1864

The coach turned onto the avenue of oaks for the first time since Savannah fell. James McBain fumed as he handed his pass to a soldier to gain access to his own property. A few seconds later he said, "Good Lord" when he saw the sea of tents covering his corn and wheat fields. "There must be a thousand men camped here." The sisters and Danny glanced nervously at each other, but didn't say a word as they felt Mr. McBain's anger. Farther down the road a crowd of about fifty slaves sat in front of their cabins and waved at them. James saw his temporary overseer and called for Dante to stop. Roman hurried over. James got out and said, "Roman, what's happening?"

The negro said the Yankees had told them that they were free and didn't have to stay. If they remained and continued to work, they had to be paid. Seven families with forty-five people had left, including Solomon and Noah, the sons of the former overseer Isaac, and moved to the city or other plantations to live with relatives. One hundred twenty-five men, women, and children remained at the Heritage. Roman also reported that the Yankees were using the lumber mill to repair their pontoons, gun carriages, and wagons, and had hired fifty men at thirty cents a day. He stressed to McBain that the people were anxious to hear about his plans for them. McBain told Roman to have all the people gather at the church in an hour and he would address them.

They drove on and passed the overseer's house, where several Union officers sat on the front porch, chewing tobacco, smoking pipes, and chatting. Dante stopped in front of the big house. James told Danny and the girls to wait for him. He walked up the stairs and said to the two guards standing by the front door, "I'm the owner of this plantation and I'd like to see the commanding officer."

One of the soldiers said, "Yes, sir. Follow me," and led McBain into the house and down the interior stairwell to his office.

A general with short black hair and a neatly trimmed black beard looked up from the desk, leaned back in the chair, and said, "How may I help you?"

McBain handed over his pass. "Good morning, General. I'm Mr. McBain. This is my plantation. I'd like to know my rights to my property."

The officer studied the document, stood, and said, "I'm General Diamond, Mr. McBain." The men shook hands. Diamond continued, "May I compliment you on your plantation. It's the nicest one I've seen in all Georgia, very orderly and clean, including the slave cabins. Please, have a seat." James sat where so many of his guests and customers had over the years. He noticed the small United States flag on his desk and took a deep breath. "Your property is under occupation and at present you have no rights to it. After you take the oath of allegiance to the Union and we leave, your property will be restored to you, except your slaves, who are now free. You may negotiate with them to work for you."

McBain liked the calm, reasonable manner of the general. "Are you saying that I can't run my plantation?"

"For now, that's correct. We should be gone in three or four weeks. While we're here, we'll take care of your property. I've been employing many of your workers at the lumber mill and all your house servants. After we leave you may prepare a list of items that we have taken or consumed and apply for compensation from the government."

James looked around his office. Everything seemed to be in order. "I'd like to speak with my negroes to explain the situation. May I do that?"

"Yes, of course. Do you need anything else?"

James didn't expect the general to be so accommodating and rubbed his chin in thought. "I have a book in the top drawer of this desk listing all my negroes. I need to confirm who are still here. Also, I'd like a pass to come out each week, check up on things, and see that they're getting their food ration."

The general looked at the pass again. He took out a piece of paper, wrote a note, and handed it to McBain. "Give this to General Wilbin. He'll arrange a weekly pass for you with the provost marshal." The general pushed back his chair, opened the drawer, pulled out a cloth-covered book, and handed it to McBain.

James thanked him and returned to the coach. He found Dante talking to a group of about thirty men. They immediately surrounded "ole Massa" and exclaimed how glad they were to see him. He greeted each one by name and told them to bring their families to the church.

Dante told McBain that Danny and the girls had walked to the river. McBain had Dante first swing by the stables. McBain walked in and closed the doors behind him. He went to a stall on the right, led out the horse, kicked away the hay, and saw the undisturbed dirt and heads of three nails that he had put in the ground after he buried the largest portion of his gold. Satisfied that the box was still there, he replaced things as they were. He returned to the coach and told Dante, "Let's find Danny and the girls."

Dante drove towards the river and wondered when he would get an opportunity to go inside the stables to see if his gun was still hidden in the rafters.

They stopped by a crowd of about twenty soldiers who were laughing and seemingly enjoying themselves. Danny and the sisters emerged from the middle of the pack and crawled into the coach. James asked, "What's going on?"

Katherine said, "We took a stroll. Those Yankees said they wanted to meet some southern girls."

Pauline said, "I was scared of them at first, but they were very polite. One said he wanted to marry me." She held her stomach and stuck out her tongue.

Katherine smiled and said, "Stop that, Pauline. He was nice looking."

"Yes, for a toad."

Mary said, "One promised to come back for me in seven years, when I'm fifteen. But I told him I'll be married to Danny by then."

Danny slapped his cheek and said, "Oh, brother."

Dante drove to the church. McBain left the youngsters and entered the building to address his negroes as he had done so many times before at marriages and funerals. But this time was different. He no longer owned them. He could no longer tell them what to do—now he had to ask them. But he also knew that they needed work and were dependent on him.

The packed hall fell silent. James could hear his own footsteps squeak on the wood plank floor as he walked to the small pulpit. He looked out at the people and saw serious, lined faces. "Good afternoon." He paused and they all replied in unison, "Aftuhnoon, Massa."

"Much has changed since I last saw you," he continued. "As you all know, the Union army now controls this area and I am subject to its laws. Slavery no longer exists in Savannah. You are free and may leave the plantation, as some already have, or you may stay. I want you to stay. I've always told you that I'll take care of you, and I say so still. If you remain, you may live in your cabins and once the Yankees leave, which I am told will be in about a month, I will pay you thirty cents for each day worked. Gang drivers will get forty cents. I understand that many of you are now employed by the Yankees. For those who aren't, Roman will assign you to other jobs." He looked at his overseer, who nodded. "Once the soldiers leave you can return to your regular tasks. Until then, I will continue to furnish food rations. That is all. I want to see each one of you at the door as you leave."

McBain walked to the front and checked off the people's names in his slave register. As each family passed by, the men smiled, shook his hand, and told him that they were glad he was back. The women asked about the missus, not knowing that she was missing, Master Joseph, and Mistess Amy. McBain felt vindicated that these folks, most of whom he had known all their lives, had decided to stay with him, at least for the time being. He thanked them for their loyalty. Afterwards, the family returned to Savannah for a quiet Christmas supper.

Joseph jumped from the chair and embraced Danny and his father when they entered the visitor's room at the Savannah jail, now a Union prison. The guard allowed the contact. The three sat and Joseph told James that he would be tried before a military commission for executing seven soldiers of the Foreign Battalion, but wasn't given a hearing date. He assured them that he didn't give the order nor was he present, and asked his father to hire a lawyer to defend him. Danny told his pa about the return of Katherine, Pauline, and Dante, bringing a smile to Joseph's face. When James told him about Chloe, he slammed the table with his palm, then apologized for the outburst.

James explained that he still hadn't received word from Sarah and described the situation at the Heritage. He also told his son about the officers living in the Pulaski and Monterey Square houses and life in Savannah under Yankee rule, which, after five days, had been civil, with few insults or acts of lewdness or drunkenness from the soldiers.

Joseph asked his father about Katherine and Pauline. James replied that they were in excellent spirits considering all they had been through, as beautiful as ever, though a bit thinner, and elated to be back home with Mary and Danny. Joseph wanted to ask his father to bring the sisters the next time he visited, but thought better of it. The guard tapped his rifle on the floor. Their fifteen minutes were up. He took Joseph away.

James and Danny returned home with their spirits lifted by Joseph's confidence in his case. Danny ran off with Mary and Pauline to find Truvy while James did some paperwork. A few hours later Katherine entered the house. James invited her into his study and described his meeting with Joseph. She breathed a sigh of relief and wondered how she could arrange to visit Joseph alone. McBain asked her how she spent her day.

"I visited a few hospitals—they're all under Yankee control—and applied to be a nurse. The surgeon at the Massie School hospital asked me to come back tomorrow."

McBain tapped the desk blotter with his letter opener. "You know you don't have to find employment. I'm holding your reward money and the cash you received from your mother's estate, all of which I converted to gold, about seven hundred dollars worth. That will go a long way in these times, and your expenses are quite low."

"I thank you for looking after my funds, but I want to work. I feel more useful."

"Whatever you wish." He put down the letter opener. "I have a surprise. I've invited Mr. Lippman and Mr. Cohen to supper tomorrow evening. They're looking forward to seeing you."

That brought a smile to her face. She hadn't seen either in many months and liked them both. "That's wonderful news, sir."

General Wilbin stuck his head in the door. He tipped his hat to Katherine and said, "Mr. McBain, do you have a few minutes? I have a matter I wish to discuss." Katherine excused herself and went upstairs. Wilbin sat and said, "I met a gentleman today at General Geary's headquarters—a New Yorker named Colonel Julian Allen. He just arrived from Hilton Head and is an acquaintance of the treasury agent in charge of this area. He sees how impoverished the place is and asked me if I knew any businessmen in town to discuss a proposition to bring food here. I told him about you."

James nodded. "Of course I'll meet with him if it will help Savannah, although I'm probably not the best person. Do you know anything about his proposal so I can invite the appropriate men?"

The general shrugged. "Very little. He said he wants to go to New York with the authorization to trade the local rice stored in the warehouses and controlled by the Union army for provisions needed here. That's all I know. I'll see him in the morning."

James drummed his fingers on the desk as he thought of a response. "Why don't you invite him for supper here tomorrow night at seven o'clock. Tell him to bring the treasury agent. I'd also like you and Colonel Simmons to attend. I'm having some friends over, including an alderman on the city council. I'll also ask our mayor. If they like the proposal they'll be able to convince the city council."

Wilbin said, "Excellent. I have a positive feeling about this."

McBain snapped his fingers. "In fact, I'll have Katherine host the affair with me. She'll put everyone in a good mood."

"Even more excellent."

The next evening Pauline and Mary spent two hours combing Katherine's hair, and helping with her make-up and dress. Pauline said, "Katherine, you are the most beautiful woman in all Savannah. The men will hover so close you won't be able to breathe. Bring your fan. Mary will teach you how to use it."

Katherine laughed. "They're businessmen and won't even notice I'm there. Mr. McBain thought it would be beneficial to have a woman's presence and I feel honored that he would invite me. After the meal they'll smoke segars and talk about business and I'll excuse myself. Now, you two go downstairs and have supper with Danny so you'll be out of the way." She returned to her mirror and practiced smiling, trying to look more confident than she felt.

Katherine met Mr. McBain, General Wilbin, and Colonel Simmons in the study before the other guests arrived. McBain said she looked beautiful and the officers nodded. The general then told them what he had learned about Colonel Allen. The man had emigrated from Poland to New York in 1848 and owned a segar shop and warehouse in New York City. When the war started he helped raise a brigade consisting of mostly Polish Jews. He served as the purser of a U.S. steamer, which frequently docked at Hilton Head, before returning to his business in New York in 1863. By the summer of 1864, with the war dragging on, he traveled to Central Europe and raised over one thousand volunteers for the Union army, gaining the gratitude of President Lincoln. When Savannah fell, Allen came south at the invitation of his friend Treasury Agent Albert Browne to investigate business opportunities.

Colonel Allen and Browne arrived next and William took their heavy overcoats and hats. General Wilbin introduced the men to James and Katherine. McBain held Katherine's hand and claimed the young woman "is just like a daughter to me." Katherine smiled and leaned gently against McBain. Mr. Lippman and Mr. Cohen came next, followed by Mayor Richard Arnold, who looked twice at Katherine when introduced to her, as she looked vaguely familiar. Katherine remembered the name Dr. Arnold as the man who had cared for her at the Savannah Poor House and Hospital after she collapsed on the street, although she didn't recall his face and was relieved when the doctor didn't seem to remember her.

After William served drinks and the guests exchanged light banter about the unseasonably cold weather, even for December, McBain escorted everyone to the dining room. He sat at one end of the table and placed Katherine at the other, as Wilbin and Simmons both rushed to hold her chair. While Lilly and Patty served the food, Mr. Lippman said, "Miss Downes, Mr. Cohen told me about your work in Marietta. Apparently, you performed admirably and made a favorable impression on everyone."

Cohen added, "Miss Downes cleaned and dressed wounds and administered medicine as well as any man. She also diagnosed some of the injuries. The surgeon in charge told me he trusted her completely."

Katherine blushed at the compliments. Dr. Arnold asked her where she acquired her skills. "Here in Savannah while volunteering in the hospitals. On my breaks in Marietta I read the Manual of Military Surgery. Of course, I didn't perform operations or enter an operating room, but the book helped me understand the injuries that I had to treat." Katherine glanced at Mr. McBain, who wore a big smile.

Colonel Allen asked, "Miss Downes, is medicine a field that you want to pursue?"

She replied, "I don't know how to pursue it any further than I already have. I find treating people—helping them heal and giving them comfort—very rewarding, but I only got the opportunity because of the shortage of male nurses. Once the war ends, there won't be a need for women in hospitals, except to cook and clean."

Allen said, "You mustn't give up so easily on something you're passionate about. Times are changing—slowly, but they are changing. Women in the North are demanding more opportunities to enter the field of medicine. They claim that women want to be treated by female doctors, as men don't understand the afflictions that women alone experience. My wife agrees wholeheartedly. It may take time, but their role is bound to grow. There's a medical college for women in New York. That's something you might consider."

Katherine noticed the other men staring at her, awaiting a response. She felt that she might float off her chair at hearing a stranger suggest that she should think about attending a medical college. "I don't know, Colonel. You have to be very smart to be a doctor. I have no formal education. My mother taught me to read and write at home."

Colonel Allen wouldn't give up. "Miss Downes, you're an articulate and bright young woman and that's what's important. If you applied, you would have to be interviewed by the college president, a delightful woman and personal friend of mine, and you'd need several reference letters. I'm certain you could get those just from the gentlemen sitting at this table." All the men nodded vigorously. "Think it over. If you're interested, I'll be happy to make inquiries."

Katherine said, "Thank you, Colonel Allen, for your encouraging words and willingness to help me. I will certainly consider it."

Treasury Agent Browne spoke. "Miss Downes, there's a woman doctor now in Beaufort. Dr. Hawks has been teaching freed slaves but she had her own practice in New Hampshire before the war. I'm certain she would be happy to talk to you if she visits here. I think you would enjoy her in any event."

McBain, who had felt like a proud father at all the praise that Katherine was receiving, became concerned when the men started suggesting that she consider leaving Savannah. "Gentlemen, please don't be too quick to take Miss Downes from me. I would never stand in the way of her dreams, and I know she could accomplish anything she sets her mind to, but for the time being, with my wife missing, I need her here."

Colonel Allen said, "I certainly understand why you wouldn't want to lose her, sir. But if circumstances should ever change—if Mrs. McBain returns, as we all pray she will—my offer still stands."

Lilly appeared at her side and said, "Not hungry tuhnight, Mistess?"

Katherine realized that she had been so involved in the conversation that she hadn't eaten. "Not really, Lilly. But it was delicious."

As the servants cleared the table, Allen clasped his hands together and said, "Gentlemen, I thank General Wilbin and Mr. McBain for arranging this fine gathering. I have been so impressed by the willingness of the people of Savannah to rejoin the Union that I would like to make a proposition to help alleviate the suffering of your citizens. Simply put, with your approval, I will travel to New York as your city's representative to trade local confiscated rice for provisions much in need here. That would include beef, lard, sugar, potatoes, vegetables, bread, and the like. I'm confident that this can be accomplished in a matter of weeks. If I'm able to leave here in the next few days, I could be back by late January and the poor will have proper food."

Mayor Arnold raised his eyebrows at Alderman Lippman. "Colonel, your offer would be most beneficial to our citizens. It will also help rebuild the old ties
between Savannah and New York. As you may know, General Sherman has gen-
erously released the seized rice, about two hundred fifty thousand dollars worth,
to the city council for distribution to our destitute residents. We would have to
obtain his approval to divert some of it for this purpose. Do you have a dollar
value of trade in mind?"

"About fifty thousand dollars."

Mr. Lippman nodded his approval. Arnold said, "I've already called for a
special meeting of the citizens of Savannah at Masonic Hall tomorrow to discuss the city's future under our new circumstances. I'll present your offer to the
other aldermen and get word to you immediately. They'll want to know what you
charge for your services."

"There will be no cost, sir. I'll do this for free."

Mayor Arnold said, "That's most kind of you, sir." McBain and the other locals voiced their thanks. Arnold continued, "Once General Sherman approves
the plan, you can leave for New York. It will be none too soon. Again, you have
our utmost gratitude for your proposal."

The men lifted their glasses and toasted. Katherine rose and said, "Gentlemen, I've enjoyed meeting you. I'm sure you have many details to discuss. I'll bid
you all goodnight."

The men stood as General Wilbin held Katherine's chair. She thanked him
and went upstairs. Mary and Pauline were reading in bed. They put down their
books and stared at her. Katherine put on her nightgown, washed, and crawled
under the covers.

Pauline said, "We're not going to sleep without hearing of your evening."

Mary added, "What did you have for dessert?"

Katherine lay back and rested her head on the pillow. "The evening was very
exciting, and the Yankees were perfect gentlemen. One of them volunteered to go
to New York to trade Savannah rice for food needed here."

Pauline said. "That's nice of him. Did the men tell you how beautiful you
are?"

Katherine smiled at Pauline. "They told me something better than that."

Pauline turned on her side and shook Katherine's shoulder. "Like what?"

"One man from New York thinks that I should study to become a doctor."

Pauline's eyes widened. "A doctor? He must have been teasing. Women can't
be doctors, can they?"

Katherine kissed Pauline's forehead. "That's what I thought, but he says attitudes are changing in the North."

Mary said, "We aren't leaving Savannah. You promised."

"Don't worry. Nothing will come of it, but it was nice hearing someone say
that. It made me feel good—special even." She kissed her sisters good night,

turned out the lamp, and closed her eyes, but she couldn't sleep. She wondered if she really could be a doctor. The idea exhilarated her. Unfortunately, to do so would require leaving the McBains, something she could never do. ⁓

CHAPTER FORTY-SEVEN

❧

The Cookie Sellers
December 28, 1864 – January 7, 1865

Mayor Arnold had to bang the gavel seven times to call the meeting to order. Just about every male resident of Savannah of any means or status was there. Despite a general despair from the occupation of their city and a deep resentment of the Yankees, most citizens understood the realities of the situation—that they had been defeated and were at the mercy of their conquerors. The smart and prudent course of action dictated that they accept their fate, deal cordially with the Union soldiers and officials, and try to obtain the best possible treatment from them. Accordingly, the gathering passed resolutions to bury differences between the two sections and live under the U.S. Constitution; try to bring the state of Georgia back into the Union; and work to restore the former prosperity and commerce of Savannah. When the mayor adjourned the meeting the attendees cheered and tossed their hats in the air. McBain left Masonic Hall satisfied that the city was on the road to recovery.

The tone of cooperation apparently pleased General Sherman. He approved an agreement in which the city council authorized Colonel Allen to be Savannah's agent, travel to New York City, and procure provisions for the city's destitute populace in exchange for up to fifty thousand dollars worth of rice. The general's ruthless reputation appeared to be overblown, at least in Savannah.

On the last day of the year Colonel Allen sailed for New York. Before he left, James McBain found him at the treasury department's offices in the Bank of Commerce and asked him to post a letter to his daughter when he arrived there. Allan said he would be glad to do it. James thanked him and the men shook hands.

The sense of hope that emerged from the public meeting grew as the new year began. The Union navy made steady progress towards removing obstructions from the river, the first step in a resumption of the trade that had once made the city so prosperous. A postmaster arrived and started to make arrangements to renew postal services. Major General John Geary, under Sherman's direction, instituted a military administration that McBain considered just and fair, and made Savannah more livable than it had been since the war began. He instituted patrols to keep the peace and protect private property; implemented price controls to prevent gouging; reopened schools; and allowed the mayor and city council to continue to run city affairs. Citizens usually received prompt approval to reopen their businesses. And while there were occasional incidents of soldier rowdiness, order and public safety prevailed. For those residents who couldn't tolerate living under Yankee rule, mostly wives and children of soldiers still fighting for the Confederacy, Sherman shipped them beyond enemy lines.

Still, deep-rooted problems existed. Commerce remained stagnant because so many people were without work or money. Many residents existed on a diet of rice and shivered because of a shortage of firewood. Many negroes, once so strictly controlled by the whites, loitered in the streets and taunted their former masters.

⌘

Amidst the changes taking place in Savannah, Katherine Downes got a job as an attendant at the Union hospital in the Massie School. She changed bedding, cleaned the ward, and served food to patients. It wasn't true nursing, but she felt comfortable in the environment, and received one Yankee dollar a day for her efforts.

James McBain began the new year by signing the oath of allegiance at the City Exchange. In doing so, he pledged to support, protect, and defend the Constitution of the United States and the Union of the States thereunder. He felt a twinge of guilt as he returned home afterwards and sat at his desk, but knew that the Yankees could have been much harsher. As a U.S. citizen again, he felt he had a better chance of tracking down Sarah, his top priority, and reclaiming his plantation. McBain stared at Pauline's drawing of his family, framed and sitting on his desk, and wondered when they all would be together again. Then Danny stuck his head in the door and said, "Grandpa?"

James looked up and said, "Danny, come in." Danny, Mary, and Truvy marched single-file and stood side-by-side at attention in front of his desk. James asked, "Who's in trouble now?"

Danny shook his head. "No one, Grandpa. We're here for a business meeting."

James laughed out loud. "And what business might that be, Danny?"

"We were walking on Broughton Street today and Mary was eating one of Miss Patience's cookies. Three Yankees stopped her and wanted to know where they could buy one. Truvy said his ma made it and that's all we had. Mary gave the soldier a piece and he said it was the best cookie he ever ate. After they left, Mary said we should have Miss Patience bake cookies and cakes for us to sell to the Yankees. They haven't eaten them for months."

Truvy said, "I went home and asked Ma. She said she would. She thinks she needs about five dollars for the ingredients to make fifty cookies. That's ten cents each."

Mary said, "If we sell them for twenty cents we'll double our money."

Danny added, "We need a loan to buy the stuff."

James's eyes shifted from child to child as they peppered him with information. He sat back in his chair. "I like the idea, but some of the ingredients are scarce and expensive once you find them. Here's what I'll do. Truvy, have your mother see me. I'll give her the things she needs from my stores and I'll charge you five dollars. Keep in mind that you must pay her for her services and repay me. I'll also lend you some Yankee coins to make change."

The children chimed, "Yes, sir," and ran from the room. As far as James was concerned, he had already been compensated.

That evening, Patience laughed with Mr. McBain in his study. "Yes, sir, they explained it all to me. I'll bake fifty cookies for them tonight. Miss Mary told me we're all going to be rich."

James smiled, "She's a bundle of energy. This will be a good experience for all of them. Lilly is expecting you. Tell her what you need and Dante will drive you home. I'm certain I'll get a report tomorrow. How are you getting along?"

"We're all fine, sir. Thank you. Of course I know about Master Joseph. We're hoping that he gets out soon."

"I do as well, but not so soon to be able to rejoin the fighting. Now that you're free, I want you to know that when he's able, he'll transfer title of your house to you. You'll own it, along with all of your other possessions."

Patience smiled and pressed her palms together under her chin. "Thank you, sir. I can't tell you how grateful I am."

The next afternoon the three children returned to McBain's study. Danny said, "We went to Forsyth Place where two Yankee regiments are camped. They just got three months pay. We sold all fifty cookies in two hours."

Truvy stepped forward and emptied his bulging pockets on the table. "There's nine dollars in Yankee coins, plus the two dollars you gave us for making change."

James blinked at the pile. "Fifty cookies at twenty cents is ten dollars, not nine."

Danny said, "Right, Grandpa. I ate one and so did Truvy. Mary ate three, but we approved. She walked up to the soldiers, told them we were selling delicious cookies, and pulled them by the arm to our blanket."

Mary hopped up and down with excitement. "Grandpa, Miss Patience is the best baker in the world. We could have sold hundreds."

McBain noticed golden crumbs at the corners of her mouth. He asked, "Nine dollars is a lot of money. What are you going to do with it?"

Danny said, "We're going to pay Miss Patience two dollars and pay you one dollar of your loan. That leaves us with six dollars, and we still owe you four.

We're each going to keep twenty-five cents and give the rest to Miss Patience to bake more cookies. I'm going to save my money."

Mary said, "I'm going to carry my twenty-five cents with me all the time so I feel rich."

Truvy said, "I'm going to give my share to Miss Pauline for drawing all those buildings for me. I wish I could give her more. I will some day."

McBain said, "That's very thoughtful of you, Truvy." He wondered if he should introduce the youngsters to the concept of interest, but decided to delay it. "It looks like you're on your way, but Mary, the more cookies you eat, the less profit you'll make."

Mary lowered her head. "Sorry, Grandpa. I couldn't help it. They're so good!"

McBain said, "Go ahead and sell more cookies. Ask Lilly to give you the same ingredients that she gave to Miss Patience yesterday and take them to her." The kids left in a chorus of giggles. McBain wished he could tell Sarah and Joseph about them.

The next night at supper Mary and Danny reported on the day's business. Katherine patted her sister on the back. Mary said, "Pauline, you could sketch soldiers. I bet you could get fifty cents each. They just got paid and have lots of money. You can sit on our blanket."

Pauline, who was waiting for school to open and spending her time reading and sketching buildings and gardens, looked at Katherine, who nodded with a smile. Mr. McBain said, "It sounds like it's worth a try." Pauline kissed Mary on the top of the head.

Katherine thought of Joseph constantly but didn't know how to get a pass to see him. She thought of asking General Wilbin, but worried that he would mention it to Mr. McBain, and she didn't want anyone to be suspicious of her and Joseph. One day while on a break from the hospital, she took a stroll around Forsyth Place and entered the Hall Street prison. She asked a sergeant sitting at the front desk for permission to see Captain Joseph McBain. He asked for her name and relationship to the prisoner. Flustered, she answered, "Miss Katherine Downes, his step-sister." The soldier wrote it in a register and told a guard to take her to the visitor's room. Her heart started to flutter.

A few minutes later, Joseph entered the room followed by a guard. He smiled, said, "It's my favorite step-sister!" and hugged her.

The guard ordered, "Captain, no touching!"

They parted and sat across from each other at the three-foot-wide table. Joseph said, "You're more beautiful than ever." Katherine smiled. "Father told me about your journey—and poor Chloe. It's remarkable that you and Pauline made it."

She glanced at the guard, who sat in a chair against the wall and looked blankly at them. "We wouldn't have made it without Dante. How are you?"

"I'm getting by—much better than so many of my fallen comrades. I assume father told you that I'm going to be tried by a military commission." She nodded. "I'll be transferred to the prison at Fort Pulaski soon. Visitors won't be allowed." He held her hand in both of his. "I miss you," he said softly.

The guard said, "No touching!" Joseph pulled back as if he had grabbed the handle of a hot skillet.

Katherine whispered, "I miss you, too, Joseph, more than you can imagine." They stared at each other for a few seconds. Then she told him about Mary, Danny, and Truvy selling cookies. "In just one week they've made ten Yankee dollars. They don't want the soldiers to leave. Mary suggested that Pauline draw portraits for fifty cents and in just a few days she's made twenty dollars! Soon Danny and my sisters will be supporting us all!" Joseph laughed.

She continued, "The Savannah School for Young Ladies is opening soon and I'm sending the girls. I guess you know that Danny's going to the Classical School for Boys." He nodded. "Danny's so cute. I love him. He's as handsome as his father, if not more so." Joseph laughed again. "He's so excited to be a businessman and talks constantly to Mary and Truvy about cookies and cakes. Each night at supper he gives us an accounting of the day's activity. With school starting, they'll sell the treats after classes and on weekends."

Joseph admired her exuberance. "I wish I could be there with you to see all this."

Katherine felt her entire body glow at Joseph's words of affection. She leaned closer. "Joseph, I think about us all the time, but you know how I feel. You're married. In Macon you said that you had already decided to leave your wife. Did you mean it?" She heard the guard snort a sarcastic laugh, but she ignored him.

Joseph clasped his hands on his lap, straining not to touch her. "Yes, I did."

"Does your wife know this?"

"She knows I was upset about her staying in New York, but I haven't been able to write to her for over a year—since my sister Amy left."

"Joseph, what if she comes here after the war—to reunite? You haven't seen her or your daughter for so long. You don't know how you'll feel."

"I do know. She left me—her husband. She made vows. What's worse, she left Danny motherless. I can't understand how a woman could do that. I'll start the divorce and child custody actions as soon as I get out of here."

"When will that be?"

"I can't say. I don't have a trial date and the Yankees may wait until the war is over. It could be a year or more. But after that, you and I will be together."

The guard tapped the wall. He pointed to his pocket watch and said, "Time's up."

Katherine stood and stepped to the door. She said, "I'm not telling your father that I came here today. I don't want him to know about us yet."

The guard laughed as he led Joseph back to the cell and said, "Some step-sister."

Joseph wondered how he would tell his parents and Danny of his intentions.

Katherine was so engrossed in her thoughts about Joseph that she walked past the Massie School before realizing that she had to return to work. While she loved him, she couldn't overcome her fear of his reaction when he saw his wife and daughter again. Still, the thought of being Joseph's wife—of being a real McBain and Danny's mother—thrilled her. She wanted to tell Pauline in the worst way but knew she would have to keep her engagement secret.

While preparing for bed that night, Pauline asked Katherine, "You've been smiling all evening. What are you so happy about?"

Katherine said, "Don't I always look happy?"

Pauline scratched her head in thought. "Well, sometimes."

Katherine lay in bed thinking of Joseph, and of becoming his bride. She thought back to the first time they met, when she had an ugly black eye and felt so poor and dirty in his family's presence. She recalled the second time, when he spoke to her in the family parlor about Willie, and he looked into her eyes. And of course, she remembered fondly the time they danced together at Dante's wedding and their first kisses in Marietta. Katherine finally fell asleep. She dreamed that she was walking along the Strand on a sunny day with Joseph, Danny, and a girl about Danny's age. Danny and Joseph were laughing as the girl skipped beside her. Joseph said that he was taking everyone for ice cream and he and Danny ran ahead. She and the girl followed. Suddenly, the little girl started to cry. Katherine stooped and asked her what was wrong. The girl pointed down the Bay. Katherine saw her father, grinning and trotting towards them. She took the girl's hand and they started to run the other way, but her legs were too heavy to move. Katherine called for Joseph, but he was nowhere in sight. Zebudiah caught up to them, wearing only underdrawers. Katherine screamed and tried to shield the child from her father, but Zeb easily took the girl away and held her in his arms. Zeb kissed her on the cheek, told her how pretty she looked, and started to leave. Katherine crawled towards them on her hands and knees, pleading with her father to return the girl. The girl looked back at Katherine over Zeb's shoulder with outstretched arms, begging for help. Katherine heard her father say, "Don't worry Katherine, I won't hurt my little angel." He kissed the girl again. ✎

CHAPTER FORTY-EIGHT

Food for Savannah

January 1865

That next morning a messenger delivered a letter to Katherine from treasury agent Albert Browne. He wrote that the woman doctor from Beaufort, Mrs. Esther Hill Hawks, had stopped in Savannah on her way to Jacksonville and would be in town for a few hours. If Katherine wanted to meet her, she should come right away to his office at the Bank of Commerce. Katherine immediately dressed and walked to Johnston Square, intrigued by Dr. Hawks and flattered by the attention she was receiving.

Browne greeted her and introduced the two women. Dr. Hawks was as tall as Katherine and looked about twenty years older. Browne asked Katherine to tell Dr. Hawks about her interest in nursing. Katherine sat straight and folded her hands on her lap, wanting to look as professional as possible. She explained her experiences in Savannah, Marietta, and Macon and ended by saying, "I'd like to continue in nursing, but as a woman I'm not sure I'll have the opportunity. Colonel Allen suggested that I consider going to a medical college for women. I didn't even know they existed."

Dr. Hawks looked Katherine straight in the eye, as if trying to gauge the girl's internal fortitude. She said, "There are colleges in Boston, New York, and Philadelphia. Your work during the war will serve you well in your education if you choose this path, but you must be ready to defend your presence. It's a man's profession and you'll be discouraged by most of them at every turn." Hawks opened and closed her fist, as if she were squeezing juice from a lemon. "The meaner ones will try to crush your aspirations. It takes a resolute female to face so much opposition and carry on." Hawks leaned a little closer to Katherine. "I'm not trying to frighten you. I'm telling you this now because you'll have to devote three years to complete your studies. You don't want to waste the time if you aren't willing to put up with the aggravation and insults."

Katherine tried to stay calm in the face of the Northerner's intensity, and held Dr. Hawks's stare. She explained, "I've faced much opposition from male nurses and doctors in some form. It's disappointing, sharing the same mission of helping our boys, and having to deal with their fear that we might do the job just as well, if not better. But I endured it because nothing was more important than healing the sick and injured."

Dr. Hawks reached over and patted Katherine's arm. "Very well put, Miss Downes. I think you understand the challenge you face."

Katherine shifted in her chair. "However, a few men were generous with their time and went out of their way to help me. They taught me most of what I know and I'm forever thankful to them. I have to take advantage of any opportunities I get to learn."

Dr. Hawks smiled at Katherine and said, "I admire your determination. I think you'll do quite well. Are you willing to move to the North?"

Katherine's shoulders slumped ever so slightly. "That's my dilemma, Dr. Hawks. My two sisters and I were orphaned early in the war. A family here took us in and they treat us like their own. Leaving them would be so difficult."

Dr. Hawks replied, "Well, it's no different than daughters going off to college. They return."

A loud knock on the door interrupted them. Browne answered it and Katherine heard the visitor shout, "Mr. Browne! Your men are shipping my cotton to New York. You have no right to do that. I demand that you order them to stop at once."

Katherine looked up and froze. It was Gazaway Lamar. She could see Mr. Browne's face turn deep red.

Browne said, "Mr. Lamar, if you don't mind, I'm in a private meeting."

Lamar's voice rose. "I took the oath and President Lincoln says that I'm entitled to keep all my property except slaves! You're violating his word."

Browne crossed his arms across his chest. "You'll be able to file a claim after the war. Now, please. Take your leave."

Lamar flushed as red as Browne. "Your men have removed all the markings on my bales. It will be almost impossible to prove which of mine have been taken."

Browne took hold of the door, ready to close it in Lamar's face. "I'm done arguing, sir. I repeat, you may file a claim with the government. But make no mistake, we're taking your cotton. I demand that you leave me and my guests in peace."

Gazaway peered into the office and did a double-take. His voice softened. "Miss Downes! I didn't know that you were here. Please excuse my interruption."

Katherine glanced at Dr. Hawks and Mr. Browne, worried about their opinion of her familiarity with the visitor. She said, "Hello, Mr. Lamar. It's good to see you again."

Lamar said, "It's good to see you, too." He then looked at Browne. "I'll take my leave, sir, but you haven't heard the last of me. I will sue you and the government for stealing my cotton. I know my rights under the Constitution." The angry Confederate tipped his hat to Katherine, did an about face, and left.

Browne dropped into his chair and said in disbelief, "Did I hear that correctly? He knows his rights under the Constitution? He did all he could to separate from it."

Dr. Hawks told Katherine that she had enjoyed their chat but had to return to her ship. "Before I leave I'm going to write a reference letter for you. I do hope you find it of use one day. The medical profession needs women like you." Mr. Browne passed her paper, ink, and pen.

Katherine thanked her and Mr. Browne and walked to Forsyth Place to meet the cookie vendors and Pauline. She stopped three times to read the letter. Dr. Hawks said that she believed Katherine to be of the highest character with the ambition, intelligence, and compassion to become a doctor. The lure to pursue her dream was greater than ever, but not greater than her desire to become Mrs. Joseph McBain. Was there any way, she wondered, to accomplish both.

⚬❧⚬

That night at supper Mary reported, "We sold seventy cookies today, our best day ever. Miss Patience said she doesn't have time to make any more than that. And getting wood for the oven is very difficult."

Danny said, "You mean we could have sold seventy if you hadn't eaten five."

Mary raised her chin. "I said I'll pay for them, Danny McBain."

Danny gripped his knife and fork in his fists. "Yes, but at our cost, not at the soldier's price, which we would have gotten if you didn't eat them."

"Truvy said I can eat as many cookies as I wanted," Mary paused to pat her hair, "because my beauty attracts the soldiers."

Danny closed his eyes, shook his head, and groaned, "Oh, brother!"

Katherine said, "Mary, don't you understand that you're in business and you can't be eating the product? It's not fair to your partners."

Mary clasped her hands under her chin and made a pleading face, "But Katherine, they're sooooooo good. You should have tried one when you came by. I could have eaten ten, but I didn't. I should be thanked for not eating more."

McBain asked Katherine, "How did you spend your day?"

Katherine nervously took a mouthful of rice, knowing that Mr. McBain would not be happy with her answer, as he did not know she would soon marry Joseph. She chewed slowly and swallowed. "Treasury agent Browne invited me to his office to meet the woman doctor from Beaufort. Her ship stopped here on the way to Florida."

James raised his eyebrows. "No doubt to talk of the medical college. And?"

Katherine needed to change the subject. "She was friendly and told me of all the challenges facing women who enter the medical profession. But something unsettling happened while I was there. Mr. Lamar walked in and started to argue with Mr. Browne." Katherine described the incident.

McBain shook his head and said, "Mr. Lamar has a short fuse where Yankees are concerned. He's making too many enemies of people who can do him harm. I know his cotton was seized, but so was the cotton of other men. There's nothing he can do about it other than file a claim. He has to learn to accept the Yankees." James paused to sip his wine. Then he asked, "And how about you, Pauline? Did you sketch any portraits today?"

Pauline held up five Yankee dollars. "Yes, sir! Ten."

Katherine relaxed, grateful that she had successfully diverted the conversation.

⌇⌇⌇

Two days later Lilly knocked on the bedroom door after Katherine returned from work. "Mistess Katrin, dat hansome Yankee soljuh at de do'. He wan' tuh see you."

Katherine smiled to herself, happy to see the man who saved her and Pauline. "Thank you, Lilly. Please show him to the garden. I'll be right down."

Ten minutes later Katherine walked down the back stairs. "Captain Bowen! What a pleasant surprise."

Bowen said, "Good evening, Miss Downes. Shall we sit?" They retired to the bench. He said, "I'm leaving tomorrow. I want to say goodbye and wish you and your sisters the best of health and good fortune."

Katherine thought the man truly was a gentleman. "Where are you going?"

"With General Sherman into South Carolina. Our soldiers can't wait. They hold that state responsible for starting this war and are anxious to exact revenge." The captain fiddled with his cap, then looked at Katherine. "May I write to you?"

Katherine didn't think that would be a good idea, considering her feelings for Joseph, but she couldn't refuse an innocent request after all the captain had done for her and Pauline. "Of course. You can reach me here, care of the McBains in Savannah."

Bowen said. "Hopefully, this war will soon end. I'd like to return to the South in peacetime."

The back door opened and Mr. McBain stepped out. Katherine and Bowen stood and she introduced the men. McBain said he was glad to meet the officer, but Katherine noticed that his smile seemed forced, as if invisible fingers were pulling at the corners of his mouth. She said, "Captain Bowen is the officer who rescued Pauline and me from the soldiers. He's leaving tomorrow and is saying goodbye."

McBain's attitude changed. His smile showed teeth and he pumped the Yankee's hand so vigorously that his hair vibrated. "I can't thank you enough, Captain. I trust those soldiers will face justice."

"These things take time, sir. They're in custody. I've submitted my report. The military commission might contact Miss Downes and her sister to testify."

McBain accepted that answer. "I'll leave you and Miss Downes now. Thank you again for coming to her aid."

After McBain left, Bowen said, "He's obviously very fond of you."

Katherine glanced at the house. "He's as close to a father as we've ever had, much more so than our real one. We'd be living in the poor house without him."

The captain half-bowed and said, "I must be going now. Meeting you has brightened my experience here. I do hope you will answer my letters."

Katherine said, "I will, Captain. And thank you again for everything. We'll never forget you. I'll see you to your horse."

They walked to the front of the house. Bowen bid her goodbye and rode off. Katherine waved until he was gone from sight. As she walked through the front gate, two women dressed in black approached. One said, "It's not becoming of a southern girl to consort with the enemy. You should know better."

Katherine recognized them as residents of the neighborhood, though they had never been introduced. She cocked her head and replied, "I don't think it's any business of yours with whom I consort."

The woman nodded, "Oh, but it is, young lady. How many of our sons, brothers, and fathers did that Yankee kill? How many Georgia homes did he vandalize and burn? How many women did he rape? That makes it every Southerner's business."

Katherine closed the gate. "For your information, that Yankee saved my life, and I'll speak to him or any other man if I choose. Good day."

As she climbed the front steps, she heard one of them hiss, "Mr. McBain will hear about this!"

Katherine felt steam rising up from her neckline as she entered the house. It was all she could do to stop herself from telling the two women to go to Hades. As she walked past the family parlor, General Wilbin called her in. Both he and Colonel Simmons greeted her. The general said, "Miss Downes, we're leaving tomorrow. It was a pleasure meeting you. Whatever the future holds, we wish you the best. We've each written a reference letter for you in case you decide to apply to the medical college."

Katherine gazed at the two envelopes that Wilbin placed in her hand. "Thank you so much! It was an honor to have met you." She curtsied and went to her bedroom to read the letters. They made her forget about the nosey women.

⸙

Dante parked the carriage at Johnson Square, unable to get any closer to the City Exchange building with the streets so mobbed. James stepped from the coach and called up, "Stay here, Dante. I'll be back in about an hour."

McBain walked towards the blaring music of the army band playing in front of the Exchange. The excitement had been brewing for weeks, ever since reports filtered back to Savannah of Colonel Allen's efforts. When he arrived in New

York in early January, instead of offering to trade Savannah rice for provisions, he convinced members of the Chamber of Commerce and the Produce Exchange to contribute money to assist the citizens of Savannah, who he claimed had welcomed Sherman's army and were eager to return to the Union fold. The two organizations raised over thirty thousand dollars. Allen then traveled to Boston and made the same appeal, which generated about the same amount. The city of Philadelphia heard of Allen's efforts, rallied to the cause, and collected almost as much. In a matter of weeks close to one hundred thousand dollars for food for the poor of Savannah had been donated. Colonel Allen also convinced shipping companies to transport the goods for free. Towards the end of January the vessels, which carried the representatives from the organizations that had raised the funds, docked in Savannah harbor. Their cargoes were brought to the City Store at Bay and Barnard streets amidst a crowd of cheering locals.

In anticipation of the delivery, the mayor had appointed distribution committees to canvas the wards of the town, identify the families in need, and issue certificates allowing them to obtain seven days rations on a weekly basis. James McBain represented the committee for Pulaski Ward. A jubilant mayor held a public meeting at noon on January 25, to express thanks on behalf of the citizens of the city to the people of New York, Boston, and Philadelphia. Speakers included the mayor, officials from the committees, and Colonel Allen, who arrived on the ship from Boston. The council chamber was packed to overflowing and James was the last person allowed in, while hundreds more thronged Bay and Bull streets.

After the event ended, James fought through the crowd to reach Allen, who pumped his hand. "Mr. McBain, I have fabulous news! I personally delivered the letter to your daughter and your wife was there! She's alive and well!"

McBain grabbed the colonel by the shoulders and gently shook him. "Yes?" Allen nodded. James hugged the man. "Thank you so much, Colonel. Did she say when she's returning?"

"Travel is still somewhat restricted for civilians, but I applied for a pass for her, which I'm certain she'll get. She should be boarding a ship any day now. Here." Allen handed him a letter. "This is for you."

James's heart thumped at the sight of his wife's handwriting. He stuffed it in his jacket pocket, slapped Allen on the back, and thanked him again. Allen said, "Do you mind if I have a word with Miss Downes? I know she's committed to Savannah, but I had supper with the president of the women's medical college and would like to tell her about it, if she should ever change her mind."

McBain, exhilarated at learning of Sarah's safety, said, "I see no reason why not. She's at the Massie School hospital during the day or my house in the evening."

The men shook hands just as Colonel Allen was swallowed up by the crowd. James hurried to the coach to read his wife's letter:

January 15, 1865

My dearest husband:

I read your letter to Amy and I cannot tell you how relieved I am to hear that you, Danny, and the girls are safe and well. Colonel Allen has to leave soon and as I want him to deliver this to you, I have only a few minutes to write.

Rebecca and I were arrested for treason under General Sherman's order and shipped to Indiana. The barbaric conditions and Rebecca's depression from the death of Francis caused her to go insane and stop eating. She died in Indiana a week after we arrived there. I thank God that her nightmare is over.

After burying her in August I took the cars to New York and have been living with Amy and Bob ever since. They are all well. The charges against Bob were dropped and he is in New York, working for the paper, but not covering the war in the field. Jimmy is more adorable than ever.

I meet Emily and Charlotte weekly in a nearby park. The girl is precious. Emily says she's anxious to reunite with Joseph, but when I ask if she'll return to Savannah, she equivocates. I feel there's a wall between us, but she's the mother of Danny and Charlotte and I must find a way to get along with her. I miss Joseph and pray for him daily. I agree that he is better off not fighting. I just hope he gets a fair trial from the Yankees.

I'm thrilled that Katherine and Pauline are safe at home, and I am most anxious to hear more about their trip from Roswell.

Colonel Allen is trying to secure a pass for me to return to Savannah. I hope to have it in a week and will book passage immediately. There is so much to tell you, and so much to hear.

I must close now, my dear husband. With God's help, I'll see you in a few weeks. Please know that you have my love and devotion forever.

Your loving wife, Sarah

James McBain sat back in his seat, closed his eyes, and thanked God for protecting his wife. He prayed that the war's end would bring back all the thousands of people who had left the city so that life could return to the way it was—prosperous, happy, and united.

On January 30, 1865, with passport in hand, Sarah McBain climbed the gangway of a ship bound for Savannah and gave a final wave to Amy, Bob, and Jimmy. After eight months, she was finally going home.

Hercules went to the sergeant in charge of the Union stables at Hilton Head Island and asked for permission to return to Savannah to see his family. The soldier approved. Hercules informed Jehova of his plans, packed his belongings, and caught a ship. After two years and three months, Hercules was returning home.

After failing as a highway robber, Willie Sloan once again needed cash. The remaining ransom money in Confederate dollars that he got from McBain was worthless. He decided to return to his old profession, stealing horses and related equipment. With residents returning to their homes in Savannah, Willie thought the pickings would be as good as ever. He laughed to himself at the thought of stealing from the Yankees. More important to his immediate needs, he knew where fifteen hundred Yankee dollars were hidden. This time nothing would stop him from getting the treasure, even if he had to tear the overseer's house to the ground and kill old man McBain. And he would finally get his revenge on McBain's coachman. He couldn't wait to get back to Savannah.

CHAPTER FORTY-NINE

The Most Beautiful Sight
She Had Ever Seen

January – February 1865

Katherine walked to the foyer of the Massie School when told she had a visitor. She smiled the moment she saw him. "Colonel Allen! Mr. McBain said you were back. Everyone in town is praising your efforts."

Allen bowed. "I'm happy that I could help this loyal town. Come. Let's talk outside." They stepped onto Gordon Street. "My trip paid other dividends, as well. I assume you know I visited Mr. McBain's daughter and found Mrs. McBain there, waiting to return to Savannah."

"Yes! Mr. McBain is so relieved. We all are."

Allen led her across the street into Calhoun Square. "She's a remarkably strong woman considering her years. I told her that you and your sisters were safe in Savannah, which made her very happy, and she sends her love. She should arrive here in a few weeks." Allen paused to tip his hat to two Union officers strolling by. "I know you're reluctant to leave Savannah and Mr. McBain wanted you here as long as Mrs. McBain was missing, so I didn't plan to make any inquiries on your behalf regarding the medical college. But after seeing Mrs. McBain in New York, I had supper with friends, including the president of the New York Medical College for Women. I told her about you and she encourages you to apply for admittance whenever you feel ready. She's confident, based on all I've told her, that you'll have no problem being accepted. In fact, she's particularly interested in having a southern woman attend. The new term starts in a few weeks."

Katherine wanted to tell the colonel that she expected to get engaged to Joseph McBain after his release from prison, but she had to keep it a secret. "Sir, you've been so kind. I'd love to go to the college, but there are so many other issues. I simply can't leave the McBains now. And I have two younger sisters. We'd have no place to live in New York. I have some savings, but I don't know if I could afford the tuition and support the three of us while I attend classes."

Allen laughed. "These are minor issues, Miss Downes. I have an unused floor in my townhouse. You and your sisters would be welcome to stay there until you find other quarters. My wife would love the company. The tuition is minimal and it's only a short walk to the college. And as a student you could find a job in a doctor's office rather easily. But I agree that now is not the time. You must be entirely comfortable with such an important decision and you have reservations. If you should resolve them and still have an interest in a medical career, feel free to write to me and I'll help you then."

Katherine gazed at the fire engine house in the corner of the square as she considered the colonel's words. He made the transition sound so easy. But she was committed to Savannah. "Thank you, sir. I appreciate your generosity. When are you returning to New York?"

"I sail a week from today, next Monday."

"Colonel, please have a safe voyage and thank you for your encouraging words. I'll never forget your willingness to help me."

Allen took her hand in his. "You're most welcome, Miss Downes. You are a special young woman and I wish you the best." He tipped his hat and left. Katherine watched him walk away, wondering how she would have fared in a medical college.

⌘

Sarah stood at the railing and gazed at the Savannah harbor—the cupola of the City Exchange building high on the bluff and the brick warehouses lining River Street. It was the most beautiful sight she had ever seen. Her ship docked and she walked down the gangway, followed by a porter carrying her luggage. They had to avoid teams of negroes pushing large carts piled with bales of cotton to docked ships, all under the supervision of shouting, blue-jacketed soldiers. She looked towards River Street and saw a man in a top hat with flowing silver hair towering above the other people. She trotted, sidestepping the workers, and embraced her husband. "Oh, James, I thought I'd never see you again."

McBain held his wife for a full minute before releasing her. "Welcome back, my dear wife. It's so good to see you again."

Sarah studied his thin but handsome face for several seconds. She asked, "How did you know I'd be on this ship?"

James took her arm and walked towards the coach. "I didn't. I've met every ship from New York and Hilton Head since Colonel Allen told me you'd be returning."

Sarah squeezed her husband's arm tighter. "I had a nice chat with the colonel at Amy's house when he delivered your letter. He told me about having supper with you, and how you aided his efforts to raise food for Savannah." Sarah stopped in her tracks by the coach and shouted, "Dante!" She grasped his arm. "I had heard that you and the girls arrived here safely. I knew you could do it. I had faith in you and you didn't fail me!"

Dante stood straight and puffed out his chest. "Ah done wut you tole me tuh do, Missus. Ah lub dem gu'ls."

James and Sarah entered the cab. She said, "How is Joseph?"

James shrugged. "The Yankees are treating him decently. There's no date for his court martial yet. It may be a while. He's confident he'll be cleared."

Sarah shook her head and said, "I was devastated to hear about Chloe. What happened?" James told her all he knew.

He said, "I'm so sorry about Rebecca. It sounds as if she suffered unbearably."

Sarah rested her head on James's shoulder. "Yes. After the war I'll have to return to Roswell and close her affairs. I also have to notify her boys." She wanted to talk about happier topics. "What's this about Danny in the cookie business?"

James laughed. "You won't believe it. He's so proud of all they've accomplished. Mary seems to have a natural inclination for business. You must hear about it from them. They'll talk your ear off. Katherine will tell you about her trip, but she must do it without the children around. They went through hell. My words won't do it justice."

Sarah sat up. "When Colonel Allen came to Amy's house, he couldn't stop praising Katherine. He said he suggested to her that she consider attending a women's medical college in New York."

James swiped at some cat hairs on his jacket sleeve. "Yes, all the men that night were taken by her. She was flattered by their compliments and initially showed some interest, but I know she doesn't want to leave here. This is her home."

The carriage stopped and Dante opened the door. Sarah stepped down and asked, "Has Isetta had the baby yet?"

Dante flashed all his teeth. "Yessum, Missus. Li'l 'Zekiel, he muh boy!"

Sarah said, "I'm so happy for you. You must bring him here for me to see."

Dante nodded. "Yessum. Ah sholy do dat."

James took Sarah's arm and led her into the house. She stopped and looked around, savoring every square inch. She closed her eyes and inhaled, smelling freshly baked cornbread. The servants stepped into the hallway to greet her. During her five months in New York, the few Northerners with whom she had conversations had sneered at her when she explained that she loved her negroes and thought of them as part of her family. But seeing them again after so many months, she never felt that was truer.

Sarah and James sat in his study. He asked about the family in New York. She glanced at the daguerreotype of her son and daughter on the side table and replied, "Amy, Bob, and Jimmy are well. I was fortunate to be able to spend so much time with them. Amy misses Savannah, but she loves Bob and Jimmy and is truly happy. She'll be happier when she can visit us freely. Jimmy is almost four years old. It's hard to believe. He sings psalms in church. Charlotte is such an adorable little lady. I wrote you that I sense a lack of commitment on Emily's part to return to Savannah after the war. I had supper at her house one night. Her parents strained to be civil. We talked mostly about Danny, a safe subject. They weren't interested in how I got from Georgia to New York. I couldn't wait to leave them. I fear Emily and Joseph will never resolve their differences, and it breaks my heart to think that we may never see Charlotte again. When I left New York, I cried the hardest saying goodbye to her. I'll have to lie to Danny when he asks when his mother and sister are coming home. Speaking of Danny, where is everyone?"

James closed his eyes and tried to clear the news of Emily and Charlotte from his mind. "Katherine works at a Yankee hospital in the Massie School. Danny, Mary, and Truvy are hard at work, selling cookies somewhere in town."

Sarah stood and stretched. "I can't wait to see them, dear. But now I'd like to go upstairs and rest a bit. I'm very tired from the trip."

"Of course. They'll be home soon." James got up and escorted her upstairs.

Sarah woke up later with someone shaking her arm. She saw her grandson kneeling beside her on the bed. "Danny!"

"Grandma! You're home. Grandpa said not to wake you, but I couldn't wait."

Sarah sat up and hugged the boy. "Danny, I think you've doubled in size."

Danny grinned. "Thanks, Grandma. I'm a businessman now, just like Pa and Grandpa."

Sarah released the boy and tousled his hair. "I heard. I want you to tell me all about it over supper."

Danny flopped back on the bed. "Did you see Ma and Charlotte when you were in New York?"

"Yes. They both miss you and can't wait to see you." Danny smiled and clapped his hands. Sarah kissed his forehead and said, "Now, get ready for supper and I'll see you downstairs."

Sarah squealed when she entered the dining room and saw the sisters. James stood by patiently as she hugged each one. Then he held the chair for his wife, relieving William of that duty. Over the meal, Sarah talked about her time in New York. She knew that her journey from Roswell to Indiana was too dark for the children and would tell James and Katherine about it at another time.

Sarah asked Danny and Mary about their cookie business. Both talked over each other to answer the question until Sarah said, "One at a time, please. Mary, you go first." Danny scrunched up his lips and sat on his hands.

Mary smirked at Danny. Then she said, "I gave a piece of my cookie, which Miss Patience baked, to a soldier on the street. I didn't want to give him any—I wanted it all for myself—but something made me break off a chunk. He ate it and he smiled like he was the happiest man on earth. That's when I thought that we could sell cookies to the soldiers. We couldn't have done it without Miss Patience, or Grandpa, who sold us the ingredients. And Danny's been a big help to me."

Danny almost levitated off his chair. "A big help? I'm a partner. I do as much as you do! And I eat less than you."

Katherine scolded, "Marrreee! Don't be disrespectful of Danny."

Mary frowned. "I'm trying to be nice to Danny."

Danny glared at Mary. "Nice? I do all the bookkeeping and help sell to the soldiers and carry things to the park." He looked at his grandma. "If I wasn't there, Mary would eat every cookie by herself and we wouldn't make any money."

James clapped his hands once to get the youngsters' attention. "You two haven't argued for weeks and now you're doing it on your grandmother's first night home. I'm sure she'd rather not hear it. Now Mary, let Danny talk."

The cookie sellers finished their stories without incident. Sarah told them how proud they made her feel. The two finally grinned at each other.

James asked Pauline to tell Mrs. McBain about her portrait business. As the girl spoke, Sarah couldn't help but think how she had changed. She lacked some of that sparkle of youth in her eyes. She didn't even offer to say a pre-supper prayer. Sarah had to have a talk with Katherine and learn of their trip from Roswell.

Pauline explained sketching the faces of soldiers. She showed some excitement for the first time in the evening when she boasted of earning ten dollars in one day. Sarah went to the girl, gave her an extra long hug, and said she loved her.

Pauline seemed to soften a bit. "Thank you, Mrs. McBain. I love you, too."

Sarah sat and asked James, "What's happening with the Yankees?"

James took a long sip of wine and explained, "I must admit, General Geary has been quite fair. The town is cleaner and safer now than since the start of the war, and the soldiers have been well behaved. Our mayor and city council still manage city affairs. Commerce is slow, but it should improve once the river is completely cleared and trade picks up. We're fortunate. We got off easy compared to Atlanta."

Sarah narrowed her eyes. "And Roswell."

James nodded. "Yes, and Roswell." He rested his elbows on the table. "I was at the Heritage yesterday. The Yankees are leaving for good in two days—early Saturday morning. Then it's ours again. Our negroes are free and I have to pay those who remain, but it shouldn't take much time to get things in order. Roman is running the operations for now and is doing a commendable job."

Sarah glanced at the dining room doors to see if any of the negroes were lurking. "What about the Heritage house servants?"

"The Yankees have been employing all of them since they occupied the place. They seem happy to be making some money."

Sarah replied, "I'll wager that after being a home to soldiers for six weeks, the house is a shambles. Tomorrow I hope to visit Joseph, but Saturday I'll go out and get the people started cleaning up the place. James, will you join me?"

He shook his head. "I can't. I have a meeting with the Union quartermaster about supplying bricks and lumber to repair Fort Pulaski. If I'm successful, it will keep us running at full capacity for at least a year."

Sarah looked at the others. "Who wants to go to the Heritage with me on

Saturday?"

Danny pleaded, "Grandma, that's our best day for selling cookies."

Sarah said, "We'll be back in the early afternoon. You can sell cookies then."

Danny reluctantly said, "Well, I guess so."

Pauline and Mary raised their hands. Katherine said, "I guess we'll all join you."

Sarah smiled and waited as William appeared and filled her and James's wine glasses. "Good. Now, Danny, Pauline, and Mary, I want you to go to bed so I can talk with Katherine and Grandpa."

Pauline glanced at Katherine, who said to Mrs. McBain, "I think Pauline should join us. She's old enough. Many of the experiences are best told by her." Sarah agreed.

That night, after hearing of the sisters' journey, Sarah fell asleep weeping.

☙

The next day after school, the cookie sellers set up their blanket on the Strand. No one using the stairs to or from River Street could evade Mary. Late in the afternoon, with only three unsold cookies, she leaned over the railing and saw a black man with one arm climb the stairs. When he reached the top, she pounced with her standard pitch. "Hello, mister. I'm Mary. Do you want to buy a fresh cookie? They're the best in Savannah." The man stared at her while he caught his breath. He hadn't seen many pure redheads. "They're only twenty-five cents each. I'll make a deal and give you three for seventy cents. Don't walk away and regret it later."

Mary stopped talking when Truvy and Danny ran past her and hugged the man. Danny shouted, "Hercules, you're home!"

Truvy wrapped his arms around the man's waist and said, "We missed you, Mr. Hercules. Are you here for good?"

Hercules smiled and rubbed Truvy's head. "Maybe. What are you two doing?"

Truvy pointed to the blanket spread on the grass. "Selling cookies, mostly to soldiers. Ma bakes them for us every day."

Hercules laughed. "Very smart." Hercules nodded at Mary. "Who's your friend?"

Danny explained, "This is Mary. She and her two sisters live with us. They have for a few years now, soon after you left."

Truvy stared at Hercules's empty sleeve tucked in his pants and said, "Master Joseph told us that you'd been shot and hurt bad."

Hercules squeezed the boy's shoulder. "It's all right, Truvy. I've learned to get along. Let's go see your ma. Danny, tell your grandpa I'm in town and I'll come by tomorrow morning to see him."

"I sure will, Hercules. And thank you for saving me. I missed you."

Hercules patted Danny on the shoulder and he and Truvy walked away. Mary stared at the two and asked Danny, "Who's that man?"

Danny shoved his hands in his pockets and said, "He's been our coachman forever. He saved my life. My whole family loves him. Come on. Let's sell the rest of the cookies and go home. Grandpa will be happy to hear he's back."

⚜

Truvy opened the door and called out, "Hey, Ma. I have a surprise."

Patience stepped into the family room, dropped the towel she was holding, and ran to Hercules. She held him and he put his one arm around her. He said, "Let's sit."

They retired to the sofa as four-year-old Gully walked out of the bedroom. Truvy lifted his little brother and sat on a chair holding him on his lap.

Patience said, "Master Joseph told me you got shot on St. Simon's Island and were taken to Hilton Head by the Yankees. He said they were keeping you there."

Hercules realized that Joseph didn't want to tell the other negroes that it was his decision to stay on Hilton Head. This provided a cover for him, as he had promised Patience that he would never leave her and the boys. Maybe one day he would tell her the truth, but this was not the time. "The Yankees did help me recover from the injury and gave me work at the stables. Once Savannah fell I came back as soon as I could. And now we're free, just like we wanted."

Patience thought how difficult it must have been for Hercules to adjust to life with one arm. She stroked his back. "Thank God you're here. I've been praying for you. Have you thought about what we should do—where we should go?"

He shrugged. "Where else can we go? You and the McBains are the closest things to family I got. And we need to work. We can get that here better than anywhere. I always said I'd be happy to work for Massa as a free man."

"Will he hire you?"

"I don't know. I'll see him in the morning. Joseph left me a letter saying I could come back anytime. How is he?"

Truvy broke in. "He was captured by the Yankees. He's in the Savannah jail. But Danny says he's not hurt or anything."

Patience added, "Master McBain said that Joseph will transfer title of the house to me once he's out of prison."

Hercules said, "That's good. What about your parents? Are they staying?"

"They still want to work for Master Low. They've been with him their entire lives. I assume he'll take care of them. He always has."

Hercules put his arm around Patience. "Let's see what Massa has to say." He looked at the boys. "Truvy, can you take Gully for a walk and tell Massa McBain that I'd like to see him tomorrow morning?"

Truvy said, "You already asked Danny to tell him."

"You ask him, too, in case Danny forgets."

"Ma, can we stay and play with Danny and Mary?"

Patience smiled and said, "Yes. Of course."

Truvy lifted his brother off his lap, took him by the hand, and left the house.

Hercules waited for the door to close before asking Patience, "Danny said Massa took in three orphan girls?"

Patience laughed. "That was two years ago. Lilly tells me Mrs. McBain had to convince Massa to take them in after their boarding house burned. Now he loves them like his own. The oldest is twenty now and quite beautiful. The folks at the McBain house are wondering when Joseph is going to grow eyes for her, if he hasn't already. Pauline is fifteen and very pretty. She's an artist. Then there's Mary. She's eight, almost Truvy and Danny's age. She makes everyone laugh, whether she means to or not. She came up with the idea of selling cookies to the Yankees, and the three of them make money every day—good money, too—and they pay me two dollars to bake for them. That's more than I get from Master Hartridge."

Hercules laughed and said, "Missus always wanted a bigger family." They looked at each other without speaking. Hercules ran his finger over her lips and said, "It's been a long time." She nodded. He took her hand and led her to the bedroom.

❧

On Friday, as Hercules and Patience were reuniting, Willie told the Yankee guard at the White Bluff Road post that he was coming home to Savannah to sign the oath of allegiance. He claimed that he never wanted the war in the first place, refused to serve in the rebel army, and celebrated when he heard the news of the fall of Savannah. The guard told him to get off his horse. He checked Willie's passport, searched his saddle bags, bed roll, and carpetbag, and let him through. He said nothing of Willie's revolver or the knife hanging from his belt. Willie went to the City Exchange, signed the oath of allegiance, and took a room at Benoist's boarding house. It was late afternoon and he was anxious to get started.

He decided to ride to the Heritage first, but was turned back at the Augusta Road guard post, where he was told that he couldn't go to the plantation without a pass until the next day, after the soldiers evacuated. Willie returned to town and rode by the McBain house on Pulaski Square a few times, but didn't see the coachman. He went to the boarding house and lay on his bed. He would take care of his business once and for all the next day—find the cash and kill the coachman and anyone else who got in his way.

For the first time in ages, Willie fell asleep with a smile on his face.

❧

The next morning, as they rode to the plantation, Danny and Mary talked more about selling cookies. Sarah looked at them in a new light. They were aware of many of the issues, though in the most basic terms, from purchasing, baking, finding customers, and bookkeeping. She thought Mary must have been the driving force as Danny had never shown an interest for business, though few nine-year-olds did. Whatever caused it, Sarah was delighted to see this new dimension in her grandson's personality.

Sarah talked about New York City, especially Central Park, as big as Savannah itself, with open fields, walking paths, lakes, and trees. Danny asked if she went to the park with his sister and mother. Sarah said she did, and described how much Charlotte loved it. Sarah also told him how badly his mother missed him, which caused Katherine to start chewing on her lip, as it reminded her of the possibility that Joseph might reunite with his wife when he saw her again.

Dante parked in front of the big house and everyone exited the cab. Sarah announced, "Katherine and I are going inside. Danny, Pauline, and Mary, you can go to the river if you'd like. We'll be here for about two hours. I want everyone back by then for dinner." She told Dante, "Take the coach to the stables and water the horses."

Dante said, "Yessum," and drove off.

The servants were lined up in the hall, all smiles, and greeted the women one by one. Sarah hugged each of them. Katherine squeezed their hands. Then Sarah addressed them. "I'm so glad to be back and with you all again. I understand we had some visitors, and you took excellent care of them." The servants laughed. Sarah asked the head female house servant, "When did the soldiers leave, Ophelia?"

"Fus' ting dis mawnin', Missus, at sunup. Dey act like gemmen, many ub dem, but dey make uh mess, Lawd hab mussy, an' move de funachuh all obuh de place."

Sarah said, "Ophelia, come with Miss Katherine and me. We're going to inspect every room, closet, and hall, and we'll decide how to get the house back in shape. In the meantime, the rest of you can start cleaning up. You know what to do."

Ophelia said, "Yessum. Dey be no sign ub no soljuh by dis ebnin', Missus.

Dante drove to the stables, anxious to see if his revolver was still there. He climbed up a ladder to the rafters and saw the box in which he had stored the weapon after shooting Sam. He took it down, opened it, and inspected the revolver's chambers. Three were still loaded with percussion caps on the nipples, just as he had left them. He didn't know if the powder was still dry, but he didn't care as he planned to sell the gun in town, hopefully for more than the fifty dollars he had paid for it. There were so many things he could buy for Isetta and Zekiel. He hid the box on the shelf under the driver's bench.

⁂

Soon after Sarah left for the Heritage, Hercules walked up the driveway to the back of the Pulaski Square house, where the McBain slaves surrounded him and stared at his empty sleeve. They wanted to hear about his fight to rescue Danny and his stay at Hilton Head. He didn't know what they had learned in his absence and decided to speak to Massa before revealing anything. William took Hercules to McBain, who stood, shook his hand, and greeted him like a long-lost friend. "Hercules, thank God you're back." James studied the man. There was more grey sprinkled in the coachman's hair, and more lines on the face, but there was still that air of dignity in his raised chin. McBain had been bitterly disappointed when he learned that Hercules had chosen the Yankees, but he wanted, even needed, him back. "I can't thank you enough for protecting Danny. Please sit. You must tell me about Hilton Head."

Hercules described the past two years with the exception of his encounter with Kitt. He claimed that God had told him to stay with the Yankees. He revealed that he worked at the soldiers' corral and was able to perform almost all the functions of a stableman and coachman, although just a little slower.

McBain nodded slowly as Hercules spoke, impressed by the man's ability to overcome the loss of an arm. He said, "Hercules, Joseph told you that you could return here anytime and we would take care of you. That offer still stands. Come back. This is your home."

"I want to come back, sir, as your coachman."

McBain, who had doubted if Hercules's would return, exhaled in relief. "I'm glad to hear that, Hercules. But I do have a favor to ask. Mr. Donnelly was drafted last summer and Roman runs things when I'm not there. Dante has been my coachman for the past month, but I plan to make him my cook in a few weeks. I'd like you to manage the Heritage until I can get Mr. Donnelly back. It shouldn't take long. I'll pay you thirty dollars a month plus full rations. You can live at the overseer's house."

Hercules considered the offer. He wanted to live with Patience, but the money was good, and the job wouldn't last long. "As long as it's not more than a month or two, sir, I'll do it."

McBain stood shook his hand. "You have my word. Do you need anything now?"

Hercules said, "Can I take one of the horses and ride out to the plantation? I'd like to say hello to the folks and see how things are."

"Go right ahead. Barney will help you. You might see Mrs. McBain there. She left a short while ago. I have an appointment in town. I'll see you later."

Hercules went to the stables, already feeling better about being back.

James McBain sat at his desk, jubilant at seeing his coachman back home. He took care of administrative matters feeling quite relaxed. He even whistled a tune. An hour later he dropped his pen and froze in his seat. Hercules would soon run into Katherine at the Heritage and recognize her as the girl responsible for his arrest. There would be hell to pay. James put his face in his hands and felt a headache coming on.

Willie woke up as he had gone to sleep—with a smile on his face. He had waited a few years for this day. After breakfast, he rode to Pulaski Square, but didn't see the coachman around. He did see another black boy in the driveway and rode up to him. He asked, "Excuse me, boy. Is old man McBain here?"

Barney answered, "No, suh. He gwine tuh town."

"What about Hercules, the coachman?"

"No suh. He jes' leab fuh de plantation."

Willie gave a mock salute and headed for the Heritage. Things were progressing right on plan.

CHAPTER FIFTY

∞

Settling Old Scores
February 4, 1865

Hercules rode along the avenue of oaks and through the Quarter. He smiled at the children playing in the road and waved to the old folks who looked after them until the workers returned at one o'clock—quitting time on Saturday. He arrived at the overseer's house, across the avenue from the hospital. He climbed the three steps to the front porch, which was littered with three old chairs, a few empty cans with brown slime at the bottom, several segar butts, and a single boot.

Hercules opened the door and called "Hello," knowing that no one lived there. The large front room looked abandoned—no items of a personal nature lying about, with a worn, stained, two-seat sofa, an upholstered chair, and a dining table with five wooden chairs around it. He gave a thorough search to the first floor, peering in each room and even walking through the weed-filled vegetable garden. Seeing no signs of recent activity, he climbed the stairs to the top floor and inspected each of the smaller bedrooms, which were all barren except for bed frames and mattresses. Just to be sure, he got on his knees and looked under each one, but saw nothing but dust balls.

Hercules took deeper breaths as he stepped into the master bedroom, where he had felt the loose bricks over the fireplace two years earlier, but couldn't remove them because Mr. Donnelly was with him. The bed, a small dresser, table, and chair were the only furnishings. He approached the fireplace and started tapping bricks over the mantel until one moved. He slid it out as well as the two underneath it, reached in with a flattened palm, and wiggled his fingers. One by one he pulled out three wads of United States greenbacks tied in rolls. He murmured, "Good Lord."

He sat at the table. Using his right hand and teeth, he untied one of the wads, spread it out, and counted five hundred Yankee dollars. Hercules froze when he thought he heard a noise downstairs. He closed his eyes and concentrated, but detected nothing more. He then untied the two other rolls and thumbed through the bills. Fifteen hundred greenbacks in all! A small fortune. No wonder Willie wanted to get into the house so badly. Hercules carefully retied the rolls, shoved them into his trouser pocket, replaced the bricks, and tiptoed downstairs. He reached the main floor, turned towards the front of the house, and faced a gun pointed at his chest.

"Well, what do you know? It's my old friend Hercules. I hoped that was you riding ahead of me coming out here." Hercules cursed under his breath as he glared at the man. Willie looked him over. "Seems like you had an accident." Hercules didn't respond. Willie also saw the bulge in his pants pocket. He motioned with his gun, "Step over to the table and empty that pocket. If you don't, I'll kill you." Hercules did as he was told.

Willie's eyes blossomed like sunflowers at the sight of the cash, which he quickly scooped up. "You knew all along where that money was hidden, didn't you? Now, I want you to lie flat on your stomach by the wall." When Hercules was prone, Willie pulled his knife, cut a strip of cloth from the upholstered chair, holstered his gun, and quickly tied Hercules's ankles together. He pulled his revolver and said, "Now, roll over and sit against the wall." Willie stood five feet from him. "We have some unfinished business. Remember, you wondered in front of all your nigger friends if I had any balls left? Well, you're about to find out."

As Sarah gave instructions to the servants about restoring the house, the Heritage butler entered the parlor and said, "Missus, Camellia at de hospital say dat a white man jes' walk intuh de obuhsuh's house. Twasn't Massa Donly. Dey two hosses outside."

Sarah looked at Katherine. "Who in the world could it be? No one comes here without an invitation. Let's walk over." As they passed through the front gate, Danny and Mary came up. Sarah asked, "Where's Pauline?"

Danny answered, "She's coming. She runs fast but walks slow." Katherine laughed at the accurate observation.

Sarah said, "We're going to the overseer's house. We'll be right back."

Danny said, "We'll go with you."

As they started to walk over, Mary grabbed Danny's hand, but he pulled it away.

Hercules scanned the room, searching for some way to escape, but his only chance was to lunge at Willie before the man could fire a shot. Willie noticed Hercules's roving eyes. "You got no way out, boy, so look at me. I want you to see the ball as it leaves the barrel before it smashes into your head, right where you shot Sam."

Hercules looked at the gun as his mind raced for a way out.

As they approached the overseer's house, Sarah recognized one of the two horses as her husband's and relaxed. Danny, Mary, Katherine, followed her in the door as she called out, "Hello?" In the dim light, Sarah saw a stranger with a gun in his hand and Hercules sitting against the wall. She froze. Willie kept the gun on Hercules, dashed to the intruders, and shoved them into the room, shouting, "Get in here, all of you, or I'll kill the old lady!" He pushed them towards Hercules. "Sit on the floor next to the nigger."

Sarah asked, "Who are you?"

Willie barked, "Move it!" Katherine's heart stopped.

Mary immediately started to bawl. Katherine hugged her sister and said softly, "It's all right." She sat next to Hercules with Mary at her other side. Sarah sat next to the girls and Danny next to his grandma.

Willie's jaw dropped. "Whoa! Penny Savannah! What are you doing here?"

"Not to see you, Willie."

Sarah said, "So this is Willie."

Willie laughed. "Guess I'm real famous around here. And you must be Granny McBain. Now keep your mouth shut." He looked at Katherine. "Penny, you show up at the damnedest places. I'm about to kill my friend Hercules, and while I'm at it, I'm going to kill you, too, for what you did outside Macon."

Mary howled louder, her open mouth taking up most of her face. Hercules glared at Katherine and said, "You! You accused me of attacking you. You sent me to jail!"

Sarah leaned forward and spoke past Katherine. "Hercules, Willie paid her to do it. Willie put you in jail."

Willie bellowed gleefully at the negro's discovery of the truth. Hercules asked Sarah, "What's she doing here?"

"We took in Katherine and her sisters. They're orphans."

Hercules looked at Mary and said, "She's the sister of the cookie girl?"

Willie broke in. "Shut up, all of you. I thought your name was Penny. Did you tell Mrs. McBain how we met—when you stole from the drunk at the hotel? I suppose I made you do that, too."

Katherine's face turned beet red. "Damn you!"

Willie smiled. "You have a fresh mouth, Penny, or Katherine, whoever you are." He turned to Danny. "Look at this! It's young Danny. I see you made it home safely on the train. You were a good boy then, and I want you to be a good boy now. And tell your little girlfriend to stop crying, fer Chrissake."

Danny shouted, "She's not my girlfriend."

Mary yelled through her tears, "I am, too!"

"You are not!"

"QUIET! Jesus, Danny, you just can't shut up. There's only one thing I have left to do before I leave. Prepare to die, Hercules. You too, Penny." He took a step forward and aimed his gun at Hercules's chest.

Hercules drew his knees up, ready to spring to save his life.

The butler told Pauline that Missus and the others had left minutes ago for the overseer's house. She went to join them and passed Dante, who had just parked the carriage in front of the big house. Dante asked her if she wanted a ride, but she declined. He leaned back, propped up his feet, and watched Pauline walk up the avenue of oaks.

As Pauline approached the overseer's house, she heard Mary crying at the top of her lungs. Then she heard a man shouting at Danny and became frightened. She tiptoed onto the porch and peeked through the window. A man was pointing a gun at her sisters, Danny, Mrs. McBain, and a negro, who were all sitting on the floor. The man took a step towards the group and steadied his gun. Pauline's legs started to wobble. She spotted a can next to her, grabbed it, opened the door, flung it at the gunman, and collapsed.

Willie turned towards the door, ducked to avoid the object hurled at him, and fired his gun. Danny, Mary, Sarah, and Katherine all screamed and lay flat on the floor. Hercules pushed himself up and took one hop towards Willie, who turned back and fired at the negro. Hercules yelled in pain as he barreled into Willie, causing both men to hit the floor. Hercules rolled on his back and clutched the left side of his chest. Willie straddled Hercules, with his back turned to the others. He punched Hercules in the face with his left hand, cocked the gun, and pointed it between Hercules's eyes.

Danny leaped to his feet, ran to Willie, and grabbed his arm, but Willie back-handed the boy with his gun hand so hard that he knocked him halfway across the room. Danny sat on his rump as blood trickled from his nose and his eyes rolled around in his head. Sarah crawled over and held him.

Hercules grabbed Willie's right wrist and pushed the gun away, leaving him defenseless against the man's blows. Willie kept pummeling the negro in the face with his left hand. Hercules's grip began to weaken. Willie strained to stick the gun in Hercules's eye.

Katherine crawled on her hands and knees to push Willie off and spotted the knife on his belt. She pulled it from the sheath, raised the blade over her head, and plunged it into Willie's back. He jerked up and screamed as the gun blasted, splintering the floor next to Hercules's head. Katherine stood and dashed to the other side of the table to hide.

Willie struggled to his feet, his teeth bared in pain, holding the gun in one hand while trying to reach for the knife with the other. His eyes met Katherine's and he fired just as she dove behind a chair. Willie staggered backwards and nearly tripped over Mary. He picked up the little girl, held her in one arm, and pressed the gun to her temple. Katherine rose to her knees and peered over the dining table.

Willie gasped, as if out of breath, "Your sister dies for that, Penny."

Katherine stood and screamed. "NO! LEAVE HER ALONE! SHE'S DONE NOTHING TO YOU!" and slowly stepped towards Willie. She saw Willie pull the hammer back with his thumb, and heard it click to full cock.

Willie backed out of the house with Mary squirming in his grip. Katherine and Sarah followed. He tried to speak but coughed, spraying blood on Mary's dress. He finally gurgled, "Say goodbye to little sis."

Dante whipped the horses the moment he saw Pauline throw something into the overseer's house, and reached for his revolver when he heard the first of two gunshots. As he pulled up, a man with a huge dark blotch on his shirt, carrying Mary, backed out of the front door, with Mrs. McBain and Katherine following him. He heard Katherine scream, "Willie, put her down! Just leave. We won't follow you."

Dante, realizing who the man was, jumped off the coach, and ran to Willie, who stood at the top of the stairs with his back to him. Dante ascended one stair, put the barrel an inch from the back of the man's head, whispered, "Dis fuh Andrew," and prayed that the gunpowder was still dry. BAMMMM!

Willie was dead before he hit the ground. Mary, splattered with blood, sprawled on top of him at the bottom of the stairs.

Katherine picked up Mary and fanned her little sister with her bonnet.

Mary opened her eyes, rested her head on Katherine's shoulder, and sobbed. Katherine told her, "You're safe, dear sister."

Sarah stared at Willie's body and said, "Dante, I won't ask where you got that gun, but thank you."

Danny called from the door, "Grandma, come quick! Hercules isn't moving."

Katherine handed Mary to a revived Pauline and ran inside with Sarah and Dante. Hercules lay on his back. Blood ran from his nose and eyebrow and dripped on the floor. Katherine knelt next to him, tore away his shirt, and saw the bullet wound by his armpit. Katherine and Dante gently pulled Hercules by his feet to the front door so she could see the injury in the daylight. Sarah told Dante to get clean towels, rags, and a basin of water from the hospital. Katherine pressed gently around the torn flesh. Hercules moaned. She saw one hole above the nipple and another below the armpit and breathed easy realizing that the ball had passed through him without breaking any bones. With her fingers, she picked out the pieces of clothing in the wound. When Dante returned, she washed the gashes, covered them with a rag, and tied a towel around Hercules's chest. She took another rag, wet it, wiped the blood from Hercules's face, and held the cloth gently over his nose. His eyelids fluttered. She said, "Willie's dead. You're going to be all right."

Hercules blinked his swollen, bloodshot eyes and said, "Money. Willie's pocket."

Sarah said, "I'll look. Then we need to get Hercules to a doctor in town." She went outside and saw Pauline holding Mary, Danny pressing a kerchief over his nose, and Dante gesturing wildly as he talked to a group of workers who had just returned from the clay pits. Sarah knelt next to Willie and removed the cash.

She said, "Dante, we have to bring Hercules to town. Have some of the men carry him to the coach." She stood and held out her hand. "I'll take the gun."

Dante bowed his head and handed over the weapon. Then he and three other men moved Hercules to one of the padded bench seats inside the coach. Katherine, Mary, and Sarah sat opposite him while Danny and Pauline shared the driver's bench with Dante.

Sarah stuck her head out the window and said to Roman, "Tell the folks in the house that we had to leave. I'll return in a few days."

Roman pointed to Willie. "Wut 'bout de body?"

Sarah closed her eyes. Her first thought was to bury him somewhere or send him through the lumber mill. "Get two blankets from the hospital. Wrap him in one and tie him to the top of the coach. Give me the other. Please hurry."

Ten minutes later they were on their way. While Sarah tugged the blanket around Mary so the traumatized girl wouldn't have to see Willie's blood on her dress, Katherine concentrated on Hercules, gently holding the damp rag on his eyes and nose until the bleeding stopped. During the ride, Sarah whispered to Katherine, "I hope you don't mind me asking, but why did Willie call you Penny Savannah?"

Katherine said, "It's a name from the past, Mrs. McBain. I'd like to keep it there."

Sarah nodded. "I understand."

When they arrived at the negro hospital on the east side of Forsyth Place, two orderlies carried Hercules to a bed. Sarah and Katherine followed them in. Sarah told the doctor that Hercules had been shot and punched repeatedly to the head and to spare no expense in tending to him.

The doctor inspected the wrapping and said, "The wound looks clean and the bleeding has stopped. Who administered to him?"

Katherine said, "I did, sir."

"Nicely done," the doctor said. "What about the ball?"

"It passed through him. I didn't detect any broken bones. I cleaned out the other debris. I think he needs a poultice."

The doctor nodded his approval. "I'll apply one and bandage him up. I'm concerned about the beating he took to the head. He should recover but he needs to rest. You may visit him in the morning."

The women left the hospital and Dante drove to the police station, where Sarah described the shooting of Willie to Chief Goodwin. Two deputies removed the body and the family finally returned to Pulaski Square.

Danny, Pauline, and Mary ran to their rooms. Sarah told Katherine, "Look after your sisters and Danny. I'll come upstairs in a few minutes."

Sarah walked into James's study, collapsed on the sofa, and said, "Willie's dead."

James bolted up in his chair. "What?"

"Willie's dead."

James moved next to her and held her hand. "How? When?"

Sarah recounted the day. "Danny, Pauline, and Katherine saved Hercules without a second to spare. Dante shot Willie and saved Mary."

So many questions flashed in James's mind that he didn't know which to ask first. He finally uttered, "Da . . . Da . . . Dante has a gun?"

Sarah said, "Had a gun." She placed it on the table in front of the sofa.

James stared at it for a few seconds as if it were a cottonmouth. He went to the liquor cabinet. "I need a drink! Let's call Danny and the girls."

Sarah said, "James, please sit." She waited until he poured himself a brandy and returned to the sofa. "They need to rest. They're all in a state of shock, and I feel a bit unsteady, too. We have a few matters to discuss. We learned why Willie was so intent on searching the overseer's house." She reached into her purse and placed the greenbacks between them. "Apparently, this was from their heists. Sam must have hid it in the house and died before he had a chance to remove it or tell Willie or Harold where it was."

James counted it. "Good Lord! Fifteen hundred Yankee dollars! What do we do with it? It's not ours."

Sarah said, "We don't know whose it is and we'll never learn. I suggest splitting it among Hercules, Dante, and Katherine."

James stared at the wads. "I guess I can't think of a better distribution. Where is Dante? I have to thank him."

"He went to tell Patience about Hercules. Speaking of Dante, the gun he used to shoot Willie—he says he bought it years ago to avenge Andrew's murder. My guess is that he probably used it to kill Sam, too. He told me he wants to sell it. I suggest you buy it from him and forget this entire episode."

James sat back and looked up in thought. He was shocked that one of his men would do something as illegal and dangerous as to buy a gun with the intent to kill someone—even if he was a criminal. "Sarah. I can't just let it go at that."

Sarah reached over and took his hand. "Yes, you can. He killed Sam and Willie and saved Mary. And he delivered Katherine and Pauline. What more could you ask of him? Buy that gun and let's be done with it."

James sighed. "All right. There's not much I could do about it now, anyway, other than send him away, which I won't do."

Sarah stood. "Good. I'm going to tend to Danny and the girls and get some rest. We'll see you at supper." She took a sip of his brandy and left.

◈

Four hours later Sarah led Danny and the sisters into the family parlor. James stood with his arms outspread and declared, "My company of heroes!" He stooped to inspect Danny's red nose and said, "I heard you helped save Hercules. I'm very proud of you." James rubbed the boy's hair and hugged him.

A pale Danny said, "Thank you, Grandpa."

James hugged Pauline and picked up Mary in his arms. He kissed her on the forehead and beamed, "I heard about your bravery, young lady." She rubbed her red eyes with her knuckles, still too upset to speak, and buried her face in his shoulder. James kissed the sad girl again and put her down. He held Katherine's hands in his. "My dear girl, yet again I'm so grateful to you." He then announced, "This calls for a celebration."

James took out a bottle of Madeira and three glasses. He poured two of them half-full and one with a few drops. He handed that one to Katherine and said, "You must try some in honor of the occasion. A small amount won't turn you into a drunkard." He, Sarah, and Katherine raised their glasses and drank. Katherine smacked her lips and said, "Oh, that's good! Could I have a little more?"

Everyone but Mary laughed. James poured more for Katherine and the adults clinked glasses. James toasted each one of them, taking a healthy swallow each time. Sarah saw color in his face that she hadn't seen in years.

The family filed into the dining room. William, Lilly, and Dolly greeted them with broad smiles. Lilly said, "Deese McBain gu'ls fuh suhtin." Katherine and Pauline could not have felt more proud. Mary still frowned.

During the meal, Pauline and Danny grew more relaxed and recounted their day. Pauline admitted she was so scared after she threw the can at Willie that she couldn't get up until she saw Willie leaving the house with Mary. She said Mary was the bravest of all. The young girl finally managed a trace of a smile.

Danny said he was about to attack Willie again to save Mary just as Dante shot him. Mary asked, "Really?"

Danny looked at her and nodded. "Really."

Mary's smile grew a little wider.

Katherine wondered when she could tell Joseph about Willie. She couldn't think of anything that would make him happier—and want her more.

Sarah said, "I have to send word to Amy about the demise of Andrew's murderer. She'll be delighted. Knowing her, she'll come down and celebrate with us."

James said, "That would be wonderful."

Danny said, "Grandma, can Ma and Charlotte come, too?"

Danny's eagerness to be reunited with his mother and sister once again put

Sarah in an uncomfortable position. She lied to make him feel better. "Your mother can't wait for the war to end so she and Charlotte can move back here and be a family again. I saw your father yesterday. He can't wait, either."

Danny clapped his hands. "I hope it will be soon, Grandma."

Katherine looked down at her plate. For the next few minutes she played with her food. Then she patted her lips with her napkin, said she had a headache, and excused herself. James stood, helped her out of her chair, and asked, "Are you all right?"

"Yes, sir," she replied. "Just a little dizzy. I think the excitement of the day has caught up to me." She thanked him, said goodnight to everyone, and went upstairs, where she fell on the bed and buried her head in a pillow.

Sometime later, Katherine felt a hand on her back and heard Pauline say, "What's wrong, Oldest Sister?"

Katherine rolled over. "I have a headache. I'll feel better after a good night's sleep."

Pauline and Mary donned their nightgowns, kissed Katherine goodnight, and crawled under the covers. Katherine stared at the ceiling with her head spinning. Joseph's wife wanted to return to Savannah to reunite with him, and he welcomed it. He had lied to her. Katherine didn't have the strength to watch the man she loved live with another woman, even if that woman was his wife. Katherine couldn't reside with Joseph's parents, who would share suppers, church, and holidays with Joseph and his family. She blamed herself for falling in love with a married man. Now, it seemed so obvious. Once again, she regretted her choices.

Yet she had trouble accepting that Joseph would be so devious. He seemed sincere when he confessed his feelings for her. She felt it in the way he held and kissed her. She loved him too much to give up without a fight and decided to confront him the next day—Sunday—after church. She had to have an answer—one that she could completely believe. She would decide on her and her sisters' future after that. ❧

CHAPTER FIFTY-ONE

Where Angels Go To Cry
February 1865

On Monday afternoon Katherine met her sisters after school and asked them to walk with her to Madison Square. Mary said she was supposed to meet Danny and Truvy to sell cookies. Pauline had planned to complete her class assignments and then sketch the Pulaski Monument in Monterey Square.

Katherine told them those things could wait a few minutes. She sat them on a bench with Mary in the middle, and tried to put on her best face. "I have some very exciting news," she said. Both girls focused on her with raised eyebrows. They loved surprises. "Do you remember Colonel Allen, that nice man from New York who had supper with Mr. McBain in late December and raised money for food for the poor people of Savannah?" The sisters nodded slowly, wondering what he could have to do with the exciting news. "That evening he learned of my interest in nursing and medicine. When he went to New York he spoke to friends and prepared the way to have me accepted to a medical college for women." Katherine smiled and clasped her hands together. "We're moving to New York! I'm going to study to be a doctor."

Mary stared at Katherine to determine if she were serious. Then she broke down in tears. "I don't want to leave! I love it here. Danny and Truvy are my best friends."

Pauline looked as if she had seen a ghost. "Oldest Sister, we live with the best family in the whole world. The McBains are like parents to us. We love them and they love us. I'd die without them."

Katherine expected their reactions and had planned an answer, even though she knew it might be untrue, at least as far as she was concerned. "We're not leaving forever, just a little while, and we'll visit every chance we get."

Mary said, "I won't go. You go without me."

Pauline put her arm around Mary. "Yes. You go and we'll stay here."

Katherine bowed her head. Through all the turmoil in their lives, she had to be strong for her sisters. But hearing them say that they could live without her cut like a knife. She pulled out her kerchief, dried her eyes, and regained her composure. "I want you both to listen to me. You may not understand this now, but one day you will. I love the McBains every bit as much as you do, and always will, but we can't depend on them to take care of us forever. What happens when they pass? Then where do we go? Do you expect Captain McBain and his wife to care for us—let us live with them? I have to think about these things and plan for our future. We can't rely on other people all our lives. I have an opportunity to do something important with my life, and if I succeed I'll always be able to get a good job—maybe even have my own medical practice. And I'll have done something that few women ever have. I don't want to regret passing this by, but I can't do it without my sisters. I need you with me. Nothing can ever separate us."

Mary said, "I'll make lots of money selling cookies and Pauline by drawing. You don't have to become a doctor."

Katherine's decision puzzled Pauline. She knew how much Katherine adored the McBains. Then it dawned on her. She had always suspected that Katherine loved Captain McBain and the other night at supper Mrs. McBain revealed that his wife was planning on returning to Savannah and restoring their marriage. Maybe Katherine was running from a broken heart. Pauline ached for her older sister. "I'll do whatever you say, Katherine," she said softly, "as long as you promise we can visit."

Katherine responded, "I promise we will, the first chance we get."

Mary said to Katherine, "You also promised that we'd never leave Savannah, and now we're leaving. You lied to us."

Pauline shook Mary's arm. "Hush, Mary! Don't you sass Oldest Sister like that. Ma said we must always obey her."

Mary wiped her eyes on her coat sleeve and said, "Sorry."

Pauline asked Katherine, "When are we leaving?"

"The day after tomorrow. I have to be in New York for an interview and the start of classes."

"What did Mr. and Mrs. McBain say?"

Katherine hesitated for a few seconds. "They don't know yet. I'll tell them when we get home." Pauline and Mary sat silently and stared at the ground. Katherine stood, took each girl by the hand, and returned to Pulaski Square. Her sisters went to their room.

Katherine found Mr. McBain in his study. He invited her in, walked around the desk, hugged her, and said, "Dearest Katherine, I'm still walking on a cloud. Please, sit."

Katherine remained standing. "I'd like to speak to you and Mrs. McBain, if I may. Is she available?"

McBain's smile faded. "This sounds important," he said. "She's in the garden. I'll get her."

James left and Katherine looked around the room. She thought about the first time she was in it—scared, beaten, and broke. Sarah walked in and took Katherine's hands in hers. "Good afternoon, Katherine. You're home early from work." They all sat.

Katherine said, "I resigned this morning, ma'am. I want to let you know that Colonel Allen was able to get me into the New York Medical College for Women, pending an interview, which he says is a formality, and submission of references. The colonel even has an empty floor in his townhouse where my sisters and I can live while I find us other quarters. He says I'll have no trouble getting work in a surgeon's office. Everything seems to be falling in place. It's a great opportunity for me. I have to try it, as much as I hate leaving you. I beg you to understand."

James turned pale. "Katherine, we discussed this at supper. Even Colonel Allen admitted there are very few women doctors in the North. You'll be wasting your time. You have so much to live for here. You already have a good job and, with your experience, you'll always be able to find employment in a hospital. And I don't mind saying that soon, after the war ends, there will be wealthy young men returning here who will compete for your hand in marriage. You must know you'll never have to work again. We think of the three of you as daughters. You belong here with us, as McBains."

Katherine silently asked God to get her through this. "Sir, you've been like parents to us—the best we could ever hope for. You couldn't have given us more love or care, and you saved us from a life of poverty and Lord knows what else. I can't tell you how much we appreciate it or how much we love you. You must understand that we're not leaving forever. Please think of us as daughters going off to college, like Amy—Mrs. Carson—once did. We'll come back on breaks, and when I finish my studies in three years, we'll return for good. But I have a chance to become a doctor. Who would have thought a few years ago, when I was cleaning rooms at a hotel, that I'd be in this position? I have to pursue this opportunity, which I have because of both of you."

James pleaded, "Things could happen in New York that would prevent you from returning. You could get a job there or meet a man and get married."

"Sir, marriage is the last thing on my mind. Taking care of my sisters, becoming a doctor, and making you proud of me are first." Katherine stood, walked around the desk, and embraced McBain from behind. "No matter what happens, if I ever get married, I'll want you—my true father—to give me away." She kissed his cheek, said, "I love you," squeezed him tight, and returned to her seat. James swallowed hard.

Sensing that Katherine was determined to pursue her dream, Sarah leaned over and held her hand. She said, "I know you'll succeed. I just know it. I'm so proud of you already. Imagine, a McBain woman going to medical college. I want you to show those Yankees what southern girls are made of." They sat quietly for a moment. Then Sarah asked, "When are you leaving?"

"On Wednesday. Classes begin next week."

Sarah said, "Oh, goodness. So soon? Have you considered letting Mary and

Pauline stay here while you're acclimating to New York? It might be easier on them until you're settled."

"Yes, I have, but it would be unbearable for me without them. They're my sisters, and you know how much I love them. However, if I see that they're miserable after a few months, I'll send them back here, if you don't mind. I don't need to tell you that they're both very unhappy about leaving."

James said, "Why don't you live with Amy? You'll be with family. There's plenty of room in their townhouse and I know they'd love to have you. Amy spoke so highly of you when she was here."

Katherine knew that if she lived with Amy, she'd constantly hear about Joseph. "That's kind of you to offer. I'll contact her once I get settled in New York. But Mrs. Allen is expecting us, and I should keep that commitment, at least in the beginning."

James also saw that Katherine's mind was made up, and now he had to look out for her welfare. "I have about seven hundred dollars in gold of yours from the reward money and your parent's estate, and five hundred Yankee dollars that we took off of Willie. I'll give you another five hundred dollars just in case. I don't think you should work while you're attending classes. And you have to send Pauline and Mary to school up there. Seventeen hundred dollars should support you for a long time, but you must write me if you need more. I'll wire it."

Sarah said, "We're going to miss you, Katherine. The three of you have added so much to our lives. You're McBains as far as I'm concerned, and always will be. Danny will be devastated—the servants, too. Joseph will also be very disappointed when I tell him."

Katherine squeezed Sarah's hand. "Mrs. McBain, if you don't mind, I'd like to tell Captain McBain myself. He's been so good to us."

Sarah glanced at James. "No, of course not. When do you plan to see him?"

"I'll try tomorrow. I hope the officer of the guard will be in a good mood."

Sarah nodded. They stood and embraced. As Katherine started to leave, James held out an envelope and said, "I almost forgot. This came for you today."

Katherine stared at the letter for a moment, then took it. She noticed the sender's name as Captain P. Bowen. "Thank you, sir. I'll see you at supper."

James closed the study door and Sarah began sniffling. "James, I feel like something has been cut out of me. Amy attended college in Georgia and I never thought that she wouldn't return. However, the girls are going to New York and I have this terrible feeling we won't see them again. I don't want to lose them, but I can't challenge her decision. She's a young woman now. If she wants to make something special of her life, we can't stand in her way."

James walked to the window overlooking the square. "Most girls would feel fulfilled finding a successful husband and raising a family. For some reason, she wants more, like Amy did at her age."

Sarah wondered, "Why do you think Colonel Allen is so anxious to help her?"

"I don't think he has an ulterior motive. When we had supper here that night, all the men were taken by Katherine and urged her to pursue her studies. I think it's his nature to help people. Some men in town criticized him for going beyond his authority when he raised money to buy food for Savannah. They said he was sent to New York to exchange rice for food, not to make Savannahians look like they were on their knees begging for charity. Still, he did great good for the city. And for you, when he got you on a ship back home."

Sarah stepped next to James and held his arm. "Do you find it strange that she wants to tell Joseph of her decision?"

"No. He was always very fond of the girls, and they of him. Why?"

"She seemed to know about the officer of the guard at the prison, as if she had been there before. I never told you this, but one night on the trip from Roswell to Indiana I dreamt that Joseph and Katherine got married." She wrapped her arms around herself and shivered. "I'm sorry. I'm letting my imagination get the better of me. I'm going upstairs. It's almost time for supper."

The meal that night was subdued. Danny, Pauline, and Mary hardly spoke. James felt uneasy and broke the silence. He told everyone that eight soldiers had stormed into Gazaway Lamar's house on Sunday, arrested him without charges, and sent him to the Old Capital Prison in Washington City. Sarah asked if they could do that. James shrugged and said, "Well, they did it."

Towards the end of the meal Danny said, "I know, Mary. You can visit my ma in New York before she moves back here. Maybe she can bake cookies for you."

Mary perked up. "Is she a good baker, like Miss Patience?"

Danny looked at his grandparents before answering. "I don't know." Then he added, "I don't think so," ending that line of conversation.

Mary didn't even touch her rice pudding. The meal ended with the usual embraces, but without the happiness.

The guard led Joseph to the chair. He smiled at Katherine. "You look more beautiful than ever. It's torture not being able to hold you."

Her heart rose to her throat. "Thank you, Joseph. I wish I could hold you." She glanced at the guard, who sat slumped in the chair with eyes half open, ready for a nap. "I have good news. Willie's dead."

Joseph almost fell off his chair. He shouted "What? When?" startling the guard. Katherine explained the events at the Heritage.

He leaned over the table and held her hands. The guard barked, "No touching!"

Joseph sat back. "You're incredible. Danny, Pauline, and Dante, too. How is Hercules?"

"His wound isn't serious, but he lost a lot of blood and took a severe beating to the face. He's still in the hospital. Patience is taking care of him."

Joseph leaned over the table as far as he could. "I love you more than ever." Katherine looked down. Her heart was breaking. "Katherine, is something wrong?"

She looked at him for a few seconds before saying, "Joseph, I have other news. I'm moving to New York to attend a medical college. We're leaving tomorrow."

Joseph's jaw dropped far enough to let a small bird fly in his mouth. "What do you mean? We're getting married when I get out of here."

She shook her head. "No, Joseph, we can't, because you're married. You have to get divorced first and resolve custody of your children, and you can't start that process until you're released from prison, and you have no idea when that will be. It could take several years, and you might change your mind once you see your wife and daughter. You must know I couldn't live in Savannah if your wife returns. I couldn't bear it. And I don't want to lose this opportunity while waiting for something that might never happen."

Joseph grabbed the edge of the table with both hands. "It will happen, Katherine. Why don't you believe me?" She didn't answer. Joseph then asked, "Why didn't you speak to me before you made this decision?"

She rested her hands on the table. "That was my intention—to see you Sunday after church and convince myself that you really planned on marrying me. But I thought of all the obstacles that you have to overcome. They'll take years to resolve, and even if they work out for the best, and you still want to marry me, I could be a doctor by then. So I visited the man who can get me admitted."

Joseph said, "What do you mean, 'If I still want to marry you?'"

"As I said, you may change your mind about your wife." Katherine took a deep breath before continuing. "Joseph, there's another thing that I feel the need to tell you before you make any decisions about me—about us."

Joseph tensed up, wondering what other bad news awaited him. "Of course, Katherine. You must feel free to discuss anything with me."

Katherine looked at the guard, who was wide awake and staring at her. Her hands started to tremble at the prospect of confessing her most painful secret, no less in front of a complete stranger. But it was now or never. She pulled her handkerchief from her sleeve, held it tightly in her hand, and looked Joseph in the eye. "When I was ten years old, my father started sneaking into my bedroom at night and taking liberties with me." Tears started to run down her cheeks. She dried her eyes and said, "I'm sorry. This isn't easy to say." Joseph reached across the table and touched her arm. The guard allowed it. She took another deep breath and continued. "He touched me and made me touch him. Joseph, I was so scared of him. I didn't know how to make him stop. I wanted to kill myself to end it." She lowered her head and her shoulders quaked.

The guard stood and said, "Miss, Captain, I'm going to stand outside so you can talk in private, but I'm going to keep the door open a slit and I'll be watching. Promise me you won't hand anything to each other."

Katherine looked up and said, "Thank you, sir. You have my word." The guard left the room. She continued. "It went on about once a month for five years, until my ma found out and shot him." Joseph sat still. His mother had told him about Katherine's confession of her father being evil to her, but he had no idea of the appalling details. Katherine's words left him speechless. "You know the rest—my mother dying, the three of us living with Mr. Wells, and our escape to Savannah." She stared at the table for a few seconds. "I'm telling you this now, Joseph, because you may not want me—knowing this about me."

The guard walked into the room and placed a glass of water in front of Katherine. She thanked him as he left and drank. Joseph said, "Katherine, of course I still want you. You were a victim of a terrible crime. That's all in the past."

Katherine shook her head and the tears started to flow again. "No, Joseph. It's not in the past. I wish it were, but he's still with me, not when I'm awake, but when I sleep, when I'm defenseless. He torments me in my dreams after I've seen you—been excited by you: the night that we danced at Dante's wedding; the day we kissed in Marietta; the first time I visited you in this prison."

Joseph felt empty at seeing Katherine in so much pain. "You just need time. It will pass. I know it will. And I'll be there to help you through it."

"Joseph, I don't know if I can be a wife—a real wife. Your kisses arouse me. I want to have your children. But I just don't know if I can make love to you like married people do. And I can't marry you unless I'm convinced I can. It wouldn't be fair to you."

Joseph took her hand and kissed it. "That's a gamble I'm willing to take."

She finally smiled. "I had a dream last night—a good one. I dreamt that I became a doctor and we had a celebration. You and Danny and your parents were with me. Mary and Danny were selling cookies to the other doctors."

Joseph laughed. The door opened and the guard entered. "I'm sorry, miss. You're already ten minutes past your time. I must ask you to leave now."

Katherine dabbed at her tears. "Joseph, no matter what happens, I want to thank you for being so kind to me and my sisters, and making us feel welcome and secure in your home. I love you." She could no longer speak. She walked from the room.

Joseph slumped back in his chair.

Katherine next went to the negro hospital. A black male nurse led her to Hercules, who was sitting up in bed and talking to Patience. "Hello, Patience. Hercules, you're looking much better. The swelling has gone down."

Hercules said, "I'm feeling better, thanks."

Patience stood. "Good afternoon, Miss Katherine."

Katherine said, "I wanted to let both of you know that I'm leaving town tomorrow for New York. I came here to say goodbye, and to apologize."

Hercules said, "We heard. Miss Katherine, I want you to know that I've buried the past. I know why you did it. You saved my life and helped kill Willie. I'll never forget that."

Patience said, "Truvy is very sad to see you and your sisters go. He cried last night when he learned the news."

Katherine felt compelled to say something that would make Truvy feel better. "Make sure he knows we're coming back."

Patience smiled. "That will make him happy."

Hercules said, "It makes us all happy."

Katherine stepped to the bed, squeezed Hercules's hand, hugged Patience, and said goodbye.

Sarah dominated the conversation at supper, trying to keep everyone in a good mood. She talked about how excited Amy will be when she learns the sisters are living near her. She also suggested that Katherine contact Joseph's wife. "You can't have too many friends in a big city like that." Sarah also promised that as soon as the war ended, she, James, Danny, and Joseph would visit. The conversation temporarily lifted everyone's spirits but James's, who hardly spoke during the meal.

No one slept well in the McBain household that night.

As Dante and Barney carried the luggage to the carriage, Mary stood by the bedroom door, holding and kissing her cat. She said, "Danny and JD will take good care of you, General Lee. And I'll be home soon." General Lee rubbed his head against her face and purred. JD sensed something was happening and came up the stairs. He lay on his back and fluttered his tail, inviting belly rubs. Each sister took a turn.

Katherine looked around the room in which she and her sisters had slept for more than two years—a safe and warm womb from the harsh and abusive world from which they had escaped. For a moment she questioned her decision, but she kept repeating to herself, "You're doing the right thing." She said to her sisters, "It's time to leave."

They walked downstairs and said goodbye to the servants. Lilly said, "Don' you go messin' wid any ub dem Yankee mens. You sudden' gu'ls." The sisters followed Danny, Truvy, Sarah, and James into the coach as Dante held the door.

Katherine stopped, clutched Dante's arm, and thanked him for all he had done on the trip from Roswell to Savannah and at the plantation. "I'll never forget you, Dante. You'll always be more to me than just a great turkey hunter."

Dante laughed. "Jes' come back home, lahk you promise."

That they stood by the gate to the pier, sharing their last goodbyes. Mary and Pauline's faces were soaked, but Katherine remained composed. James said to her, "Remember, if you need anything, write to me and I'll take care of it immediately. And deposit your money in a bank as soon as you get up there."

Katherine stood on tip toes and kissed his cheek. "Yes, dear father, I will."

James held her. "And if things don't work out for any reason, you're always welcome back. You know that."

Sarah hugged her. "Dearest Katherine. We love you and will miss you. You'll never know how proud I am of you."

The ship's horn tooted and the McBains gave the sisters one last embrace. Danny said to Mary, "I guess we'll have to wait to sell more cookies together."

Mary pulled out her kerchief and blew her nose, sounding like a honking goose. She said, "I guess. I'm going to learn how to bake them and sell them in New York. They have plenty of Yankees there. I'll write and tell you how I do. Will you write to me?"

Danny kicked at the ground. "I guess."

The horn blew again. Katherine kissed Danny, told the boy she loved him with all her heart, and took Mary's arm. The sisters walked through the gate, along the pier, up the gangway, and stood by the railing of the promenade deck. Katherine rubbed Mary's back, trying to soothe her pain. She looked up she saw Hercules, Patience, Truvy, and Gully standing on the bluff high above River Street. They waved to each other.

Then Danny walked inside the gate, half-way down the pier, and stood. Mary broke away from her sisters and dashed down the gangway. Katherine yelled, "MARRREEE!" but the girl ran until she and Danny faced each other.

Mary said, "I'm going to miss you, Danny McBain. Tell me that you love me—just a little."

Danny gulped, looked at his feet, and said, "Well, maybe just a little, I guess."

Mary bent slightly forward, closed her eyes, and pursed her lips. Danny scratched his head, closed his eyes, and bent slowly from the waist until their lips met. They both jerked back as if hit by an electric shock.

Mary said, "I love you, too, Danny McBain," and ran back to the gangway, where Katherine stood with her hands on her hips. She took Mary's hand and they returned to the top deck.

The horn blared, the engines roared, smoke billowed, and the ship eased away from the pier. Mary leaned against Pauline. The sisters waved as they watched the town and the people they loved slowly disappear. Katherine wondered if she would ever see them again. As sad as her sisters, but excited about the journey that lay ahead, Katherine sat on a nearby bench. She called, "Mary, come sit on my lap."

Mary shook her head. "I'll never see Danny or Truvy again."

Katherine repeated, "Please, let me hold you." Pauline picked up Mary with a grunt and placed her on Katherine's lap, and then sat next to them. She pulled out a book and started to sketch the Savannah harbor.

Katherine said to Mary, "Don't cry. We're going to have a grand time in New York. I'm going to become a doctor, Pauline is going to become a famous artist, and you're going to make thousands of dollars selling cookies. And before you know it you'll be back here with Danny and Truvy. But you must have hope."

Katherine kissed the top of Mary's head and said, "You know, when I was a little girl and I cried, Ma would tell me a poem to make me believe that better days lay ahead. Do you want to hear it?"

Mary rubbed her cheeks on her jacket sleeve, leaned back against Katherine, and squeaked, "I guess."

Katherine stroked the hair from Mary's forehead.

There's a place deep in the sky,
Known only to a few,
A special place, by and by,
Where angels go when feeling blue . . .

APPENDIX A

Author's Notes and Sources

Chapter Two – Blind Tom

Thomas Wiggins, aka Blind Tom, was born on May 25, 1849 to Domingo and Charity Wiggins, who were purchased by General James N. Bethune shortly after Tom's birth. General Bethune employed music teachers to develop the boy's natural talents, and by age eight Tom was performing on stage.

After the war Tom's parents gained their freedom and legal custody of their son, who was by then a teenager. Almost certainly at the urging of General Bethune, the Wiggins signed a contract with him whereby he became Tom's legal guardian on the condition that he support the boy, continue his music education, and pay him twenty dollars per month plus two per cent of the net proceeds from his performances. Bethune also agreed to provide Charity and Domingo Wiggins with a good home, subsistence, and five hundred dollars a year as long as Bethune managed Tom. This contract was endorsed by the general superintendent of freedmen for the state of Georgia. (*New York Evening Post*, July 24, 1865, and the *Houston Tri-weekly Telegraph*, August 30, 1865.)

At some point early in Tom's musical career, General James Bethune turned over the management to his son, Colonel John T. Bethune. John established the Blind Tom Tour Company and became the effective guardian, living and traveling with Tom. John died in a train accident in 1884 and Tom again went to live with James Bethune in Warrenton, Virginia. (*Philadelphia Inquirer*, February 19, 1884, and the *Evening Star* (Washington, D.C.), February 19, 1884.) However, John Bethune's widow, Elise Stutzbach Bethune, with the support of Charity Wiggins, successfully sued for custodianship of Tom in the New York State Supreme Court in 1887. (*Cleveland Leader*, November 27, 1886, and *Philadelphia Inquirer*, August 1, 1887.) Tom lived with Elise Bethune (who remarried and became Elise Lerche) in Hoboken, New Jersey, from 1887 until he died in 1908. (*New York Times* [hereinafter cited as *NYT*], June 15, 1908.) General James Bethune died on February 13, 1895 at the age of ninety-one. (*Baltimore Sun*, February 14, 1895.) Historians and reporters frequently confuse General James Bethune with Colonel John Bethune, as well as their relationship with Elise Stutzbach Bethune Lerche, which made researching these individuals challenging.

For reports of Tom's exploits on stage, see the *Charleston Mercury*, January 31, 1860, the *Commercial Advertiser* (New York), November 14, 1860, the *Cleveland Plain Dealer*, April 12, 1861, and the *Providence Evening Press*, April 23, 1859.

After the Civil War several lawsuits were brought by different individuals contesting Tom's custody and earnings. Tom, who reportedly never matured mentally beyond five or six years, was apparently oblivious to them all. Music was his life.

Tom gave concerts in Savannah on November 7, 8, and 9, 1861. I have changed the dates to coincide with the first battle of Manassas. The *Savannah Daily Morning News* (hereinafter cited as *DMN*) did not say who accompanied Tom, and I chose to use General James Bethune.

James Lord Pierpont, a native of Massachusetts, moved to Savannah in 1853 at age thirty-one. In 1857 he copyrighted "A One Horse Open Sleigh," which later was reissued as "Jingle Bells." He remained loyal to the South when the war broke out and wrote the patriotic tune, "We Conquer or Die," as well as several others. He joined a Georgia militia unit and served until the end of the war. He lived in Valdosta and Quitman, Georgia, before moving to Winter Haven, Florida, where he died in 1893.

I'd like to thank my friend and neighbor, Dieter Boes, for helping me with the music scale of "Dixie."

For accounts of the mustering, parading, and departure of the Oglethorpe Light Infantry from Savannah, see *DMN*, May, 22, 1861 and Lindsey P. Henderson Jr., *The Oglethorpe Light Infantry: A Military History* (Savannah, Ga., Civil War Centennial Commission of Savannah and Chatham County, 1961): 4-7.

I substituted the fictional Joseph McBain as second lieutenant of the company for A. F. Butler.

Chapter Three – Breakfast in Virginia

For the journey from Savannah to Manassas, see Muriel Phillips Joslyn, *Charlotte's Boys: Civil War Letters of the Branch Family of Savannah* (Gretna, La.: Pelican Publishing Co., 2010): 11-44; Henderson, *The Oglethorpe Light Infantry*, 17-20; and B. M. Zettler, *War Stories and School-Day Incidents for the Children* (New York, Neale Publishing Company: 1912): 43-59. For the soldiers breakfasting on their march to Manassas, see ibid., 55-57.

For the dispute between Governor Joseph E. Brown and Captain Francis S. Bartow, see the *Augusta Daily Constitutionalist* (hereinafter cited as *AC*), June 28, 1861, and the *New York Herald*, July 12, 1861.

General Beauregard's Confederate Army of the Potomac became the Army of Northern Virginia under General Robert E. Lee and should not be confused with the Union Army of the Potomac, which maintained that name throughout the war.

Chapter Four – "Never Give Up the Field, Boys"

The specifics of the battle of First Manassas are complex and I omitted or changed a few actions or movements to make it more understandable to the reader. There are several accounts of the Eighth Georgia's role in the battle of First Manassas. I relied primarily on the officers' reports in *The War of the Rebellion: A Compilation of the Official Records of the Union and Confederate Armies* (hereinafter cited as *OR*) (130 vols. Washington, Government Printing Office,1880-1901) as presented in volume 1, series 2; F. D. Lee and J. L. Agnew, *Historical Record of the City of Savannah* (Savannah, J. H. Estill: 1869); and Joslyn, *Charlotte's Boys*: 44-49.

Colonel William Tecumseh Sherman commanded a brigade of five regiments that participated in the battle. For his account, see William Tecumseh Sherman, *Memoirs of General W. T. Sherman*, Michael Fellman, ed., (New York, Penguin Books: 2000): 168-172. His brigade suffered more casualties (killed, wounded, missing) than any other in General McDowell's army. See *OR*, S1, v2, 327.

Chapter Five – The Wagon
See the Introduction for comments on the use of slave dialect, the "N" word, and the term "negro."

Chapter Six – Port Royal
The scene in which Jehova is chased by Mr. Williamson and subsequently defended by Mr. McBain is based on an interview of former slave Benjamin Johnson as recorded in the *Slave Narratives*, which can be accessed online at:
http://memory.loc.gov/cgi-bin/query/D?mesnbib:10:./temp/~ammem_0hdF::
(Accessed January 21, 2006)

For official accounts of the Union navy's attack on Hilton Head Island by Union General Thomas W. Sherman and Confederate General Thomas F. Drayton, see *OR*, S1, v6, 3-16.

Chapter Seven – "They Cannot Breach Your Walls"
For General Lee's tour of Fort Pulaski and his comment that the fort's walls could not be breached by the enemy's guns, see Lilla Mills Hawes, ed., "The Memoirs of Charles Olmstead, Part VI," *Georgia Historical Quarterly* (hereinafter cited as *GHQ*) 44 (March 1960): 63-65.

My thanks to Hugh Harrington of Gainesville, Georgia for instructions on how to load a Civil War era revolver.

Chapter Eight – "If Only For One Day"
For a discussion of issues facing Savannah River planters during the war, including the disloyalty of their most favored slaves, see Albert V. House Jr., "Deterioration of a Georgia Rice Plantation During Four Years of Civil War," *The Journal of Southern History* 9 (February 1943): 98-113. For another comment on the disloyalty of favored slaves, see Aaron M. Boom, "Testimony of Margaret Ketcham Ward on Civil War Times in Georgia, Part II," *GHQ* 39 (December 1955): 376-377.

For the voyage of the Fingal, see Thomas R. Neblett, "Major Edward C. Anderson and the C. S. S. Fingal," *GHQ* 52 (June 1968): 132-158.

The spiritual "Trouble Done Bore Me Down" was taken from the online website, http://www.negrospirituals.com/songs/trouble_done_bore_me_down.htm

(Accessed January 2014).

For a description of a slave's lantern-lit funeral procession, see Sarah Hodgson Torian, ed., "Ante-Bellum and War Memories of Mrs. Telfair Hodgson," *GHQ* 27 (December 1943): 352.

The concept of slaves "wearing the mask" was taken from Whittington B. Johnson, *Black Savannah 1788-1864* (Fayetteville, University of Arkansas Press: 1996): 161.

The slave superstition of the screech owl signaling death was taken from the interview with Julia Brown (Aunt Sally), *Slave Narratives*, available online at: http://memory.loc.gov/mss/mesn/041/145152.gif. (Accessed January 22, 2006).

Chapter Nine – "Dis Chile Will Receeb Him Lubingly"

The reprint of the advertisement that ran in a northern newspaper mocking southern slave holders can be found in the *Savannah Republican* (hereinafter cited as *SR*), January 3, 1862.

The Heritage plantation is based upon the Hermitage plantation, which produced the Savannah Grey brick, and was owned by Henry McAlpin. Life on and descriptions of the plantation were obtained from the Savannah Unit of the Georgia Writer's Project, "The Hermitage Plantation," *GHQ* 47 (March 1943): 55-87; *Souvenir of the Hermitage*, General Vertical File—Savannah-Historic Houses-Hermitage—at the Georgia Historical Society, Savannah; *DMN*, December 1, 1929.

Colonel Charles Olmstead wrote in his memoirs of firing a cannon and hitting a Union soldier as he and two others frolicked on the beach at Kings Landing. This is confirmed by a report in the *DMN*, January 13, 1862.

For a master punishing a slave other than by whipping, see the interview with Bob Mobley, *Slave Narratives*, available online at: http://memory.loc.gov/mss/mesn/043/139136.gif. (Accessed January 21, 2006.) He said, "Grown Negro men, in those days, wore their hair long and, as a punishment to them for misconduct (etc.), the master cut their hair off."

Chapter Ten – The Negro Ball

For an advertisement announcing the ball to be held on January 22, 1862, by "The Colored People of Savannah" for the benefit of the sick and wounded soldiers in the service of the state of Georgia, with permission of the mayor and aldermen, at St. Andrew's Hall, see *DMN*, January 17, 1862. No description of the ball could be found in subsequent editions.

The advertisement announced the music to be played by Ross's Brass Band of Macon. The band was almost assuredly comprised of black musicians, as it would be doubtful that white musicians would play at a black ball.

The description of the Cakewalk was obtained online at the Xroads Virginia website. See http://xroads.virginia.edu/~ug03/lucas/cake.html. (Accessed January 2, 2013.)

Chapter Eleven – General Lee's Mistake

For an account of the March 4, 1862 enrollment in Savannah and the poor response by the locals, see *DMN*, March 7 and 18 1862.

For the Confederate sequestration laws, see Daniel W. Hamilton, "The Confederate Sequestration Act," *Civil War History* 52 (Winter 2006): 373-408.

For the Ladies Gunboat Fund, see Mark Swanson and Robert Holcombe, "CSS Georgia Archival Study. Report to US Army Corps of Engineers Savannah District, Savannah, from New South Associates, Stone Mountain, GA.," *The MUA Collection*, accessed July 1, 2013, http://www.themua.org/collections/items/show/967. The Savannah newspapers regularly published lists of the donors.

There are several first-hand accounts of life at Fort Pulaski leading up to and during the assault by Union forces in April 1862: Lilla Mills Hawes, ed., "The Memoirs of Charles Olmstead Part VI," *GHQ* 44 (March 1960): 56-74; Spencer Bidwell King Jr., ed., "Rebel Lawyer: The Letters of Lt. Theodorick W. Montfort, 1861-1862," *GHQ* 49 (March 1965): 89-97 and (June 1965): 200-216; the *Private Journal of E. W. Drummond* and the *L. H. Landershine Diary* kept at the Fort Pulaski National Monument, Savannah, Georgia. I would like to thank Park Ranger Gloria Swift and her staff for allowing me access to these diaries.

For the Union strategy and actions in capturing the fort, as well as the terms of surrender, see *OR*, S1, v.6.

For a technical but understandable discussion of the difference between rifled and smooth-bore guns, see *Columbian Register* (New Haven, Connecticut), May 17, 1862.

Chapter Twelve – The Reunion

Details of the trip from Fort Pulaski to New York, and the prisoners' arrival in New York and Fort Columbus, are taken from Hawes, "Memoirs of Charles Olmstead," *GHQ* 44 (March 1960): 73-74, and *GHQ* 44 (June 1960): 186-190; King, "The Letters of Lt. Theodorick W. Montfort," *GHQ* 49 (September 1965): 324-333; Whitefield J. Bell Jr., ed., "Diary of George Bell, A Record of Captivity in a Federal Military Prison, 1862," *GHQ* 22 (June 1938): 169-184; The *L. H. Landershine Diary* and the *Private Journal of E. W. Drummond*.

Union authorities at Hilton Head gave the slaves captured with their masters at Fort Pulaski the option of accompanying them to prison in New York. This reflects the feeling at the time (April 1862) that the North was still not of the mind of abolishing slavery and respected the private property of the Southerners. Eight of the slaves chose to go with their masters.

In his memoir, Charles Olmstead refers to the taunting boys as "street Arabs."

Chapter Thirteen – Sam Bannister

For a history of the Confederate draft, see William L. Shaw, "The Confederate Conscription and Exemption Acts," *The American Journal of Legal History* 6 (October 1962): 368-405. For Governor Brown's proclamation on the draft to the people of Georgia, see the *DMN*, February 27, 1862. For an editorial on the debate over the draft, see *DMN*, March 18, 1862. For the process of transferring state troops to Confederate service, see the *DMN*, April 17, 1862.

For the formation of the Southern Rights Vigilance Association in Savannah, see *DMN*, December 22 and 24, 1859, and January 2, 1860. For activity of the association in the early years of the war, when residents suspected of disloyalty to the South were put on trial, see *NYT*, January 16, 1861, and *DMN*, September 27, 1861.

For the tar and feathering of the British Captain Vaughan of the Kalos, and the rewards offered, see *SR*, February 5, 1861 and *AC*, February 8, 1861.

For the establishment of ward patrols, see Minutes of City Council (May1857-June 1863), City Hall, Savannah, 604. For General A. R. Lawton's request for a system of passes to prevent entry into the city by the enemy, see ibid., 610. For notice to the public of the requirement of passes and the hours of the passport office, see *DMN*, April 17, 1862.

For March Haynes's role in smuggling slaves to Union ships, see Clarence L. Mohr, "Before Sherman: Georgia Blacks and the Union War Effort, 1861 – 1864, *The Journal of Southern History* 45 (August 1979): 340-341; *DMN*, April 28, 1863.

Chapter Fourteen – "Look Like You've Lost Your Balls, Sir"
For the request by General Pemberton to the city council to declare martial law and to evacuate the women and children from the city, see Minutes of City Council (May 1857-June 1863), 662-663.

Chapter Fifteen – Just Plain Dumb
Charles Olmstead told a poignant story of Sport, a dog that the prisoners found and adopted on Governors Island. Sport formed the basis for JD. See *Charles H. Olmstead, The Story of a Rebel*, read before the Confederate Veterans Association on September 6, 1892, available at the Georgia Historical Society, Savannah.

For the transfer to Sandusky Island and prison life there, see Hawes, "Memoirs of Charles Olmstead," *GHQ* 44 (June 1960): 186-196; The *L. H. Landershine Diary* and the *Private Journal of E. W. Drummond*.

Newspaper articles mimicking the Irish brogue were used to produce Colleen's accent. For example, see *Frank Leslie's Illustrated Newspaper* (New York, N. Y.), May 1, 1858; and the *Cleveland Plain Dealer*, March 6, 1857.

Chapter Sixteen – "The Perfect Person for the Job"
The Confederate army made many calls on slaveholders in Chatham County to hire out their slaves to help strengthen fortifications in the area. General Hugh Mercer constantly complained of the local planters' lack of support in this effort.

Chapter Seventeen – Regrets
In researching the justice system for slaves in Savannah, I came across a case

of a white woman who accused a slave of rape. The slave's owner hired a defense lawyer, a trial was held, and the slave was found not guilty by a white jury. See State of Georgia v. York (a slave), Superior Court of Chatham County, Civil Minutes Book 24, September 1859 – November 1863, 474.

Chapter Eighteen – "Decent and Respectable Girls"
For a description of the African American colony on St. Simons Island, see George Alexander Heard, "St. Simons Island During the War Between the States," *GHQ* 22 (September 1938): 249-272; and *OR*, S1, V12, 590-1, 613-4, 633-4, 689, 727, 756; S1, V13, 19-21, 144-145. This last reference is the most descriptive of life on the island. It mentions a man named Hope, and states that the commanding naval officer placed freed slaves who neglected their work in irons for punishment.

Chapter Nineteen – Penny the Pretender
The Second Baptist Church of Thomasville is fictional. For an excellent description of Thomasville and Thomas County from their founding to the War Between the States, see William Warren Rogers, *Antebellum Thomas County 1825 – 1861* (Tallahassee, Florida State University: 1963).

On August 30, 1862, Thomasville citizens held a town meeting in which German Jews as a group were denounced, current German Jewish residents banished from the town, and non-residents prohibited from visiting. However, it appears as if the resolutions were never enforced. See the *Augusta Daily Constitutionalist,* September 12, 1862; *Augusta Chronicle*, September 23, 1862; *Macon Telegraph,* September 26, 1862; Ron Block, *Southern Antisemitism: The Case of Thomasville Georgia*, (n.p.; n.d.) located in the Judaism File of the Thomas County Historical Society, Thomasville. On September 13, 1862, the German Jews of Savannah held a meeting to protest the Thomasville action. See *SR*, September 15, 17, and 20, 1862.

Delores Downes's poem of hope was inspired by a song by the SteelDrivers, "Where Rainbows Never Die." Check it out at: https://www.youtube.com/watch?v=fpA6Xk4KUdU

Chapter Twenty – Escaping Thomasville
Information on the Savannah Female Asylum was obtained from the Admission Book, July 6, 1841 to August 14, 1879 of the institution, as found in the Parent and Child Development Services records, MS # 1920, Box 11, located at the Georgia Historical Society.

Chapter Twenty-One – "Trying to Get to Savannah"
For prison life on Johnson's Island and the journey to Vicksburg, including the food toss in Memphis, see Hawes, "Memoirs of Charles Olmstead, Part VI,": 186-201; also see the *Private Journal of E. W. Drummond*, 53-78.

For the destruction of Randolph, Tennessee, see the *Memphis Bulletin*, September 25, 1862, as reprinted in *NYT*, October 5, 1862.

For Sherman's command at Memphis and the interaction between the Union Army and southern commerce and travel, see Joseph H. Parks, "A Confederate Trade Center under Federal Occupation: Memphis, 1862 to 1865," *The Journal of Southern History* 7 (August 1941): 289-314; A. Sellew Roberts, "The Federal Government and Confederate Cotton," *The American Historical Review* 32 (January 1927): 262-275; E. Merton Coulter, "Effects of Secession Upon the Commerce of the Mississippi Valley," *The Mississippi Valley Historical Review* 3 (December 1916): 275-300; *OR*, S1, V17, Pt. II and S3, V2. Also see the *NYT* for various articles between July and December 1862.

Chapter Twenty-Three – "I'm Probably Doing Your Old Man A Favor"
The best illustration of the roads leading to Savannah, its surrounding forts, and two rings of artillery is the "Map of the Vicinity of Savannah," compiled from the old County Maps of John McKinnon, MS1361 – MP 031, Georgia Historical Society. For a diagram of the individual gun batteries of the interior line of defense, see *OR*, s1, v14, 859. For a description of the forts surrounding Savannah, see ibid., 645-648.

Chapter Twenty-Five – The Poor House and Hospital
For a history of the Poor House and Hospital, see the *Savannah Morning News*, March 29, 1959, contained in the Candler Hospital Vertical File at the GHS. Also of interest is the rare pamphlet, *Rules and Bye-Laws of the Savannah Poor House and Hospital Society* (Savannah: Printed by Philip D. Woolhopter, 1810) at the Georgia Historical Society.

At some point during the war (the above referenced article says 1863), the hospital used some or all of its beds for sick and wounded soldiers. For the scenes in this chapter (October 1862), I assumed that it was still used as a hospital for the poor.

Chapter Twenty-Six – "It Feels Like Another City"
I would like to thank Park Ranger Talley Kirkland for an excellent tour of Fort McAllister. For a daily journal of life at the fort in 1862, see Roger S. Dunham, *Blues in Gray: Civil War Journal William Daniel Dixon* (Nashville: University of Tennessee Press, 2001), 82-125.

For an account of a Georgia citizen rowing out under a flag of truce to request the return of his runaway slaves, see *OR*, S1, V13, 196-197.

During a bombardment of the facility in 1863, Tom Cat, the fort mascot, was the only Confederate casualty.

Chapter Twenty-Seven – The Negro Colony
See the references for Chapter 17.

Chapter Twenty-Eight – Danny's Prayer

The Union navy controlled the coastal waters of South Carolina, Georgia, and Florida and patrolled them regularly. Ships often picked up abandoned slaves and brought them to Hilton Head and St. Simons Islands.

Chapter Twenty-Nine – Mitchelville

For a description of the Hilton Head village before and after the occupation of Union forces, see *AC*, February 28, 1863, quoting the correspondent of the *New York Herald*. For the life of freed slaves on Hilton Head, see *NYT*, July 19, 1862.

For the history of Mitchelville and a profile of General Mitchel, see the *Hartford Daily Courant*, November 6, 1862, *Public Ledger* (Philadelphia), November 7, 1862, *Philadelphia Inquirer*, May 18, 1863, *Liberator* (Boston), May 12, 1865, and *South Carolina Leader*, December 9, 1865.

Chapter Thirty – "Jutth Two"

For The Language of the Fan, see the "Social Life and Customs" Vertical File at the Georgia Historical Society.

Chapter Thirty-One – Dante's Wedding Day

The celebration of a slave wedding was at the discretion of the owner of the bride, which left a wide range of options, from no ceremony or party to a relatively elaborate affair. For example, Congressman Alexander H. Stephens, future vice president of the Confederacy, wrote home to Mississippi regarding a male slave who wanted to marry his female slave, Eliza. "I have no objection, and tell Eliza to go to Sloman and Henrys and get her a wedding dress including a pair of fine shoes etc. and to have a decent wedding of it. Let them cook a supper and have such of their friends as they wish." See Spencer B. King Jr., *Georgia Voices: A Documentary History to 1872* (Athens: University of Georgia Press, 1966), 193. Another example of a lavish celebration, the model for Andrew's and Patience's wedding in Savannah Grey, can be found in Gerald J. Smith, "Reminiscences of the Civil War By J. W. Frederick," *GHQ* 59 (Supplement 1975): 159. "I remember the marriage of my nurse, Charity, and Handy, a likely looking couple. The negro quarter homes were some 300 yards from our house. On the evening of the marriage, the broad, raised walk from their quarter to our dwelling was brilliantly lighted with piles of lightwood knots at frequent intervals, on each side of the walk. The bridal couple was preceded by torch bearers. . . . The couple was followed by all the quarter. . . . Arriving at the 'White House,' Father, from the back porch, impressively read the ritual that made them man and wife."

Chapter Thirty-Two – A Cake for Harold

For a description of the festivities on Hilton Head on January 1, 1863, see the *New York Herald* (hereinafter cited as *NYH*,) January 7, 1863. For the Emancipation Proclamation, see *NYT*, January 3, 1863.

For the order drafting Negroes in the Department of the South, see the *Portland Weekly Advertiser* (Maine), March 28, 1863. For the reaction of some blacks to the order, see the *Daily Eastern Argus* (Portland, Maine), March 17, 1863. According to *NYH*, April 1, 1863, the blacks employed by the Quartermaster's and Commissary Departments were drafted into a regiment called the Third South Carolina Volunteers, though they performed the same duties as before. They were drilled and subject to military discipline to make them more efficient laborers.

For positive responses of white soldiers to the drafting and training of black soldiers, see the *Portland Daily Advertiser* (Maine), July 17, 1862, and the *Springfield Republican* (Massachusetts), August 9, 1862. For a negative response, see the *Daily National Intelligencer* (Washington, D.C.), August 11, 1862.

By July 1863, there were three black regiments in the First South Carolina Volunteers: First Regiment (Col. Thomas Higginson) at Port Royal Ferry; Second Regiment (Col. James Montgomery) camped near Beaufort; and the Third Regiment (Col. Augustus Bennett) camped on Hilton Head. See *NYT*, July 15, 1863.

For General Hunter's defense of his controversial actions organizing the regiment of fugitive slaves in his department, see his letter to Secretary of War Edwin M. Stanton, June 23, 1862, in the *Sun* (Baltimore), July 4, 1862.

For reports of the early expeditions of the First South Carolina Volunteers, see the *Milwaukee Sentinel*, April 3, 1863, *New Haven Palladium*, June 24, 1863, and *NYH*, June 19, 1863, as reprinted in the *CM*, June 29, 1863.

Chapter Thirty-Three – "I Believe You've Met My Son"

For an overview of blockade running, see Stephen R. Wise, *Lifeline of the Confederacy: Blockade Running During the Civil War* (Columbia: University of South Carolina Press, 1991).

Chapter Thirty-Four – A Little Dark Cloud

For a history of women's roles in Confederate hospitals see Jane E. Schultz, "The Inhospitable Hospital: Gender and Professionalism in Civil War Medicine," *Signs* 17 (Winter 1992): 363-92. For the order providing for women matrons in Confederate hospitals, see *OR*, s. VI, v. II, 209-10.

For a first-hand account of the women serving in Confederate hospital, see Kate Cumming, *Kate: The Journal of a Confederate Nurse*, ed. by Richard Barksdale Harwell, (Baton Rouge: Louisiana State University Press, 1959). This diary of a Civil War nurse from April 1862 to May 1865 provided inspiration for several scenes in the book. For example, she writes of a dying soldier who gave his watch to a male nurse for his kindness (p. 110), though the nurse was not later accused of stealing it. She also describes the opposition women faced in hospitals (p. 12, 38-9, 63, 135-6, 226). Cumming occasionally contradicts herself, as on pages 135-6, where she says surgeons have every right to exclude women from hospitals. Interestingly, although a nurse for two years, she never dressed a wound until Atlanta in May 1864 (p. 198). Her comments on southern society are as interesting as those on nursing life. For example, she writes, "If the negro should be set free by this war, which I believe he will be, whether we gain or not, it will be the Lord's doing. The time has come when his mission has ended as a slave, and while he has been benefited by slavery the white race has suffered by its influence. . . . That the South has not fully done her duty by them I do not believe any good southerner will deny; but who does his whole duty, and whose fault is it that she has not done so in this respect? None but the abolitionists" (p. 158).

For more experiences of a woman nurse, see Fannie A. Beers, *Memories: A Record of Personal Experience and Adventure During Four Years of War* (Philadelphia: J. B. Lippincott Company, 1888).

Other good sources for Confederate hospitals include Glenna R. Schroeder–Lein, *Confederate Hospitals on the Move: Samuel H. Stoudt and the Army of Tennessee* (Columbia: University of South Carolina Press, 1994); H. H. Cunningham, *Doctors in Gray: The Confederate Medical Service* (Baton Rouge: Louisiana State University Press, 1958).

For the names and locations of Savannah hospitals under the Confederacy, see J. David Griffin, "Benevolence and Malevolence in Confederate Savannah," *GHQ*, 49 (December 1965): 347-368; and the *Macon Telegraph* (hereinafter cited as the *MT*), February 26, 1864.

For the resolutions of the Savannah Vigilance Committee, see the *DMN*, August 22, 1861.

Chapter Thirty-Five – "We'll Be Back Before You Know It"
For an advertisement of a wayside home and the services it provides, see AC, July 23, 1862. The homes were usually funded by public donations. For a financial report and a plea for financial help, see the *MT*, November 24, 1862. For the rules and regulations governing a wayside home, see ibid., February 24, 1864.

There are many sources for Sherman's North Georgia campaign from Chattanooga to Atlanta. I used the accounts in the New York Tribune (hereinafter cited as *NYTR*), from May 7 to July 30, 1864. Also helpful were Joslyn, *Charlotte's Boys*, 220-275; Wilfred W. Black, ed., "Marching with Sherman through Georgia and the Carolinas Part 1: Civil War Diary of Jesse L. Dozier," *GHQ* 52 (September 1968): 308-336; and *OR*, s1, v52, pII.

Chapter Thirty-Six – "This Used to be the Loveliest Town in North Georgia"
For descriptions of Marietta, its hospitals, and the relief committees during Sherman's march, see the *Richmond Whig*, September 25, 1863; *DC*, October 10, 1863, June 30 and July 2, 1864; *MT*, September 30, 1863, June 1, 4, 6 1864; *NYTR*, July 14, 1864.

For a history of Marietta, see Burnette Vanstory, "Marietta," *The Georgia Review* 12 (Spring 1958): 41-49; and Sarah Blackwell Gober Temple, *A Short History of Cobb County, In Georgia* (Marietta: Cobb Landmarks and Historical Society,

1989). I would like to thank Brad Quinlin for an instructive tour of Marietta and Kennesaw Mountain.

The wayside home on Church Street is fictional.

The details of the amputation that Pauline witnessed were taken from an article in the *MT*, June 4, 1864. Special thanks to Susan D. Hoffius, director of the Waring Historical Library in Charleston for providing me with much medical-related reference material.

Chapter Thirty-Seven – "Protect Those Girls With Your Life"
Two excellent sources for the saga of the Roswell women are: Mary Deborah Petite, *"The Women Will Howl": The Union Army Capture of Roswell and New Manchester, Georgia and the Forced Relocation of Mill Workers* (Jefferson, N.C.: McFarland & Company, Inc., 2008); and Michael D. Hitt, *Charged With Treason* (Monroe, N.Y.: Library Research Associates, Inc., 1992).

Chapter Thirty-Eight – "Hell Would Be an Improvement"
The most comprehensive sources of information for Andersonville prison are Edwin C. Bearss, *Andersonville National Historic Site Historic Resource Study and Historical Base Map* (Washington, D.C.: Department of the Interior, Office of History and Historic Architecture, July 31, 1970); and "The Trial of Henry Wirz," *Executive Documents of the House of Representatives, Second Session of the Fortieth Congress, 1867-68*, Washington, D.C., Government Printing Office: 1868. William Marvel, *Andersonville: The Last Depot* (Chapel Hill: The University of North Carolina Press, 1994) is also well written and comprehensive. I would like to thank Alan Marsh, Cultural Resources Manager of the Andersonville National Historic Site, for his time and assistance and furnishing diaries of Union prisoners and other reference materials.

I also used the diary of Private William H. Smith, great, great-grandfather of my friend Bob Goss, proprietor of the Inn at Monticello, in Charlottesville, Virginia. See William H. Smith, Civil War Papers, 1864-1866, Accession #13164, Special Collections, University of Virginia Library, Charlottesville. The diary was particularly revealing for a prisoner who worked in the hospital outside the stockade and didn't suffer like the other prisoners. Some of the most remarkable revelations occur during his trip from Andersonville to the North. In the entry for February 4, 1865, Smith writes from Columbia, S.C., "Five of us go into a saloon to get something to drink and [lose] the rest of the boys. Go into a house to enquire. The Lady gives us a good warm supper." Could five Union prisoners simply walk into a bar for a drink in the middle of Dixie with the war still raging, and not get shot on the spot? Would a rebel woman then invite the enemy into her home and serve them supper? Fascinating!

For a first-hand account of the execution of the raiders, see the *NYT*, December 11, 1864.

Henry Wirz was born in Switzerland and moved to New England as a young

APPENDIX A

adult. He traveled south and worked for several doctors. He soon joined a Louisiana infantry unit and after the first battle of Manassas was assigned to guard Yankee prisoners. He ran military prisons thereafter, including those in Richmond. He was then transferred to Andersonville.

Chapter Forty – "I'll Wait for Francis"
See references for Chapter 36.

Chapter Forty-One – "De Lawd Bin Lisnin'"
For the history of Macon during the war, see Richard W. Iobst, *Civil War Macon: The History of a Confederate City* (Macon, Ga.: Mercer University Press, 1999). For a description of the Macon hospitals, see the *MT*, September 28, 1863. For surgeons' views on the presence of women in their hospitals, see ibid., June 7 and 16, 1864. For a soldier's view, see ibid., July 20, 1864; for a description of the Macon wayside home, see ibid., June 10, 1864. For a call to citizens to take wounded soldiers into private homes, see ibid., July 23, 1864. For General Stoneman's raid on Macon and his capture, see ibid., August 2 and 3, 1864. Also of interest are William Sanders Scarborough, *An American Journey from Slavery to Scholarship*, Michele Valerie Ronnick, ed. (Detroit: Wayne State University Press, 2005) and *Citizens, Soldiers & Sites of 1860's Macon, Georgia*, compiled by Cheryl Bloodworth Aultman, (Sesquicentennial Commemoration 2013). My sincere thanks to Muriel Jackson of the Genealogy and Historical Room at the Washington Memorial Library in Macon for her assistance and advice.

Chapter Forty-Two – Mrs. Price
For an incident where marauding Union soldiers dug up a grave, found a body, and didn't rebury it, see Mark H. Dunkelman, *Marching with Sherman: Through Georgia and the Carolinas with the 154th New York* (Baton Rouge: Louisiana State University Press, 2012), 76. This book presents an excellent, balanced picture of Sherman's march and is highly recommended.

Chapter Forty-Three – "Us Lookin' fuh de Rainbow"
The incident at Ebenezer Creek took place on December 9, 1864. A similar incident occurred at Buck Head Creek on December 3, 1864. See Chaplain John J. Hight, *History of the 58th Regiment of Indiana Volunteer Infantry: Its Organization, Campaigns and Battles from 1861 to 1865*, compiled by Gilbert R. Stormont (Princeton: Press of the Clarion, 1895) especially pages 426 and 432; James A. Connolly, *Three Years in the Army of the Cumberland*, Paul Angle, ed. (Bloomington, 1959), 354-5, 362-3, 367; Robert G. Athearn, "An Indiana Doctor Marches with Sherman: The Diary of James Comfort Patten," *Indiana Magazine of History* 49 (December 1953): 419-20. Connolly says that five to six hundred black women, children, and old men were involved, but doesn't say how many died. All these accounts express revulsion at General Davis, but none report any effort to help the blacks as they struggled in the creek. See also James P. Jones, "General

Jeff C. Davis, U. S. A. and Sherman's Georgia Campaign," *GHQ* 47 (September 1963): 242-5. Secretary of War Edwin M. Stanton visited Savannah in January 1865 and questioned General William T. Sherman about the incident. Sherman defended Davis. Stanton subsequently interviewed Davis and dropped any further investigation of the matter. See Jones, "General Jeff C. Davis," 244-5.

For the order given by the soldiers to the freed slaves following the Corps, see Sherman's Special Field Orders, No. 120, VII, available online.

For an account of General Davis shooting General William Bull Nelson in a Louisville hotel, see *NYT*, September 30, 1862.

Chapter Forty-Four – The Foreign Battalion

A foreign battalion of "Galvanized Yanks" was sent to Savannah. A number of them tried to escape to the Union side, and got caught. A court martial was held and seven ringleaders were executed by firing squad. Brigadier General George W. Mercer was arrested after the war and tried by a court martial in Savannah. He was cleared of the charge of murder. For a report of Mercer's court martial, see the *Savannah Daily Herald*, January 19 and 20, 1866.

One of the members of the Foreign Battalion said that the incident took place near the "Augusta Pike" or road, on the Confederate right, so I placed the incident there.

For an account of the siege of Savannah, see N. C. Hughes Jr., "Hardee's Defense of Savannah," *GHQ* 47 (January 1963): 43-67. For a more detailed account, see Charles Colcock Jones, *The Siege of Savannah in December 1864 and the Confederate Operations in Georgia and the Third Military District of South Carolina during General Sherman's March from Atlanta to the Sea* (Albany, N. Y.: Joel Munsell, 1874), available online at docsouth.unc.edu/fpn/jonescharles/menu.html.

Chapter Forty-Five – "Ain' uh Slabe No Maw"

The Union occupation of Savannah was relatively civil. I'm often asked why Sherman didn't burn down the town. The question is predicated on the assumption that his army destroyed every town during his march to the sea. There is no question that his men did considerable damage, especially to private homes and plantations, but reports of total destruction are questionable. While buildings were burned in Milledgeville, there is an entire section of the city with stately houses in the Federal and Greek Revival styles, including the Governor's Mansion, all pre war, still standing. Madison was also visited by Union troops yet boasts many pre-war houses. Some believe that Sherman saved the town for the vast stores of cotton in the city warehouses. But if Sherman wanted to burn the city, he could have easily removed the cotton and then torched the place.

Sherman didn't destroy Savannah because it was a vital strategic location on the Atlantic coast. He explained to General Grant in a communication soon after the occupation, "The capture of Savannah, with the incidental use of the river, gives us a magnificent position in this quarter. . . ." (See W. T. Sherman to U. S.

Grant, December 22, 1864, *OR*, S1, v44, 6-7.)

Depictions of Savannah life during the Union occupation are taken from "Fanny Cohen's Journal of Sherman's Occupation of Savannah," ed., Spencer B. King Jr., *GHQ* 41 (October 1957): 407-416; Caro Lamar to Charles Lamar, December 24 and 28, 1864, Charles Augustus Lafayette Lamar Papers, Georgia Archives, Morrow, Georgia; Dunkelman, *Marching with Sherman*, 93-109;

Chapter Forty-Six – Colonel Allen's Proposal

Union forces took control of Savannah hospitals soon after they gained control of the city. According to an account in the *Savannah Daily Herald* of March 24, 1865, the U. S. hospitals in Savannah were located at the Screven House building at Bull and Congress Streets; the Marshal House building on Broughton between Drayton and Abercorn; the Pavilion House, which had been the wayside home, at Bull and South Broad streets; and the Savannah Medical College building at Habersham and Taylor streets. It could not be determined how long the old Confederate hospitals remained in operation after the occupation. However, there were still Confederate sick and wounded troops in Savannah and it could be assumed that these facilities continued to treat them.

Colonel Julian Allen did indeed visit Savannah on December 27, 1864, and subsequently volunteered to obtain much needed provisions for the suffering and destitute citizens of Savannah. A description of his efforts can be found in John P. Dyer, "Northern Relief for Savannah during Sherman's Occupation," *The Journal of Southern History* 19 (November 1953): 457-472. His efforts were also chronicled in the three major New York newspapers (*Herald, Tribune,* and *Times*) in January and February 1865. Colonel Allen moved to North Carolina after the war and died there. For an obituary, see the *Charlotte News*, February 10, 1890.

The New York Medical College and Hospital for Women was chartered by the state legislature in 1863. The first term started in October of that year. For a description of the college, its courses and professors, and a graduation ceremony, see *NYH*, March 3, 1865. Following the opening of the college, a debate raged by letter writers in the pages of the *New York Times* over the propriety of women becoming doctors and their insulting treatment by male students. See *NYT*, December 11, 18, 25, 1864 and January 1 and 8, 1865. Information on admission requirements or tuition could not be found. However, the course of study lasted three years.

Chapter Forty-Seven – The Cookie Sellers

For a report on the public meeting held on December 28, 1864, and the resolutions passed by the committee, see *NYT*, January 5, 1865.

Chapter Forty-Eight – Food for Savannah

Esther Hill Hawks graduated from the New England Medical College for Women in 1857 and opened a practice in Portsmouth, New Hampshire. During the Civil War she joined her husband Dr. John Hawks when he served in Union controlled territory of Hilton Head and Beaufort. She taught freed slaves, but did not practice medicine during this time. She did visit Savannah after the war. For more on Ms. Hawks, see *A Woman Doctor's Civil War: Esther Hill Hawks' Diary*, ed., Gerald Schwartz (Columbia: University of South Carolina Press, 1989).

Chapter Forty-Nine – The Most Beautiful Sight She Had Ever Seen

No record could be found identifying the date when the Savannah River plantations were returned to their owners.

Chapter Fifty – Where Angels Go To Cry

Gazaway Lamar was arrested without being charged by the Union authorities on the order of the assistant secretary of war and spent three months, from April to June 1865, in the Old Capital Prison in Washington, D. C. There have been several articles written about Lamar. One of the more interesting accounts of his incarceration is found in his angry letter to President Andrew Johnson detailing his travails after the war. See *G. B. Lamar, Sen. To Ex – President Andrew Johnson* (n.p.: n.d.), Box 1, Folder 16, James Jordan Collection of Lamar family papers, MS 2549, Georgia Historical Society, Savannah, Georgia.

List of Real (R) and Fictional (F) Characters

LAST NAME	FIRST	R/F	DESCRIPTION
Allen	Col. Julian	R	NY businessman in Savannah after occupation
Anderson	Edward C.	R	Confederate officer sent to Europe to buy arms
Arnold	Dr. Richard C.	R	Savannah doctor and mayor
Bannister	Sam	F	Partner in crime of Willie and Harold
Bartow	Francis S.	R	Confederate officer from Savannah
Barney		F	Stable boy in Savannah
Benoist	Mrs.	R	Owner of boarding house in Savannah
Blair	Lieutenant	R	Confederate officer of the guard at Ft. Pulaski
Bowen	Capt. Patrick	F	Officer on staff of U.S. General Jeff C. Davis
Branch	Charlotte	R	Mother of John, Sanford, & Hamilton; volunteer
Branch	Hamilton	R	"Hammie"; Confederate soldier
Branch	John	R	Oldest of Branch brothers; killed at 1st Manassas
Branch	Sanford	R	"Santy"; captured at 1st Manassas
Browne	Albert	R	U.S. treasury agent in Savannah under occupation
Brown	Joseph E.	R	Governor of Georgia during war
Burns	Mrs.	F	Hosts Katherine and Pauline for one night
Carson	Jimmy	F	Son of Amy McBain and Robert Carson
Carson	Robert	F	"Bob"; husband of Amy; newspaper reporter
Chloe		F	House slave & seamstress of McBain in Savannah
Cohen	Isaac	R	Volunteer for Savannah Relief Society in Marietta
Dante		F	Slave cook of McBain family
Davis	General Jeff C.	R	Commanding officer of U.S. 14th Army Corps
Delpha		F	McBain house slave at plantation; wife of Isaac
Dillon	Mr.	F	Thomasville lawyer
Dolly		F	House slave & seamstress of McBain in Savannah
Donnelly	Robert	F	Overseer at Heritage plantation
Downes	Delores	F	Mother of Katherine, Pauline & Mary; wife of Zeb
Downes	Katherine	F	Oldest of Downes sisters
Downes	Mary	F	Youngest of Downes sisters
Downes	Pauline	F	Middle Downes sister
Downes	Zebudiah	F	Father of Downes sisters; husband of Delores
Duffy	Mrs.	F	Owner of Savannah boarding house

Geary	General John	R	Commanding officer of Savannah after occupation
Goodwin	Lyde	R	Savannah police chief
Hardee	Gen. William	R	Confederate officer commanding troops in Sav.
Hawks	Dr. Esther Hill	R	Woman doctor from New Hampshire
Haynes	March	R	Slave boat pilot in Savannah
Hercules		F	Slave coachman & head stableman of Jas. McBain
Holcombe	Thomas	R	Mayor of Savannah in 1861
Hope		R	Leader of Negro colony on St. Simons Island
Hulett	Laurence	F	Emily McBain's brother; U.S. seaman first class
Isaac		F	Slave overseer at Heritage; husband of Delpha
Isetta		F	House slave of Charles and Caro Lamar
JD		F	Danny McBain's dog
Jefferson		F	Slave stableman of McBain in Savannah
Jehova		F	Slave brick worker at the Heritage
Jinny		F	Slave cook of McBain in Savannah
Kitt		F	Slave brick worker; third son of Isaac & Delpha
Lamar	Caro	R	Wife of Charles
Lamar	Charles	R	Savannah businessman, slave trader & rebel officer
Lamar	Gazaway	R	Savannah businessman; father of Charles
Lewis	Pastor	F	Minister of Second Baptist Church in Thomasville
Leyland	Harold	F	Partner in crime of Willie and Sam
Lilly		F	Kitchen slave of McBain in Savannah
Lippman	Joseph	R	Owner of dry goods shop; makes soldiers' clothing
Long	Captain	F	Union ship captain
McBain	Amy	F	Daughter of Jas & Sarah; wife of Bob; lives in NY
McBain	Charlotte	F	Daughter of Joseph & Emily; lives in NY
McBain	Danny	F	Son of Joseph & Emily; lives in Savannah
McBain	Emily Hulett	F	Estranged wife of Joseph; lives in NY
McBain	James	F	Patriarch of McBain family; owner of Heritage
McBain	Joseph	F	Father of Danny & Charlotte; Confederate officer
McBain	Sarah Potter	F	Wife of James; mother of Amy & Joseph
McBain	Andrew	F	Murdered husband of Patience; friend of Joseph
McBain	Patience	F	Wife of Andrew; owned by Joseph McBain
McBain	Truvy	F	Son of Patience & Andrew; best friend of Danny
McBain	Gully Palladio	F	Youngest son of Patience & Andrew
Mercer	General Hugh	R	Confederate officer; served in Sav. & No Georgia
Mullins	Colleen	F	Irish servant of Amy McBain Carson

Nannie		F	House slave of McBain in Sav; wife of Jefferson
Noah		F	Heritage slave; second son of Isaac & Delpha
Olmstead	Col. Charles	R	Confederate commanding officer at Ft. Pulaski
Ophelia		F	Head house slave at the Heritage
Patty		F	Kitchen slave of McBain in Savannah
Pope	Mrs.	F	Resident of Macon; hosts Katherine & Pauline
Price	Mrs.	F	Pregnant women living outside Millen, Georgia
Roman		F	Slave brick worker at the Heritage
Rowland	John	R	Owner of March Haynes; served at Ft. Pulaski
Saunders	Dr. Dudley D.	R	Surgeon in charge of Confed. hospitals in Marietta
Simmons	Colonel	F	Union officer living at McBain house in Savannah
Sims	Frederick	R	Captain of Oglethorpe Light Infantry, Co. B
Sloan	Willie	F	Partner in crime of Sam & Harold
Smith	Peyton	F	Businessman visiting Savannah in 1862
Solomon		F	Slave brick worker; oldest son of Isaac & Delpha
Tanner	Johnny	F	Owner of stables in Savannah
Thorne	Rudy	F	Jewelry thief in Bryan County; friend of Harold
Tilda		F	House slave of Rebecca Toll in Roswell
Toll	Francis	F	Owner of shoe factory in Roswell
Toll	Rebecca	F	Sarah McBain's sister; Francis's wife
Tyler	Parker Lee	F	Friend of Danny; son of post office director in Sav.
Venus		F	Slave following Union army; wife of Cyrus
Wells	Mr.	F	Farmer in Thomasville, Georgia
Wells	Mrs.	F	Wife of Mr. Wells
Wells	Jonas	F	Son of Mr. & Mrs. Wells; soldier serving in VA.
Wilbin	General	F	Union officer living at McBain house in Savannah
William		F	Butler for McBain family in Savannah

ABOUT THE AUTHOR

Photo: Melinda Welker

JIM JORDAN researches and writes about the colonial, antebellum, and Civil War South. He lives in Okatie, South Carolina, with his wife Kathleen.

The novel *Penny Savannah: A Tale of Civil War Georgia* is the sequel to *Savannah Grey: A Tale of Antebellum Georgia*, published in 2007. His non-fiction book, *The Slave-Trader's Letter-Book: Charles Lamar, the Wanderer, and Other Secrets of the African Slave Trade* will soon be published by the University of Georgia Press. Mr. Jordan has published articles in the *Georgia Historical Quarterly* and the *Journal of Military History*.

Comments or inquiries should be sent to tours@savannahsojourns.com.

Visit the author's website: SavannahGrey.com

Made in the USA
Charleston, SC
25 November 2016